MW01058297

THE MOON BENEATH THE MOUNTAINS

MATTHEW JOHN SCHELLENBERG

ISBN-13: 978-1450553384
ISBN-10: 1450553389

Moon Beneath the Mountains

TO MY WIFE CAROLYN

Contents

Page

Key to map and tribal divisions

The swamp-dwellers
(Shushunushu)
1.) Tanaka- the Clan of
the Lynx
2.) Daimadunva- the Clan
of the Painted Turtle
3.) Shabbasa- the Clan of
the Dragonfly
4.) Zevi-Zevi- the Clan of
the Muskrat
5.) Ek-Rignara- the Clan
of the Heron

The marsh-dwellers
(Mamarra)
11.) Pagam-Atohka- the
Clan of the Badger
12.) Chichmolar- the Clan
of the Black Bear
13.) Ek-Kuntai- the Clan
of the Red-Winged
Blackbird
14.) Ek-Mamoo- the Clan
of the Loon
15.) Ek-Birin- the Clan of
the Flicker

The mountain-dwellers
(Kanattar)

6.) Hitasha- the Clan of
the Rattlesnake
7.) Ek-Makatin- the
Clan of the Eagle
8.) Kumuchska- the
Clan of the
Wolverine
9.) Demnaza- the Clan
of the Elk
10.) Ek-Dividawa- the
Clan of the Osprey

The forest-dwellers (Krim-
Krim)

16.) Ek-Kuntez- the Clan
of the Cardinal
17.) Chadza- the Clan of
the Timber Wolf
18.) Melumblumblar- the
Clan of the Fox
Squirrel
19.) Mitsa-Mitsa- the Clan
of he Salamander
20.) Murinal- the Clan of
the White-tailed Deer

Matthew John Schellenberg

Moon Beneath the Mountains

Long after the Creator sang his song of creation, but not too long after the trees began to fall, the woodpeckers of the forests in the land began to complain. The Downy Woodpeckers complained that their beaks were too short and because of that, the process of pecking holes in the trees to find beetle larvae to eat was too long. By the time they had reached one larvae, they were hungry again. If things were to continue this way, they would have to peck all day to keep from starving. The Pileated Woodpeckers complained that because they were so large and their beaks so heavy, by the time they landed on a dead branch and began hammering on the wood, the larvae had long since been alerted to their presence and were able to hide. If things were to continue this way, they too would have to hammer and search all day to keep from starving. The Red-headed Woodpeckers did not complain for the same reasons the other two woodpeckers complained because their beaks were longer than the Downy Woodpeckers' and yet their bodies were not so large as the Pileated Woodpeckers'. If the Red-headed Woodpeckers had been the only type of woodpeckers in the land, they would have no complaints. But they were not the only type. And they complained that because the Downy Woodpeckers were continuously pecking in the forest, it was difficult for them to find dead limbs where no bird was already pecking. And when they did find unoccupied limbs, often the larvae had already hidden because the Pileated Woodpeckers had just been there. As a result, the

Red-headed Woodpeckers also had to search for food all day to keep from starving.

The unrest continued until finally all the woodpeckers convened to discuss their problem. They then chose delegates to send to the Great Spirit to voice their complaints. The Creator listened attentively to their stories. When they had finished, the Creator asked a question. "Where are my children the Flickers? They are also of the Tribe of the Woodpecker, are they not?"

The other woodpeckers did not know how to answer the Creator. Actually, this was the first time they themselves had realized that the Flicker was absent. In fact, the more they thought about it, the more they realized that it had been a very long time since any of them had seen the Flickers.

"I wish to continue our discussion," said the Creator "but I wish to do so with your brothers and sisters the Flickers. Find them and return to me."

The woodpeckers returned to their places and began to search for the Flickers. They searched the oaks and the maples. They looked in the hickories and walnuts and birches. They went to the pines and firs, the poplars, the ashes, the spruces, and the cedars. But they could find the Flickers nowhere among the trees of the forests.

"Maybe they have left," said the Downy Woodpecker.

"Maybe they were all eaten by the Hawks," suggested the Red-headed Woodpecker.

"Or maybe," mused the   Pileated Woodpecker as he peered down to the forest floor, "maybe those birds down there in the grass are not chickadees or wrens or thrushes as I previously thought. Maybe the Flickers are down there now."

The Downy Woodpecker was quick to fly down and discover if what the Pileated Woodpecker had surmised was true. He found that it was true. The Flickers were all on the forest floor. The Downy Woodpecker alerted them to the fact that the Creator would like to see a delegate from the Clan of the Flickers at the Council of the Woodpeckers.

Later that night, the council reconvened. The Creator began with a question. "My Flicker child, why is it that your brothers and sisters have not seen your clan among the treetops of the forest where your fathers and mothers have lived?"

The Flicker was a bit afraid to answer the Creator because he thought that perhaps his people had done something wrong. "Great Spirit," he began hesitantly "as you know, for you are the Creator of all and you know all there is to know, before the trees began to fall, the woodpeckers of every clan ate the berries and nuts that grew from every bush and every tree in the forest. But since that fatal day, the woodpeckers have pounded their holes in dead limbs and branches in search of the beetle larvae they need to survive--for now not enough berries grow on the bushes and not enough nuts grow on the trees to sustain all the people. Like the rest, we also bored our holes, searching for our sustenance. But soon, we noticed that the

Downy Woodpeckers had to peck all day long to keep from starving. And then we noticed that the Pileated Woodpeckers also had to work all day. But when we noticed that the Red-headed Woodpeckers also had to work all day to keep from starving, we realized that if we were to continue along that same path, we would cause all of the woodpecker clans great hardship. It was then that we decided to search for a new path."

"Each of us went a different way to find some place where we could hunt for food and not bother the other woodpecker clans. Some went to the pine forest, others to the maples, others to the oak woods, and still others to the walnut stands. When we met again that night, no one had good news to report except one Flicker. She had decided to go somewhere she thought no one else would go. She flew to the forest floor and wandered around until she found something the Flickers might be able to eat that would not cause a shortage of food for the rest of the woodpecker clans. After an entire day of searching, she stumbled upon a huge ant mound. She thought to herself, "Maybe we could eat ants." She immediately captured one and ate it. It did not taste nearly as good to her as the beetle larvae that live in dead branches but she felt that her people would do well to begin hunting ants on the ground. There were so many of them that the Flickers would never starve. And they would also not be competing for the same food as the other woodpecker clans. Upon hearing the She-Flicker's report, our council decided that this would indeed be the best new hunting ground for our people. We have hunted there ever since." The Flicker representative said humbly. "We hope this does not offend you, O Creator. We did not choose to hunt the ants because they taste better or because they are easier to hunt but because we believed our sacrifice would benefit the other clans."

At that, the Creator was very pleased, saying, "My dear son. Do not fear. You have not offended me in the least. Stand tall now and receive my congratulations. Your sister clans came to me with complaints, seeking my help to solve their problems. You on the other hand, have taken the initiative and have solved your own problem. Your ingenuity and humility have caused you to be blessed among the clans of the woodpecker. As a reward, I will adorn you with brown and yellow where your sisters and brothers are adorned with black and white. And may all birds look to your example as they live and struggle in the land I have created for you all."

This is how the Flicker came to eat ants on the ground even though he is a woodpecker.

I.   There are those whose eyes drink of the night as some eyes sip of day's light; those whose waking labor wades through shades as deep as the dreams of others who soak sun while plowing the scabs of the skin of the earth; those whose glistening orbs glow red with the blood of remembrance while others mask bloody memory with half-feigned ignorance or countless decades of selective truth--truth extracted from an epic fully pregnant with heroes for both the light of the sun and the light of the moon. And the blood of the past fills the veins of all the living. With vengeance and pity it floods the sea of life with the food of destiny.

CHAPTER 1

He drew his cupped hands to his mouth and sipped from the stream. The rush threatened to numb his submerged feet but it shocked his throat to pleasure. Stooping, he drank until he was satisfied. Then he drank more. The sun beat on his reddish-brown skin and his back drank its warmth as he drank from the icy stream. When he was finished, he stood up and watched his brother hop down the embankment to join him in the water.

As Damowan's bare foot contacted the mountain brook, he exclaimed in ridiculously over-dramatic tone, "O, Temmonin, this is the meaning of life!"

"That and her kiss upon your brow when we return," Temmonin answered, his tone equally as feigned.

Damowan chuckled at his brother's false formality but his laugh was soon doused by the water as he plunged his head beneath the surface. He swished it from side to side for a moment before pulling it out and panting. Then he dropped to his hands and knees and, dipping the lower half of his face into the surge, sloughed like a dog.

As Temmonin watched, he was warm with satisfaction at the sight of his brother's exaggeration. That characteristic was one they had always shared, he in his over-determined approach to master every aspect of his life and surroundings and Damowan, his brother, in his unintentional yet uncanny ability to make rude remarks and ridiculous boasts. Throughout their lives, both had excelled among others their age but, somehow, unlike himself, Damowan seemed not to have stripped himself or his essential innocence. By comparison, even

1

Damowan's playful method of drinking seemed to shroud Temmonin's calculated cupped hands with over-thoughtfulness. The sudden sting of droplets on his chest jerked Temmonin's thoughts back to the present.

"Eh, brother, look out fer the demon of the mountain stream! I hear the ugly jerk lives around here." Damowan splashed sarcasm at his brother's concentration.

Temmonin was angry for an instant. But he smiled as he shouted a mock warning and leapt from the water, "Look out fer the demon of the older brother! He's about to rip yer hair outta yer head!" Then the two clasped arms and wrestled each other into the stream like two bear cubs.

Days later, their footfall was all that informed the surrounding forest that the two were still traveling through its shade. Their glee had turned sour as they traversed the North Wood in an unsuccessful search for elk. More than two weeks previous, Damowan, Temmonin, and the other young men of the village had been sent out in pairs to supply the people with meat. After nearly ten days of hiking, the two brothers had secured the permission of the Chadza to hunt in Krimma-Dentl. The people of the Timber Wolf had celebrated their asking and sent them into the northernmost woods with a soul-gripping dance around a hair-singeing fire. The mien of this wolf clan seemed to translate into human utterance the stark deliberation of the ragged, stone-cleft forest. And their bare subsistence complimented the trees' ability to suck life from granite and shale. Their smiles had filled Temmonin and Damowan with hope.

But six fruitless days of stalking had drained most of that hope from them. The brothers now walked with a carelessness that spat at the elders who had trained them. Only one day remained in which to find their wapiti. If they could not find one by then, they would have to return to their village empty-handed.

They traveled in an afternoon sun wedged between an eventless morning and what they predicted would be a boring evening. At the onset of their journey, laughter bubbled from their smiles at the sight of every nervous chipmunk and chickadee. But now, if humor perched nearby, they did not notice.

The trail was typically rugged for one in the shadow of Imnanaw-Kanat. The cedars in these craggy foothills seemed to test a traveler's alertness by baring their bony roots at unpredictable intervals in the trail. Every time one of the brothers stubbed his toe, the other could not refrain from chuckling. At this point, only violence could conjure laughter from their disappointment. When they had found a small creek, they stopped for the day. Both dropped to the mossy stones and released disheartened sighs.

Damowan tore the sling of his quiver over his ebony head of hair and let his spear, bow, and arrows clatter on the shale.

"Chaneerem and Jemalemin're most likely floatin' in the moisture of kisses by now." Damowan made a grandiose gesture as he spoke.

Temmonin's thoughts smacked of similar sarcasm. Using his most poetic tone and attempting not to laugh at how ridiculous he sounded, he continued Damowan's thought. "And those same, wet-lipped women are dressing them for their victory dance this evening." Then, recalling an important fact, he shook his head. His voice lost its poetry. "No. Wait. They'll wait fer the dance."

"Yea, until we, the grovelers, get back!" Damowan cuffed himself in mock rebuke.

"They'll touch their feathers to the fire and blow the smoke into our faces." Temmonin's tone was proverbial again.

"And the fireflies will cringe and lose their glow at such forsaken brotherhood," Damowan concluded the verse.

They both smiled.

"Alright, enough of this high-falootin' mumbo-jumbo. It's time to git down to the nitty-gritty." As Temmonin peeled his moccasin from his right foot, he noticed a cracked and bleeding toenail which had recently hammered a root. Upon touching the nail, he hissed.

"I'll betcha those two idiots spent their first huntin' days beggin' the trees in our path to raise their roots in greeting," Damowan edged.

"Why, Damowan, my boy," Temmonin again returned to his sarcasm, "I'm sure those virtuous warriors meant no ha..." Temmonin stopped and raised his nostrils to the breeze. Immediately, Damowan mimicked the gesture. Blood. Not far. And something burning..

They had sat down in a small bowl of shale, the rim of which was thick with ferns, knee-high maple saplings, and lilies-of-the-valley. As they stood, it was through this undergrowth that they peered. No movement. Evening shrouded the view. No sound.

Together, they climbed the short bank and stepped slowly forward. The odor grew. The blood smelled fresh. And something was still burning. They spied a clump of blackened Osage orange trees not a stone's throw away. Branches and leaves were so twisted, they formed a wall and blocked vision from the height of the brothers'

4

waists to a point far above their heads. As they approached, Damowan pointed to the source of blood. Temmonin recognized the form of a bull wapiti beneath a black tree. It lie silent on its left side facing away from them. Its massive rack curved toward the sky, crying for justice. As the brothers looked further, they saw a ragged yaw of ribs and hide and flesh through which a delta of crimson elk blood spilled. The blood was still wet and the bark of the trees was still smoldering. Temmonin scanned the area, senses peaked with apprehension. No movement. No sound. With extreme caution, they crept beneath the brittle branches, begging the silence to yield its answer.

They found that the orange trees encircled a small clearing. The wapiti must have wandered into the circlet before it had been attacked. Temmonin and Damowan both knelt to examine the beast. Its side had been gouged open by something with huge claws, which had plowed the hide in all directions. Most of the organs were absent. The hair was charred as far as a hand's length surrounding the gash. Temmonin turned nervously before continuing. No movement. No sound. He had to clench his fists to keep from howling at the stillness.

After another look at the carcass, Temmonin stood up. He whispered half to himself, "Fire." Still, no movement. No sound.

And, glancing up at his brother from where he knelt, Damowan's eyes suddenly swelled with shock, "Temmonin!"

Then the silence screamed between Temmonin's ears. Adrenalin surged and threatened to burst his chest. He clutched his heart long enough to wriggle his stone dagger from its sheath and wheel around. He saw a burning blur, took a mind-wrenching clawed cudgel-blow across his

5

chest and neck, and slammed to the earth. Blinded with delirium, he groped about himself as if searching for his senses. He had lost his knife. The attacker bellowed again with the rage of an insane bear and that rage kicked Temmonin's sight back into his skull. He raised his head to see that Damowan had retrieved his dagger and was crouched like a cougar in front of the assailant. Temmonin could see it clearly now and it was a bear. Its shaggy black hulk towered twice as tall as Damowan's cat-hunch and its face was a mass of chipped granite. From its jowls jutted two fangs, each a hand long and glistening with saliva. And strangely, its paws were burning.

Without warning, Damowan rushed into the monster's hot breath, driving Temmonin's knife into the folds of its throat. Then, he was swallowed in greasy fur.

Temmonin stood and pulled his spear from where it hung on his back . He gripped the shaft and thrust it into the forest of fur. His plunge slammed to a nerve-shattering halt. The beast seemed to have been carved from oak, as if created and controlled by some angry wooden spirit. And Temmonin had collided with it. His arms vibrated as if a red squirrel had screamed through his heart and the echoes were still roiling in his veins. The instant he had sorted through the debris in his mind, he focused to see another firebrand streaming for his face.

His hair burst into flame as the paw struck his temple. Again, he sprawled to the ground. He heard only sporadic groans of effort and pain from Damowan, but he felt that he himself had emitted a continuous moan since he had first been hit. Then his nose gripped the reek of his own burning hair.

Gathering moss and leaves to himself, he rolled his head until the flames subsided.

He rose and hacked the stench from his lungs. The odor of roasting hair stung him to a pointed rage. Swinging his weapons from his back, he grasped his bow and notched an arrow. As he raised his eyes, he saw that Damowan was furiously arcing his blade in and out of the creature's bloody chest. Temmonin shifted to the left and found a broad swath of fur into which he let his stone-tipped shaft fly. When the arrow hit, the fire-bear reeled on its left leg and wretched an obscene gout of blood and flesh but quickly regained its balance and its grip on Damowan.

Neither Damowan nor the bear had lost any fervor as Temmonin drew his bow the second time. The elder brother circled his target but the bear seemed to sense his position and began placing Damowan between itself and the bowman. Temmonin countered and leapt, aiming in mid-flight. But he was forced to shoot low as Damowan's leg dropped in front of his intended target.

Circling like a bothersome deerfly, Temmonin notched a third arrow and, as he did so, he heard Damowan shriek. He jerked a glance upward to see the fire-bear slapping his brother's bare back with palms of searing flame. After three of the mammoth blows, Damowan released his grip and dwindled to the stone, exhausted and emptied of will. Immediately, Temmonin's arrow slit into the bear's heart as the monster bent to pulverize Damowan's head. The creature held. Then a fourth arrow entered. The bear seemed to forget its intent. Then a fifth. The creature lurched, stood motionless for an instant, then crashed like a rotted willow over Temmonin's senseless brother.

The archer breathed deeply for a moment. He again scanned the area. No movement. No sound. He dropped to his knees next to the lifeless hulk and heaved it onto its back and off of Damowan. He was startled to his feet by a growl and he stared, tense and anxious, into the bear's glowing, orange orbs. But the glow flickered and faded and what remained of the giant's spirit sank with its blood into the moss. Relieved, Temmonin wiped his face and pushed his hair from his view.

Damowan slept through that night and the next day. His breathing grew steadier and gentler as the day progressed. As evening again grayed the air, Temmonin washed his brother's body with water he had carried from the creek. Kneeling beside him, he whispered prayers to the Creator,

"Great Spirit, You who crafted the flicker and every animal, You who formed the marsh and every land, You who shaped my brother and every man, let this water, the lifeblood of Your footstool, now add life to his fallen body that he might walk again in the shadow of beauty and sweat again in the sun of life."

Temmonin had used his moccasins as water skins. Now, pouring the icy balm over his brother's chest and face, he cleared away the congealed blood and bark and hair. Damowan smiled groggily as if he were pleased that evening's kisses were finally able to caress his skin. Somehow, he had managed to land on his back. Fortunately, this position made for the easiest breathing. Temmonin was hesitant to move him for fear of hindering his healing. Having completed the cleansing by rinsing the warrior's arms and legs, hands and feet, he lay down alongside Damowan with his feet to the fire he had built. His heart rode the wings of a brown-backed woodpecker to dreams of laughter and tears.

Moon Beneath the Mountains

He was roused from slumber by a ghostly
breeze that danced in his nostrils, scattering
cinnamon as it passed. Without moving his body,
he slit one eye to find the last of the fire's embers
bidding each other good night. The sky was pitch
and pierced with stars. He was about to lift his head
to look around when a column began to materialize
from the smoke-wisps of the departing fire. He
held his head still and continued to view through
slitted eyes. The whirling column split into six
smaller cylinders which moved to points equidistant
from one another in a circle around the charred
wood. As more wood breathed into the chill air,
another form began to appear in the center of the
fire and, as it solidified, Temmonin felt the gutting
of a drum in his ears. The six shapes began moving
in circular motion to the beat of that drummer.
They were men with beaks and eyes like flickers and
they danced. They arced and swirled, half-stepping,
half-floating in translucent sentiment to the hollow
rhythm. Entranced by the six spirit dancers,
Temmonin hardly noticed that the drummer had
gained clarity.

She stood in gorgeous raiment, her pale
dream-wings were vague hints of black and yellow
and around her neck hung a wide, black necklace.
Her arms were laden with bracelets strung with
mollusk shells that shook and clattered as she
drummed. Her obsidian hair gathered stars that had
fallen to the ground at the sight of her beauty. They
swam the glossy stream to her compelling face. She
wore the beak of a woodpecker as gracefully as any
spirit could and the stars flooded her eyes with
glory. A red hairpiece hung on either side of her
stately head.

The dancers began to call, "When to give the blessing? When to tell the tale? When to give the blessing? When to tell the tale?" they repeated.

But then Temmonin realized that he had been hearing something else throughout the drummer's chant. A high-pitched, grinding whine had threaded its way through the forest and, when he traced it to its source, Temmonin found that it came from the woman spirit. She was creating two melodies simultaneously, one a silvery, feminine glide and the other something nasal, almost crude. The first outlined a wordless counterpoint to the dancers' questions while the second whispered and sung and chewed some distorted language. When Temmonin concentrated, he could understand.

"When the heart is humble and the tongue wanes soft, then draw we strength from the wise sons' spirits. For, until that moment, our voices are silent while discipline's river continues its course."

Her speech-song and its pulsating accompaniment echoed through his amazement for what seemed to be an hour. He felt he would become a stiff addition to the shale beneath him if he did not move soon. But he gritted his teeth in an effort to remain still. Relief followed quickly.

"The time has come," the angel's voice was thick with layers like a crosscut of sandstone. "The wise sons have awoke."

With this, the six discontinued their dance and arranged themselves in a semi-circle facing the brothers, each less than an arm's length apart, three to either side of the bird-woman. But she had said, "The wise sons have awoke". Glancing to his right, Temmonin found Damowan locked in slumber. The elder son sat up. The echelon focused their attention on him.

"Temmonin of the clan of the Flicker, from youth to manhood, your submission to the Creator has shone brightly to the spirits that guard the marshes. You must know that whether in each given task you succeed or fail, in the end, you will have accomplished much for the sake of honor. Be comforted in this."

His cheek stung with wetness. Startled, he snapped his eyes open to find a circlet of Osage orange trees, half full of dawn's yellow-grey mist. Damowan lay still beside him. Where the woman spirit had stood, the embers of the fire had long since dissipated. A light rain pattered the charred wood and moistened Temmonin's mossy surroundings. He blinked. A sigh of disappointment slipped through his lips.

"And dreams led them to the heights of frenzy," Temmonin recited a lament as if he had lost a friend.

"And left their bones to the vultures and birds of prey," Damowan concluded the verse Temmonin had begun. The voice startled Temmonin. But after instantaneous surprise at the fact that his younger brother was awake, Temmonin smiled.

"Eh, sleeping mole, wake soon or join the river. This rain's gittin' pretty nasty." Temmonin jested.

Damowan rolled back his eyelids, "Go easy on us woun. . ." The scarred warrior choked and tensed in mid-sentence as pain halted his attempt to right himself. Grimacing, he eased his torso prone again. As if invisible strings connected their faces, Temmonin's expression matched his brother's.

"My back," Damowan hissed, "Did you use my ribs fer kindling or somethin'?" His spirit was indomitable even when saturated with blood. "Was

11

that thing the Gorma from Uncle Ammon's fire-beast stories?"

Temmonin shrugged. "I guess. I always thought he was jus' tryin' to scare us 'cuz we loved to be scared. When we got older, I figured he'd exaggerated all the details. Guess we jus' learned fer ourselves." Temmonin paused. "But it's strange. He always told us the Gorma were almost extinct and they lived too far north fer us to meet one even if we hiked fer months."

"I can't believe how hot those paws were!" Damowan had covered his eyes with his hands to deflect raindrops. "My skin's still burnin'."

"I almost cried when he started burnin' you. I could hardly get a decent shot."

"How many times did he hit me?" Damowan winced.

"Three, I think." Temmonin wondered why his brother always took the worst wounds. Could it be carelessness on Damowan's part? Was Temmonin himself so much more wise? Or was Damowan just more adept at shirking the ever-present temptation to cowardice? "D'you think you could roll over--or let me roll you over so I can wash those burns?"

"I don't know. Guess I could try. Steady my roll, would ya?"

Temmonin gingerly lifted Damowan's right shoulder and lower back so as to avoid strain on his brother's frame. Then, as Damowan's roll continued, Temmonin reversed his hands and lowered the younger man's chest to the shale. Then the wounded man ground his vocal chords as if to eradicate his reopened pain through vibration. Temmonin's eyes stung with disgust and his face contorted as Damowan's roasted flesh glistened in

the drab dawn. Temmonin could not contain a
rueful sough.

Damowan stopped groaning to ask, "How
bad is it?"

Temmonin hardly heard the question. He
stared in unbelief at the dead hulk of the fire-beast.
Its raven black hide lay silent on the ground. The
bear glared wide-eyed through the trees like a shrine
of violent destruction, daring the clouds to thunder.
Even dead, those eyes made him shudder with
memories of blaze and blood.

"Temmonin, how bad is it?" Damowan
was more insistent.

"Wha?" Then Temmonin jerked his gaze
back to his brother's wound. "Bad. Jus' stay here.
I'll be back soon." And he loped away to retrieve
more water.

Temmonin wondered how much granite
had been mixed with flesh to form Damowan's
body. As he neared the brook, his mind traversed
the distance to Kemkemmayam, their village in the
territory of the clan of the Flicker. He watched as
his fifteen-year-old brother was borne blindfolded
through a small hole in the ice of a frozen lake and
pushed about two body lengths away from that
hole. He remembered the suffocating paradox that
gripped his heart as he watched his brother flailing
beneath the stoic ice. And, although Temmonin's
mien matched the stoicism of the lake, inwardly he
writhed and trembled, yearning to drive his thoughts
through the ice to guide Damowan to safety and
manhood. But like the other warriors, he watched
and waited. Damowana became Damowan that
day. He had endured the week long rites of passage
which culminated in this final test. After heaving
himself from the black water, he was honored with
the shortening of his name.

When Temmonin's feet reached his goal, his mind returned to the duties at hand. He dipped his moccasins in the stream. Still, his thoughts were restless. With arms elbow deep in the chill, he tried to imagine his brother drowning under the frozen lake or melting in the clutches of the fire-beast. He was unable to do so.

Damowan's wound beckoned to be cleansed. It stretched across most of his back. Temmonin lowered himself to his knees and chided his brother,

"Damowan, this habit of yers is gonna kill you one of these days. Someday yer muscles're gonna rebel and start runnin' you away from anything that looks even the least bit dangerous."

Damowan responded slowly and with feigned congeniality, "Temmonin, I am deeply indebted to you for such timely, practical advice."

The elder chuckled at the face his brother had made. Damowan's stomach quaked then constricted to hold his laughter. He groaned regretfully.

"My back is killin' me. Don't make me laugh!"

Temmonin could not resist the temptation. He pursed his lips and spoke in the high-pitched, teasing voice a child would use, "Well, don't make me laugh." And the brothers shook.

"Temmonin!"

Temmonin concentrated on controlling himself. He knew it must hurt for Damowan to laugh. His lips quivered as he spoke, but he managed to avoid another trigger, "Hold still and let me wash this rot away."

After removing numerous sticks and lichen with his fingers, Temmonin poured some water across the wound and rinsed away any imbedded dirt and sand. Damowan remained tense throughout the cleansing. When the elder was satisfied with his work, he sat upright and scanned the knoll with eager eyes.

"D'you remember seein' or smellin' any semsaweva on our way in here?" Temmonin spoke half to himself.

"Temmonin, I don't remember much of anything right now."

But the elder had not waited for an answer; had not expected one. His eyes were intent on the trail to the stream. He remembered having smelled some of the healing herb on his trips for water. He retraced his path and, not a stone's throw away from where his weary brother lay waiting, he spied several of the plants. After having gathered two handfuls of leaves, Temmonin raised his arms and face to the sky for a moment, then drew his hands to his mouth and kissed the greenery three times. Content, he returned to Damowan. Upon reaching the edge of the knoll, he announced, "Now we'll put to flight the demon of infection."

"Quickly, brother, for the flies are commencing their feast."

Temmonin had to cringe to keep himself from laughing at the situation. Damowan had just received what might have been the most serious wound of his life. He was lying on his stomach and could barely move. Yet he was making fun of the kinds of things the elders of the tribe say as they speak at council. And he was twisting his face to accompany his words. As he whisked the insects from Damowan's wounds, Temmonin remarked, "Y'know if you'd stop usin' that stupid Mr. Sophisto-voice, maybe I wouldn't laugh at you so much and then you wouldn't end up laughin'."

Temmonin moved quickly. Immediately, he found a large, flat section of shale and swept clear an area in which to work. He then stacked the leaves in the center of the spot and covered them with a stone that was the size of one hand and roughly egg-shaped. With a twist of the stone, he began to crush the leaves.

"It's too bad the autumn sun hasn't dried up these leaves yet. But they're still pretty potent when they're green." And when he had finished, he added a few drops of water and kneaded the mixture until it was the consistency of a loose putty.

Damowan jerked rigid as his brother smeared the medicine across his back. Temmonin imagined the pain his brother must be feeling--as if his skin were being flayed and his ribs being exposed to fire once again. Damowan continued wincing as Temmonin continued the treatment.

The elder sought to comfort his brother but stopped short for lack of the right words. As he completed the application of the herb paste, he found them. "The soul that thirsts in the summer sun is warmed by the heat of the winter sun."

Pain had raked the humor from Damowan's tone but there was no anger in his voice as he completed the verse his brother had begun, "And the self-same sun drives a man to both passions." Within breaths, the wounded man fell asleep.

Damowan's healing stretched for several days. By the third day, he was able to sit up and eat some of the meat Temmonin had hunted and cooked. Both realized that they had long since missed the appointed day of return to the Mamar and that realization drove their thoughts in circles. By now, their rivals, Chaneerem and Jemalemin may already have been celebrated with a victory dance.

They frowned at what their mother would say when they returned.

Several times, Temmonin began to explain a dream he had a few nights before, but even its simplest details slipped like frog eggs from his view.

Two days later, Damowan was willing to try walking. Because of his wounds, he was only able to carry what his hands could hold, which included the spears, bows, and quivers. As a result, Temmonin was laden with two bundles, two grey fox hides, one large opossum hide, and a porcupine pelt, all of which were slung from his shoulders. They left the dead wapiti because decay had already set in. Their pace was much slower than usual but, in three days, they stumbled through the foothills of Imnanaw Kanat and into the region of the Kumuchska; the clan of the Wolverine.

By midday, a small band of Kumuchska hunters spotted them from a hill overlooking the valley through which Temmonin and Damowan plodded. With a shout, they sheathed their weapons and, bare palms raised, ran down the slope to greet the Ek-Birin. Temmonin and Damowan were glad to see them.

The leader of the Kumuchska party spoke a short, ceremonial greeting in the guttural tongue of the Kanattar tribe then followed by raising a stocky right arm until it was perpendicular to his frame, palm facing Temmonin. The animal-laden brother responded by mirroring the Wolverine's right arm with his left. When their palms aligned, both men drew their free hands to touch their lips.

The two spoke in Mokhamoyuba almost simultaneously, "Peace and beauty."

Then, as if a drama had ended, the formality fell away and smiles of welcome appeared. After the leader introduced himself and his

17

companions, Temmonin introduced Damowan and
explained their reason for being here. At that, six
Wolverines reached for the game and supplies the
Ek-Birin were carrying and turned to guide them to
their village. The Kumuchska were also returning
home from their hunt, gladly burdened with food
for their people. Two of the men carried a large
white-tailed buck on a wooden pole. The other four
carried fox, raccoon, opossum, and geese. As the
party moved forward, one of them noticed the
burns on Damowan's back and assured him,

"Our healer'll fix ya up right." He was near
Damowan's age and his features resembled the bark
of a clean aspen, gently tanned and rugged against
the harsh winters of Imnanaw Kanat. His eyes and
hair and nostrils were black like the place where
limbs reach from the aspen's trunk. And his soul
danced through his expression like quaking leaves in
a rush of wind. He must already have endured the
rites.

"My name's Gegmogar." Temmonin was
right. His name held only three syllables, the sign of
a man.

"And I'm Damowan."

Gegmogar explained that their village was
not far and that the Ek-Birin could rest there. The
walk was refreshing. They passed under and beside
huge stands of hemlock and white pine dotted with
aspen, birch, maple, and basswood. Chattering red
squirrels announced the passing of the group to the
rest of the forest. Then, the ground grew more
rocky and, as they crested a hill, they could see a
village in a long valley at the base of the North
Mountains.

The leader, whose name Temmonin had
discovered was Shegra, spoke in a reverent tone to
the thin air, "This valley is Shemtootoo: the mouth,

and our village is Demdegumshannatez: where rivers meet." He then cupped his hands to his mouth and trumpeted, "Shegra returns. All is well."

Moments later, the company walked through the trees on the outskirts of the village and were greeted by a crowd of women. Several older men leaned or sat against a number of wooden huts and watched with ambiguous interest. Each of four of the Kumuchska hunters was met by one woman approximately his age; probably his wife. But Gegmogar was greeted by two, one who seemed by her age and manner to be his mother and another who was beautiful and roughly two years younger than him. While his mother fussed over him, the younger woman smiled shyly and waited.

Her eyes surged with excitement as Gegmogar gazed past his busy mother to honor her with his attention. When his mother could see that he was unharmed, she relented from her gaudy affection. Her son grasped his opportunity and knelt on one knee before the object of his adoration. Still kneeling, he stretched his right arm toward her in a manner reminiscent of the greeting between Shegra and Temmonin. As he bowed to her, the young woman bent to the ground and gathered sand, leaves, and pine needles into her hands. Rising, she sifted the mixture through her fingers until it sprinkled the ground, first to the left of his outstretched arm, then to its right. When her hands were empty, she displayed them before him. At this signal, he drew his left hand to his lips and spoke with passion,

"Menna, in peace and beauty, I honor you."

Drawing both of her hands to her lips, she replied, "By honoring the earth which is our mother, you honor her who replenishes its life."

At the sight of the familiar ceremony, Temmonin turned to Damowan. It seemed the flame in Damowan's heart was threatening to overstep its bnoundaries. He could see how much his younger brother longed for the moment of his return home when he would participate in similar exchanges.

As Gegmogar turned to Damowan, Damowan flushed. Temmonin felt that the Kumuchska might reach to wipe away the sentiment that dripped like pine sap from his brother's face. Instead, he gestured for Damowan to come nearer. Damowan obliged. Gegmogar presented the Ek-Birin,

"This is Damowan of the Ek-Birin; the clan of the Flicker." Then, turning to Damowan, "And this is Menna, she whom I will serve. She will lead you to our healer who will tend to your wounds." Damowan obviously felt lavished. He bowed in thanks.

Temmonin smiled and watched his brother follow Menna. Although he was two years Damowan's elder, he had still learned little of the arts of healing. But his brother's back did not need much help. Damowan had already forged through pits of pain twice as deep.

Shegra turned from his wife to face Temmonin, "My friend, pardon me while I seek quarters for you and your brother." The thick-boned Wolverine passed him and approached the sixth member of their hunting party. The hunter was very young and very embarrassed at the amount of attention his mother was paying him. All of the others had been greeted by spouses or, in Gegmogar's case, his fiancee, but this novice seemed to wish the nearby birches would gather more shade around him so no one would notice him. His mother, however, being entirely insensitive to the intricate workings of the male ego, continued to strip him to boyhood with gentle motherly care. He was relieved when Shegra interrupted.

"Dear mother, your concern is evident and necessary at the return of your son but, if you'll excuse my intrusion, our guests from the Ek-Birin are in need of shelter for the night. Might they come to know the hospitality of the Kumuchska through the wealth of your home?"

The subtle sarcasm with which Shegra emphasized the word 'necessary' appeared to be intended to assure the young hunter rather than to insult his mother. Mischievous enlightenment lifted the corners of the boy's frown. The fact that he himself had understood this subtlety seemed to encourage him. This, coupled with the fact that his mother had not been offended by the remark but was blushing at such an honorable request seemed to restore the boy's hope for a place among men.

When the woman gave her response, Temmonin did not hear it. He caught sight of a figure walking toward him from the center of the town and was surprised to recognize a face. He smiled widely but he held his tongue as the elder neared him.

"Nephew Temmonin, peace and beauty. Nigh five years go did I hear of and rejoice at the word of a boy's rites of passing. And now before me stands a man--and no less than his mother bore." He raised a burly right hand in greeting.

"Uncle Nosh, peace and beauty. You honor me with your attention." Temmonin mirrored Nosh's movements. Both raised fingers to their lips as their eyes exchanged the invisible blood of kinship.

His uncle gleamed approval. Temmonin almost quivered at the weight of such honor. Even though he rarely saw him, he had always respected his father's younger brother. And now his respect multiplied as he noticed a wide swath of mottled skin across Nosh's shoulder. Nosh followed his nephew's gaze.

"Ah, the greeting of the fire-bear. I hear Damowan was likewise greeted." A playful grin crept into the chief's cheeks. Temmonin felt suddenly ashamed that he himself bore no burn marks. He responded to his uncle's jest with an awkward grimace.

"And I suppose you stopped it short of a full welcome?" Maybe his uncle understood his embarrassment. Maybe he was just being merciful. Before Temmonin could muster a reply, Nosh spoke again, "Temmonin, we've got a lot to discuss but the center of the village isn't a very good place fer lengthy conversation. C'mon. Let's go to my place and we can eat while we talk." Looking past his nephew's shoulder, he raised his voice, "Shegra."

Shegra turned from the woman to whom he was speaking, "Yes, my chief?"

"We. . ." Nosh stopped short, remembering his manners. He righted himself and raised his arm. "Shegra, my son, peace and beauty. How was the hunt?"

"Nosh, my father and my chief, peace and beauty. You honor me with your attention. We are laden with bounty for our people. And we have brought with us two men of the Ek-Birin."

"My son, you have brought with you two of your cousins."

For a brief moment, Shegra studied the Ek-Birin, "Cousin Temmonin?" At that, the whole group laughed heartily.

"Cousin Shegra, peace and beauty," Temmonin announced in mock formality.

"Peace and beauty."

"Well now that you two have gotten to know each other again, why don't we go and eat. Then we'll tell some stories until we fall asleep." Nosh began to walk away.

"But, Father, I've already approached this mother about them sleeping at her house." Shegra looked slightly embarrassed.

"Ah, I am truly sorry Indamma," Nosh apologized to the woman. "Please continue the arrangements, Shegra. We wouldn't want to steal an honor already offered to an able hostess. Perhaps the guests will stay another night, in which case they will be welcomed into our home."

"Yes, Father."

"Your cousin and I will be at our hearth for supper."

Nosh's mien puzzled Temmonin. He seemed extremely anxious to speak in private. He hid his anxiety well but, like his own father, Nosh was not unreadable--his thoughts often slipped through cracks in his speech. As they strode alongside each other, the chief shot his arm around his nephew.

"Ah, Temmoninek, my young Temmoninek. We so often offer peace and beauty and are given only strife and blood in return."

The Ek-Birin withheld his questions. He studied his uncle. Changing winds of extremity had riven channels into his face. Fierce jowls guarded his mouth--a mouth accustomed to the exorbitant emotional ordeal of leading a clan. His thin, umber eyes sat like a dual eclipse on the glowing copper foothills of his cheeks. The nose of a hawk separated the two powers. His terra cotta hide covered muscles that snaked around his bones like the rope of life's passion. And he wore his porcupine quill headdress with the lean pride of a white pine. Turning into his longhouse, he motioned Temmonin through the doorway and into the chief section of the dwelling.

Upon entering, Temmonin was greeted with a barrage of surprised smiles. His aunt and grandfather and cousins jumped up in welcome. They were sitting in a circle around the fire but rushed to exchange kisses with their relative.

He recognized Nosh's second wife, his Aunt Zemma, and his own grandfather from his father's side of the family. His cousins, however were images from a dream. Dendaminek was thick and bristling like his father and brother and as he reached out his welcome, he pushed aside the plump child that held his space in Temmonin's memory. Then, as Dendaminek moved away, Temmonin stood dumb and awed at the sight of his two female cousins. He wondered if every Kumuchska virgin were so beautiful. He silently thanked the Creator that they were actually not Nosh's daughters. Zemma's first husband had died when her two girls were quite young. When Nosh's wife died and left him with two boys to care for, it seemed best to all concerned that the two families be joined. Yet even if Temmonin were not allowed to marry them, he would still be entranced. His words spilled randomly from flaccid lips as his cousins drew near to kiss his cheeks. Kneeling like a man losing control, he extended his arm and touched his fingers to his lips. After a moment, he rose to perceive the residue of a knowing smile on his aunt's face. As he met her gaze, she flushed and shifted her eyes to Zheva, her eldest daughter.

"It's good that we're dear to each other,"
Nosh chuckled, "Seems distance kindles kinship."
Then, after a short pause, "Zemma, our nephews
Temmonin and Damowan'll be joinin' us fer the
evening meal. Until then, I have to talk to this boy."

"Oh, don't worry. I'll take care of
everything." Zemma's eyes flashed between
Temmonin and Zheva.

"Thank you, my love."

The family returned to their places around
the fire and Nosh invited the Ek-Birin to join them.
Nosh began to sit but quickly righted himself and
walked to the corner of the room and gathered four
fire logs into his arms and brought them to the fire.

While his uncle did this, Temmonin began
to search his memory for recollections of Zheva.
Through the mist, he caught vague glimpses of a
gangly, unproportioned child whom he seemed to
have disliked. He had not even remembered her
name. But that was ten years ago and he had spent
most of that visit with a juvenile Shegramennin in
the forest hills, not in the village where the young
females stayed. Something in him wished he could
have seen the future.

"Temmonin," Nosh interrupted his
thoughts, "Bad news has reached us from yer
mother's tribe. Jus' last night, a Demnaza
messenger brought us the story of three deaths; a
woman and two young children. All from
Kemkemmayam." He waited. Temmonin's eyes
widened. They asked questions for which his
tongue had no words.

"Temmonin, it seems that all three were
clawed and stabbed. The marks from the stabbings
were those of a knife--no animal could've made
'em." Again, Temmonin was silent. His uncle
related the information as if feeding a child.

Temmonin began slowly, "Who?"

"Bezhava, the wife of Mantaw, and their only two children."

At that, realization surged into the Ek-Birin's eyes. The thought of his father's friend losing his entire family stung him to tears. The small room and its occupants watched Temmonin in stillness.

"And they don't know who did it? An outsider?"

"Not a trace of the killer except fer the marks on the bodies."

"They were stabbed and clawed? Clawed by what?"

"Nobody knows, Temmonin. Maybe fingernails but prob'ly claws or talons. It's really weird."

Temmonin spurted decisively, "Our people need us. We have to go."

"Your chief and your people'll understand, Temmonin. Damowan needs rest. Why don't you two stay here a couple nights?" Nosh was not patronizing his nephew. He spoke as a friend. Temmonin knew that too often he had countered his elders' advice only to watch his impulsive arguments melt away in the dawn of prudence. He acquiesced with a shrug.

"The healer might want another day anyway."

"And we'll take advantage of the time to hear some stories and to tell some." Although his uncle allowed only a half-smile to tighten his cheeks, Temmonin knew he was overjoyed. This was the man who had offered Temmonin's father to find a wife for him among the Kumuchska. And this was the man who had offered to travel to the Mamar in the harsh January winter to perform Temmonin's rites of passage.

"Tell us about yer scuff with the Gorma." As he finished his sentence, he was distracted by a noise. He turned with the rest of his family to watch a figure move through the hide-covered doorway.

"Make sure ya tell 'em who the hero was!" Damowan's jest burst into the room like the spirit of a flash flood. And bodies, grins, and laughter rose to greet him like waves rush to greet the shore. Temmonin watched his younger brother kissing and sparking lights in the eyes of his relatives. The two exchanged an easy grin as the younger found a seat near the fire.

"And how have the miracle poultices of the North Woods treated your wounds?" Nosh seemed to have an affection for the harshness of life.

"Uncle Nosh, your healers wade through herbs that exist only in the dreams of the healers in the marshes. I feel so much better, I could start back home right now. But I'll wait fer a meal and a night's rest so's not to offend my hosts." Facetious politeness rolled from his frolic. "Now, brother Temmonin, what was that you were sayin' about me?"

The elder brother began amidst waning chuckles, "Damowan and I had been huntin' fer elk fer almost two weeks when we smelled blood and fire nearby. We went to investigate and we were ambushed by the thing. It's almost as if it gored a wapiti and laid it out for us as bait. I took the first fire-paw across my face and, when I got up, Damowan was on him slashin' at his neck. My spear was useless--one lunge and I was on the ground again. Then I used my bow. With Dama's woodpecker arm shreddin' its neck and five of my

27

arrows goin' into its side, it lost its grip on brother, here."

"But I think he wanted me to have somethin' to remember him by." With Damowan's interjection, the family began to fill the air with a multitude of questions. As he answered each one, Temmonin began to feel emanations from his cousin Zheva. More than once, he gazed across the fire to meet her admiration. As they ate, she served the family. And it seemed as though she had requested this task just for the privilege of serving Temmonin. After the meal, he and Damowan retired to the longhouse of their hostess.

A clumsy scraping stirred Temmonin from sleep. From his place next to the outside wall, the noise seemed to be only inches away. He rolled to his side, his right eye hugging the dirt, and peered through the crack between the earth and the wall of the house. Although the moon was bright, he could decipher only abstract shadows--but something was moving. He rolled to his back again and lay still for a moment, trying to decide how curious he had become; whether the risk of waking his hosts was worth stealing outside to glimpse a shadow dashing into the brush.

As he pondered, his eyes followed the pale smoke which rose from the dying fire. Temmonin spat a syllable of realization. Then, he held still. How could he have forgotten that dream?

From what he could tell, Temmonin had not waked anyone as he crept from the room and down the hall. He slipped as quietly as he could into the night. The moon was nearly full and greeted him as if it had been waiting. Moving slowly so as not to be noticed, he bent and peeked around the aspen corner post of the longhouse.

A grunt from behind him shot adrenaline to his extremities. He snapped his head back toward the door.

"Shhh." His brother's half-shadowed face gleamed a ridiculous smile, interrupted by the thin finger he had raised to his lips.

"What're you doin', Damowan?" Temmonin whispered.

"Investigatin'."

"Did you hear it too?"

"No, I didn't hear a thing 'cept fer you."

Then the scraping was much nearer.

Temmonin motioned Damowan to stillness and moved his head until his right eye broke the plane at the edge of the house. Before he could stop it, a spurt of laughter leapt from his lungs. Damowan rushed to see the object of his brother's amusement and the two watched as a large porcupine lumbered into the relative safety of the underbrush. They laughed whispers at its clumsiness. And Damowan laughed at Temmonin's exaggerated interest in the noises of the night forest.

"Damowan, you woulda done the same thing if you'd've heard it."

"Prob'ly not."

"Oh, yea, how could I fergit. I could cut yer arm off while you're sleepin' and you'd think you'd had a bad dream."

"Well, let's jus' hope we don't bug as many people on the way in as you did when you left, Mister 'I carry thunder in my moccasi. . .'"

"Damowan, wait! Wait!" Temmonin was ecstatic.

Damowan was already half-way through the entrance to the house, "What?"

"Damowan, I remembered somethin' jus' before I came out here. A dream. It was the night after you were burned."

Silent, Damowan stared at his brother, using Temmonin's eyes as mirrors with which to search his own memory.

"There was a woman spirit--Ek-Birin. And six dancers. . ." Temmonin began.

"'When to tell the blessing? When to give the tale?' er somethin' like that, eh?" Damowan's trance broke.

"What? But you were asleep, Dama.

"In my dream, you were asleep."

"I can't believe I forgot this until now."

"Neither can I."

II.   And of this food we partake often not
knowing in what way it will cause us to grow or if it
will be, in fact, a detriment to our destinies or to
those who through no choice of their own bear the
consequences of our decisions. For surely the foot
that races to aid a brother in peril often, in so doing,
crushes the threshold or the dwelling or the lives of
others to whom, at the time of its passion, it gave
little thought. And in our casuistic ignorance, we
serve this food to others who, in their time, may
again serve us. We, as often as they, flee the foot of
the approaching giant.

CHAPTER 2

As they left the village, Damowan lifted satisfied eyes to the horizon. "I don't think Uncle Nosh'll ever change. At least he hasn't since we saw him last time."

"But his daughters have."

"Hmmn. I didn't notice." Damowan responded. But Temmonin's cocked eyebrow drew a smile from his brother's feigned ignorance.

After four days, they passed out of Imnanaw Kanat and into the foothills that stepped down to the vast swamp region of Shushunu. Having spent nearly a week in mountain air, the marsh-dwellers were gladdened at the sight of low land. And, three days later, even ghostly autumn showers could not douse their joy as they gained the north shore of Zazamma and surveyed their beloved fen for the first time since just after the last full moon.

They arrived home five days later than the last of the other parties. They were welcomed by an amalgamation of relief, disappointment, excitement, and, as the brothers had anticipated, derision. Certain rivals seemed to have been born to fulfill a destiny of prohibiting others from fully enjoying the life of the tribe. From what Damowan and Temmonin could gather, this was the decree to which Chaneerem and Jemalemin were devoted. Throughout the barrage of questions, kisses, and playful scoldings that the two late arrivals received, the other two stood as sad commentaries on social grace, aloof and half-drunk with mocking condescension. For the most part, Temmonin and Damowan ignored them. When their mother and father found them, the two sons had completely forgotten about the scoffers. And when Damowan's eyes focused on the shy approach of the woman of his affections, he probably would have had to have been reminded that they existed at all.

Temmonin watched as Damowan knelt before Nawana. Although his own attention was divided, the elder thought he saw his younger brother trembling from the strain of harnessed passion. He wished he might always feel as close to Damowan as at that moment.

Temmonin's mother and father kissed and hugged him. Both consoled him for the lack of an elk. Feeling as if he were creating excuses for his and his brother's idleness, he related the facts of Damowan's injury. At that, both parents turned to their youngest son and left Temmonin to his thoughts. After a moment, he went to relieve himself of his burdens and to find his sister.

Tutumora sat with her back to the door pulling her bone needle through overlapping pieces of deer leather--probably a coat for the coming winter. She sat in a chiaroscuro drawn by the afternoon sun that slipped through cracks in the longhouse wall. His sister had found a fairly broad beam in which to sit. There she sewed, deaf to the presence of her onlooker. Temmonin drew his lips together and whistled the call of the cardinal. With the tension of a startled chipmunk, she chirped an alarm and swung her head. Her brother shattered her tension with a howl of laughter that quickly fell silent as his body continued to shake. She lay down her work, ran to him, and beat his chest with her fists.

Temmonin allowed her to beat until he felt it proper to greet her, at which time he held her fists and kissed them. She laughed. Then they hugged.

"What're ya makin'?" Temmonin asked.

"Oh, a coat for Papa. His old one is totally worn out. Y'know, the one Mama made for him out of elk hide at least eight winters ago," she answered.

"Ah, the spider web coat." They both chuckled.

"Did you two git a wapiti?"

"No, girl, but there's plenty from the other hunters to feed us fer a little while. But I got some skins." And as Temmonin finished his sentence, he shifted his shoulder to display his take. He walked to the fire pit and lay the four skins on the ground. "This porcupine's pretty big. Plenty of long needles fer us to make stuff with. And two more fox tails fer yer dancin' shawl."

"Thanks, my wonderful brother who stays on hunt almost a week longer than he's s'posed to."

"Yea, but idleness has its advantages. We stayed at Uncle Nosh's fer two nights. It was a blast. Dama's back was killin' him—he got burnt by this fire-bear thing—but don't worry, he's already doing way better-- but it was great."

Tutumora's face dropped, "Maybe I could be idle fer a while and go somewhere and see someone or do somethin' someday."

Temmonin remained silent long enough to let her know of his empathy. He wondered, had he been born a female, would he be a frustrated fawn like Tutumora or a willful doe like his mother, Semarda. Or might he be as daring as the women known to him only in stories--those young women who, being entirely unwilling to submit to watching their brothers ride the rapids of life into the heart of history and, being entirely uninterested in manipulating the man to which they were to be married and, being entirely disgusted by the prospect of raising daughters who would surely look on as their brothers succeeded or failed attempts to live out their mother's aspirations; those young women who had left their families and tribes to learn, with sisters of similar spirit, the ways of the deer. Would he have the courage of the Chavva? Had he, in having been born male, been excused from such decisions? And was his conformity to the conventions of tribal manhood even a whisper of valor when compared with the passion of those women?

His sister punctured his swelling thoughts, "And here comes our wolverine of a brother."

Temmonin heard the rest of the family chattering their way down the longhouse hall and then through the door flap. In their wings, they carried that comfort by which he recognized home. Except for the relation of the story of the Gorma and the rest of the hunt, their meal and the ensuing evening might have been one of hundreds they had shared. It was good to be back.

And the following day stirred in Temmonin a rush of anticipation reminiscent of other days he had waited for victory dances. Although he had not always tasted victory, he had usually found it extremely natural to participate in the celebrations. Tonight, however, he and Damowan would swallow defeat. They had returned home late and empty-handed. Had he and Damowan been first to return with an elk and had any of the others been wounded or arrived late or unsuccessful, Temmonin and Damowan would have felt the need to share the victory. Chaneerem and Jemalemin surely would not feel such mercy.

That evening, he sat and forced himself to watch as several older men began to beat leather drums and to chant. These elders had not been hunting this time but they had gained victory on many occasions before and knew exactly what would arouse the dance in those who had just returned. The twelve victors began circling the bonfire. Glancing sidelong at Damowan, Temmonin saw a frustrated warrior, eyes averted from the dance and even from the affectionate stares of his beloved. But the dance called to Temmonin and his curiosity was too great. Although he hoped he might avoid Chaneerem's glare, he was prepared for the embarrassment that would certainly follow.

For a while at least, all twelve dancers seemed engrossed in their performance. The fire shot from the ground as if molten anger from a pore in the earth's skin and this fury sparked passion in those who felt its breath. The twelve moved counter-clockwise, the younger men dipping and twirling, the older men focusing their energies on less elaborate expressions. Each held a long staff in his right hand and a wand of feathers in his left. Their shoulders, arms, and legs were draped with leather fringe, squirrel tails, and yellow flicker feathers. Their forearms and ankles were laden with bracelets and anklets of shells, twigs, and clay beads, the clatter of which mimicked the choral pounding of the deer hide drums. The slow, deliberate crescendo of the chanters provoked the party by degrees until, like water gradually boiled, they seethed with frenzy.

The fire grew only hotter and the dance only wilder. For a moment, Temmonin imagined that Chaneerem and Jemalemin had forgotten him and Damowan. They he saw the cue. Amidst a heated crowd of Ek-Birin gathered and enveloped in the glory of clan life, two adolescents continued their heedless course toward undermining all that was sacred. In snide symmetry, Chaneerem and Jemalemin touched their feather wands to the flame and, in contrast to the motion of the other ten dancers, whirled away from the fire pit and toward Temmonin and Damowan.

Temmonin watched as a familiar attitude crept across Damowan's face--an attitude that had always told the elder when to stop his brotherly jests. But Chaneerem and Jemalemin were not Damowan's brothers. And they had spent far too little time with him to recognize in his eyes the livid promises of pain that balanced now so treacherously between the suppressions of discipline and the release of fury. Blind to the signs, the two dancers carried their taunts dangerously close to the waiting volcano.

Temmonin had often felt as he did now. Countless times, he had wished he could transfer his composure to his brother. Yet, at the same time, he had always coveted his brother's abandon. If he had his brother's ability to ignore propriety, however, he would also need Damowan's ability to forget so as not to torment himself with endless regret. As it was, the elder had already harvested fields of regret from experiences the whole world had surely forgotten. Memory was like a leech that sucked at life. But to remove the monster, Temmonin might also lose his heart. Damowan was in no such danger.

Both Chaneerem and Jemalemin had converged on him. Temmonin snapped from thought just in time to watch them raise their smoldering feather wands to their mouths and blow cinders at his brother. That was all Damowan needed. Before Temmonin could stop him, his younger brother leapt and drove his right fist at Jemalemin. Temmonin jumped forward.

Damowan's left fist, intended to add to the damage done by his right, pounded into Temmonin's chest as the elder tackled the younger. The two fell to the dust and rolled heavily away from the taunters. Damowan struggled momentarily but eventually desisted; his older brother knew the wisdom of restraint. Lying beneath Temmonin, he turned with him to view the results of his outburst.

Jemalemin's nose was bleeding. His hands, now doused in red, could not quell the stream that washed his chest and arms like the residue of regret. But he seemed oblivious to regret and to the one who had just caused his pain.

But if Jemalemin were oblivious to Temmonin and Damowan, Chaneerem was oblivious to anyone but those two brothers. As they rose to their knees, he leveled a glare at them that seemed to be fed from subterranean chambers of lethal steam. He stood with a rush. Some of the dancers had attempted to continue their celebration. Now all of them had halted and, with the remainder of the village, watched Chaneerem. He, as if insuring the attention of all present, shifted his eyes from side to side while reaching into the pouch attached to his loin cloth. From it, he withdrew a large, black talon. Breathing malice, he turned to his wounded brother and, dropping to one knee before him, smeared the claw with the blood glaze on Jemalemin's chest. He stood again.

Like an announcement, he raised the glistening talon in his right hand far above his head for the village to witness. Then he plunged the point down into his left palm. He held it there until red rivulets threaded his fingers and gathered on the back of his hand to drop to the ground. Temmonin begged his memory for interpretations. Chaneerem answered his silent question as he drew the claw to his mouth and licked it clean. The crowd gasped in concert.

"Let my blood be added to his whose blood I shall avenge. Let not this blood pass from me until his offender's pride is slighted in similar manner." Most of the villagers who watched were appalled that Chaneerem would mark so minimal an offense with such gravity. But he continued, "And let the blood of Damowan rot in the stomach of the Mitsa-Mitsa!"

"You have no right!" One of the elders could hold his rage no longer. Behind him slunk his wife, bearing the natural birth inscriptions of a Mitsa-Mitsa half-breed. As Chaneerem turned to rebuke, she hid her blotched tan and umber flesh in the folds of her robe.

"I have every right," Chaneerem spat, rabid with vindication. He turned from the elder to see his mother and two sisters assisting Jemalemin to their longhouse. He passed them by as the circle of onlookers made way to let them through.

Temmonin and Damowan exchanged concerned glances. The village contemplated in silence and whispers. Temmonin shifted his gaze to his father Amowz. Amowz was staring with disgust at Chaneerem's and Jemalemin's father Zevil and asking with his eyes how Zevil could have allowed such behavior from his eldest son. Zevil stood unscathed in body and spirit and returned Amowz's questions with apathy. But as he turned to join his family, he let a vague look of delight slip through his congealed visage.

Vagueness emanated from his person like the light of the moon over the marsh on a foggy spring midnight. To Temmonin, it seemed that Zevil must have fashioned a mask of vagueness for himself and worn it often. It was not unusual that he wore it to the clan council the following night.

During a tedious discussion about the death of Mantaw's wife and his two children, the mask hung loosely on Zevil's face--a glob of frog eggs might have looked better. Temmonin was drawn to study his slitted eyes and that slitted mouth and those slitted nostrils. Zevil was closed to the council. He was closed to the world. And those slitted apertures to his soul were open just wide enough to glean from the world that which he needed to survive, but closed tightly enough so as not to allow out even the slightest drop of tenderness his heart might bleed. Temmonin was sure Zevil could feel his stare.

"It is clear that Mantaw does not plan to come to council; he still mourns his family. But, my elder, we need his knowledge. He is the only one who studied the death marks upon the victims' bodies before they were raised to their rest." Amowz's urgency drew Temmonin back from his analysis.

Desh, the clan high elder had arrived from his own village that afternoon to conduct the council in Kemkemmayam. "Amowz, you are correct in saying this. But we cannot steal a man's tears from him. If he wishes, he will offer his aid. Besides, we have countless words to speak concerning other matters," he answered Amowz.

Desh was correct about countless words. Temmonin found it very difficult to focus his thoughts on the river of speech that was fed by the tributaries of each village leader. His mind continually climbed from the banks of that river up to the valley of remembrance. He pictured Chaneerem and Jemalemin dancing so near to Damowan's anger. He pictured himself holding

Damowan back from violence. He pictured duplicating on Chaneerem what Damowan had done to Jemalemin. He even pictured the death-blow he would drive at Chaneerem if that fool were to retaliate. Every time a distraction pulled his mind back to the clan council, he found that the muscles of his back were tensed almost to the point of aching. By the end of the meeting, his thoughts had nearly drained his energy.

Then, not far off, there was the sound of a man exerting much effort dragging something. Most of the council turned to see. This new disturbance, like the rest of the conversation, hit Zevil's mask and dripped off as if it were so much rain water.

"Hold the council!" the man's voice called from the edge of the firelight. He was moving toward the gathering.

"Mantaw, what're you doin' here?" Amowz was the first to recognize the new arrival.

"I have some important evidence the council should see."

Several men rose to help Mantaw. Together, they lifted his burden and carried it into the light. It was a body. In the center of the council of elders, Mantaw and the two others laid what appeared to be a costumed corpse of an extremely muscular man. His back was a matted mass of black and brown hair segregated by two broad, vertical yellow stripes which joined at his rump. These markings were almost identical to those on the back of a wolverine. Most of his skin was hidden by hair. From where fingernails and toenails should have grown, ebony claws curved and tapered to threatening points.

Temmonin and the crowd of elders and clansmen huddled closer. Some tugged at the fur,

41

perhaps to discover whether or not it were attached to the skin beneath. Others touched the talons that suddenly reminded Temmonin of Chaneerem's oath the night before--they were very similar. He glanced quickly at the oath-taker. Chaneerem stood beside Zevil, his arms crossed, too proud to be inspired to awe by the terribleness of the creature. Again, Temmonin's thoughts lunged into knolls of dark thought.

"Look at that face." Damowan nudged his brother. "This thing's as nasty as the Gorma."

"Only thing is the fangs aren't as long," Temmonin answered.

Mantaw, who had observed quietly until now, stepped up to the monster and pushed it onto its back with his moccasin-clad foot. Its stomach was dotted with several puncture wounds.

"While the most of you thought me mourning, I tracked the destroyer of my family and destroyed him. The Kumuchska will hear of this!" A glint of revenge tinged Mantaw's eyes as he looked to Desh, the high elder.

"Maybe they already know of it," Chaneerem spoke through impassive lips.

Desh turned to the oath-taker then back to Mantaw, "My son, how did you single-handedly ensnare and lay to rest so fierce a beast?"

"I erected the sign of three bloodied stones and the blood fire which causes all evil spirits to materialize and drink. When he entered my triangle and dipped his paws into the flame, I pierced his belly with arrows from my hiding place in the brush."

"And whose blood was on the three granite stones and in the stone bowl feeding the fire?" Desh seemed to be steering Mantaw.

The younger man hesitated, then stiffened and leveled his eyes at the high elder. "My family's blood stained the stones." He lifted his left arm and pointed to a long scar on the back of his wrist. "With my own, I fueled the fire in the bowl." He braced himself and waited for Desh's reaction.

Desh did not respond immediately. While the council watched, he scanned the strange corpse of the wolverine man. His eyes were troubled. Although everyone wanted to break the tense silence, no one dared speak. When the elder finally spoke, his words were enveloped in a sigh.

"Will our new purpose be to destroy all of the traditions upon which our people depend?" And as he finished, he glanced at Chaneerem then back at Mantaw. He must have learned of the talon-licker's oath from Da, the leader of Temmonin's village. Da was a timid leader. Because of this, he would choose not to confront Chaneerem directly. Temmonin wondered if anyone would confront him directly.

"Mantaw, you are right in saying that the Kumuchska will hear of this. They must be questioned as to their dealings with the evil spirits and with the forbidden tradition. But let us not wax proud lest we too find ourselves consumed by the fire we ourselves set!" Temmonin guessed that this last comment was intended not only as a warning to Mantaw but also to Chaneerem. Desh was a master of discreet rebuke. Often, that skill saved him from more extreme measures he would need to administer had he no such resource. But some people were too slow to recognize the mercy in his subtlety or too impetuous to offer him respect.

"Is it so terrible a thing to serve to others as they have served to you?" Chaneerem asked in ridiculous haughtiness.

"And if every time the puma wished to eat, he killed one of his brothers to reach the deer, how many puma would still roam the hills?" Desh countered.

"Only as many as were worthy of life."

Two nights later, Amowz, Damowan, and Temmonin lay awake on the floor of their longhouse with Semarda and Tutumora. The mother was always curious about council conversations and, as the three men discussed the implications of their clan meeting, they were often forced to explain every detail and the entire context of those conversations to her. For the most part, Tutumora listened and remained silent, her eyes reflecting the dying firelight.

"D'you think they're gonna deal with Chaneerem?" Damowan asked his father.

"With all respect, I doubt that Da will ever say a thing to him. And I don't think Desh got a chance before he left."

"Amowz," Semarda began excitedly, "Do we have to live in fear of Chaneerem's threats as long as we live?"

"No, mother, only until he dips his knife like a cup into the spring of my heart," Damowan punched out his quote and turned to Temmonin.

"And drinks his fill of the juice of revenge until his bowels burst from the potent fermentings of corruption." Both brothers laughed aloud, hardly noticing their mother's demands that they be quiet. Tutumora welcomed the rest from analysis and joined her siblings. But, as Semarda became indignant at her sons' lack of consideration for neighboring families, Tutumora became increasingly annoyed, especially when her mother attempted to enlist Amowz's aid to reprimand the boys. The young fawn slunk back into the folds of her blanket. Eventually, Semarda and her sons settled again.

"Temmonin, Damowan," Amowz spoke slowly, "Da asked me to talk to you too. It's about another trip to Kumuchska territory."

"To question 'em about the forbidden arts?" Damowan asked.

"Among other things," Amowz answered.

"And what? Are we expected to carry that Kumuchska monster's head up to show 'em what killed one of our families?" Temmonin said sarcastically smiling at Damowan.

His father stopped his sons short of laughter, "No Temmonin, the whole body."

"The whole body!? What?" Damowan continued in spite of his mother's renewed efforts to calm him, "Dad, it took three guys to carry that hulk into the firelight. And we're s'posed to hike with it fer ten days?"

"Damowan, you'll have help." Amowz held for a moment. "I'm not really worried about that aspect of the trip."

"Ah, it's once we get to Wolverine territory that bothers you. Dad, don't worry. We know Uncle Nosh's village. We can jus' steer clear of the other villages and go straight there. Besides, we just passed through Imnanaw Kanat without any trouble from. . ."

"No, it's not the Kumuchska that worry me either. It's who you'll be goin' with--who's gonna be sharin' yer load." Amowz seemed to think he needed to say nothing more. Temmonin and Damowan twisted their eyebrows in an effort to conjure names of men who might be hard to deal with. It took less than a moment.

"No way, Dad, not Chaneerem and Jemalemin." And as his father nodded, Damowan spat, "What the heck does Da think he's doin'? Chaneerem might try to kill me out there!" Then, as his mother began to object to the explosiveness of his reaction, "And no, Mama, that's not an exaggeration!"

This time, even Temmonin begged his brother to be quiet. But the froth of Damowan's heart had already spilled beyond the boundaries of his will. Somehow, he managed to contain his passion to a fiery whisper.

"I won't do it! I will not do it! Da can throw me out of the Ek-Birin. I'm not goin' anywhere with that claw-suckin' demon!"

Damowan seemed to be finished. Still, Temmonin paused before he questioned Amowz, "Dad, why would Da ask us to do such a stupid thing? What could he possibly be thinkin'?"

"Temmonin, you know Da almost as well as I do. I'd already destroyed all his excuses even before he could argue with me. But that man is as stubborn as the North Mountains. Once he's convinced of somethin', he doesn't even know how to change his mind."

Semarda gritted her teeth and wondered aloud, "How can the same man be so weak-willed and so stubborn at the same time?"

Amowz responded with empathy, "I don't know, Semarda, but he does it better than anyone I've ever known in my life."

"But, what could he be thinkin'? What good could he possibly think would come of this?" Temmonin asked.

"He thinks Chaneerem was jus' spittin' steam when he made that vow the other day. He thinks the four of you'll work things out while yer out there in the woods."

"He thinks that flesh-eater and his crowfoot brother'll stick knives in both our backs one hazy midnight and blame it on the cougar of the foothills!" Damowan sliced. "There ya go! No more rivalry!"

Semarda objected, "Damowan, I don't think Da would be that ridiculous!"

"I can hear it now: 'Da, what a lovely village you have. No lack of food or shelter, always a host of pleasant smiles--and no nasty brotherhood rivalries! So Da chows the corn without the sweat of the plow. What a gallant chief we have!"

During a short pause in the conversation, Temmonin wondered if, had he been the village leader, would he be any different.

Tutumora interrupted his thought. She spoke shyly perhaps unsure if her question would be worthy of being asked. "Dad, why do those boys hate Temmonin and Damowan so much?"

Actually, Temmonin could think of no question more worthy of being posed.

"Tutu," began Amowz, "it's hard to say really. But I'm pritty sure it stems back to the time when their father Zevil and I were about your brothers' ages. Well maybe even farther back than that 'cuz Zevil's dad was a tyrant. You think Zevil's hard on his sons, you shoulda seen their grampa." He whistled and shook his head. Semarda added her assent with a strong nod of her head. "But anyway, I think the present state of affairs goes back to when Zevil and I were young warriors and I first visited the Mamar to call on yer mother here. I was here fer most of a month and, y'know, tryin' my hardest to impress the woman of my dreams." He raised his eyebrows quickly a couple of times as he glanced at Semarda before continuing. "I think I went a little too far fer Zevil's likin'"

"What'd ya do Dad?" asked Temmonin. "Steal his sweetheart too?" Everyone laughed at that.

"Actually, yer not too far off, son," said Amowz slightly embarrassed. "It seems that while yer mother here was playin' all hard-to-get, Kemlanna--you know Saffaloon's and Tatakemm's mother?" He paused. "Well, it wasn't anything I was plannin' on doin' but I sorta won Kemlanna's heart in the process of tryin' to win yer mother's heart. Y'know, all the young men would be spear-fishing and showin' their stuff with a bow and arrow and of course all the young ladies're tryin' to be all secretive but ev'rybody knows they're checkin' us out the whole time. Come to find out, Kemlanna's takin' longs looks at yer dear ol' dad here. But I don't even think I had to try too hard to git her to turn her head. She flitted from man to man like a butterfly. As soon as I left to go back home to Wolverine territory, she fell in love with Geshar and married him a couple of months later."

"Yea, but what does that have to do with Zevil?" Tutumora asked.

"Well, that's just it," explained Amowz, "Kemlanna was sweet on Zevil before I stole her heart. I had no idea what I was doin'. I was young. I can't say that I minded the extra attention." He glanced quickly at his wife and smirked. "And actually, I was able to use the situation to my advantage to git ol' stoneheart over here to move my way a little." At that, Semarda punched him in the shoulder as their children laughed. "But I had no idea that I was steppin' on Zevil's toes. You know me. I wouldn't've planned somethin' like that."

Damowan's face twisted. "So jus' 'cuz of that Chaneerem and Jemalemin hate us?"

"Well, it's a little more complicated than that, Damowan. Ya see, as time went on, I still had no clue as to what was goin' on with Zevil so I never apologized. And I guess I kept doin' stuff to irritate him. By the time I figured out what was goin' on, I had a full-fledged enemy on my hands. And nothin' I said made it better. So I stopped tryin' to make it better. I jus' tried to avoid the guy. And after a while I could see where he got his attitude from. His dad was still alive fer a while after I came here and married yer mother and all I had to do is watch how he treated Zevil to figure out why he turned out the way he did. The problem is that when he had his two sons and we had you two, well he just did what he was raised with--he passed on his grudge to his kids. You guys never did anything in particular to git 'em to not like ya. But you know how it is. Ya pritty much believe the stuff yer dad and mom tell ya."

"So there's no use in tryin' to talk with 'em-- maybe with some of the elders?" Temmonin asked.

"Some people ya jus' can't talk to." Amowz answered with a sigh.

That statement seemed to close the discussion. Silence saturated the room; dark and swollen silence that spread plump hands across the mouths of the family so that each was left to his thoughts until sleep persuaded him away from reason. Temmonin, however, lay watching his family slip into slumber.

Damowan's breath elongated so rapidly that his older brother imagined he had fallen asleep the instant he had stopped speaking. And probably with sleep came the settling of his heart. In part, Temmonin envied him for that ability; to forget the impetus for anger as soon as it was expressed. Damowan was like a geyser that spat its scald often, but gladly invited the sun to dry its skin after the ritual of emission was complete. If Damowan were a geyser, Temmonin was a tepid swamp where thoughts like stagnant water mingled and remingled in ever-changing confines of sameness. Often, it seemed that no new thoughts drifted in and that nothing would ever trickle out to nourish the rest of the forest. Of course, Temmonin knew that he had been of some benefit to others. But he felt that this could only have been possible because those expressions had escaped his concentration as he stirred his contained pool of comparisons, guilt, and regrets. If he could read his older brother's thoughts, Damowan would surely laugh. Oh, to fall asleep.

Moon Beneath the Mountains

III.   But shall we bring this giant to trial, knowing full well that whatever jury we might choose to choose his fate would be equally or to a greater degree stained with that same tar of ignorance from which at some point all with the slightest inclination toward knowledge flee? And were we to view the evidence that accused this giant and reconstruct the myriad of civilizations and cultures inscribed into his monstrous heel, could we not, by offering our own heels for study, mirror those deaths in microcosm? And might not those we scrape from our heels also raise their heels to mirror those of their banes? And, upon careful examination, might we not find an infinity of dissected mirrors; facet upon facet, held together only by the fragile capillaries that diffuse the blood of history to those who stalk its forests? And when held to the light, might not these countless facets resemble the bewildered reflections of mica or the coruscated eyes of the dragonfly? Being overwhelmed by such a multitude of images, dare we condemn the giant? And who among the images is the giant?

CHAPTER 3

Since their father had relayed Da's decision to him and Damowan, Temmonin had spent most of his emotional energy accepting the fact. Now, two mornings later, as ripe Osage oranges began to drop from the trees, he knelt with Damowan and ceremonially kissed the ground of their birthplace. The anxious fingers of autumn cold had coaxed from the surrounding marsh waters wandering throngs of steam that played with the dawn sun. Some of the sunbeams danced through the fog to splash the cedars with rosemilk. The nourishment of such sights and smells and sounds strengthened Temmonin and Damowan against their impending duty.

Chaneerem and Jemalemin arrived at the meeting point without their family and, since Temmonin's and Damowan's family had already left them, the four faced each other alone across the wrapped body of the Kumuchska monster. Damowan's eyes avoided the others. Instead, he studied the slender aspen trunks that his father had lashed together to form the drag-trailer with which they were to transport the dead beast. As Temmonin gathered himself to meet Chaneerem's stare, he was met with slate. Stone frigid eyes sliced at Temmonin and stirred queasy unrest in his stomach. Looking away, he pictured three weeks of tedious anxiety; continuous strain that would steal from all four of them the joy they might feel if Chaneerem knew how to forgive. Jemalemin seemed less interested in revenge than he did in avoiding his present situation. As the two younger brothers stole glances at each other, Chaneerem blurted a rough directive and began northwest

53

toward Zazamma. Jemalemin followed after a short hesitation. Temmonin and Damowan waited, allowing enough space to fall between them and the other two that they might converse freely. Because the drag trailer was built for only two couriers and the others had ignored it, Temmonin and Damowan each hefted an end of the yoke. Damowan's shoulders had for the most part been spared from the paws of the Gorma so he was able to join Temmonin in carrying the load. His older brother knew better than to wonder if Damowan was fit to do this. The two pulled away from the village.

The next three days passed with little event. Being proud and unsociable, Chaneerem avoided any village on their path. And because of the distance between them and the other two, Temmonin and Damowan could not question his choices. Except for occasions when the oath-taker would grunt that it was time to hunt for a meal or to sleep for the night, few words passed between the two parties. Traveling in this formation eased strife while they hiked, but did nothing to relieve the awkwardness of eating meals together. Temmonin wondered if their separation during transit might even have added to the frustration of coming together again. But propriety and safety demanded that they camp together each night, especially since Chaneerem was avoiding the safety of friendly villages.

Damowan was nervous as evening grayed the air the third day. "Temmonin, I think we should take watches," he said.

"That wouldn't be too obvious, would it?" Temmonin responded with sarcasm.

"Well, it's not like it's a mystery that Chaneerem'd like to see me dead. You'd better watch it too. You're not exactly his buddy."

"What, 'cuz you couldn't control yerself at the victory dance, now I have to lose half my sleep ev'ry night?" Temmonin started loudly but quieted himself so as not to reveal the subject of their speech to the others.

"Well, thanks for all yer sacrificial brotherly love, Temmonin."

The elder held his tongue after his brother's pronouncement of mock gratitude. Although he felt justified in refusing to keep watch, he soon recognized a familiar inflection in his emotions. Was it really so much to ask of him to guard his brother's life? Was sleep and comfort so very precious? And how would he himself have reacted if, at the victory dance, Chaneerem and Jemalemin had approached him instead of Damowan? Could he have remained objective? Temmonin felt the press of reason driving him to agree with Damowan. But he could not yet bring himself to discuss his error with his brother. They strode in silence until Chaneerem called for a halt. As they approached the talon-licker and his brother, Temmonin mumbled apologetically to Damowan,

"Maybe if we jus' lay down like we're sleepin' but one of us stays awake at all times."

"That'd be good." Damowan's disappointment subsided somewhat.

Chaneerem was the only one of the four who seemed to desire to speak and it appeared that he enjoyed the dominance he held over the others. He called for rests, meals, and hunts. Up until this point, he had also indirectly assigned to Temmonin and Damowan the task of hauling the drag trailer. This, however, hardly bothered Temmonin and Damowan--Chaneerem and Jemalemin would soon take their shift.

"We'll camp by these rocks tonight. Zazamma is only a short hike farther north--we can fill our water skins t'morrow mornin'. We'll use the rest of the rabbit fer dinner." Chaneerem's tone was as flat as shale. Surely it was intentional that he had failed to recognize that Temmonin had hunted this rabbit.

As Temmonin collected brush and a couple of fallen birch logs for a fire, Damowan prepared their tent-skin. He tied the ropes attached to the upper corners of the squarish skin to a pair of cedars that stood some fifteen feet apart. He then found two raccoon-sized stones around which he wrapped the ropes connected to the bottom two corners of the skin. He adjusted the position of these stones until all four ropes were taut and the skin they suspended hung high enough off the ground for Damowan to crawl beneath.

Temmonin was arranging stones for a fire pit when he glanced at the lean-to. "The Creator has sent a mother elk to shelter us in her belly should the sky be sad tonight." It was Temmonin's first attempt at humor since they left their village. He knew it was a painfully weak attempt.

Damowan poked his head from behind the elk hide tent, "And so long as our mother's waterproofing job holds," He pointed to a pair of seams where the three wapiti skins were sewn to make one; they were smeared with translucent pine sap, "Mother elk here will save us from those sad tears of the clouds."

They laughed fabricated laughs. Both knew their comments were not at all humorous, yet they were tired of the ruthless seriousness that hung like dead salmon from their shoulders. Temmonin saw Chaneerem look up from where he knelt stretching his and Jemalemin's shelter. He felt as if the talon-

licker had slapped him. Chaneerem's expression
was the embodiment of pompous sarcasm.
Temmonin immediately looked away, feeling more
like a child than he had since before his rites of
passage. Perhaps he had never felt this childish
even when he was a child. He busied himself with
the fire and ignored his urge to spit at Chaneerem.

From a nearby tree, Jemalemin had
gathered enough chestnuts to fill eight hungry men.
He lay his harvest near the fire Temmonin had
started. Damowan had begun unwrapping the
remains of the rabbit in Temmonin's pouch when
he spied the inviting nuts. He reached for one.

"There's a whole tree full of those within
easy walkin' distance," Chaneerem interrupted
Damowan.

"What? Y'mean..." Damowan's objection
was cut short.

"Yea, I mean you can git yer own!"
Chaneerem gritted.

Damowan started to rise.

"Damowan," Temmonin whispered
anxiously, "Jus' go get yer own."

Damowan was incensed. "I can't believe
this!" His arms flailed through the air as he
stomped off into the brush, head down.

His older brother fumbled with the leather
sack in which the rabbit lay. He wondered if he
looked as much like a child as he felt.

Damowan returned empty-handed. He was
not chewing anything either. Temmonin concluded
that he had not gone to collect nuts but to calm
down. As Temmonin cut the remaining rabbit meat
into four portions, Chaneerem, Jemalemin, and
Damowan joined him at the fire. Each grabbed a
stick and, jabbing it through the meat, used it to
roast his meal over the blaze. Except for the cracks

of the flames and an occasional hiss when juices spilled on the hot rocks, silence shrouded the camp.

Chaneerem looked and ate with stern decisiveness, as if trying to impress upon the others that even in such simple aspects of life, he was superior. Sitting between the talon-licker and Damowan, Jemalemin looked more uncomfortable than ever and Temmonin thought the boy would either burst from tension or disappear altogether. Temmonin was confused at Jemalemin's behavior. He had never spent much time near the boy but he had never seen anything like this before. Damowan ignored the others while he ate. When he had finished, he leaned back on his right arm and accidentally scattered a number of the chestnuts Jemalemin had collected.

Jemalemin surprised the group as he offered quietly, "You can have one if ya like."

The others stared at him for a moment. Damowan had begun to decline the offer when Chaneerem bent his brow and rasped, "What, can't he git his own?"

"Can't he speak fer himself?" Damowan protested.

"Damowan's right, Chaneerem. Let Jemalemin make some of his own decisions."

"Seems t'me, you sound a whole lot more smart when you keep yer mouth shut, Temmonin!" Chaneerem blasted across the fire.

"And we'd all be a whole lot happier if you'd get rid of some of that lava you're carryin' around in yer gut!" Damowan was half-squatting and ready to stand as he spoke.

Chaneerem reached for his stone knife as he blurted, "Ya wanna talk about the lava in my gut?"

But before either Damowan or Chaneerem could stand, Jemalemin leapt up and screeched at his brother with unprecedented abandon,

"I was jus' offerin'! I didn't mean nuthin' by it! Ya don't have to pull out yer stinkin' knife!" Then he slumped to the ground as quickly as he had risen, head in his hands.

A moment passed.

"Well, if you like bein' made a fool of. . ." Chaneerem started.

Jemalemin's voice hissed like the juice on the hot rocks, "It doesn't have nuthin' ta do with me being made a fool of!" And he scrambled away to his shelter.

Chaneerem was notably disturbed by his brother's actions. As stars began to materialize between the charcoal clouds overhead, he shifted his eyes between Temmonin and Damowan. "We all know Jemalemin hasn't become a man yet. Both of you better believe I'm not gonna let either one of you take advantage of that." He too left the fire.

Temmonin and Damowan spoke in whispers.

"Damowan, 'member when we were cubs and we used to run through the squash fields and trip and break the vines?" Temmonin smiled.

"Yea, I remember," Damowan replied, amused.

"And remember how upset Mama and Papa would be at us, and how bad we felt?"

"Yea."

"I think I liked that feeling better than this one."

Damowan thought for a second, "Well," he added, "At least we could make up with Mama and Papa."

They talked long into the night about their youth and how easy life seemed then. But at that time how they yearned to be free from the boundaries of youth to don the shackles of manhood. Finally, they fell asleep. Both forgot to keep watch.

Having slept for several hours, they woke to the splash of rain. Early morning darkness surrounded them and the clouds were dousing the land. As Temmonin shifted from his side to his back, he felt the cold seep of water beneath him. Both his and Damowan's sleeping skins were damp with mist that had drifted beneath the shelter skin through the three exposed sides. He shifted again to discover that the seam overhead was dripping into a puddle just next to his left cheek. He soughed. Damowan groaned. They shifted several times in attempts to avoid the influx of moisture. After an hour of unsatisfied rest, they forfeited their efforts to squeeze comfort from the situation and began packing their camp. Chaneerem and Jemalemin eventually did the same.

Appallingly and yet predictably, Chaneerem again ignored the responsibility of the drag trailer and began north, gulping a wet chestnut. Jemalemin's spirit was as water-logged as his drooping pack. He followed without lifting his head. Damowan shouted a curse that was driven to the mud with the pelting rain. He and Temmonin bent and lifted the inundated trailer to their shoulders.

They caught up to Chaneerem and Jemalemin at the bank of the river Zazamma in a half an hour. The river was vaguely perceptible through the deluge. It almost seemed to encompass them. Temmonin was irritated at the fact that the others were simply standing and watching the rain.

As they stared blankly ahead, he barked through the weather,

"You two have to help us cross!"

Chaneerem responded with an abstract assent.

Surprised at the oath-taker's agreeability, Temmonin and Damowan slipped slowly into deeper water. More than once, one or the other lost his footing in the sucking mud of the river floor. Soon they trudged waist high, then chest high in roiling murk. All four strained against the pressing wall of water.

Temmonin stepped into the heart of the current first. His feet were flung from beneath him and he collided awkwardly into Damowan, his right cheek scraping against the bark of the trailer. Not having expected such violent increase in the speed of the river, he lost his grip and, had it not been for his brother's dexterity, he would have been lost to the other three. Damowan held firmly to his older brother's forearm and drew it back to where Temmonin himself could again grasp the wooden yoke. Then Chaneerem and Jemalemin were ripped downstream and Temmonin and Damowan yanked with them.

Damowan choked on gritty water and hacked profusely as he surfaced. Through the soak, Temmonin could see that the other three had managed to retain their holds on the trailer. Jemalemin was wheezing and spitting and perhaps crying--Temmonin could not decide. Chaneerem's resentment at his own helplessness dominated his attitude but, as Temmonin peered at him, another emotion sweltered in his eyes. He followed the oath-taker's stare downstream for interpretation. Then, like the crash of remembrance, they collided with the gurgling froth of the rapids of Zazamma.

They were blinded with spray. Granite jutted between gusts of foam. Mud reeled and moaned. The river pounded the four meager bodies. Temmonin felt as if he were witnessing the birth of chaos. Or, at least, that he was passing by the ragged wound in earth's veins through which chaos enters the world. For restrained within every life, he thought, there seemed the desire for destruction which, when released, ravaged what usually kept it at bay.

The grinding of his vertebrae against sharp stone wrenched him from this ridiculous poetry. He had no time to curse his wandering mind. Forced by the current, the trailer and the other three carriers pressed him into the rock and pivoted on that focal point of pain in his back. Temmonin clenched his entire being at such pressure and burst into a scream. The weight shifted and he was jerked again into the liquid melee. Before he could reconsider, he relaxed his fingers. The trailer and his companions slipped away from the grey numbness that gradually shielded his mind from the throb in his spine. Then, grey numbness seeped into umber and crimson, muck and blood, and soft, rhythmic pattering.

He swam easily through the tide of evening. Over ancient stands of fir and cottonwood, he floated like a swan of passion. He laughed at the fact that, until now, he had not known how to mimic the osprey and the kestrel. But now the chill after-winds of sunset urged him higher. Zephyrs whispered to his spirit in forgotten phrases only the inflections of which Temmonin understood.

He was startled by an overwhelming exploding of light behind him. And before he could maneuver to improve his view, a blazing comet shattered his vision.

Damowan's sweaty forehead and hair hovered over Temmonin as he woke from sleep. A spark erupted near his left cheek and his body jumped. As he lay back down again, consciousness reorganized the barrage of memories in his mind. There was no comet--only Damowan striking stones to start a fire. But the thought of the stream and the unmoving fact of the rock he had been wedged against presented itself in undeniable terms as he settled to his back. His spine felt as if a spike had been driven into it.

"You up, Temmonin?" Damowan chirped. "How's yer back?"

Temmonin breathed harder but could not speak.

"What were you jus' dreamin' about? Ya shoulda seen yerself." Damowan continued clicking his stones.

His elder brother roused himself, "Where're we at, Damowan?"

"'Bout a stone's throw north of Zazamma. We had to carry you here. You've been out a whole day and a whole night. The sun's up again, but it's cloudy. And it ain't rainin' so much now."

Temmonin glanced around himself at the bed of pine needles on which he lay and then at the branches that hung over him and his brother.

"I can't get this stupid fire started!" Damowan threw down his stones and shifted until his back rested against the trunk of the white pine that gave them shelter. "Everything's wet--our tent, our cloaks, our food-everything!"

"What happened?" Temmonin managed another question.

"Oh, you must've passed out in the rapids. We lost ya fer a second there. But then we all fell a long way down a waterfall. When we surfaced, you were layin' on that Kumuchska thing. We had to ride the rapids fer a long time until we could git to shore. I had to carry you here--and that was no berry pick--the others lugged the monster. It rained fer most of the night and it's been gittin' colder. Jemalemin's been sneezin' and coughin' a lot. I think I might be gittin' sick too."

"You? Sick?" Temmonin was too exhausted to laugh at his own comment and Damowan didn't seem to think it was very funny either. The rain had water-logged everything including his sense of humor. They huddled in damp deer and elk hide and occasionally glanced across the small clearing to where the other two huddled. They had also failed to spark a fire.

So the day passed, muffled by a saturating fog that deadened their voices as they spoke. The smell of moss and shelf mushrooms meandered through the pines and silver maples and cedars. Although the rain eventually ceased, the ever chilling air arrested the moisture where it had seeped, denying comfort to the four battered travelers. They ate, sat, talked, hunted, and slept in the afterdew of the storm that, like a droning mosquito, followed them into the night.

The next morning, Chaneerem's piercing commands ripped Temmonin from slumber. His mind sloshed within the confines of his skull as he strained to comprehend why the oath-taker was talking so loudly so early in the morning. He could not believe that Chaneerem wanted to leave so soon. Temmonin had only one and a half days to recuperate. His back was still throbbing.

"Shall we wait until next spring for the sun to dry our packs?" the talon-licker sliced a verse through the haze as he bundled his skins together. He was obviously intent on leaving immediately.

Moon Beneath the Mountains

Temmonin searched his conscience for reasons to continue on with those other brothers. To his disappointment, he could not allow himself the relief of separating from them. He realized that if it were physically possible for him to begin hiking again, propriety and honor constrained him to the task.

Damowan had not yet moved when Temmonin began to sit up. But as his older brother strained and groaned, Damowan woke in full question.

"Temmonin, what're you doin'?" he asked through his grog.

The elder had righted himself and was preparing to kneel as Damowan scurried out of his covering to stop him.

"Damowan, don't try to stop me!" Temmonin was rife with determination.

"Temmonin, you're gonna kill yerself tryin' to git up! Cut it out!"

But for all of Damowan's pleading, his brother continued through the pain. Movement to Damowan's left momentarily stole his attention. Chaneerem had finished packing and he stood in front of Jemalemin. He spoke loudly enough for Temmonin and Damowan to know that it was actually to them that he was speaking,

"When is it that we should leave, Jemalemin, my brother? When all of life smiles upon us?" Chaneerem's younger brother had no answer to the grandiose question. "Others may choose as they wish. When life decides to smile upon us, at least we'll be closer to our destination." And he dropped to his knees to lift his side of the drag trailer.

"Idiot!" Damowan nearly screamed.

65

Chaneerem halted. With precision, he turned his head in their direction and laughed like an insane crow. The sound thudded without echo into their ears and into the fog. Then the two hefted the drag trailer and pulled away from Temmonin and Damowan.

Temmonin prepared to stand up. Damowan started to help his brother when an awkward series of scuffs and grunts again drew their attention to the others. Damowan could not refrain from snickering then laughing aloud. Temmonin had to limit his amusement to a taut grimace. Somehow, Chaneerem had lost his balance and lay sprawled on the muddy shale, half-pinned to the ground by the yoke of the trailer. Jemalemin had managed to avoid falling but stood dubiously over his partner. The talon-licker gurgled curses at the earth and at Damowan and Temmonin. He then howled at Jemalemin,

"What're you waitin' for? Git this piece of junk off me!"

Jemalemin stooped to ease the pressure and Chaneerem flung the yoke from himself. He gruffly repositioned the burden on his shoulder. Hardly giving Jemalemin a chance to predict his intentions, he again began forward.

"So mister smooth stone has rough edges after all. I thought the guy would never make a mistake," Damowan spoke as his brother circumspectly lifted his body. "That is besides the mistake of bein' the biggest jerk in the whole world."

Temmonin brought himself rigid and, as if groping for health, stretched his arms far over his head. "I don't think I can carry a pack but I guess I'm decent fer travel. I hate to make you lug everything, but. . ."

Damowan interrupted Temmonin, "Well, you did it fer me after I played my little game with the fire-bear. This'll pay ya back fer all yer drudgery. Besides, yer not the one who decided to move on today anyway."

They packed quickly and followed the lead. As was his habit, Chaneerem skirted the villages that lay on their path. Temmonin could only guess that he would not allow himself to need anyone, not even those of his own tribe. But soon they reached the Shushunu and he had never traveled through that region before. They often chanced upon villages there. Still, he painstakingly avoided them.

The path was muddy and the pines and maples soon made way for a growing number of weeping willows. These brooding giants gathered at the edges of the myriad swamps and streams and licked the water with a thousand tongues in the perpetual silence of the autumn fog. And their roots poked up through moss and spongy soil. Smells that seemed to have accumulated for decades wafted from bog to bog and the gargling voices of algae-covered swamp dwellers bubbled through the mist.

Chaneerem and Jemalemin labored with the drag-trailer. Temmonin was grateful that they were so slow; the easier their pace, the less pressure on his back. But he found his pain to be less than he had anticipated--the morning and afternoon passed almost without discomfort. He mentioned his relief to Damowan.

"That hardly excuses that demon from goin' ahead without askin' if it was all right with you."

"Dama," Temmonin replied, "We both know he's an idiot. But the more you hold this grudge, the more right he feels he has to destroy you and the less regret he'll feel if he ever does it."

Damowan halted in front of Temmonin and wheeled to confront his brother. Squinting in exasperation so that he looked as if he were looking directly into the sun, Damowan asked, "How can you say that?"

Temmonin did not answer but raised his shoulders and cleared his face.

"How can you say that, Temmonin?" Damowan repeated loudly. "How can you sit there and bend at every joint? When're you ever gonna stop lettin' that cowbird steal yer nest?"

"What?" But Temmonin could not gather a rebuke or an explanation.

Damowan turned and continued. As he resumed his careful gait, Temmonin thought he saw Chaneerem flash an imperious smile. Embarrassed and insulted, the last in line shook his head and tried to concentrate on the path.

Some time later and before the overcast sky darkened at evening, they came to a place where a well-worn path dissected two large lakes. If they passed between the lakes, they would be clearly visible to anyone on shore. But, because it would take too long to circumvent either body of water, Chaneerem risked an encounter with the Daimadunva and started across the isthmus. They had passed the mid-point of the land bridge when, to their leader's dismay, they heard the rumor of a large group of people ahead. Within moments, a column of Painted Turtle warriors manifested itself through the mist.

The first of the Daimadunva warriors was startled and sent up a sharp chirp to report an encounter to those behind him. Others assembled next to him, curious to share in his find. Seeing that

Chaneerem had not yet lowered the yoke from his shoulders, Temmonin forced himself past his companions and met the leader of the other party. They exchanged the traditional greeting of the members of the four-tribe confederacy as Temmonin had with Shegra of the Kumuchska. And, as before, after they had greeted formally, each leader introduced the remainder of his party.

Temmonin felt ochre with self-consciousness as he spoke, "This is Chaneerem, son of Zevil." The oath-taker looked directly at Temmonin's chest. "And this is Jemalem, brother of Chaneerem." Jemalemin shot an awkward glance at Temmonin then at Chaneerem. "And, finally, this is Damowan, my brother."

His chest was hot and his mind clouded as the Daimadunva led them to their village for the night. Between conversations, he began to ask himself why he had lied about Jemalemin's manhood but he was invariably interrupted. As a result, a sickly unrest nagged his gut. He could not compel himself to look back at his brother. Damowan too must have been wondering why Temmonin had done it.

The ten warriors of the tribe of the Painted Turtle surrounded the Ek-Birin as they walked. This polite gesture eased Temmonin's unrest somewhat. After a whole day of hiking, he was drained but his legs still had enough energy to walk to the small clearing in the center of a village.

Devhamar, the Daimadunva guide, spoke with obvious affection, "This is Mestaumdelmez: Mosshaven, and these are our people."

Clearly, this host of warriors had not been absent from their kin as long as Shegra and his company had been from theirs--no one greeted them. In fact, they bore no bounty, only weapons.

Matthew John Schellenberg

Temmonin suddenly realized that it was odd that no
questions had been asked of him concerning their
purpose or destination. But the Painted Turtle
leader and his fellows were as gracious as Shegra
and his companions had been; perhaps more so.

This village itself was an acme of
graciousness. It was so polite to the swamp and the
forest surrounding it that Temmonin could hardly
feel its intrusion on the landscape. The clan that
had settled here had chosen hillocks as dwellings.
They had excavated them through tunnels in their
sides, leaving their appearance relatively unchanged.
Temmonin noticed women and men entering and
exiting through these openings and imagined turtles'
heads emerging and retracting from within the
confines of their shells. Most of the willow strands
in the area were trimmed to a height just above a tall
man's head, allowing freedom to move beneath
them, but the trees themselves towered massively
overhead, filtering most of the light that fell upon
them. Several Daimadunva stole through this
perpetual, green dusk between the weed-covered
dwellings. None acknowledged the arrival of the
party. Rarely did anyone look their way. Except for
the arguments of crows overhead and bands of
rasping blue jays that wandered through the
overcast, all was at a hush.

An ensemble that now approached them
did so in keeping with the sedated attitude of the
entire village. Two warriors appeared first. Their
chests were painted with crimson, ocher, and olive
to form faces and designs that jiggled in rhythm to
their regular steps. Their actual faces, including
their lips, were smeared with the black mud found
on the floor of certain swamps. To their arms, they
had lashed reeds that hindered any bending at the
elbows. Of all the inhabitants of this village, only

these two warriors wore these strange reeds.
Temmonin recognized these trappings as those of
official mourning. But they were not the signals of
the mourning that follows an accident or an
expected death. These men announced the intent
of justice. The acting leader of the Ek-Birin felt a
nervous apprehension slink into his spirit.

The two sentinels were followed by one
who was obviously the chief of Mestaumdelmez.
From his temples hung strands of heron feathers
that reached to his plump belly. Black mollusk
shells clicked in whispers from his headband and
arm bands as he strode forward. His face was
blackened by mud except for his mouth--the chief
of any clan must speak for his people even in
mourning. Like the two preceding him, he wore a
special loincloth of hanging willow strands; a
garment that covered very little. The Shushunu
men wore these sparse drapings when in mourning
to symbolize the fact that those who had passed
into death could not hide themselves. From the
willow bough staff he carried hung three hollow
turtle shells.

The clams and clay beads on his anklets
rested as he stopped in front of the arriving party.
"Mok, the leader of the Daimadunva that dwell in
Mestaumdelmez greets those who pass through this
place. Be welcome in our midst."

Temmonin thought his tone less inviting
than his words and searched his expression for
other signs. Nothing but wrinkled eyelids and
cheeks and jowls stared back. Before an
embarrassing amount of time could pass,
Temmonin returned his greeting, "Mok, peace and
beauty to you and your clan."

At that, the chief and his sentinels returned
the way they had come. The ten who had found the

Ek-Birin began to follow their leader, motioning for their guests to join them. Temmonin mulled over his impressions. This chief had not offended him-- those who mourn were not obligated to raise their arms and touch their lips in formal greeting. But something told the Ek-Birin that Mok was warm with preoccupations other than death.

As they crossed the clearing, they entered forest thick with pines and cedars and undergrowth. The path they traveled, however, was well-trodden and led to another clearing, a clearing carefully groomed and shrouded with gravity. A treeless hill marked the center of the circular glade. White pine gathered around the edges. The green growth on the hill was trimmed so short that as Mok and the sentinels walked across it, Temmonin could not see evidence of where they had just passed.

The chief halted on the opposite end of the clearing at a considerable oak stump. The tree had been cut at eye level and a seat with a back and armrests had been carved into the grain. Three holes near the bottom of the stump acted as a ladder and, with the aid of his two accomplices, Mok climbed these steps and adjusted himself in his throne. He lay his staff across his knees. The turtle shells clattered. He snorted.

One of the sentinels spoke, "Will those in question now step forward." This was not an invitation but a command in polite words. The four young Flickers hesitated.

"Will the four Ek-Birin now step forward and face Mok."

Without speaking, Temmonin and Damowan proceeded to the crest of the hillock. Chaneerem and Jemalemin, still bearing the drag trailer, met them there. For the first time since they had encountered this clan, they lowered the trailer

to the ground and stood beside the other two. Mok
glowered down at them from his place.

The chief opened his wide mouth and
several slithering and gulping sounds slipped out.
The sentinel immediately followed with an
imperative in Mokhamoyuba,

"State your purpose in passing through
these lands."

"Wha. . ." Damowan cut his own objection
short. They stood entirely vulnerable upon this rise
and they were grossly outnumbered.

"My chief," Temmonin responded, "Your
servants, the servants of the Creator, we of the Ek-
Birin, travel through the land of Shushunu and that
of the Daimadunva with urgent concerns for the
Kumuchska of Imnanaw Kanat. We thank you for
your gracious hospitality."

Mok again garbled and sipped several
sounds. The sentinel again interpreted, "Of what
nature are the concerns of the Ek-Birin?"

Temmonin guessed that the leader of the
Painted Turtles was speaking Shushunushu but he
never remembered the language of the swamp tribe
to be so foreign. "The Ek-Birin carry messages of a
very serious nature to their sister clan, the
Kumuchska, to the village of Shemtootoo where
Nosh leads the clan."

Mok showed signs of irritation at
Temmonin's elusive answers. He spat a string of
slimy words directly at the Ek-Birin.

Almost as if to retract his chief's anger, the
sentinel translated in his insipid tone, "Of what
specific nature are the concerns of the Ek-Birin?"
Even in his flat interpretation, he emphasized the
word 'specific'.

Temmonin held for a moment. He looked
at Damowan. Inadvertently, he clenched his fists.

"We of the Ek-Birin wish to honor the trust of the confederacy and ask that the Daimadunva also honor that tru. . ."

Mok sizzled and hit his chest with his right fist. His body roused from side to side in the oak throne. He sliced several sentences, rife with rage.

Then the sentinel, "The trust that kills will be killed."

Temmonin stood steady but his heart was groping through the bars of his ribs for more air. The sentinel had obviously been selective in his last translation. What else had Mok threatened? Why did Mok refuse to speak to them directly? What had caused this suspicion? This hostility?

"Gracious Mok," Temmonin began, "Your servants wish only to honor their own clan and the clan to which they bear news."

Silence dropped around the glade like a thousand maple seeds. Mok no longer shivered with anger; no longer frowned. He spoke stoic words into the soft swamp air.

And the sentinel, "Then you will die."

Damowan could no longer restrain himself, "How can you do this!? You have no respect for our people! What are you accusing us of? How will you explain this to our families? Will you tell them you executed us because we accepted your hospitality?"

"Infidel!" The sentinels were as surprised as the rest that Mok was suddenly speaking directly to the Ek-Birin and in Mokhamoyuba, "What rightful price shall a man pay for the ravaging and murder of my eldest daughter!?"

Awe constricted the throats of the Ek-Birin. Now they comprehended the object of Mok's mourning. They also understood the reason for his offense.

"Kill them!" Mok spat.

The men crowded around them, pressing sense-giving air from their lungs. Temmonin stumbled through the bracken that cluttered his mind. A flush of fear reddened his vision and he swooned. The Daimadunva closed. His eyes shivered. Damowan lurched forward and pivoted.

Then Jemalemin whispered to Temmonin, "Temmonin, let's show 'em the monster thing!"

Temmonin turned and flashed a grateful look at the boy. In the heart of his panic, he had forgotten that they did have a good reason to be traveling this way. "Mok, my chief." With that, the warriors held their approach. Temmonin straightened himself and continued. "Since you have so clearly demonstrated the need to know the specific nature of our communications with the Kumuchska, it can only honor your servants to reveal that information to you. Forgive us for our obstinance."

Jemalemin was fumbling with the leather that covered their burden. Damowan stooped to help remove it. The talon-licker stood stone silent, his pride aching but unexpressed. Temmonin glanced quickly at his harsh brows and those poisoned brown eyes, averting his gaze before Chaneerem could respond.

As the two younger brothers pulled back the last of the wrappings, a putrid gust of decay permeated the glade. Those surrounding the four winced and stepped back. Mok dropped from his throne and made his way forward. With the rest, he stared at the wolverine man. Gangrene had soured the leather of its hide, but the Painted Turtle chief needed to examine this evidence. He nudged its side with his foot.

"My chief," Temmonin explained, "This monster stole the lives of three Ek-Birin--a woman and two children, Mantaw's family." As Mok knelt to move the monster's head, he shifted the bloated corpse enough to release a rank miasma from its mouth. He stood and retreated a step as Temmonin furthered his explanation, "We have been sent to the Kumuchska to inquire as to their dealings with the forbidden arts." The Ek-Birin could think of nothing more.

The chief dwelt long on this. When he spoke, he did so with obvious repentance of his fury, "You were wise to reveal your mission to us." Mok's congenial tone relieved Temmonin. "My daughter may have been slain by some corruption similar to this. Her body was covered with blisters and burns and char marks." He looked again at the heap of hair and hide. "Please, stay with us this night and may our hospitality heal what wounds I have created."

Temmonin was shocked at this man's capacity to convert his thunderous ravings into such refreshing gregariousness. Somehow, in spite of what could be interpreted as vacillation on the chief's part, he felt he could trust this Daimadunva leader. Damowan and Jemalemin had begun recovering the corpse when Mok spoke again,

"Please, my friends, when you are finished, leave the trailer and its burden here. It will be safe. We will post two warriors here for security against the creatures of the night."

"And what of our security?" Chaneerem slashed. All present focused on him. These were the first words he had uttered since the four had found the village. "Moments ago, we prepared for our final breaths and now you wish us to lay ourselves and our possessions in your trust? Are we fools? Are we gullible opossums in the blinding sun, waiting for guidance to the fire pit where we will be roasted?"

"Chaneerem," Temmonin blurted in Ek-Birin, his brow tensed, "Don't insult the gracious hand of repentance."

"The gracious hand of repentance?" Chaneerem mimicked him to scorn. "You're gonna lead us to our death!"

"Not that it'd pain you too much to see us git killed." Temmonin mocked.

"Enough!" Mok inserted. "I am deeply troubled at this talk of distrust. I can assure you that my anger was based solely on what I now know to be untrue. The event has passed and, because of my mistake, I am doubly indebted to fulfill my duty to you as your host." Then he peered directly at Chaneerem, "My son, I am disappointed in you, a fellow member of the tribes of the confederacy, and in your suspicion that breeds suspicion. Should we all react similarly; we should again see the blight of war upon our land."

Chaneerem simply glared at his rebuker.

After a moment of uneasy silence, Mok motioned the Ek-Birin back into the village. The evening was calm and warm and a glorious fire helped them forget the grating chill of the previous two nights. Although Temmonin almost forgot the aching in his back, every time he moved he was reminded of it. Sleep was a balm.

They woke the next morning beneath an unfamiliar roof of pitch sod. Nothing was distinguishable except the outline of dawn around the log their hosts had used to plug the round entrance to the hill house. At present, this log was being wrested from its place by the silhouette of a child. As the plug dropped to the floor, sunlight gushed onto the moist soil beneath the child's feet. The boy, entirely naked, drew his hands to his lips and lifted them to the sky. Temmonin felt himself grinning.

"Well, Dama, we're still alive." Temmonin received no response so he rolled from his back to his stomach and rustled the elk hide nearest him.

Chaneerem's snarl leapt from the folds of the cover, "Well, isn't our little leader full of wisdom." Temmonin was ravaged by embarrassment. Chaneerem heaped coals higher, "What's yer prophecy fer today's fortune?"

Temmonin shook his head and heaved himself from the shelf of earth on which he slept. Now that the morning sun was shining in, he could see the interior of the hill house clearly. The single chamber was circular, roughly three body lengths in diameter and, at the center, almost tall enough for Temmonin to stand in. Carved into the side walls were several sleeping-shelves like the one he had used and the one from which Jemalemin now slipped. Covering each of these platforms was a canopy of muskrat fur. The vaulted ceiling was supported by randomly placed willow log pillars and occasionally dripped moisture from the spongy peat above.

This clan lived in moisture. When it rained, the house must be afloat. Then Temmonin saw the method by which the house drained itself of water. The muskrat canopies which hung above each of the sleeping-shelves carried runoff from the edges of the ceiling and dripped it into channels dug into the floor. Two such channels, one for each half-circle, sloped down and met at a point opposite the entrance where a hollow log carried the stream through the earth and outside. Bending low,

Temmonin glimpsed yellow warmth at the end of the tube.

But in winter, he thought, the heat of their fires must surely cause the snow on the hill to melt and seep into the house. And the smoke; there were no vents here. Temmonin could imagine how hard it would be to breathe. He glanced at his hosts, some of whom were still quiet in sleep while others were rising and dressing, and wondered at their ability to endure such constant dampness.

The morning was cold in spite of the sun, so Temmonin grabbed his elk hide and wrapped himself in it as he exited. He crouched through the portal and into a bath of brilliance. Squinting, he stretched his arms far above his head. Jemalemin scraped the side of the opening as he pulled himself through, his eyes tightening upon meeting the light. Temmonin was surprised to see Jemalemin alone and, unconsciously, he expected to see Chaneerem follow his younger brother. The talon-licker did not come.

"Beautiful day," Temmonin offered.

"Yea," Jemalemin said quietly.

"I might be able to handle the trailer now."

"I think me and Chaneerem're gonna go another day." Jemalemin snatched glances at Temmonin but never held his gaze.

"Well," Temmonin admitted gently, "I guess I could use s'more time to heal up." He watched as the boy fumbled with his belt and loincloth. Temmonin had never before spoken to Jemalemin alone. Like this glorious sun after two days of gloom, the conversation was refreshing yet slightly uncomfortable. "Thanks, Jemalemin."

Jemalemin looked into Temmonin's eyes as if hearing some esoteric phrase, then nodded and dropped his gaze.

Damowan emerged from the portal next. He was followed by two Daimadunva women and Chaneerem, who preferred a bland drooping of his eyelids to squinting. He also preferred silence to speech; at least in this village. At breakfast, Temmonin spoke more with Mok and the other Painted Turtle warriors as did Damowan and, to a very limited extent, Jemalemin. But the oath-taker held himself as if confining within his soul some smokeless raze. And his pupils were ebony ducts to pits of bitterness. How Chaneerem had not already destroyed himself, Temmonin could not fathom.

The man of tension was anxious to drive north and, moments after he had eaten, he stood and made his way toward the tribunal glade. Without looking back, he called, "You comin', Jemalemin?"

Jemalemin had not finished his meal but grudgingly joined his brother. While they were gone, Temmonin and Damowan inquired as to the best route through Shushunu during the rainy autumn.

Mok seemed eager to help, "Stay on the north path from here 'til ya reach the feet of Imnanaw Kanat. To the west of North lies Zubzza, the Great Gorge. Flash floods're common near there. Even from a big distance away, yer whole camp can be swept down into the gorge. Some say Zubzza's hungry fer the hearts of humans--that's why our forefathers gave the bodies of their firstborn daughters to appease the obese god of the gorge. But that was before the confederation. Even now, the grass doesn't grow too close to the lips of the hungry glutton. Stay away from the banks of that gorge.

When you reach the territory of the Zevi-Zevi, they'll help you from there." The other two now approached with the drag-trailer. "And, my friends," Mok lowered his voice and shifted his back to Chaneerem, "Woo this dissident into fellowship with the people." With a wry smile, he turned and met the others.

Damowan and Temmonin laughed polite laughs and avoided Chaneerem's gaze so as not to alert him to the fact that Mok had just spoken to them about him. They slung their packs over their shoulders as the trailer passed in front of them. Then they bid Mok and his village good bye and thanked them for their hospitality.

Not one of the Ek-Birin spoke throughout the morning. Since Chaneerem and Jemalemin had ventured north, Temmonin felt no need to repeat Mok's advice. Instead, he relished the increasing heat of the sun and the decreasing pain in his back and pondered the quick emotions of the Daimadunva chief.

When they stopped for lunch, Chaneerem ate nothing before he probed Temmonin, "Did he say anything about the fat gorge?"

"Only to steer clear of it," Temmonin answered flatly.

"And where is it that I might not mistakenly stumble into it?" Chaneerem was obviously annoyed at Temmonin's brevity.

"Let's put it this way--we're not heading for it now," Damowan interjected.

Chaneerem widened his expression in mock surprise, "So leadership runs in this family. Maybe when we get back home, you two could organize the next hunting assignments. Maybe we could hunt fire-mice."

Damowan growled at this. Then Chaneerem demanded their attention as he pulled his knife from its sheath and drove it deep into the trunk of the fallen willow upon which he sat.

"Where's the gorge?" he shot.

No one answered.

"Where's the gorge?" this time more intently.

"Who are you--some kinda god in an elk hide?" Damowan reacted.

"Where is the gorge?" Chaneerem rasped. He stood, pulled the knife from the bark and cut his finger with the jagged stone tip. He then proceeded to wag the finger at Damowan, shaking droplets of blood across Damowan's chest and face. "Where is the gorge?"

Again, the volcano erupted. Damowan sprang at the talon-licker like the birth of lightning, punching the dagger from Chaneerem's left hand and ramming his shoulder into his diaphragm. Then he was in on top of him, pounding with hot fists and cursing. But if Chaneerem was startled, the bewilderment did not last long. He quickly drew both arms to his right side and swung a double-fisted club at Damowan's cheek. For an instant, Damowan desisted his poundings. Chaneerem bucked and threw him off. He looked around himself for his knife only to see it cradled in the crook of Temmonin's arm some feet away. He compressed and sprang, intending to recapture his weapon, but Damowan intercepted him in flight and they struck the tall grass entwined. Chaneerem drew his extended right leg forward and nearly shattered Damowan's chin with his knee. Damowan's entire consciousness seemed to gather at the fresh pain in his teeth and jaw and he lost his hold on the oath-taker. Chaneerem then drove several punches at Damowan's abdomen.

Confident in his victory, he stood and peered at Temmonin.

The veil of Damowan's anguish drifted open just wide enough for him to watch Chaneerem stand up. With what was left of his waning concentration, he shifted and swung his legs at Chaneerem's. Chaneerem gurgled his words as his feet were flung from beneath him. He crashed to the earth. His vertebrae crunched and his skull clapped a small stone in the grass. He could not restrain himself as his lungs wrenched a hoarse roar. He rolled to his stomach and stopped. Damowan lay also, cradling his chin in his hands, lacking the energy to lift himself. He was lying on his side, trying to avoid the wounds on his back. And he was dabbing his mouth, checking for blood.

Temmonin smiled at Jemalemin across the fray, "Well, I'd like to know where the doe is--that was quite a display, but it's a little early fer the rut, wouldn't ya say, Jemalemin?"

Jemalemin would not say but he did smirk.

"D'ya think you can handle the knife again, Chaneerem? Or should I keep it to avoid any unnecessary accidents in the near future?" Temmonin wondered why he was taunting the talon-licker. He decided to stop. At this point, neither fighter was interested in talking.

"Are you two all right?" he inquired, voice void of sarcasm.

"Kinda," Damowan moaned, "You might have to help me find my jaw."

Temmonin then remembered his partially eaten meal. Flies had already assembled on the glistening juices of the cooked muskrat meat. He swished them away and sat down to eat. "I pity you, Damowan. It'll be tough to finish yer meal without a jaw."

The two fighters slowly found comfortable positions in which to sit and eat. Jemalemin had finished by that time. He observed and listened as his older brother reconvened.

"So where's the gorge?" he asked.

"Chaneerem," Temmonin wrinkled his brow, "Mok told us to. . ."

"Temmonin, what's the difference?" Damowan interrupted. His face was strangely fulfilled for having just been assaulted.

"What?" Temmonin sneered at the younger.

"What's the difference, Temmonin?" Damowan repeated, then smiled eagerly, "Why don't we go and see it? It's on the way."

"Damowan, what're you. . ?" Temmonin stopped before he could embarrass himself. He was suddenly overwhelmed by the heat of a host of unwelcome emotions. Did Damowan recognize the awkward position into which he had placed Temmonin? Had some new alliance been struck between blows? Temmonin could not imagine that Damowan had been subdued; he seemed excited and curious, not eager to appease Chaneerem.

"Temmonin," Damowan broke into his brother's thoughts, "We could save some time too. The gorge is right on the path to the Kumuchska. If we go around it, we'll prob'ly take an extra day-- and think what this monster's gonna smell like by that time."

Temmonin shot glances at each of the others, "Alright. If that's what you guys want, but if we get into trouble, I'm not takin' the blame." Somewhere beneath the scattered ruins of his confidence, he felt an easy elation in this defeat. Actually, he wondered why he so often found himself upholding standards to which he had little attachment. But at least he had waived his responsibility. Now, after having taken his stand and having lost, he could join the rebels free of accusation. His own integrity, however, was calling for his attention, chiding him with the same shake of the head his father would give could Amowz read his thoughts now. But these ethereal pleadings soon dissipated in the light of anticipation.

They ate quickly. Now that they had decided to go see the gorge, even Jemalemin showed signs of excitement; it was more than either Temmonin or Damowan had ever seen from him. Their pace was spritely and, except for the fact that Chaneerem and Jemalemin were dragging a trailer, they may have been young boys playing out some imaginary adventure. By the time the sun was setting over the yellowing autumn willows, they thought they could see the beginning of Zubzza's long slope. Although no immediate danger presented itself, the four back-tracked and camped about a stone's throw away from the edge of the slope.

"Who's gonna dip their foot in first?" Damowan laughed over the fire.

"Who's got a leg as long as a pine tree?" Temmonin laughed back.

Chaneerem seemed to have lost some of his aggression. He at least allowed himself to pay attention to each of the others as he spoke. Jemalemin must have sensed this; his tongue was more free than usual.

"Is it true that the fat gorge is fifty trees deep and filled with the white breath of giant bats?" Jemalemin posed his question, eyes sparked by the fire.

"No one's ever returned from it to tell the story," Temmonin answered over Chaneerem's snicker.

"Some people say it doesn't have a bottom," added Damowan, "Or at least none a man could reach in his lifetime. Some say the fat god's mouth is a swamp bigger than any swamp on the whole earth and anyone who wanders along his lips is swallowed up in a fat second."

Even Chaneerem laughed at that.

"And the fog that fills the chasm is actually the stench of breath so rotten you can see it!" Temmonin spurred the laughter on. And their laughter spurred him on, "It's almost as if Damowan laid down and opened his mouth wide and fell asleep for a few hundred years."

"What was that?" Jemalemin hushed the others with his hands. His eyes were jerking back and forth.

"Where?" Temmonin whispered.

Jemalemin pointed to a black swatch between two white pines behind Damowan. Damowan turned his head slowly, following Jemalemin's finger. There was a sharp scattering of pine needles and a fleeting glimmer like pebbles in a shallow stream.

"And there!" Jemalemin sliced the night, creating a similar reaction in the shadows of a wrinkled willow trunk several feet from the fire.

Jemalemin, Temmonin, and Damowan began searching the surrounding shadows. Chaneerem would not allow himself to appear curious. He poked the fire and scoffed more than once.

"Zubzza's sending his messengers to escort us to the evening meal." Damowan jested. "Please," he raised his voice to the black woods around them, "Be a little more polite than this. At least let us see our escorts!"

"Damowan!" Temmonin scolded, "You're gonna scare 'em away."

"Scare 'em away?" the younger questioned. Who's them?"

"I don't know but I'd like to find out so quiet."

Again they gazed at the black under-images of the trees. The undulating crickets accompanied the silent song of the stars and katydids hanging in the elms and oaks responded in weird counterpoint. But Damowan's sudden, silent concentration begged the others from this symphony to observe him as he moved. He crawled across Temmonin's lap, his wide eyes fixed on the thorny bracken behind Jemalemin, purposefully crawling toward a tiny pair of eyes that watched his approach. As Damowan drew closer, Temmonin and Jemalemin pressed his shoulders. The eyes in the brush began to squirm rapidly. Damowan reached one hand through the vines. The movement of the eyes increased to violent shakings and the air was threaded with squealings. Damowan spread wide the clogging vines that shaded the owner of the minute yellow orbs. Caught and held stationary by thorns twisted into its shaggy, olive green fur stood a weird hybrid of a squirrel and a man. Its head was little higher than a hand from the ground. Except for a grey and pink flesh area across its chest and abdomen, its entire body was lavished with oily, moss-colored hair, much of it now tangled in the encroachment around him. Those shining beads of light set in its skull were stretched with fright. Its mouth, like the spot on a leopard frog, gaped at the three giants above him. The squealings stopped. The shakings stopped. Four paws hung in vine shackles that any child could have kicked through.

"What'd you find?" Chaneerem called from behind the three.

"Shhh!" Temmonin hissed.

Damowan cautiously reached to loosen the grip the vines had on the creature. As his hand neared its nervous abdomen, it jumped away and further into the thick. Damowan forced himself closer. With a jerk, he clasped his hand around its body and began disentangling its fur from the thorns that so jealously clung to it. It howled such frantic howls and resisted with such fervor that Temmonin thought there may have been several creatures sharing this body. It fought against its own rescue like an infatuated adolescent. But soon Damowan had freed both legs and an arm and had kept the animal from re-entangling itself. Then it was loose. Its rescuer released it, backed away and stared in wonder.

By this time, the creature seemed to have comprehended the mercy involved in Damowan's actions. Certainly, it had lost several patches of fur to the bracken. And, although the pain of being freed had been caused by the huge, red hands of the giant before it, it relinquished its squirmings and whinings and stared in return.

"What'd you three find?" Chaneerem repeated.

No one answered him.

The three were mesmerized by this squirrel-man so full of emotion. Its nearly indistinguishable facial features were now shifting and it appeared that the thing was attempting to communicate. It ground infinitesimal vocal chords and chattered curious announcements to its rescuers. Then it waited.

"What was that?" Chaneerem bothered again. Why the talon-licker refused to cross the clearing to see the creature himself Temmonin could not understand.

"Come over here and see if ya want," Temmonin answered.

At the sound of a human voice, the squirrel man again began to chatter. The timber of its squeaky chirps rose with impatience as the giants in front of it gawked misunderstanding and silence. It proceeded to flail its tail wildly. As its frustration escalated, Temmonin heard Chaneerem's footfall behind him.

Suddenly, a grey blur sailed and landed next to the creature, spitting dirt at its body. Then another rock flew and nearly crushed the thing. Temmonin, Damowan, and Jemalemin turned to see Chaneerem aiming another missile.

"Chaneerem, stop!" Temmonin bellowed as he shot out his hand to catch the newest rock. He withdrew his hand quickly as the stone slapped his palm. After cursing at the pain, he yelled, "That coulda killed the little thing!"

He and the others returned their attention to the creature only to see a mottled clump of bracken and two stones lying in the dirt. Further into the undergrowth, a bushy, green tail whisked away into oblivion. Jemalemin crawled back to the fire. Damowan and Temmonin soughed almost simultaneously. Temmonin glared at the oath-taker and, disgusted, questioned,

"What is yer deal Chaneerem?" He shook his shoulder-length, ebony mane. "Why do you have to destroy everything? I mean, you don't have to be like this. Yer life could be way different. And you'd prob'ly feel a lot better about yerself too. I know ev'rybody else would." He did not wait for a response.

Chaneerem stood his ground as the other three situated themselves around the fire. He blurted a spitting laugh before he answered Temmonin's rhetorical questions.

"What do you know about how to make my life better?" The talon-licker scowled. "But I do know one thing that's gonna feel real good—makin' sure the Kumuchska pay for their mistakes."

Moon Beneath the Mountains

IV.   Or rather, shall we attempt to appease the giant by stirring within him some curiosity or amusement or sympathy or sentiment causing him to notice or befriend or even to cherish those he might otherwise unknowingly have slaughtered? And, in so saving ourselves from impending doom, shall we distract our new guardian long enough to cause him to neglect his watch for those who have made his home their footpath? And should his fall shield us from a death of and for which he certainly would be equally as ignorant as responsible had we not aroused his conscience, shall we then escape free of guilt? Or shall we consider our souls stained with that same blood which, beneath his careless step would stain our bodies, our families, and our houses? And were we to weep tears for every stain of blood, would not the sea of life drown all those living with the backwash of their own penitence? But were we not to weep, might not that same sea shrivel and stagnate? Perhaps we, so imprisoned in paradox, should pray that the moon draw tribute from our eyes and, in so doing, unite us with the ever revolving law of the tide

CHAPTER 4

The passing of a cloudless night could not scrape away the distaste Chaneerem had left in Temmonin's chest. But the mellowing of dawn and the promise of an uninterrupted robin egg sky stirred in him renewed excitement. Today they would visit a forbidden place; one that had been inscribed into their dreams. His elation reminded him of his first hunting trips with his father and how easy it was to wake up on those mornings, how impossible it was for him to sleep.

"Damowan, you up?" He shook his motionless brother.

Damowan murmured into the folds of his elk hide blanket. He always slept with his head beneath it. Temmonin wondered if that was why that granite-jawed warrior could forget; perhaps the recycling of his own breath every night caused his mind to concentrate only on things at hand rather than to think and rethink every one of his experiences. True or not, Temmonin could not bear to breathe anything but fresh air at night.

"Damowan it's time to greet brother sun."

"Temmonin," Damowan whined.

"And our fat friend Zubzza," Temmonin taunted.

At that, the younger found enough reason to push away his lethargy. Slowly, he forced himself into a sitting position and faced his older brother.

"So today we git to see it." He coughed and rubbed his eyes with the heels of his thumbs. Then his tone became formal, "Will we find that ancient race of magic that dwells...?"

"Wait, Damowan, that's what that creature was last night--one of the Chrebin!" Temmonin chirped excitedly. The other two woke.

"That little bump?" Damowan laughed, "That thing could hardly have 'stolen the voices of an entire clan', or 'drank swamps dry'."

"No, Damowan. It's not the size of the body. It's the size of the magic! That was a Chrebin, I know it."

"Temmonin, you don't know. It looked like a deformed squirrel to me. How do you know it wasn't just a freak of nature?"

"I jus' know, Damowan. How do you know I'm not right?" Temmonin felt a rush of indignation swell his neck.

"I never said I know yer not right. I just said you don't know fer sure that it was a Chrebin," Damowan countered.

"Well, why did you have to say that?"

"Why do you always have to get mad when I say you might be wrong?"

"I don't always get mad." Temmonin was sneering now.

"Well, most of the time."

"Shut up Damowan, it was probably a Chrebin."

"But you don't know," Damowan insisted.

Temmonin's face contorted and, as he spoke, his lips pouted, shaped by sarcasm, "Yes, I don't absolutely know for absolute certain absolutely. But it prob'ly was. Now would you jus' shut up about it!"

Temmonin had not been this forceful with his brother in a long time. Across the fire pit, Chaneerem and Jemalemin were gathering their gear. During the argument, Temmonin had lost sight of them as the haze of self-righteousness

94

crowded his vision but, suddenly, he was exposed and he almost quivered at his shame. During the spat, he felt as if Chaneerem were storing arrows with which someday he would wound Temmonin. And, for some strange reason, he felt as if he had greatly disappointed Jemalemin. Then Chaneerem began to whistle the song of the cardinal. Temmonin was sure he was doing this just to spite him and his treatment of Damowan. Of course Chaneerem would have no difficulty recognizing such arrogant behavior; he had perfected it. Yet, not only was Temmonin embarrassed at having revealed aspects of himself that mirrored distasteful flashings in the oath-taker's teeth, but he now feared that his outburst might also cause Jemalemin to close what little he had opened of himself. It was no longer clear where Jemalemin stood in his relationship to his brother. And if the boy had hoped to find trust in Temmonin, perhaps Temmonin had just dashed those hopes to the floor. But he could think of no way to explain away his aggressive behavior and he knew that if he were to try to explain, he would only increase his embarrassment and Chaneerem's amusement. And he was in no mood to apologize. He held his tongue and began to pack his things.

Chaneerem walked first and Jemalemin followed quickly and quietly. The talon-licker neglected the trailer, indirectly assigning the transport of the fly-covered thing to Temmonin and Damowan. The two were forced to rush to prepare and to take up their burden. Temmonin gazed directly at his brother as they stood astride the bundle of the Kumuchska monster.

"I think my back's ready now. Still hurts a little," he said quietly. Damowan assented without looking at Temmonin. He bent to lift the yoke.

"Damowan," Temmonin said, "You're right. I do always get mad when you confront me."

"Well, not always," Damowan admitted, eyes still down.

"A lot," Temmonin returned. "I'm sorry. Forgive me." He was relieved he had pushed through his discomfort and addressed the issue.

Damowan could not yet face his brother. He let go of the trailer and tested one of the ropes that held the monster down. Temmonin repeated himself,

"Damowan, I'm serious. I'm sorry."

Damowan raised his shag to expose an awkward grin. Then, in a spasm that pitched his body over the trailer, he fell upon Temmonin. They rolled to the moss, laughing.

"You little bobcat!" Temmonin exclaimed. "Ow, my back!"

"Yer not gittin' me with that one this time!" Damowan exclaimed as he began punching his abdomen. The elder grabbed his brother's ears and pulled them apart until Damowan had to reach to stop the pain. As Chaneerem had done the day before, Temmonin bucked. But Damowan was prepared and clamped the elder's sides with his knees. For a few moments they locked grips on one another's forearms and struggled for leverage. But, like crows trying to balance at the tops of saplings in the winter wind, neither could gain control. Eventually, they both gave up. Temmonin was relieved to discover that his back still felt well enough to lift the trailer.

"We'd better hurry up or we'll never catch the others."

The slope was almost undetectable except that the vegetation on the soil here was much thinner here than in the swampland through which they had just traveled. Still, plants pushed into the filtered green sunlight from paths carved by flash floods and from between exposed roots of cedars and oaks and maples. The soil to which they clung was a dull orange clay mixed with gravel and large stones. All else must have been swept into the gorge. Vines whose tenacity had surely been tested by rushing waters showed signs of stress. Some meandered haphazardly but most grew straight in the same direction as the channels in the clay. A number of times, Temmonin and Damowan had to wrest the runners of the trailer from the clutches of vines or channels.

For most of an hour, the brothers kept Chaneerem and Jemalemin in view. The slope remained slight and the vegetation short and even distant movement was easy to detect through the multitude of tree trunks. But then they lost sight of the others. As Temmonin and Damowan discussed the possibility that they might become totally separated from them, the slope increased beneath them. Ahead of them they saw more and more of the sky and the autumn sun through the thinning trees. Soon they reached the point where they had last seen the other two.

Here the dry channels had widened into ravines which spilled air over a steep, barren embankment. Was this the lip of Zubzza? Although they were close enough to toss stones into the gorge, neither was very impressed by what lay in front of them. All they could see was a soggy fog that dissipated only after it had risen above their heads. Then something moved on the embankment below them. Temmonin recognized a pair of pale figures through the mist. Apparently, Chaneerem and Jemalemin had discovered a second lip some twenty feet beneath the lip where the newcomers stood.

Suddenly the damp edge of clay on which Temmonin and Damowan rested lost its hold on the cliff and, with the swiftness of a panicked deer, rushed them down the embankment and toward the gorge. Urgency overwhelmed the two as they flailed to find a handhold. Damowan roared and Temmonin panted. Clay, granite, and the drag trailer pushed them toward mysterious death. Damowan somehow managed to snag Temmonin's left arm and each gripped hard to the other. When their feet met the narrow strip of level earth between the inner lip of the gorge and the slope down which they now rushed, Damowan attempted a final maneuver to stop their cascade. But as he pushed up into the dirt slide, his feet peeled back a thick layer of mud that allowed him no support against the onslaught that so furiously pressed their death. Temmonin sprawled face first into the mud as the drag trailer raked across his back and slid into the fog. Like a stone sinking into a pond, the trailer and the monster disappeared into the grey gorge. Damowan's feet pushed into the mud for only a moment. Then his whole body slipped over the edge. In a panic of effort, he caught himself by entangling his arms in the roots that protruded from the lip of the gorge. His eyes and nose and mouth were pounded with dirt and clay and stones. He was nearly blinded and deafened by the rush, but screamed for his brother through the fray as he groped for him with his free arm. He felt flesh but could not hold on to Temmonin. He needed both arms to hold himself up.

Amazingly, the roots held his entire weight as he dangled from their mesh. The avalanche quieted and Damowan opened his eyes to search for

Temmonin. In spite of his own exhaustion, he
lifted himself to the edge of the cliff. His older
brother was lying unconscious on the ledge half-
buried with debris. Damowan reached to uncover
his head to allow him some air but found he could
not get himself in good enough position to do so.
He tried to pull himself over the edge without
disturbing the loose dirt above. His feet, however,
had little from which to push--the cliff fell away
from where he clung to its edge. Nervous
adrenaline surged through his heart as he pictured
his situation. Again, he struggled to lift himself only
to return to his desperate position. The top of the
cliff offered no solid handhold. Exasperated, he
searched the cliff's edge to his right and then to his
left.

"Damowan." Jemalemin's quivering voice
shocked Damowan so that he almost lost his grip
on the roots. "Damowan, hold on." The boy was
only feet away from the other two. "We'll figure
somethin' out here." Then Jemalemin slipped on
the mud. He barely caught himself. "Chaneerem,
help me out here!" the boy nervously beckoned.
"How're we gonna. . ?" He glanced over his
shoulder to see Chaneerem leisurely picking his way
up the slope a stone's throw away. Damowan saw
him too.

"Chaneerem! What're you doin'!? These
two need help right now!!"

The oath-taker reeled and returned his
brother's stare. For an instant, Damowan
recognized the ashamed flush that crossed
Chaneerem's cheeks. Then the rapid gathering of
thoughts in his eyes. Then the darkened visage and
cruel tongue.

"Whaddaya think I'm doin'? I know they
need help right now! I'm goin' up top to lower

some vines!" His tone was patronizing. "Better than all four of us slippin' over the cliff, don't you agree?" Then he continued up the slope to the outer lip.

Damowan could see the humiliation in Jemalemin's tensed shoulders, "Damn you, Chaneerem!" Jemalemin screamed, "You don't care about nobody! Nobody!" And as he released his anger, he lost his balance. His bare back slapped the mud heavily. Shaking, he found a good grip nearby with which to secure himself. As he struggled to right himself, Chaneerem spat over his shoulder,

"Be careful little brother, we wouldn't want to drop over the side now, would we?"

"Shut up!" Jemalemin raged.

At that, Chaneerem halted and, without turning to face his brother, called out, "D'ya want my help or not?"

His younger brother gasped in disbelief, "Chaneerem, these two are hangin' on to life by a corn husk!"

"So do ya want my help or not?" the talon-licker repeated.

"Of course." Then his tone melted into a plead, "Chaneerem, please hurry!"

"Then shut up yerself and lemme git to work!" And he began up the embankment again.

Damowan stared at Jemalemin as the boy turned and crawled over the mud toward him. Jemalemin was hissing his frustrations as he neared Damowan. Damowan only understood pieces of his cursings: "Can't believe him," or, "...gonna leave." Then, Damowan's muscles began warning him of his limits.

"Jemalemin, I can't hold on much longer."

"I know, Damowan," Jemalemin answered with empathy, "But we gotta wait fer my brother."

"Well," Damowan remembered, "Until then, could ya dig Temmonin's head out. I can't reach him."

"Good idea." And Jemalemin cautiously removed the dirt and mud that covered Temmonin's face.

"Jemalemin, what about Chaneerem? Was he gonna leave?"

"Yea. He was gonna leave you two here. He was gonna leave me here too. I know it!" The oath-taker's brother's eyes were red. "He was gonna leave us here." Tears dripped from Jemalemin's cheeks--not whimpering tears, Damowan could see, but the juice of bitter realization. "I can't believe he was gonna leave us here." More clearing of debris. "If I didn't notice him, he woulda left us here."

The thump of a vine landing near Jemalemin's head startled him. He looked up just in time to shield himself from several more as Chaneerem flung them over the cliff. The boy gathered the ends together and tied them into a loose knot. Then he handed the knot to Damowan. He whispered to the one who had once covered his face in blood.

"You're gonna have to trust him, Damowan. There's nothin' else you can do."

Damowan gazed up at Chaneerem who was now bracing himself against a tree, preparing to pull him up. Realizing he could cling to the roots no longer, he resigned himself to trust Chaneerem and tugged on the vine rope. The talon-licker had wrapped his end around a thick cedar and was using the bark to help grip the rope. As he pulled, he rewrapped the tree trunk with the new slack. He continued this process until Damowan knelt beside Jemalemin in the splayed mud around Temmonin's unconscious body.

Together, the two younger brothers gingerly wriggled Temmonin from beneath a blanket of mud and clay. The unconscious man was breathing the uncomfortable breath of having been laid to rest against his will but he showed no signs of deep injury. They lifted his body and carried him up the embankment far from the dirt slide.

They met Chaneerem some feet from the upper lip of the smoking gorge.

"Looks like ya hardly needed my help anyway," he began.

The other two had just eased Temmonin to the soil. Jemalemin heaved himself from the ground and spewed venom at this older brother, "You were gonna leave us! You were gonna leave us!" he spat at Chaneerem's feet, "You and your coward gut were sneakin' off into the forest!! If I didn't call you, you woulda been gone!" His entire body was jittering as if all of his composure had spilt out with his boiling accusation.

"What? Didn't you want my help?" the oath-taker returned, but the tension of his voice did not equal that of Jemalemin's.

"Yer help? Yer a. . ."

"Didn't you want my help?" Chaneerem interrupted sternly.

"It's not gonna work this time, Chaneerem. I saw where you were startin' to cover up yer tracks. You were gonna let yer two worst enemies die and then you'd be the greatest young Flicker warrior in the village."

"Well, next time I won't give you my help. Maybe next time our two worst enemies will die!"

"No," Jemalemin replied, his voice more controlled. "No, Chaneerem, maybe next time yer three worst enemies'll die!"

Temmonin rose from sleep shortly.

"Oh man, am I dyin'," he slurred. "Jus' barely git over one massive injury and along comes another one."

"Well, if you'd watch where you put yer foot," Damowan offered.

"Oh, man!" Temmonin moaned, gripped with knowledge, "The drag-trailer!"

"Yea," Damowan replied, quickly stripped of his smile.

An uncomfortable silence pervaded the forest. Damowan and Jemalemin had found relatively easy positions in which to rest. Chaneerem, however, had stood leaning against a tree trunk or had paced a wide circle since before Temmonin woke. It seemed that his disinterest was intended to punish his younger brother for his vindication. Yet Jemalemin hardly let himself be affected. Or, if he were affected, he showed little evidence that he had been.

From what Temmonin could glean from the mixed lines of Damowan's expressions, his younger brother wanted to tell him something but felt he should wait. Through subtleties in his own eyes, Temmonin let Damowan know that he understood.

"Well," Temmonin said, "No trailer, no Kumuchska monster, no mission. What do we do now? Ow, my back!" He shifted into a more comfortable position.

"We could keep on explorin' Zubzza," Damowan jested.

"If we could see it," Temmonin responded. The wall of fog was still as high as the tops of some trees. The gorge was a shrouded dream and the four Ek-Birin were as helpless to scale its cliffs as dreamers without eyes or hands. "No, guys. I say we gotta keep on going to Uncle Nosh's—at least until we come up with some better plan." No one replied.

"Maybe the gorge is only a few feet deep. Maybe we were scared fer no reason." Damowan always grew playful when situations became ridiculous.

"How'd you get me outta there anyway? Somethin' musta really knocked me out, huh?" Temmonin asked Damowan.

"Yea, the drag-trailer went right over yer head. But then Chaneerem dropped some vines from the upper cliff here and pulled me up. Then Jemalemin and I carried your limp flesh up here. You felt like a clump of corn silk."

"All right, all right, Damowan. Jus' remember you sleep sometimes too." Temmonin blurted. "And jus' remember that I'm awake sometimes when yer sleepin'."

"Ooo!" Damowan feigned being threatened, "I think I'll set traps around my bed tonight."

"You could never outsmart yer older brother," Temmonin boasted playfully and then rubbed his ear. Dirt dropped from his hair.

Although he attempted to shade his reaction, Jemalemin jerked his gaze to Temmonin and immediately shifted it away again. Temmonin hoped his fun had not offended the boy, but he guessed it probably had. Jemalemin had probably never been allowed to feel good about himself except in the context of being Chaneerem's younger brother. Temmonin was reminded of how overbearing he himself had often been toward Damowan. He remembered times when he had manipulated situations to keep from marring his own image and how Damowan, although never entirely losing respect for his older brother, had slowly learned to uphold a certain defense when dealing with him. Eventually, however, and unlike the talon-licker, Temmonin was forced to face himself. Through a series of painful conversations with his father, mother, and brother, he began to recognize that his actions were far from the clandestine maneuvers he had envisioned them to be. In fact, as time went on, he felt more and more naked and ashamed. He did enjoy the advantages he won for himself but soon his embarrassment at being exposed made him hate what he had become.

Change was often as excruciating as holding an unclenched hand over a searing fire. For a time in his life, pride, anger, and frustration collided within him so frequently, he felt like a victim and was greatly tempted to use that feeling in further manipulations. Yet he allowed his shame to steer him to the place where Damowan rarely distrusted him, where incriminating confrontations became fewer, and where he submitted more quickly to his limitations. Now, as he glimpsed fragments of his past, he hurt for Jemalemin as he had finally learned to hurt for Damowan.

V.   And shall we see ourselves and our people as unlike the law of the tide? Do we, in fact, possess even slightly more liberty than the cyclic wanderings of the ocean's perimeter? Or does the moon now draw us, now release us from the lap of mother earth while the stars and comets vie for some food for their emblazoned egos? Has the Creator, his lips quivering with sadism, placed us amidst worlds as small and as plentiful as sand, leaving us not with the choice of if we shall destroy but with that of whom we shall destroy? And should we, in seeking never to maim or kill, choose to withhold ourselves from all activity and all thought, and should we, in so doing, fall in death from our own self-neglect, would we then drown forever in the guilt of our own blood? And would that eternal drowning judge us for the death we had allowed or rather for our failure to take our place in the infinite killing and being killed that like breath infiltrates the boundaries of the living? Or have we misjudged the awesome act of killing? Have we, in our fear of enduring the exorbitant ordeal of dying, assigned to this ultimate violence inherent immorality? Do we manipulate facets of truth to avoid the realization that this horror laces our very existence? Do we dream of worlds that may have been in order to cushion the blows of our pressing reality and, in so doing, do we, being molded clay, attempt to mold that which molded us?

CHAPTER 5

They were far from the disappointing gasp of Zubzza, picking their way through depleted blackberry bracken on the path leading to Demdegumshannatez when Damowan felt that they were finally a safe distance from Chaneerem and Jemalemin. Although they were no longer dragging the trailer, both sets of brothers again drifted apart. And, although they could see the others through the thick forest, Damowan felt he could talk without being overheard. Temmonin was not altogether surprised that Chaneerem might leave them to die. But he was shocked and rather pleased as Damowan repeated Jemalemin's reaction to his older brother. In muted tones, they discussed the implications of what had happened and soon realized that in leaving Jemalemin alone with Chaneerem they may have allowed a dangerous situation. They decided to catch up to the other two.

The sun intensified its outpouring on bristling evergreens and the variegated leaves of oaks and elms and maples. But the four rarely stopped to notice the red, orange, amber and brown glory that surrounded them. Temmonin wondered how long they could remain together without another explosion of violence. And they had experienced enough violence already to make him believe that the next instance might result in at least one death. Because of this, he actively attempted to steer conversation from potentially hazardous subjects. To some extent, the others did also. But the offensive abandon with which Chaneerem related to the rest seemed gradually to force them toward an inevitable confrontation.

Eventually, however, the persistent grandeur of the late harvest sky and the late harvest air stole Temmonin's attention. Rasping bands of blue jays shredded his concentration and caused him to remember the threads of pure pleasure that had woven together all of his life, even in times of extreme pain. At one point, Damowan stopped and coaxed a mustard-colored dragonfly to mount his finger from its perch on a sumac leaf. Chaneerem and Jemalemin obviously could not comprehend the hearty laughter this caused the other two. The forest was alive with distractions and Temmonin and Damowan spent the remainder of the afternoon stopping, perusing, and then rejoining the others. At times, when the trees gave way to swamps and marshes or, increasingly, to small meadows, they could see the glazed tips of Imnanaw Kanat. They smiled widely at such sights.

By this time in autumn, evening let its presence be known with occasional slices of shivering breeze. After an entire day of soaking their bodies and loincloths and moccasins in sweat, they felt that same liquid evaporate with the evening breeze and fly from them, leaving them salty and chilled. Temmonin had never grown to enjoy the sensation of clammy leather against his skin, but he knew the others had to cope with the same discomfort and so voiced no complaint when they stopped to don elk hides for the remainder of the day's travel.

The waning sun burnt a gorgeous farewell across the western sky and soon the four found a suitable camp. Temmonin and Damowan were enthralled with the passing of bats overhead and spent a few moments watching them arc between the silhouettes of cedars. By the time they began to think about preparing for the night's rest, Jemalemin had already finished stretching his and his brother's tent. And Chaneerem was lighting the fire.

Temmonin almost cursed aloud for not having started the fire himself. He hated when Chaneerem had control over any aspect of their social functions. He could only guess what manipulations might be brewing behind those demented eyes. But every thought of Chaneerem's domineering calculations only reminded him of himself and again of Jemalemin and what that brave young brother was thinking. Damowan, however, had already reached for their packs.

"Temmonin, where'd you pack the tent-skin?" his younger brother inquired.

"I don't know. Where'd you pack it?" said Temmonin, slightly irritated at the insinuation of blame. "How could you not find somethin' that big?"

"Temmonin, you packed it this mornin. . ."

"Well, I don't know. . .oh, no. Damowan, I lashed it to the drag trailer." The elder stood and stared into the shadows.

"Well, what're we gonna do now?" Damowan released his pessimism.

"Hope it doesn't rain 'til after the moon hides half his face again."

"Temmonin," Damowan leveled a knowing eye at his brother, "we both can be sure that it will rain every single night until then. And it will be very cold in the mountains and we will die of frostbite."

"Then at least we won't have to explain how we lost the Kumuchska monster over the lips of the forbidden Zubzza," Temmonin said.

After a moment of silence, Damowan spoke, "So should we trust the clouds and sleep near the fire or should we be wise and use these cedars as a canopy?"

109

"The trees, Dama. We still have a few more days. I'd like to stay as dry as possible."

As they finished preparations for the night's rest, Temmonin and Damowan left their evergreen canopy to face a welcome and warm blaze over which the ambivalent hunch of Chaneerem roasted a chunk of turkey meat. It looked as though he were only cooking enough for two so Damowan moved to cut another piece for himself and his brother. He did so without objection. Temmonin again admired him for his ability to forget. Temmonin himself may have spent an hour deciding whether or not it were worth the risk of confronting Chaneerem about the turkey he had killed. In many ways, he was tired of confrontations. And, when he thought more, he realized he was afraid also. It would take some thought before he knew which emotion were more prevalent but he was certain that he would never possess Damowan's liberty in facing tense situations. That young puma either never remembered the uncomfortable past or he was not even slightly threatened by it or he thought it amusing to test Chaneerem's limits. In any case, the event passed without significance and soon all four surrounded the fire, mouths full of saliva.

The meat was some of the best they had ever eaten. When they had finished eating, they settled near the fire and chewed spearmint leaves.

"I really don't see why we're still here," Damowan said. "We're gonna walk into Uncle Nosh's village and gawk like idiots. Who's gonna believe our story?" He held his eyes away from Chaneerem but addressed the whole group.

"Damowan, he's our uncle. And besides, remember that, as a village and as a clan and as a tribe, they've pledged themselves to the same code of integrity that we have. They have to accept our story or we don't have to accept theirs," Temmonin reasoned.

"That's just it! They don't have a story fer us to accept. But we've got the great grandpappy of all the most stupidly unbelievable stories in the world!" Damowan countered.

"Yea, but they're also not travelin' ten days to take a message all the way to Flicker territory," Temmonin said. After a moment of silence, he continued, "Don'tcha see, Damowan? The fact that we're makin' this trip adds weight to our story. Why would we go through all this trouble if we were lyin'?"

"Well, it'd all be much more sensible if we were bringin' some simple story of rape or murder-- but some weird monster? Half human, half wolverine? Temmonin, without any evidence, there's a good chance this whole thing could turn back on us. We could git totally messed up!" Damowan returned.

"But," Jemalemin entered the conversation, "if Nosh is yer uncle, he'll believe you guys, right?" His voice was tentative but not quavering.

"Yea, but Nosh's bound by code to impartiality," Damowan replied gingerly. "He's not gonna kill ev'ry adult male in the village because his two nephews suspect the dark arts."

"We're not talkin' about killin' anybody, Damowan," Temmonin broke in. "We're gonna ask for a thorough investigation beginnin' with Nosh's village and then throughout the Kumuchska territory. Is that too much to ask? Who said anything about killin' anybody?"

The crackling fire spoke its opinion as the brothers thought.

"I don't know," Damowan added. "It still seems kinda ridiculous."

"Well, we gotta do somethin' and this seems better than goin' back." Then he followed an impulse, "What d'you think, Chaneerem?"

The oath-taker looked mildly surprised at inclusion in the conversation. His gaze crossed the flames and met Temmonin's with strange ambiguity. Did Temmonin's boldness conjure in Chaneerem some vague respect? Would the talon-licker use this opportunity to mock him? Surely this kind gesture had not caused Chaneerem to soften.

"Whatever," he spoke softly. "It's fine." And nothing more.

Then they sat in silence for a time. Perhaps because of Chaneerem's gentle answer, perhaps because their conversation seemed to be of no use, perhaps because they had all spent enough time away from the village, Damowan felt it necessary to recreate an evening at home. His story began as so many they had heard the elders tell.

"In the beginning, the Creator created. In His mind, He thought His thoughts of worlds, of cosmos, of creating, and by His song which is heard and is no dream, He created. And His thoughts were no dreams but more thick and more real than quartz and more solid than granite. And his thoughts, the first of which a world of men could not explore in a thousand generations, His thoughts compelled His song. And His song, like the infinite strokes of the carver's tools in a thousand lifetimes, His song carved from the nothingness all that breathes and all that grows and all that burns and all that dreams. And His song created all that is soft and all that is hard and all that shines and all that soothes. And His song created all that flies and all that slithers and all that crawls and all that walks or runs. And when the. . ." Damowan's stopped suddenly.

Jemalemin was staring at the edge of the clearing. Temmonin looked and saw several of the olive-furred creatures they had seen the night before. Then twigs snapped behind Chaneerem and he, with the others, turned to see hundreds of the things emerging from the shadows. Within seconds, the four realized that they were encircled by a horde of tails and fur and glimmering yellow eyes. And those infinite eyes, like the fireflies that dance over the hot summer marsh, stared and shone their odd light on the four in the center. Temmonin could gather nothing from their positioning--no one of them looked to be their leader. He could see no obvious intent. They approached randomly and without comprehensible emotion. Recalling the audible violence with which the other had protested Damowan's manipulations, Temmonin was impressed by the absence of all expression now. Then the horde halted.

Temmonin glanced at Chaneerem. The talon-licker sat still, scanning this miniature legion. Temmonin recognized no panic in his eyes. Damowan met his brother's eyes and they exchanged adrenaline. Temmonin thought he saw him smile.

Then Jemalemin clenched his hands to his ears and splayed to the dirt near the fire. Writhing like a salmon on a spear, he tore at his hair and screamed his throat into the fire and into the hollow black sky. Temmonin and Damowan dove to keep him from burning himself. The elder slammed into Jemalemin. His head recoiled as Jemalemin's elbow swung into his upper lip. Blood spurted onto Jemalemin. Temmonin voiced his pain through the

warm wash that suddenly covered his face. But he
and Damowan held firmly as Jemalemin convulsed.

"Jemalemin, what're you tryin' to do?"
Damowan yelled.

"In my head!" Jemalemin roared. "My
head! My head!"

"What's in yer head?" Temmonin pressed
his face against Jemalemin's chest to avoid being
wounded again.

Jemalemin redoubled his flailings and rolled
Damowan over himself and into the fire. Singed
and wild with shock, Damowan released his grip
and flung himself out of danger. He turned back to
see Jemalemin pointing at the horde and bellowing
accusations. He was sitting up and entirely free of
Temmonin's grasp. Temmonin observed him from
the ground where he lay.

"Them! They were in my head! Git out!
Stay outta my head!!" Jemalemin was still holding his
skull with his left arm but was no longer catatonic.

Then screams again burst open the ears of
the night. Across the fire, Chaneerem tensed and
gurgled and rasped at some unseen marauder.
Before any of the others could react, the oath-taker
thrust his left arm into the fire and held it there.
But it seemed as if he were doing so against his will.
His screams focused and intensified and, as
Damowan leapt to help him, the younger had to
scream himself to counter the raging in his ears. As
Damowan landed, Chaneerem kicked him off. The
oath-taker sat up, pulling his arm from the flames,
and extended that mottled, fuming appendage in
front of him as if waiting for some kind of healing.
His lungs continued to rake his throat with
vehemence even when one of the squirrel men
stepped forward and placed its hand on the flesh
above his wrist and upturned palm. The creature

stayed a moment, then removed itself from the talon-licker as a priest removes himself from an altar.

Another of them proceeded toward the fire with one oily arm extended. It stopped just as the blaze licked its palm. Although the flames crept up its arm, it did not rescind. Then it turned and walked ceremoniously to where Damowan was kneeling, a small flame now glowing around its palm. It stood waiting. Damowan was entranced by the thing and silently stared question after question at the tiny sentinel. It did not move. It simply returned Damowan's stare and continued to extend its fiery arm toward the giant. Then several of those near Damowan stretched their twig-like arms forward in a manner reminiscent of what Chaneerem had done moments before. Damowan continued to gape wonder. The creature with the flaming arm addressed him with a series of bird-like chirps and a long whining squeal. Again, the group mimicked Chaneerem's movement and followed with a chorus of some foreign command. With a shrug, Damowan moved his left arm forward, palm up, exposing the light skin of his wrist to the burning sentinel.

"Damowan, don't!" Temmonin spurted.

But, if Damowan could hear Temmonin, it seemed he did not care. Something may have possessed him--Temmonin could not tell. He continued to expose himself.

Panic blackened Temmonin's vision, "Damowan, what're you doin'?" And he sprang from the earth. But, as he jumped, something entered his head. For an instant, every dream he had ever dreamt collided in the rapids of his mind and, fruitless, he crashed and spilled his stomach onto the ground. Through spasms of blindness and

115

torturing pain, he watched Damowan receive on his left wrist the brand of the creature's palm. From what he could decipher of his brother's mien, Temmonin guessed that Damowan was torn between fright and curiosity; between haplessness and discretion. But Temmonin himself had been invaded entirely against his will, as Jemalemin and Chaneerem had been. Then, as a knife is pulled from a melon, the presence left him. He twisted his neck to view his brother. Damowan's face showed no signs of manipulation or pain.

"You all right, Temmonin?" Damowan spoke in a normal tone, without affectation.

Temmonin could not yet bring himself to answer. But his brother did not seem at all offended by the silence. He did not repeat the question.

Jemalemin stood up. From beyond the fire, Chaneerem produced muffled sobs, surely not intending that they be heard, yet not being able to restrain them. Soon, all four noticed that the legion of squirrel-men was slowly retreating. Although their eyes showed no sign of emergency, they systematically left the clearing and, within a moment, were swallowed by the innumerable shadows.

As the last of them faded from view, Damowan laughed lightly as if having just discovered some amusing fact, "You were right Temmonin, they are the Chrebin."

Temmonin looked again and noticed Damowan holding something in his hands. It was one of the creatures. It made no motion to escape but sat with its legs folded and its hands in its lap staring up at its holder. Damowan reciprocated. Temmonin crawled over the vomit he had spilled on the ground and moved to his brother's side. Jemalemin followed, hesitant but curious.

"Damowan," Jemalemin began, "that thing almost killed me." Even in warning, he was as meek as a spotted turtle.

"I know, but it hasn't done nothin' to me. I think it's thankin' me."

"What?" Temmonin objected. But then he noticed the bare patches on the Chrebin's arms and legs. These were sections where its fur had been pulled away, exposing minute scars and scrapes. "It's the same one you freed last night," the elder admitted apologetically.

"And I think it plans on stayin'," Damowan said. "I think this mark is somethin' rare." He pointed to the brand on his forearm.

The three stared at the weird creature. Its salmon-colored chest and abdomen rippled as it moved and its placid yellow eyes glinted firelight. It seemed to have no specific interest in Damowan, yet held itself as if it had felt his touch all its life. The Chrebin gurgled and chirped but demanded no attention. It seemed overly occupied with contentment. Damowan and Temmonin could not contain their laughter and, for the first time since they had known him, Jemalemin laughed.

Chaneerem, however, rarely found humor in trivial matters. He rose from his bed of pain snarling with bitter disgust. Tensed and fiery, he rushed forward, biting words from his tongue and spitting them at Damowan.

"If you think yer gonna keep that thing, yer more than stupid. You're dea. . ." As the oath-taker reared to swing his unwounded arm, he choked on his words. Instead of clubbing the Chrebin from Damowan's hand, Chaneerem was crushed to the earth and immobilized by the re-ignition of his left

forearm. He lay cradling his coal black limb as if it
might crumble and blow away. The brand of the
Chrebin on his wrist glowed a morbid crimson in
the shadow of his embarrassment. And his sobs
returned; hopeless, humiliated sobs. The talon-
licker raised his head and, through dripping tears,
slashed hatred at the Chrebin,

"Demon!" he cried. "Demon from the
heart of Hell!"

Then he rolled over and pressed his charred
arm against his chest.

If, in Chaneerem's case, the brand of the
Chrebin were intended to rehabilitate him from his
egotism, it failed. On the contrary, it seemed to
have further ingrained in him the code of bitterness
he had practiced all his life. But at least he had now
learned that the Chrebin had control over his
attacks. He did not repeat his advances on
Damowan or any of the others. The talon-licker
seemed, like his febrile left forearm, to fume a
lingering stench that alienated him not only from his
fellow travelers but, apparently, from all of creation.
He fumed through the remainder of the Shushunu
and the foothills of Imnanaw Kanat and into the
shivering late autumn mountains.

As Damowan had so pessimistically
predicted, rain soaked their camp the first night out
of the swamp land. The hiking, although
uncomfortable, was immensely less uncomfortable
than the dank, uncompromising night he and
Temmonin had endured. If they slept at all through
that infiltrating deluge, they could not recall. And,
although the rain did not cease, they welcomed the
gradual grey of dawn. The temperature dropped
steadily as they ascended into the mountains and the
precipitation vacillated between several varieties for
the remainder of the morning. The clouds offered

sleet. They then returned to rain. Then to an icy drizzle. As the party gained the first pass, snow began to cover the trail and the surrounding landscape. The four pulled their elk hides even tighter to their necks and shoulders and often danced the nervous dance of chill as icy gusts slipped through their coverings, caressing bare skin.

Yet snow carried with it certain uplifting connotations. Temmonin and Damowan were gladdened that the rain had stopped. The Chrebin seemed unaffected by the cold but often shielded its relatively large eyes from falling snowflakes. It had situated itself near Damowan's neck and had wrapped its oily hide in Damowan's coarse, ebony hair. It chirped and whined at irregular intervals and Damowan laughed often. At noon, the snow ceased.

For lunch, they finished eating the turkey they had begun eating the day before. Temmonin and Damowan pressed especially close to the fire, a position to which the Chrebin objected, nearly leaping from Damowan's shoulder to sit in the snow behind him.

"I think my feet fell off back at that last crag." Damowan jested, "It's colder than Mama gets when we tease her about her moles."

"It's very cold, Damowan," Temmonin shivered and laughed, "but not that cold." Temmonin glimpsed Jemalemin laughing again. He shot a wide grin at the boy. Jemalemin received it with warmth and, from what Temmonin guessed, slight embarrassment.

"I 'member one winter that was colder than any other in my life. Remember when the snow drifts covered the west side of all the longhouses in the village?" Jemalemin reminisced excitedly.

119

"And we made tunnels ev'rywhere!" Damowan interjected. "It was our little paradise."

"That was the winter when almost ev'ry mornin', Papa and the other men had to dig us outta the house, the wind was that strong ev'ry night." Temmonin's eyes waned romantic. "And the ice was almost two feet thick. Oh, and . . ." Temmonin was suddenly shaking so hard he could not speak. His smile strained his face almost to the point of shattering.

"What, Temmonin?" Damowan begged, he himself infected and starting to chuckle.

Finally, his older brother was able to control his laughter. "That was the winter when you were on the thin ice near the river tryin' to make ev'ryone laugh by actin' like a goose and you fell through!" And all four burst into bellows. Jittering like an aspen in the wind, Damowan fell back into the snow and nearly crushed the Chrebin.

"And," Temmonin added after catching his breath, "You were doin' it to try to impress that girl, Felvanna!" They all shook until they were exhausted.

They finished lunch and, in spite of their desire to stay there and remain warm, they doused the fire and continued into the chiaroscuro of snow and evergreens and grey crags. That night and the next, they halted at Demnaza villages to eat the evening meal and to sleep. They found the clan of the Elk a tremendous comfort. Not far from the village where the four stayed the second night was a cave with a hot mineral spring. Several young warriors accompanied them to the cavern where they shared an evening of soothing heat and enjoyable conversation. When they finally exited the cave, stars bit through the blackness so intensely that they rivaled the light of the glowing, pregnant moon. Temmonin felt as if his swelling heart might burst through his ribs. Even the burning cold of snow beneath his bare feet could not threaten his joy. The thoughtful hospitality, the welcome camaraderie, the extensive feast, the grandeur of the mountain air, and the forest--all this led his heart to the heights of elation. This night was the first of its kind they had in over a week.

At dawn, with great reservation, they packed and left the oasis of comfort to face what the villagers described as the Lonely Valley. The village elders explained that the traveler's path would descend into a deep chasm which none of the clans of the Kanattar had ever populated in winter. All those of the Demnaza who lived in the valley during the warm months had left two weeks previous at the sign of the first snow. And snow was the reason they left. Snow--an arm's length deeper every day--was the only obstacle to permanent dwellings in the valley and a significant source of concern for those who passed between the cliffs in winter. To pass around it, however, would add days to their journey. Fortunately, the Demnaza had graced each of them with a pair of snowshoes. The four had not thought to pack any because Temmonin and Damowan had encountered no snow on their previous trek and, at least in the lowlands, most of the leaves were still on the trees. The Demnaza also supplied them with extra deer and elk hides.

Very soon after departing, they encountered the gorge. When they began the rapid descent, only sparse flakes of snow meandered through the expanse before them. But, as they arrived at the floor, which may have been several body lengths higher than the floor in summer and spring, the thick clouds concentrated their efforts and increased

their production of white blindness. Within
moments, the four were tying ropes between one
another to remain connected. Temmonin and the
others skied with little knowledge of their
surroundings for over an hour. Temmonin led. He
struggled to hold a straight course and, in spite of
the difficulty of the task, succeeded. In the midst of
his labor, his mind continually returned to the
nagging question of why this cavern, being so near
to the Demnaza village where they had spent the
night, received so much more snow than that
village. But the urgency of the storm never allowed
him to focus his thoughts for any length of time.
As a result, the nagging accompanied him all day
and he was unable to come to any conclusion about
the matter.

It stopped snowing for a time and this
allowed the travelers the luxury of opening their
eyes and enjoying the scenery. From all
appearances, this valley was relatively narrow and
tremendously long. It might take more than a single
day to travel its entire length. As evening fell, it
brought with it the certainty that this was the case.
They found a configuration on the west valley wall
that most resembled a cave and set up their camp
there. Over the evening meal, Temmonin and
Damowan discussed their proximity to Shemtootoo
and Uncle Nosh's village. At this, Temmonin's
mind carried him to thoughts of that entrancing
cousin with whom he had recently been
reacquainted. He continued his conversation with
Damowan and Jemalemin but intermittently
returned in his mind to fresh memories of beauty.
And his memories followed him into the grey and
black of sleep.

But the grey and black of sleep lingered
long and coalesced with a multitude of colors and

sights and sounds. Dreams elongated and changed
into epics of worlds and of histories as foreign and
as familiar as the death of mountains. Evergreens
bowed and caressed Temmonin's face and drew
from his eyes lamentations for the death of entire
races. He danced through parades of macabre
creatures and watched as their tongues twisted and
undulated, attempting to impress upon him the
overwhelming urgency of their plight. But suddenly
they were his mother and his father and Damowan
and Tutumora. His family smiled at him, their eyes
glistening with expectation, their arms extended in
greeting, but he could not reach them. They were
estranged by a cavern--the gorge small at first--
almost small enough to cross with a leap, then
expanding, then carrying his family so very, very far
from him. And then he was alone with the snow
falling so gently about his eyes and ears. And then
he was in the gorge staring into the overcast above,
hoping Damowan would soon leap from the cliff to
join him. But then he was the gorge; within himself,
granite and shale and receiving into his belly so
much snow. And he felt his family as they walked
about upon his eyelids and searched for him and he
could not call for them because his tongue was
laden with so much snow. In his panic, he ground
his vocal chords--his deep, molten larynx--begging
them to stay. But with his plea, he woke the
quakings of his tormented belly. Guilty and
immobilized, he watched his family plummet into
his stomach.

Then his legs returned and his arms were
dappled with feathers; the lithe, blue-grey feathers
of Ek-Rignara, and on the wings of the great heron
he flew to where the osprey glides through island
clouds. He knew then that Ek-Dividawa held the
wisdom to free his family and unite them again. But

the clouds were too numerous and the maze they
formed too extensive and Temmonin flew and flew
and turned and turned until he was certain he had
returned to the entrance to this maze of mist--
though if he had, he would not have recognized the
place. And again, panic flooded his heart as the
feathers drifted from his arms and he, with his
family concealed in his bowels, and perhaps by then
dead, dropped to earth--not like a rusted, brittle oak
leaf in a playful spring breeze but like an acorn or a
walnut with direct and fatal intent.

Temmonin never saw the earth. There
were only pools of ocher and veridian, of magenta,
of chestnut; concentric circles, imbricated and
translucent and gradually focusing to harsh black
and breathing and random evidence of movement
and. . .

Temmonin was now sure he was awake.
But the situation that greeted him was unlike
anything he had ever experienced. He had often
woken in strange places and been confused as to
where he was. But that confusion had always been
temporary. Within seconds of waking, he would
look around and quickly recall the previous evening
and regain his bearings. But now, after several
seconds, he realized he was not wrapped in his
sleeping skins beneath the lean-to he and the others
had erected. He was not surrounded by snow and
cold. He was not outside at all.

It was warm here. He felt that his skin was
directly exposed to the air around him but he was
not chilled in the least. He could not move his arms
or legs. He was bound to what felt like a large log,
the bark of which had imprinted itself into the back
of his skull, the length of his spine, his elbows, his
calves, and his heels.

These inscriptions throbbed. He smelled the pungent, sickly salt of neglected bodies--of his and possibly others. He could see very little in this feeble light, only a multitude of shadows like the premonition of an eclipse. And his eyes began to ache from straining. Something or some things were moving in the same unpredictable pattern as one starting a fire or preparing a meal. Frightened by what might happen if he were to make a noise, yet too curious to remain silent, he decided to signal for his companions.

He began with a quiet, short sough. He continued this seemingly unintentional sound intermittently for quite some time, feigning the signs of dreaming. Something brushed by his leg. Something bristling with hair. He heard a low-pitched groan from the air above his feet and, tensed in blindness, he prepared himself for the shock of contact. None came.

All was quiet for a while. Then, in a very tentative voice, someone called his name. Wanting to be sure of himself, he waited. Then the voice repeated itself,

"Temmonin." It was Jemalemin.

"Jemalemin?" Temmonin replied. "D'you know what's goin' on?"

"No, I thought you might."

"Keep it down over there, eh?" Damowan's voice drifted from farther away.

"Damowan?" Temmonin jumped as far as his bonds would allow. "What's going on here? Do you know where we are?"

"No, Temmonin. It's dark in here and I'm not a bat."

A low groan suddenly emanated from somewhere to Temmonin's left. All three were still for a few moments. Scufflings and grunts soon filled the area. He could still see very little. He then noticed that his shoulders and upper back were sore from tension. His head began to feel pain to the rhythm of his heartbeat. Any of his attempts to relax were futile. Sounds. Endless anonymous sounds.

Eventually the activity ceased.

"So nobody knows anything?" Temmonin whispered, "Chaneerem, you here?"

"Yea," he answered, "lashed to a tree trunk."

"I think we all are," Damowan added.

"Is anyone hurt?" Temmonin asked.

Two negatives returned. Temmonin assumed that even if Chaneerem were wounded, he would probably not admit the fact.

"So no one saw or heard anything?" Temmonin inquired again.

"Temmonin, d'you think we'd hide it if we did?" Damowan replied quickly, "we're in this too, y'know."

"Tshhh! Quiet, Damowan." Temmonin whispered.

The admonition was tardy, however, for the scrapings and gruntings and moanings returned. More bristling hair. More sounds of observation and perhaps congregation. But this time, Temmonin felt hot, salty breath. A bear? Then he felt warm, over-large hands touch and manipulate his face. Too gentle to be a bear. Yet this unannounced intimacy almost caused him to scream from embarrassment. Controlling his tongue during the ensuing inspection of his entire body sucked monumental emotion from his bewildered mind. Within minutes after the completion of the manipulation and the withdrawal of the inspector, Temmonin slunk into sleep.

He could not be at all certain how long the four had spent in this dark world where it seemed they dreamt more often than they were awake.

He would have liked to have been fed less often. The four received undercooked or burnt meat, bitter leaves including needles from pine trees, and several varieties of gnarled, fibrous roots all soaked in or rolled in gross amounts of salt. At first, the salt was a sort of consolation for the brackish subsistence that was forced upon them. Soon, however, their tongues were lumped with canker sores and they loathed meals more than any other event in this world of insistent midnight. And their bodies swelled in the humidity.

Whoever was keeping them here was not any animal they had come to know during their relatively short lives. Much too intelligent. They were obviously communicating to each other but none of the four Ek-Birin could make any sense of anything they were saying.

Any attempt at communication with their invisible captors was met with silence. Either these keepers could not speak Mokhamoyuba or Ek-Birin or they refused to do so. Temmonin tried any words from any dialect that he knew. Still, no response.

Temmonin's dreams seemed gradually but persistently to gather at an inexplicable focal point. He saw a face, grotesque and not overly human. The face snarled and coughed, whimpered and cooed. As he dreamt, the presence pressed him with urgency and dominated his awareness. To his increasing frustration, however, he could not define his vision after he woke. He grappled with his clotted memory for hours, repeatedly failing to master it. He wanted to discuss the phenomenon with Damowan but was too embarrassed to do so

with Chaneerem nearby. Like the moth that lands
and takes flight again as a child rushes to capture it,
so this morsel of thought eluded Temmonin's grasp
until his mind was tired of the pursuit.

His conversations with the others were
tediously repetitive as were the spasms of disgust at
having to lay on his own refuse and smell the reek
that filled this chamber. After a time, he wretched
at the vaguest aroma of salt. Fortunately, he was
free to move his head and so could avoid choking
on his vomit. This still did not exempt his face
from congealing and eventually crusting over. On
occasion, his body was drenched with great amounts
of icy water. Their keepers surprised all four of
them with these random cleanings. But they were
never scrubbed or turned and so the results were at
best only vaguely satisfying. Their muscles whined
to be moved. Their skin slowly evolved into
chambers of discomfort from which they could not
remove themselves. They could not scratch their
irritations and they could not ease the penetrating
fire of rashes or the stinging descent of infection.
Their captors repeatedly probed their bodies. The
grunts and scuffles and the food and the dreams and
the pain and the futility returned again and again in
a cycle that led their imaginations into the center of
howling tornados.

"What're you doin' to me!?" Damowan
tore the air apart.

Temmonin woke from a stupor.
Questioning whispers filled the room.

"What're you doin', you sick, jerk demons!"
Damowan railed again. His voice was ragged and
obviously tired, but he could not refrain.

"Damowan! What's happenin'?"
Temmonin yelled back.

"You demons! You bastards!" Damowan continued, "Git yer salty, grimy paws off. . ."

"Damowan!" Temmonin screamed.

But ambiguous shadows offered no response. Damowan was quiet again.

"Damowan!" Temmonin whispered. And upon receiving no answer repeated his question with more fervor, then again in panic. He cursed his captors.

After a period of silence, he spoke again, "Jemalemin? Chaneerem?"

"Yea?" Jemalemin answered.

"What's goin' on over there, Jemalemin?"

"I don't know, Temmonin."

Temmonin desisted. He stared at the starless sky of nothing and wished for some sight other than the abstract splashes of color that chased each other across the inside of his eyelids. Then, even these blurred as tears gathered in his eyes. He let them wash salt and sweat from his temples. He sobbed without sound but with a tense face and clenched fists. Because there was nothing else to do, he again gave in to sleep.

He knew he was dreaming as the twittering of nuthatches permeated the air over his head. He lay immobile in his smoldering awareness hardly caring if he had finally passed from life. Salt vapors tickled his nose hairs. Without opening his eyes, Temmonin rolled from his back to his right side. His muscles, congealed with lethargy, protested against the slightest of his movements. Opening his eyes now, he was flooded with perception. Dawn's vague light outlined for him impressions of trees, of mountains, of undergrowth, of mist and scattered clouds that dotted the pastel orange sky, of earth and granite and shale upon which he lay. And of

Jemalemin, then Damowan and Chaneerem. He was awake.

But for the second time in his life, he had no idea where he was.

In spite of his protesting muscles, he sat up, propped by his right arm, and scanned the area. Snow was quite present beneath most of the surrounding trees but had apparently been melted away from the areas where the sun could shine. Where he and the others huddled, all was brown and rusty earth with a light covering of yellow maple leaves. He was very cold. He inspected his body.

His arms and legs were a pale, pale mauve-- much more pale than the palms of his hands had ever been. And he was gaunt. His legs looked like rotten birch limbs from which the bark had been haphazardly torn. And his feet were tangled in several lengths of thin vine that had been smeared with pine sap or tar. He studied the vines and found that the feet of his three sleeping companions were also tangled. He could see a small field of these sticky things laid like a mat across the clearing into which they must have walked. But he could not remember having walked here. All he could recall was black and salt and sweat and vomit. He reached to rouse Damowan.

"Damowan, we're out." He startled a chipmunk with his speech. The rodent scurried noisily away through the maple leaves. "I don't know where out is but it's cold and we're almost naked and somethin' really, really nasty happened to our bodies." Damowan squinted at Temmonin who proceeded, "How can you sleep in this freezin' cold?"

"What's goin' on here?" Damowan asked, rising. In the midst of a moan, he continued,

"We're out? Temmonin, where are we? And what happened to my arms?! Ugh and my legs?!"

"I have no idea, I jus' woke up myself," Temmonin answered. "One thing's fer sure. We haven't been taken to the land of perpetual summer."

"Temmonin," Damowan moaned heavily again, "You are always so very funny."

Jemalemin and Chaneerem had awoke. Now, all four gazed in confusion at each other and at the clearing.

"Temmonin," Damowan burst out, full of laughter, "You are one ugly Flicker!"

Temmonin laughed too, "Looks like they made us up real good." He paused. "We'd better get outta these trappings before some new adventure eats us fer breakfast."

But as they worked at freeing themselves, they heard the forest shiver with the presence of men. Damowan saw a group of three warriors, fully clad and hefting spears, approaching from their rear. He motioned to Temmonin. Jemalemin was startled by a group entering the clearing from the direction of the rising sun. Others soon followed and stood around the four Ek-Birin. They were clad in Kumuchska gear and their faces were painted for war, solid black on the left cheek and jowl, solid red on the right.

"Men of the Ek-Birin," one warrior announced, "Know that treachery is not tolerated among the tribes of the confederacy nor among the clans of the Kanattar, nor even among sister clans from the marshes."

Suddenly the familiarity of these faces made sense to Temmonin. These were warriors from his Uncle Nosh's village. It must be near. How did they get here? And what was this aggression? Was the whole confederacy infected with this corrosive suspicion? Had Mok sent Daimadunva messengers ahead to warn the Wolverine clan? How had the four gotten this far north? Temmonin stared at their new captors, grateful that at least he and the other three would soon be warm again. He decided to submit to these warriors and wait to speak until he and the others were brought before Nosh.

The Kumuchska helped loose them from the vines that clung to their ankles. Then they stood by as the four Ek-Birin contorted their faces in efforts to avoid tearing their own muscles from their bones as they stood up. Every move conjured fresh surges of pain in Temmonin's legs and back. When he stood, he almost lost his balance. His feet recoiled as he stepped on twigs and sharp-edged stones. He had lost his callouses. How long had they been tied to those logs?

The whole party plodded toward Demdegumshannatez, the Ek-Birin picking their way across a field of pain, the Kumuchska patiently preceding and following their new captives. Before the sun had pulled itself over the eastern mountain ridge, they entered the waking village. The four naked men needed help to cross the numbing, knee-high stream that marked the east border. Temmonin's soul stirred at the comforting thought that, within minutes, he would see Nosh's smile. And as they climbed the west bank, he glimpsed his cousin Zheva. Blood warmed him to the limits of his appendages. Hundreds of dreams clouded his vision as he saw that woman and, not paying attention to where he was stepping, he stumbled over a rock. He righted himself in a flush. But as he continued on, he could not force himself to look at Zheva again. His limbs were white and covered with rashes and sores and he was as thin as a

cornstalk. Perhaps she did not even recognize him.
He thought he heard the sound of giggling from
where she and her friends sat tanning hides.

Their captors shuffled them into a small hut
set apart from the cluster of the village longhouses;
the prison hut. Temmonin expected at any moment
to see Nosh come and reprimand these haughty
young soldiers for capturing his nephews of the
sister clan. The chief never appeared. After a short
while, the door flap slipped open and four skins
were deposited near the door.

"For your comfort," the bearer announced
with at least some notion of a sneer.

Damowan, who sat closest to the door,
eagerly distributed the hides and wrapped himself in
his, "Oh, man!! I can hardly believe how good this
feels. But my muscles. What happened to our
bodies? I know this doesn't make any sense but
could it have somethin' to do with those mineral
springs?"

"Mineral springs?" Temmonin squinted as
he lay down beneath his fur. "Damowan, this is
Nosh's village. We're a million miles away from
those mineral springs." His voice weakened as
warmth soothed his shiverings. " It musta been that
place, Dama. That. . . place." His sentence trailed
off.

"What. . .place. . ?" But soon Damowan,
like the others, was sleeping.

They slept for most of the day. Chaneerem
woke first and sat up. The sound roused
Temmonin.

"When's that uncle of yers gonna git here?"
Chaneerem asked.

"I don't know," Temmonin answered.
"Maybe he's out huntin'."

"A chief?"

"I know it's not normal but, maybe." Temmonin was actually happy to be talking to Chaneerem.

The talon-licker rubbed his eyes with the heels of his thumbs.

"Did they do anything strange to you back there?" Temmonin asked.

The oath-taker looked at Temmonin for a moment. "You were there the whole time," his voice sharpened slightly. "They got us unstuck from those vines and led us across the river and into this hut. What's so strange about that? I mean I have no idea why they stuck us in a prison hut, but what do I know? It's yer family, not mine."

"No, I mean before that," Temmonin continued, "in the cave or whatever it was."

"The cave?" Chaneerem's tone was puzzled and harsher. "What, with those Demnaza warriors last night? Nothin' strange to me about sittin' in hot mineral springs. And I don't know about you but none of those guys so much as touched me. So what's yer problem?"

"Last night?" Temmonin interjected.

"What about last night?" Chaneerem replied as the other two woke, Damowan more slowly than Jemalemin.

"You said last night we were at the Demnaza mineral springs."

"Yea, I was jus' statin' a fact."

"A fact? That wasn't last night! I don't know how long ago it was but it sure wasn't last night! It takes at least three or four days to git from that village to here, Chaneerem. At least."

Chaneerem scoffed, "What're you talkin' about?"

It seemed to Temmonin that Chaneerem refused to agree with this statement because he knew Temmonin was more experienced in this region. That fact seemed to irritate the talon-licker.

"Y'mean you don't remember a cave and salty food and. . .look, yer body is just as emaciated as mine. And you've got sores on yer mouth, too. From the salt." Temmonin's voice tightened. "And look at yer left arm. They musta burned it."

"Look," Chaneerem's tone was detached, "I told ya I remember the cave. And I'd imagine those mineral springs had some salt in 'em and I have to admit I'm as much in the dark as you are about what happened to our bodies, but what are you talkin' about?"

"What am I talkin' about?" Temmonin wheezed. "Y'mean you don't remember bein' tied to a log fer days and. . .aww, fergit it, Chaneerem!"

"A log?" Chaneerem asked, eyes cocked.

"Fergit it," Temmonin repeated.

Damowan was awake enough to comprehend at least the last few sentences his brother spoke. The younger scratched his leg as he leaned on his right elbow,

"Temmonin, what're you talkin' about? Back there in the clearing, you were sayin' how we were out and that somebody made us up real good. Now you're talkin' logs and salt?"

Temmonin was taken back. "Damowan please don't tell me you don't remember either."

"Remember what?" Damowan echoed Chaneerem's sentiments.

"Damowan, look at yer body!" Temmonin paused and blinked and shook his head. "Fergit it. I don't know what's goin' on here."

The air was filled with rufflings and scrapings and, once again, the door flap opened to permit a gush of evening sunset into the bark hut. The four could see only the outline of the woman who carried their food. Her head fully eclipsed the sinking sun. But, as she knelt to place the birch-bark tray on the floor of the prison, Temmonin and Damowan recognized Zheva.

Her eyes were shadowed with gravity and her movements sullen and disappointed. As she lifted them to greet Temmonin, tears splashed the food she carried.

"I am forever sorry, my brothers. I will pray to the Creator that he will shut the ears and nose of pain that you may not hear the screams of the eagle of death nor smell its wicked burnings." And she rose to depart.

"Wait! Zheva!" Temmonin's pleading halted his cousin. "Zheva, what're you doin' prayin' the prayer fer men about to die? What's goin' on in this village? And where's yer dad?"

"I'm sorry, Temmonin." More tears washed her cheeks, "I can't say any more. Shegra'll be here. He'll tell you." And she whisked out into the fiery sunset.

"Shegra?" Damowan questioned after her, "What about Nosh?"

Shegra entered the tent soon after sundown. His voice was padded with the same apology that escorted Zheva's words.

"My brothers, I am here to greet you because Nosh, my father, left over seven moons ago for Ojeb-Mawitez."

"Ojeb-Mawitez?!" exclaimed Damowan, "The high council?"

"Why the high council?" Temmonin added.

"You didn't know about the high council?" Shegra asked and paused, perhaps waiting for some sign that his cousins were jesting. When he was sure they were serious, he began his explanation. "Brothers, I'm sure you know the moon has danced almost three times since that family in yer village was killed. And since that time, a bunch more weird things've happened."

Damowan's boisterous objection stilled Shegra, "Three months!?"

"Yea," replied Shegra, "it's been at least three months, hasn't it?"

"That long?" Temmonin's tone was somewhat introspective. "We've been away that long?"

"Temmonin, shut up!" Damowan was angry as he questioningly looked at his brother and his cousin. "What the heck is this three months stuff!?"

Shegra paused before continuing. "It's pretty much been common knowledge fer a while now that you four've been lost--or, some say, hiding. It's been about three months, Damowan. The last you were seen was when you left the Demnaza village of Gamnashta near the mouth of the Lonely Valley a week after you left from the Mamar."

"Last night," Damowan spoke with certainty, "that was last night, Shegra."

"I'm afraid not, Damowan," Shegra returned. "It was months ago."

"What? Do you think we're a bunch of idiots? It was last night!" Damowan steamed.

"Damowan, quiet!" Temmonin burst out, "I wanna hear the rest of this."

Shegra hesitated, hampered by the concern he had for his cousins and their companions. He spoke slowly, "There've been incidents like the killing in yer guys' village all over the North and East of the confederacy. In fact, they went ahead of yer guys' trail all the way here. It started with the Chichmolar, then among the clans of the Shushunu-

-the Daimadunva, who you guys encountered, the Tanaka, the Zevi-Zevi, and then, after you guys left their territory, the Demnaza. Since you four were last seen, a bunch more Kanattar villages lost good people. The problem got so big they called the high council out of season to talk about how to deal with it." As Shegra paused, silence licked their ears like the whispering of venomous snakes. "There's been lotsa talk about the Ek-Birin message party—about you guys." At that, Damowan threw up his arms in disgust. Shegra proceeded. "Some people think you guys got killed jus' like the rest. But most people think you've been secretly involved somehow."

"I can't believe this!" Damowan shouted.

Temmonin met Shegra's eyes. "Shegra, you gotta believe us, we haven't killed a single person. I mean back in one of the villages in Painted Turtle territory, they accused us of raping and killing the chief's daughter but we told 'em why we were traveling through and it seemed like they believed us. They even helped us on our way." He could not help but glance over at Chaneerem to see how he would react. Fortunately, the oath-taker remained silent.

"Temmonin," Shegra started, "My friends, almost every death happened at night and the wounds almost always included scratches like those a bird claw would make. And the faces were almost always part eaten, especially the eyes, as if a beak had pecked them out. On some occasions, feathers were layin' around, larger than any bird could carry-- but Flicker designs. Not Eagle or Heron or Cardinal feathers. Flicker feathers."

"A man from yer clan has been taken to council. I think his name's Mantaw. He admitted that he used the forbidden arts to capture and kill the monster you four were s'posed to bring here from yer village. Some say that what he did started this whole sequence of events and now there's this bloodlust in the land."

"So what does all this have to do with us?" Chaneerem asked, annoyed.

"The most recent killing happened here in this village: Two nights ago a man and his wife were killed and their five children were left orphans. That warrior must've fought well before he died; Flicker feathers were all over the floor of the longhouse. As other people came to help, they saw this huge bird-monster run away from the village and into the mountains. The men saw it tryin' to fly but one of its wings was wounded so it had to run. The next day, yesterday, we worked all day to lay out those clinging vines that trapped you guys. All our warriors started patrollin' the perimeter before nightfall. In the mornin', we found you guys. Ya have to admit it doesn't look very good."

The four Ek-Birin sat motionless, soaking into themselves the severity of their situation. Silence thickened the air in the hut, causing Shegra's final words to sound as if they were spoken through fog.

"The elders of a bunch of Kumuchska villages're gonna meet here tonight. They're gonna talk 'bout yer guys' capture and. . ." He held himself steady, "And maybe yer execution."

"I have to warn you, brothers. You don't have too many friends in the Kanattar. And I'm s'posed to stay impartial." With that, Shegra left.

As he departed, the four Ek-Birin stared at the inside of the hut and at each other. Damowan released his breath first, "What's this three months stuff, Temmonin?" he asked, exasperated.

"We musta been in that cave fer the whole time," Temmonin answered, "but I can't believe it was that long."

"The cave," Chaneerem scoffed. "Here we go again."

"Why don't any of you guys remember? What am I s'posed to do if none of you even knows what I'm talkin' about?" Temmonin cried.

"I remember," Jemalemin said.

"You remember what?" Chaneerem sneered.

"I remember darkness fer a long, long time. And salty, grimy, prickly food-and I remember bein' tied to a log, and I remember dreams."

"Dreams?" blurted Damowan. "Why don't I remember any of this?"

"I don't know, Damowan," Temmonin said, "But look at us. We're emaciated. Our muscles're so sore we can't even walk. And feel yer back. You still have the marks of the bark on yer spine." Temmonin heaved himself to his knees. "Damowan, Chaneerem, how did you feel when we walked outta those mineral springs? Not like this, I'll bet. How do you think we got this way?"

"I don't know what's goin' on but this whole thing is startin' to make me mad!" rasped Damowan, "I mean, I have no idea how I got this way and it's driving me crazy tryin' to figure it out but how could I fergit three months of my life, Temmonin, three months?"

"You know I wonder if any of this really matters when the fact is that we're gonna git cooked like opossum tonight," Chaneerem reminded them of their situation.

"Aw, come on, Chaneerem, think about it! What if they ask us where we been and we give four different answers? That'll look fairly convincing, won't it?" Temmonin was moving his hands as he talked.

"Look," Chaneerem cut, "if they're as ready to kill us as yer two cousins say they are, we wouldn't have to say a single thing and they'd have us tied up and roastin' before the raccoons're out."

"Well, there's no harm in talkin' about it. It's not as if we have anything else to do right now?" Temmonin argued.

"Well, far be it from me to stand in the way of progress," Chaneerem stated ambivalently. He pulled his left arm from beneath his deer hide and fondled with it. The abstract burn marks that had blackened his skin looked even more hopeless than his withered muscles. Then Temmonin noticed the crimson brand of the Chrebin on the oath-taker's wrist. For the first time since their long dream had ended, Temmonin remembered the night with the squirrel-men. "So how come none of you guys got burn marks?" the oath-taker asked.

"None of us was stupid enough to throw rocks at the Chrebin," Temmonin retorted. Then, as Chaneerem's face showed signs of confusion, he added, "Oh, no. Don't tell me you don't remember that either."

At first, Chaneerem's face was blank. Then Temmonin watched subtle signs of remembrance creep into the talon-licker's eyes.

Damowan raised his eyebrows and wagged his finger at the oath-taker like an old woman at a child, "Don't mess with the Chrebin!" he teased.

The inside of the hut was almost black when Shegra returned to take the four to the clan council. He led them but a few steps from the prison to the bonfire in the center of the circle of elders. As they were seated, Temmonin noticed a large hole dug near the fire and, lying next to it, a massive oak timber. He was sure that the pole would soon be dropped into the hole with the four Ek-Birin lashed to it. Adrenaline singed his eyelashes and churned in his stomach; perhaps the fire was calling for his soul, perhaps his spirit was preparing to leap from his charred corpse. Perhaps his Creator was imbuing him with new blood to sustain him through the rage that was to follow. In any case, Temmonin was as anxious as a gnat struggling to pull itself from the surface of a stream before the bass notices it.

The circle of elders closed behind them and one of them invoked the presence of the Creator. Directly afterwards, he gazed around at his fellows and began,

"My brothers, peace and beauty. We come together this chill evening for one purpose only--to discuss the fate of these four intruders. We do not yet decide that they are guilty of the murder which took place only two nights ago, but we do know that they are those of the Ek-Birin which were followed by a long series of strange murders through marsh and swamp and, finally, into our mountain forests. These are those which early this morning our warriors found entangled in the vines which we laid out to trap any intruders. Now they stand before us awaiting our word." He looked around the entire circle of men. "But first, we await their word. Speak to us Ek-Birin. Let us know your minds."

The four traded glances in an attempt to decide who would speak. Finally, Temmonin and Chaneerem began simultaneously. Chaneerem continued as Temmonin subsided.

"What eloquent myths might we conjure to sway such strong opinion?" he spoke deliberately, inviting rebuke.

The elders were markedly surprised by such impenitence. The leader asked, "You would not speak a word in self-defense?"

The four stood silent. A thousand speeches crowded Temmonin's thoughts, each crawling over the others for preeminence but, in the end, all lay broken and unable to be heard. He stared at his accusers.

"Have you no words, Temmonin, nephew of the high elder of Demdegumshannatez?"

Temmonin began slowly. "My fathers, my brothers, we are emaciated. We are exhausted. We have sores on our entire bodies. We can barely walk. When the patrol found us this morning, we were naked and shivering. If I were among the jury today and not among the accused, I could hardly imagine how four men such as us could carry out such devious plans."

It seemed to Temmonin that his words had had some effect on the circle of elders. All was quiet for a moment. Then one elder stood and cleared his voice to capture the attention of the gathering.

"Finely chosen words to conjure the pity of the clan of your uncle. But," a short, bitter laugh slipped from between his lips and he shook his head, "let us not forget the reasons why the forbidden arts were forbidden. I and several others sitting here this evening have been fortunate. . .or unfortunate enough to have witnessed the fate of several men from our own village who were foolish enough to succumb to the temptation of the power that those arts offer a man. When these men were finally caught, they too were emaciated. They too were exhausted. They too had sores on their entire bodies. They too could hardly stand up. But they were not to be pitied. On the contrary, these men, in their inability to control their passions, caused the death of a six-year-old girl." He paused and looked around. "No, my Flickers, such words do not stir the pity of those who have seen the destruction of beauty."

If Temmonin's call for reason had swayed a single man to sympathy, he was sure that now none remained on his side. What had seemed to be his most convincing argument for their innocence had just been blown aside like a small feather in a light breeze. The four stood waiting for the breeze to get stronger.

"Temmonin of the Ek-Birin, have you nothing to say in reply to the words of our brother?"

Temmonin breathed deeply and spoke the only words he could think of. "I can only say that if you execute us this night, you will stain guilty knives with innocent blood."

This reply stung the council to outrage. Some of the elders spat into the center. Others hurled insults. Others slandered among themselves. The acting high elder stretched his arms far above his head, wielding his fur-covered staff some twelve feet into the air. The gathering quieted again.

"Now we await your words, my brothers." His eyes followed the circle, "Let us know your minds."

Beginning with the man to the leader's right, each elder stated his advice concerning the fate of the four Ek-Birin. With every vote, Temmonin felt the gloom gather and rumble in his heart. These men had truly made their decision. Very few had mercy on him and his companions. Suddenly, amidst the swirling anticipation that circled the four, Jemalemin began whispering vehemently,

"That face? I see that face again?" he swooned and Chaneerem caught him by the arm.

The others said nothing, awaiting his explanation.

"Salt," was all Jemalemin said.

Temmonin's eyes bulged. He moved closer to Jemalemin, "Jemalemin, a huge, hairy face, the smell of salt?" He was sweating with excitement, "Is the face sayin' somethin'--some strange language?"

Jemalemin looked directly at Temmonin, but his glazed eyes seemed to focus on the pale moon behind the older Ek-Birin. "Yea, a strange language. . .but, I understand it. . .how?" Jemalemin slapped his hands over his face, "This is so weird!"

On the crest of a strange elation, Temmonin spewed a string of grinding words and stared at Jemalemin, just as surprised at himself as the other three were at him. Jemalemin nearly laughed,

"Temmonin, you understand too."

"What was that?" Damowan asked, eyes like hungry cisterns, "'The world of the night howls its outrage?'"

Temmonin swung around and clutched his brother's shoulders, "Then you understand too?"

"Yea, but what is it?" Damowan asked.

"It's from the cave!" Temmonin was jittering. He turned to Chaneerem, "Chaneerem, do you understand?"

The talon-licker looked as if this admission were as humiliating as being unjustly burned. But when he answered, he did so with surprising tenderness, "Yea, I do. I remember the cave now too."

In a frenzy of confidence, Temmonin leapt away from the other three. He ran to the leader of the council before anyone could intervene.

"My chief!" He fell to one knee and extended his right arm, "You must delay these judgments. I have proof of our whereabouts these last months."

Temmonin's words were splintered like oak twigs as a group of yelling warriors emerged from just outside the circle of longhouses. They were preceded by a flailing, winged monster. The monster was half-running, half-flying directly toward the circle of elders and, as it crashed through the perimeter, it made clear its intentions to plunge into the bonfire. But three Ek-Birin stood in its path. Temmonin was about to call a directive to Damowan when he recognized that his brother was thinking the same thing.

Damowan had stolen a large branch from the burning pile and, with what little strength he had, was pointing the charred, tapered end toward the monster. As the thing rose in an attempt to leap over Damowan, Temmonin noticed the yellow and black of its broad flicker wings and its heaving, speckled chest. Damowan swung his lance weakly but managed to bother the monster's flight just as its claws cleared his shoulders. Screaming, it crashed and pinned Damowan's thin figure to the ground a body's length from the blaze. The Flicker monster drove its needle-like beak at Damowan's head. The massive blade struck the dirt just to the right of his cheek. Jemalemin leapt to his companion's aid. The monster was about to pull its beak from the soil and correct its aim when Jemalemin slammed into its side, causing it to lose its clutch on Damowan. With little effort, the thing flung the boy far from him. As it concentrated on

Jemalemin, however, Damowan kicked it from himself. He looked for his spear. But Chaneerem had already retrieved the spear and had committed its deadly tip to the space the monster had just left. As Damowan began to sit up, the branch grazed Damowan's shoulder with stinging slivers and black soot. Damowan glared a blank question at the oath-taker.

"I was aimin' fer the monster!" Chaneerem yelled, "Look out!"

Again, the Ek-Birin creature pressed Damowan to the earth. By that time, however, the group of Kumuchska warriors was upon it and they pulled the vicious assailant from the fallen warrior's back. Jemalemin and Temmonin tried to help control the writhing, undulating mutant. No one noticed as Chaneerem reached again for the spear he had thrown. The talon-licker drove the javelin between two warriors and directly into the creature's chest.

Temmonin burst out, "Don't kill it, Chaneerem!" But his command was doused by the roaring wave of death as the Ek-Birin monster rasped its last. Within seconds, the entire circle of elders had converged upon the bleeding mass of feathers, claws, and wings. Then the head released its tension and rolled back away from its body and onto the ground. The thick gel of its tongue slipped through its beak as it sunk into death.

Even though they had previously seen the Kumuchska monster, the four Ek-Birin were as appalled as the elders at the carnage. Like the other mutant, this flicker was partially human. Grotesquely clawed arms poked from beneath the limp wings. The eyes were vaguely mannish and moved Temmonin to compassion. Red, thick blood streamed like a spider across the massive breast and

abdomen, slowing but still running. Temmonin felt
tears gathering.

"Chaneerem, how could you do that?" he
asked. "We needed that thing alive!"

"Come now," called one of the elders,
"How convenient of this thing to interrupt our
council that you might destroy it for all to see! A
clever plan to convince us of your innocence. But
not clever enough."

"What're you talkin' about?" Damowan
roared, forgetting his respect.

"Ah, and would you have it that we should
now release you," the elder continued, "that you
might again hide amidst dark caves, conjuring new
demons to guide into our camps? Kill these guilty
murderers!" A surge of voices glutted the crowd as
Temmonin groped for comprehension.

"How could we have staged all this?"
Damowan raged, the veins of his neck roiling,
demanding silence. "How in Hell's name can you
think I liked bein' sliced to ribbons by this thing!?"

Another elder spoke in defense of the Ek-
Birin, "It would be very difficult to arrange such
specific events. We must reconvene and vote
again."

And another rebutted. Soon voices piled
upon each other like branches in a beaver dam.
Before too long, however, the high elder again
called attention to himself by raising his staff. The
arguments trailed off.

"All here listen well," he spoke sternly,
"these matters are far to intricate for hasty decision.
Injustice awaits behind every tree. Judgment in this
case shall be reserved only for the highest council."
The men murmured amongst themselves. "And
since the high council is meeting at this very time
and is discussing this very issue, we shall send a

party south to Ojeb-Mawitez tomorrow morning."
His tone was final. "Who would escort these Ek-Birin to the island?"

As the volunteers advanced toward the acting high elder, Temmonin caught Damowan's eye. He saw there the relief he himself felt. They would see Nosh. They would see Desh. Perhaps Amowz had been chosen to accompany Desh. The brothers smiled at each other through the crowd.

VI. Or is it our intention to best our maker, to reveal the weaknesses and limits of Him who so precisely knows our weaknesses and limits, to discern the actions of Him who made us able to act, to demand an answer from Him who demands our very lives in service to Himself. Shall we, like spiders feeling the tremble of the web, like rabbits gazing through bracken-covered passageways, or like embryos sensing the stirring of the dawn, curl our brows at Him who made us? Having fully assessed the manner of all things within our minuscule scope of vision with our truncated capacity of perception, shall we then take this hand print of knowledge and, with it, cover the face of the universe? And shall we, after having covered the face of the universe, then attempt to cover the face that made the universe? And shall we, after having rid ourselves of our burden of accountability, then use the minds He has provided and the compassion with which He has imbued us and the energy with which He has laced every living thing to create a new world less offensive to our thirst for comfort. In our blindness, do we thirst for that which, in the end, would, like salt water, drive us to insanity?

CHAPTER 6

"I want you guys to know," Shegra apologized, "that I didn't mean for anything bad to happen to any of you." Doubt danced with the corners of his mouth. "You guys know that the son of a chief has gotta stay impartial. It ripped me apart inside to see so many elders yellin' fer yer death."

"Shegra," Temmonin spoke for Damowan and himself, "we woulda had to do the same. Don't beat yerself up."

"I prob'ly woulda started screamin' at those idiots," Damowan interjected. "They didn't even listen."

"But, Damowan, we didn't even say anything," Temmonin said. "What were they s'posed to go by?"

"Well, still," Damowan sulked, "they didn't even think."

"My brothers, you guys'll be in really good hands. These guys are really honorable and wouldn't dream of harmin' you without direct authority," Shegra assured them.

"And if the authority happens to change its mind?" Damowan cocked an eyebrow.

"Damowan!" Temmonin was irritated.

"They have their orders, Damowan," Shegra returned. "Nothin'll happen to you guys while you're in their care." He turned with the four Ek-Birin to watch the remainder of the escort arrive, about twenty warriors in all. "I wish I could go with you guys. I wanna hear your story. But I've gotta stay here. I'm Nosh's son."

"Shegra," Temmonin answered, "We don't even really know our whole story ourselves. We're

151

hopin' we can piece it together on this trip." The escort made motions for the four to begin walking. Ahead of them, two Kumuchska warriors were carrying the Flicker monster which was wrapped and tied to a drag-trailer. As they withdrew from Shegra, Temmonin leaned in close, "Pray fer us, would ya?"

His cousin's smile lingered in Temmonin's memory for most of the morning. He knew Shegra was as honest as any man in the confederation and he truly had done all he could have done to help them. Temmonin would not have wished to be in his place.

Temmonin guessed that this trip would take three or four days and, judging from the twisted knots his muscles had become by the midday meal, each day would be like walking through briers. He and his companions winced at the thought of the pain they would feel the next morning. Although Chaneerem's face was carefully controlled so as not to reveal his distress, his equally careful movements betrayed his pride.

"At least they gave us moccasins and hides and snowshoes," Damowan said.

"Some comfort for such achin' bodies," Temmonin added. "I wonder if we'll have any feet left when we reach Moza-Imsaw." He smiled at Jemalemin who had acknowledged his comment.

He thought that Jemalemin wanted to express his own discomfort but was intimidated by Chaneerem. It must be very difficult to be a boy among those who had already endured the rites of passage.

"Were we gonna to try to figure out our dreams?" Jemalemin asked Temmonin.

"Yea," Temmonin answered. He thought for a moment, "Well, why don't you start, Jemalemin?"

They were interrupted by the warriors behind them who told them they must pay attention to their speed. Pricked by this goad, the four concentrated on moving more quickly and, because of the pain that effort caused, they momentarily forgot their conversation. They also ignored much of their changing surroundings. The forest through which they struggled, which previously consisted mainly of maples, oaks, and birches, was at this point thick with cedar and hemlock. Although the change had been gradual, the Ek-Birin had not noticed what they normally would have had they not been so burdened with pain.

Not far ahead, they would be forced to decide between moccasins and snowshoes. The powdery snow was now a hand deep and soon, at the pass between two very prominent mountains, they might even need ropes for climbing. The overcast that had hidden the moon after the council the previous night still hung high above them. At times, it sprinkled thin snow around them. The pale forest was shadowed with the same sleepiness that shrouded the mountain peaks; the entire landscape had been translated into terms of white, grey, and grey-green.

The cold wind was less of an intruder here than in the valley where the rivers met. In random gusts, it tossed leaves and snow across their path and tugged at their cloaks. But it was far less insistent. All four were able to relax somewhat and clutch their wraps less tightly. After they had walked for some time, they began discussing. Damowan spoke first.

"So, we're in this dark pit, or hole, or whatever it was," Damowan began, his heart still light in the midst of his pain, "and we're lashed to logs and we're dreamin'. And we're understandin' some language we've never heard before and, Temmonin, help me out. I really don't remember any of this crap. I mean the language, yea. But the rest?"

"It musta happened sometime after we camped in the valley," Temmonin said. "We musta been captured that night and taken somewhere underground fer three months."

"Maybe these people are some guys from the Kanattar tribes tryin' to make a secret society or somethin'?" Jemalemin suggested.

Temmonin turned to Damowan. "Did that language sound anything like Ek-Makatin or Demnaza or Kumuchska to you, Dama?"

"A little bit," Damowan answered. "I don't know, Temmonin. D'you think they coulda made up a new language?"

"Well, yea. But, why? Who would go to all that trouble?" Temmonin asked.

"I don't know, maybe the good harvest last year left 'em with nothin' better to do than create new languages and capture young travelers," Damowan said.

"The harvest wasn't that good," Jemalemin cut, then, unsure of how his jest would be received, added, "Was it?"

Damowan smiled wide at the youngster, feeling, from what Temmonin could gather, uncomfortable that Jemalemin would fear poking fun at him. It was odd to be conversing so freely with Chaneerem's younger brother. The talon-licker himself seemed almost to have accepted the boy's demand for distance. Temmonin tried to remember if it was as hard for himself when Damowan pulled away. He did not think so.

"What d'you think, Chaneerem?" Temmonin asked as a particularly strong gust of wind blew snow down their necks. Regathering his voice, he continued, "What d'you remember? Any of the language? Anything?"

The warriors to their rear again prodded them forward. Temmonin waited for a moment to see if Chaneerem would still answer. When he did not, he repeated his question.

"No," the oath-taker mumbled, "nothin' specific."

"Alright. What're the possibilities of where this place was and who these people were that had us?" Temmonin asked.

"Maybe they were men sent from the high council to investigate our trip," Jemalemin offered.

"No," Damowan said, "they called fer the council after we got captured back in the Lonely Valley. That couldn't be it."

"What about another council?" Jemalemin added, "A different one that got called before that."

"Which one?" insisted Damowan.

"Hold on, Damowan. He might be right," Temmonin inserted. "If those tribes that had murders happen to 'em--if those tribes, or even clans met and discussed us. . .maybe the painted turtle tribe told the Demnaza villages on our path. Maybe Mok told 'em."

"Y'mean the village where we sat in the hot springs?" Damowan remembered. "Gamnasn. . ?

"Yea, Gamnashta," Temmonin was excited, "maybe they followed us into the valley and took us somewhere."

"They were the last to see us," Damowan stated conclusively.

Temmonin thought for a moment, "But, I don't know if Mok would be like that. He jus' didn't seem like that kind of a guy."

"Didn't seem like that kind of a guy?" Damowan spat. "That kind of a guy almost killed us, Temmonin."

"Damowan, I'm not an idiot. I know he almost killed us. I jus' feel like he was straightforward. Once he found out what we were doin', he really changed," Temmonin argued.

"Anyone can act polite, Temmonin," returned Damowan. "The fact is, his change in attitude doesn't help us conclude anything about his motives. Maybe he was bein' polite to relieve our suspicions long enough to set this abduction thing up."

"Why would he go through so much trouble? We were right there. Why wouldn't he have jus' held us captive." Temmonin moved his hands to emphasize his frustration. "Or, better yet, why not jus' kill us when he had the chance?"

The conversation paused. Ahead, the leaders were crossing a fairly wide stream by means of a fallen oak. They were gingerly carrying the Flicker mutant across. This took some time. Suddenly, Temmonin found his thoughts in Demdegumshannatez and with Zheva.

But Damowan reconvened, "I guess I just can't swallow this whole conspiracy thing. It just seems too big to orchestrate. And anyway, why?"

Jemalemin voiced his own frustration, "But what else could it be?"

No one answered the boy. They crossed the stream with more difficulty than the Kumuchska warriors did. The ice that filled the grooves in the bark of the fallen tree made balance tedious and that tediousness taxed the muscles of the four Ek-Birin

almost more than the morning's hike. They were
not at all conditioned to exerting themselves after
having been immobile for so long. In fact, not once
in their entire lives, had they experienced a single
day in which they refrained from either hunting,
hiking, or dancing. This complete invasion of pain
was a new sensation and one not easy to accept.
But soon they and all the Kumuchska stood on the
other side of the river.

They continued their trek toward higher
ground. The Ek-Birin did so in silence until the
mid-day meal, which consisted of strips of dried
venison. The meal was brief but it afforded the four
a chance to talk with some of the Wolverine
warriors. Damowan spoke with the one who had
followed directly behind him.

"How soon 'til we reach Mitsa-Mitsa
territory?

"First we'll pass through the villages of the
Ek-Makatin." This man was somewhat older than
Temmonin and spoke with an ease that betrayed no
prejudice against the four Ek-Birin. "We're almost
there now--another day, I s'pose. Then the Mitsa-
Mitsa. Why? Haven't you seen one yet?" he
concluded with a quick laugh.

Damowan seemed puzzled by the laugh but
answered, "Actually, one of the elders of our village
is married to a Mitsa-Mitsa half-breed. She's the
daughter of a Salamander who married into our
clan. He died not long ago." Damowan glanced at
Chaneerem. "Not too many people in our village
hold on to the old prejudices."

Another wolverine, who sat nearby, laughed
as he addressed Damowan. "So you know all there
is to know about these Salamanders?"

Damowan shrugged as if to ask what there
might be that he did not know.

"So you know about how bad they smell and how rotten their food tastes?" a third Kumuchska entered the conversation.

"And how lazy they are?" the first warrior added.

"I've never known 'em to be particularly lazy," Temmonin said.

"And how many of 'em have ya known?" the man across from him asked. He then pointed at Damowan, "As many as this one here?"

"Nobody's ever seen as sad a hunter as a Mitsa-Mitsa warrior," the first warrior spoke again. "All they know how to do is sit by the shore and wait for fish to spear--and that's so easy, they even let some of their women do it."

This comment sparked a surge of laughter from the group. Chaneerem laughed along. Jemalemin did so hesitantly. Damowan and Temmonin did not join them. Temmonin would have liked to have objected more strongly but felt he should avoid stirring antagonism against himself and his companions. He tried to keep a neutral expression on his face. Damowan, however, shook his head and glanced sidelong at the mocking men. The man across from them smiled as he spoke,

"What, do we have an altruist here?" More laughter.

Temmonin was relieved that the wolverines did not continue. He would have hated to see Damowan's spirit squelched by their tauntings while his body was too weak to respond. The party finished their meal and again moved toward the mountains.

The four Ek-Birin said little for most of the afternoon. Each strained against his hampered muscles and his confusion over their recent experiences. They traveled with their pain and their thoughts through deepening snow and increasingly large foothills. Soon after their meal, they stopped to don snowshoes. The white powder was a sea on which they skated. They walked on its surface and it cloaked their bodies with its purity. It clung to their eyelashes and revealed to them the direction of the wind. After the sweltering heat and the blind blackness of the cave where they had been held captive, this cold whiteness was refreshing to the four. Yet it was abrasive. Shivering in this wind only multiplied the tension in their muscles. And the brightness was often overbearing to their unaccustomed eyes. As he struggled, Temmonin's mind returned to thoughts of their captivity.

"I remember hair, bristly--like pine needles," Temmonin spoke into the wind. "When we first started talkin' to each other, and when we tried to talk to them, they brushed by my leg. I have no idea why they thought they needed to wear skins in that heat, but they did."

Jemalemin remembered too, "And d'you guys remember--or did any of you guys git touched all over?"

"Now that I do remember," Damowan voiced his disgust. "That was sick! I remember those sweaty, smelly hands! Oh, man, that was sick!! I could do without rememberin' that!" He paused as if it might help him forget. "But y'know what I wanna know? How in the world're we able to speak and understand this language. Say somethin' to me, Temmonin."

Temmonin thought for a moment then uttered several words.

Damowan laughed and translated into the language of the Ek-Birin, "From the sea of salt were we formed. . .and of its fruits we partake."

"They're right about the salt part," Jemalemin said. All three laughed.

"Alright," Damowan spoke again, "Jemalemin, you say somethin'."

They had just come upon a knot of fallen timbers and were working their way through. Jemalemin had to delay his response until after they cleared the obstacle.

"I got one," the boy said.

"Well, go ahead," Damowan urged him.

So Jemalemin spoke his sentence.

"You guys," Temmonin's face was solemn, "this is gittin'a little serious if you ask me."

Damowan obviously thought his brother over-dramatic. "What? Don't ya think maybe yer readin' a bit too much into this stuff, Temmonin?"

"You heard what Jemalemin said, Damowan," Temmonin returned. "'You who have pushed us ever down, you shall find your blood among the roots of the cedars that so long have shaded you!' Doesn't sound like kids' rhymes to me."

"Temmonin, we have no idea what any of this means."

"I'm not so sure, Damowan," Temmonin replied. "I wonder if this maybe has to do with the Chrebin or the Gorma or maybe even these weird monsters that seem to be killin' people ev'rywhere. I mean, look, you and I killed that Gorma not too long ago. And how do we know if that species of creature isn't just as intelligent as we are--only in some different way. You remember Uncle Ammon telling us how the Gorma once covered this entire land, but when our ancestors moved east and north, they pushed the fire-bears out of this land and into the North. Maybe they're outraged at the death of one of their own kind."

"Well, then why didn't they do any of this before we killed that one?" Damowan criticized. "Somebody else musta killed one of 'em at some point in history."

"I don't know, maybe when we killed that one this fall it was the first time it happened in a long, long time." Temmonin posed. "Maybe it rekindled their hatred of the people--and maybe they know how to follow their brothers' killers. Maybe that's why we were captured."

Damowan opened his eyes wide in order to let his sarcasm flow, "Now that doesn't sound like too contrived of a story."

"Not too contrived for the weirdest experience we ever had in our whole lives." Temmonin was irritated. "Look, Damowan, Uncle Ammon said the Gorma were really smart creatures--look at how the one we killed lured us into that clump of trees and managed to keep itself hidden until the last second." He paused and looked away. "Anyway, I'm jus' tryin' to think of as many ideas as I can."

They skied in silence for a few minutes. Not far away, a woodpecker hammered for food. Chickadees chased each other through the branches of the evergreens near the trail and, more than once, the stark red of a male cardinal glided past Temmonin's view. Looking up between the trees, he watched a raven labor against a wind that was much stronger at such heights than beneath the cover of the pines through which the party traveled. As the day progressed, the trees became increasingly taller and eventually masked the overcast sky. The party was very near the base of the mountain now.

Temmonin wondered if they would have enough of a story to present to the council. Although Damowan's comments about the ridiculousness of their situation bothered him, the elder found himself slowly adopting the same point of view. Their understanding of their own experience was so paltry. Why would the council of elders consider such slim evidence? And if these four Ek-Birin had no story, what judgment awaited them?

"If they were some of the people," Temmonin began again, "if they were men of one of the four tribes of the confederacy, what language does their language sound closest to? Demnaza?"

"Maybe they're not from the confederation," Damowan argued. "Maybe they're from the northern tribes that hunt the white bear."

"All the way down here?" Jemalemin asked.

"Yea," Temmonin answered Jemalemin. "Once in a while they send exploration and trading parties south." Then he turned to Damowan. "But that's so rare, it hasn't happened once in our lifetime." He shrugged and furled his eyebrows, "and what would they want with us?"

"I don't know," Damowan said. "It's just that they speak a strange language."

"Nosh knows some of the words of the northern tribes. We'll have to ask him when we get to the island," Temmonin concluded.

Their conversations revolved around similar thoughts for the remainder of the afternoon. At nightfall, they camped near a bluff in the shadows of the snow-covered granite pyramid that had loomed in their vision for half of the day. Sleep pulled them from consciousness like large stones tied to their limbs.

Morning was offensive. The slightest of movements incited rebellion in Temmonin's muscles. But at dawn the Kumuchska were ready to leave this bluff and were not at all sympathetic to the Ek-Birin warriors' pain. They prodded the four with quick, insistent words. Temmonin, Damowan, Jemalemin, and Chaneerem all responded with tremendous effort and hid their anguish as best they could; they knew that at least two more days lay ahead. As soon as Jemalemin had risen and walked a few feet, he fell to the snow. Damowan went to help him up.

A Wolverine warrior approached with their rations. "You'll have to eat 'em while we're walkin'," he said. "We've gotten a late start." He began to leave, then held for a moment. "We'll be climbin' the pass. Leave yer snowshoes on yer pack."

As the four rushed to pack, the Kumuchska who had slept near them began to urge them on. "Today we'll see what yer really made of." This was the same man whom Damowan had asked about the Mitsa-Mitsa.

"And let's move," another added, "before my feet freeze."

Damowan stopped packing his sleeping hide and sneered at them. "You guys obviously have no idea what it's like to not use yer muscles fer months and then to walk all day." Temmonin wished his brother had not said that.

The eldest Wolverine chuckled, his voice tinged with warning. "Well then, today'll be yer second rite of passage," his eyes laughed without cruelty, "and if you four can make it through the storms we're sure to meet, and the climbin' you'll have to do and the fightin', you'll be twice men in every Wolverine's eyes."

"The fightin'?" Jemalemin asked, "who's to fight?"

"Not who," the second warrior corrected the boy, "what."

"Haven't you guys heard stories about the Shetatantaw?" the first explained.

"Snow serpents?" Damowan exclaimed.

"They love mountain passes," said the second, "and you can try as hard as you like not to, but you'll always walk right into a nest."

"And they don't seem to like that too much," the third commented.

"But if you four don't hurry, we won't see any 'til t'morrow," the first motioned urgently with his hands as he spoke. "Let's go."

The Ek-Birin hefted their packs to their tender shoulders, winced at the weight, and fell in behind the first Kumuchska warrior. The other two Wolverines followed the Flicker tribesmen.

"The Shetantantaw're only aggressive when they're nestin', right?" Damowan asked.

The first warrior answered without turning around, "Well, I'd give you my four best arrows if you come upon one that's not matin' or givin' birth or nestin'. Passionate things." Temmonin could not help but laugh at this warrior. "But if you're not ready for 'em, the only passion you'll feel is fangs and cold, white death."

"How big are they?" Jemalemin asked, his body contorting to keep from pulling any more muscles as he walked.

"Some as long as five men--that's a female," the man replied. "The males're a little shorter. Big around as two of ya and able to make a meal of one of ya in a few minutes."

"Well, can't we avoid 'em?" Damowan asked.

"Be my guest if you feel like climbin' to the peaks of these mountains and hoppin' down the other side," the man said, "Y'see they love the passes--maybe 'cause that's where the people travel."

"Then we'll have to pray to the Creator to protect us," Damowan concluded.

The second warrior spat a laugh from the end of the line. "The Creator made them too. You s'pose He'll be lookin' to play favorites today?"

As the Kumuchska laughed, Damowan lowered his voice and leaned back toward Temmonin. "We didn't see a single serpent when we passed through the mountains this autumn."

"Yea, but it hadn't snowed by then either," Temmonin answered. "Remember?"

"Yea, I remember. So what?" Damowan replied.

"Damowan," Temmonin whined, impatient at his brother's ignorance, "snow serpents?"

"Oh," the younger was embarrassed with realization. He rolled his eyes, slapped himself in his face, and shook his head as he hiked on.

They traveled with the bluff to their left, the forest to their right, and the low, grey sky overhead. The morning sun was a pale ghost in the recesses of their minds. Although no snow was falling and no wind was blowing, the dead air was icy. Cold permeated their cloaks and loincloths like thick oil. The novelty of this cold had already passed from Temmonin's mind; the discomfort he now felt rivaled that of the three months he had spent in sweating atrophy. And he felt the beginnings of a familiar ache in the back of his throat. How much more would his body accept before he became sick?

Only an hour had gone by when the party reached the broken cliffs beneath the pass. All twenty Wolverines and the four Flickers drew together to await the leader's directions.

Several warriors produced coiled ropes from their packs. From what Temmonin could see, the ropes were woven of vines, fibers, and strung animal intestine. Ek-Birin had little use for such strong rope; the marshes afforded them only rare occasion for climbing.

He was fascinated by the rope but more interested in what the leader would command. He looked again at that man. The leader and two others were pointing up the cliff and discussing their plan of attack. Temmonin gazed at the top with them and was relieved that these men were expert climbers. This was no gradually sloping mountain pass. The cliff wall, although sporadically veined with vertical channels, was an uninviting entrance to the high saddle between the mountains. And it was the only entrance.

As they had done the day before, the Kumuchska spoke to each other in their own dialect except when speaking directly to the four Ek-Birin. But because Amowz had grown up as a wolverine, Temmonin and Damowan both understood some Kumuchska. So they were able to follow some of the conversation between their leaders as they tied ropes together and judged the ascent.

They seemed to be focusing on something but Temmonin could not ascertain what it was. Then one of the warriors threw a hand-sized stone attached to the end of a long rope. The stone rose about twenty-five feet up the wall and arced over a thick branch that protruded perpendicularly from the cliff face. As the stone cleared the post, the trailing rope caught on it, causing the stone to swing like a pendulum beneath it. The man holding the end of the rope then released his grip and allowed it to slip through his fingers. He tightened his hands again when the rock on the other end reached the height of his head. Gathering both ends of the rope, he tugged to test it. Then, he turned to the group.

"Well, who's first?"

A young warrior responded. His shoulder was laden with more rope and a leather pouch was strapped to his waist. He leapt onto the hanging rope and scaled to the post in seconds. As he reached the branch and perched upon it, Temmonin noticed several shorter branches protruding from the wall next to the post. The warrior stood up with one foot on the long branch and the other foot on one of the stubs and drew a stone from the pouch on his waist. He tied it to the end of the rope on his shoulder. Then he checked his balance and swung the rock up another twenty feet. The arc of the trailing rope missed its intended target, a post similar to the one on which the warrior stood, and dropped too far away for him to catch. But he gripped the end of the rope and quickly gathered up the slack until he again held the rock in his hand. His second toss caught. Then, another warrior climbed the first length of rope and joined the warrior who stood on the cliff face. This first warrior steadied the rope as the second climbed to the next set of protrusions. Soon, a series of four cords stretched up the escarpment and several warriors had climbed the entire length and stood on the cliff above.

Then the leader motioned to the four Ek-Birin. Temmonin was dreading this moment; he knew his arms were almost useless. He glanced at Jemalemin and saw in the boy's eyes reflections of a bruised confidence. Temmonin felt worse for Jemalemin than he did for himself. If the boy could not scale this cliff, Chaneerem surely would use the failure as a weapon for further harm.

The talon-licker scowled at the other three as he walked to the rope. His ascent to the first post was surprisingly quick. Perhaps it was fueled by his ever-expanding bitterness, perhaps by his limitless arrogance. As Chaneerem climbed to the second post, he showed signs of weakening. He reached the third post and almost lost his hold. The warrior there had to help him to safety. After three furious attempts to scale the final length, the oath-taker was forced to admit his inadequacy. He was tied and hauled up to the top.

Damowan flashed a clever smile at Temmonin and grabbed the rope next. He gained the third post much more quickly than Chaneerem had but then stopped to breathe. Temmonin imagined that he had over-exerted himself and that he would have to be pulled up. But Damowan only rested a moment. In a flurry of determination, the young warrior heaved himself up the final span.

Temmonin looked at Jemalemin. "Jemalemin, you go," he offered, "I'll follow."

"No, Temmonin, please," the boy was riddled with inner turmoil. "You go, please."

Temmonin wondered how he would feel if he were this battered soul. Would he be able to continue resisting an older brother whose every word exuded treachery? Would he have been able to push a yoke of such thorough dominance from himself? Temmonin's respect for Jemalemin began to multiply as he gave the boy his gentle answer,

"Sure, Jemalemin," he smiled. "See ya up top."

Jemalemin's smile was more polite than heartfelt.

Temmonin began his climb. His biceps caught fire as he scaled and his mind was clogged with amazement that Chaneerem and Damowan had done this so easily. When he gained the first post, he could not imagine himself going any further. But, somehow, his muscles remembered their old habits and he soon found himself at the second post. He climbed almost to the third post and realized that Jemalemin probably would not make it this far and that the brunt of the boy's failure might be softened by companionship. Temmonin hoped his act would be convincing. He slowed and feigned exhaustion just out of reach of the warrior at the third post. He held for a long moment. When his biceps were truly incapable of continuing, he eased himself back down to the second station. From there he was tied and hauled up as Chaneerem had been.

Having reached the top of the cliff, Temmonin turned and, with Chaneerem and Damowan and the rest of the Kumuchska, watched Jemalemin reach the third post. He did so at the expense of much energy. Like Chaneerem, he submitted to help after spending himself trying to scale the final length.

"Not bad overall," said the elder Kumuchska who had spoken to them most, "for Ek-Birin." He smiled without malice.

"Not many cliffs like this in the marshes, eh?" called another.

The Ek-Birin were silent amidst Kumuchska chuckles. They were still chuckling as they secured the Flicker monster and hoisted it to the top.

Finally, the remainder of the warriors crested the cliff and gathered their ropes to themselves. As they did so, a light snow began to dance over the cliff. The sun sliced through the overcast and nearly blinded the party but those who kept their eyes open saw the spectacular procession of winter. Flakes gathered and separated and whirled in intricate patterns across their field of view. They could hardly distinguish the trail from the air around them. But the sun was not persistent. Soon, the clouds reconvened and they could see the pass directly in front of them. The snow still shrouded the view but they could continue traveling without fear of losing the way.

Temmonin started to watch the sides of the trail. His stomach began to tingle with anticipation.

"One of 'em's gonna come up behind ya and swallow ya whole," Damowan interrupted his older brother's watch.

"What!?" Temmonin was irritated at being accused of fear.

"But, of course, I'd split its belly and you'd walk free jus' like ya walk outta the longhouse ev'ry morning," Damowan finished his thought.

Temmonin's tone became near scolding, "I'll betcha yer gittin' a bit nervous, too."

"Who wouldn't be," Damowan replied. "At least my eyes aren't shakin' like a perch on a spear."

"Yea. We'll see who's shakin' when I save yer life from some white-eyed snow-worm."

"Now yer gittin' funny, Temmonin," Damowan fed the banter.

"Not much funnier than you, Mister 'I let the Gorma build a fire on my back'." At that, both Damowan and Temmonin laughed more heartily than they had since they had left their village so long ago.

"What're you guys tryin' to do, invite 'em?" a young Kumuchska warrior sliced through the snow flurry.

Temmonin suddenly felt childish.

But, Damowan snapped back, "I thought the fact that we're here was invitation enough."

"I'd rather surprise a snow snake than be surprised by one of 'em any day," the young warrior's voice sharpened.

"Well, fine," Damowan cut.

Answers like Damowan's were so unsatisfactory for Temmonin that, after many years, he had learned never to make them. He wondered if they were sufficient for his younger brother. Perhaps Damowan felt as if he had equaled his opponent by issuing such an insubstantial retort. Perhaps the expression of the anger on which it rode was enough for him. Perhaps Damowan was not satisfied; maybe he was just more skilled than Temmonin at hiding his embarrassment. The elder brother was much quieter as he resumed conversation.

'I think I remember learnin' that the Shetatantaw do some kinda reverse hibernation. When summer comes, it's too hot for 'em so they dig down and sleep 'til winter comes again."

"I'm kinda excited to see one of those things," Damowan said. "Time to use my muscles again."

"My arms're like muck," Temmonin commented. "Ya sure yer gonna be able to fight?"

"I don't know, I made it up the ropes didn't I?" Damowan paused. "Course you only reached what, the second post?" He smirked.

"Well. . ." Temmonin started then stopped short and glanced back at Jemalemin. Seeing that the boy could not hear him, he continued. "Things aren't always what they seem."

Damowan was puzzled at his brother's comment. But he answered sarcastically. "What, ya actually made it all the way?"

"No," Temmonin chided. Then, looking again at Jemalemin, "I'll tell you later."

Damowan feigned seriousness. "Yes, we are quite busy now. Later would be much better. Some time when we don't have so much time to talk, eh?" Damowan's chuckle caused Temmonin to realize how humorous his own answer must have seemed to the younger. But even though they had plenty of time to talk, he could not risk destroying Jemalemin's self-esteem. He could not allow Jemalemin or Chaneerem to know that he had held himself back simply for the boy's sake. As he thought more, he was glad that Jemalemin had reached the same height his older brother had. He would not have predicted it. This boy who had not yet seen his rites of passage was shattering every underestimation Temmonin had concerning him. He wondered how frustrated Chaneerem was. How much longer could the talon-licker control himself?

After the party had stopped for the midday meal, they quickly resumed hiking. The snow continued to fall on a path that grew increasingly rugged and they soon reached a place where the slope was too steep for snowshoes yet not steep enough to climb with ropes. They packed their snowshoes and picked their way up through the continuous flurry of snow.

Although Temmonin's muscles were strained, his emotions were busy remembering--and this white flurry that encompassed him was reflecting his youth. He remembered hunting with his father and the other men of the clan. He remembered trudging through snow two feet thick and how, since he was only ten years old, he was allowed to ride the sled on top of the moose they had killed. He remembered the smells of wet wood and his sweaty parka and even the faint odor of blood from the carcass below him. He remembered sitting backwards on the sled so that he did not have to squint to keep snowflakes out of his eyes. He watched the albino kaleidoscope that trailed away behind the sled and wondered if this was what the crayfish saw as it propelled itself through summer streams. Snow always mesmerized him. It always made him remember. It always made a part of him ache; made him long for something he could not name. He did not entirely desire to return to his childhood. And, although he was often anxious about the future, he did not relish losing his youth. Perhaps he ached for places to which he could not return even if he wanted to. And for people he would never again see in this life. Perhaps the ache was only the residue of boyhood dreams. Perhaps it was a longing for the return of Spring and warmth and leaves and flowers. He might never know.

Damowan scrambled up a tall, square boulder. Temmonin waited until his brother had reached the top before following him up. The elder brother would have preferred a rope for such steep climbs. Handholds were few and the muscles of his fingers, wrists, and forearms were almost too weak to support his weight as he hung and felt below himself for footholds. As he drew himself over the upper edge, a gust of wind blew snow through the fold of his hood and onto his chest. Shuddering, he slipped his leg onto the top of the boulder and jumped up. He thought the weather may have worsened but soon realized that this gust was just one of the inconsistencies of mountain air circulation. But then a violent whirlwind ripped his hood off of his head and blinded him.

"Whoa, no!" he heard an anonymous shout ahead of him. "Jus' when ya don't expect 'em!"

"And sometimes even when ya do!" another voice joined.

When the commotion cleared, Temmonin saw Damowan in front of him amidst a group of Kumuchska warriors. Each of the men had a weapon ready, one a bow and arrow, another a knife. They were all tense. They were all scanning the surrounding crags. Temmonin scanned with them, wondering what the eyes of a snow serpent looked like. One of the Kumuchska spoke through a grimace,

"Looks like they're jus' smellin' us out," he resheathed his dagger, "but don't worry, brothers of the marsh, they'll be back soon."

Temmonin could not understand how the man could have inferred so much from so little evidence. As they resumed the hike, he drew near the warrior.

"What kinda signs did you jus' read?" he asked. "How'd ya know they were nearby?"

"Signs?" the Kumuchska asked back. "Oh, you mean the whirlwind--they do that all the time-- with their tails. A lotta times, when the snow settles, one of yer buddies is in a worm's mouth. Some tactic, eh?" They walked side by side for a while. "You fellas don't mind lookin' like ya don't know much, do ya?" the Kumuchska interrupted the silence.

"When I wanna know somethin', I ask about it," Temmonin answered.

"Smart man," the man smiled widely. "My name's Shemshem." And, as they pushed through the snow, he brought his left hand up and touched his fingers to his lips.

"My name's Temmonin of the tribe of the Flick. . .but you already know that."

Shemshem smiled again. Temmonin could see now that this was no bitter man. But he was no weak man either. He was a little younger than

Temmonin's father Amowz and it appeared that the years he had lived had only served to refine his body and his tongue. The Ek-Birin did not appreciate his prejudice against the clan of the Salamander but he imagined Shemshem had had enough bad experiences with certain members of that clan to warrant some ill feelings. Temmonin was hesitant to inquire about this issue but his curiosity was too great.

"How do you know about the Mitsa-Mitsa?"

Shemshem was surprised at the question. He waited before he answered. "There're times in ev'ry man's childhood he'll never fergit." Snowflakes curled around his hood and he brushed a strand of hair from his lips." "I was seven years old when I stood on the north shore of Moza-Imsaw. I was watching my father--I really don't know what happened to him--he wasn't a bad swimmer. He was a good stone's throw out from shore in a birch-bark canoe he borrowed from the Mitsa-Mitsa. It capsized and he went into the water. He musta got tangled in somethin' or bit by somethin'–nobody really knows. Anyway, he was flailin' around and yellin' fer a really long time when I realized somethin' musta been wrong. What did I know? I was just a kid. I'd never seen him do nothin' like that before There were a couple of Salamanders on shore spear-fishin' and they didn't even swim out to help. They jus' kept hoppin' from rock to rock spearin' their fish. So I started swimmin' out to him. By the time I got to him, he wasn't movin', jus' floatin' face-down in the water. I screamed fer help and finally some of the men dropped their spears and swam out to us. It was too late though. My dad was already dead."

They walked in silence for a moment, shrouded by the whispers of winter. Temmonin's head was full of questions but he restrained himself. He could not bring himself to interrupt Shemshem's contemplation.

"The part I don't git is how they could jus' stand there and watch a man drown. I mean I know my father didn't hold 'em in the highest regard but he woulda saved any one of 'em from drownin'." He shook his head. "Lazy as turtles on a log."

Temmonin looked away from Shemshem to find that they were approaching some sort of crest. The warriors ahead of him were climbing over and disappearing beyond it. He turned to Shemshem,

"All downhill from here, eh?"

"No," the man replied, checking his foothold. "We'll cross a few of these small valleys before we start down again--and this is only the first pass. There's two more passes ahead."

Temmonin looked over the crest as Shemshem turned to let himself down the other side. "What's that?" He pointed at what appeared to be a long snowdrift. The majority of the party was hiking single file alongside it. But the drift had begun to move.

"Mesha! Shetatantaw Mesha!" Shemshem roared in Kumuchska. Temmonin did not have to ask what he meant.

Suddenly, snow distorted his vision. Even Shemshem was hard to distinguish, but the Ek-Birin saw him jumping down the slope, dagger in hand. Temmonin followed as quickly as he could. As he reached the valley floor, he steadied himself against a snowbank to his right. The whole thing shifted beneath his weight and he was thrown to his face. His heart surged as he felt the pressure of something huge moving over his legs. Holding his breath, he kept himself as rigid as possible and waited for the thing to pass over him.

Temmonin knew that during this trip he would meet a snow snake but he never expected to feel one before he saw one, or to lay beneath one as it slithered past. Although panic was clutching at his chest, he could not allow himself to scream for help. He was a weaponless prisoner and, if he called for help, he would have no defense should the creature notice him before one of the Kumuchska came to his aid. The thing moved across his legs for so long Temmonin thought he would burst from the suspense. The second he felt the weight lift, he spat out his breath and inhaled hard. He lifted his head, panting. Snow continued to blur his vision.

Though his eyes were useless in the confusion, he could clearly hear the cries of men fighting all around him. He then realized he had been hearing them all along. But until he was free, his fear had demanded his full attention.

"Damowan!" Temmonin cried. His words were swallowed in snow. "Shemshem!" Nothing. "Jemalemin! Chaneerem!"

"I gotcha," a voice called from behind him as a hand grabbed him by the armpit. "Stand behind me," it was Shemshem, "and don't go anywhere!"

The initial whirlwinds were waning and Temmonin could now see his Kumuchska friend. The man held a long hickory spear in both hands and stood in a defensive hunch, spear pointed into the dissipating white cloud. Temmonin squinted to decipher. Suddenly, foot-long fangs stormed toward Shemshem like a shocking nightmare. He leapt to his left, leaving Temmonin gawking. But the serpent did not see Temmonin until Shemshem had moved away. It shifted in the air, turning its pink mouth toward the Kumuchska and, because it had not done so soon enough, it bumped into Temmonin with the side of its enormous head and knocked him to the snow. It hissed and snorted as it faced Shemshem. The warrior thrust his spear at the snake's neck. Dodging this attack, the thing plunged at him and lanced his shoulder. Fortunately, its fangs did not hold, but the Wolverine fell as the weight of its head glanced off of him.

Half-buried in the snow, Shemshem drove his spear between several of its icy white scales and pulled out again as the serpent reeled. Temmonin could see blood seeping into the fur of the warrior's parka. But the fact of that wound was insubstantial when compared to the urgency of Shemshem's attacks. He stabbed and connected twice more before the snow worm could counter. When it snapped at him again, it sliced the warrior's cheek from ear to nose. He bellowed. But as he turned again toward the Shetatantaw, he roared with renewed viciousness. It was as if this fresh blood had saturated his nostrils with fury. He threw his spear down and dove at the worm's neck, clinging to it like a wolverine to the neck of an elk. He drew his dagger and began stabbing. The worm started to flail its head but it could not reach its assailant because that Kumuchska was just beneath its jaws. Clutching with his right hand, Shemshem continued to stab with his left. But his accuracy was greatly hindered by the spasms of his target; the snake was becoming reckless.

Then Temmonin remembered the Kumuchska's abandoned spear. He scooped it up out of the snow and drew back to thrust. He pierced the worm's side deeply and, for the first time, blood surged from the snake. The liquid was a murky ocher that quickly drenched Temmonin's mittens and the forearms of his parka. None of Shemshem's blows had dug this deep. As he withdrew the spear, Temmonin glanced up to see more ocher blood spattered across the Kumuchska's face and arms and running down the neck of the beast. Perhaps they had both succeeded simultaneously.

Suddenly, the snake swung its head, and with it Shemshem, toward Temmonin. The two warriors collided and the Kumuchska lost his grip on the monster. He fell in a heap onto Temmonin and groped awkwardly for his bearings. But the Shetatantaw struck before he could regather himself. Just as Temmonin felt Shemshem's weight lift, the monster pinned them both to the snow again.

Temmonin writhed and shifted beneath overwhelming pressure. He felt he would burst if he did not wrest himself free. But he could do nothing. Panicked, he screamed.

Then the pressure eased. Shemshem pushed himself away from Temmonin and threw the limp head and neck of the dead snow-worm from his back. The Kumuchska stood and looked behind himself.

"That thing almost had ya there, eh?" another Wolverine jested. Shemshem did not respond. "Would ya mind handin' me my spear before it gets too bloody? I mean, savin' yer butt is one thing but losin' a good spear to old acid-blood here is another thing altogether."

Shemshem hopped up onto the worm, grasped his fellow Wolverine's spear with both hands and yanked it from the corpse of the monster. As he turned to give it back to its owner, he began in formal tone,

"Our lives were yours to save and you saved us fr. . ." Then his eyes stretched wide and he pivoted and prepared to cast the javelin in the direction of his fellow Kumuchska. "Duck!" he blurted.

The other warrior had raised his hands in front of himself in fear of Shemshem's new aggression but quickly understood his intention and dove away at his command. Shemshem yelled as he shot the spear into the face of another snarling snow worm. The spear was swallowed into its nostril and the worm halted. Enraged, it doubled its speed. This worm was larger and moved toward its dead kin with vehemence in its hot, crimson eyes. Although the other Kumuchska had stood directly in its path, it seemed less interested in him than in Shemshem who now stood on the corpse of its sister.

Temmonin had been lying in the snow since his friend had pushed himself away. At the sight of this new attacker, he scrambled behind a boulder. Turning as he gained its cover, he watched the worm engulf Shemshem, its massive jaws expanding to clear his flailing arms. Temmonin's eyes bulged. He gulped too quickly and began to cough.

When he had finished clearing his throat, he looked again at the white behemoth before him. At first, he tensed thinking the worm was now coming for him. But he had mistaken the vacant look in its eyes for a look of attack. Actually, it was swallowing. It seemed not to notice him. It seemed not to notice even the band of Wolverine warriors that crept up behind it. It concentrated solely on forcing Shemshem further down its throat. Temmonin cringed.

The first lance pierced its armor and it
turned to discover its new enemies. Shrieking
almost like a hawk, it bit furiously at the sliver in its
side, all the while watching the echelon of warriors
that cautiously approached. Several arrows flew
simultaneously. A spear grazed its neck. The
monster reared, hot fog trailing from its mouth and
nostrils into the chill mountain air. More arrows
flew, some glancing off the snake's hide, some
sticking. As the Kumuchska warriors attacked,
Temmonin noticed the worm's tail forming itself
into a tight coil.

The tension released and the tail raised a
cloud of snow between itself and the company of
Kumuchska. But the screen did nothing to thin the
barrage of arrows and spears that continued to
shower the beast. One lance fell very near to the
boulder behind which Temmonin crouched. Again,
he seized his opportunity. He sprinted into the
snow worm's side and used his momentum to drive
the shaft through its armor. Temmonin held his
grip and began wresting the spear from its place
when the monster's entire body began quaking. The
vibration was so strong, he had to let go of the
shaft. Then the gory shaking stopped. The snake's
body went limp. The snow flurry thinned.

Standing solitary next to the beast,
Temmonin greeted a host of Kumuchska warriors
and his fellow Ek-Birin. He thought nothing of his
audience as he bent to retrieve his spear but when
the crowd began to cheer, he flushed. The worm
was bristling with arrows and spears and
Temmonin's contribution had probably done little
to kill it, but since the Wolverines were offering
their adulation, Temmonin decided to accept it. He
ripped the spear from its skin and held it
horizontally in front of him. Then he raised his

chest and furled his brow and curled his tongue to make the call of the Flicker. When he had finished the ceremony, the howls of the Kumuchska doubled in volume and some of the warriors danced a few steps. Temmonin flashed a smile at Damowan so that at least his brother knew he had not taken credit for killing the worm. Damowan had trouble restraining his laughter.

Suddenly Temmonin remembered Shemshem. "Shemshem," he blurted, "he's still in this thing!" And he leapt over the snake and began pushing to roll it onto its back. "Help, please! Shemshem!"

Others rushed to his side. Together, they rolled the albino behemoth until its underbelly faced them. One Kumuchska stabbed with a long wooden knife and slit the plates lengthwise for at least a body's length. Amid gushing ocher and stinking green gel, several hands reached in and pulled back the hide.

"There's his leg," Temmonin called.

More cutting. More pulling. Shemshem's leg was moving. Then his body was free. The men worked to clear his body of the slime while Temmonin tried to revive him. His clothes had been reduced to rags by the worm's acidic saliva and his bare skin was covered with burns. He worked hard to breathe. Some time passed before the Wolverine could speak.

"Are you alright?" Temmonin asked.

"Of course I'm not alright," Shemshem labored. "What d'ya think I am, a young buck or somethin'?"

"But are ya gonna make it?" Temmonin persisted through the laughing of the rest of the warriors.

"Who killed the worm?" Shemshem asked.

Temmonin flushed again as he looked around at the others but then he smiled, "My brother Damowan, here. A clean shot too. Right through. . ."

"You killed it, didn't ya?" Shemshem whispered. He winced before continuing. "Temmonin," he winced again, "yer humility and yer courage are like the smell of cedar in the nostrils of the Creator." He was silent against his pain but all the warriors could see that his pain was great. No one was laughing now. "Did you lose the Flicker monster?" One of his fellow Wolverines shook his head. "Then the mission hasn't failed. That's good." And soon Shemshem died.

Matthew John Schellenberg

VII.   And are we insane or is our terror and
confusion at and about the monumental pain of
death and corruption and decay--which like a
cascade cuts the gorge from the earth through
which it flows--is our repulsion the only normal
reaction we might have chosen? And is it, in fact,
our choice in the least to be or not to be repulsed.
Rather, is our reaction like the result of drinking
poison, the reaction varying from person to person
not in kind but in degree--but strong poison that is
always fatal; never to be ignored? Is our offense not
healthy, our situation unhealthy? Do we not
perhaps offend the Creator when we accept such
horrid conditions as the conditions in which He
intended us to live? In so doing, have we not forced
ourselves against the spikes of bitterness like the
pulling of a frog from the mouth of a snake. And
have our efforts only served to add to the putrid
reek that rises from the refuse mound of history?

CHAPTER 7

As they hiked through valleys and climbed escarpments for the next two days, passing and stopping for meals at various villages of the Ek-Makatin, Temmonin could think of nothing but Shemshem's death and his own foolish display of pride. If he had opened the worm immediately after killing it, would Shemshem have lived? Was Temmonin's embarrassment at being hailed as victor just another sign of his preoccupation with self-introspection? If he could ever become truly selfless, would he someday save a life rather than lose one? Regret taunted his conscience like the whirling snows that shrouded this southward journey.

The villages of the clan of the Eagle were hospitable enough but, while the party stayed with them, Temmonin often felt the weight of vindictive stares. He wondered if the rest of the confederation would be so suspicious. He also hated how those stares of condemnation always directed his thoughts back to his regret about Shemshem. If he was guilty of any death, It was Shemshem's.

That Wolverine, in spite of his lasting bitterness toward the Mitsa-Mitsa, seemed content with his part in life. He seemed not to judge anyone--except Salamanders--prematurely. He was the only Kumuchska besides Shegra and Zheva who had spoken kindly to the four Ek-Birin since their long dream and their capture. As the holy man sang the final chants and wrapped Shemshem in his elk hide to be raised to his rest, Temmonin loved that dead man's placid, terra-cotta face. Shemshem's raw humor and unpolished yet insightful wisdom reminded Temmonin of his own Uncle Ammon.

Perhaps their personalities had been shaped in similar ways by the fact that they had both lost dear family members; Shemshem his father and Ammon his wife and his only son.

How often Uncle Ammon had let Temmonin and Damowan suffer through undesirable situations just to teach them discipline. And how the two brothers were grateful to their uncle for such training. Most often, the man expressed his affection through those things he withheld from his nephews rather than through what he gave to them. If Shemshem had nephews, Temmonin was sure he would have treated them in like manner.

But Shemshem was no more. Temmonin had helped build the snow mound on which they lay the dead man. And when he had done his part in covering the Kumuchska with more snow, he could hardly keep from crying. This was not his family--to cry would be an embarrassment. But Temmonin asked himself why he felt such emotion. Was he really so attached to a man he had just met? Or was the guilt for his foolishness pressing sorrow onto his heart?

Two nights after Shemshem died, they camped at the southern base of the mountains on the edge of Mitsa-Mitsa territory. Their progress had been hindered by heavy snows. Since they had killed three Shetatantaw, they had enough fresh blood to smear on every man's parka--the tribes discovered long ago that snow-snakes always avoid the smell of their own blood. And even though the blood did some minor damage to their coats, they were able to move ahead without fear of attack. But the storms were vicious enough to add much time to their trek.

The four Ek-Birin felt their muscles harden as they journeyed across Imnanaw-Kanat. Now only traces of pain lingered in their legs, somewhat more in their arms and chests and backs. The fact that their bodies were demanding less attention would have allowed them more energy to discuss their defense had the storms not been so persistent. But, finally, the snows stopped. The rest from the domineering weather allowed all the men much needed conversation.

"Thought I saw Moza-Imsaw jus' before sunset," Damowan began. He was roasting bear meat over a fire at the evening meal. "Maybe we'll make it by t'morrow night. Then the next day there'll be council fer sure!"

"How can you be so excited?" Temmonin asked. "That council might be our death sentence."

"Temmonin, ya don't have to cover ev'rything with mud. Nosh'll be there. And Da and Desh. And maybe Papa and Uncle Ammon." Damowan waved his hands confidently. "They'll understand--and they can stick up fer us."

Chaneerem interjected a rare comment, "Now that's somethin' ya don't hear ev'ryday, the younger brother tellin' the older brother not to worry." He laughed a short laugh.

Temmonin and Damowan did not know how to interpret this observation but both smiled and laughed politely. Chaneerem did not respond further. He just looked into the fire and away from his fellows. He fidgeted with his burnt left arm.

"Well, Damowan, yer right about one thing," Temmonin began again. "I guess we prob'ly don't have to worry about dyin'. It was different back at the Kumuchska council. We didn't have any friends there 'cept Shegra." He paused. "But we still have to sort through this stuff." He looked quickly at Jemalamin and Chaneerem. "Now, we've all had some time to think. Did you guys come up with anything new about the dreams or about the language or about those people?"

"Tell ya the truth, I didn't really think about it Temmonin," Damowan said casually.

Temmonin could not understand how anyone could spend two silent days hiking without a single thought about such an urgent issue. But he restrained his anger. "How 'bout you Jemalemin, Chaneerem? You guys remember anything new about anything?"

Jemalemin looked squeamish.

"Jemalemin, you got somethin' ya wanna say?" Temmonin repeated.

"Not really," Jemalemin admitted, "it's stupid."

"Jemalemin, no idea's stupid right now. We need all the information we can remember," Damowan encouraged the boy.

"But it ain't information. It ain't nothin'. It's stupid." Jemalemin dropped his head and fumbled with his parka.

"Jemalemin, please. This is really important," Temmonin urged him. "Whatever you say, it's not gonna be stupid."

Jemalemin would not speak.

"Jemalemin," Temmonin pleaded.

Still, the boy would not raise his head.

Temmonin waited before continuing. "O. K. fergit it. I got an idea. Let's talk about this language. Y'know, the one we all speak. When I think about it, I guess I really never heard anybody talk like that. . .I really can't figure out who it could be. And the things they did to us. Can't really figure out anything from that either. I guess. . .well, I guess I really don't have anything either." He was

suddenly relieved that he had not expressed his
anger at Damowan for not having thought about
their captivity.

They ate without talking for some time.
Temmonin began to think about the trip ahead of
them and about the fact that soon they would be
encountering more Salamanders than ever before in
their lives. He and his brother had always been
extremely curious about them. "Damowan,
t'morrow we git to eat with the Mitsa-Mitsa."

"I know," Damowan, like Temmonin spoke
low and away from the Kumuchska. "We gotta
make sure we ask 'em everything."

"'Specially about the fishin' magic,"
Temmonin added.

"Especially."

Temmonin thought he heard scoffs from
some of the Wolverines nearby but when he turned
to confirm, the warriors were laughing amongst
themselves.

Jemalemin leaned in close to Temmonin
and asked, "Why does ev'rybody hate Salamanders?
What'd they do that's so bad?"

"Our dad says people jus' seem to need
somethin' to hate," Temmonin answered.

"But Dad hates it when people hate other
people fer no good reason," Damowan added. "He
says, 'If ya can't explain the reason fer yer hate in
less than five words, ya jus' wasted a great emotion—
ya spread it too thin and it don't mean nothin'."

"D'you 'member. . ." Temmonin stopped to
think for a moment. "I'm sorry Jemalemin, you
wouldn't remember. You weren't there. But you'll
remember, Damowan. Dad picked Mayban, the
Salamander from our village who's dead now, to run
one part of our rites of passage. And his decision
made a strong impression on the rest of the men

from our clan--news spread across the whole
territory of the Ek-Birin. Nobody else'd ever done
such a bold thing before. Prejudice was dyin' away
in the village–'specially since Mayban married
Teshamasaw and came under the longhouse of her
grandmother--but what Dad did started a new
acceptance of the Mitsa-Mitsa. Course some people
still kept on hatin'. . ." He tried not to look at
Chaneerem. He thought he succeeded. "But at
least things started changin'."

"So it doesn't have nothin' to do with some
war or crime they did in the past?" Jemalemin asked.

"Prob'ly more with color of skin than
anything else," Damowan answered, "but that's
what makes the Creator's work so awesome--endless
variety."

Something slid out of Chaneerem's mouth.

"What's that?" Damowan turned to the
talon-licker.

"Color of skin, color of skin!" Chaneerem
stood. "Dirty, stinkin', lazy, slimy cowards! There!
I summed it up in exactly five words. Good enough
for ya Damowan?" And with that he walked a few
steps and squatted facing a cluster of Kumuchska
warriors.

Jemalemin lowered his voice. "He's always
like that. I think my dad made him that way."

"It's easy to blame somebody else,"
Damowan responded. Temmonin wished he had
not.

"No, but you should see how my dad treats
him," Jemalemin continued, "then you'd know fer
yerself." He bent his head, began again, "Mama
says. . ." Jemalemin's words trailed off. It was
obvious that he was trying to decide if he should
continue. He glanced uncomfortably at the other
two and remained silent in the end.

Temmonin was glad Jemalemin stopped. He was encouraged by the boy's openness but he did not want him to reveal more than he should. He reached out his hand and touched him on his shoulder.

"Anyway. T'morrow we git to see the clan that's raisin' all this controversy," Temmonin summed up the conversation.

They slept and woke the next morning beneath a frigid winter wind that buried their hide tents in snow. After digging themselves out, they ate breakfast and packed. During the meal, the snow thinned and eventually stopped falling. Within minutes, blue sky pushed the clouds eastward and away from the company of travelers. Black-green pines cut into the pungent azure above, painting a scene that caused Temmonin's blood to surge. As they began their descent through the southern foothills of the Northern Mountains, they skied between boulders and sporadic clumps of trees. After an hour, they reached a broad, barren swath that gave them a panoramic view of the forest before them and shimmering Lake Moza-Imsaw beyond. Less than a day's hike away, snow-covered ice stretched from horizon to horizon, covering the largest lake in the territory. The party halted for a moment to look.

"Is that Ojeb-Mawitez?" Damowan nudged Temmonin.

"Where?" Temmonin asked.

"That little dot out there."

"I don't know, Damowan," Temmonin was slightly irritated, "this is my first time seein' it too."

"Jus' askin', Temmonin."

Although he felt compelled to retort, Temmonin held himself and fell in behind

Damowan as the party resumed skiing. The urge subsided.

The forest through which they skied was fairly orderly and the paths clear of debris. Skiing was smooth and took little effort. As the sound of their snowshoes in the powder found a rhythm, Temmonin's mind slipped away from the trail and began picturing the future.

He imagined himself and the other three Ek-Birin trying to explain their experience to the council. He saw elders from many clans and villages railing accusations. He imagined Nosh and Amowz defending their family. He saw the other elders rejecting their defense as favoritism. Then flames sucking his feet into a black pool. His mother and father and sister mourning Damowan and himself. Zheva crying for days. Zheva. . . He imagined bursting out upon the elders with a decisive speech that could not be ignored. He saw himself leading a search party to the place of their abduction. He imagined discovering a secret plot laid by Chaneerem to kill Damowan and himself. He saw himself honored as a great man. Then his marriage to Zheva. Their children. Their grandchildren. Himself telling them stories. He and Zheva old together. . . He imagined breaking free of their Kumuchska escort. He saw himself and Jemalemin and Damowan fighting off Ek-Makatin warriors while on their way to the Lonely Valley to discover their captors. Again he was a hero. Again he married Zheva. . . He imagined the devastating evidence used against them at the council. He argued like he had never argued before; like an old man, laden with wisdom. He argued. . .

"What was that?" Damowan penetrated his thoughts.

"What?"

"What'd you jus' say to me?"

"Oh, nothin'," Temmonin laughed, "jus' talkin' to myself."

More skiing. More rhythm. More thinking.

The party passed several villages before stopping for the midday meal at a very small one deep in the forest. They were welcomed politely; this village was directly on the path regularly used by northern clans to reach the shore of Moza-Imsaw and the Mitsa-Mitsa who lived here were accustomed to travelers. The party was offered a meal from the stores of the village. The Kumuchska politely declined. They had enough and more in their own packs. And since the clan of the Salamander was the keeper of Ojeb-Mawitez, the traveling party would be eating Mitsa-Mitsa stores for as long as the council convened. They did, however, eat with the villagers, a decision, Temmonin thought, was difficult for the Wolverines to make. But Temmonin and Damowan were ecstatic.

"I am Temmonin of the clan of the Flicker," Temmonin began with a Salamander who sat next to him. "And this is my brother Damowan, my fellows Jemalemin and Chaneerem." With his nose, he pointed to each respectively.

"And I am Kashtawa of the clan of the Salamander." This warrior had not met the party when they first entered the village. He had joined them at the fire. His skin was a rich red-brown like that of the leaves of a silver maple. The blotches that meandered across his face and neck and hands were a similar color, only lighter and more red. Temmonin had always been intrigued by the skin of the Mitsa-Mitsa, but had always been too polite to study Mayban. And he had to work at being polite now.

Damowan leaned over Temmonin's lap and said quietly, "Don't worry, we don't hate you. I mean Mitsa-Mitsas in general. We don't hate you guys. We're not prejudiced."

Temmonin blushed. He smiled as uncomfortably as Kashtawa did. Damowan received a piece of meat from the meat-carver at the fire and immediately began eating, unaware of the discomfort he had caused. Of course, Temmonin knew that his younger brother meant well, but he could see how Damowan's comment had unsettled the other warrior. Temmonin and Kashtawa took their meat and also began eating. For the most part, communication was limited to small talk between members of the same race and, after a few bites, Temmonin felt the bile of disgust crawling in his throat. He detested traditions of hate.

"Kashtawa," he said, "d'you know a guy named Mayban who married Teshamasaw of the clan of the Flicker?"

"D'you know which village he lived in before he got married?" Kashtawa returned the question.

"I think by the shore. Maybe here on North Shore. Maybe on the peninsula." Temmonin's brows were furled in thought. "I don't think he lived on any of the islands but I'm not sure."

"I might know him," the Mitsa-Mitsa answered. "It's a bit rare that a Salamander marries out of clan." Temmonin thought he sensed a vague hint of humor in the man's voice but he could not be sure. "When did he get married? A while ago?"

"Oh, he died an old man not too long ago." Temmonin suddenly realized how improbable it would be that the two would know each other. "His

wife's still alive. His daughter married one of the
elders in our village."

"Might know him," Kashtawa nodded.
"Prob'ly seen him once."

"Jus' thought ya might." Temmonin could
think of nothing else.

After a few minutes of eating, the
Salamander turned to Temmonin, "Is this yer first
time to the Mitsa-Mitsa forests?"

"Yea," Temmonin answered, "I've been. . ."
He turned to Damowan. "We've been to
Kumuchska territory. West through Shushunu, but
never along the coast. The closest we've come is
Zazamma."

"So is it all you guys've dreamt of?"
Kashtawa's mouth bent with a laugh. Several
Wolverines and Salamanders turned for a moment.

"We haven't hardly seen anything yet,"
Damowan interjected.

"I'll show you guys all ya need to see." The
Mitsa-Mitsa was smiling. "All a couple of 'fair ones'
need to see."

Temmonin and Damowan looked at each
other and laughed heartily. The younger leaned into
the elder's lap again.

"If we could jus' shake these Wolverines
from our necks," he jested.

Temmonin explained, "We're prisoners.
We're gonna be tried at the high council fer
murder." Kashtawa's eyebrows rose. "If we're
found innocent, maybe we'll come right back and
accept the full extent of yer hospitality."

Kashtawa waited. "Murder," he said,
"pretty serious stuff. What'd you guys do--or not
do?"

"We've been accused of bein' involved in a bunch of murders that've been happenin' in the Shushunu and the Kanattar," Temmonin answered.

"And do we look like murderers?" Damowan leaned over again. "Hunters, yea!" He flexed is sad biceps. "But murderers? Somebody's got their head in the mud."

"Anyway, we'd love to stay, but we can't," Temmonin added.

"You're big and strong." Damowan seemed to like this Mitsa-Mitsa. "Maybe you could help us fight these Kumuchska off, eh?"

Temmonin looked around at the Wolverines as he chuckled. He did not know how to interpret their stares. Most of them were probably accustomed to Damowan's sense of humor but he could not be sure whether or not some were offended. Kashtawa already seemed to have adjusted to Damowan's quick tongue. He laughed loudly.

This Mitsa-Mitsa was tall and thick, not obese but not overly thin either. And not entirely muscular. His chin was square but padded. His agile mouth was quick to answer and to smile. Deep-set eyes were shaded by his overgrown eyebrows. But a jutting nose dominated his visage. That nose, like that of a raven, appeared immense not only because of its size but also because of the large burgundy blotch that seemed to have been painted across it. The design began a broad swath just under his left eye and, after folding over his nose, tapered and trailed off his right cheek onto his neck. The blotch was unusual in that the markings on Salamanders' bodies were typically symmetrical. This mark was not. But it was not ugly. And he was not ugly.

Lunch was brief. Temmonin expected it would be. As they prepared to leave the village, Temmonin and Damowan heard Kashtawa speaking to his elder in the language of the Mitsa-Mitsa. Then he saw him disappear into a longhouse near the fire. Temmonin was disappointed that he would not be able to tell him good-bye. But he did salute the elders as the company departed, a gesture only the leader of the Kumuchska party was polite enough to offer; and he only because it was proper for him to do so.

Just as they withdrew from the village, Kashtawa joined them. He was dressed for traveling and was wearing snowshoes. He passed the four Ek-Birin, who were near the end of the formation, and skied directly to the leader of the party. Moments later, he slowed until Temmonin and Damowan caught up to him.

"I wanted to say good-bye to you." Temmonin smiled, "Where'd ya go?"

"I asked if I could escort you guys and yer party to the shore," Kashtawa answered. "My chief said he didn't think it was too good of an idea but if I really wanted to, it was up to me." He adjusted the bundle of skin on his back. "So here I am. I know Wolverines don't especially love us but it's just a short trip and it's through my own territory. They're not gonna do nothin' to me."

"Brave soul," Damowan said.

"Bored soul," Kashtawa countered. They all laughed.

Temmonin wished he and Damowan knew the language of the Mitsa-Mitsa. He did not enjoy that their conversation with Kashtawa was so transparent to the Kumuchska. But he resigned himself to the fact and decided he would ask and answer as he wished, without discretion. He would rather befriend one open-minded Salamander than a hundred indifferent Wolverines, even though the Kumuchska were his father's clan.

"So are you gonna get married soon?" Temmonin began.

"No," Kashtawa laughed. "Nobody's available in my village. Maybe my mom's gonna look fer me in another village. Maybe on the shore. That'd be good." He paused, "But I ain't in no hurry. Who is?" They skied for a while. "So what's yer guys' story again? Yer suspected of murder or somethin'?"

"There was this string of murders--maybe twenty--and ev'ry one of 'em was along the same route we took north to visit our uncle's village, Demdegumshannatez. I can see how people think we've got somethin' to do with it but, no matter how far-fetched it sounds, it had to be a coincidence--a huge coincidence--but, still, a coincidence."

"What were you guys doin' on the trail?" Kashtawa asked.

"This is the weird part," Damowan interjected.

"Yea, what's ironic is that we were carryin' evidence--a body actually. . ."

"This huge monster thing," Damowan again.

"There's a guy in our village and this thing killed his whole family. Our elders sent us to the Kumuchska to question them about their dealings. . ." Temmonin lowered his voice, ". . .in the forbidden arts."

After a moment, Kashtawa looked puzzled. "What do the Kumuchska have to do with a murder in your village?"

"Three murders," Damowan slipped in.

"Well, that monster thing was some kinda mutant: half human, half wolverine. Nothin' was conclusive--we were headin' north to ask questions, not to accuse 'em of anything."

"You'd think we'd at least git a chance to ask a few simple questions, wouldn't ya?" Damowan jested and complained in the same sentence.

Temmonin looked around. The looks Damowan drew with his statement were not as difficult to interpret as before. These Wolverines were now obviously agitated at his brother. But Temmonin felt they deserved to be taunted. And he was glad Damowan was more prone than himself to voice his opinions.

"So who'll be at council to defend you guys?" Kashtawa asked.

"Our dad, maybe Jemalemin's and Chaneerem's dad, our Uncle Nosh--the chief of Demdegumshannatez, the town we were headed for. Maybe some other elders from our clan." Temmonin thought for a moment, "Oh, and maybe a chief from this village in the Shushunu--Mok of the Daimadunva."

"Ha!" Damowan spat a laugh almost as loud as Chaneerem did. "Temmonin, you might be my brother and I'd trust you with almost anything but, in this case, you're jus' like the man in November who keeps on waitin' fer the snow to melt before leavin' his longhouse to go huntin'; yer hopes're completely in vain."

"Dama, what's yer problem. Do we need to talk about the meaning of the word 'maybe'." Temmonin stopped and stood still in his tracks. The Wolverine behind him almost fell trying to avoid colliding with him. That warrior spewed what must have been curses in Kumuchska and angrily pushed Temmonin ahead. Temmonin immediately

200

resumed hiking, moving his hands through the air as he continued rebuking his brother. "I mean, I never heard myself say, 'It's certain' or 'I'm absolutely sure that Mok'll be there cheerin' us on.' Man, can't a guy say somethin' around here without his words bein' twisted around his head?"

At that Damowan puckered his lips and exaggerated his face and began mocking Temmonin with garbled syllables. Temmonin glanced at him and immediately roared with laughter. Damowan and Kashtawa joined him, amused as much by Temmonin's ridiculous change in emotion as by Damowan's face. When he regained control of his vocal chords, he spoke with a smile,

"Damowan, jus' now, I was about as mad as I've ever been at you, but that was the most hilarious face you've ever made," Temmonin laughed more, "You win. I say no more."

Some time passed before anyone spoke again. By the time Damowan re-initiated conversation, he did so with apparent affinity towards Kashtawa.

"Kashtawa," he said, "what's it like to be a Mitsa-Mitsa? I mean, the prejudice?"

The Salamander raised his brows. "We only have another coupla hours 'til we reach the shore." Temmonin looked at the serious expression on Kashtawa's face which suddenly melted into a wide smile. Temmonin and Damowan both joined him in laughter.

"Kashtawa," Temmonin offered, "ya don't have to answer that if ya don't wanna."

"I wasn't bein' rude," Damowan reacted.

"No," the Mitsa-Mitsa shook his head, "you two're the first people who've ever asked me that. Maybe you could tell the rest of the world that there really is real, red blood underneath this strange, exotic skin," he spoke loudly enough for all the Kumuchska to hear. He then dropped to a normal level. "It's like wonderin' where everyone else learned their logic from. See, among the Mitsa-Mitsa, a guy's judged by his love fer his family, fer his skill as a hunter, fer his loyalty to his people, fer his submission to the Creator. When a Salamander meets somebody fer the first time, he can't make a judgment about the guy's character or about the relationship he might have with the guy 'cuz he doesn't know the guy's heart. When he sees this guy a buncha times and in a buncha different situations, then he can make a judgment. Maybe he's right, maybe he's wrong. But the color of his skin, the amount or shape of the spots on his body, the length of his hair; all this stuff is useless as far as his judgement is concerned. I mean, tell me, when you trust a guy with the same color skin as you got and he ends up rapin' yer sister and steals yer best huntin' arrows, are ya usin' logic? And when ya distrust a guy with different colored skin and this guy respects yer sister and maybe might give ya his best huntin' arrows, are ya usin' logic?" He hunched his shoulders and turned to the two Ek-Birin in full question. "And what kinda person teaches their children this kinda logic?" He slapped his forehead and sighed, "Right there's how it feels to be Mitsa-Mitsa."

Kashtawa's frustration rang in Temmonin's ears until they arrived at the shore village. The sun set on Moza-Imsaw as the party entered the circle formed by longhouses. A fire was already burning in the center. Around that fire stood several people, none of which greeted them for some time. Then, as if suddenly remembering his manners, one of them came toward the newcomers. He raised his arm and touched his lips with his fingers in greeting.

The Kumuchska leader did the same. When the Wolverine had finished, the Mitsa-Mitsa warrior knelt in the snow at the other's feet and untied the traveler's snowshoes. Temmonin saw the leader's discomfort even from behind the man. Such graceful measures were rarely extended even among friendly clans and tribes, but this Salamander served with no apparent malice or sarcasm.

Stepping out of his snowshoes, the leader turned and signaled his party to do the same. They did. Kashtawa leaned toward Temmonin and Damowan, "I'll meet up with you guys a little later. There's some people here I wanna see." And he walked to the fire.

The company of travelers was led through the circle of longhouses to another longhouse just beyond. The Mitsa-Mitsa warrior led them to the door and, just as he did so, a young boy met him. The boy was carrying a burning torch which he had obtained from the village bonfire. The warrior accepted it and entered the house through the door flap. Within seconds, he returned. He then invited the travelers to unload their packs, make themselves at home in the longhouse and to join the villagers later that evening for the dance of the full moon.

The Kumuchskas filed into the longhouse to find a fire glowing and a clean-swept room leading to three others beyond. The elm bark walls were in good repair. They were even decorated with mollusk shells and painted hides and wood carvings. These Salamanders were experts in the field of hospitality. They were escorts to the Island of the Council for most of the northern clans and so, in spite of the prejudice they often felt, they returned only welcome. And they were supported well for their service. From each of the clans they served, they received skins, meat, and weapons. Temmonin wondered if it were this agreement that caused outsiders to see the Mitsa-Mitsa as lazy.

After he had entered the house, he waited until the last of the Wolverines had followed and then he peeked his head out of the door. From what he could see, he guessed that Moza-Imsaw lay a stone's throw away from this longhouse behind a thin wall of pines. He saw faint silhouettes of canoes stacked near the shore. He was glad the party had finally reached the lake.

The boy who had brought the torch returned after they had eaten and again invited them to the dance. The look on the boy's face told Temmonin that acceptance of his offer was not at all expected. And acceptance was not given. The Kumuchska remained seated long enough for Temmonin and Damowan to realize they did not plan on attending the dance. Temmonin looked at his brother,

"Wanna go?"

"Yea, c'mon." Damowan started out the door.

"Can I come with you guys?" Jemalemin called after the other two.

"Sure," Temmonin smiled and waved his hand, "c'mon."

"Hang on there, Ek-Birin!" called the leader of their party. "You can't just take off without an escort." The man motioned to two of the youngest wolverines in the room. "You two keep an eye on the prisoners." The two seemed irritated that they had to accompany the flickers but they submitted.

They followed the Mitsa- Mitsa boy into the night.

At the fire, they saw Kashtawa and several young warriors dressed in full dancing gear and waiting for their cues. The drummers around the circle began pounding just as the three Ek-Birin and their guards joined them and, as if predicting the moment, the dancers moved forward. They wore thick leather moccasins that covered them from their feet to their knees. The boots had been polished black. Below the knee, the men had wrapped leather thong from which pine cones, feathers, mollusk shells, and deer bones were hanging. Their thighs were bare except for a layer of grease they had applied. They wore loincloths of shiny black bear hide. Thick layers of leather were wrapped around their waists and from these wide belts hung more bones and shells and feathers and pine cones. All of them were wearing several necklaces. Some of the necklaces were made of bear claws interspersed with clay beads. Others were made of porcupine quills and pine cones. Still others were strung with bones or shells or twigs. Several dancers wore bearskin arm bands and bracelets of leather thong and feathers. On their heads they wore fans of turkey tail feathers that made them appear more than a foot taller than their actual height. And in their hands, they held rattles and pine branches that they shook as they danced.

They danced in single file around the fire, slowly, carefully. As two more dancers entered, several of the drummers began working a new rhythm on higher-pitched drums. Chanters offered their voices to the liturgy and their melody, coupled with the new rhythm, seemed to animate the two new characters. These men, greased with black-pigmented oil and wearing grey fox loincloths, moccasins, and mittens, carried large maple limbs which had already been smoldering when they had first engaged the circle. They ran to the fire and lit the branches again.

As the new arrivals left the fire, branches arcing in a blazing stream, Temmonin noticed that a thin rim of blood red had been painted around their eyes. The two wove fiercely through the circle of dancers. They began to scream. The host of dancers continued plodding to the driving, steady pounding of the deep drums while the two black men became furious, waving their firebrands through the air like crazed dogs. The fire streamed dangerously close to the elder men, women, and children who stood on the perimeter. But no fire escaped the circle.

Then a flute sounded. The high-pitched drums stopped. The black dancers stopped their flailings and moved together in a sheepish attitude toward the perimeter, still facing the fire. Rising higher as it sang, the flute finally found its highest note and fluttered there for several moments. The circle of dancers began to wave their arms to mimic the fluttering. Soon, the high-pitched drum reconvened with a spritely, bantering meter that, if it had had a melody, might sound like a forest full of chickadees and cardinals. Now, the host of dancers responded as the two black men stomped in place. The line broke and dancers whirled everywhere in the circle. And as each desired, he neared the fire and caught his pine branch ablaze. More whirling. More pounding. As he looked around, Temmonin suddenly noticed that all of the onlookers were holding pine branches. Then he noticed a pile of branches near him just outside the circle. He retrieved three branches and handed one each to Damowan and Jemalemin. The dancers began lighting the branches that the onlookers were holding and soon the circle of light roared its harmony to the thin melody of the flute. The black men had been stepping toward the fire as if their feet were tied together. They now dropped their dying torches into the coals and turned to face the perimeter. They bowed their heads. They fell to their knees. They fell prone and rolled onto their backs.

The host of dancers gathered at the two men like flies to a carcass, their steps shortening as they approached. The flute melted into a languid dirge. The deep drums accompanied the melody quietly. The entire crowd of villagers converged on the fire and the dancers. Temmonin, Damowan, and Jemalemin followed, their branches, like all the others, no longer burning but trailing black and grey smoke. Eventually, the drumming was too quiet to hear. The flute continued its lament in spite of the lack of accompaniment. Soon, it too calmed to a whisper. Then, all was quiet.

Silence wrapped the dance like the stark cold of a deep cave. Temmonin closed his eyes and listened. He heard only the hushed breathing of the evergreens. He felt something rise within him, something too glorious to express; an incapacitating awe that saturated his soul. He felt he could not move even if he wanted to. The quiet and the cold weighed upon him so heavily he thought he would explode from ecstasy. But he did not. The presence of so many others enthralled with the same silence fed the inferno that raged within him. He opened his eyes to see the fire-licked faces of his brother and of Jemalemin and of the Mitsa-Mitsa village. Still serene. Still silent.

The host of young dancers quietly bent and helped the black men to their feet. The entire crowd began to sway. A chant grew: Mitsa-Mitsa. Temmonin loved hearing such gradual crescendo. But the drone never outgrew a murmur. The three Ek-Birin swayed and listened, watched as foreigners.

The drums crashed the silence with ten loud booms and rested again. At the tenth hit of the tom-toms, the whole crowd threw their branches into the fire. The blaze surged. As the sudden burning slowed, the chant started again, gently as before. The people danced so little, their feet did not leave the ground. Silence again rose to subdue all sound. When all had been quiet for several moments, the crowd turned and stepped into their longhouses.

Temmonin, Damowan, and Jemalemin stood and watched. Kashtawa walked near them, heading for one of the houses. Temmonin touched his shoulder,

"Kashtawa, what. . ."

Kashtawa raised his hand and covered his mouth. Temmonin nodded. The Mitsa-Mitsa proceeded into his lodge and the Ek-Birin to theirs.

Moon Beneath the Mountains

VIII   And of this putrid reek from the refuse mound of history, this reek from which we must conclude the pervasive presence of defecation--Shall we use such evidence as foundation for thoughts of judgment against the one who made history and defecation possible? Shall we, the thumb prints of the Creator, now decipher His intent through examination of that which we with our thumbs have printed. Shall we be as the gluttonous squirrel who, having himself stripped the trees of food and having filled his stomach to the point of bursting and having become ill to the point of death, then burns with anger against Him who created trees and food and stomachs and hunger? And the choice to eat or not to eat? And if we judge the one who makes all standards, by which standard shall we judge Him. If we accuse him of being the giant and of creating us simply for the pleasure of stepping on us and on those we have stepped on--and if His actions seem to us a defecation, from what source do our judgments come? If the giant is the source and we the stream, how is it that we flow with different water?

CHAPTER 8

Kashtawa met them at the boats in the morning. During the night, the temperature had risen and fog had settled into the forest and onto the shore. They sky was no more than a reflection of the snow on the ice-covered lake. Temmonin had to squint as he looked at the travel-ready Salamander. Kashtawa would leave this morning also.

"They're good hosts, eh?" Kashtawa said. "A guest in a Mitsa-Mitsa village is treated like a chief'd be treated in any other village."

"Ya got that right," Temmonin said. His heart was sore. He did not fully understand why but he was ready to cry at the thought of leaving Kashtawa. That Mitsa-Mitsa warrior seemed content enough. "Well, friend, I guess we'll see ya when we git proven innocent."

"Why?" the Salamander patted his bundle of supplies. "I'm goin' with you guys. Just in case that Painted Turtle chief doesn't show up."

Temmonin and Damowan laughed with him. Temmonin had thought Kashtawa was packed and ready to return to his village. But this was a great surprise. Although those around him would not know it, Temmonin was ecstatic. And although the four Ek-Birin faced a death trial within the next two days, he felt an inexplicable sense of peace. Kashtawa would be with them.

"Great!" Temmonin said.

"Move," one Kumuchska barked from behind them, "we wanna reach the island by nightfall."

The Salamander and the Flickers began skiing across the snow-covered ice. Ahead,

211

Temmonin saw several Kumuchska bearing the
Flicker monster and, at the front of the column,
their Mitsa-Mitsa escorts. They skied in double-file
at a steady, medium pace. The strain of
Temmonin's initial strokes was considerable but
once the group had traveled for some time, his
muscles were almost free of pain. This was ideal
skiing snow, easily packed yet not heavy.
Temmonin smiled at the thought that soon his body
would have recovered completely.

"So what's yer guys' chief gonna think?"
Damowan shouted in order that Kashtawa could
hear.

"Not much," Kashtawa shouted back, "he's
a good chief, not too interested in controllin'
ev'rybody's life."

"What?" Damowan asked, pulling the parka
back from his ear.

"I said, 'He's not interested in controlling
ev'rybody.'"

The company spread across the ice for
lunch. Their pace had been a good one; they had
passed the halfway point an hour before. If no
storm hit, they would reach the island before dark.

"Sorry I couldn't talk with you guys last
night," Kashtawa spoke genuinely, "but the full
moon ceremony is really sacred to our people.
We're supposed to meditate silently before fallin'
asleep." He looked into Temmonin's eyes, "You
understand, don't ya?"

"Oh, yea, Kashtawa, totally," Temmonin
raised one hand as if to hold back any apology, "I'm
glad you let us know."

"What does it mean?" Jemalemin asked.

Kashtawa prepared himself. "We do the
dance of the full moon--prob'ly like in yer guys'
village--every full moon. But I think it means

somethin' different to us than to any other clan in the whole confederacy. It's an ancient dance and I think the meaning's changed over the years--like everything else--but a lot of it's the same as it was a thousand moons ago.

"At the start, the big group of dancers represents the common man--like you and me— normal people who don't see themselves as more than they are, although sometimes we all fergit how easily our lives can be taken away from us. Anyway, that group is supposed to be humble people. The two guys painted black represent the haughty and the proud—y'know, people who fer some reason feel more worthy of life than others. There ain't enough time right now to talk about how those kinda people git that way. These haughty guys are all boisterous and pompous at first. They dance real freely and don't even take the time to think about the others that're dancin' around 'em. Pritty soon the moon's almost covered and there's no more light in the darkness.

"But then there comes a time when righteousness cuts into the pride of the darkness like the flute in the dance and when this righteousness starts cryin' out fer humility, the proud're stopped in the middle of their dance. The music of humility is simple and little but it's so beautiful that haughtiness has to listen to it. And the melody says two things; a dif'rent message fer each kinda person. Humility embarrasses proud people. It exposes 'em, accuses 'em, y'know? But to humble people, the melody reminds 'em who created 'em and what an honor it was that they were created by such an artist as the Creator. So the melody inspires humble people and fills 'em with joy and soon the moon burns bright in the sky; it becomes the thing we're celebrating.

"But then comes the paradox of humility--it even helps proud people see their beauty--it lifts the proud ones to their feet and teaches 'em a new dance, a dance of silence before their Creator, a dance of waitin' on their Maker, a dance of quiet dependence on the one who sustains ev'rything.

"But a lot like the moon, history's like a cycle that goes through dark times and light times. It's kinda like we control the light sometimes. Sometimes we shine as bright and beautiful as the full moon and other times we're more disgusting than feces. We dance ev'ry month hopin' fer the day when humility and honor'll reign forever. And we always remember that even the light we shine comes from the Creator Himself."

Kashtawa finished his explanation in time to gulp the remainder of his meal. The others had finished as he spoke. Although they were well within schedule, Temmonin still felt a hurried attitude among the Kumuchska. Perhaps they did not enjoy walking across ice. Perhaps they were anxious to return to Demdegumshannetez. Whatever the reason for the rush, they began hiking as soon as they could finish their small lunch.

And traveling continued to be easy. Aside from the monotonous albino landscape, they saw nothing as they crossed the lake. Soon, a black needle lay far ahead on the horizon. Then, as if an ebony eye were opening, the line broadened, rose from the surface, and became Ojeb-Mawitez, the Island of the Council.

Temmonin's heart pumped harder. He was excited that they had finally reached their destination but anxious about what would happen there. His stomach tingled as it did before almost every dance and every hunt. The intensity of this tingling, however, had been rivaled on only one other occasion--the weeks before his rites of passage.

He remembered the snow packing beneath his bare feet, so cold it felt as if he were walking on coals. He remembered the helpless darkness beneath his blindfold, his inability to stop shivering, his longing for Damowan to share his fear. He remembered being led across snow-covered meadows first, then rushes and cattails. Then he remembered sensing the shore of the lake, the smoothness of the ice beneath the snow on which he stepped. And cold. Cold. He remembered thinking that the only warmth left in his body was near his groin and how that thin heat had made his scars ache--groin scars he had received only two days earlier as part of his rites. He remembered not feeling his feet, his hands, his nose, his ears. Then he remembered being stopped. How elated he was that he had finished! He remembered waiting for the removal of the blindfold and for the announcement of his manhood and for the howling of congratulations. He remembered the quietness of the crowd of men that surrounded him. Then again the tingling in his stomach--there was still more.

He remembered four hands, the brusque shifting of his position, and the lifting and plunging into the panic of cold. Those last words engraved themselves into his memory like the sound of his mother's voice: "Find your way from the darkness to manhood." He remembered almost not getting a full breath before he broke the surface of the lake, the anger he felt at the man who dove with him and swam him away from the opening in the ice, the raging in his lungs even before he could remove the blindfold. Then the overwhelming panic at so foreign a sight. He remembered trying to

understand what he was looking at, whether he was
looking up or down, whether he could last another
second without exhaling. Then he saw the opening,
a white tear in the grey wall above him. Finally, he
remembered his lungs exploding into the air and his
gasps and his weak climb from the hole in the ice,
the final cut near his groin--without pain in his
numbness--and the announcement of his manhood.

Why could he see Zheva? Why, in all his
thoughts, was he always performing for her? And
why, before he had met her, was he always
performing for the female to whom he was
attracted? Would he ever live life for himself,
simply because he enjoyed it?

Sometimes he wished he could stop
thinking.

Then the party reached the shore of the
island. Mitsa-Mitsa guards stood and greeted the
escorts in their own tongue, then in Mokhamoyuba
for the benefit of the Kumuchska and the Ek-Birin.
The first guard moved past his fellow Mitsa-Mitsa to
the Kumuchska leader and bent to untie his
snowshoes. As the leader stepped out of his skis,
his party did the same.

As he and his captors followed their
Salamander escorts, Temmonin looked around
himself. The clan of the Salamander had done
much work on this island. The path was broad
enough for three fully-laden men to walk abreast
and was lined on both sides with sculpted poles.
Each was somewhat taller than Temmonin and
shaped like a cross from the crux of which hung an
oversized mask. Every mask was different.
Possibly each was a contribution from a young
Mitsa-Mitsa warrior newly initiated into the folds of
manhood; the carving being a part of the rites of
passage. The carvings themselves were not

masterworks but the collective aesthetic was glorious. And it was accented by the fog. The path was revealed slowly as if it were a net being pulled from the water and with each pole another nuance of Mitsa-Mitsa culture was expressed. If Temmonin were not so preoccupied with anxiety, he thought he might be able to enjoy the scene more. Yet maybe this situation had intensified his perceptions. He could not decide.

Temmonin gazed beyond the masks at the massive fir trees that lined the path. The huge sentinels padded the small channel in which the men walked; no wind whistled or threatened to pull away their parkas. Temmonin heard snow crunching and fur rubbing and noses sniffling like he never had before. And he smelled wet leather and fish and bear grease as if the smells themselves had originated inside his nose. Anxiety had multiplied his awareness. Adrenaline made him swallow hard and clench his fists.

He looked at Damowan. His younger brother shot him a half-smile that betrayed a similar nervousness. Temmonin knew that Damowan must be as anxious as he was. But he must also be just as thrilled at the prospect of this experience; they would tell such stories if they lived through it. Something in him would not let him doubt their survival.

When they halted in the center of a clearing, Temmonin overheard the Mitsa-Mitsa guard say that the council had been alerted to the presence of the Kumuchska envoy. The guard explained that the council would wait until the next day to consider the new evidence. Then he turned and led the way through the darkening fog to the lodge for the night. Temmonin knew it would be useless to ask if he could see Nosh and his father sooner than the next morning. He held his request.

"Well, Temmonin," Damowan sighed as they found their bedding in the longhouse. "I guess we got either one more day. . .or a whole lifetime together."

"Guess so," Temmonin's mouth was dry from endless pondering. He swallowed before continuing and felt the annoying soreness in his palate. His sinuses were clogged and his head ached. Still, he spoke poetry into the air above the place they were lying, "Perhaps the Creator will see fit and we will both hunt together and dance together in a new land where no one can accuse us falsely." Silence. One of the Kumuchska put out the torches. Several men began conversing with each other in muffled tones. And Kashtawa and the Ek-Birin felt comfortable enough to continue their conversation as well.

"Ek-Birin believe in an after-life?" Kashtawa asked into the darkness. "After we die, I mean." Damowan laughed loudly at that. "Alright, I guess that was kinda redundant. But seriously, d'you guys believe in a life after this one?"

"Yea, don't the Mitsa-Mitsa?" Temmonin answered.

"I thought everybody did," Jemalemin added, a question in his assertion.

"Well, I guess we believe in a sort of after-life," Kashtawa said, "but more like a re-creation--a righting of wrongs. Remember what I said 'bout the dance of the full moon?"

Temmonin was feeling very comfortable with this new friend. He mused casually, "That makes sense given the kind of oppression yer people've felt." Kashtawa did not respond.

Damowan seemed to sense the uneasiness of the silence. "Makes some sense at least. Doesn't it?" Kashtawa did not respond immediately.

"If you four weren't in such nasty circumstances, I might be more likely to tear you guys in half fer sayin' that kinda crap," the Mitsa-Mitsa stated slowly. "But I can see what kinda trouble yer in so I'll only say this: Don't assume ya know how somebody else feels."

"Well, I don't think we were really assumin' anything," Damowan returned.

"I'm sorry, Kashtawa," Temmonin responded. "Forgive me."

After a moment, the Salamander spoke, "I forgive you." He paused, "Maybe yer even right about why we believe what we believe. But maybe the clan of the Salamander believes the way it does because it's the truth, not 'cuz it fits our desire to see our enemies punished." Temmonin was learning how to interpret this Mitsa-Mitsa but was still not certain how much more he would have to learn. "Now, I'm still interested in how you guys plan on defendin' yerselves. I think the last time you started tellin' me about it, we were interrupted by a little spat." Temmonin and Damowan chuckled. "Y'told me you guys'll have relatives here to testify as character witnesses, but ya never told me what you guys're gonna use as evidence to prove yer innocent."

"Well, that's 'cuz our evidence is about as thin as the ice on Zazamma," Damowan said.

"Damowan's right," Temmonin seconded, "we hardly know anything about what happened to us fer the past three months. One night in October, we were sleeping in the snow in the Lonely Valley-- you know which one I'm talking about?" Kashtawa grunted his assent. "And the next thing we remember is wakin' up emaciated and almost naked on a freezin' January mornin'."

"It took us a while to figure out how long were out of it," Damowan inserted.

"Yea, and durin' these past few days of hikin'. . ."

"And achin' unbelievably," Damowan again.

"Yea, and achin' unbelievably. Durin' this trip, we've tried to piece together our story. But we ourselves can't even come close to understandin' this three-month gap in our lives. We have no idea what the council'll say. I mean, one day you're in a Demnaza village enjoyin' hot springs--the next you're being burned at the. . ."

"Temmonin?" Damowan was oddly dreamy.

"What, Damowan?"

"I jus' remembered somethin'."

"Yea?"

"I got this little scar or--it feels like a brand--on my forearm?"

"Yea?" Temmonin was irritated at having to encourage Damowan to continue.

"Well, these past few days, I been tryin' to figure out where it came from."

"And?" Temmonin was growing impatient.

"Well, I think I 'member what it's from."

"What, Damowan? What?"

"Don't laugh--but a little squirrel-man-thing." At that, Temmonin burst into laughter and Kashtawa with him.

"No, Temmonin, I'm serious," Damowan insisted, "there was this thing and. . ."

"I know Damowan," Temmonin assured his brother, "I remember. I'm jus' laughin' at how funny that thing was--the Chrebin, right?"

"Yea, I remember," Jemalemin laughed in agreement.

"Man, you guys, this is weird. I mean, why didn't we remember this back when we were in the prison hut at Shegra's when we were talking about Chaneerem's arm?" Temmonin questioned.

"Wait! What's all this about?" Kashtawa asked, suddenly realizing that their laughter was for a different reason than his.

"A Chrebin–this little thing about as tall as your head or a little smaller," Damowan chuckled, "it made friends with me. . . what--a coupla days before we got captured. And it branded me. It was some kinda bond of loyalty, I think. But we haven't seen it since we got out. Actually, I fergot all about it."

"Wait. You got captured?" Kashtawa was confused. "You got out?"

"Oh, I was gittin' to that," Temmonin explained. "Right now we're pritty sure that we were captured while we were sleepin' in the Lonely Valley. But we have no idea who did it, though."

"And those three months were Hell," Damowan spoke slowly and emphatically, "or at least the closest thing to it you could imagine."

"Somebody was holdin' us. Studyin' us or somethin'. It was really uncomfortable," Temmonin continued.

"Salt and pine needles. And sweat was all over," Jemalemin added.

"Y'know what, the Chrebin wasn't with us back then either, was it?" Damowan asked.

"I don't think so," Temmonin said. "You'd be the one to know. It was on yer shoulder."

"Oh, but tell him about the language, Temmonin." Damowan.

"Yea," Temmonin remembered, "we all know a new language but none of us knows how we know it."

"A new language?" Kashtawa doubted. "I've heard almost ev'ry language in the confederacy. Lemme hear this."

"Alright. Well, how should we do this?" Temmonin asked. "Kashtawa, why don't you whisper a sentence to Damowan and he'll tell it to me in this new language. Then I'll translate back into Mokhamoyuba. Good?"

"Good." Kashtawa thought for a moment, then leaned over near Damowan.

Damowan garbled a long sentence out loud.

Temmonin was quick to respond, "And should I dream of peace in my life, I would only wish a night in the swamp without mosquitos."

Kashtawa spat, "I can't believe it!" He laughed. "Damowan, say it again."

Damowan obliged.

"Sounds a little like Hitasha but I'm not an expert. There'll be elders from that clan here on the island though," Kashtawa said. "This is amazing. So you guys never knew this before?"

"No. But somehow we know it now, though."

"But, Temmonin," Damowan changed the subject, "where'd the Chrebin go?"

"I don't know, Damowan. I was asleep when we got abducted--jus' like you."

"I jus' thought ya might have an idea."

"This Chrebin thing," Kashtawa interrupted, "was it one of those magic things like in the stories? Some kinda spirits?"

"No, not spirits--well I'm pritty sure they had spirits," Damowan explained. "No, the one that chose me was a little clump of swamp-green fur. It had yellow eyes--big fer such a small thing. But I'd never wanna be its enemy." Temmonin gazed through the dark room to where he knew Chaneerem lay. Perhaps the talon-licker had not heard Damowan's comment. Perhaps he was sleeping. Perhaps he did not care. Damowan continued, "One night we were surrounded by hundreds, maybe thousands of 'em. That's when the one kinda chose me to be a blood brother. At least that's what it seemed like. See, a coupla nights before--or the night before--I untangled it from a thornbush."

"They can git into yer head, too," Jemalemin entered. "They got into mine and almost killed me. I hated it."

"Yea," Damowan said. "I think that's how it found out who rescued it and who threw a. . ." he trailed off.

"Who threw a what?" Kashtawa mimicked.

"A rock," Temmonin finished for Damowan. "Chaneerem threw a rock at it and scared it away."

"Why?" Kashtawa asked.

Silence.

"D'you think you guys could find yer way back to where those things live?" Kashtawa asked.

"We don't really know where they live exactly. They jus' filtered in through the forest. Mysterious things," Temmonin mused, "but, I think I remember where we met the first one." He did not want to mention Zubzza if he did not have to. Since the Mitsa-Mitsa did not ask him to elaborate, he continued. "The place we saw the whole group of 'em was north of there, though."

In the darkness, their tired bodies began to relax and slip toward sleep. Just as Temmonin was succumbing, he thought he heard Kashtawa comment, "Maybe I oughta start spendin' some time with you Flickers. Might enjoy life a little more."

Then Damowan, through the ebbing greyness, "Might get killed."

And sleep.

Temmonin found himself beneath the ice again. But now he was not at all cold. In fact, he was warmer than he had ever remembered being; as if wrapped in the hide of a freshly killed wapiti-- warm like dying blood. But this was no death. He was finally alive. And he had finally mastered the simple skill of breathing water. How it had eluded him before, he did not know.

The water beckoned him to its depths. He could hear its voice now, soft, echoing, drumming from far below him. And as he swam deeper, he was surprised to discover that the murk did not swallow him. Rather, it began to illuminate his way. And now he could see such sights. Schools of silvery minnows engulfed him and danced through and around his limbs; with his hair. Bluegill and sunfish and perch glided past his eyes unafraid of his intrusion into their realm. They seemed almost pleased that he would join them in this fluid dance of life.

Then he realized that they were unafraid because they had no reason to be--he was not a man. He was a fish. His heart surging with delight, Temmonin whirled in the water, testing his new fins and tail. He moved his tail fin and began swimming hard. Pleased by the scintillations of the water as it passed by him, he increased his speed. He was a comet and now he could travel faster in water than he had ever been able to travel as a man on land. He plummeted ever deeper into the lake to where the water grew colder and darker. But there at the bottom was the light he knew he must reach.

Suddenly, an ominous shadow passed across his destination. A gargantuan pike, lithe and burgeoned with teeth, guarded the light. Temmonin hid among the weeds and rocks of the lake floor. But this cover was insufficient and the gar pike drove towards him, mouth open and now more like a fire-bear than a fish. And when the monster pounded into the mud, Temmonin's eyes were strewn with filth. He wanted to view his adversary but needed to keep his eyes closed because of the pain. He rubbed viciously at his eyelids.

No teeth pierced his chest, only something tender, gentle. He opened his eyes to find himself on the shore in mid-summer and the Gorma was his pet. He himself, no longer a fish, lay wrapped in the silken folds of the fire-bear's black hide. He reveled in the cyclical heaving of its belly. He hung motionless, suspended between sleep and wakefulness, almost unaware of himself, almost unaware of the others around him.

The others around him! His heart roared into flame. His accusers stood in a circle awaiting his word: why had he killed the Gorma, the last one of its kind? How could he have destroyed such a gentle, amiable beast? But they did not understand--the Gorma was not dead. It was asleep. And he had not killed it. He had befriended it. And now it would benefit the whole confederacy. But why could they not see it breathing? Why was he the only one who knew the truth? And why would no one believe him--not his friends, not his uncle, not his mother or his father--not even Damowan!?

Accusations stormed his ears and drove him into himself. And he waited for his death.

Death did not come, but his eyes opened to a blackness that made him question whether it had come. He was awake. The inside of the longhouse was still pitch; no dawn seeped through the cracks in the bark. He felt the presence of the others sleeping near him. Lying on his back, he stared into the shadows until his eyes were able to decipher the vague outlines of bent birch rafters and roof supports.

He again began reworking scenes of the high council. In some, he won the arguments. In others, he lost. Although he did not want to die, he felt an odd satisfaction in the pity he felt for himself; a pressing hopelessness that was fed from visions of his passing. This comfort tugged at his heart and begged him to revel in the glory of such an untimely and unjust fate. He saw the faces of his family, his friends. He heard their words, saw their tears. And again Zheva. And Zheva never married after Temmonin died. She walked shrouded in loneliness until the day she died.

Temmonin was glad it was dark in the longhouse. He could not face his brother after having bathed in such self-indulgence. He could not understand why his mind continually reverted to such thoughts. But it seemed that the most difficult task in all his life was to pry open the door to this cave of introspection and escape its dank emotions. The introspection promised him his dreams. But in the end it left him aching.

Temmonin was weary now, but sleep still eluded him. He shifted several times to find a more comfortable position. He noticed his throat becoming more sore and dull pains behind his eyes. It caused him to remember the signs of illness he had felt earlier in the trip; almost never did he feel the onset of sickness without soon finding himself completely within its grasp. He was surprised, however, that he had remained healthy for so long. In fact, now that he thought about it, he was surprised that he had not had a sore throat during the entire underground captivity. Perhaps that was because there had been no drastic temperature changes there. But there was all that salt. In the end he concluded that he would never be able to understand his own body. Again, he rolled to his side, drawing his hide-blanket around his neck.

"Temmonin," a voice called from behind him.

Temmonin rolled over, eyes glaring into the blackness. None of the others were awake. But this was not a man's voice. "Damowan?" Temmonin whispered, hoping.

"Temmonin," the eerie voice repeated. Then a pale figure melted through the wall of the longhouse. It was the same spirit he had seen in the vision he and Damowan had on their elk hunt. Temmonin looked around at the others.

"They will not awake, Temmonin," the she-spirit said, her voice shimmering. "I have come to talk with you this night. Do you feel fear, child?"

Somehow, the fact that she addressed him as a child did not make Temmonin feel any less of a man. He simply felt honored by her presence. "Yes, I feel fear. . .and other things."

"What other things?" The shells on her wrists clattered but did not disturb the others in the room.

Temmonin was embarrassed but felt that he could not hide anything from this spirit. "Pity, hopelessness, anger, anxiousness. There's so much."

"Yes, Temmonin, there is much. More than some would be willing to continue suffering."

She bent and touched Chaneerem's shoulder.
Temmonin was afraid the oath-taker would stir.
But he remained asleep. As she rose, Temmonin
marveled again at her ornate beak. "Temmonin,
there is still so much more to be done. Your
submission to the Creator is what has given you
strength thus far; continue in this. And remember,
my brother, when you are falsely accused, trust in
Him who made you. Even if He is the only other
who knows the truth, it is sufficient; He is the
Maker." She bowed as she dissipated. Tears
gathered in the corners of Temmonin's eyes as he
fell back to sleep.

Morning came quickly.

"Well, this is it, eh?" Damowan commented
as he rose.

"But you know how long this stuff can take,
don't ya?" Kashtawa asked.

"Well, you're right about that," Damowan
agreed. "Maybe this isn't quite it. Not yet anyway,"
he stood and raised his brows at Temmonin, "but,
soon."

Along with the Kumuchska envoy, they
were shuffled out of the longhouse by their Mitsa-
Mitsa hosts into a morning less foggy than the
previous day. Still, they could not see very far ahead
of themselves. Their hosts led them to the pavilion
where the morning meal had already begun. There,
Kashtawa excused himself, saying he wanted to see
some Salamanders he knew. Temmonin did not
want him to leave but smiled as he walked away.
But as he and the others moved on, his heart
jumped. In the clearing, he saw small groups of
men eating together. Would his father and his
uncles be there? At first, he did not see them, but
when the host had led them past the initial
scattering of elders, Temmonin noticed the

headdress of flicker feathers that always adorned his father's head at formal activities.

"Father!" Temmonin leapt from the line and ran to Amowz. Damowan followed, laughing.

Their father turned and stood, eyes wide and brown, "Temmonin! Damowan! My sons!"

All three forgot the formality of the occasion and embraced each other without considering those around them. Temmonin did not care how inappropriate the action was. His father was here. This might be the last time they would ever embrace.

Amowz pushed them away in playful brusqueness. "My sons, you should be embarrassed at yourselves." His eyes switched back and forth as if afraid of something. "Don't you know how to behave in the presence of elders?"

"Yes, my rebellious nephews!" Nosh appeared at Amowz's side.

"Uncle." Temmonin suddenly could not decide whether or not to greet Nosh formally. He raised up his arm hesitantly.

"Temmonin." Nosh grabbed his nephew's arm and pulled him into his own arms. "Don't worry, my friend, the world'll see what the world wants to see. But God help the osprey when the salmon skims the surface."

"'Specially since this might be the last time," Damowan scoffed in jest.

"Not if I can speak my mind," a gruff voice entered the circle, "and I will speak my mind, whether the moon rises or not."

"Uncle Ammon!" Damowan's eyes lit. But before he could move to hug his uncle, Ammon stretched out his arm in greeting.

"Peace and beauty," he said.

Temmonin and Damowan raised their arms in formal greeting. Ammon was ever aloof, even at such an intimate moment. Of course, he was their master, their trainer. His duty was to discipline them in the ways of tribal manhood, a task that demanded his aloofness. It was not that Temmonin and Damowan had never seen him smile or laugh or show affection. It was just that he had never allowed those emotions to enter their public relationship. Often, he refrained from giving them approval even in the privacy of the longhouse. Yet the two brothers had grown to understand the creases in Ammon's face. At this point, they recognized in his stoicism the suppression of the pleasure they often shared with him in private dealings.

In comparison to Ammon's thin release, Amowz and Nosh poured out their hearts. Amowz and Nosh were so quick to smile, their cheeks were permanently piled with wrinkles. But Ammon's wrinkles gathered at his eyes, as if fortifying themselves against the tears that had so frequented his life. Amowz's hair had already begun greying and now hung in mingled strands down to the middle of his back. Nosh and Ammon, however, still possessed coal black manes. A stack of wrinkles, Amowz's forehead stood taller and wider than his brothers'. Theirs were less worn than his. Ammon's eyes had been placed deeper than his brothers' had been and were shadowed by oversized brows. And his mouth and chin were as strong as a muzzle. But, in spite of the differences that distinguished the three, they were obviously born of the same parents. Temmonin and Damowan bore the resemblance too. Damowan actually looked more like Ammon's son than Amowz's. Temmonin had his father's mouth but otherwise reflect his mother's features and some of Nosh's as well.

Many times, Temmonin had felt the security in these resemblances but never, he thought, as pungently as now. If nothing else gave him comfort at this moment, this did.

"C'mon, join us fer breakfast," Nosh motioned. "You'll need a good meal fer today's proceedings. And this stuff's prob'ly much better than you've had fer a while now."

"How's Mom?" Temmonin asked Amowz, "and Tutumora?"

"Good," his father returned, "but last I saw 'em was the last full moon. I'm sure they're fine. You know yer Mother." He smiled. "C'mon, sit down and let's eat."

They sat in a rough circle and Nosh immediately passed the young men bowls of steaming wild rice soup. As Temmonin reached to receive his meal, he noticed a familiar face across from him. Mantaw smiled.

"Peace and beauty, Temmonin, Damowan," he nodded to each.

Temmonin also greeted Da and Desh and one other clan leader in the circle. Just behind Mantaw, he saw several other Flicker elders in another circle. Temmonin studied them as he chewed. But the hot fish and wild rice was as succulent as any he remembered and he soon forgot his interest in placing names with those faces. He ate his soup in a few minutes. When they had finished the meal, Amowz leaned in to Damowan and poked his shoulder,

"A little gaunt there, eh?"

"A little sore!" Damowan snapped playfully.

"A little undernourished too!" Temmonin added.

231

"What? D'you guys fergit how to hunt?" Ammon bent his upper lip.

Temmonin knew the comment was a joke but he suddenly felt his emotions ride to his throat. "Actually we didn't even git a chance to hunt. We couldn't do nothin'. We got captured." Not far away, a head snapped toward Temmonin. From the corner of his eye, he could see that it was Chaneerem. The talon-licker and his younger brother had remained with the Kumuchska envoy and sat eating some feet to his left. Apparently, they had heard Temmonin's comment. Da noticed Temmonin's distraction and he himself caught sight of Zevil's sons.

"Chaneerem and Jemalemin too?" he exclaimed. "Why aren't they eatin' with their people?" He stood and waved the other two Ek-Birin to the Flicker congregation. Within seconds, Zevil's sons came and sat with their people.

"So now that yer all here--" Nosh stated, "and before the council convenes again at midday--tell us ev'rything that's happened in these past three months."

"How much do you know, Uncle Nosh?" Temmonin asked.

"Word of yer whereabouts reached this island only yesterday. We only knew that a Kumuchska envoy was escortin' you guys here."

"Then it's really important that all of you understand what a weird experience we had." Temmonin glanced around the circle. A couple of the men nodded. The rest stared at him, eager to hear his words. "We traveled through the marshes and through the Shushunu until we reached the Kanattar. After hiking all day, we spent a couple of nights at Demnaza villages. We were captured the night we left the last Demnaza village up by the mouth of the Lonely Valley. That night, we sat with the young warriors of the village in the hot springs in the caves of Imnanaw-Kanat. They gave us furs and snowshoes. The next time we saw the sun was a week ago. Here's the real weird part, though. We have no idea where we were durin' those three months. We know exactly what it felt like. It stunk, it was totally uncomfortable, and everything was so dark we couldn't see a thing."

"Somebody was down there with us," Damowan interjected. "It was always hot but then somebody'd walk by every once in a while--usually when we were tryin' to talk to each other--and whoever they were, they were hotter than the air. You could feel the heat of their skin when they came up close to ya."

"It was like they were studyin' us," Jemalemin added.

"Touchin'. They kept touchin' me." Damowan wrinkled his face. "That was sick."

"I'm pritty sure we were underground," Temmonin said.

"Or in a forest so thick ya couldn't see the sun," Damowan said.

"Underground." Temmonin twisted his mouth and slit his eyes at his brother.

"So how d'you guys get there?" Amowz asked. "You must remember somethin' about that."

"No, actually, I don't," Temmonin answered, "but I do remember some really strange dreams. In fact, I 'member a lotta really strange dreams. Seems like most of the time we were down there, we were dreamin' or swoonin' or coughin' or pukin' or bein' touched or massaged or somethin'."

"Sounds like these guys were really checkin' you guys out." Nosh half-smiled.

Damowan burst into laughter. Temmonin thought he saw Chaneerem's face sour. Jemalemin laughed some but not overmuch. Temmonin smiled as he answered his uncle. "I think it was somethin' else. They never tried to have sex with us or nuthin' like that. Somethin' else was goin' on down there. There's prob'ly even more to it than this but all four of us, for some weird reason--we can all understand and speak a new language."

"A new language?" Amowz asked. "Y'mean you worked out some kinda code so these people couldn't understand ya?"

"No, Dad. We can all speak a language we never heard before. We didn't even know we could do it until we got captured by the Kumuchska." Temmonin's face was transparent, his shoulders high. "It doesn't make any sense at all."

"This language," Amowz was excited, "what does it sound like? Nosh knows all the languages of the Kanattar. . ."

"A little of each," Nosh tempered his brother's boast.

"But you know all the dialects of Kumuchska and Demnaza, right?"

"Most," Nosh replied. "Lemme hear this, Temmonin, Damowan."

Temmonin thought for a moment, then spoke a long sentence.

"Sun and moon!" Nosh exclaimed. "This is really weird. Damowan you say somethin'."

Damowan complied. Nosh shook his head.

"This isn't Kanattar–not even close. And I'm sure it's not Mitsa-Mitsa. I don't know. I've never heard anything like it." Nosh threw up his hands.

"So you guys jus' know this language all of a sudden? How does somethin' like that happen?" Amowz was perplexed.

"What about the tribes from way up North--the ones that hunt the white bear?" Damowan asked, ignoring his father's question.

"I really doubt it--but I guess maybe," Nosh answered. "Wait, say somethin' else--somethin' long."

Damowan spoke enough to grow bored of speaking.

"No, not the white tribes. And I don't think it's Shushunushu either. Or Melumblumblar," Nosh spoke while thinking hard. "Could it be one of the southern tribes? I jus' can't place it."

"Who would be in the Lonely Valley in the middle of winter?" Amowz asked not expecting an answer.

The circle was silent. After a moment, Nosh reiterated, "So, you guys have no idea who these people were?"

"No," Temmonin and Damowan spoke together. "Not a single clue."

"And no idea where they took ya?"

The brothers shook their heads.

"I think it's wise not to bring up this language-thing," Nosh asserted, "at least not right away. It's just too weird. Prob'ly jus' confuse the issue." Amowz and Ammon nodded assent. "But maybe there'll be a time for it. Just don't be too hasty to start babblin' in front of the High Council."

"Well, what're we gonna say then?" Damowan asked.

"The truth. Even though yer story sounds like a story, it's the only thing you'll be able to say with any kind of integrity." Ammon smiled.

Kashtawa spent the entire morning with his fellow Mitsa-Mitsa. He rejoined the Ek-Birin at the council that noon. Temmonin felt his own smile jitter as the Salamander took the place next to him in the circle. His belly was seething, roiling with anticipation. Naturally, he felt secure in the presence of his father and his uncles, Damowan, Jemalemin, Kashtawa, and even Da, but the fellowship of his kin could not quench the burning of his adrenaline.

He had always pictured the council to be an awesome gathering of men. He had never imagined, however, that the weight of that awe would press fully upon himself. And the weight increased with every new arrival. As each member entered the circle, he stepped to the Flicker mutant that was displayed near the center. Some scrutinized. Others stared. Then they eased away and moved to their seats. Soon, over one hundred elders sat in an extravagant circle of justice. Temmonin sighed.

"Overwhelming, isn't it?" Kashtawa nudged.

Temmonin just shook his head. He stared at his feet for a moment, then turned to Kashtawa, "Thanks," he whispered.

The warrior's face wrinkled, "Fer what?"

Temmonin wrestled with his tongue for an instant. "Well," he began hesitantly, "I know we haven't known each other long, but--fer yer friendship."

Kashtawa nodded, the corners of his mouth bending down. "Sure."

Across the circle of trodden snow in the center of the gathering, Temmonin saw a group of five men enter. Blood surged in his chest as he recognized the second in line as Mok, the chief of the village in the Shushunu. Mok did not return the Ek-Birin's stare and, apparently unaware that Temmonin was looking at him, sat down exactly opposite him so that the fire in the center of the clearing distorted his expression. Temmonin could not tell what the swamp chief was thinking.

Soon, a small entourage of Salamanders led the mediators of the council to the edge of the fire. As the Mitsa-Mitsa returned again to the outer circle and the four mediators moved to their places, Temmonin turned to Damowan who was sitting just on the other side of Amowz. Damowan stared at Temmonin and raised his eyebrows. Then he clapped his hands together softly and looked with Temmonin at Jemalemin. The boy was searching the snow at his feet, not interested in meeting anyone's eyes. Chaneerem's face was escarpment.

At the center, the four mediators had positioned themselves at points equidistant from each other around the fire. Just as they did so, the sun seeped through the mist, struggling to be recognized. Many heads rose and smiled, kissed with yellow warmth. The mediators, however, were intent on their ceremony. They faced outward from the fire to the four cardinal directions and raised their arms to reveal wooden bowls in each of their hands. Then the chanting.

"Our Creator, You who formed us from the fire and brought us up through the earth and up through the lake and up into the air that takes the osprey high and the vulture. You who rages in winter wind and roars in summer thunder, who burns leaves in autumn and paints flowers on the heels of the retreating snow. You whose blackness is deeper than the dark forest at night, whose whiteness pales the most brilliant of clouds, whose yellowness burns brighter than the sun at highest summer, and whose redness is that of a hundred cardinals. We call You now. We ask that You sit among us." The four turned inward. "We offer You fire." They bowed. "We offer You earth." They emptied the soil in the bowls in their left hands. "We offer You water." They emptied the water in the other bowls. "We offer you air." At that, all of the elders including Amowz, Ammon, and Nosh blew breath up into the fog.

"Be with us, we ask You," the whole congregation whispered.

Three of the mediators sat down in the snow facing the outer circle. One remained standing and began to speak. He faced South, in the direction of the shrouded noon sun. He was dressed predominantly in red and wore on his head the large rack of a white-tailed deer. Feathers and deer tails shook from his deer-hide cloak as he spoke,

"My brothers, we have discussed for some time now the terrible offenses that have caused outrage in almost every clan of the confederacy. We have strived for understanding but have fallen short of any conclusions. Today we add four to our number. We have also viewed a new piece of evidence--the body of a monster killed by one of the newcomers. Let us listen to their stories with an ear of sound judgment and impartiality." He faced the Ek-Birin. "Temmonin, Chaneerem, Damowan, and Jemalemin of the clan of the Flicker, rise and address the council." The four stood and moved forward. When they had advanced several steps, the mediator signaled for them to halt. "Speak to us only truth and your hardships will be few." The man paused as if gathering to himself the questions of all the elders present.

"My brothers, your elders have informed
you of the events the council has been discussing,
am I correct?" The Flickers nodded assent to his
question. "And you are aware that our questioning
of you four is not only to discover more about this
situation, but also to determine your involvement, if
any, in it?" Again, the Ek-Birin nodded. "Then we
begin." He paused. "It has been determined that
the last your party was seen was at the Demnaza
village of Gamnashta. There are some here who
have testified to that fact. It has also been
determined that the next time you were seen by any
of the confederation was when you were captured at
the edge of Demdegumshannatez where the
Wolverines of that village escorted you to their
council. Please, tell us of your whereabouts and
your actions during the months of the interim."

The four Ek-Birin looked at each other.
Temmonin felt that the others wanted him to speak.
He did so, "My fellow people, our story this day is
as true as the mountains which rise from the sea.
But, understand, it is short and it is simple. Please
do not let its brevity steer you from belief."
Temmonin glanced at Damowan and Jemalemin
and Chaneerem before he continued. "My brothers,
the morning we left Gamnashta was sad for us
indeed, for their friendship and hospitality warmed
the chill in our toes. Not only did they share their
food and companionship, but they also supplied us
with much needed snowshoes and sleeping furs to
continue our journey north. For this, we were and
are extremely grateful." He had noticed some elders
present from the clan of the Elk. He nodded at
them. "But, still we left. We knew our destination
was days north. That entire day after we departed
from Gamnashta, we fought a storm in the valley
they called Lonely. Finally, when darkness fell, we

found a partially sheltered spot against the cliff wall
and set up our tents there. Sleep did not come
easily. Winds rampaged as if demanding that we
remain awake but, eventually, we fell into the soft
hands of slumber. That night, however, we fell into
other hands as well. None of us are able to
remember the actual event but we were all four
taken captive that night and we were taken to a dark
place. We were tied tightly to logs and studied for
the entirety of the time we were missing. We do not
know who did this. We do not know where we
were taken. We do not know why this was done to
us. And we have not been able to determine
anything by discussing our memories of the
experience. All that we remember is the evening at
Gamnashta, the day in the midst of the storm, this
extended nightmare, and waking up entangled in the
vines near Demdegumshannatez. Everything else is
vague, dark, and distorted. We wish to know what
happened to us as much as this council does."

The council stared at the Ek-Birin and at
the red-clad mediator. The fog around them
padded their ears and their minds. None spoke for
some time. The mediator began slowly,

"This is all you would say?"

"Yes," Temmonin replied.

"And would none of you add to the story?"
the mediator asked.

Damowan and Jemalemin shook their
heads. The talon-licker may as well have had no
tongue; he seemed to have forgotten how to use it.
The mediator stood even taller than he had been
standing,

"My brothers, we have heard the story of
our fellows. What questions would you now ask of
them? Remember that we, of all congregations, are
devoted to impartiality. Let us cling to the

principles of our ancestors as a child clings to its mother's breast."

The elders sat silently for some time. To the left of and beyond the mediator sat Mok. Temmonin could see him clearly now. The Daimadunva chief met his gaze without hesitation. At least there was no violence in those eyes. Mok was not the first to stand.

"Mosh of the clan of the Rattler," announced the red mediator, "please speak your mind."

Mosh spoke as directly as any man Temmonin had ever heard. That fact, if nothing else, made Temmonin warm. "My fellow people, as a chief of a village that has suffered no ill from this situation, I would caution this company to patience." Damowan raised his eyebrows at Temmonin. "But in view of such a weak story, I must say that my heart laughs at these four Flickers." He sat down to the rustle of cloaks and a wave of murmurs.

Not long after that, the mediator introduced an elder from the clan of the Eagle, Chash. "And as an elder of a village that was visited with death four times over, I must disagree with my Hitasha brother." He paused, it seemed to Temmonin, for effect. "I would not caution this assembly to patience. This confederation has had its fill of waiting. We wait like a mother waits for her stillborn son to cry. And if this mother does not soon leave the land of dreams, she will hold in her arms a dry skeleton. Must we wait until other young men of the confederacy follow the deceitful imaginations of their childish hearts. Must we allow the disciplines of our forefathers to slacken from neglect. Must we bind ourselves with the vines of so-called prudence and watch as our people are eaten away as the shore is eaten away by pounding waves?" He clenched both fists and held them in front of himself. "With my heart and my lips, I say no!" Chash looked directly at the four Ek-Birin. Then he turned and sat down. The council was silent.

The mediator scanned the circle. "Would any of my brothers ask questions of these our brothers of the Ek-Birin? Is there an issue that has not been addressed? Let us not ignore any thought that leads to thoroughness."

Several elders were introduced and these men asked questions the Ek-Birin could not answer. As questions were repeated, the council seemed to sigh impatiently. Each question added to the frustration that pressed like granite against the will of these elders. And Temmonin had to breathe deeply and slowly to hold his anger. Why did these men continue asking about the very things of which the Ek-Birin themselves were ignorant? Why could they not gaze at the earnest eyes of the innocent young warriors and see only the love these four had for their brothers and sisters? Why could they not see? This was not guile.

"Perhaps these four sincerely do not know of their recent whereabouts," began a chief of the Melumblumblar, "or of their recent actions." A flash of confusion unsettled the circle. "Perhaps there is some deep magic involved here that has masked these four Flickers from their own consciousness. Similar things happen when any of us chances upon a peace eddy. Men have been known to walk for miles and wake in other villages. Perhaps. . ." As this elder sat, another stood and objected vehemently.

"And now, on such simple grounds, we will excuse this multitude of crimes--the murder of our people?!" This outraged Ek-Makatin chief had been sitting next to Chash, the elder who had called for immediate action. "All of us know that no man can be overcome by a peace eddy unless he is willing and pure before the eyes of the Creator. And surely, you would not believe that a man--or three men and a boy--caught up in a peace eddy caused by the Creator would murder his brothers and sisters." Many heads nodded their assent to the Eagle. "Yes, perhaps these monstrosities were committed while these warriors were caught up or possessed. But not by my Creator or by yours! No, and if they were possessed, it was not by any good thing!" More assent and growls of anger, "And, given the fact that no man can be caught up but by that into which he is willing to be caught up, these four, should they have been caught up at all, must have submitted themselves to all that we as a council detest. No, we will have no waiving of responsibility on these grounds."

An elder of the Kumuchska stood, one whom Temmonin did not recognize. "I am insulted by this banter! I want action. Six of my villagers were destroyed and, whether these four committed their murders in a trance or if they are lying to us like children--whether conscious of their sin or not, these four must die!" He beat his chest with his right fist.

Voices crawled over voices and, as Temmonin's head reverberated with the bellows of death, he pleaded silently with his father and his uncles. Ammon gave Temmonin no assurance; he sat as stoic as Chaneerem. With their eyes, Amowz and Nosh let him know their empathy but they did not move to speak. He turned to the mediator. Nothing but a blank stare.

Then, across the fire an elder stood. It was Mok, the Daimadunva chief who had almost killed them. Suddenly, Temmonin's defense of this man was feeble; a naive intuition. His heart pushed at his chest as if it wished to escape its inevitable fate. The mediator introduced the Painted Turtle.

"My brothers, we of the swamps greet you. And, although I understand the anger you feel, I would again caution this council to patience and to prudence. And lest any of you object to my warning, I wish you to know the context of my words." No one spoke. All eyes watched Mok. "I was in deep mourning when these four were discovered near our village. My daughter was she whom I mourned. She had been ruined the night before by something hideous and demented. But the marks on her body did not match those described by any of my brothers here--except those described by Mantaw of the Ek-Birin. The death-marks on my daughter were not made by this dead creature here. No feathers were scattered on the floor of my house. But there was hair; fur." He paused. No whispers from any of the elders. "When these Flickers arrived, we questioned them. They did not want to incriminate the Kumuchska so, at first, they refused to reveal the burden they bore. But when they understood the gravity of our need for information, they peeled back the covering on their trailer and showed to us the monster that Mantaw, Da, Amowz, Ammon, and Desh have described to this council. I cannot be certain, but I would guess that a similar monster killed my daughter. These Ek-Birin carried the Wolverine creature through our village. It could not have been the same one that had killed my daughter. It had decayed at least five days and stank horribly. When our elders had discovered the integrity of these men,

they were welcomed to stay with us and they acted
honorably until they left the next morning. I have
no complaint regarding their actions or their
character. And since it is my daughter that has died,
for whom I still mourn until this very day, I believe
my testimony weighs heavily upon this council." As
Mok finished, he was staring at Temmonin. His
eyes spoke only encouragement and respect.

Temmonin was so relieved at Mok's words,
he wanted to run and hug the chief. But he knew
he could not. Instead, he returned respect and
gratitude with a bow of his head. But as he did so,
the Wolverine chief who had insisted on death
stood and spoke.

"And where is this carcass?"

Temmonin's warm heart went cold. His
sudden embarrassment almost caused him to shiver.
He looked at Damowan and Jemalemin. They were
staring at the snow. He had hoped this issue would
be neglected but he knew the council needed the
information. He drew a deep breath before he
spoke.

"I am greatly embarrassed to admit that I
do remember what happened to the carcass of the
Kumuchska monster." He paused to conjure
resolve. "The four of us left Mok's village intending
to skirt the great gorge of Zubzza and to travel
north to Imnanaw-Kanat and through the
mountains to Demdegumshannatez where we were
to show our evidence to Nosh, the chief of that
village. On our way through Shushunu, however,
our curiosity became great and we decided to stop at
Zubzza and investigate." Murmurs among the
council. "Our decision," Temmonin spoke loudly,
"was foolish for we saw nothing and both
Damowan and I were almost killed in a fall that
nearly took us over the edge of the gorge. It was

during that fall that we lost our hold on the drag trailer and the monster. The gorge was filled with fog and the monster was completely lost to us. We never heard it hit the floor of the gorge. I am sorry to say that we have no other explanation."

Temmonin was afraid to look at his father or his uncles. Along with Damowan, Jemalemin, and Chaneerem, he looked at the white blanket that stretched between the edges of the forest. He was cold from having spent his heart on the shameful truth--much more cold than he would have been had this not been the high council. Now the story would be told to children and grandchildren. Temmonin's acts would be numbered with every act that taught the people the meaning of foolishness. And they deserved to be. Temmonin wondered how his face could be so hot while the rest of his body was so very frigid.

After much silence, the mediator spoke again, "Are there still more questions?" And after more silence, he concluded, "Then we must part and meditate on these things. This evening, we will reconvene for the evening meal. At that time, we will give our word as council. The four mediators will remain at this fire that each of you might bring us word separately."

At least these men did not harangue. Had Temmonin's mother been present, he would have been asked the same questions several times and would have been much more likely to flame into rage. Then he realized that these men had done exactly that. Probably, it was just easier for him to become angry at his mother. A good number of these men seemed to take him at his word. Or, if they did not believe him, they were content to allow him to lie instead of feeling that they must manipulate him until he contradicted himself.

Although Temmonin knew his tension should increase, thoughts of this high council comforted him. He wondered if there were other tribes that were this level-headed.

In the back of his throat, however, Temmonin felt the burning. The sickness that had flirted with him for a week had now settled in his tonsils. He spent the afternoon bewildered, his thoughts vacillating between the joy of seeing his family again, the rawness in his palate, and the ambiguous anxiety of waiting for the final council. And he could not exactly understand why Kashtawa stayed with them but the presence of the Mitsa-Mitsa almost made him laugh.

This was a moment like only a few others in Temmonin's life when any emotion he felt, no matter how slight, became so intense he could not ignore it. He shook his head at himself. Even his joy and his laughter were weighty. Like stones, they could be tossed into the air and he could feel unbelievable elation, but they were always quick to descend; always ready to return him to his thoughts. He saw Damowan and how that man, engorged with laughter at a joke Amowz had just told, had already forgotten the gravity of their situation. Temmonin struggled to be free of his stagnant swamp of thoughts. But the stones only drew him down. Again, he shook his head at himself.

Temmonin only caught the last sentence Nosh spoke. "Oh, yea, we had fun when we were yer guys' age," he laughed, "but never as much as yer havin' right now." Temmonin wondered if Nosh knew what vultures were circling in his nephew's head.

After the council had eaten the evening meal and had reconvened for their final meeting, the red mediator stood. He now wore over his other clothing a full length black vest of bear fur that was tasseled at the shoulders with dyed yellow eagle feathers. He addressed his brothers, "I speak for you, my people, as I give the judgment of the four mediators. We have heard from you as a council and we have heard from you as individuals. We now give our judgment as any of you would give in our place." He bowed with the three other mediators. "Heed the words of the high council. Temmonin, Chaneerem, Damowan, and Jemalemin of the clan of the Flicker, we do not call you responsible for this multitude of crimes. And yet we cannot completely call you innocent. There is a depth to the situation at hand and only time can reveal what we as humans cannot. Our judgment is that you four travel home with your clansmen and that you remain in your village until the snows leave and return again. You are not to leave your village to hunt or to carry messages nor for any other reason." He raised his staff and his head and bellowed, "Heed the words of the high council."

IX.   Or is that we have grown fond of the putrid reek from the refuse mound of history? Perhaps we do not seek truth at all. Perhaps, like children playing with their own excrement, we do not recognize our own grotesqueness or the danger that we draw so near to our lips. Or perhaps, unlike those children, we do recognize the grotesqueness but are so enamored with our own creation that we cannot bring ourselves to part with it. And so we manipulate the defecation into shapes that please us, we dress the defecation with costumes that make us marvel, we name the defecation with names that connote honor and dignity. In our passion, we create dishes from the defecation and we imagine that their aroma reaches the ends of the earth. But we do not eat the dishes for, if we know nothing else, we know at least that all we have created is in fact only defecation. Yet, when confronted with this fact, do we not most often raise our chests and sing the praises of the manipulations and the costumes and the names that we have done and made and given? Do we not strive against any who would call attention to the hideous stench? And, in the end, will we truly learn anything from the refuse mound of history? Or will the reek steal from us our ability to reason so that, finally, we can be as children playing with our own excrement, entertained, decaying and damned?

CHAPTER 9

Damowan was on the trail nearest the lake when he noticed Temmonin sitting on the shore. "Eh."

"Shhh," Temmonin slowly turned his head inland. "Gourdfish."

Damowan made his way to the rocks and sand, found a dry spot near his brother, and gingerly lowered himself. Several gourdfish lay on the beach, their tail fins still dipped in the lake, their shoulders glistening in the steamy sun. They squirmed for an instant as Damowan broke the serenity. But they remained.

Since spring broke, Temmonin and Damowan had spent most of their time studying gourdfish. Temmonin had already been scolded for trying to help the women of the village process hides for clothing. And the village elders held strictly to the rule of the high council. As a result, Temmonin had grown to know this stretch of shoreline like he knew no other. Now gourdfish were spawning.

Temmonin whispered to Damowan without moving his head. "I think this is gonna be a big colony--a good year." He pointed to a long swath where the gourd-like egg-sacks were clumped along the edge of the lake like miniature pumpkins and squash in an autumn field. "Man, look at those colors. Unbelievable." Another fish squirmed onto the shore, nudging the others aside.

"Y'know Temmonin," Damowan whispered, "I love the beauty the Creator's given us but I must admit that I'd like to use the muscles he made fer me."

"Well, think of it this way, Damowan. We now have the best archer's aim in the village, maybe in all the marshes." Temmonin attempted to console him.

"And it certainly is a useful skill to have when ya aren't allowed to hunt, isn't it?" Damowan shook his head and glanced irritated toward the village.

"But ya gotta think about their side of it, Damowan." Temmonin wrinkled his face. "What else were they s'posed to do? We were framed--we know that. But they weren't there. They can only make a judgment based on what they know, right?"

"Temmonin, there's not a single person more positive and understandin' than you." Damowan paused. "And nobody I'd like to kick in the teeth as much as you either."

Temmonin burst into laughter. Damowan followed. All the gourdfish scrambled back into the water. Temmonin wiped tears from his eyes. When he noticed that the fish had scattered, he punched his younger brother in the thigh. Damowan's expression begged for an explanation.

"You scared my buddies away," Temmonin chided with a smile. "Now, I gotta wait all mornin' before they come back."

"Not half as long as we have to wait until we can live normal lives again. Another summer and another fall." Damowan looked skyward and turned his palms upward. "Come quickly snow."

"Never thought I'd hear you say that," Temmonin laughed.

"Neither did I."

They sat in silence for a long time, the summer sun drenching their backs, the cool water licking their bare toes. Some feet from shore, gourdfish began to peek their eyes above the surface of the water. Not long after that, the bravest wriggled onto the sand again. Soon they lined the

beach as they had before. These were all males.
The female gourdfish had lain on this same sand
two weeks earlier and had deposited their eggs. Not
until today had these eggs been large and ripe
enough to emit the juices that attracted the males of
the species. And the males would lie here,
stimulated by those juices, until they were ready to
fertilize the gourds.

"It's jus' like the males're lyin' here checkin'
the place out before they make their move,"
Temmonin whispered.

They sat quietly for a long while.

"Y'know," Damowan broke the silence,
"All due respect to the beauty of this moment but I
think you and I have checked this place out long
enough." He slapped Temmonin's leg with the back
of his hand. The gourdfish once again splashed
back into the water. "Maybe it's time we made our
move." Then he stood and walked away from his
older brother.

Temmonin felt his stomach stir. "And
disobey the high council?" he shouted after
Damowan. Damowan did not answer. Temmonin
settled back into his view of the shoreline,
pondering possibilities.

Since Shabba was not in his longhouse and
it was midmorning, Temmonin knew where to find
him. The young warrior began down the trail to
where the elder would be. As he approached the
crest of a hill that overlooked the gourdfish bay, he
felt his stomach rise. He knew that Shabba had
always sworn confidence. But Temmonin had
never come to him for advice about whether or not
to obey the high council. Temmonin dropped onto
a small shale platform.

"Hmmn," Shabba grunted, turning his head
but not enough to meet Temmonin's eyes.

"Peace and beauty," the intruder spoke softly, "I am Temmonin."

"Peace and beauty," Shabba answered. "Let me see you."

The elder was as thin as a birch sapling except for his prominent belly which, as Temmonin circled around the man, slowly showed itself. And his skin was as deep and glossy as polished walnut shell. His face was pleated a thousand times to make room for each new sorrow, every new joy. His hands had long since been crippled into claws and were little more useful than his swollen ankles and knees and hips and elbows and shoulders. Arthritis had conquered most of his youth but Shabba's stubbornness had wrestled from the illness what little agility he retained. Sometimes Temmonin would watch the old man cross the clearing in the center of the village and marvel at his determination. And he refused help. Now he was sitting with his back against a tree stump, legs extended straight in front of himself.

"Please sit with me," Shabba motioned.

Temmonin situated himself directly in front of the elder, crossed his legs, and released a heavy sigh.

"Temmoninek, my son," Shabba ignored Temmonin's subtle plea for pity. "What have you learned from your meditations and your watchings?"

Temmonin cleared his throat. "I've been watchin' the gourdfish, Shabbamassa. I've seen the gourds grow, but I didn't watch the she-fish lay their eggs because you told me not to. The gourds've grown and they've spilled their juice. The he-fish've come to bask in the juice and in the sun."

"And they have not yet taken their part, have they?"

"No, Shabbamassa." Temmonin answered.

253

"They will do so soon," the elder half-whispered. "You think so?"

"Yes." Temmonin was waiting for the right moment to shift the subject of the conversation to Damowan and himself and their decision.

"What do you glean from your watchings? And what does the way of the gourdfish tell you about the one who created them?"

Temmonin was enthralled with Shabba's ability to question without shaming his pupil--to be wise without ridiculing the naivety of those younger than himself.

"I've seen that a woman and a man give of themselves and that what comes from this giving is more beautiful than what was before," he paused, "and I've seen that a man has to be patient with a woman 'cause, if he isn't, he'll destroy the beauty they can make together."

Silence.

"Temmoninek, my son," Shabba said, "you are right in saying that a man must be patient with a woman. In fact, a man must be patient with the whole world. And the whole world often makes him wait. But there is another lesson in the way of the gourdfish." He shifted and winced. "What did you see before the she-fish came to lay their eggs?"

"Nothing, Shabbamassa." Temmonin was perplexed. "You told me not to watch the she-fish."

"No, my friend. I only told you to avert your eyes when the she-fish lays her eggs. No, there is more to the lesson of the gourdfish." Shabba shifted and winced again. "And I will tell you what it is." He shifted again and recoiled as violently as Temmonin had ever seen him do. "Damn this rotted oak of a hip!" Then, with a smile tugging at one cheek, "pritty soon the chipmunks'll be nestin' in here. But I must tell you of the gourdfish.

Temmoninek, if you had watched in the water
before the she-fish covered the shore, you would
see that it was the he-fish who initiated the spawn.
When spring warms the waters, the he-fish grows a
bony spike on his forehead. When it is time to
spawn, the he-fish pushes his spike into the egg-sack
of the she-fish. Then he waits until she can close
her sack around the spike. When she has a grip, he
pulls violently away, breaking the spike from his
own body and leaving it in her sack. And if you are
observant, you will notice that it is around this spike
that the gourd grows on shore." Shabba coughed.
"But this is not the lesson I would teach you. Now
I will tell you the lesson of the gourdfish. The he-
fish does not wait for permission from the she-fish
to plant his spike in her. He gives himself for her--
and not without great pain. Pain that lasts until he
finally receives the fruit of his suffering--the day the
juice flows from the gourds the she-fish plants.
Only by this juice will his wound be healed. And
only then may he release his seed over the eggs.
Only then does the blood stop flowing from the
place where the spike broke off his head. Hear this
Temmoninek. You are a man and, like the he-fish,
you are to sacrifice, to give. Do not think of your
own pleasure, but that of your mate. Love and
serve her without thought of yourself and, in the
end, you will know the pleasure of love. And
remember, my friend, this is how our people are
made strong. It is not through your skill with a
bow, or with a mace in battle. It is not through
your skills as a tracker or in the hunt. No,
Temmoninek, it is not with these that our people
become great. It is with the sacrifice of blood for
our women that we men become strong. For a
single man is nothing, but he and his people, when
tied by blood and by love, are the most powerful

force on the earth. If you learn nothing else from the he-fish, learn this."

The two sat on the shale for a long time, neither desiring to speak above the summer heat that kept their skin moist with sweat. Temmonin almost forgot why he had come. The black stone beneath him cooled the backs of his legs while the sun baked his knees and thighs and shoulders. He felt as if he were sandwiched between two layers of heaven. And his mind, like his eyes, wandered through the trees around him. Although his need for Shabba's advice had been urgent, he now saw little reason to ask his questions.

He and Shabba had often sat together in silence and Temmonin had learned long ago how to feel the wordless comfort of another soul. But this time, something strange was happening.

Something about the trees. The first thing he noticed was the oak in front of him, then the group of firs to his left. His focus on them was blurring--or sharpening. He could not decide which. Then, everything around him seemed to grow, to swell, to pulse. Looking to where Shabba sat, he saw only what he thought was a shadow. Somewhere inside of himself, he felt that he ought to be careful but no part of him responded to that dim plea. He was engulfed by his stillness. And the stillness, along with the trees and hills and marshes was growing and pulling him from himself so that he could hardly differentiate between his fingers, which lay on the shale, and the roots of the trees surrounding him. And it was as if he could see each individual leaf and trace its veins to a source within the branch and further to the trunk, and then further to the roots. And the roots were sucking moisture from the soil. And the soil was sucking moisture from the marsh and the muggy air above.

And the air was sucking moisture from Temmonin's skin.

And everything was laughing. Everything was laughing. Temmonin was sure he was laughing too, but his hold on himself was like a cloud dissipating. His thoughts were still the glue that bound his senses together but these thoughts seemed slowly to loosen their grip and to find a way to meld with the mirth around him. The mirth was deep and lasted long and the world was enormous to him.

Then he began to cry. And with those tears came the remembering of his self. Then, more tears. The trees, the marsh, the shale seemed to take notice of his pain and came to him quietly, their laughter controlled for his sake. Soon, as if they had realized the reason for his sorrow, they too began to weep. And the weeping that joined him encompassed his own tears and he longed to end the separation--the chasm that split him from that from which he was made--the chasm that estranged him from all that now shared in his mourning. To Temmonin, that mourning lasted much longer than the laughing. As it began to wane, Temmonin felt a withdrawal. Was he pulling away from them? Or were they shrinking back from him? No matter. The meeting was ending and, although his tears were drying, a dull ache like a stone in his gut replaced them. His throat hurt.

The sun was half-swallowed by evening's horizon when Temmonin finally found himself again. Shabba was still sitting against his tree. The old man was peering directly at Temmonin, his yellowing eyes questioning.

"I'm alright, Shabbamassa," Temmonin anticipated the elder's words. "Don't worry, I just. . ."

"I know. The first time almost killed me. But then, I was a lot younger then than you are now." Shabba smiled suddenly and coughed a laugh.

Temmonin was still groggy. "You've done this a lot?"

"My son," the old man laughed again, "see these crevices in my face? They didn't git there from watchin' gourdfish."

"We've been here since midday," Temmonin realized aloud.

"You never know when you stumble into a peace eddy," Shabba raised his brows, "somehow, I've never seen that as the best name for it, but. . ." He shrugged.

Temmonin rubbed his eyes once more. "So that was a peace eddy? You're right, it's not the best name fer it."

"Perhaps the person who named it experienced only the first part," Shabba mused.

"I gotta admit, that woulda been nice." And as he swallowed, he remembered the ache in his throat.

"Ah, but Temmoninek! All honor is lost the day that comfort is valued above truth."

Temmonin thought for a moment. "Shabbamassa, thank you fer givin' me such an experience and fer givin' me not only the pleasure, but also the painful truth."

"Temmoninek, my son. . ." Suddenly, the elder's face tightened and he ground his vocal chords, scolding himself for having attempted to move his arm across his chest. "No, Temmonin. Don't thank me. I have no power over such things. Your hands should be raised upward."

Temmonin had shifted to his knees and stopped. "You mean you didn't plan this or ask fer it?"

"This is why I said we 'stumbled' into a peace eddy," the old man repeated. "I don't think I've ever heard a satisfying explanation for any of it--except that it involves the Creator and the creation and that something happens."

Temmonin laughed aloud at this vague description and was gladdened when Shabba joined him. As their laughter faded, Temmonin stood and watched the elder struggle to his feet. The young warrior was careful not to move to help him.

"Temmoninek," Shabba held an arm against a nearby cedar for balance, "remember the lesson of the gourdfish."

And they walked slowly back to the center of the village, the last glow of evening lighting their path.

Matthew John Schellenberg

X.   What is it that causes us to cling to the canoe that falls over the edge of the waterfall? Is it that we do not know of the waterfall? As the river becomes a rapid and the spray douses our hair and the churning froth pummels our boat against boulders that threaten to destroy us, do we not read the signs? Are we so involved in accusing the waves and lambasting fate that we do not even realize the deeper danger that lurks so near? Or perhaps we are so inebriated with the sensation that can only be conjured by such lethal proximity to death that we are not concerned about the consequences. Perhaps, when compared with the enormous task of escaping the rage around us, even the acceptance of the final act of violence is preferable. But, no matter how faint our knowledge of the danger, no matter how vague our understanding of the truth, no matter how distant our relation to the Creator, are we left with any alternative but to seek Him and to give ourselves fully to what we find? Is there a mediator who will audience our complaints against the Maker? Or is there only One who listens, who creates, who sustains, who judges, who loves. And if we choose to refuse the path that leads to this absolute truth, will we only be eternally confronted with the Harsh face of reality?

CHAPTER 10

Damowan was smiling as if he had just punched Chaneerem in the face. Then he shook his head. "Y'know, Temmonin," he grinned, "I really thought you were gonna keep me in check. And, I gotta admit, I prob'ly woulda jus' stayed here too. But, now. . ." Damowan stopped short when the bush behind him rustled.

Jemalemin thrust his head into the small clearing among the birches. "Is that you guys? I can't see real good." He gripped Temmonin's shoulder and quickly released when he realized that it was not a tree branch. "Uh, sorry. I didn't know. . ."

"It's alright, Jemalemin," Temmonin replied. "Sit down--nobody followed you here, right?"

"I didn't see anybody," Jemalemin whispered as he sat. He pushed several twigs aside to make his seat more comfortable.

"Well," Temmonin announced, "we can't make this long or someone'll suspect us."

"Yea, prob'ly Chaneerem," Jemalemin added.

"Yea," Damowan agreed.

"Right, but anybody could. So Jemalemin, jus' so ya know, we're plannin' on goin' back up to the cave in Imnanaw Kanat," Temmonin said.

"You guys're goin' back up there?" Jemalemin almost lost control of his voice.

"Yea, yea! Calm down, Jemalemin," Damowan warned.

"Why're ya goin' back up there?"

"'Cause we gotta find out what happened to us," Temmonin explained. "In fact, I jus'

'membered somethin'--let's use the language so
nobody can overhear us and understand."

"Temmonin," Damowan countered, "that's
stupid. Why don't we jus' talk normal? I mean. . ."

"What if somebody hears us?" Temmonin
answered.

"Out here?"

"Look, Damowan, we don't have much
time," Temmonin pleaded.

"Alright, we'll use the stupid language."

"Actually, if ya think about it, it's kinda
good we know it. I mean there're a whole buncha
good uses for it. We might as wel. . ."

"Weren't you the one who jus' said we don't
have much time?" Damowan frowned.

"Right, right. Sorry." Temmonin stifled his
pride and shifted languages. "Now, Jemalemin, the
thing is, ya don't have to come. We jus' wanted ya
to know what we were doin' in case ya wanted to
come too."

"But if they catch us, they'll kill us, won't
they?" Jemalemin's voice quavered.

"We don't know that," Temmonin said.

"Prob'ly," Damowan added.

"Yea. Good chance of it," Temmonin
admitted. "But if we don't get up there before the
snow falls, we'll have to wait 'til another year from
now. And how do we know what'll happen to the
place between now and then. And a whole year
from now, we might forget the little bit we
remember about the Lonely Valley. It's jus'--we
gotta do it now."

"I'll go," Jemalemin said quickly.

"Jemalemin, you don't have to," Damowan
repeated.

"I want to," Jemalemin said firmly.

They sat in summer night silence for a few seconds.

"Well, we'll leave late tonight," Temmonin concluded. "Meet here. We only need hip or shoulder bags and weapons. It's a good thing it's summer." A pause. "Alright, Jemalemin, see ya late tonight when I go out to relieve myself." Damowan snickered at the emphasis Temmonin put on the word 'relieve'.

"You guys go back now, okay?" Jemalemin offered. "I'll leave in a minute."

"Now, not a word to our families tonight," Temmonin said nervously, "and, Damowan, not a word to Nawana, either."

"Get goin'." Damowan slapped his brother's back.

Temmonin was noticeably restless at the fire that night, noticeably at least to himself and, he thought, to Damowan. Eshtawana, the high mother of his longhouse, was telling her story of creation-- the one Damowan had learned so well. Temmonin could hardly keep his eyes on her. He continually glanced at those sitting around the circle, wondering if they suspected. His stomach roiled in him and, like an erratic wind tears oak leaves from the forest, his emotions sent leaves of anxiety tumbling through his insides. Sometimes he would look at Chaneerem. The talon-licker never returned the glances. But Temmonin knew the man noticed and, as he did, Temmonin felt a rush of adrenaline in his arms and legs. If anyone suspected what he and Damowan and Jemalemin were planning, it would be the oath-taker. In fact, Chaneerem had probably developed several excellent plans to make the same journey himself but, since he had no one to manipulate along the way, he had not actually decided to go.

"And His song created all that is soft and all
that is hard and all that shines and all that soothes.
And His song created all that flies and all that swims
and all that crawls and all that walks or runs,"
Eshtawana continued, the young children at her feet
giggling at her hand motions and the way her eyes
widened or squinted at various points in the story.
"And when the Creator created, He did so slowly,
not wanting any detail to be left to chance. And he
pushed layer upon layer up from beneath the lakes
and onto the dry land. And with each layer, His
deep voice broadened--for the Creator is not a man
or a woman whose voice can sing only one pitch at
a time. And as His song expanded, so did the
young world."

Temmonin almost lost himself in the high
mother's story. But, since he himself was not
reciting it, he did not need to concentrate on it. So,
in his mind, he continually wandered from the trail
and into the thick forest of anxiety that kept his
stomach hot.

"And when the Creator sang too close to
the bear's ear, the great black mother scratched
there and from her fur came a family of wolverines
which scampered into the brush. And when the
Creator sang too close to black mother bear's other
ear, she scratched there also and from her fur came
a family of squirrels which immediately climbed the
nearest tree to avoid being stepped on. And when
the Creator sang too close to mother bear's feet, she
began to stomp to stop the itching and where she
stomped were valleys and in between where she
stomped were hills and mountains. And some of
the valleys filled with water and became the Green
Lake, the Turquoise Lake, the Black Lake, and the
River Zazamma. And when the Creator sang too
close to the great bear's eyes, she began to cry from

the wind and when she rubbed her eyes out came a family of trout from the left eye and a family of pike from the right eye. All of the fish quickly found a stream and swam in it until they found the Green Lake, the Turquoise Lake, the Black Lake, and the River Zazamma. And. . ."

But Temmonin could concentrate on the story no longer. When Eshtawana mentioned 'valley', he could think of nothing but the Lonely Valley. And when she mentioned Zazamma, he could only think of how they had crossed and once again would cross that river. Without realizing it, Temmonin stared blankly at the fire in the center and, as his high mother spun her tale, he spun his own tale of possibilities. It wasn't until she had finished that he regained control of his thoughts.

"Temmonin," Amowz spoke from behind him as he moved to sit between his sons, "Damowan, I've got some good news." He situated himself comfortably on the ground. "I jus' talked to Da today. Jus' this afternoon, he got back from the tribe council and he says there haven't been any more complaints from any of the marsh clans about Flicker demons or murders."

"Really?" Damowan's face showed such a ridiculous mixture of happiness and false excitement that Temmonin wished he had not said anything. He sent his younger brother a mild warning through slits in his own eyes.

"Yea," Amowz returned, "and what's more is that Da seems to think that there aren't any more complaints from the Shushunushu either."

"Well, how would he know that?" Temmonin asked, wondering if his face were as flushed as Damowan's. Did his father know? How could he have guessed that they planned to leave?

"Elders from both the clan of the Black Bear and the clan of the Blackbird told him that they hadn't heard anything bad from their neighbor clans in the Shushunu."

Damowan's face suddenly lost all its pretense. "Well, this could be good news and it could be bad news."

"What do ya mean?" Temmonin curled his brow.

"Well, maybe some people'll take this as a sign that whenever me and you leave the village, murders start happenin'. But when we're stuck here, they stop."

"Yea, but it doesn't seem like that's what people're thinkin'," Amowz countered.

"Right, but just wait 'til winter when we're free to roam again." Damowan's chin was high. "The first murder that happens within three days' hike'll be blamed on us. Jus' wait."

"Well, Damowan, maybe." Amowz was always the pinnacle of objectivity. "But people tend to fergit. I think the circumstances'll have to be pritty incriminatin' before you four ever git blamed again. And anyway, the moon still has to dance at least four more times before the snow falls. That's a lotta time fer people to fergit."

Temmonin glanced past their father at Damowan who met his eyes with slight alarm. Could Amowz know? Was this a subtle fatherly warning to stay in the village? Gazing away from both of the others, Temmonin focused on a few pebbles at his feet to keep himself from asking his father if he knew about their plan to leave that night. But Damowan obviously thought talking was the best method of distraction.

"Well, it's best to be prepared fer that minority of very vocal, vengeful people who don't like to fergit." Damowan was over-acting again. "We all know they're out there."

"I'm jus' really happy that Da seemed to think things were smoothin' out--at least in this region. I hear there's still problems in the North Mountains and farther north in Krimma-Dentl and Krimma-Norba but there's no way to link those murders to you two. Of course, it's not that I'm glad that people're dyin' but it kinda gits you guys off the hook." Amowz raised his brows and took on a strange grin, "I jus' wanted you to know how proud I am of the both of you fer stickin' this thing out and controllin' yerselves. I know it can't be easy."

At that Temmonin almost burst. Some saliva caught in his windpipe and he began to cough furiously to remove it. Even as this violence overtook him, he was grateful that he did not have to continue holding his expression to hide his heart from his father. But as his body relaxed and he could breathe normally again, he began to feel a familiar dread. Not an intense, impending dread that prepared him for battle or for argument, but a more common, more irritating dread that, in this particular case, could picture his father's disappointment tomorrow upon discovering his sons had left the village. It seemed that this dread was Temmonin's closest companion throughout most of his adult life. The dread had become so pervasive that it could no longer distinguish between Temmonin and anyone else with whom he came in contact. When Damowan offended people, Temmonin probably felt more fear of rebuke than his younger brother did. When Chaneerem said vicious things, Temmonin somehow felt responsible, as if he needed to explain why the talon-licker was the way he was. It was as if the dread had become a whirlpool which sucked guilt and blame into itself and shot it at Temmonin. And he hated it.

But this time, his fear was for himself alone. If anything destroyed his well-being, it was his father's disappointment. He could face an army of Gorma if Amowz smiled upon him. But if the elder had any reservations, Temmonin always felt himself floundering for any approval he could find. He was never truly at rest until he could look straight into his father's eyes and laugh like a child.

He had learned, however, that his father was not a man to take many risks. In fact, Semarda had taken far more risks than Amowz probably ever would and she seemed to enjoy it. All too often, Temmonin found himself loving the thrill of the leap yet hearing the worried voice of concern whispering in his ears. Somehow Damowan had inherited all of Semarda's abandon and none of Amowz's reticence. But Temmonin had inherited enough from both of his parents to tense his stomach for life.

"You alright, son?"

"Yea, yea." Temmonin shook his black hair. "Jus' somethin' in my throat."

"Well, don't die on us before yer allowed to leave the village again!" Amowz smiled wide.

"Yea, Temmonin," Damowan grinned, "wouldn't wanna have to travel the world without ya."

Temmonin could not help but smile at his brother's brashness. But he felt he could not stay with his father any longer or he would surely say something incriminating. He stood and went to his mother who sat not far away from him around the fire. She was talking and laughing with two other women and, as he approached, he recognized the story she was relating. It was about he and Damowan as boys tripping over and uprooting pumpkin vines. Semarda noticed her son and slowly reached out her hand to greet him, still speaking and smiling as she did so.

"He's not so clumsy now, though." His mother grinned widely and grabbed his hand.

Temmonin brought his other arm around her, bent his torso, and hugged her from behind and kissed her cheek. Then, he raised his head and greeted the others, "Hello, mothers. Don't believe her. She's completely biased and has nothin' good to say about our farming ability."

At that, the other two laughed in playful shock as Semarda turned and, equally as playfully, gave Temmonin a slap on the chest.

"Yer mother already boasts too much," she defended, "I'm jus' tryin' to balance things out a bit."

"Well, you go ahead balancin', Mama." He kissed her again, this time on top of her head. "I'm gonna turn in early tonight."

"But it's so early. We've only heard a coupla stories."

"I'm kinda tired fer some reason. I'll see ya tomorrow." Inside himself, Temmonin cringed. He could force himself to disobey the high council but was not at all accustomed to deceiving his parents. He hugged Semarda once more and bowed his head to the other women before turning to the longhouse.

Inside the longhouse, he found Tutumora.

"What're you doin' in here?" he mimicked the question his father and mother would have asked. They could never understand her desire for so much time alone, but somehow Temmonin could. He twisted his face, "Shouldn't you be out with the others?"

Tutumora laughed and threw an ear of dried corn at him. "What're you doin' in here?"

Temmonin caught the corn and tossed it back to her. "I'm tired. It's time to go to sleep and I, fer one, am gonna do so." He sat down on his sleeping fur. "Besides, what else is there to do? I'm not allowed to do anything but work in the fields and skin the animals that the other guys bring back from hunt. Sleep can be pritty exciting--at least I can dream."

"Yea," Tutumora scoffed, "I'd know about that."

"Yea, well I guess I'm not the only one, eh?" He slipped beneath his cover. "I guess it's the first time I really understand what you've been sayin' all this time. If ya liked farmin', skinnin', and cookin', it wouldn't be so bad." He paused. "I think I could handle this fer a while--as long as I could get out and hunt quite a bit too."

Tutumora was sitting with her back against the partition which separated their section of the house from their aunt's and uncle's section. She sat now with her hands in her lap, staring at the small fire she had built. The deer hide she was supposed to have been tanning was lying on the dirt next to her. She brooded some more.

"Well, if ya wanna talk, jus' wake me up 'cause it's still early and I'm sure I'll get enough sleep." And Temmonin closed his eyes. Tutumora never woke him.

Matthew John Schellenberg

XI.   And so we rush toward the waiting foot of the giant in our canoe filled with defecation, worshiping the work of our own hands and bathing in the relative comfort we have found in ignoring our fate. We cling to the familiar as if anything else would be poison to us. We lay dreaming in the dusk of death, hoping to avoid the imminent intrusion of that insistent reality. And in our refusal to acknowledge this reality, do we not gather our children into the same canoe, scolding them if they entertain any thoughts which differ from our own? Do we hate death or do we love it? And, if we say we hate it, do we not betray ourselves by wallowing in the excrement that kills us slowly every day? Or by so viciously proselytizing all who disagree with us? Is it that we are supremely convinced that we are right? Or is it simply that we do not care to die alone?

CHAPTER 11

Temmonin's eyes snapped open. The entire longhouse was black and silent. He lay still for a moment, picturing where he had left his pack and his weapons and how he should grab them without being able to see them. He listened through the multitude of breathing noises for Damowan's. He could not decide whether or not his brother was sleeping. He thought he would be.

The elder brother rose quietly. He tried not to sound overly careful as he stepped near Damowan and kicked him lightly in the thigh. Damowan murmured something. Temmonin kicked him harder.

"What? What're ya doin'?" the younger protested. "I'm still slee. . ."

"Sorry, Dama," Temmonin whispered, "I was jus' goin' out to relieve myself."

The chorus of breathing was interrupted by sniffs and swallowing sounds as the other members of the family slipped to the edge of consciousness. Temmonin hoped at least someone had heard his explanation. He reached the wall and gingerly lifted his things and passed through the doorway, careful not to let the arrows clatter against themselves.

Exiting the longhouse, he let out a long sigh. He had not realized that he had been holding his breath. He stood just outside the doorway long enough to be certain that no one else was moving in the village. The half-moon peeked from behind clouds that clambered to pass one another. The light it gave made walking easy. Temmonin crossed the clearing behind the longhouse and entered the birch woods.

Jemalemin was already waiting at their meeting place. Temmonin was startled by the boy and almost tripped over him.

"Sorry, Jemalemin. I didn't think you'd be here already."

"I was pretty nervous," Jemalemin answered, "didn't sleep too much."

"Tell ya the truth, I'm surprised I slept at all," Temmonin whispered a laugh. "I can't believe we're doin' this. Damowan, I can understand. But, you and I?"

The moon was completely covered for a few moments.

"We have to move at night only, right?" Jemalemin asked.

"Most of the time, yea," Temmonin answered, "but when we're in the deep woods, we'll have to be really careful, but I think we can move by day in there."

"I hope we can make it." Jemalemin's voice quavered slightly.

Temmonin smiled in consolation but then realized Jemalemin could not see his face. "Yea, me too."

The clouds parted and closed over the moon several more times before either of them spoke again. A breeze rustled some of the leaves above their heads. From the swamp behind them, they heard the repetitive rhythms of spring peepers and bullfrogs as those animals enjoyed their rest from being hunted by heron and bass. Katydids undulated their counterpoint. At sporadic intervals, nighthawks or bats screeched or buzzed through the blue-black backdrop that changed according to the whim of the wandering clouds. Scratchings in the trees overhead caused the two warriors to look up. Several small objects dropped around them.

"Prob'ly a raccoon," Temmonin mused, handling a piece of bark that had fallen onto his shoulder.

"No," Jemalemin responded, "just a porcupine. Here's a quill that jus' fell on me."

Silence for a moment.

"I hope I woke that brother of mine up," Temmonin worried aloud. "It's been a really long time. I mean, we said we should wait a while between when we each of us left, but this is a really long time." He soughed. "I think I'll go and. . ."

But before Temmonin could do anything, Damowan was upon them.

"It's me," he whispered, "sorry, I fell back to sleep fer a bit there."

"Alright. Let's git goin'. We gotta lotta ground to cover tonight." And Temmonin led the way through the birches.

The first night was exhilarating. They had not hiked so far since they had returned from Ojeb-Mawitez. At times, Damowan nearly leapt for the joy of this release. And since they all three knew this marsh land so well, they were able to choose their path with assurance that they would not be seen. They traveled through uninhabited areas where they did not have to worry about being very quiet. As a result, Temmonin allowed himself to laugh at Damowan rather than scold him.

They decided to jog through the forest and had done so for quite a while, when they began to discuss whether or not to sleep at dawn and, if so, where. They shortly resolved to continue through that day and try to find a good hiding place in the evening. At this pace, they would surely reach Zazamma before anyone would be sent to alert the surrounding areas of their escape. And although Amowz, Da, Desh, and Chaneerem would have a

good idea that the three warriors would be headed
for the Lonely Valley, they could not be certain of
the route the three would take, nor necessarily that
the valley would be their goal. Temmonin,
Damowan, and Jemalemin would also be two or
three days ahead of any search party--at least until
the three had to slow down and travel only by night.
Hopefully they would be able to outrun news of
their flight.

"It'll be dawn soon, Temmonin," Damowan
said between large breaths. "Which way?"

"Why don't we stick to the birch forest and
stay away from the rivers and lakes and marshes.
There's hardly any villages directly north of here in
the deep forest."

"We gotta watch out fer huntin' parties
though. Somebody's bound to recognize us,"
Damowan noted.

"Once we're outta Flicker territory, it won't
be bad to be seen, right?" Jemalemin asked.

"No, Jemalemin," Temmonin answered,
"we've been to too many tribal councils. Black
Bears'd know us fer sure."

"We might be able to git away with skirtin'
the villages near the mouth of Zazamma,"
Damowan said. "There're so many people from so
many clans there that we'll prob'ly jus' blend in."

"But what happens if somebody from
Flicker country just happens to be there?"
Temmonin argued. "And besides, it's Chichmolar
country. They still might recognize us."

"Yea, yer right, we'll prob'ly jus' have to
stay hidden all the way."

As Temmonin turned his head to assent, he
stopped short and swung around. He grabbed
Damowan's arm as he peered through the dead, grey
dawn. "I could swear I jus' saw somebody back

there." All three searched the forest behind them, their breath hot and heavy.

"I can't see anything, Temmonin," Damowan concluded.

"Guess it was jus' my imagination." He looked once more. "Sorry."

They turned to continue.

Damowan whispered like a rattler, "Down!" And he dove to the dirt.

Jemalemin and Temmonin followed quickly, trusting his judgment. Damowan crawled to the side of the path and scanned the woods for a place to hide. But it was Jemalemin who first sighted a group of fallen trees. He pointed. All three crawled as quickly as possible in that direction. When they had reached the spot, they rolled themselves over the trunks and situated themselves for a look at the trail.

Damowan's eyes were very keen. The Flickers had had enough time to hide and the hunting party he had spotted was still far up the trail from where the three had exited.

"They're gonna see our tracks," whispered Damowan.

"Maybe not," Temmonin returned, realizing mid-sentence how wrong he was.

"Temmonin, they're hunting. They'll be lookin' fer tracks. Besides, they'd have to be blind not to see the scuffle we jus' left behind."

"Yea, yea. I know. I jus'. . ."

"They're gonna come this way. You know they are. We might as well jus' build a bonfire right now and tie ourselves up so all they have to do is throw us into the fire." Damowan was shaking his head.

"Well, jus' be quiet for a bit."

The party was definitely Flicker and from a village both Temmonin and Damowan knew.

"There's Mend. . .I always fergit that guy's name. Oh, and Shemdaman." Damowan was anxious. "Temmonin, we're dead--this is it."

"They're noticin' our tracks," Temmonin said as the other Flickers reached the place on the trail from where Damowan had first noticed them.

"Told ya," Damowan said, still shaking his head. "We are dead."

"What're we gonna do?" whispered Jemalemin.

"Die," spat Damowan.

"Damowan, shut up." Temmonin's face was red.

"Well, first they'll find us and then we'll die."

"Jus' calm down. They haven't seen us yet," Temmonin cautioned. Then, "I got an idea! All of us kneel. Make sure they can see the backs of your heads and your bows."

"Are you crazy?" Damowan snarled.

"No, Damowan. They'll think we're huntin', which we prob'ly oughta be doin' by now anyway, and they'll leave us alone," Temmonin explained, "but jus' wait 'til they're not lookin' this way before ya pop up."

All three exposed themselves to sight. Damowan had an arrow notched in his bow. Jemalemin did likewise. Temmonin was facing the trail, keeping enough branches between his face and the other party to distort his features. One of the others noticed them and pointed, calling his fellows' attention to the spot. Temmonin promptly waved as if begging them not to interrupt the silence. He breathed relief as the other five Flickers waved understanding and courtesy to the three. As they moved on, Temmonin whispered to Jemalemin and Damowan,

"Good actin'. You guys do a really good job lookin' like hunters." He smiled.

"Well, Temmonin," Damowan laughed, "I gotta give it to ya, you've discovered at least one good method of keepin' people off our backs."

"It worked perfect, too," Jemalemin interjected.

"Yea, but I really don't think it'll work outside the marshes. By the time we reach Zazamma, we'll have search parties after us. And news'll prob'ly reach Imnanaw Kanat before we get there."

"You're right," agreed Damowan, "any Flickers caught wanderin' in Shushunu're gonna be suspect—even if they're actin' like their huntin'."

"Well, at least we're safe fer a bit," Temmonin assured. They waited until the other hunters had disappeared before traveling on.

They set a fast pace for the morning. They ran in single file, rotating the lead to keep fresh concentration on the trail ahead. It was not until noon that they could bear their hunger no longer. Plenty of squirrels had been leaping through the branches above them so they decided to hunt some of them for lunch. It did not take long before they had several of the black and grey creatures hanging from their belts. They built a small fire far from the trail and roasted all of the meat.

"I can't help thinkin' this is a waste of time," Temmonin said.

"Temmonin, we have to eat or we'll never keep up our stamina. And at least we got enough fer a coupla days," Damowan countered. "We don't gotta do this again 'til we hit Shushunu."

Temmonin realized that his brother was right.

To their surprise, they had no other encounters with Flickers or Black Bears for the next two days and nights and they soon found Zazamma waiting like a silver snow snake, glistening in the midnight sun. They hunted on the south side of the river and cooked two opossum, a raccoon, and a porcupine before crossing. They were well into Ek-Rignara territory before dawn began to wash the sky again.

"They're searchin' for us now. Aren't they?" Jemalemin wondered.

"Fer sure," Temmonin answered.

"They'll be breathin' down our necks tomorrow night or the next day," Damowan added. "Message-runners can fly like crows--and then they relay to another message-runner when they're too tired."

"Yea, they should be able to cover the same distance we jus' did in less than half the time. That means we really gotta move it now," Temmonin urged.

"But right now we gotta find a good hidin' place and git some rest. I'm dead," Damowan said.

After a short search in the early morning shadows, they found a thick clump of thorn trees and briers. They worked their way into the uninviting cover to see a suitable resting place into which they all could fit. Although the spot was partially visible from the other side, they were able to arrange themselves and their sleeping skins so as to camouflage their bodies. Temmonin took the first watch. Several hours later, he woke Jemalemin for the second watch.

As Temmonin settled in for sleep, he drowsily stared at the thorns above him--so thick and overlapping that, even in the midday sun, they blocked almost all light from his eyes. As his eyelids began to shut, his mind decided that he was looking at a midnight sky; the pinholes of light that forced their way through the maze of vines and branches became stars. And as sleep pulled his eyes shut, he saw a more magnificent sight.

The stars were now bubbles on the surface of the swamp, glinting the blazing sun's rays. Painted and spotted turtles gathered on water-soaked logs that half-floated in the duckweed. Frogs, their bead-eyes shimmering like permanent ripples in the water's surface, added their stone-silent commentary to the dream before him. The heron waded like the apogee of the hunt--careful and exact. A thousand birds, chickadees, wrens, swallows, crows, blue jays, cardinals, robins, and thrushes celebrated the madness of the summer sun and the feast of insects it afforded them. And Temmonin was dancing on the swamp.

If the turtles and the heron had noticed him, they did not seem to mind. They simply continued in their stillness. But Temmonin could not be still. In spite of the sweat that ran in rivulets down his torso and his legs, he could only dance harder. And since the duckweed beneath him did not give way, he began to swirl and leap across the swamp, tumbling and rolling when he desired. He reached a frenzy as his hair swung around his head like a net that tried to catch his emotion. But his emotion was not to be captured. He was as wild and as real as he had ever been. He was the creation and he played for his Creator in the brilliance of the day.

Then he began to sink. For a moment, he panicked. But then he remembered how to breathe in the water. Although he was not swimming, he moved wherever he wished. He glanced up to see the bellies of the frogs floating on the surface, the bellies of the turtles hanging over the edge of the logs. Perhaps his own body no longer existed; he seemed not to disturb anything as he passed by. Perhaps the water had dissolved his flesh, leaving him a disembodied mind wandering through this shallow muck hole. No matter. This was like the elation he felt when he saw Zheva.

Zheva. She was here now too, he knew-- she also without a body. He could sense her near him, but there could be no connection. She was at once as near to him and as far away as she could ever be. He cried for her. And she for him.

Then they were together, both with bodies, both naked, clothed only by the duckweed that covered them up to their stomachs. They kissed. They kissed ten times. They kissed a hundred times. And they were one like no two people had ever been one before. They were at one with themselves, at one with each other, and at one with every creature in the swamp.

But some monstrous crow covered the sun and descended upon the two. Suddenly, they were cold. They hugged each other to keep warm, but the black intruder sucked the heat out of the air. The turtles had all dipped back beneath the surface. The heron tried to fly away but was pulled into a fold in the black shadow-bird. And its screeching was incessant, as if it did not want to allow Temmonin to think another thought.

All he could do was wake up.

It was evening in the open air and almost midnight beneath the briers where he and Jemalemin lay. Temmonin was so comfortable he did not want to get up. But nearby a gang of crows was cackling as loudly as any gang of crows had ever cackled. Their silhouettes traded places in the multitude of branches overhead as their voices interrupted the sunset. Temmonin shifted onto one elbow and glanced at Damowan's silhouette just outside of the hiding place.

"Hey, Dama," the elder brother spoke groggily, "anything interesting happen the last watch?"

"Huh?" Damowan's muffled voice came from directly next to him. "What Temmonin?"

"What?" Temmonin jumped and caught his hair on the briers above him. Pulling away, he continued, "Did Jemalemin take both watches?" But as he looked beyond his brother, he saw the boy waking up. "Jemalemin, you fell asleep? Well, who's out there then?" He pointed to the figure outside.

The shadow was crouched as if it were about to flee. Temmonin, who had been speaking Ek-Birin, spoke directly at it in Mokhamoyuba,

"Who are you?"

A young boy answered, "I am Zemmandidek of the clan of the Heron. And I would also ask, who are you?" His voice trembled.

"I am Temmonin of the clan of the Flicker. Here also are my brother Damowan and my good friend Jemalemin. We have traveled far and were in need of rest and so we stopped and chose this place. Where might we be, Zemmandi, my fellow?" Temmonin was probably more nervous than this boy. He selected his words as carefully as if he were walking barefoot over pine needles. He even shortened the name hoping to flatter the child and to keep him from running away.

"You have reached Eshtashezeshta, the village where I live. The village of my mother and

father and of my grandmother and her mother."
His voice was noticeably more stable.

"Peace and beauty to you and your family,
Zemmandi," Damowan said.

"Peace and beauty," repeated Temmonin.

"Peace and beauty," Jemalemin and
Zemmandidek spoke in harmony.

"What brings three Ek-Birin to Shushunu?"
Zemmandidek inquired.

"We are on a very special journey to find
something of great value to our people that was lost
in. . .Krimma-Peltl." Temmonin hoped the pause
did not cause the child to guess his bluff. He
realized that he had already told him enough of the
truth. "May I ask of you, my friend Zemmandi,
how far are we from the village of your
grandmother? You seem to be an intelligent young
man. What is your estimate?"

The flattery seemed to work quite well.
Zemmandidek's voice soon became very relaxed,
"Probably twenty stone throws away--maybe a little
more."

"And what, my friend, brings you to this
small place so far from your village? An adventure,
perhaps?" Temmonin was nearly nauseated by his
own patronizing.

It seemed Zemmandidek did not grasp the
patronization. "I came to the place that I will call
my secret place someday--the place where I will pray
to the Creator and meditate. But when I arrived,
you three were here. I thought you might be spirits
who would speak to me. For the wise elder of my
village, he who is named Cha, has spoken to me
often of spirits and peace eddies and of submission
to the Creator. But, when you woke, I discovered
you were not spirits at all but warriors from another
territory."

"But perhaps we are spirits," Damowan interjected.

"Yes," added Temmonin, holding himself from laughing, "we never told you we were not spirits. Perhaps we are here to teach you or to encourage you."

"Would not a spirit make himself known so as not to deceive?" Zemmandidek asked innocently.

Temmonin was surprised at this child's ability to express himself in formal language. "That one is not necessarily a liar who does not reveal his entire self. Has Cha not taught you this yet, or your mother or your father?"

"I understand this, although I have not been taught it specifically. I have been taught that only a fool tells all his stories to the whole world."

"May I say, Zemmandidek, that you are the wisest young man I have ever met," Damowan noted.

"Thank you, sir," Zemmandidek replied and paused. "May I ask what you might teach me if you were spirits?"

At that, Temmonin could hardly keep from laughing. He was glad that dusk had fallen around them and the child could not see his shaking. "We would teach you and encourage you to continue in your submission to the Creator and to your village elders and to your parents. Remember that evil wants to destroy your soul but that in doing good and in making your clan proud of you, you destroy the evil that would destroy you. This is what we would teach you."

"Then I am grateful for your teaching."

"And we would ask one thing of you, Zemmandi," Temmonin said.

"Please, ask."

"We would ask that you not mention our presence here. It is very important that our mission remain secret and we would be forever indebted to you if you would treasure this meeting only in your memory and not upon your lips."

"I can do this," the boy promised. "Now I should go back to the village. My mother will soon worry for me." He promptly rose and began to walk away. Then he stopped and turned. "And should you ever need my secret place again, please feel at home there. Thank you once again."

"And thank you, Zemmandi. Peace and beauty to you and your family," Temmonin concluded. The child was gone.

Suddenly, Damowan snapped, "We gotta git goin'!"

Temmonin and Jemalemin did not need to respond except to roll up their sleeping skins and load themselves for travel. They crawled out of the opposite side of the briers and looked around to make sure they were alone.

"Sorry I fell asleep in there," Jemalemin mumbled.

"Jemalemin, don't beat yerself up," Damowan assured him. "I've done the same thing hundreds of times before."

"Yea, it's no big deal, Jemalemin," Temmonin added.

They found the trail and set a steady jogging pace to which they held for most of the night, stopping, only when necessary, for water. They ate while running. They talked while running. They breathed the muggy air of summer midnight. Like salmon returning to the place of their birth, the three Ek-Birin proceeded to the cave where their confusion was born. By some inspiration, they increased their speed throughout the night. Perhaps it was the waxing moon, perhaps the fireflies over the swamps and marshes. Perhaps Temmonin was trying to impress Zheva. He was always trying to impress her.

To their surprise, by morning they had reached the fat gorge of Zubzza. Temmonin forced his thoughts from the woman in his dreams to the matter of breaking camp. They decided that sleeping close to the gorge was the best idea. Since the rainy season was over, the chance of a flash flood, although possible, was not probable. And the inhabitants of the Shushunu made it a practice to avoid the gorge. So the Ek-Birin would not need to worry about being discovered by a casual passerby. Although they knew that search parties would certainly suspect the edge of the gorge as a hiding place, they felt they would have to assume that news had probably not yet reached this far north.

After eating, they bedded down. They slept relatively well that day. The mosquitos and black flies did not enjoy the pine tar the Ek-Birin had smeared on themselves and, consequently, did not interrupt their sleep at all. Temmonin had to cover his head with a skin in order to keep the light from his eyes. This left his head and his cheeks swelling with heat but allowed him sleep he would never get otherwise. He woke as the sun was on its way down. But it would still be some time until dusk. He waited at least an hour for the others to awake.

Behind him, a twig snapped. He turned his head slowly to investigate. He saw nothing in the pine forest but green needles and mottled black shadows. The others were still asleep. Careful not to make a sound, Temmonin stood and stepped toward the woods in the direction of the noise he had heard. A robin warbled its ridiculous territory song over his head. Several chickadees were

laughing and chasing each other through the pines
ahead of him. In the distance, he could hear a crow
ripping out its own throat. But there was nothing
snapping twigs. As he reached the forest edge, a
chipmunk startled him. The rodent splashed pine
needles in its panic and took cover beneath a fallen
log some feet away. Perhaps a chipmunk had made
the first noise. Temmonin thought not. It could
have been an animal. But he knew that the time
when he and his companions would be pursued was
too quickly approaching to excuse anything
anymore. Yet he could see nothing and the sound
did not repeat itself. Still shifting his eyes, he
returned to the others.

He woke both of them quickly. "I think it's
time we see more of Shushunu."

"Mmmm," Damowan groaned, "I was
kinda enjoyin' the insides of my eyelids myself."

"Yea, well, we wouldn't want that to be a
permanent situation now would we?"

"I could think of worse things."

"No, Damowan, I'm not talkin' 'bout naps,"
Temmonin explained as he rolled up his sleeping
skin. "I'm talkin' 'bout dyin'."

"I don't see any clouds," Damowan argued,
rolling from his side to his back, "only blue sky."

"I'm not talkin' 'bout flash floods either. I
heard a noise in the forest--a twig snapped. It jus'
makes me a bit nervous. I think we should keep
movin'."

Jemalemin was now packing. "I'm pretty
rested now anyway."

"Alright," Damowan agreed begrudgingly.
He sat up and began to roll his skin as well.

When all three had finished, they stood and
faced each other. Then they headed northwest
along the outer rim of the fat gorge. To their right,

through the myriad of birches, elms, oaks, and cedars, they could see the mist that shrouded Zubzza.

"Someday," began Damowan, "when nobody's on our tail, we're gonna go down there."

"I'm with ya," said Temmonin. "As soon as all this junk is over."

Temmonin turned to include Jemalemin. The boy simply smiled. They continued in silence until the sun set.

Evening shadows infected the color of the trees and the color of the sky until all that surrounded the three Ek-Birin was merely a shade of grey. It was then that they slipped out of the dried mud outer rim of the gorge and into the pine forest. Using the stars to point them, they headed directly west in search of the trail that led to Imnanaw Kanat.

"We're not far now," Damowan said as he stepped over a fallen log. "If we can make it to the mountains tonight, we should only be one more day away from the Lonely Valley. All the joggin' and runnin' we been doin' sure has made a big difference."

"Yea, and not carryin' a drag-trailer," Temmonin laughed.

"And not goin' in rainy season," Jemalemin added.

"That's right," Temmonin smiled, "it hasn't rained one time since we've been out."

"Ahh. Shouldn't've said that, Temmonin," Damowan chided playfully. He gazed into the clear sky. "I feel sprinkles already."

"No problem, bro'. Only two days left--in fact, rain right now might really help hide us from search parties." Temmonin said, stepping sideways to avoid a small maple sapling. "But let's git back to the trail and hightail it to the mountains before we have to depend on rain to cover our tracks."

Suddenly, Damowan was slammed to the ground. Temmonin hunched like a mountain lion, searching the dusk for signs of the aggressor. Then Jemalemin was in the dirt. Temmonin yelled. Then he was on his back. He could not move. Then he felt something crawling on his legs. And it was on his arms also. What was it? He could not decide. Damowan and Jemalemin must have encountered the same fate; neither of them spoke. But the crawling continued across his torso, his groin, his neck. Then over his face--they were vines! And they were pressing hard over his nostrils and lips. He could barely breathe. Next to him, he heard the same wheezing from Damowan. Then all three began to cough violently. The vines only held more tightly and constricted their diaphragms closer to the ground. Temmonin's head went insane with panic but nothing he did changed his inability to control his body. His brain clouded over. He saw flashes of color. His body slowly stopped rebelling and, along with his will, slumped as far as it could into the soil.

But then he felt more crawling, this time on his entire body at once. He was so far away now that he did not care. This new crawling was tickling his abdomen but he was much too comfortable to laugh. He slipped further into the black abyss of his delirium.

The vines came away from his nostrils and his mouth and he was torn from the gorge of his dying like a perch on a line. And he hacked and sputtered and writhed like a perch on the beach, his panic rudely reopened. Tensing his every muscle, he roared his frustration into the night air, without a single thought of the secrecy of their mission.

When he finished, his vocal chords were as ravaged as if he had swallowed a pine cone whole. He held his throat in his hands and panted. He rubbed his blood-hot face. He rubbed his itching eyes.

"Temmonin," a voice called from his left.

"Yea," he answered hoarsely.

"You alright?"

"No. . ." Temmonin moaned. "Why? Are you?"

"Well, no. Not really." Damowan laughed weakly. "But guess who's back?"

Temmonin blinked several times before he could keep his eyes open. When he could, he deciphered Damowan's chest and on it a small figure.

"The Chrebin?" Temmonin gawked.

"The whole tribe." Damowan smiled through the starlight. Temmonin scanned the area to see the entire forest floor covered with thousands of squirrel-men. "They saved us from these carnivorous vines. This stuff woulda killed us fer sure."

"Are they peaceful?" asked Jemalemin.

"Of course, Jemalemin," Damowan assured the boy. "Last time, they were after Chaneerem. This time, my little friend here's jus' found me again."

"Are they sayin' anything?" Temmonin asked.

"How should I know? I can't understand a sound this thing is makin'--could be words, I guess."

"Well, I figured, since ya had this special connection and all. . ." Temmonin trailed off.

"I'm jus' guessin', Temmonin. Same as you," Damowan answered. "Oh, and there they go again."

"Where?"

"Yer guess is as good as mine." He looked at the creature on his chest.

"I wonder where they live," Temmonin mused. "Wanna follow 'em?" But then he was not sure if he really wanted to follow them himself. His mind was still swirling.

"No, I don't think that'd be a good idea," Damowan warned. "I don't think they'd want that."

"Alright Mister 'I don't understand a sound they're makin'"."

"What, now jus' 'cuz I said that means I can't have any ideas, Temmonin?"

"Whatever." Temmonin got to his knees. Rubbing his throat again, he continued, "We should really git movin' anyway. This scuffle could've attracted a lot of attention."

"Yea, Mister 'I roared louder than the beast that wanted to eat me'."

Temmonin could not help but laugh, "I couldn't help it. I was dyin'," he paused, "but it was pretty stupid of me. If anybody's around, we're caught fer sure."

"So let's git outta here. The moon's already peekin' out." Damowan had already started as he spoke.

They wasted no time finding the trail. Another clear moonlit night escorted them to the foothills of the North Mountains. The Chrebin seemed completely content on Damowan's shoulder. Aside from occasional attempts at communication, the midget clung quietly to his hair as the three jogged through the moonscape. None of the Ek-Birin spoke. Perhaps the weight of the mountains in their eyes held their mouths shut. It was not until they felt a cool mountain breeze that dawn softened the harsh black of the sleeping sky and they began to talk about looking for a campsite.

They found a small cave in the forest quite a way from the trail. It appeared to have been a fox's den at one point but there were no signs of it having been used recently. They crawled beneath the shale platform and ate the remainder of the meat they had roasted two nights earlier. Within moments, they were all asleep.

Temmonin woke with a start. He looked at Damowan to his left. The younger was on his belly and alert, peering out of their hiding place.

"Wake up, Temmonin," Damowan whispered. He held his bow flat against the ground with an arrow notched.

"What is it?" Temmonin asked.

"Demnaza hunters--warriors. Real close. Shhh."

Voices of several men reached the small cave. Temmonin wriggled up to get a better view. There were six of the Elk warriors. Given the fact that the party was so far away and the fact that they were speaking their own Kanattar dialect, the brothers could understand none of their conversation. But they were obviously searching. Could it be for rabbit? For quail? Perhaps for snakes. Their method was not normal.

"They're searchin' fer us," Damowan said flatly.

Temmonin thought for a moment and recognized his brother's assessment. "Have they been by this way yet?"

"That's the problem--I don't think so," Damowan said, "but I was only awake a little before you two. They mighta been by."

"What're we gonna do?" Jemalemin asked. "Fight?"

"If we don't, we're dead," answered Damowan while watching the six.

"Yea, let's jus' hope that no more murders have followed our trail," Temmonin whispered.

"Do we wanna wait 'til they strike," asked Jemalemin, "or do we wanna git 'em with arrows first?"

"I don't know," Damowan answered.

"Well, we better figure this out pritty soon 'cuz they're definitely headed this way," Temmonin spoke as he turned to look at the cave more carefully. They had not chosen the cave imagining that they would need a real hiding spot, merely a place that would not attract a passerby. But now they needed to conceal themselves completely.

After staring out at the white overcast beyond the trees, Temmonin could only see black in the cave. He allowed his eyes to adjust and soon was able to distinguish between shallow and deep shadows. After a moment, he found a configuration in the rock worth investigating. He slid down to the rear of the cave. Reaching deep into a narrow slit ncar the ground, he discovered that it opened up into another cave further in. Hurriedly, he cleared away enough dirt so that he could squeeze through. Then he did so.

Damowan had not turned to see what his brother was doing. "Temmonin, what're ya. .?"

"Come on in, you two." Temmonin's voice was muffled.

Jemalemin went immediately to where Temmonin was waiting and, after he had handed his bow and arrows to the elder, slipped through the small opening.

"Scared little opossum," Damowan jested as he made his way into the second chamber. "Yer just afraid we couldn't take 'em all."

"Yea, shut up." Temmonin laughed as he pulled Damowan's loincloth and, with it, Damowan through the opening. Jemalemin laughed too.

Then, Temmonin mounded the dirt back in front of them. He left only a thin horizontal slit through which they could observe. The space was tight. None of them could stretch out and, in no matter which position they chose to situate themselves, knees were in backs, elbows against chests, packs and bows and arrows on top of everyone.

"Hope we don't have to spend the night in here," Damowan complained, a half-smile in his voice.

Temmonin and Jemalemin chuckled. "Actually, we might end up finishin' off our naps in here. I don't think it's much past noon. But with an overcast, it's a bit hard to tell." Temmonin finished covering the entrance.

All three quieted themselves and prepared for the fact that the Demnaza search party might enter the cave at any time. It was not long before they heard voices. Then came scuffling. From the deep shadows where the Ek-Birin lay huddled, Temmonin could see searching eyes. One of the Elk warriors looked directly at him. Adrenaline spilled through his torso but he clung to the fact that it was much too dark for them to see through to the rear of the cave. He was right. The eyes of the searchers skimmed past their chamber. Two others bent and peeked in briefly but they, with the two who had spent a few moments looking, soon backed away from the crevice and stood up to continue their search.

Temmonin was just about to shift from a sitting to a kneeling position when he heard two more voices. He pressed his face against the rock to his right in order to expand his view to his left. This position gave him a glimpse of one of the Demnaza warrior's backs. He could hear their conversation very well but he wrestled with their dialect. From what he heard, however, he confirmed the suspicion that these warriors of the clan of the Elk were hunting Ek-Birin from Kemkemmayam. He settled back as comfortably as he could.

After some time, the search party was gone and Damowan and Jemalemin had somehow fallen asleep in the cramped coolness. Temmonin could not sleep. Every noise tensed his shoulders. Ground squirrels, chipmunks, even a dried oak leaf kept him awake. He abandoned his hope for more rest and began to picture the Lonely Valley.

At this point, they were only a day from their destination. Now Temmonin remembered how difficult the task of finding the cave would be. He realized that the opening might be as high as ten feet above the valley floor and completely hidden. In fact, they had never actually seen any opening-- even the idea that there was an opening in the valley wall through which they were abducted--even the idea was conjecture. He began to question the reasonableness of their assumption. He hoped they would have enough time to search out the place and recognize it without being sighted.

The fact that they had not been sighted yet was amazing to Temmonin. Aside from the young boy near the Heron village, no one had a good chance to look at them. But he knew that this was no time to relax. At this point, the Lonely Valley might be swarming with search parties. But perhaps the false information the three Ek-Birin had given to Zemmandi would steer at least some trackers from the trail. So many variables made Temmonin's neck tight. He had to concentrate to relax.

To his surprise, he awoke after having slept for several hours. The grey of evening had settled among the trees of the forest and Temmonin glimpsed an occasional firefly dance across the cave mouth. He stirred the others and began clearing dirt from the opening. They crept cautiously from their hiding spot and, still kneeling, scanned in all directions. There was a noise from behind them; from on top of the slab that formed the roof of the cave. Then the night erupted in orange.

Temmonin was cudgeled in the back of the head and between his shoulders. He was slammed to the earth, his right cheek pressed into the forest floor. A knee pinned him to the ground and threatened to crack his spine. As he grunted his alarm, he could hear more signs of struggle beside him. Damowan was hitting someone. Jemalemin was breathing hard. He heard fists thud dully into chests or arms or ribs. The knee in his spine crunched harder.

He gathered all his strength and bucked. In great pain, he managed only to roll to his side before he was pinned again. His right arm was immobilized beneath his body and his attacker had his left with both of his hands. He bucked again and freed his right arm but kept it tight against himself in order not to alarm the attacker. But the man on top of him released one grip from Temmonin's left arm and reached for his right. Temmonin waited until the man touched his wrist and then exploded at him with all his strength. He connected with the intruder's nose. Blood spattered across Temmonin's face and chest. He directed another punch at the silhouette above him. This time, he was sure he struck the man's jaw; Temmonin's knuckles hurt. But then the man rammed Temmonin in the eye with his elbow.

Temmonin had to cover his face. He took a blow
to the ribs and, almost instinctively, bucked again.
As the man caught his balance with his knees in the
dirt and his hands on Temmonin's chest and
shoulder, the Ek-Birin drew both of his own knees
up hard into the man's buttocks. And when the
man lurched forward, Temmonin closed his eyes
and swung his forehead into the intruder's teeth.

At that second, he felt the attacker swept
from him. Damowan rolled with the man across his
brother and, within the blink of an eye, was
pounding the bewildered warrior. Temmonin
jumped to his feet. He heard a footfall to his left
and hunched in defense.

'It's me, Temmonin!" Jemalemin exclaimed.
"There's only two of 'em. Damowan already
knocked the other guy out."

"That's it!" Damowan stood in victory.
"Shouldn't've sent only two."

Then they heard more footfalls--at least two
people running--to the south.

"Let's git outta here!" Temmonin whispered
hotly.

They ran north through full dusk that soon
entered night. Dodging trees and ripping up
undergrowth, they fled heedlessly through the
woods. It was not until a good time later that they
found the trail again. Even then, they were hard-
pressed to decide whether the faster travel that the
trail would allow them would be worth the risk of
being sighted. But they had so little time. They
took the trail northwest and up the first mountain.

The emergency of the moment fed their
pace and they had added many miles to their
journey before they slowed at all. Still running, they
reached into their packs for food. They found
none, but continued running. Some time later, they

crossed a small stream and, before continuing, satisfied their thirst. But they paused only for a moment. The forest seemed alive behind them, teeming with the sounds of the hunt. Perhaps it was only the normal chatter of brooks and owls and crickets but, for them, everything had become the hunter.

The sweat that glazed them and soaked their leather loincloths seemed to lubricate their drive through the dim woods. They pounded the trail over several smaller mountains, dodging roots and jagged rocks in the trail, occasionally slapping deer flies or mosquitos. They all sensed the nearness of the Lonely Valley.

It was still dark when they reached Gamnashta for the second time in their lives. This time, however, they would make no acquaintances and enjoy no hot springs and no hearty conversation with Demnaza warriors. Temmonin wondered if these people hated them now. Would they supply them with skins and snowshoes now? Or would they kill them in their sleep? They skirted the village in silence and drove down into the valley of their abduction.

Moon Beneath the Mountains

XII.   Yet even if we were able to clear our vision of the fog of lethargy and pride that we in our constant efforts to maintain the sick standard of impurity that we have become so very fond of, even if we were able to glimpse beyond this self-exuded veil, this fog that we have so diligently sweated into the air around us--if we could see the pressing threat of pain ahead of us, if we could hear and recognize the shouts and shrieks of death that rally around our demise, if we could feel the rumble of finality that calcifies our joints with fear, and were we to bend and bow beneath such a weight of truth, would we not still be pushed just as heatedly to our end. To what avail does the oak recognize that the wood-cutter's axe is sharp? Does the knowledge bring it any comfort? What profit do we gain from lingering in the wake of the prophecies of doom anticipating with every snap of a twig the crash of the cosmic hammer on our heads? Or do we in fact possess the means by which we might somehow escape the fall into the abyss? How difficult would it be for us and how long might it take for us to unravel the seemingly endless riddle that from birth echoes in our skulls? Has the Creator hidden the answers in a place accessible to souls as filthy or as preoccupied as ours? Or is any effort we might make just as futile as the sled-dog that chases the meat that dangles before it, never to know that its master is he who holds the stick and string to which the meat is attached? And if we ourselves, entirely convinced of the necessity to wake from our childish fetishes, if we cannot convince the others in our rotting canoes of the emergency that broods ahead of us, are we not now still more like the striving sled-dog and the knowing oak. Does the woodcutter dangle the meat with one arm and swing the sharp axe with the other?

CHAPTER 12

All three were restless as they descended into the canyon. Jemalemin looked over his shoulder continually. Damowan kept slapping his thighs lightly with his fingertips. The sound did nothing to endanger them but it annoyed Temmonin. The elder held his tongue, however, and led them down the steep path that would soon connect with the valley floor.

To their surprise, the place was thick with evergreens, some as tall as fifteen feet, and through the center of the bowl flowed a fairly wide river. All this was entirely hidden to them during their winter trek and the Demnaza had not warned them of the presence of the river. Temmonin shuddered as he thought of the last time they were here. He pictured the four of them dropping through the snow into cold, liquid death. But somehow, even without trying, they had avoided the water. And the snow must have completely covered the trees, allowing the travelers to walk on top of the forest.

As they reached the bank of the river, they looked around. No movement. No sign of a fire or a camp. Only the drone of the river echoed in their ears. Dawn was still a short time away. Feeling fairly secure, they drank for a while.

Between slurps, Damowan mused. "Y'know, I betcha this cave or the opening we're lookin' for isn't very far at all." He shifted his head in an attempt to see the cavern wall through the pines. "I mean, we prob'ly hiked fer half the day in that snow storm--and we couldn't't've been goin' fast at all." Before Temmonin could add to his comment, Damowan continued. "Of course, we did have good skiing 'til nightfall after that."

"Yea, but you're right," replied Temmonin. "It might not take us all day to reach it."

"It's gonna be really hard to find it isn't it?" Jemalemin posed.

"Ya had to bring that up, didn't ya?" Damowan contorted his face ridiculously, probably, Temmonin thought, to insure that the boy knew he was joking. Jemalemin knew and smiled warmly.

"What're we gonna do about food?" Jemalemin again. "I'm really hungry."

"Well, I'm gonna wash up first--they could smell us a mile away," Temmonin replied through the greyness. "But if we hurry, we can prob'ly catch some rabbit or quail before there's too much activity down here."

They all stripped and bathed. They carried their loincloths with them to wash as much of the scent of sweat from them as they could. But they were hurried by the approach of dawn and quickly exited the river. The heat of the morning had already descended into the valley and, as they dressed and entered the forest, they were already fairly dry. Within minutes, they came across a pair of raccoons that served as their breakfast. They built a fire as the sun appeared over the mountains.

"Prob'ly, the only camps down here durin' the summer're along the river," Damowan said. "Why make it hard to go fer water?" He bit off a piece of the fat raccoon meat they were cooking.

"Yea," agreed Temmonin. "I think we should prob'ly stay to the cliff edge of the forest." Damowan and Jemalemin both nodded. "And if I 'member right, it was the south cliff where we slept that night, right?" Damowan and Jemalemin nodded again. Damowan cut a small piece of meat for the Chrebin. The little thing rejected it and quickly jumped down to grab a pine cone to gnaw on.

"I sure hope we can find what we're lookin' for," said Damowan. "'Cuz if we can't, we're gonna be three sad woodpeckers."

"With nothin' to do but hide fer the rest of our lives," Temmonin shook his head.

They ate quickly, dousing the fire as soon as it had served its purpose. Then they dug a hole, buried the ashes, and spread pine needles over the dirt until the spot resembled the surrounding area. Satisfied with their work, they began hiking to the south wall.

They soon reached a place in the pines from which they could easily view the cliff face. From here they could also see some distance through the trees toward the river. They used a path that appeared not to have been used for quite some time and jogged a light pace through the shadows of the morning sunlight.

Temmonin felt the heat swab his head. Even in mid-morning, sweat was beading on his brows and dropping onto his cheeks and eyelashes. At times, he felt the sting of salt in his eyes. If the morning in this shade were this hot, he imagined how uncomfortable noon might become. And his mind was craving rest. But black flies continually reminded him that this was not the time nor the place to sleep. Eventually, the haze behind his eyes cleared. He was fully awake again.

Twice they heard the distant sounds of camps on the river. Not once, however, did they notice any hunters or even any sign of people near their path. In fact, the two raccoons they had eaten for breakfast were the only things they had seen move all day.

At noon, they began to pay closer attention to the valley wall. Not long after they had paused for their midday meal, they began sighting spots to investigate. At each new site, two of them kept watch while one climbed the face of the cliff and explored. But after a while, the trees began to cluster at the base of the wall and blocked the view from where they walked on the path. As a result, they decided they should all walk as close to the edge of the forest as possible. There was no real path this close to the cliff and because of this progress was very slow.

They took a short rest in the shade of a group of cedars as the sun blazed its strongest that afternoon. Damowan drank from his water skin like a dog from a creek. When he was finished, water was still running down his chin and neck.

"I hope we find that thing pritty soon," Damowan wiped his lips. "Almost outta water." He offered some to the Chrebin who drank heartily.

"If you'd ration a bit, ya might still have some," Temmonin smiled.

"Hmpf," Damowan raised his brows. "Never had to ration before. Course, we've never been hunted lawbreakers before either. Normally, I could jus' saunter on down to the river and charm all the ladies into fillin' my water skin."

"Well, Mr. Lover boy, if you need some more before we get a chance to refill, I still got some," Temmonin offered.

"I still got some too," added Jemalemin.

"Well, there's still a bit in here." As Damowan raised his skin, it slipped from his hand and dropped to the rocks, spilling its entire contents. Damowan almost yelled a curse. Somehow, he managed to stifle his frustration. He bent to pick up the limp pouch and immediately brought it back to his mouth to salvage what little remained in it.

"Wouldn't wanna waste a single drop now, would we?" Temmonin snickered. Jemalemin smiled.

"Wait a second!" Damowan called. "Woah? Tastes like salt."

"Prob'ly sweat, Damowan," Temmonin answered.

"No, Temmonin, this is salt."

"It's here" Jemalemin's eyes bulged.

"What's here?" Temmonin.

"The entry," Jemalemin.

"Y'mean the cave? Where?" Damowan.

"We gotta look!" Jemalemin said as he licked his finger and touched the ground near him. After tasting it, he exclaimed as quietly as he could. "It's salty here too!"

"I'm gonna look over here," Damowan explained as he stood and headed through the cedars and toward the wall. After a moment, he called. "Yep, salt here too. And stronger."

Temmonin's mind was like water when robin's bathe. So many thoughts were splashing against each other, he could not keep himself focused. He searched with Damowan and Jemalemin but did so absently, almost as if he could not control himself. Visions of their imprisonment took him to that black dream and he felt hot breath and vomit saturate his nostrils. He wondered how they would be able to face their abductors. He wondered if they would even have the chance to face them. Still, he continued to search for the opening.

"Temmonin, I got it!" Damowan whispered. "Jemalemin, Temmonin, come here!"

The two reached Damowan's side to see a narrow slit approximately eight feet tall. The slit was created by a slab that leaned against the cavern

307

wall and was barely wide enough for a man to pass through walking sideways. Temmonin peered into the shadow.

"How're we s'posed to be sure this is it?" the eldest asked.

"Look at the ground, Temmonin," Damowan answered, pointing to a myriad of footprints and porcupine quills. "Must make their headdresses outta quills. This's gotta be it." They stood silent for a long while, staring at the cave entrance as if it were the hole in the ice at their own rites of passage. Finally, Jemalemin spoke.

"D'you wanna go in?" he said.

Temmonin shrugged. "May as well. That's why we came."

Being nearest, Damowan went in first, turning his body and reaching his right hand as far ahead of him as he could. The Chrebin flattened itself against the side of his head. Temmonin saw in Damowan's hesitant steps the fear that expects to touch a gar pike while swimming or to step on a snake when walking at night.

"Damowan, wait a second," Temmonin grabbed his left arm. "We need torches. Whoever those people were, they musta known their way around in there 'cuz they didn't seem to need any light--but we're not gonna be able to see nothin' without torches. C'mon."

They found suitable branches and divided the fatty hide of a raccoon among themselves as fuel for the torches. Then they secured the skin to the sticks and made a small fire with which to light them. Within minutes, they were at the cave mouth again.

"Y'sure ya wanna go first, Dama?" Temmonin offered him an out.

"Oh, I guess I don't mind," Damowan

made his brows hop twice. "Here goes." And he and the Chrebin were in.

Temmonin and Jemalemin followed quickly. The slit remained thin for two body-lengths but soon widened so that they could walk normally. Yet the floor of the tunnel was by no means easy to navigate. The tunnel rose and sank over boulders and slabs and rocks, providing a never-ending variety of obstacles. Their bows often caught on the walls and they had to be very careful not to turn their ankles on the uneven floor. Every once in a while, they noticed a wad of hair or a porcupine quill or a feather. This fact assured them that they were moving in the right direction. The air, which had grown steadily cooler since they entered, now began to feel warm. In fact, at times, gusts of heat blew at them. Temmonin imagined that they were making their way down the throat of some enormous snake--perhaps a snow-snake--and the serpent's hot breath was rising to greet them. What poison might lie waiting in its belly?

"It was hot where we were at, wasn't it?" Jemalemin looked to Temmonin.

"Yea," Temmonin nodded. "We might be close now."

"Whew," Damowan soughed. "Smell that salt. And get ready to puke."

"Don't remind me, Dama," Temmonin smiled and shook his head.

They traveled in silence to a place where the heat became constant and they began to sweat again. They continued another hour. Their torches began to lose power. Jemalemin spoke again.

"Don't turn around," he whispered. "Jus' keep walkin' and lookin' ahead. We gotta git to the shadows when we pass this rock ahead of us."

"Why, what's goin' on?" Damowan asked.

"I think somebody's followin' us." Jemalemin explained.

"I think I been hearin' it too," added Temmonin.

They passed the boulder and slipped into its cover before stopping. Damowan handed his torch to Temmonin and motioned that the other two continue on while he waited behind the rock. The other two assented and moved ahead very slowly, glancing back as they walked. After a short distance, the tunnel curved to the left. Temmonin was irritated because, if he and Jemalemin continued, they would not be able to look back and see anything. He reached to stop the boy.

"Jus' walk in place," the elder directed. "Act like we're movin' ahead but jus' walk in place. I wanna see what's goin' on back there."

"Chaneerem!" Temmonin heard Damowan blast. "What're you doin' here?"

Temmonin swung his head around to see the talon-licker materialize out of the shadows.

"What?" Jemalemin cried.

"I can't believe this!" Temmonin slapped his own forehead. "That's what I kept hearin'. I musta heard him ten times back there. I kep' thinkin' I was jus' nervous."

"Yea, I know," replied Jemalemin. "That's why I jus' said we were bein' followed."

"No, I mean in the forest back in the Mamarra--and near Zubzza. And I heard noises a coupla other times too." Temmonin shook his head as he started back toward his brother and Chaneerem. "I was right. Somebody was followin' us!"

"Yea, the whole time," Jemalemin shook his head too.

Temmonin and Jemalemin walked back and

met the other two at the boulder. Temmonin
looked into the oath-taker's eyes.

"Why didn't you jus' join us, Chaneerem?"
he asked, annoyed.

"I don't know," Chaneerem returned.
"Guess I may as well now, though."

"Well, yea," Damowan laughed. "Or, if ya
really want to, you could jus' keep followin' us." As
Damowan spoke, Temmonin saw Jemalemin point
further down the tunnel where they hadn't yet
traversed. "Course, we wouldn't wanna give ya any
of our torches 'cuz we'd wanna make like..."

"Damowan, shut up," Temmonin
interrupted. "Somebody's here."

Damowan turned his attention to the hot
black hole ahead of them. The dying torches in
their hands revealed movement in that direction.
Several pairs of eyes reflected the light. And, in
spite of the shadowed obscurity in which the eyes
floated, Temmonin thought he could see curiosity in
them. Slowly, bodies came into view and forced the
eyes of the four travelers wide open.

These were giants. Temmonin thought
they might even be as tall as the fire-bear. He could
count at least six of them and it appeared that more
might be following. As the men approached,
Temmonin recognized the face of the leader. He
had dreamt this face a hundred times. And the
other faces were similar. They appeared to be
wearing masks with snouts and whiskers and slits
for nostrils and their eyes were small round pebbles.
The masks were huge and covered almost entirely
with porcupine quills. One of the giants turned to
look behind himself and exposed what appeared to
be a ridiculous backdress of quills.

"Who are these people?" Damowan asked,
his dagger already in his hand. The Chrebin stood

on his shoulder and gazed with him. It seemed nervous somehow.

Temmonin did not answer his brother. Neither did Chaneerem or Jemalemin. They just stood with arrows notched in their bows.

The giants were now close enough so that Temmonin could see them clearly. They carried no torches and no weapons. As they approached, their long, sinewy arms hung almost limp at their sides. Their legs were overgrown with brown and gray hair that was matted in several spots. Although they appeared to be human, the only parts on their bodies that weren't covered with hair or quills were the middles of their faces, the palms of their hands, and their chests and abdomens. And they stood at least a head taller than the four Ek-Birin. When they had come to within a few feet of the Ek-Birin, they stopped.

"We still got time to git outta here," Damowan whispered. "I think we can outrun 'em."

"Are you crazy?" Temmonin pinched his face together. "This is what we came here for."

"What? To fight a buncha giants?" Damowan argued, adrenalin forcing his hand tighter around the stone dagger he held in his left hand.

"Who are you and what do you want?" the talon-licker demanded in Mokhamoyuba. "And why are you dressed like that?"

Then, one of the giants opened its mouth and spoke, "So, you have returned," he said in a voice as deep and as thick as a boulder. He spoke the language the four Ek-Birin had mysteriously learned.

Temmonin suddenly felt himself teetering on the edge of a dream. He felt the pain in his back from being lashed to that log for three months. And his nostrils quivered, reignited by a salty insanity. These men were their captors.

"We wished that you would return and we welcome you. Please know that any pain we have ever caused you was only because we saw no alternative. If we had, we would have avoided making you uncomfortable."

Temmonin's mind was swirling. This language was at once so strange yet so very familiar--almost as if he had known it in his mother's womb. The very presence of these huge men threatened him. Yet he was entirely comfortable with them and he seemed to understand every nuance in their expressions. The other Flickers seemed equally as dazed by this welcome.

"Now, our friends," the giant began again. "Please join us in a welcoming feast which we will prepare in your honor." They turned and motioned for the Ek-Birin to walk ahead of them.

Damowan glared at Temmonin as if to ask if this was still the reason they had come back. Temmonin made a face that asked if anything could be more obvious. Damowan shook his head to communicate the fact that he was not entirely convinced that they should proceed. Then he turned and went ahead anyway. As the young Flicker passed the spokesman, the Chrebin stood as tall as it could on Damowan's shoulder and looked directly at the giant as if daring the thing to attack it. But, in keeping with all of his actions, the speaker was as gentle as a mother raccoon. He watched the tiny creature with a mild curiosity.

The other three Ek-Birin followed Damowan and walked for several minutes, surrounded by their towering, bristling escorts. Temmonin glanced at his brother several times and was met with a reservation that told him that if this situation were to turn sour, Damowan would take no blame. Temmonin shrugged and continued. Yet in his gut was a simmering nervousness which warned him that his brother could be right. But his curiosity was huge.

Soon they came to a place where the tunnel curved to the right and narrowed until only two people could pass through simultaneously. Damowan took the opportunity to lean in close to his brother.

"Can we at least tell 'em we brought our own food?" he asked, still protesting. He did not want an answer.

Temmonin shook his head and had to laugh. But Damowan's sarcastic question reminded him of how difficult it would be to eat this welcoming banquet. As their hosts led them through the tunnel, he felt his stomach begin to protest the ensuing feast. But he overruled his desires and followed.

He noticed that the walls in this new section had been worked more precisely than those nearer the surface. He noticed patterns, subtle and weirdly beautiful, carved and scraped into every available space, including the ceiling. They appeared to be scars or twisted worms or perhaps the inside of a snow snake. Temmonin was impressed with the amount of time it must have taken to create such intricate patterns. He nudged Damowan and pointed. Damowan nodded in such a way as to inform his older brother that he had already noticed. Jemalemin followed Temmonin's finger and began to study the walls as well.

Soon their awe was cut short as the quill-men motioned for them to enter the very large chamber that was opening ahead of them. Stalactites hung from it in random groupings.

Temmonin thought he saw bats hangings in several crevices. Moisture permeated the air. The surrounding walls were so far away that they were almost indiscernible but in the center of the place was something that demanded their attention.

A fire was burning and over it, on a spit, hung a number of turkeys that had obviously been roasting for some time. Around this fire sat a group of some forty of the giants, all eagerly watching the new arrivals. Temmonin recognized on each of them the same array of quills their escorts wore.

These people were definitely not dressed like people from the four tribes of the confederation. Temmonin recognized none of their customs or mannerisms.

"Please," said the one who seemed to be the leader, "Please take your place at the fire of our people. We apologize deeply for the obvious discomfort we caused you by our previous cuisine. But we can assure you that we have taken great pains to prepare this feast according to the tastes of your people. We hope you enjoy it."

The four Ek-Birin took their places slowly. Because they knew that the feast was being prepared in their honor, Temmonin and the others accepted the seats nearest the fire without argument. But the situation was odd. The strange people stared at them without shame and did not avert their eyes until Temmonin gazed directly at them. One of them raised a knife to the meat over the fire and began to cut chunks and distribute them to the crowd, beginning with the guests and continuing until everyone had a piece in his hands. Then, to Temmonin's surprise, the whole crowd raised their food in front of them and spoke the traditional blessing of the confederation in stilted Mokhamoyuba.

"Great Creator, you who like rain replenish us, we bow in your honor." Temmonin and Damowan and Jemalemin looked around as they ate. Chaneerem allowed himself to satisfy his curiosity on occasion but generally ate watching the fire. The Chrebin refused any food Damowan offered. At times, the noise the quill-wearers made as they ate swelled to the point that it seemed they were competing to discover which of them could eat most loudly. Somehow, even while eating relatively dry meat, they managed to slurp and gurgle. In contrast, there were moments when they sounded as quiet as the four Ek-Birin. Temmonin began to wonder if these crescendos were orchestrated. But he could see no sign of communication between these people that would lead him to conclude that this was more than coincidence.

When the turkeys over the fire were finished, they were removed and more fully cooked birds were placed on the spits to warm. These animals were also divided and devoured. By the end of the meal, at least six turkeys had been consumed.

The crowd seemed satisfied. Again, the multitude of eyes converged on the Flickers. Temmonin began to feel ridiculously self-conscious. He was relieved when the leader spoke again.

"Our friends," the man said as much to the whole crowd as to the Ek-Birin. "It is good that you have returned. It is as we wished. Please know that, had you not returned willingly and of your own accord, we would not have forced you to do so, even though such a thing is within our power." The words of this mystery language danced with Temmonin's understanding. Yet he followed every thought the quill-man conveyed. Damowan raised his left eyebrow and tightened his lips. "We understand the temptation to fear. The mere sight of our people is probably frightening to your people. Our powers would only add to that threat. But we would ask of you still more patience of the sort you have displayed thus far. For we are not a violent people. We are not a cruel or vicious people. We are a peaceful people who have waited long and have suffered much. And, like your people, we want only what is rightfully ours."

As Temmonin glanced at his brother, Damowan lightly shook his head. "So what do these people want?" he whispered to Temmonin.

"Yea, and what does it have to do with us?" Temmonin returned.

"There is so much we wish to explain," the quill-man continued. "And we welcome your questions as well. But let me begin by offering you my name. In am Ejuarginginshawagin." And as the man introduced himself, he raised his left arm until it was parallel to the earth and raised his right hand to touch his lips with his fingers. "Peace and beautiful," he said in Mokhamoyuba with a strong accent. Damowan raised his eyebrows and peeked at Temmonin who was equally curious. "And," the man continued in the mystery language, "These are my people, the Ginginmarin."

Chaneerem sat up and spoke in Mokhamoyuba. "Who are you people? Why would people of the confederation dress themselves so strangely?"

Ejuarginginshawagin bowed his head gently and spoke the weird language. "We of the Ginginmarin are not of the confederation. In fact, we have never been a part of it," he answered. "In reality, our people were here long before the confederation existed--long before any of the tribes of your kind ever came to this land. The name

'Ginginmarin' means literally 'those here before'."

Temmonin gathered the courage to speak in Ginginmarin. "The tribes of the confederation have lived in this land for hundreds of years. How is it that you can claim that your people have been here longer?" A murmur passed through the crowd and Temmonin could see approval emanating from the faces of the Ginginmarin as he spoke their language.

Ejuarginginshawagin's eyes appeared to comprehend Temmonin's objection. He answered in Ginginmarin. "Temmonin, your people have lived in this land for 938 years. It was at this time that the first of your kind arrived here. Our traditions record that the first act your people did to ours was one of violence. They killed the first Ginginmarin they saw."

Damowan cleared his throat and tried his Ginginmarin. "Your people are not the only people who have traditions. The people of the confederation also have their traditions and none of them include any mention of giants who dress themselves with porcupine quills." In spite of the aggressiveness of Damowan's tone, a new murmur of approval made its way through the crowd.

Temmonin was embarrassed, "Ejuargingi. . ?"

"You may call me Wagin."

"Wagin," Temmonin began again. "Please do not be offended by my brother's rash comments." And as Temmonin continued, Damowan twisted his brows and framed a wordless question with his lips. "We do not in any way insult your way of clothing yourselves or your tallness as a people. But what Damowan means is that your people appear in none of our stories. We have never even heard of people who dress as you do."

318

"My friends," Wagin smiled like a grandfather to his grandchild. "There is so very much to explain." He waved his arm as if revealing the crowd for the first time. "The Ginginmarin are not of your kind. We do not dress ourselves in quills." He tugged at a few of the quills attached to his cheeks. "These grow from our bodies. They are a part of us just as your hair is a part of you. Our race is an ancient one and one that does not easily forget. Our scratchings preserve our history in a way that your verbal traditions cannot."

The four Ek-Birin looked at each other and then back at the Ginginmarin. Somehow, Temmonin was not extremely surprised that these people were not wearing costumes. He was not sure why but it seemed natural that a race like this one existed. He was so involved in his thoughts that he did not notice the last thing that Ejuarginginshawagin said.

"Your scratchings?" Damowan interjected.

"Yes," Wagin answered. "This word is not readily translatable into your language because the concept does not exist among your people. The best word would probably be 'picturing' or 'word-picture-talking'. And we have pictures--or words--which we have scratched into copper sheets. Some of the sheets were completed long before the first of your tribe set foot on this soil."

"And do the speakers bite these copper plates to leave their words on them?" Chaneerem snickered in Mokhamoyuba.

"No." Wagin obviously did not catch the sarcasm. "They scratch or imprint them using sticks or sharp stones. Some who do this even become artists at their work."

"We also have many great artists who paint on deer and elk hides. But we do not say that they put their words into the hide." Damowan was skeptical.

"But," Jemalemin entered the conversation speaking Ek-Birin. "Maybe that's what they're talkin' about."

"Then why not jus' say it?" Damowan shrugged his shoulders. "Why make up some new word for it?"

"It is difficult to explain without showing you," Wagin said. "If you wish, we will take you to our library--the place where we store our scratchings."

"This is why we have come," replied Temmonin in Ginginmarin. "Please, take us."

Damowan gave Temmonin another look that begged the elder not to be so confident. Temmonin soughed and shook his head at his brother's persistent reticence. "Y'know Damowan, fer bein' the braver of us two, yer bein' a little over-cautious, don't ya think?" Temmonin laughed. "C'mon."

Wagin lead the four to a chamber just down the hall from the large chamber where they had eaten. Four other Ginginmarin followed them. These four carried new torches that allowed the Ek-Birin to see their way. After walking for some time, they turned left into a fairly large room that was filled with stacks of copper plates. Once in the room, Wagin chose a copper plate from one of the stacks and laid it on the stone table that stood in the center of the room. Jemalemin stepped up close and the other three flicker warriors followed him. The Chrebin climbed down Damowan's arm and onto the table to inspect the plate. The torch-bearers moved in and Damowan asked to hold one of the torches. As the light made the details on the surface of the plate visible, the four saw what appeared to be vertical lines and regular scratchings. They stood and scrutinized for some time before Damowan could not contain himself any longer.

"I'm sorry, but I could easily do something like this," he scoffed in Ginginmarin.

"It may not be what you think," Wagin objected. "You see, when Ginginmarin look at these plates, we receive a message."

Damowan was irritated. "What: the message that somebody spent a long time scratching with a sharp stone?"

"No, Damowan. Look here." Temmonin nudged his brother and spoke in Ek-Birin. "This stuff looks pritty intentional and pritty regular."

"It says, 'Let us not dream of the world beneath the soil. Let us leave the dream. Let us again find the land where the moon lights our way!'," Wagin spoke reverently.

"I know that!" Damowan exclaimed. "How do I know that? Temmonin?

"I do too--clear as day."

Chaneerem slapped his open palm on the stone table. Then he pointed directly at Wagin and spoke in Mokhamoyuba. "How do we know yer language and how d'you know ours. And why? Fergit this scribblin' crap. I wanna know what's goin' on! Why did you torture us fer three months!?!"

All five Ginginmarin were silent for a moment. The torchlight flickered on their quills and on the rough granite walls surrounding them. Wagin moved to a place directly in front of them and stretched both of his arms onto the table. Then he spoke in Ginginmarin.

"We have studied your language for many, many years and have worked toward the day when we would use it. That day has come. Our final preparation has lasted at least a hundred years and we now feel ready to begin negotiations with you and your people."

"Negotiations!?" Damowan snorted.

"Yes," Wagin replied. "The Ginginmarin once lived on the surface and enjoyed the light of the moon. But one day, your people came and stole our places. At first, there were few of you. But soon it was dangerous for us to live anywhere near your villages because, when we were discovered, we were feared as monsters and invariably killed. In the beginning, we felt that it might be possible for our two races to live together and share the land--for your race sleeps by night and ours by day. But within a few very short years, our ancestors were driven to find another solution. Your people destroyed hundreds of our people and, since we have never been a war-like people, we were forced into deep caves for protection. Now, only rarely does one of you wander into our places. And even now, the result is often the death of one of our own. Fear is a very volatile force among your tribes."

"Wagin," Temmonin protested. "I am sure that your people could find a place among our confederation." The talon-licker spat out a condescending laugh that entirely disagreed with his fellow Ek-Birin. Temmonin did not let that wordless comment steer him from his train of thought. "Are there many more of you than those we saw at the welcoming feast?"

Deep laughter rumbled through the five Ginginmarin. The sound startled Temmonin and he readied himself for action. But the smile on Wagin's face relaxed him again.

"Temmonin, please forgive the outburst, but your comment was extremely humorous to us.

There are too many of us to count. Our places stretch beneath the entire land. We in no way believe that this problem will be easily resolved. It is for this reason exactly that we have prepared for so long. And it is for this reason that we have chosen you. We are forever sorry that initially we did so against your wills. We understand that few men would choose to undergo what we put you through, especially without any knowledge as to why we did it. This that we put you through--this training--was the best way we could think of to introduce our cause to your people. During the three months that you spent in our chambers, you were infused with the history, the culture, and the language of our ancestors. This is why you speak and understand us. This is why you knew us even before you met us face to face. And we wish you to stay here still one more week that we might stir up and further explain what you have already been taught. To stay or to leave is, at this point, however, your choice. We merely ask that you consider the importance of the issues at hand."

"One week is enough?" Damowan's Ginginmarin was more and more fluent.

"As I have explained, you have already been infused with all that we know. This, among other things, is a skill of our race--the ability to give the gift of knowledge. The week ahead of us will serve mostly to remind you of what you have already learned and to embed that knowledge into your minds. In addition, you may have questions that we ourselves could not foresee. We will also use this time to answer any of these." Wagin paused and bent his head. "Embarrassing as it might sound, we beg you to stay, to learn, to ask, and eventually to act as liaisons between your people and our people."

Temmonin glanced at each of his

companions. Damowan and Jemalemin both assented with a nod. Chaneerem's face was neutral; he met Temmonin's gaze with neither animosity nor disdain. Before he turned to answer for the four Ek-Birin, Temmonin smiled gently at the talon-licker.

"Wagin, we are honored that you have chosen us as recipients of so large a gift. We must, however, delay our decision to negotiate on your behalf until we have asked all we wish and until we have learned all you wish to teach us. Please understand our position."

"Then it is settled,." Wagin announced. "But before we speak further, we would be remiss were we not to offer you a room."

"A room?" Damowan repeated as the Chrebin climbed from the stone table to his shoulder.

"Yes, Damowan," Wagin replied. "A private chamber to which you may retreat to discuss, to ponder, to rest." The quill-man motioned for them to follow as he walked from the library. As they walked, he continued. "The five of us have chosen to alter our schedules to accommodate you. We will sleep by night and be here for you during the day. We will feed you, answer your questions, show you through our place, help you in any way we can." He stopped before an archway that led into a small room. But he did not enter. Instead he extended a hand to one of his fellows. "We do not expect you to remember our names immediately, but it will eventually be helpful in communicating. This is Chabin--I am using names you will be able to remember. Next to him is Chemgar . Behind him is Olangash and to his right is Mishchag. Now, it is late. We will begin in the morning after we have all rested. Sleep well, my friends."

After the quill-men had left and all the Ek-Birin had entered their quarters, Damowan sat on the sand floor. "Well, at least none of our confederation brothers'll find us here. And if these porcupine people wanted us dead, they coulda done it anytime--so I guess we're pretty safe, huh?" He was already preparing a spot to sleep on.

"As safe as we'll be fer a while, I think," Temmonin assented.

Jemalemin and Chaneerem did not assent except to lie down and quickly fall to sleep. Damowan's breathing lengthened as soon as he stopped wriggling in the sand. Temmonin stared at the blackness for some moments before he too fell asleep.

His dreams were more pungent than ever. He again saw the faces of the Ginginmarin as clearly as if they had not left the room. The faces were riddled with channels of injustice. They cried out for vindication. They wept. They pleaded for the return of what was originally and rightfully theirs. And they demanded to be heard. Their insistence was not overbearing but pervasive, like the smell of the swamp. And, like the swamp, they gave their story slowly, not only intent upon reaching the lake--like the river--but focusing on every detail and congealing those details and their implications into a massive unified force of logic that drives to conclusion--not like the haphazard splashing of the river as it passes--but with simple, persistent presence.

Temmonin began to feel the burden of those hundreds of years beneath the earth without the freedom to wander through hills and forests and lakes. He began to understand the urgency with which this people ached for the night air. He began to know their depression, their need. He was full of the knowledge of the Ginginmarin, almost as full as he was of the knowledge of his own people. And his understanding led him to the place in his heart where allegiances are born. Then, the burning.

There was a burning where the realization had entered--somewhere between the soul and the spirit. It made the corners of his eyes wince. Then he woke up.

Damowan was already sitting, rubbing his eyes.

"We never got a answer about how they know Mokhamoyuba if they never lived on the ground," Jemalemin said.

"You're right, Jemalemin," said Damowan. "They kinda started to answer and then we got sidetracked."

"Well then, we'll have to ask 'em again," added Temmonin. "And what else? I was thinkin' of somethin' before I fell asleep last night. Or maybe it's still last night. At least we got a torch on."

"Yea, Wagin or one of those guys came in and lit it for us. I don't know how we're s'posed to tell 'em apart." Damowan spoke as he stood to his feet and leaned against the smooth granite behind him. The Chrebin sat silently at his feet.

"I know what we gotta ask 'em," Temmonin remembered aloud. "We gotta find out what they'd want us to say if we ever decide to negotiate. I mean, if there's as many of 'em as they say there are, what're they gonna ask us for?"

"Seems to me we're jus' gonna go through this week and then jus' have to refuse 'em anyway," Damowan said. "I mean if there's as many of them as us, there's no room for 'em. Excep' maybe way up north."

"They seem to be doin' jus' fine down here if ya ask me," Chaneerem added as a sound entered the archway from the hall.

Jemalemin walked to the exit just as the Ginginmarin appeared.

"Good morning." Temmonin guessed that the one that greeted them was Wagin. He spoke his own language. "We have brought you breakfast. We have also prepared enough for ourselves if you do not mind our company. May we join you?"

Jemalemin looked back at the others.

"Sure," replied Temmonin.

The two parties sat and ate together. They discussed several issues, including the method by which the quill-people had learned Mokhamoyuba.

"Long before your people came to this land," began Wagin. "The Ginginmarin had developed a magic by which we could alter our shape. And, although we probably have the ability to obtain many forms, long ago we settled upon one shape which we have used to observe your people and not be noticed. What was more of a fancy and an amusement before the red man's coming became a necessity after his coming. All of the Ginginmarin have now learned to gain the shape of what you call a porcupine."

Damowan gasped in surprise. The Chrebin on his shoulder gazed up at his face. Realization flooded Temmonin's eyes.

"You mean that that is what our ancestors killed?" Jemalemin asked.

Wagin paused, his brows betraying his confusion. "I'm afraid I don't underst. . .Ahhhh! I see. No, my friends. This is not what I am speaking of although it is true that some of the Ginginmarin have died as porcupines. In fact, it could be argued that all porcupines are in some way

Ginginmarin. But this is not what I meant when I said earlier that our ancestors were feared by your ancestors and killed as monsters. No, those that were killed had not yet seen the need to alter their shape. It was their deaths that led the rest of us to perfect our skills. The shape-changing was and is a survival skill. We have used the form to come near to your villages and meetings. We have spent hundreds of years listening and observing. Your languages changed and became similar. Then they became different. Then a common language--Mokhamoyuba--arose and united you. This made our work simpler. We abandoned the study of several dialects and tongues and decided to concentrate only on this form to communicate with you. Now that we have nearly perfected the use of the language of your confederation, we have made steps to begin negotiations. And that, of course, is why you are here."

"What do you mean by saying that all porcupines are Ginginmarin?" Damowan asked, his mouth half-full of food.

"Well," answered Wagin. "When our race began to learn the shape-change, some of us enjoyed the surface so much that they refused to return to the caves. As far as any of us knows, they either never again wanted to return, or they reached a point from which they were unable to return. They quite obviously discovered how to survive without the rest of us. Through the centuries, others joined them. Yet, as the years have past, the number making that choice has dwindled. Perhaps the desperate need for the outside has been diluted with time. Perhaps most of us have become, for the most part at least, accustomed to the new life that we now have. Whatever the reason, fewer of us leave these days. And this is good because once one leaves, all communication is broken with him. We believe the others--the half-brothers as we call them--we believe they may be able to communicate with each other but we do not know to what extent. However, none of us has ever been able to make any sense with any of them. To us, they are as all other animals--they live purely from instinct."

"So why would they stay porcupines?" Temmonin asked. "Are you sure they just refused to return? Maybe something happened?"

"Some of us believe they could not help themselves. I believe that they refused." Wagin was strong. "I have changed shape many, many times and I know the feelings that begin to come over one as it becomes time to return. All those who leave do not do so after their initial change, nor after their second or third change. But each time, they linger longer--perhaps out of curiosity to see what will follow, perhaps out of desire for a pleasure that grows with each changing. In any case, they do not use wisdom and they eventually wander into the trap that robs them of their senses altogether and renders them powerless to do anything but eat and mate. I could hardly call this a helpless choice."

"I understand the pull toward this senselessness," interjected another of the quill-men. Wagin looked at him and hesitated. Then he nodded as if giving him permission to continue. "When I first changed shape, I observed one of your villages for almost one week when the sensations came. They frightened me deeply and I immediately set about the reversion process. But with each of my subsequent changes, the sensations became more appealing and less alarming until I had to stop changing because I knew the next change might be my last. You see, as the pleasure increased, my reasoning power decreased and the

329

last reversion was extremely difficult. The others
probably just ignored the danger in their desire to
feel those feelings and, after a time, lost either the
will or the reason to revert. No one has ever
returned after remaining for more than three
weeks."

When the quill-man had finished,
Temmonin noticed on his face what seemed to be a
look of embarrassment. But like a ripple on the
surface of the river, it dissipated as quickly as
Temmonin could focus. This new quill-man would
not gaze directly at Temmonin or any of the
Flickers. At times, however, when all of the
Ek-Birin were concentrating on Wagin, he thought
he saw the other giant stealing glances. Perhaps this
one reminded him of Kashtawa.

The ensuing days were a blur to
Temmonin. The four learned and remembered so
much about the culture of the Ginginmarin that he
thought he now knew more about them than his
own people. He began to be able to distinguish
between the five quill-men. The one who reminded
him of Kashtawa was named Mishchag and
Mishchag gradually revealed more of his
sensitivities. Soon, Temmonin wondered if that
giant were not more like himself than Kashtawa.
None of the other Ginginmarin seemed especially
interested in making themselves known. They
answered questions politely and thoroughly but
offered little more. At times, Wagin seemed to be
quite relaxed and friendly. Then suddenly, as if
prodded by some unseen slave master, he
regathered his composure and remained aloof. But
Temmonin was beginning to enjoy Mishchag. From
what he could glean without asking directly, he
thought Mishchag reciprocated the feeling.

Yet, in spite of this developing relationship,

Temmonin began to feel the weight of decision press his shoulders again. Finally, the evening arrived on which the four Ek-Birin must commit to represent the Ginginmarin or decline the request.

"If ya ask me, this whole thing is stupid," Damowan shook his head. Some of his hair slapped the Chrebin in its face and the tiny squirrel-man raised its hands to shield itself. "I mean, I know I keep sayin' this but, even if we do start talks and the confederation accepts our plea on their behalf, where're we gonna put all of 'em? Chaneerem said it right--they're gittin' along fine down here." He glanced into the hallway to insure that none of their hosts were listening.

"And what happens then," asked Temmonin. "I mean, these people've waited forever. They're not jus' gonna sit back and say, 'It's too bad the confederation isn't nicer--guess we'll jus' have to wait for a nicer high council'. If we say no to these guys, who knows what they might do."

"Yea, but they said they weren't violent people," Jemalemin interjected.

Chaneerem's eyes lit suddenly as he turned to his brother. "That's exactly what the puma said before he ate Grampa! I don't know if I can trust a single line they're feedin' us. For all we know, this whole thing is a nice little fantasy they've cooked up to swindle away some of our land."

"And if what yer sayin' is true, Chaneerem, then we better figure out some way to deal with 'em," Temmonin warned. "'Cuz if we don't, it sounds like there's enough of 'em to start somethin' pretty nasty."

"So what do we do?" Damowan asked. "What're we s'posed to believe? Who're we gonna trust?"

"D'you guys think our elders know about

this already and never told us?" Jemalemin said.

"Don't be stupid!" cut Chaneerem. "Why would the council keep somethin' like this secret? Y'know, there's a better chance that there aren't even enough of these things to do anything to us. They're prob'ly jus' bluffin'."

"And if they aren't bluffin' and we ignore 'em, then what?" Damowan asked.

"We find out which of us're men and which of us aren't."

"So what do we do? Negotiate or no?" Temmonin attempted to unite the Flickers. "And if no, what do we tell 'em?"

"We got 'til tomorrow mornin', don't we?" Damowan asked and shrugged his shoulders, the Chrebin bobbing along with that movement.

"Yea, but we gotta sleep too. We don't have much time. We gotta figure this out tonight." Temmonin was moving his hands as he spoke.

"Yea, well right this second, I gotta go take a pee, thanks. I'll see you guys a little bit later," Damowan blurted as he stood..

"Me too," added Jemalemin. He followed Damowan out of the archway.

When the younger two had been gone for some minutes, Temmonin spoke again. "I guess if we don't wanna say yes to 'em, we could jus' tell 'em we need to talk to the council before we give 'em our answer."

"Yea. That's good," Chaneerem agreed. "That way, if we don't feel like comin' back, we got our butts covered."

"We have to come back," Temmonin countered. "If nothing else, these people're worthy of respect They've acted towards us with complete honor."

"Once again, yer twisted sense of honor

surfaces," Chaneerem half-scoffed. "Do I need to remind you ev'ry day of our 'honorable' three-month stay in these incredibly comfortable halls?"

"I'm talkin' about this time, Chaneerem," Temmonin reasoned.

Pause.

"Well, this whole thing hangs on whether we can even make it past one village on the surface," Chaneerem said. "Remember, we're still wanted by the confederation. It's only been a week."

An anxious scuffle in the hallway suddenly caught their attention. Like two pumas, Damowan and Jemalemin sprang into the room. Both were panting and could hardly speak. The Chrebin clung desperately to Damowan's black shag. Temmonin stood up quickly.

"What's goin' on?" he asked, his brows wrinkled in confusion.

"These people're the ones," Damowan drew another breath before continuing. "The ones who created those monsters."

"Created those monsters?" Chaneerem asked haughtily.

"What's that supposed to mean, Damowan? What monsters? What're you talkin' about?" Temmonin paused. "Oh, you mean the mutants, like. . ."

"Like the Flicker monster and the Wolverine monster. We jus' saw. . ." Damowan stopped short and looked to the entrance. Wagin and two other Ginginmarin entered the archway and stood still before them.

"Is everything all right?" the huge quill-man inquired in Ginginmarin. "We heard running." Mishchag peeked around Wagin's shoulder. The other porcupine-man was Chemgar and he stood next to Mishchag almost out of view.

"Oh, that was just a game we play," Jemalemin spoke hesitantly after an uncomfortable silence. "We do it all the time up top."

Temmonin looked at the Ginginmarin, carefully pretending to chuckle at Jemalemin's explanation. But anxiety sizzled through his chest as Wagin continued to question.

"You play a game without the use of playing tools?" the giant asked.

"Yes," Chaneerem stated with subtle sarcasm. "We have many games without tools."

"So late at night?" Wagin's persistence began to worry Temmonin.

"Well, we had to go relieve ourselves," Damowan explained. "We thought of the game while we were walking back."

Wagin looked to be in thought for a moment. Mishchag whispered into his ear. Temmonin saw Damowan tense for action. Then the leader bowed his head toward the Ek-Birin. "Please excuse our inquisitiveness but, in our culture, games are played only by boys--not men-- and always with sticks or balls or other playing tools. You can understand our difficulty in understanding. But please, if anything should alarm you or displease you, let us know. We do not wish you any discomfort."

"Thank you," Temmonin assured Wagin. "No, nothing has been a problem in the least."

"Then we wish you a pleasant rest this night." The three porcupines moved from the archway.

After they had gone, Jemalemin leaned out of the entrance and scanned the hallway. None of the giants had remained. Temmonin closed his eyes and sighed.

"Damowan," he said softly. "What'd you guys see?"

"Temmonin," Damowan shook his head. "These Ginginwhatevers make those mutants. We saw a room where they had people like us--humans--tied to logs. And all kinds of animals and stuff. And there were mutants too. It was not a pleasant sight. They were torturin' people and all kinds of stuff. This must be one of their abilities."

"Yea, some peace-lovin', non-violent people," Chaneerem blurted. "They jus' let somethin' else do their dirty work for 'em."

"Whaddaya mean?" Damowan asked before thinking.

"Obvious, Damowan," Temmonin answered. "These people're sendin' those mutants out to kill our people. That's how Mantaw's family died. That's how Mok's daughter died."

"Peaceful people," Chaneerem sneered.

"We gotta git outta here!" Damowan whispered urgently, the squirrel-man still watching him. "What're we gonna do?"

"We gotta wait 'til tomorrow," answered Temmonin.

"What?!" Damowan's face contorted.

"We're gonna have to play along like we didn't see anything. If we leave now, they're gonna know somethin's wrong." Temmonin looked around. "We'll give 'em our answer at breakfast like we planned and then we'll leave and alert the high council."

"Yea, but you didn't see 'em--those mutants!" Damowan argued. "I can't sleep knowin' they're jus' down the hall. What happens if somebody recognized us?"

"Y'mean somebody saw you?" Temmonin's eyes enlarged.

"We're not sure," Jemalemin.

"Whaddaya mean, yer not sure," Chaneerem was typically cutting as he spoke to his brother. "How'd you get into this place yer talkin' about anyway?"

"It's not far--and you go through the wall," Jemalemin started. "And prob'ly nobody saw us."

"You guys went through a wall?" Temmonin.

"Yea, it's like an illusion," Damowan answered. "Like when it's really hot and the air above the lake looks weird."

"I gotta see this." Temmonin's face was determined. "Take me there, Damowan!"

"Temmonin, you're crazy!! We gotta go the other way--outta here. Somebody mighta seen us! We don't got any time to waste!" Damowan was almost yelling.

"Shhh! Damowan, jus' 'cuz yer speaking Ek-Birin doesn't mean they can't hear you," Temmonin scolded. "Damowan, I wanna go and see this place. I want to go. Now, come on." And with his last words, the elder walked from the room and to his right.

"Temmonin!" Damowan pleaded as he followed his brother out.

Chaneerem was behind Damowan and Jemalemin followed last. Damowan looked back and rolled his eyes at the sight. He spat an exasperated sign of frustration and turned to catch up to Temmonin.

"Temmonin, wait," he whispered. "Once we get to the end of this hallway, the torches end. But we took the spur off the main way and, jus' when we got to the place where the light stops. . ." He was feeling along the wall with his right hand and sniffing intensely. "Here!" he whispered excitedly as his hand melted into the carved stone.

Temmonin squinted. "How'd you guys find this?"

"Well." Damowan mimicked the act of relieving himself against the wall and with his finger traced the line the stream of urine would travel to hit stone, then he continued through. "It jus' looked really weird, y'know." He stood again. "Now, I don't know their reason but they got this inner cave lit with torches. Maybe they want the humans in there to be able to see or somethin'. I don't know. But anyway we can only go in a little bit or we might be noticed."

Damowan nodded curtly at Temmonin before dipping his face into the wall. Temmonin almost laughed as the forward half of his head disappeared into the rock but the elder controlled himself and followed Damowan's example. Chaneerem walked around both and did the same. Jemalemin continued looking down the hall.

Temmonin closed his eyes on instinct as his nose penetrated the wall. Once he had pushed through a short distance, he squinted tightly and slit them open. The cave in front of him was lit dimly but that light allowed the three to see all they wished to see. There were two rows of men and women lashed to tree trunks, some of whom had lost parts of their bodies. The air reeked of the blood that leaked from their wounds. Around the rows of people were cages and pens that housed racoons, fox, bear, deer, blackbirds, eagles, and other animals. From these animals came sporadic appeals against their captivity. Off to the left was where the fusing took place. There, Temmonin could see mutants of several varieties and at several stages of mutation. Wings, arms, legs, fur, horns, blood, writhing faces.

He had to close his eyes again to keep from retching. When he looked again, he saw that Damowan had retracted his face.

At the end of the cave where the mutants were tied to logs, a quill-man moved through what appeared to be another illusion entrance. The creature glanced in Temmonin's and Chaneerem's direction. Temmonin winced and caught himself but could not stop a small noise from escaping his lips. Suddenly, one of the women directly in front of him screamed in Mokhamoyuba.

"Help!!" She was staring at Temmonin and pulling desperately against her bonds. "Don't leave us here!"

Temmonin froze, then shifted his gaze to the Ginginmarin, The quill-man was advancing toward he and Chaneerem, its neck outstretched and its eyes concentrating on their red-brown faces.

"Dammit!!" Chaneerem raged and ripped his face from the light. Temmonin pulled himself away and instantly all four were sprinting back toward their quarters. Damowan and Jemalemin were asking questions, trying to understand what had ignited this blaze of panic.

"They saw us!"

"Oh, man!!" Jemalemin and Damowan cried in unison.

"Wait," Temmonin commanded as he crunched to a halt and grabbed two torches from the wall. "Take these. We'll need 'em farther up."

"But they'll give us away!" Damowan protested. The Chrebin watched calmly from his perch.

"We're already given away!" Temmonin exclaimed as he shoved a torch into his brother's face. Then he immediately began sprinting again. They were seconds from the entrance to their quarters.

"D'we need our stuff?" Jemalemin coughed.

"No!" Temmonin replied. "We jus' need to git outta here. Let's go!"

They passed by their room and ran further. Hot breath and sweat beginning to bead. Four heaving chests and grease dripping from the torches. In minutes, they entered the corridor that led to the meeting hall where they had first eaten with the Ginginmarin. Over Chaneerem's shoulder, Temmonin noticed ahead of them two quill-men with their backs toward the Flickers.

"Chaneerem, slow down!" Temmonin whispered as he extended his arms to hinder Jemalemin and Damowan.

As best they could, the four fell into a casual walk and attempted to mask their emergency. The two quill-men eventually turned and greeted them. Damowan whispered to Temmonin.

"This is when they all wake up."

"Yea, like the mornin' time fer us," Temmonin added. Then he spoke louder and in Ginginmarin to the giants, neither of which they recognized. "Good morning, friends. How was your rest?"

"Very fine, friends," the larger of the two answered. He had obviously not missed many meals in his lifetime. "And is it not the time for our guests to be retiring themselves?" He laughed and his plump belly shook. Apparently, these two had not been alerted to the fact that the mutation room had been discovered. Still, the Ek-Birin had not even thought of an excuse for their activities and so they fumbled through their response, the entire time realizing how incriminating their awkwardness was. Damowan finally came through.

"Actually, we're waiting for Wagin and the

others to come." He hesitated. "They asked us to wait in the main hall." He shrugged his shoulders. "They said they would be there soon."

"Well, fine," the porcupine-glutton spoke with no apparent sarcasm. "Allow us to escort you."

Damowan and Temmonin answered simultaneously, the elder saying, "That won't be necessary.", the younger, "Sure, thank you."

The Ginginmarin seemed only to recognize Damowan's acceptance and led the way to the large cavern. "Isn't this usually when you surface-dwellers sleep? It's dark above, correct?"

"Normally, yes. But Wagin told us there was something special he had for us tonight," Temmonin started, hardly knowing where his mind would take him. "He said he needed to gather many of the Ginginmarin in the meeting place and we should come also." He felt heat in his neck like he never had before. And he had no idea where this new lie would lead them. What would they do once they were in the main cavern?

"Ah, this is good!" laughed the rotund quill-man. "Many have already assembled for breakfast. You can eat some while you wait." The other quill-man said something that Temmonin could not understand. "Oh," said the fat one. "But it's only Ginginmarin food--you probably don't like it. You've only been here a week. Have you tried much?" The porcupine-glutton did not seem to care if Temmonin answered. He turned away before the Ek-Birin could speak. "And here we are," he announced suddenly.

The hallway opened into the meeting cavern and Temmonin felt a storm of hopelessness shower his heart. At least thirty Ginginmarin were gathered and eating breakfast, their conversation swelling with each step the Ek-Birin took in their direction. He looked at Damowan and Jemalemin who both reflected his wilted spirit. Even Chaneerem showed graphic signs of desperation. The two quill-men led them through the crowd to a place directly next to the fire--the place of honor. Several of those already seated stopped eating to greet the four warriors as they passed by. As he sat down, Temmonin's heart threatened to constrict itself. Damowan's nostrils flared in a silent, impatient, wide-eyed demand to know how Temmonin's plan would unfold. But Temmonin had no plan. He only knew that they were now completely surrounded by creatures that might want to use them as subjects for mutation. Damowan, Jemalemin, Chaneerem, and he himself might be made into tools which the Ginginmarin would use to kill the people of the confederation. His head was wild with implications. A quill-woman at the fire handed him a bowl of food.

Across the room, a group a Ginginmarin entered. They used the same arch through which the Ek-Birin had entered. Chaneerem leapt up, splaying his bowl of food onto several of those nearby. He plowed through two females and tumbled over the leg of another. Temmonin stood and looked toward where the Ginginmarin had just entered. It was Wagin, Chemgar, and several others. Next to Wagin was another quill-man Temmonin did not recognize and this one was pointing at the Flickers. It must have been the one who had seen them at the mutating cave. The porcupine-men began to jog toward Chaneerem who was now running like a wild boar toward the hallway that led to the surface. But the talon-licker had no torch. Only Damowan and Temmonin had torches and Damowan's was flickering. Suddenly, Jemalemin grabbed Temmonin's torch and drove to his

brother. Temmonin and Damowan then decided to
join them and began dodging Ginginmarin. The
whole crowd seemed to stand simultaneously to
block their way. Temmonin slammed into the side
of one of the giants and felt several quills puncture
his chest and abdomen. He pulled away and found
he could not separate himself--the quills had bitten
deeply into his skin and, in some areas, into the
muscle. He braced himself and pushed harder.
Pain seared across his skin. Still no separation.
Finally, he redoubled his effort and heaved away
from the beast. Several points of fire flared where
the quills had bitten into him as he fell heavily to the
ground. He felt his vertebrae crack in sequence.

As he opened his eyes, he fully expected to
find torn flesh across his torso. But instead, the
quills had pulled away from their roots and now
their foot-long shafts hung from Temmonin's flesh
by thorny barbs. He squeezed a glance through his
pain and through the legs of the Ginginmarin to see
Damowan and Jemalemin fighting to catch up to
Chaneerem. There were so many voices echoing off
of the walls and off of one another that Temmonin
could not understand anything that was happening.
Grimacing, he rolled to his knees and then rose to
his feet. The Ginginmarin were moving as one
toward the other Flickers. Temmonin moved with
them. As he carefully forced himself between giants
to get a better look, he felt one of the quills in his
chest become entangled. Without thinking, he
grabbed it and ripped it from himself. His face
contorted in regret. But he had no time to
concentrate on that searing fire. He had to see
where Damowan was. He contorted his face again
and, as tears streamed down his cheeks, he groaned
and lurched forward.

Temmonin spilled to the dirt between two

Ginginmarin to see Damowan and Jemalemin
completely surrounded. Chemgar and two others
had already grabbed Jemalemin and Wagin was
commanding those nearest Damowan to do the
same to him. Chaneerem was out of sight.
Jemalemin was not struggling in the least.
Damowan, however, was spreading his arms out,
warning the beasts to keep their distance. But they
continued to close. The two that straddled
Temmonin bent down to lift him to his feet and to
hold him steady. They seemed polite and somewhat
confused as to what was taking place. They clung
loosely to his armpits and watched the rest of
Damowan's performance. Damowan was snarling
and slowly shaking his head to ward off this attempt
to contain him. One of the Ginginmarin reached
for his arm but only touched his wrist. Damowan
recoiled as if he had an open sore in that spot and
screamed as loudly as Temmonin had ever heard
him scream. Then, simultaneously, three of the
quill-men grasped him.

When Temmonin glanced at Jemalemin,
something odd occurred. Without explanation, all
of the porcupine-creatures let go of the three Ek-
Birin and, along with those who looked on, raised
their hands to their ears and clutched the sides of
their heads. Then they began to create a low,
growling noise, the collective effect of which almost
caused the ground to rumble. At first, Temmonin
could see no reason for their actions but as he
looked at Jemalemin and then at Damowan, it
occurred to him that the giants were all cowering
away from Damowan. It was the Chrebin.
Temmonin was elated. He smiled widely at his
brother who seemed oblivious to the source of the
Ginginmarin's overwhelming discomfort.

The entire crowd was now kneeling or

curling on their sides in fetal position, trying to hide their heads as completely as possible. Damowan shook his head and wiped his brow with the back of his wrist. Then he too seemed to realize who was causing this sudden reversal. He craned his neck to look at the Chrebin on his left shoulder. He spat a laugh.

"Let's go!" Temmonin blurted. "They're all down." And with that, he ran a pair of steps to join the other two as they turned to exit the chamber.

The Flickers hopped over several hunched figures, careful not to be pierced by the quills on their backs. Temmonin halted abruptly and grabbed Damowan's arm.

"Wait! Where's Chaneerem?" He scanned the cavern. Some of the Ginginmarin farthest from them were beginning to lower their arms and to look around.

"I don't see him. C'mon!" Damowan said, pulling his brother toward the exit.

"I think I saw him reach the tunnel before these guys could get him," Jemalemin added.

Temmonin was slightly relieved at the news. Just as they gained the tunnel, he glanced back over his shoulder to see a few of the quill-men coming to their senses and kneeling or standing. Then the three Flickers were in the snake's belly. Jemalemin had picked up his torch again after having been forced by his captors to drop it. It too was now losing strength. But they ran as quickly as possible. They dared not hesitate even for a moment.

The flickering light only partially exposed rocks in their path. Sometimes the irregularity of the path floor was entirely disconcerting and the Ek-Birin were forced to slow down and feel their way through the tunnel. But emergency was urging

them to rush and, more than once, Temmonin
rammed his toes into obstacles.

Then, ahead of them, the tunnel became
lighter. For an instant, the Flickers jumped at the
thought of the surface and sunlight. But Temmonin
immediately realized that they had not traveled long
enough through this hallway to reach the end. Then
he remembered that it was night anyway. Although
the new light confused them and they were tempted
to stop, they knew they could not.

"Yea, see if they can stop us." Damowan
renewed his effort and rushed toward the surface.

And as they rounded the next gradual
curve, they saw the source of this new light. It was
another torch. It was held high in the air by a single
Ginginmarin. Temmonin could not entirely
decipher the shadows behind the beast, but he could
see no more quill-men. He and Damowan and
Jemalemin continued running toward it, taking
advantage of the light. They could think of no
other option but to charge forward. Jemalemin
tossed his useless torch to the side. Temmonin and
Damowan drew their daggers. Like salmon
swimming upstream, the three raged into the fire,
ignoring the pain that awaited them.

Then the Ginginmarin began to wave his
heavy hand in front of himself. "Damowan,
Temmonin, Jemalemin! Wait!" he cried in
Mokhamoyuba. The words brought the Ek-Birin to
a bewildered halt. "Friends, it is the me, Mishchag.
Please to wait!"

"Mishchag?" spat Temmonin.

"Whaddaya want?" Damowan railed in
Mokhamoyuba. "To trap us?"

"No, no! Please to wait! I have wished to
wanted to talk to you! There was never not a good
time."

"Well, you sure picked a stupid time to confess that!" Damowan was wildly attempting to view Mishchag and the hall behind himself simultaneously.

Temmonin was angry that he could not resolve the factions in his mind. He felt as if he were suspended in a cloud which allowed him to see everything and yet touch nothing. The harder he concentrated, the less control he felt. Then he heard the sound of commotion behind him--the crowd of Ginginmarin!

"Hurry! Mishchag, what?!" the eldest Ek-Birin screamed.

"Well," Mishchag fumbled anxiously with his Mokhamoyuba.

"In Ginginmarin!" Damowan ripped, his hands shaking with adrenalin.

"All right, I needed to tell you that not many of the Ginginmarin know about it, but there are a small group of us--not me--but these men have been planning to sabotage the confederation! They will use the mutants you discovered just tonight. They've already started. But if my people knew, they would not support this! We are a peaceful people. It's just some of us! You must believe me-- I needed to see what kind of people you were before I told you this!"

"Good!" Damowan said sharply in Mokhamoyuba. "Thanks for the information. Now we gotta go! Outta the way!"

"Please don't leave me here," Mishchag pleaded in his own language. "I've taken a huge chance for you. They'll kill me when they find out!"

"Well whaddaya think's gonna happen to you up top?" Damowan twisted his mouth.

"I still have a chance there."

Too much information was swarming

Temmonin's head. And the giants behind them were now in distant view. He felt constrained to believe Mishchag, even if only to expedite their escape. But the nagging possibility that this was a trap lodged itself in the back of his mind. He looked at Damowan and Jemalemin.

"We gotta believe him! Let's go!"

Again they were rushing away from the darkness. Mishchag handed Temmonin the torch. The three Ek-Birin, encouraged by the new light, accelerated their pace and were soon far ahead of the crowd. But Mishchag was breathing like the sound of waves crashing on rocks. He was keeping up but barely. His thick legs were becoming hindrances.

"Are you going to make it?" Jemalemin asked in Ginginmarin between breaths.

"Yes," Mishchag sprayed saliva. "I will try."

The Flickers slowed somewhat, feeling secure the others would have as difficult a time as Mishchag. But Temmonin was not completely comfortable with relaxing. Mishchag seemed trustworthy. His story was reasonable. He saw no obvious reason to doubt this giant. Yet such a story contained all the elements needed for Mishchag to lead the Flickers into a trap. The eldest Ek-Birin began to search every crack in the walls, every shadow. He imagined every scenario that might await them. But none materialized.

Finally, they reached the outside. They squeezed through the slit and into moonlight. Temmonin immediately began beating the torch on the ground to stop the flame. When it was extinguished, the three Ek-Birin paused a moment so that their eyes could adjust to the new light. Then they scurried through the pines to find a hiding place a stone's throw away from the entrance.

They settled in and waited, hidden by a pair of fallen timbers. No sound. No movement. Several minutes later, they concluded that the Ginginmarin had given up their pursuit. Still they were cautious.

"Where d'ya think Chaneerem got to?" Damowan whispered.

"No idea, Dama," Temmonin whispered back.

"We really can't wait around though," Jemalemin leaned in and added.

"No, we gotta go," Damowan said. Then, looking at the quills hanging from Temmonin, he laughed. "Are you ever gonna git those things outta yer chest?"

"When we're really safe."

They made a wide circle through the forest, careful to keep a good distance between themselves and the cave opening. Eventually, they regained the wall of the valley. Mishchag explained that there were no more tunnels in this direction; all of them were farther east and on the other side of the valley. Temmonin was relatively reassured. He and the others agreed that the direction in which they were then headed would also be Chaneerem's most likely escape route.

They had jogged for only a few minutes when they met the oath-taker. He proceeded from behind a stand of cedars as the three other Ek-Birin passed him.

"What's this thing doin' here?" Chaneerem said in Ek-Birin. He sneered and jerked his head toward Mishchag.

"He basically saved our lives," replied Damowan in Mokhamoyuba in deference to Mishchag. "Gave us a torch. Explained about the sabotage that the rest of his race've been plannin'."

"Not the rest," Mishchag interjected in

Mokhamoyuba. "Just some few of men. I think they to see no other way."

"And you swallow it all, don't ya Temmonin?" Chaneerem said. With a look of disdain, he noticed the quills still hanging from Temmonin's torso.

"Maybe because it's all so reasonable," Temmonin answered, fearing that some time soon, Chaneerem's skepticism might be proven right. "He's given up everything to tell this to us. They'll kill him if they find him."

"Well I say there's no way to tell whether this is a trap or not until it's too late and we're all mutants ourselves." Chaneerem was strangely nonchalant as he walked up to Mishchag. "So why not make our chances better." The oath-taker waltzed up to the hulk and, without warning, drew his dagger and drove it at him.

Mishchag's reaction was too slow and the blade sliced his left bicep. Temmonin reached to grab Chaneerem's arm.

"Chaneerem, come on. We don't. . ." But Temmonin sucked in the rest of his sentence. The oath-taker had swung his dagger around and connected with Temmonin's right forearm. "Ah, Chaneerem!" Fortunately, the slash was not very deep. But it bled.

Damowan moved in.

"Don't even think about touchin' me," the talon-licker sizzled through his teeth at Temmonin's brother. "If you three wanna play games with this mutant-maker here--well, I guess that's yer stupidity, not mine. But you won't see me sittin' around waitin' to see what happens." He moved away from the rest. "I'm leavin' to go tell the high council." With that, he swung around and trotted west.

"But, Chaneerem, they're not all bad,"

349

Temmonin argued with the talon-licker's back. "In fact, most of 'em are prob'ly fine!"

The oath-taker wheeled while continuing his flight, glared at Temmonin, began to speak, and then simply shook his head and threw up his hands. As he was enveloped by the forest, the three remaining Ek-Birin and Mishchag heard him cry. "Fools!"

Moon Beneath the Mountains

XIII.   If, however, we are simply sled-dogs forever chasing unattainable objects of desire, wishing beyond logic and reason for that which is beyond us, why is it that such a concept so thoroughly saturates our vision? In a forest where a thousand generations of hunters has stalked the deer that live there and yet not a single deer has ever been slain, would not the hunters have long ago abandoned their quest? But if they continue, does their persistence not speak of a memory--however ancient and vague--a memory of a time when hunters did succeed? Could it be that the world we now embrace and reject and marvel at and despise is but a distant cousin to the world that once was and might again be? Could it be that those who long for an end to the distortion and are certain that such an end will someday come, are these not those who live in reality? And the pack of wolves that howls at and mocks the people who cling to the vague memory, the wolves that accuse those people of infantile dreaming, the wolves that draw strange satisfaction from the knowledge that such visions are the hope of the weak, is the wolfpack so vehement because they are so sure of themselves or because they are eternally bitter at a creator who would allow us to be burnt by the fire which we built intending to warm ourselves?

CHAPTER 13

They ran through the night. Mishchag frequently asked to stop and, although the Ek-Birin were eager to stay as close as they could to the talon-licker, they welcomed the rest. They realized from the start that they would not be able to catch Chaneerem, especially with the Ginginmarin in their company. But they made steady progress that night and found a good place to sleep through the day.

The next three nights, the four travelers continued without event. Occasionally, they were startled by an animal as they slept but they saw no warriors and managed to avoid detection. As they progressed through the maze of valleys that laced the mountains of Imnanaw Kanat, Temmonin became increasingly convinced that Mishchag was telling the truth. The giant often indicated places that he thought or knew to be entrances to the Ginginmarin depths. None of his suggestions seemed to steer them toward any danger and Temmonin never sensed any clandestine attitudes in the Porcupine's speech. The fact that the quill-man had previously shown himself as transparent assured the eldest Flicker. He really liked Mishchag.

On the fourth morning, they found a good cave high on a mountainside in which to sleep for the day. The dawn was still in embryo when Mishchag quietly began to speak in Ginginmarin.

"My friends, you have saved me from those who I have called my people. All my life I have called them my people. And they truly are my people. But now I believe I will be called a traitor to them. Ejuarginginshawagin, Chemgar, and the others will surely convince them that I have betrayed their cause. I am afraid that they will first go to my family and speak powerful words and oaths and curses against your people. They will show my family that you have persuaded me to side with the cause of your people and that I have turned against them entirely. They will use emotional words and manipulations to drive my family to hate me. And I will be alone."

After a short period of silence, Damowan consoled the giant in Ginginmarin. "I'm sure your family will stay with you. And your closest friends at least."

"Damowan," Mishchag explained. "You underestimate their power. I have seen them cause the entire assembly to turn against a man or a woman. And I have seen this man or woman sent out onto the surface to fend for himself. Such outcasts probably all starve to death. We need the support of all the people to change shape. Since they lose that support, they cannot change. And they are all too honorable to solicit help from the people of the confederation against their own people. They probably just find a deep cave somewhere and refuse to eat until they die of starvation. Anyway, there have not been many outcasts. It all started when Wagin and the others came to power and began planning the mutant sabotage of your confederation."

"May I ask exactly what Wagin hopes to accomplish by these mutants?" Temmonin spoke softly.

"Well," answered Mishchag. "I have been slow to tell you this. The point is that by planting these mutants in strategic places and at chosen times, Wagin hopes to send your confederation into blood war against itself. In fact, at this moment, he believes that, at least in the southeast--the Mamar. . ."

"Mamarra," Jemalemin offered.

"In the Mamarra, war has already erupted. The surrounding clans have joined together against your clan--the Ek-Birin."

"A war?" Damowan crumpled his face.

"If we do nothing else quickly as a people, we at least communicate quickly. The news arrived just a day after you arrived that the tribe just west of you, the. . ."

"The Chichmolar," Damowan aided him.

"The Chichmolar attacked your village in blood--not in honor--because they believed you four were responsible for many new deaths in their villages. It was actually Flicker mutants that killed the Chichmolar. It seems that the Ginginmarin--or Wagin and his group at least--have succeeded.

"So you know everything that happens in the villages? Is that how you know when and where to send the mutants?" Temmonin.

"Yes," Mishchag replied. "As you were told, the network of caves is extensive in this land. And our watchers are everywhere. We know almost everything."

"Are there more wars or just that one?" Jemalemin asked.

"I did say that we know almost everything," said Mishchag. "But I know only of this one war. I suspect that other places have been targeted. Very recently, many mutants were unleashed from several caves. But I do not know the ramifications yet."

"Well, so far we haven't seen any signs of war. Maybe there won't be a whole lot of ramifications," Damowan.

"We will not know for some time what has really happened," Mishchag said as the sun broke over the mountains to the east and showered him with an orange glow. "But I began this by speaking about the fact that you have saved me." He paused and shifted to avoid looking directly into the sunrise. A chickadee landed on a sapling nearby and upon sighting the four travelers immediately flew away. "I will now make a very important request of you all. I would ask you to seal our pact by performing with me the ritual ceremony of heartbond. Now is the time of day that is best for the ceremony."

"Heartbond? What's that supposed to mean?" Damowan cocked an eyebrow. The Chrebin had found a place behind Damowan to shade himself from the sun. Birds of several varieties were working their chatter in the rocks on the mountainside and in the valley far below. A turkey vulture circled high above them. Mishchag looked at all these things and breathed the mountain air before answering.

"The heartbond ceremony is reserved for those who have experienced a deeply disturbing event together and have lived to tell the story. It is the way those indebted may pledge to pay their debt and those owed the debt may understand the gratitude of those indebted. If none is indebted to the other, the ceremony memorializes the event and gives those involved a chance to pledge themselves to one another."

Temmonin glanced at Damowan in the growing dawn. "What is it you want us to pledge?"

"No," the giant immediately answered. "You are not indebted to me in the least. It is I who am indebted to you. You are not indebted to me, not even for the greatest thing that I did for you."

Temmonin was confused by these words. Was this as plain a statement as it sounded? Or was there a reason that Mishchag had called attention to 'the greatest thing' he had done for them. The

eldest Flicker certainly felt indebted to this giant. If
he had not been waiting for them in the tunnel with
a fresh torch, the three Ek-Birin would surely have
stumbled in the dark until they were overtaken.
And he could only imagine what horrors might have
awaited them if that were to have happened. Still,
the manner in which Mishchag had just spoken
seemed, at least in part, to excuse he and Damowan
and Jemalemin.

"Mishchag," he began almost apologetically.
"At this point, we are quite well-versed in
Ginginmarin culture. But I must tell you that I am
confused by your choice to ignore our indebtedness
to you. You saved our lives by bringing that torch."

"Please, my friends. It was nothing at all."

Temmonin still sensed something. "Really,
Mishchag, you know we are not very good at
understanding your nuances. And I believe we owe
you our lives. There is a slight chance we could
have escaped in the dark, but we probably would
have been caught. You know better than us what
that would have meant."

"But my part was nothing," Mishchag insisted
although it seemed to Temmonin much more
weakly than before.

"Mishchag," Temmonin returned. "You must
allow us the privilege of giving and not only
receiving."

This seemed to constrain the Ginginmarin and
he acquiesced without further argument.
Temmonin felt satisfied that he had succeeded in
discovering the giant's true intent. But suddenly it
struck him that he was not sure what he had agreed
to. How much was the quill-man asking for? Was
this the final trap? He faked a cough and glanced
back into the cave. Nothing but shadows.
Damowan spoke in Mokhamoyuba.

"I'm sorry. I don't mean to be rude but, before I pledge anything, I need to know what I'm doin'."

"Please." Mishchag seemed burdened with emotion, so much so that he did not even attempt to answer in Mokhamoyuba. "I can see that the situation for all of you is precarious. But I assure you that if I betray you, you are freed from this covenant of friendship. Because I have initiated it, I am committing myself to you for life. I may not renege under any circumstances. So do not worry, Damowan. In any case, you are safe. You are all safe." After a long silence, he lowered his head and spoke quietly. "We must all sit and face the sunrise."

The Ek-Birin situated themselves as Mishchag directed. All of them squinted in the glare. Sweat glazed their naked torsos. Temmonin could smell strong odor emanating from the porcupine-man. Over the past two weeks, the odor had become a matter of fact but this was the first time he was conscious of its presence. It was a mixture of salt, sweat, and vinegar. Temmonin licked his dry lips.

"Life is pain and pain is good," growled Mishchag. "Pain is not good because we enjoy it. Pain is good because it speaks secrets. Life is pain and pain is powerful. Pain is not powerful because we crave it. Pain is powerful because it offers us the knowledge we crave. Life is pain and pain is necessary. Pain is not necessary because we want it. Pain is necessary because we want the harvest that is ours only when pain had come and gone. Life is pain and pain is discipline. Pain is not discipline because discipline thrives on pain. Pain is discipline because only the voice of pain is loud enough to awaken discipline. No voice is louder on the land or under the land. No voice is more feared on the land and in the sky. No voice is more offensive on the land and in the rivers. And no voice works more wonders in the land of the living."

Mishchag raised both arms in front of himself, palms facing the sky. He drew his hands together and cupped them as if collecting rain. He then brought them to his mouth. Temmonin and Damowan and Jemalemin mimicked his movements. As the Ginginmarin touched his lips, he spoke again.

"We drink the juice of pain willingly--not gladly--but willingly." With that, he and the others after him drank air from their palms.

"In this land, we drink together for there is no way that we may drink apart. It is pain that has whispered this secret to us. When we have tried to ignore it, we have died. Although we drink the juice of pain together, we often serve it to one another-- sometimes with intent, other times without knowing it." He pounded his chest hard with his fist then raised both palms and extended them to face the sun. Tears were streaming down his cheeks and spilling onto his leathery chest. He framed in the blazing globe of the sun with his thumbs and forefingers. "Giver of life and giver of pain, we call you our source and our sun. We suck like cubs from your teats. We wander and wait in your garden for the day when pain will no longer be the language of wisdom. But we see no end in sight and so we live and breathe like brothers. And like brothers, we join in heartbond--no blood that spills will be less dear than that of brothers. No pain that is felt will be felt alone. No longer do we live and breathe as strangers with indifference but with knowledge and the pledge of fellowship and protection to one another."

Mishchag grabbed a handful of pebbles and sand from the granite floor of the cave and tossed it about three feet in front of himself. He then signaled for the others to add to his pile. When they had done so, the giant reached his gargantuan hands to mix the pile. He then scooped up some of the sand and rubbed it into his hair and scalp. Somewhat reluctantly, the others followed his lead. The quill-man spoke in a final tone.

"My friends, I owe you my life. My offer to you is to serve you until I die. Do not refuse my offer."

Temmonin looked at Damowan who mirrored his concern. Jemalemin's brows joined in question. Temmonin was lost. He could think of nothing to say. Mishchag's commitment was overwhelming. But Temmonin did not feel he could pledge his life in return. And even if he felt he could, he was not at all comfortable with speaking for the others. If he himself was unsure of the porcupine-man's loyalty and the continuing possibility of betrayal, he was certain Damowan would have much greater reservations. Jemalemin was probably as confused as Temmonin. Damowan spoke in Ginginmarin.

"I cannot speak for my fellows but I am willing to accept your offer on a condition that you accept the pledge of my life to you in return."

Temmonin stared at his brother. He swallowed hard. Jemalemin was equally as surprised. Mishchag stared at the sand in front of himself and began to weep. As the tears drenched his neck, he stretched and scooped up more sand and ground it into his scalp. With mucous running from his nose, he struggled for intelligible words.

"I. . .I accept your conditions."

"I pledge my life too," Jemalemin said softly and as Damowan reached for sand so did the boy.

As they rubbed it into their hair, the porcupine-man's tears gushed from his small eyes. The giant was almost shaking. The quills on his neck and back quivered with the weeping.

"And I accept your offer, Jemalemin." Mishchag repeated the sand ritual.

Temmonin felt his stomach tense. He could not see the future he so dearly wished to see. The suspense of his own decision was filling his throat with acid. He glanced at Damowan and Jemalemin and then looked away before either could catch his eyes. Then a rush of recklessness poured through his insides. Before he could rethink his impulse, he spat out the words.

"I give you my life for fellowship and protection."

At that, the Ginginmarin fell face-down onto the rock, gathered more sand and dumped it across the back of his head. His chest was heaving up and down, he coughed and doused the granite with tears. He assented to Temmonin's commitment with what seemed to be more of a groan than an acceptance. Temmonin slowly leaned forward to retrieve some sand. After he had ground it into his scalp, he leaned forward again and, careful not to prick his hand, laid it on Mishchag's shoulder.

The quill-man continued to cry for some time, during which the Ek-Birin watched patiently, not entirely grasping the reason for or the nature of his sorrow. When Mishchag had finished, all four crawled into the cave and slept until evening.

The next four days passed as if they were only a moment. The four needled their way through Ek-Makatin forests and the looming peaks of Imnanaw Kanat with new determination. To Temmonin at least, it seemed that they had all gained assurance that there would be no betrayal among them. This thought alone gave him a strange elation that completely conquered his tentativeness. He often found himself laughing as they ran. But he also began to ache for some time alone with Damowan.

Since they had left the village three weeks ago, they had not had any length of private time together to discuss any of their thoughts. They were always with Jemalemin, Chaneerem, or Mishchag. Perhaps spending the entire winter and spring with Damowan had caused him to rely too heavily on the talks they had had. Perhaps when they were old men they would again share so much time together. Then again, perhaps they would have less to talk about.

He looked ahead at Damowan as he ran. The grey moonlight glistened on his brother's hot shoulders and his shadow-black hair flapped on his back in polyrhythm to his pace. Jemalemin and Damowan were talking. Suddenly, Temmonin felt as if he were floating. He continued to stare at Damowan but barely recognized him. Yet all that they had experienced together, their common sister, mother, and father, their village and the clan--all of it pressed him to the conclusion that this was his brother. But somehow, he seemed new, fresh, foreign. Temmonin was almost in awe of him. He felt so small and insignificant in himself; almost ashamed.

But they were brothers born two years apart and at this age almost identical in build, strength, and agility. When they fought against each other and together against others, each knew the other's position at all times and each knew what the other would do next. Temmonin's only advantage was the fact that he was the older brother. Some unnameable strength accompanied the elder in all his dealings with Damowan. Even in moments when Temmonin was weak, he could always rely on subtle manipulations to remind his brother of his secondary place. Now, however, Damowan did not appear secondary in any way.

He was as bright as he had ever been, running and hiding and laughing whenever he could. Only the moon and its reflection on the lake to their left were brighter. Damowan glided through the darkness like a rivulet of water down the back of a turtle. He was sleek and as ready as an army of snakes. He was quick as an avalanche, as unable to ponder as a shooting star, and as unexpected as the glimpse of a fox in the shaded distance. Although he was a refugee of two races, he owned the world through which he was now being chased. He could swallow the confederation for breakfast and slurp the Ginginmarin from their caves for an afternoon snack. When accused falsely, he was as ruthless as a tornado and Temmonin was sure that, should he be captured, whole clans would be swept into his wrath. And Temmonin was a grain of sand next to the Chrebin on Damowan's shoulder.

They entered Mitsa-Mitsa territory that night and, as the moon slipped down and away through the forest, they reached the shore of Moza-Imsaw.

"We're gonna have to steal a canoe," Damowan whispered, gazing across the endless ripples before them.

"Borrow, Damowan," Temmonin corrected him, now only half-remembering his recent vision of his brother.

"Is one gonna be enough?" Jemalemin asked.

"Yea, I think one should do it," Temmonin.

"Well, there's that lakeside village over there we jus' avoided. Y'wanna come with me Jemalemin?" Damowan was already moving. Jemalemin joined him without speaking.

Temmonin was mildly surprised that his brother had chosen Jemalemin instead of himself but immediately decided that Damowan was only trying to involve the boy.

"These canoes," Mishchag interrupted the silence in Mokhamoyuba. "Are they to be the large canoes?"

"If yer worried about us all fittin' in one, ya don't have to."

"Then they are large enough to my size?"

"Sure, Mishchag." Temmonin was puzzled. "We've had whole families and equipment in some of 'em. But they're light enough fer jus' two of us to carry."

"So," the porcupine made a motion with his right hand beginning from tight against his abdomen and then swinging his arm toward the lake, palm facing the sand. "So, they do not never sink?"

"No, not unless there's a leak. But we usually fix those. Why?"

"Nothing. I simply had the interest."

Temmonin sensed something like embarrassment in Mishchag's reply. But the Ginginmarin were difficult to decipher. If Temmonin had been asked such a question, he would have answered quickly and looked away to hide his embarrassment. Yet the quill-man gazed directly into the Ek-Birin's eyes until Temmonin himself was forced to look away. Maybe this was some sort of intimidation act to reverse the ill feelings.

"So how do you like the surface?" the eldest Flicker began.

"It is very nice," Mishchag answered. "But to remember, I has been above quite much times."

"Yea, but jus' wait 'til you git to spend a whole day in the glorious sun." Temmonin shook his head. "Once we get to Ojeb-Mawitez, we can get back to a regular schedule again."

"This moon is enough of glorious to me, Temmonin. You forget that we are always a nocturnal people."

"Oh, yea. I did forget," Temmonin admitted and, as he looked again across the lake, a thought struck him. "What happens to you in the sun? Is it just the brightness?"

"The brightness for us is almost the blindness," the quill-man nodded. "We can to endure it but it is not to be comfortable to us. You saw the way my eyes cried when I to look into the sun at the heartbond?"

Temmonin nodded. He hesitated, then spoke. "I figured that was emotion."

"No, that is the sun." And Mishchag again peered at Temmonin until the Flicker was uncomfortable and turned away. Temmonin became more certain that the porcupine-man was embarrassed.

"Temmonin, they saw us!" Damowan's voice drove across the sand.

Temmonin and Mishchag jerked their heads in that direction to see Jemalemin and Damowan sprinting toward them, somewhat hindered by the hulk of the canoe they were carrying over their heads. Temmonin immediately jumped and ran to meet them. Mishchag was directly on his heels. The four connected at the edge of the lake where Damowan and Jemalemin had just thrown the boat into the water.

"We gotta fly," Damowan roared as he leapt in and grasped a paddle. "They saw us and they're comin' after us!"

Temmonin glanced toward the village. Several silhouettes were progressing up the beach toward the four. He took his place in the canoe.

"Mishchag, c'mon!" Damowan raged. Temmonin looked at the beast and saw him stammering at the shore. "Let's go!" Damowan's command was so cutting, Temmonin almost expected to see Chaneerem next to him. But Damowan's intensity forced the quill-man to act before the Mitsa-Mitsa warriors were upon them.

The Ginginmarin plunged through the shallows and fell upon the canoe, clutching it as if it were his dying mother. Temmonin worked to get the giant on board while Damowan and Jemalemin began paddling. Only when Mishchag was entirely in the boat did Temmonin pause his efforts to look toward the Mitsa-Mitsa. Amidst Damowan's and Jemalemin's frantic strokes and the Ginginmarin's hollow gasps and panicked grip on Temmonin's wrist, he could only ascertain that the Salamanders were too quick to outrun. Four canoes were slicing through the water on a course that would intercept them in a moment.

"Damowan!" Temmonin warned.

"I know! I know!" Damowan yelled back from the front. "Jus' get ready for 'em. You too, Mishchag!"

But Mishchag was huddled at Temmonin's feet, barely relaxing enough to look over the edge of the canoe.

"Here they come!" Jemalemin called from the rear between strokes.

And with that, the first Salamander boat pulled up alongside. Like an eruption of anger, Temmonin sprang into the three Mitsa-Mitsa warriors and capsized their canoe, sending them into the water and into the canoe that followed them. Remaining

underwater, he avoided the others who had plunged
in with him and swam as quickly as he could back
toward his own boat. When his lungs finally
demanded air, he surfaced and wiped the water
from his eyes. He discovered that he was in
between two canoes, neither of which was his
companions'. He thought he saw one of the Mitsa-
Mitsa point him out and issue a command just
before he himself gulped another breath and swam
toward the other canoe. After a pair of strokes, he
could see the boat pass over him. He lunged
skyward and broke the surface. As he grasped the
edge of the canoe, a paddle grazed his shoulder.
The Salamander at the rear gave a shout of surprise
just before Temmonin heaved and sent both of the
boatmen into the water. He sucked in deeply and
pushed back into the blackness. His leg hit a body
part. His arm hit something else. Somehow,
however, he was able to come clear and to swim
some distance before he had to surface again.

No one noticed as his head bobbed up. He
was only inches from a capsized canoe and it was
this obstacle that saved him from being recognized.
He noticed that there were also others clinging to
the same boat, Salamanders from what he could see
through the shadows. Farther into the lake, he saw
two canoes tottering alongside each other, kept
from tipping only by the fact that the men in each
were locked in struggle with each other. He could
hear shouts.

"Thieves!" Temmonin heard in
Mokhamoyuba. Skin slapped water.

"Damowan!" Jemalemin yelled as he hit the
lake.

"Jemalemin!" Damowan returned from where
he was wrestling a Mitsa-Mitsa.

"Wait!" Temmonin heard from the other side of the canoe to which he clung. And then there was an expletive in Mitsa-Mitsa. Then another sentence in Mitsa-Mitsa.

The struggle in the two connected canoes settled and the boatmen simply held each other.

"Damowan," the same Salamander called. "Is that you from the Ek-Birin?"

"Yea, but we haven't done nothin'. We were jus' borrowin' the canoes. We gotta git to the high council with important information."

"Who else is with you besides Jemalemin?"

"Who are you?" Damowan returned suspiciously.

"I am Kashtawa," the shadow answered. "Do you remember me from Ojeb-Mawitez?"

Temmonin's heart beat like a duck's wings at the sound. "Kashtawa! It's you!?"

Startled, Kashtawa turned to his left. "Temmonin?" At that, Temmonin pulled himself onto the overturned bow and reached his hand to grip the Salamander's. "I can't believe this! What're you guys doin'? Did the council let you off?"

"Who are they?" called another Mitsa-Mitsa. "Are they the refugees? The ones that started the war?"

"Yea, they're the. . .No! They didn't start any war!" Kashtawa defended.

"But they're the Flickers who left their village and broke the word of the high council!" another called.

"And they've got one of the mutants here in the boat!" one accused.

"He's not a mutant--he's Ginginmarin!" Damowan blasted.

"What's that?" said another.

"Liar!" cried yet another.

"Fellas! The whole confederation is in an uproar!" Kashtawa bellowed and commanded attention. "We don't need to add our stupidity to it!" The lake was suddenly quiet. "Let's take these four back to shore and hear their story before we judge 'em."

The party of Salamanders seemed to need a moment to consider. But soon the group turned and paddled to land. When they hit the sand, they led Temmonin, Damowan, Jemalemin, and Mishchag a few steps from the water and sat in a circle enclosing them. The four also sat down.

"Please, Temmonin, Damowan, Jemalemin, tell us yer story. Why'd you take our canoes? Did you disobey the high council and, if so, why? Where're you guys gittin' to in such a hurry? What's this creature you've caught?"

Damowan was still fuming at having been captured. As usual, Jemalemin seemed to have no desire to speak in public. Temmonin began in the black quiet that had settled around them.

"We stole the canoes 'cuz we need to git to the council before Jemalemin's brother Chaneerem does. We're prob'ly already really late. He was travelin' alone from the same place we started so, unless somethin' weird happened, he prob'ly made a lot better time than we did. We also had to adjust our pace to Mishchag's pace—and he isn't our prisoner. He isn't an animal. He's from a race named Ginginmarin and the relationship between his race and ours is the reason for our journey to Ojeb-Mawitez. Mishchag came with us of his own free will as a friend to help begin talks between our two races. Ya gotta understand that his race lives in caves way beneath the surface and that there's as many of them as us." In his mind, Temmonin had predicted the shock with which the Mitsa-Mitsa would receive this knowledge. He waited until they had again settled before he continued. "Last fall we were travelin' north to Wolverine territory when we got abducted fer three months and then got returned to the surface. We spent those three months in the hands of Mishchag's people. They taught us about their history and their culture. They did this hopin' we would be go-betweens between our two races. We don't understand why they sent us back to the surface before explainin' anything to us--to us it was like we had a dark three-month-long dream. Anyway, the Wolverines found us and took us to the high council to tell our story. During that journey, we met Kashtawa for the first time. And after he and a group of Mitsa-Mitsa took us to the Island of the Council, we were told to stay in our family's village 'til the next snow came. But we needed to know what'd happened to us that autumn and so we broke the command they gave us. We found the entrance to the caves of the Ginginmarin and we were their guests fer a week. Once we were down there, we got reacquainted with all the stuff we learned last winter. Then they told us they wanted us to be their spokespeople. But, before we left, we found out somethin' we weren't supposed to. A small group of the Ginginmarin—the leaders-- had already started a plan to create wars between our tribes and clans. They used those mutants we started seeing this past year. And the wars that are goin' on right now in the Mamarra and other places were started by these few Ginginmarin."

Temmonin cleared his throat. "But the problem is that Chaneerem doesn't believe that only a few of the Ginginmarin're responsible. He sees 'em all as guilty. That's why we gotta to get to the council before somethin' stupid happens."

"Please," Mishchag began in Mokhamoyuba. The Mitsa-Mitsa were shocked again. "My people are a good people. Most of them to know nothing for this plot to make the civil war under the confederation. Most just to wish to discuss to the sharing of the land. Only some wish to cause the pain and take the revenge. You must to believe us."

Temmonin could decipher in the eyes of these Salamanders the inability to imagine all that they had been told. But he also saw in some of them an attempt to understand. Mishchag sat before them as huge as a mystery, like the sun before it rises over the east ridge, like the kind of danger that twists a man's stomach from within him. None of them could deny that the hulk had spoken to them in Mokhamoyuba—but all of them were constrained to doubt each detail of the explanation. A few, however, comforted Temmonin in the fact that they seemed willing to use the story as a working assumption. As they talked amongst themselves in Mitsa-Mitsa, he thought he saw the mood of their entire party evolve into one of general acceptance, although still not void of skepticism. He could expect nothing more. He was sure that if he now sat on the outside of the circle, he too would be struggling to come to any conclusion.

"Whether we believe you or not," began one of the Mitsa-Mitsa. "We can still take you to the Island of the Council. But watch out. If any of you guys does anything at all suspicious, we're gonna be forced to take strong action. You're wanted by the people. Don't fergit that." He paused and nodded to the Ginginmarin. "And explain it to yer friend here."

"He already understands," Damowan answered. "He speaks fluent Mokhamoyuba." Damowan seemed to have muscled his way into the minds of these Salamanders because they did not respond further. They simply stood and once again moved to the shore and to the boats.

They entered the lake silently and slipped like muskrats across the surface. Temmonin was gladdened by the fact that the Salamanders gave him and Damowan paddles. Of course Mishchag had never had any opportunity whatsoever to develop canoeing muscles in his arms or to learn the rhythm needed for the task. Because of this, he declined to take a paddle. But the two Ek-Birin paddled energetically, grateful for a chance to show their earnestness.

To Temmonin, Kashtawa seemed reserved. Yet certain glances and half-smiles from that Salamander led the Ek-Birin to believe that this reservedness was probably an act of protection. Although they had become friends, they had not spent enough time together to trust each other completely. Still, Kashtawa had not pulled entirely away. His occasional attempts to convey assurance to the Ek-Birin comforted Temmonin.

Other than these silent communications, however, little else passed between the travelers. They were immersed in the sea above the sea; a swarming humidity that drew moisture from their skin and circulated it into that which already swam around them. The perspiration fell from Temmonin's side in counterpoint to the water that dripped from the tip of his paddle as he lifted it from the lake between strokes. Everything was deep, black rhythm.

They hit the sand of the island as the black sky warmed into morning. The noise of landing the canoes had probably alerted some of the keepers of the island because, by the time the rowers had finished pulling the boats from the water, a greeting party of four Salamanders was waiting for them just up the trail. Kashtawa and his companions discussed the purpose of the visit with the keepers of the island and, within moments, the Ek-Birin and the Ginginmarin were being led to the heart of the council village.

Matthew John Schellenberg

XIV.   If the wolves are bitter about the backlash, do they not all the more lend credence to the hopes of the people who cling to the vague memory. Who is bitter about the absence of that which he does not believe he has the right to lay claim to. Rather, does the anger not betray a deeper recognition of the limits of the one who complains and of the seeming inaccessibility of the thing he so desires? Does his frustration not demand that the world around him reform to become that which pleases him? Does it not demand that the Creator admit his inconsistencies and mistakes and cower to the howls of the wolfpack? And if the creator were to grant such wishes, if we were to obtain the ability to light bonfires in our refuse filled canoes and not be burned, if we were to obtain the power to ride the waterfall into the rocks below and never perish, if we were to obtain the license to become the idiots of the universe and yet never suffer the consequences of our own stupidity, would we then be happy? And would we truly own free wills?

CHAPTER 14

The deliberation lasted the entire day. Questions of why the Ek-Birin had disobeyed the council filled the morning. Each new question began to sound like the host of questions that had preceded it and, in Temmonin's mind, they started to resemble the lapping of waves on the beach. He soon found himself wrestling to stay awake. More than once, he was forced to use all of his concentration as one of the elders pointed questions at him. He would stare at the elder and the trees behind the man would begin to spin and blur as Temmonin pleaded with his eyes to ignore their desire to close. But his eyelids were gaining weight. The fact that the three Ek-Birin had become accustomed to sleeping at this time of the day coupled with the fact that such proceedings always bored Temmonin added pressure to his clouded brain. He could vaguely sense Damowan fidgeting next to him. Mishchag, however, had spent most of the morning squinting and wiping tears from his eyes, squinting and wiping tears from his eyes, squinting and wiping tears. The Ginginmarin's process of adjusting to daylight became a monotonous chant that called Temmonin to lie down and rest. After some time, Mishchag was able to stare at the sand beneath his feet. Jemalemin did not move. Temmonin wondered if the talon-licker's brother was asleep. It was difficult to know. To Temmonin, the whole forest wanted to sleep and this irritating interrogation was a mosquito in its ear. But he answered the questions as well as he could. He was surprised when Damowan raised his voice.

"These people're harmless." All eyes turned to him as he stood to speak. "Only a few of 'em are

involved in the conspir. . ." Damowan stopped
dead in his speech.

Temmonin was fully awake now. He wanted
to kick himself for not having told Damowan to
keep quiet about the Ginginmarin conspiracy. But
he never mentioned it because he imagined that
Damowan would be bothered by his older brother's
nagging. He was suddenly extremely angry at the
fact that life was so full of these kinds of situations.
But he had no time to reason with his frustrations.
Damowan continued.

"There's a conspiracy among some of the
Ginginmarin. But it's not among all of 'em." He
looked around. "Only a few of 'em!" No one
reacted. "Mishchag here actually helped us escape--
he's not the same. We did a ceremony of
friendship. He has family and friends down there.
And if we don't watch out, we're gonna have guilty
blood on our hands."

One of the elders moved and cleared his
throat. He was from the clan of the Badger. "My
son. Unfortunately, you have come with a
contradictory message to that of your fellow Ek-
Birin, Chaneer. . .?" He spoke the oath-taker's name
hesitantly and looked to Jemalemin for assurance as
he repeated it. "Chaneerem?" Jemalemin nodded.
"Your colleague reached our shores over three days
ago. And now he is leading an army to eradicate
these porcupine-people from the north forests of
our beautiful land."

Mishchag's eyes widened with surprise then
quickly shut to block out the sun. Temmonin and
Jemalemin joined him in his shock.

"You believed him?!" Damowan's face
twisted.

"We believed him," he answered.

Matthew John Schellenberg

"You believed a guy who tried to kill his own brother?" As Damowan stirred and grew louder, the Chrebin tightened its grip on a lock of his hair. "He woulda killed me and Temmonin too if he could've. He is not the man to lead an army and he's not a good person to take information from!"

Temmonin knew that the elders would not quickly ask Jemalemin to betray his brother, but he thought perhaps this new information might cause them to question the boy about Chaneerem. He hoped they would.

"And now you place us in an interesting situation, Damowan of the Ek-Birin," the same elder spoke. "Do we believe you three or Chaneerem? You see, this is our problem now."

"And that's exactly what yer here for mister!" As Damowan blurted his words, Temmonin almost jumped at his brother's brashness. "To figure this stuff out!!"

Temmonin wanted to grab him and shake him. Not only was Damowan totally ignoring the polite language of protocol, which was usual for him when he was angry, but now he was being obnoxious. Temmonin wished his brother could control himself. But he knew better than to try to repair the hole Damowan had torn in the fragile net that might save the Ginginmarin. The elder brother had attempted to correct such mistakes in the past. It had always hurt the situation more. He decided to sit and observe in spite of the fact that speech was collecting in his jaws, pressing to be released.

The Pagam-Atohka elder spoke with the kind of tone that told Damowan how useless his anger was. "So you see, we have this problem," he seemed slightly bored--not so much that anyone could see that the boredom was feigned. But Temmonin thought he could see the delicate

378

balance the elder was trying to keep. He wondered how much Damowan had actually disturbed the man. "As you have said, it is our duty to make decisions in such circumstances. You have spoken correctly. Yet you have just now introduced new information into our assembly--specifically an intensely strong accusation against a member of your own clan. Such bits of information add new dimensions to our discussions. These things take much time, you see."

Temmonin remembered his hope that this man would ask Jemalemin about Chaneerem before the boy finally broke and offered the information himself. He knew the talon-licker would never forgive his brother if Jemalemin volunteered incriminating evidence without resistance. In fact, Temmonin could imagine Chaneerem not forgiving his brother even if Jemalemin had suffered extensive torture before yielding the information.

"You see," continued the elder. "We must decide which story to believe about the porcupine-people--yours or Chaneerem's." Temmonin's hopes piqued. "And now we must also decide whether or not to try a man in his absence."

Suddenly, Temmonin's emotions split into two rivers--one of hope, the other of fear that the elder never intended to interrogate Jemalemin concerning Damowan's accusation. The fate of the Ginginmarin was at the edge of a precipice. An entire race might be bumped into oblivion by a single elder vaunting his language skills.

Temmonin glanced at Kashtawa to see what was in that Salamander's eyes. The Mitsa-Mitsa did not offer anything except a look of friendship. But it was a consolation to see acceptance from him, especially given the fact that his clan dominated this island. Temmonin smiled at Kashtawa and then switched his gaze to the Ginginmarin. Mishchag stared forward, a hulk of innocence.

Jemalemin stood up suddenly. Damowan raised his brows. Temmonin completely forgot about Kashtawa and Mishchag and looked intently at the boy. "You don't need to try to judge my brother in his absence. I'm here. I'll say what I know about him." Temmonin winced. Jemalemin had just given in without the least bit of a fight. The youngest Ek-Birin continued. "He was gonna leave me fall off a cliff. We had to yell at him to git him to help out. He was jus' gonna go away and leave me fall. And I'm his brother."

The presiding elder's eyes widened enough to show that he had been moved. But he loosed his grip on his stoicism for only a moment. After his face had leveled itself again, he slowly raised his hand to stop Jemalemin from speaking further. "My son, I do not forbid you to speak--we welcome such information. Yet, please. . ." The elder released an ambiguous sound; perhaps a laugh of exasperation. Temmonin sensed him trying to cover himself. Probably, this elder had expected anything but such candid innocence. "Proceed with caution."

The elders present could not control their surprise and more than one of them smiled. And though Temmonin could see on their cheeks the temptation to patronize Jemalemin, he thought he could also read a certain respect in most of them. Jemalemin had done what not a single one of them had ever imagined doing. Or perhaps they had imagined doing such a thing but had never thought they would see it happen in their lifetime. Temmonin himself had seen men die from torture without saying a word when it was obvious that they were withholding information and that they themselves were innocent. Jemalemin was probably too young to understand the implications of his actions.

"Chaneerem took a stupid oath to take revenge on Temmonin and Damowan and the whole village thought it was stupid too." Temmonin began to dread what Jemalemin would say next. "The whole village is sick of him. He's my brother but he's tortured me my whole life. He only cares about himself. If he takes an army up there, he's gonna make us look real bad. He might even hurt a bunch of his own people to git what he wants."

Temmonin was thoroughly embarrassed by this time. He imagined that the boy could now say nothing that could possibly make his own situation worse. Chaneerem, if he heard about this testimony--and Temmonin could not picture such news bypassing the talon-licker's thirsty ears--he would become a volcano. There was no longer any escape for Jemalemin. Still, he continued.

"We all got took underground to that place and Chaneerem knows the whole story. He was there. He saw Mishchag rescue us. He saw how almost everybody there treated us good. It was jus' some of 'em that made that secret conspiracy thing. Chaneerem knows that. He jus' hates everything. He jus' loves to be mad at people. Those people aren't bad. They jus' don't know how to talk to us so they picked me and my brother and Temmonin and Damowan to be helpers. Now, Chaneerem jus' wants to kill 'em. We gotta talk to 'em, not kill 'em." Jemalemin looked exhausted after having spoken. He sat down shaking.

"Jemalemin of the Ek-Birin," the presiding elder said. "In keeping with the courage you have just displayed, I must admit that you have surprised me, and. . ." He motioned to the assembly. "I would guess, the entire forum. It is never the custom of our people to doubt the testimony of blood. If your word were to be found untrue, you would lose your place in your family and in our society. As it is, you have risked much and it remains to be seen whose fellowship you will retain. But you have chosen to step into the fire and for this you will always be respected."

The elder looked as if he had just washed his hands and dried them on Jemalemin's loincloth. Then, he began again with a relieved look on his face. "My brothers," he now directed his words to his colleagues. "With this information now in our hands, we must further discuss our options. How shall we proceed? We must discontinue the advance on the porcupine-people and reconsider our course of action. But, the question is, 'How?'"

Another elder spoke. "It is customary, is it not, to send a group of warriors to signal the withdrawal of an aggression, thereby allowing them that receive the message the security of receiving such information from a variety of persons and not simply from the mouth of one or two?" Temmonin had never heard such a flowering of speech about so simple a subject. He glanced at Damowan who rolled his eyes and smirked. Temmonin almost laughed aloud. In the midst of this situation, the tension in his body had increased to the point that he was not sure he could control it any longer.

"Well said, my brother of the Ek-Rignara." When the Badger elder reacted with such enthusiasm, all of the elders added their assent with murmurs and grunts and nods. Temmonin recoiled in distaste at the council's excitement over a beautifully constructed sentence. They seemed more interested in verbiage than life. Temmonin felt compelled to look at his brother again and, as he did so, he felt as if he were looking at his own reflection. It was as if Damowan had just been pounded by a mud clod of nausea, his eyes glazed and his chin pulled back into his neck as his gaze met Temmonin's. He and his younger brother had spent years together perfecting this expression of disgust and Damowan's performance was particularly hilarious at this moment. And Temmonin knew without a doubt that his own face looked exactly like Damowan's. Laughter spurted out of his lips. He had to bury his face in his chest and bring his hand up to cover his forehead. He could not look at Damowan again. And he knew his brother was also laughing and trying to avoid being seen.

As he finally came to control of himself, Temmonin sat up again with as pale a face as he could muster. No one seemed to have noticed. He was relieved. Occasionally, he felt smiles pushing to the surface of his face but he was able to hold them down. He ignored his pressing desire to peek at Damowan. They might destroy all of Jemalemin's work if they were not careful. Why this urge overtook them in such inopportune moments, he could not decide.

The council continued. They chose a group of Salamanders from the mainland to withdraw the attack. They directed Kashtawa to lead the party and to take Temmonin, Damowan, Jemalemin, and Mishchag with them. Temmonin was pleased that there was no disagreement about the appropriateness of the Ek-Birin and the single Ginginmarin joining this mission. For a time, at least, the council seemed to have lessened their distrust in them. Perhaps, they had transferred it to Chaneerem. Perhaps not. Temmonin thought not.

Because the council did not finish until it was time for the evening meal, Kashtawa thought it best to remain on the island until morning. The travelers welcomed the idea. In fact, Jemalemin and Damowan were almost too tired to eat. But they did eat. Then they slept for almost ten hours.

Dawn came grey; overcast. Temmonin was eager to move north. He woke early and slipped out of their sleeping quarters into the summer heat. Seating himself on a stump, he began to picture what might already have happened in the caves. Part of him despised Chaneerem. The other part recognized in himself the potential to do things far more evil. Only shame had tamed him. Somehow, Chaneerem had lied to himself more often and with greater urgency than Temmonin had. Or perhaps Chaneerem was simply happy with the island he had created of himself. Perhaps he knew of no real escape and, therefore, was making everything as comfortable as possible for himself. Perhaps he thought everyone else was doing the same thing. Temmonin wished that, for once in their lives, the two of them could talk with no hostility; like the friends they could have been. He shook his head.

Without him noticing, a damselfly had landed on his shoulder, its penetrating sky-blue reminding him of what the clouds now covered. Temmonin was studying it as the others exited the longhouse where they had slept. The insect quickly disappeared as Damowan approached, the Chrebin on his shoulder. Mishchag followed, stopping to unsnag a group of quills from the doorpost. As he finished, he raised his hand to cover his eyes from the white above. Jemalemin followed him. Kashtawa came out last. The Salamander nodded and smiled at Temmonin and immediately rounded the corner of the house and walked away from the rest. Temmonin thought he was probably arranging

their departure with the other warriors who had
accompanied them. He was right.

Within moments, Kashtawa returned with his
eight comrades and directed the entire party toward
the meeting place. There, they ate a quick breakfast
of wild rice stew and deer jerky before boarding the
canoes and pushing into Moza-Imsaw.

Temmonin became slightly drunk with the
smell of the green water beneath his paddle. And
soon the early morning sun was sweltering. It
burned a hole through the veil that had separated it
from the lake and the herons that occasionally
worked their way across the water. Mishchag
squinted and wiped tears from his eyes. The rowers
began to sweat.

The sweat rolled down Temmonin's sides and
down his back. But he loved this heat because it
added to his drunkenness. His arms and chest and
legs fell into a perfect rhythm with the other rowers,
allowing his mind to float alongside the canoe and
to dream. And his dreaming meandered through a
thousand different forests, a thousand green seas.
But in every dream, he saw Zheva. She was always
watching--he performing. He paddled for her. He
sweat for her. He ran into the midst of pain only
for her. He saw from the corner of his eye how she
watched. And he knew that if he turned to
acknowledge her, her cheeks would flush like the
essence of their mutual love. As the sun intensified,
so did his dreaming.

He became a flicker and he sailed across the
olive sea in counterpoint to the waves beneath his
speckled breast. He flew forward. He did not
consider the past. He dreamt of his wife and his
children--strong sons, strong daughters, laughing
and dancing around the bonfires of the North
Mountains. He flew with direct intent into the heart

of the future. His mother and father played with their grandchildren there. Of course, Uncle Damowan threw his nephews into the lake and wrestled with them. His own sons learned to love their cousins in the shadows of the ever-present willows. But Temmonin flew through their swaying branches and beyond. He saw how his own grandchildren were born and set on his knees. He saw the honor he received for all that he had done in his life.

Then, he felt stupid.

When his daydream ended, he looked up to see that the overcast had replaced the blue sky again. At this point, the sun was only smoldering, barely visible behind its cover. And the team was still rowing. Of course, Temmonin was also still rowing. His thoughts rarely demanded the full attention of his body and this instance, like so many others, came and went without the notice of any of his companions. Some time later, they reached the shore.

In the village on that shore, the Mitsa-Mitsa spent some time gathering supplies, informing their elders of the news, and saying good-bye to their families. The stop was brief. Before long, they were traveling north through the forests on the foothills of Imnanaw-Kanat.

"Looks like we'll have this place memorized before long," Damowan spoke after the group had hiked through a familiar stretch of forest.

"I'll betcha Chaneerem purposely picked a different way back to the Ginginmarin jus' so he wouldn't have to run into us," Temmonin posed. "And I'll bet he never let the others know the real reason why he didn't take the most direct route. He probably made up some stupid story and they all believed it."

"Why does everybody believe him?" Damowan complained. "It's so obvious what's going on in his wicked, nasty head. That guy can't hide a thing from me."

"Somehow, I think he just bullies people into believin' him. Probably does the same thing to himself." Temmonin smiled.

Damowan laughed as he replied, "He's the only guy I know who could live with himself in the middle of so many lies. He's like this big, fat, warty frog sittin' in his stinkin', slimy swamp. Sittin' in his stupid swamp of lies. Just spittin' 'em out and sittin' in 'em."

Temmonin laughed loudly at such a perfect metaphor. A few Salamanders and Jemalemin and Mishchag glanced back at them but no one seemed to mind that they were having such a good time. Temmonin made a frog-face, the corners of his mouth pulled back to his ears and his eyelids drooping. Then he burped out some sounds. Damowan roared and followed with his own frog imitation. Of course, his version was more ugly and exaggerated than his older brother's. It made Temmonin laugh not only because it was funny in and of itself but also because Damowan always had to improve on anything funny that Temmonin did. Yet Temmonin was not bothered by his younger brother's competition because the results were always hilarious. In fact, he often initiated the process just to see where Damowan would take it. After a while, they finished acting like frogs and settled into their hike. Then, Temmonin saw the future.

"I hope he doesn't totally destroy their place."

Both hiked in silence for a while. The sun occasionally worked its way through the haze above them. Birds were everywhere. The pine forest breathed its fragrance into the thick, summer air. Temmonin walked and thought, only partially able to enjoy the beauty around him.

"He's prob'ly gonna kill as many as he can," Damowan stabbed into the silence. "I jus' know him. He'll surprise 'em if he can. He'll waste the place. He'll burn it. He'd love that, wouldn't he--to hear the sound of screaming women and children just on the other side of the boulder he blocked the door with. And totally satisfied as he sees the smoke comin' out, knowing that's what's killin' 'em, knowin' he started it." Damowan's shoulders were tensing and that tension was spreading into his face and into his arms and his fists. "I can't believe he can be such a jerk!"

"Damowan, we're not sure yet," Temmonin cautioned, only slightly convinced of his own statement. "Let's wait until we get there. There's no reason to git yerself all worked up."

Eventually, the tension in Damowan's shoulders lessened as his thoughts were diluted by the hike and the surroundings. After sometime, he was noticeably calmer. But in Temmonin, the thoughts began to press against each other like branches at a beaver dam. Each new possibility added to the jam. And the whole thing became a force that wedged itself into Temmonin's entire consciousness. He could not escape it. He saw the grotesque but strangely beautiful faces of the Ginginmarin all gathered into a single chamber, awaiting their own execution. Or perhaps Chaneerem would force them to come to the surface into the bright sun and torture them in their blindness. Maybe a new idea would strike the talon-licker. Maybe he would tie them to the ground and fill their mouths with salt and watch them sweat their way into dehydration. He could not even guess what other tortures Chaneerem had planned. The oath-taker could outdream Temmonin even if he were busy doing several other things at the same time. Such a huge, wicked imagination.

Yet Temmonin had to wonder why it was so easy for him to guess Chaneerem's motives and to picture his newest nightmare. He wondered really how different he was than that man. Was it just chance that took the talon-licker down the path of bitter, lonely self-preservation and Temmonin more into the mainstream of self-control. Was it anything Temmonin had done or was it only his family that had saved him. Probably it was the Creator. But he wondered if he deserved such special attention. The difference between Chaneerem and himself was only that Temmonin had stopped doing some of the things that came to his mind. Temmonin wondered how big of a difference that was.

As the days past, all three of the Ek-Birin felt their fear growing. But, as they spoke about it, they limited their conversations to their Ek-Birin dialect so that Mishchag would not understand.

"I think we gotta tell him," Jemalemin said one day as they were eating.

Damowan and Temmonin just looked at the boy.

"He should know, right?" Jemalemin asked.

"Yea, but who's gonna say it?" Damowan replied.

"I will," Temmonin said seriously.

"Why don't we all," Damowan suggested.

"When?" Jemalemin asked.

"Pretty soon, I think, 'cuz this is lookin' kinda rude, talkin' right in front of him in Ek-Birin." Temmonin was embarrassed that Jemalemin had brought the idea up in such uncomfortable circumstances.

Damowan turned to Mishchag and began in Mokhamoyuba, "Mishchag, sorry about speakin' our language and leavin' you out of our conversation but we were talkin' about the Ginginmarin." He looked to Temmonin expectantly.

Temmonin was irritated that his brother had not continued, but then he remembered that he had volunteered to explain. He swallowed before he spoke.

"Mishchag, we've gotta tell ya somethin' about Chaneerem. We think he mighta already done some terrible stuff to yer underground village. He's a crazy man when it comes to revenge and we don't know if your people'll be able to get ready fer his kinda war."

The Ginginmarin was quiet. Over the past couple of days, his eyes seemed to have fully adjusted to the sunlight. He was now able to look at the others without squinting or covering his eyes.

"Will they be ready fer this at all, Mishchag?" Temmonin's eyebrows rose higher.

"I cannot to tell you," replied the hulk in Mokhamoyuba. "I do not to know. But I do not think so much."

Temmonin glanced at Damowan with dejection in his eyes. They were now less than a day from the valley and he almost wished they were weeks away. He wanted to be there. He needed to see what had happened and to help if he could. But he could see no reason why any Ginginmarin would ever trust him after what Chaneerem had probably already done to them. He was happy that at least Mishchag would understand--his situation was the exact mirror-image of theirs.

"Mishchag," Damowan spoke again. "We'll be here fer you. You were here fer us when yer people turned on us. We'll be with you too."

"We made the ceremony of friendship," Jemalemin added.

"What're you gonna do if yer village is destroyed?" Temmonin asked. After the question left his lips, he partly regretted it.

"I do not to know," Mishchag sighed. "I never thought this would be to happen."

None of them spoke again during that meal.

Temmonin could not sleep that night. He lay on his back looking at the sky. The moon was strong and the clouds that crossed its face were thin strips of smoke rising from the paws of the Fire-bear. Somewhere, the Gorma was waiting. Temmonin was now nearing the circle of thorn-trees but he could not see where the beast was hiding. Deep beneath the mountains was that circle of thorn-trees and Chaneerem was more angry than twenty Gormas. The talon-licker was waiting there and Temmonin felt completely powerless. His heroic dreams were now frightened crickets that hide beneath rocks, no longer chirping as they had before. He knew he must face Chaneerem and the other warriors. He knew he must face the Ginginmarin. He knew he must face the disgusting truth of the world upon which this moon now shone so lovingly.

If only Chaneerem could look long enough at this moon, he would finally have to see how sad his life had become. If only one time, he could rest in its silver light, Temmonin was sure he would be wooed into compassion. If only Temmonin could push this moon beneath the mountains so that its face could shine on the oath-taker's face, on the faces of the Ginginmarin who were creating the mutants, he knew that they would cry together as he now cried.

Tears had soaked his temples and the hair above his ears but he did not care. He cried for the Ginginmarin who would never see this moon again. Then he pictured Mishchag discovering his mother and father and his whole family dead. He felt the emptiness claw at his soul like a raven pecking at the eye of a dying consciousness. But his consciousness was not sinking into death--it was being pushed farther into the light of the moon. The sadness only became sadder as it saw the beauty it might have become. And he only became more alive as he wept for the infection that now spilled out of Chaneerem's soul into the hearts of the hundred warriors who accompanied him. His tears doubled as he saw whole villages of innocent Ginginmarin scattered dead on the floors of their own caves, none of them even having a chance to hear an explanation for this untimely fate. His tears continued as the clouds drifted across the sky. He thought of his own mother and father and sister and grandparents and how much he missed them. And, of course, Zheva. But they were all far away, unaware of his tears. In his pain, he was more alive than at any other time in his life.

Damowan was sleeping next to him but there, in his pool of tears, Temmonin was alone; alive and alone. The black sky was as empty as anything he had ever known. It swallowed the light from the moon as a man swallows spit--not even noticing what he has just done. Enchanted by this empty, empty beauty, Temmonin finally fell to sleep.

They reached the entrance to the caves at noon the next day. Temmonin's anticipation was overwhelming and he could infer from Damowan's silence that his brother was also stressed. By looking at the approach to the entrance, their party could see the evidence of much activity. Quills were everywhere. Signs of struggle had imprinted the sand and had broken small branches off some of the surrounding trees. The pale memory of dried blood was smeared on several rocks. And in many places, Temmonin could see drag-marks. But he could make no certain conclusion as to what exactly had happened.

"He's definitely been here," Damowan stated.

Mishchag was already at the entrance to the cave. But he had not stepped in. He hesitated like a child does before jumping into a cold river. Kashtawa and Temmonin came alongside him and nodded as they passed him and peeked into the corridor. No sign of life. The two came back out and Kashtawa gave an order to light torches. After a moment and before Temmonin could think very much, they were out of the sun and in the passage.

He expected at any moment to see someone alive. Nothing moved. They continued at a medium pace. The leaders, Kashtawa and Damowan, walked carefully forward. From behind, Temmonin could see that his brother was holding himself back. Still no sign of life. Only shadows scurried across the corridor walls ahead of their torches. Soon, Temmonin thought he recognized the place where the passage widened.

"Is this it?" He pointed forward as he asked Mishchag.

Mishchag seemed to have been in a trance as he lumbered forward. But Temmonin's question broke him out of it. "Yes."

Temmonin stared more intensely into the black hole that grew with each step. What awaited them there? Surely Chaneerem had already left the place. But would they find any Ginginmarin still alive? Or was it possible that the porcupine-people had repelled the attack? Would they find children crying, looking for their parents? Would they find old Ginginmarin hobbling around, trying to figure out what had happened?

Then they entered the hall.

Their torches lit up the entire place. No movement. No sound. Nothing was there except for an overturned cooking pot and embers that had obviously been kicked. Temmonin took a look at Damowan. The Chrebin on his shoulder was staring intensely at Mishchag, as if waiting to stare him down. But Mishchag did not seem the least bit interested. The quill-man was scanning his barren world, attempting to make some sense of the few signs he could see. Still, the Chrebin stared.

Mishchag motioned toward a corridor. Kashtawa, Damowan, and a few others accompanied the porcupine man while the rest followed behind. Temmonin continuously glanced behind the group to see if they were being followed or ambushed. Still, no movement anywhere. They pushed forward and searched each room, only to find it as empty as the last. Temmonin pricked himself mentally to keep his guard up. It was only too easy to be surprised under such circumstances. He kept his dagger in one hand and the other hand free beside him. But the farther they went, the less it seemed he would need either.

There were items in each room on the floors or on the walls or on tables. Signs of struggle were everywhere but it was far from obvious what had happened. In certain spots, it was almost apparent that a murder had taken place. Burgundy stained the rock floor in many places. But it was so silent. Could the quill-people have known what was coming--or at least most of them--and could they have escaped before Chaneerem got here? Maybe they knew that they should abandon their village as

soon as the four Ek-Birin had escaped with
Mishchag. Their bodies and their magic were slow,
but their minds were as quick or possibly quicker
than those of the people of the tribes. It must be
frustrating for them to be so stifled by the physical
world. It must be devastating to watch centuries of
planning wasted in a moment. Temmonin felt the
tragedy in his gut like block of granite.

After having completed a search of the entire
village including all of the secret rooms that
Mishchag knew of, the party found not a single
body--no Ginginmarin, no people of the tribes. The
search party formed a loose circle in the passageway.

"So, there's nothin' here that gives you any
clues, Mishchag?" Temmonin posed in
Mokhamoyuba."Is anything missin'?" Kashtawa
added.

The Ginginmarin was silent for a while. "No,"
he said finally. "I cannot to think of what is wrong
here. It is so strange. We do not to know much
about this place."

"You mean about what happened here?"
Temmonin attempted clarify Mishchag's ambiguity.

"Yes, I mean this," said the quill-man. "Wait!"
And then he spoke in Ginginmarin quickly and
quietly to the Ek-Birin. "There are maps--they
show our villages and secret rooms and passages."

"What's he sayin'?" one of the Salamanders
demanded nervously.

Damowan turned and waved his hand. "No
big deal. He was just expressin' his frustration in
the language he knows best"

The warrior eyed Damowan suspiciously for a
moment and then relaxed a bit. Temmonin knew
that none of the Salamanders had been convinced
that Damowan had told them the truth but they

seemed to be willing to give the Ginginmarin a little room.

"Perhaps one of my people has maked marks into the room with tablets," Mishchag offered in Mokhamoyuba.

"What's he sayin'?" the same warrior asked with renewed distrust. "What's that supposed to mean? Maked marks?"

"I know it sounds weird but they do somethin' strange--every one of their words has a picture," Temmonin explained. "And they keep words from their grandfathers' grandfathers on copper plates."

"What?" Kashtawa looked irritated.

"Come see," Temmonin pointed. "Mishchag, this way, right?"

"Yes." The hulk moved down the hallway towards the main chamber. Shortly, they turned left into the same room the Ek-Birin had visited earlier that summer. There was just enough room for all the warriors.

"I think to here," Mishchag immediately began his search for the maps. "Yes, to here. . ." Then he spoke in Ginginmarin, "No! One is missing!"

"In Mokhamoyuba!" the same Salamander commanded.

"One of 'em's missin'," Damowan rolled his eyes as he translated. And, with that roll of his eyes, he had done everything short of tell the man verbally how irritated he was at him. Temmonin laughed to himself.

"Lemme see that!" The warrior pushed forward to grab the tablet Mishchag was inspecting.

"Y'know, ya may as well jus' trust us, fella!" Damowan partially barred the Salamander's way with an outstretched arm. "If we were gonna pull some kinda trick, we'd have done it by now. Jus' take it easy, eh?"

Temmonin thought this might ignite open aggression. The salamander did stop at Damowan's arm but his eyes and his nostrils flared to almost twice their size. In his face, blood danced and screamed for Damowan to move his arm.

"He's right, Mamgachin," Kashtawa interjected. "These men're fine. They're with us."

Mamgachin gathered all of his strength to control the anger that was festering beneath his chocolate and burgundy skin. But he could not repress a look that told Damowan never to do such a careless thing again. And Temmonin could not repress a smile.

"But I can see the plate, can't I?" Mamgachin asked as he moved beyond Damowan and next to Mishchag. He did not expect an answer. He gazed at the tablet for a few minutes then put it back on to the table. "I don't know what it is." He shrugged his shoulders as he backed away from the Ginginmarin and towards one of the walls.

Temmonin caught his brother in the corner of his eye. Damowan contorted his face and silently mouthed the words, "I don't know what it is." And he shrugged his shoulders so slightly that no one except Temmonin could possibly notice.

Temmonin fought to keep a stern face as he mouthed the words, "Shut up!" But inside, he wished Damowan would never stop.

"Someone has taked plates from this place-- probably my brothers. But Chaneerem also can to understand the markings." Mishchag was sorting through the copper plates as he spoke.

"Chaneerem?" Temmonin had not yet thought of this possibility. "O, man, we don't want him to have that stuff!"

"Yea, but he always gets his hands on that kind of stuff, doesn't he?" Damowan said.

"This is bad," added Jemalemin. "This is real bad."

Kashtawa looked very concerned. "He'll go to more villages, won't he?"

"As many as he can before we catch up to him," Damowan.

"But we can move quicker," argued Kashtawa. "We can reach him soon."

"Let's hope so," Temmonin said.

"But we do not even to know where he has going," Mishchag said.

"Where's the closest Ginginmarin village?" Temmonin asked.

"Or the next biggest," Damowan countered.

"Knowin' him, he'll have it all figured out how he can hit as many of 'em as he can as quickly as he can," Temmonin reasoned. "He'll go straight to the closest village, Damowan."

"That's exactly what I'm saying. He'll prob'ly go to the biggest village," Damowan returned. "That way he can nail more of 'em."

"Well, either way, Damowan." Temmonin was annoyed. "I'm just saying he'd prob'ly go to the closest place first."

"And I'm just saying he'd prob'ly go to the biggest one so. . ." And then Damowan threw up his hands as if to walk away. Suddenly, he turned back. "Okay, Jemalemin, what do you think?"

Temmonin immediately nodded and faced Jemalemin, making it clear that he saw Damowan's idea as a valid way of resolving their conflict.

"I don't know," Jemalemin squirmed a little under this kind of pressure. He obviously did not want to disappoint either of his best friends. And he was probably also intimidated by this crowd around him. "I think maybe the nearest village."

Temmonin felt an instant rush of satisfaction at having been proven right. The feeling lasted only until he looked at Damowan. His younger brother had that abashed look that told Temmonin they would not be able to feel comfortable with each other for a while. He hated these times. And, of course, they did not have time to talk the thing through.

"And which way to the nearest village?" Kashtawa was eager to prevent bloodshed, a fact that encouraged Temmonin. "We might be able to catch him there."

"Olgashchimna is to southeast of here," Mishchag responded. "One day by foot. If Chaneerem did not gone there yet, I am sure we will can to find information about what did happened there. Perhaps my people fled to there after these three and me ran away from here."

"Will you lead us there?" Kashtawa asked.

"I will." And Mishchag moved through the Salamanders and into the corridor.

The entire group continued to look into every room as they exited the caves. Still, they were not gratified by a single movement or sound. They left the main cavern and climbed out into the afternoon sun through the same silence through which they had entered.

And except for the songs of birds and the occasional whirring of grasshoppers, the same silence ruled this summer day. The party once again searched the area just outside the cave entrance as they passed on from there. By this time, Temmonin could not bring himself to expect anything. He was now sure that if they encountered Chaneerem's war party or the Ginginmarin, it would not be in this place.

Temmonin thought Mishchag would turn toward the valley floor and eventually ascend through the narrow crack at the northeast end of the valley. But the quill-man did not.

"Mishchag," Temmonin objected. "Didn't we jus' pass the trail to the valley floor and the river?"

"Yes, we did," answered Mishchag. "But there are many things about these mountains that your people have never to known."

The porcupine man continued to hug the cavern wall until, at one point, he turned and faced it. Then, he walked through it. Temmonin was surprised, but then remembered the same type of wall in the caverns below. It suddenly struck him as a bit spooky that there might be places like this everywhere in the land--all results of the patient magic of a displaced race which longed once again to own some part of the light of the moon. How much was being manipulated that he and his people could never know of? He walked through the sheet of stone in front of him. The others followed. The passage led steadily upward.

"Mishchag," Temmonin whispered in Ginginmarin as he caught up to the leader. "Why would you show so many of us this kind of a secret? I mean, why didn't you just go the long way so you didn't have to show us this secret passage?"

"None of you will never again can to find it," Mishchag answered in Mokhamoyuba.

"But it's just back there," said Temmonin. "I remember the exact trees and the way the cliff curves over your head."

Mishchag laughed a strange, hoarse, high-pitched laugh. "It is not this so simple, my friend. Slow magic takes the long time to understand."

Temmonin raised his eyebrows as they continued up the hidden passageway. Somehow,

the thing was situated in such a way that the
afternoon sun could shine into it. Although the
light was not bright, Temmonin and the others had
no problem following the Ginginmarin. In minutes,
they were at the top.

They filed out of the throat of the corridor and
gathered as a group before moving on. Behind
them was a short cliff about the height of a man
standing on another one's shoulder. In front of
them were a pine forest and the occasional glint of
the late afternoon sun piercing through it. A few
clouds smeared the otherwise robin-egg sky. As the
last of the party entered the light of day, Damowan's
face soured and wrinkled.

"What's that smell? Awww, sick!!"

Temmonin could smell it too. He almost
choked. Suddenly, the whole group was cursing and
spitting and searching for the source of the stench.

"That's the most disgusting stench I've ever
smelled in my life!" Damowan coughed and started
up the embankment to his right.

Temmonin noticed what he guessed his
brother had already noticed. Smoke was trailing
over the cliff behind them. Damowan was going to
investigate. Temmonin followed him up along with
the others. Soon, Temmonin reached his brother's
side at the crest of the small cliff.

Tears had already begun to roll from his eyes
because of the reek in the air but, when he pulled
himself over the edge, he was ripped to the heart.
He and Damowan immediately began to weep.
They could not speak. They could not warn the
others. They could only stand and cover their
mouths and noses to try to avoid the smoke.

In front of them was a heap of black, black
death so deep and horrible it would not allow them
to turn away. Hundreds of bodies were still

burning--Ginginmarin bodies. Some had been
impaled in a small circle and these jutted out of the
charred heap like frozen geysers of bitterness.
There were arms and legs lying around the
perimeter of the circle. There were small children
pinned to the unforgiving granite with spears
through their abdomens. Old men. Old women.
Bodies. So many bodies. And the smoke was still
fuming. No fire roaring. No crackling embers. Just
a slow fuming fire. The soul of this people hovered
just inches above the bodies, weeping and burning
out the wretched eulogy that filled the nostrils of the
people of the confederation. After all the
Salamanders and Jemalemin had reached the crest,
Mishchag did so also.

As he lifted his ragged head, the survivor of his
village squinted and pushed himself forward by
infinitesimal increments into the scene in front of
him. He did not look around or drop his jaw. He
seemed to have become a protrusion of the rock
beneath his feet. And his paralysis lasted forever.
After that eternity, he walked forward. First, he
passed a child. He did not actually look at the child,
but Temmonin saw that, as Mishchag lumbered by,
he held out his hand as if to collect the girl's spirit
from the shell of her body. He walked farther
through the myriad of limbs that were strewn across
the earth. He continued directly toward one of his
fellows who had been raised and roasted on a thick
stake. He stopped there about an arm's length from
the feet of the corpse. He did not raise his head to
view it. He simply stopped there. From behind
him, Temmonin and Damowan and Jemalemin and
the others could see nothing of his frozen
expression.

Then, almost unnoticeably, his head jerked to
the side. But in such stark, still, quiet anticipation, it

was as telling as the cry of a hawk. Mishchag
reached his left arm toward a black and smoldering
hump only a few steps away. His knees seemed to
be drawn with his arm and he crashed to the
ground. As he knelt there slumped on himself, the
whole world was silent in deference to him.
Temmonin's tears stopped for a moment as he
waited to see what would happen next. He waited a
long time.

Then, he began to hear something like the
sound of a mosquito whirring at the far edge of
earshot. At first, he could not decide where it was
coming from. From inside his own head? But then
it started to grow. It sounded almost like a beehive
and he could now hear that it came from Mishchag.
It built upon itself more quickly until the hulk was
howling; screaming. And Temmonin was struck so
deeply that his heart poured out its compassion like
a flash flood. Tears soaked his cheeks as he listened
to the massive sobs the porcupine-man choked out.
Mishchag heaved. He shook. He filled the sky with
such intense weeping that the clouds swelled with
blood and the mountains quivered. And, in that
moment, the world was torn a little farther from
itself. After a long time, the weeping stopped.

Temmonin approached Mishchag.

"My mother," the mourning Ginginmarin
whispered in his own language. "My grandmother."
He tried to motion with his arms to point out where
each was, but his arms were saturated with the
rancid oil of desperation and they only flopped back
onto his thighs. "And my father, my sister. . .all
here." And his sobs continued. Temmonin stood a
long time listening. Then he quietly walked back to
Damowan and the others to explain.

Matthew John Schellenberg

XV.   Or could it be that we are again like
children, unreasonably fickle about the gifts we have
been given? Is the hope in the vague memory, of
that which we have long ago lost, and the possibility
of losing such wonderful things by doing that which
causes us to lose wonderful things really so
objectively repulsive. Or is it simply that we refuse
to be pleased. Could it be that when we mature and
reflect on our obstinacy, when we ponder back
upon all that we have accepted and rejected from
the hand of the creator, when we finally paddle our
way to the island of decision where our weak vision
will be emblazoned to life by a light a thousand
times brighter than that of the sun and the moon,
could it be that then we will regret our refusal of
that which we were offered, could it be that then we
will be ashamed that we did not trust that the one
who created vision could see farther than we
ourselves could see? Perhaps he can see farther
than we can.

CHAPTER 15

It was late that evening when Temmonin, Kashtawa, and the others decided to climb back down the small embankment behind them and set up camp. Mishchag had not moved and, although the Ek-Birin and the Salamanders felt compelled to push on and to stop Chaneerem from repeating himself at the next Ginginmarin village, they could not bear to pull their guide away from his tears. The next morning, Temmonin woke early. He retraced his steps up to the massacre mound to find that the porcupine man still had not moved. Temmonin decided to join him. He walked up to Mishchag and knelt beside him and waited.

Not too much later, the quill-man spoke in Ginginmarin. "I give them to the ground. I give them all away. Only my life is mine and even that not sure. May all their enemies pay for hatred and for evil. And may all debts be counted and finished on this day.

I give them to the moon. She will not cease to shine. Her power and her memory will wash their bones in death. The vultures will be hungry and satisfy their need and take the moon into their bellies and carry them inside.

I give them to the night; the sea in which we swim. I lay my claims aside now. I walk now only to remember. And this I will remember in view of every star, that they once lived among us and passed among the pines.

I give them to my heart, like trees which fall and rot and feed the trees still standing. I will not fall as well. The world is sun and shadow, the world is noon and night, and I will cry in sorrow but I will laugh in truth.

Someday soon, the dust will settle."

Mishchag stood slowly, stretched his arms out in front of himself, and struck his chest three times with both fists.

"We can go now," the Ginginmarin said solemnly.

Temmonin was shocked as Mishchag turned and left the pyre. He did not seem concerned about raising his people to their rest. It seemed just this short poem was enough to close the lives of his entire village. But he needed to follow the hulk or perhaps he might cause offense.

"That is all?" Temmonin asked sheepishly in Ginginmarin.

"Nothing more would be proper, would it? The world is cruel. But we live on." Temmonin could sense no bitterness in Mishchag's voice, only a strange mixture of fatalism and resolve. He was struck with understanding as to how this race coped with life. After centuries, their eulogy still retained such connection with life above ground. Their ceremonies were as serious as knives and they were built like a frame around the Ginginmarin to lessen the weight of the mountain that threatened to crush them.

As far as Temmonin could see, all of the Salamanders now had enough proof that Mishchag was not a spy. None of them seemed suspicious or demanding anymore. They followed his lead without question along the eastern side of Imnanaw-Kanat and south towards Zubzza, the Fat Gorge. Chaneerem's war party had left undeniable signs behind themselves as they traveled. They were not very careful to hide their trail. And perhaps Chaneerem was so full of vengeance that he did not care.

Rain soaked the forest that day. But it was not uncomfortable to hike in. Actually, it was refreshing to Temmonin and Damowan. The smell of wet wood and leaves helped them remember that the world could indeed be a beautiful place. That smell helped to purge their noses of the smell of burning. Mishchag's grief had not noticeably lessened but Temmonin thought that at this point almost nothing short of the resurrection of his village could change that.

That evening, after they had eaten their third meal, they passed through a small valley that led to a deep ravine. The party could still see signs of Chaneerem's passing.

"This is Olgashchimna at the mouth of this ravine-place," Mishchag announced in Mokhamoyuba.

Then he moved forward again. Temmonin's blood began to heat up. Damowan leaned into Temmonin and whispered, "We musta missed him again."

Damowan was right. The smell of burning had been limited by the rain, but it rose to greet them as they rounded the crag that covered the cave entrance. There, lying in two halves, with entrails spilled on the ground between both, was a mass of quills and fur and claws. The porcupine-man had been partially burned. It looked as if the rain had halted the roast. Temmonin saw Mishchag flinch at the sight. It was as if the Ginginmarin had tried to prepare himself for this but had not quite succeeded.

The entrance to the village, which was actually a hole just large enough for a man to squeeze through, was plugged with another blackened Ginginmarin woman. Since she was sheltered from the rain, she was still smoldering.

"Through to here," Mishchag stated, the rain spilling down his nose and cheeks. "This is the entrance." And immediately he grasped the woman's arms and began to pull her from the opening.

It only took a moment for him to clear her away. He did so as if she were not one of his people; as if she were as incidental as the sand and small rocks that crumbled into the hole as he lifted her out of it. And he left her corpse in a careless heap not far from the opening. Temmonin and Damowan and the others watched stunned as he then ignored her and let himself down into the entrance.

Temmonin had to tighten his jaw to hold back a sudden urge to cry for this woman and for the mound of corpses Mishchag had left to rot on the cliff above his village. No ceremony. No respect for their bodies. Just a short poem for his own family and not a word for this woman. He felt something sour seep into the back of his mouth. As he looked around at the others, he could see that they were wrestling with the same distaste. What kind of creatures were the Ginginmarin?

Feeling almost guilty for following Mishchag, Temmonin entered the hole. He was sure that it would be strange for these Salamanders to defend such a race against Chaneerem. Of course, they would still do it. But Temmonin had seen in their faces the kind of disgust that has no interest in listening to explanations. They would obey the word of the council but with no emotional attachment to the quill-people. He too found it difficult to feel much sympathy for a race which treated their dead with such apathy.

He passed through the entrance and dropped to the floor of the passageway. He heard Damowan

just behind him. The cave was dark and full of
death. He had to hold his nose and breathe through
his mouth to avoid the smell but that did not save
him from having to cough as he sucked in smoke.
He stopped short. He suddenly realized that he and
the others would see nothing without torches. He
turned into Damowan, who was rubbing his eyes.
They bumped.

"We need some torches," Temmonin
explained. "Can't see a single thing down here."

"Well, I don't have any," Damowan said
defensively, still rubbing his eyes as if sand had
made its way into them.

"Yea, but you could ask the others,"
Temmonin replied irritated. Then he pushed past
his younger brother and called up through the
opening himself. "We need torches. It's all black
down here."

"Everything's soaked!" Kashtawa called back
through the rain. "We'll have to go search for some
dry stuff in the woods."

The two Ek-Birin brothers leaned against the
cave walls and waited for torches. As Temmonin's
eyes adjusted, he recognized the shapes of bodies
slumped against the granite along the corridor.
From the look of it, Chaneerem's group had
surprised this village too. But then it occurred to
him that the other village may not have been
surprised. Perhaps it did not matter whether the
Ginginmarin were aware of an attack or not.
Perhaps they were so slow that no amount of
foreknowledge could allow them to prepare. Maybe
they had no idea of where to hide and no possibility
to defend themselves. Temmonin felt pity rise up in
himself. And this pity began to mingle with the
disdain he had been feeling for Mishchag's lack of
respect for the bodies of his dead people.

Temmonin felt as if his stomach were a pot of stew being boiled.

"Man, I am really startin' to hate Chaneerem," Damowan said dryly. "There's no reason fer stuff like this."

Temmonin waited a moment, then replied. "You can see where it came from though. I mean you and I saw that room too--I mean the room where they were makin' all those mutants."

"What? Now yer gonna start defendin' the jerk of the century?" Damowan was incredulous.

"No, I'm not defendin' him!" Temmonin answered with a whine in his voice. "You jus' said there was no reason for this when there actually is-- it jus' wouldn't be enough reason fer you or me to do what Chaneerem's doing."

"Well, I'm glad somebody's makin' sure every word I say is perfectly logical enough fer a speech in front of a full gathering of the council," Damowan complained. "You know, you are my brother and I know you knew exactly what I meant. So why do you always have to do that to me??"

"I don't always have to do that to you." Temmonin retorted with a touch of sarcasm.

"Yer always doin' stuff like that, Temmonin, and you know it." Damowan's reply was definite and demanding.

"Not always, Damowan."

"May as well be..."

"It doesn't matter," Temmonin stated coldly.

"What?"

"It doesn't matter, Damowan. Jus' drop it."

"Oh, of course it doesn't matter to you, cause..."

"I said it doesn't matter so jus' drop it, all right!" Temmonin spat.

"All right," Damowan gave in. He said something else but his voice trailed off as he turned his head and looked up to the opening.

Temmonin could feel from the tone and the melody of his brother's last words that they agreed with what his own conscience was now saying. He had not actually heard any of the words but that was unimportant. Once again, Temmonin had avoided admitting to an obvious fault. But he was as guilty as mud. He was tempted to shove down the rising guilt and to force the issue further with Damowan but he knew that that would only worsen his guilt in the end.

"I'm sorry," Temmonin pushed himself to a point at the edge of his self-control, but then stopped himself short of an actual apology. "I guess it's jus' been too much these past coupla days. I jus' feel like crap."

"I guess that makes sense, "Damowan added, glancing at his brother for a quick moment.

Behind him, Kashtawa's burgundy Mitsa-Mitsa forearms lowered a pair of burning torches into the air above the heads of the Ek-Birin. Damowan turned and reached for them, the Chrebin clutching his hair as he did so. As he grabbed both, Mishchag called from down the corridor.

"It is no need to come." The hulk entered the light like the birth of dread, his small eyes shining crimson like two fresh wounds. "They are all dead. Everything is killed."

Temmonin and Damowan hesitated for a moment. Kashtawa leaned down and made a face that asked for clarification.

"Everything is killed," Mishchag repeated impatiently. "We must to go to the next village."

Temmonin could see from the Ginginmarin's resolve that there was no point in arguing and, since he did not particularly want to personally confirm Mishchag's report, he raised his torch back up to Kashtawa. Damowan followed. Soon, they were again pushing through mud and over the slippery rocks and roots that decorated the trail.

On their way along the western rim of Imnanaw-Kanat, they visited three more villages. There were no survivors in any of them. Just blood and burning death. With each new visit, Mishchag looked more like the corpses of his dead sisters and brothers. And something strange was happening with the Chrebin.

Until now, the tiny creature seemed entirely repulsed by any Ginginmarin it had encountered-- even by Mishchag who had saved Damowan's life. But the squirrel-man was not shrinking away from him any more. Temmonin began to wonder if the creature were simply growing accustomed to porcupine-men when, long before sunrise the next morning, he woke to witness the Chrebin with its hand on Mishchag's temple.

Temmonin did not move. Keeping his head still, he looked around to find the entire camp sleeping. Only the Chrebin had moved. And Mishchag's eyes were open wide to the overcast above him. It was as if he were dreaming without sleeping. Temmonin could not be sure how long the two had been like this, but after about thirty seconds, the Chrebin withdrew his hand and returned to his usual place near Damowan's shoulder. The eyes of the quill-man slid closed and Temmonin could see the tension dissipate from his shoulders as he sank back into sleep. The Ek-Birin could see no obvious reason to be concerned. He decided to continue observing the development of their relationship in the morning.

Temmonin probably slept for another hour when the camp awoke. As they finished breakfast, Mishchag spoke in a dull tone that matched the grey sky above them.

"We will go to Zubzza today."

No one spoke for a moment. This was a change in the plan to continue along through the foothills as close as possible to Imnanaw-Kanat and to visit the many Ginginmarin caves along the rim of these mountains. Yet the Fat Gorge was not far from their present position.

"Is there a village near there?" Kashtawa asked.

"I do not to know if the Ginginmarin live there still. It is an ancient place." Mishchag looked directly at the Chrebin on Damowan's shoulder. "It is the first ancient village of my people when they cannot to live on the land."

"You mean, that's the very first place your ancestors fled to when our ancestors came?" Damowan asked.

"Yes," replied the porcupine-man. "I have reading about this place. I know to where it is. I was never to going there."

"But what if Chaneerem isn't goin' there?" Jemalemin interjected carefully. "Or what if he didn't already go there? Won't we be wastin' time?"

"I have not asked for much things," Mishchag reasoned. "Now we must to do this for my people."

None of the others objected.

That day, as they hiked through forests of cedar, fir, oak, and maple trying to avoid the numerous puddles left by two days of rain, the sun began to find its way through the clouds. By noon, the party was hiking through a welcome bath of warmth. In spite of the fact that they were a group which was tracing the trail of destruction, their mood noticeably lightened. Temmonin came up alongside Damowan on the side opposite the Chrebin.

"I think this has somethin' to do with yer little friend, Dama." He whispered in Ek-Birin as they walked.

"Whaddaya mean?" Damowan was slightly surprised.

"I saw the little guy with his little hand on Mishchag's temple before dawn. I don't think he knew I was watchin'."

"What?"

"Don't act too strange or he'll know we're talkin' about him," Temmonin cautioned. "But it looked to me like he told Mishchag somethin'— y'know, with the hand thing, like with Jemalemin's head when we were here last time. And he communicates with you somehow too, right?"

"Yea, but not with words really," Damowan explained. "I don't even really know if he understands anything we say to each other. We might be totally safe talkin' about him right in front of his face."

"I'm not about to count on that one," Temmonin objected. "I'm jus' sayin' that somethin' happened between them early this mornin'. I don't know how long they were like that—talkin' or whatever; it wasn't with words--but you saw how Mishchag looked straight at yer little man when he was talkin' about this village we're goin' to, right?"

Damowan thought for a moment. "Yea, I guess so. At first, I thought he was lookin' at me. But then it seemed like he couldn't be. So that's what he was doin'." Damowan rolled his eyes around as he worked to put his ideas in order. "Okay, so maybe my man here put it in Mishchag's mind to come over here instead of goin' further south?"

"Exactly," Temmonin nodded. "I mean, why would he take the chance of fallin' farther behind Chaneerem? He doesn't even know if this place still exists."

Damowan's forehead wrinkled as he wrestled with this new information. "So now we have to wonder why did my little man do it."

"I don't think we'll have to wonder long, though," Temmonin added. "We'll be there before the sun goes down."

And they were at the outer rim of Zubzza by the time they were hungry enough to eat the evening meal. Mishchag was chewing on rabbit when he spoke again.

"I do not to know this place. It will to be difficult to finding the entrance."

Some of the Salamanders gave the quill-man strange looks. Temmonin himself wondered how he expected any of the party to be able to help him find the way to a village that might no longer exist. Yet, Mishchag seemed so confident in his goal that no one felt it necessary to demand an explanation for this detour. It was only a few minutes later when the porcupine-man spoke again.

"It is here!" He stood and dropped his food. "Over behind this place." He crossed the clearing where they had set up camp and, as he did so, he nearly kicked through the fire that had cooked his food. He seemed to be listening to something.

Temmonin could not hear a thing but he rose along with several Salamanders and followed the beast. Mishchag disappeared behind a small hill. When the rest of the group rounded a clump of trees to get a better view, they saw him standing and staring down at a squirrel-man. The Chrebin seemed as interested in the Ginginmarin as the hulk was in the little creature. Temmonin looked back at Damowan to see if the Chrebin was still on his shoulder. It was not.

"Guess I shoulda noticed." Damowan shrugged. "He's been right near me ever since he found me. But I didn't even catch it that he left." But at this point, the fact seemed quite unimportant.

The Chrebin stood before the fanned out root-system of a fallen hemlock. The massive tree itself was as big around as Mishchag was tall and the thing had displaced an enormous chunk of earth as it pulled itself out of the ground. It had once grown next to the large boulders it now lay upon. Between two of these crags, Temmonin could see the reason the Chrebin had led Mishchag to this spot: the mouth of a cave.

The Mitsa-Mitsa immediately prepared torches.

The way was a little narrow at first but soon it was wide enough for three of them to walk abreast. It pitched down quickly. With the Chrebin on his shoulder, Damowan led the way. The Ginginmarin and Kashtawa followed close behind. The way led to increasing slopes and, at times, the shaft opened out into caverns. But there were no signs of civilization-- ancient, new, or recently decimated. And there was no sign of Chaneerem's passing.

In one of the caverns, the ceiling was completely covered with bats. Temmonin was in awe of the sight and stopped to stare up at them. Jemalemin waited and looked a bit squeamish, but held the torch high to help Temmonin see. In shifting to get a better view, Temmonin dislodged a pile of rocks with his foot and sprawled to the dirt. Several bats screeched and flew up the corridor. He was annoyed at his blunder and was about to get up when he recognized how close to death he had just come. To his right, the cave floor fell away. Jemalemin seemed just as curious about the shadows as the elder Ek-Birin was. He held his torch as far out from the edge as he could. Temmonin was stung with fear. He could see more than a stone's throw down into the canyon and there was no bottom in sight. He slowly moved away from the edge. Standing and shaking his head with relief, Temmonin turned toward Jemalemin. Without speaking, the boy let Temmonin know that he too was relieved. They backed away from the cliff and continued down the tunnel.

They moved fairly quickly and soon they caught up to Damowan and the others in a large cavern. The group seemed to have been regathering in this chamber after having split up and having searched the surrounding passages and rooms.

"Well, it definitely was a village," Damowan spoke as if he were calling a council together. "How long ago it was abandoned we'll probably never know."

"But it's time to get back to the camp and get some sleep, I think," one of the Mitsa-Mitsa called. "The sun is fer sure down by now and the climb up'll take longer than the hike down."

"Yer right," Damowan began. "May as well get started. . ."

Then the Chrebin leapt from his shoulder and slammed onto the sand floor. He stood without dusting himself off and walked intently to a wall of the chamber into which no exits had been cut. He stood there and stretched out his arm. Damowan and Temmonin and Kashtawa and Mishchag followed closely behind the squirrel-man while the others observed.

Suddenly, the wall near the floor stirred. Then it crumbled and fell away to reveal some kind of low

418

passage. But it looked barely big enough to crawl through. Temmonin's heart spit adrenaline as he pictured the group making its way through such a tight shaft.

"Well," Damowan shrugged. "I guess plans change."

"Wait a second, Damowan," Kashtawa objected. "All of us're wasted. We've been walkin' all day and all evenin'. And we've still gotta to git outta here before we finally git some sleep. This can wait until mornin'."

"I don't think so," Damowan shook his head.

"You don't think so?" Kashtawa was as near being offended as Temmonin had seen him. "Whaddaya mean, ya don't think so?"

"The Chrebin--he gets in these certain moods and. . ." Damowan hesitated. It looked to Temmonin as if his brother had just realized how strange he would look if he continued. But he did anyway. "I can jus' tell. He wants it to happen tonight."

"Well I'm headin' up!" One Salamander waved as he turned toward the passageway that led back to the surface.

"Hang on a second, Zelmash!" Kashtawa called. Then he faced Damowan again. "Now, yer sure 'bout this, Damowan? The Chrebin knows his way through these tunnels?"

"Well, I don't know a hundred percent." Damowan's mouth twisted a bit. "But, the Chrebin live around the rim of this gorge and I'm guessin' he knows what he's doin'. I mean, look what he jus' did."

"Look," Zelmash complained. "I'm tired Kashtawa and this is obviously conjecture. Besides, we don't all have to go down that chute. I'm goin' up to get some sleep. Anybody else fer some sleep?"

Kashtawa obviously saw the need for a compromise. "Okay. Anybody who wants to miss out on the excitement can go back with Zelmash." He smiled at Zelmash. "Anybody who wants a nice, juicy leg of roast turkey can stay and crawl down this chute here and check out what's next."

"Where's he gonna git a turkey down here?" Jemalemin whispered to Temmonin.

"No, Jemalemin," Temmonin laughed. "He's speaking figuratively." And when the look of confusion lingered on the boy's brow, Temmonin clarified further. "He's sayin' this little adventure ahead of us is gonna be exciting. Y'know, like eatin' a turkey leg?"

"Ahh." Jemalemin understood.

Temmonin noticed Mishchag behind Jemalemin. The hulk simply stood and listened and watched.

"Is this all right with you?" Temmonin asked him.

"Yes." And Mishchag peered so strongly at the Ek-Birin that Temmonin could not bear to maintain eye-contact. He looked to the sand until Mishchag stopped staring. When the quill-man had finally desisted, Temmonin snuck a glance up at him. He did not study the hulk for long but this quick moment filled Temmonin with so much wonder about the Ginginmarin. He could hardly believe that he had been chosen and thrown into the middle of this thing. For a moment, he was overwhelmed by the ancient pain that seeped from Mishchag's soul. This race was like the moon; for as long as Temmonin had lived, it had been there and it had never demanded his attention. Yet now it had suddenly stolen from behind the deep clouds

that had shrouded it for so long. Like the moon,
the Ginginmarin had revealed themselves. But even
having revealed themselves, they had barely made
themselves known. Mishchag had offered his life to
the people of the tribes in hope that he might save
his own people. And he had also offered a
surprising amount of his soul to Damowan,
Jemalemin, and Temmonin. Yet at times like this,
Temmonin felt as if he knew nothing at all about
the beast and that he never would.

Only four Mitsa-Mitsa warriors left with
Zelmash. The rest joined the Ek-Birin and the giant
and the dwarf. Since the Chrebin could easily walk
erect through the shaft at the same pace that
Damowan could crawl, there was no need for the
squirrel-man to ride Damowan's shoulder. As
Damowan knelt to enter the chute with his torch in
one hand, the Chrebin raised his own hands and
waved them at the flame as if telling the man to
stop. Then he proceeded a few steps into the
tunnel and stretched his arms to the sides.
Damowan and Temmonin laughed together as the
rock walls began to glow. They lay their torches on
the ground and kicked sand on them until they
stopped burning. The others did the same.

"We can use these on the way back out,"
Kashtawa stated. But, as one of his colleagues
prepared to unload his unused torches from his
backpack and to add them to the pile on the cavern
floor, Kashtawa stopped him. "Hold on to those.
We might need 'em farther down."

Mishchag followed directly behind Damowan.
Jemalemin and Temmonin went in after them. The
dull gleam of the quartz around them allowed
Temmonin to see how difficult it was for the
Ginginmarin to snake his way through this tunnel.
The beast could not crawl on his hands and knees.

The lack of space forced him to wriggle on his belly.
Fortunately, everyone else could travel on all fours.

At times during the descent, Temmonin felt
surges of panic sizzle through his chest. The light
of the quartz walls helped him to keep calm but this
thick air so saturated with sweat and the dank odor
of fungus pushed him to the edge of himself. He
wondered how Jemalemin was handling the
situation. From behind the boy, he could see no
evidence that he was afraid. Jemalemin was not
shaking or breathing especially heavily. Perhaps it
was only Temmonin who felt this fear.

Soon, the sweat that ran down his arms and
legs was reflected by the moisture that collected and
dripped down the tunnel walls. This sweat on the
walls began to trickle in rivulets onto the sand floor
over which the party crawled. Temmonin's hands
became encrusted with wet sand that he could not
avoid. Ahead of him, Jemalemin stopped. Then the
boy started forward again.

Within minutes, they were traveling through
mud about an inch deep and, in the center of the
floor, between Temmonin's grimy hands and knees,
a small stream was running down the passage along
with them. Jemalemin stopped again. He started.
Then he stopped yet another time.

"What's goin' on, Damowan?" Temmonin
called forward.

Damowan's voice was as thin as the tiny
stream beneath him. Temmonin could only hear
the rhythm of the words.

"What?" Temmonin spoke louder.

Jemalemin turned his head. "He said they
reached water." Jemalemin listened to Damowan
for another moment. "He says to come up by him."

"How'm I s'posed to do that?" Temmonin
said, frustrated but, even as he spoke, he was

pushing past Jemalemin. The boy had also already
made way for the eldest Ek-Birin by pressing
himself tightly against the right side of the tunnel.
As Temmonin passed by, Jemalemin retreated to
where the elder had just been. Behind him,
Temmonin could faintly hear the boy explaining the
situation to Kashtawa. Ahead of him, Mishchag
was lying on his stomach like a giant clump of moss
with reeds growing from it.

"I'll never make it past you this way,
Mishchag." Temmonin tried to keep his statement
free of offensive color but he was unable to mask
his irritation. "I'll get to know ev'ry one of those
quills personally if ya can't get 'em outta my way
somehow"

"Well, what's he s'posed to do, Temmonin?"
Damowan's thin voice reached him as if it had come
from across a canyon. "There's not too much room
in here, y'know."

"Mishchag." Temmonin touched the
Ginginmarin's foot. "Roll over onto yer back."
Mishchag managed to do what Temmonin had
asked. "Okay now, shove yerself into the corner."
Mishchag just lay there. "I mean don't lay right in
the middle of the stream. Lay on an angle. Stick
your backbone into the place where the wall and the
floor meet."

Mishchag finally complied.

"What's the matter, guy?" Temmonin asked
partly joking, partly frustrated. "A little uptight
down here?"

The hulk did not answer. He said nothing. As
Temmonin passed carefully by him, he was sorry
that he had asked that last question. The porcupine-
man truly was almost frozen by fear. He was as stiff
as the quartz into which he was pressing himself.
Several times, Temmonin had to work alone to free

himself from Mishchag's quills because the beast seemed to have no ability to help in any way. The Ek-Birin felt quite uncomfortable as he moved up to where the two were eye to eye, just a hand away from each other, several of their body parts touching.

"Sorry 'bout this, friend." Temmonin hoped his weak apology was enough.

"C'mon down here, big brother." Damowan helped Temmonin out of the tunnel and into a very small cave. The place was just tall enough to crouch in and the floor was covered by two feet of water. "We have to go through there." He pointed to the wall.

At first, Temmonin laughed because he could not even see a place to go. But then he recognized that the tunnel did, in fact, continue beyond this tiny chamber. But it was almost entirely under water. The green glow faded away under the wall in front of them. Temmonin felt a raven's talon reach up from his gut and clutch his heart.

"Damowan." He shook his head. "There's no way yer gonna convince these guys to go in there. No way, Damowan! There's no way yer gonna convince me to go in there!"

The air seemed to thicken visibly as Temmonin awaited Damowan's reply.

"I'll go first and check things out." With that, Damowan started to ease himself into the pool.

"Wait, Damowan," Temmonin protested. "Whaddaya mean, you'll go first and check things out? Damowan, yer not goin' anywhere. Wait a second." He had to grab his brother's arm to keep him from laying back into the water.

"Temmonin, I know it's dangerous," Damowan argued. "And I'm just as scared as you or any of the other guys." He motioned back up the tunnel with his hand and fixed his eyes on Mishchag for a second. "Okay, maybe not as scared Mishchag. But you know what I mean."

"Damowan, just admit it and move on," Temmonin reasoned. "This is a dead end. It doesn't lead anywhere. Now, let's get outta here. It's gettin' really hard to breathe."

"Temmonin, look at the Chrebin."

The squirrel-man was lying in the water on his back and making motions with his hand from his mouth.

"See, Temmonin. He's been here. He knows the place. He knows how to git through. There's somethin' important through here. I know it."

"So what's this supposed to mean, Damowan?" Temmonin's face smashed tightly into itself as he pointed at the Chrebin. "A little squirrel-man floatin' on his back doin' some little dance with his hands? This is totally idiotic, Damowan!"

"No, Temmonin." Damowan's face was full of disbelief that his brother could not see what he himself could see. "Can't you see, he's showin' us how to get through. We swim on our backs and breathe the air above the water."

Temmonin looked sidelong at Damowan as if he did not trust him. Then he situated himself to get a better view down the submerged shaft.

"Damowan, I can't see a thing down there."

"That's why I'm sayin' I'll go first," Damowan explained slowly. "Then I'll come back and tell you what I find, okay?"

"No way, Damowan!" Temmonin spat red. "We don't even have a rope. What happens if you get caught or somethin' attacks you. You have no idea what's in there."

"The Chrebin'll be right with me, Temmonin."

"O, yea. That'll help a lot if there's an upsurge of water and it fills the whole tube." Temmonin laughed sardonically. "Yea, the Chrebin'll just create an air pocket outta nothin'."

"Temmonin," Damowan raised his voice. "I'm gonna go in there, okay?"

"You won't even be able to see where you're goin'!!"

"I'm goin' in." Damowan said calmly, resolutely. "Trust me. I'll be right back."

Temmonin glared at his younger brother for a long moment. Then he punched out his words. "Git outta here!"

Damowan's resolve slackened for an instant. "Temmonin, it's gonna be all ri. . ."

"You jerk! Git outta here before I. . ." Temmonin stopped speaking and helped Damowan lean back into the water. Nervously, he watched as his brother slipped into the murky olive stream. At first, Temmonin could see some movement, then only a pale blob, then nothing.

"They wanna know what's takin' so long," squeaked Jemalemin from just beyond Mishchag's statue.

"Tell 'em not to be surprised but that Damowan jus' went on ahead with the Chrebin to look at a special situation down here." Temmonin could barely make out Jemalemin's features but he saw the boy nod and turn to pass on the information. "Tell 'em I have to wait until he gets back and I don't know how long that'll be."

After a moment, Jemalemin called back. "He says it's gettin' hard to breathe in here! We can't stay too much longer!"

"Tell him I know! I'm in here too!" Temmonin was getting short with everybody now.

"Tell him you know what?" Jemalemin yelled.

Temmonin was confused for a moment by the question. Then he understood and rephrased his statement. "Jus' tell him I know! I understand!"

Not long after that, Temmonin heard noise from down the water tube. This was sooner than he expected Damowan to return. He dropped to his knees to see what had happened. He could barely make out the shape of a forehead, a nose, and a chin. Within a few seconds, his younger brother was back in the tiny chamber, pulling his slick, black mane away from his face and panting.

"Temmonin, this is unbelievable!" He could hardly say what he needed to say. "This is the most important thing on this trip. I cannot believe it!! O, man—it's amazing!"

"What's amazing? And where's the Chrebin?" Temmonin wondered.

"That's what I'm saying, Temmonin," Damowan stumbled over his own explanation. "He stayed back there. That's. . .that's where the Chrebin live. He's takin' us to the place where they come from. This is too much. I can't believe it!"

Temmonin pondered from a moment. "Dama, this is no time fer sight-seein'. I mean, I know this is exciting for you and all, but it's the crappiest time you coulda picked fer seein' where the Chrebin live. Chaneerem's still out there wastin' on Ginginmarin villages and you're down here playin' around!"

"But, Temmonin, he brought us here to help us!"

"How is this supposed to help us? And how do you know he wants to help us anyway?"

"Temmonin?" Damowan responded incredulously. "Of course he wants to help us. I mean, I don't absolutely know for sure. But, c'mon! So far he's only done stuff to protect us."

Temmonin was still a little unsure. Finally, the thickness of the sweaty air and the dull, green light pushed him to a decision. "All right, let's do it!" He looked up the corridor. "Jemalemin, c'mon down here. Just you." He turned back to his brother. "Damowan, send Jemalemin ahead of you. I'm sure he's gonna be scared out of his wits. But if you go right behind him, I'm sure he'll do it. I'll go back up and explain everything to Kashtawa. Then I'll send Mishchag ahead of me and Kashtawa can take care of the rest."

Jemalemin was already crowding into the pool when Damowan repeated, "Temmonin, I am serious. This is the most important thing about this trip!"

Temmonin smiled at his brother's enthusiasm, then squeezed past Jemalemin and Mishchag on his way to Kashtawa and the others. The giant was as stiff as he had been when Temmonin squeezed by him the first time. In fact, he may have become even stiffer and he had not changed his position whatsoever. Temmonin listened for breathing as he passed by Mishchag's face. The brute was still alive. And it was easier for Temmonin to get through this way. But he stopped before he was through.

"Damowan," he called blindly.

"Yea?" came his brother's muted reply.

"Don't go until we take care of Mishchag. I don't think he's doin' so well."

"All right," Damowan agreed. "We'll wait."

Temmonin reached Kashtawa and explained everything. To those who did not want to continue, he gave the option to turn back. Although tension was constricting the belly of this snake, none of them chose to leave.

"Just hurry, eh?" Kashtawa suggested.

"Okay," Temmonin turned back toward the pool. "Mishchag, you've heard all of this. Now it's time to go." The hulk did not respond. "Mishchag!" Temmonin charged. "Hey, Mishchag, it's time to go! Let's do this thing!" Still stiff like shale.

Temmonin grunted and pushed himself back down the shaft. He picked through the quills and reached the porcupine-man's chest.

"Mishchag," he said calmly. "Mishchag!" he yelled. "Mishchag!!" he screamed as loudly as he could.

Suddenly, he became dizzy. There was no more oxygen in this chute. Deciding not to scream again, he pulled his arms up from his sides. A quill pierced his left forearm and he roared in pain. He attempted to free it by pulling away. But the barb at the end of the quill had grabbed a hold of his skin. Grasping the smooth shaft of the quill with his right hand, he concentrated for a moment and then ripped the thing from its follicle in Mishchag's arm. The beast only jerked slightly. Temmonin had succeeded in wrenching the quill from its root. He immediately positioned the point of the tiny arrowhead so that it would push through his skin at another point not far from where it had entered, braced himself, and shoved as hard as he could. With his teeth tight against each other, he tensed most of the muscles in his body as fire exploded in his arm. Then, when the pain had subsided, he pushed the quill the rest of the way through both puncture holes and out.

"Mishchag!" he screamed again in frustration. Then, in spite of his light-headedness, he pounded on the hulk's bare chest. The Ginginmarin woke with a start.

"What is wrong, Temmonin?" he asked, apparently unaware of all that had just occurred.

"It's time to go on before I can't breathe anymore." Temmonin was simultaneously relieved and extremely angry.

Mishchag looked toward Damowan. Temmonin did too.

"Go ahead you two," Temmonin said to Jemalemin and Damowan.

Both Temmonin and the porcupine-man watched as the other Ek-Birin slipped into the tube and swam away. Jemalemin did not look nervous at all. As Damowan's feet disappeared, Temmonin made his way into the pool.

"Okay," he began to explain the procedure to the beast who was still lying in the tunnel. "We're gonna go through this channel in the water floatin' on our backs, breathin' the air at the top of the channel. It won't take too long and we'll be on the other side and out of these cramped quarters!"

Mishchag pulled himself partly into the small chamber and seemed to shrink back from every contact with the water. But he forced himself forward. He had been sitting in the pool for quite some time when Temmonin felt compelled to raise his eyebrows.

"You gonna be all right, Mishchag?"

The quill-man snatched his head from the tunnel in front of him and fixed his gaze directly at Temmonin. "Yes. I will to be fine."

Temmonin was breathing too little air to think logically. "What's goin' on with this starin' at me when I ask you how yer doin'?" he demanded. By this time, Kashtawa had made his way down the shaft. Temmonin continued, "I'm gittin' pritty sick of this crap! I just asked you a simple question and you look at me like you wanna fight!?"

Kashtawa's voice reached him through his swelling consciousness. "Temmonin, stop it! We gotta git outta here before we all lose it!" The Mitsa-Mitsa leader pointed at the Ginginmarin's chest. "Now, lean back slowly and git goin'. You can do it Mishchag."

And the beast did it. Temmonin followed just behind him.

"We're right behind ya," Kashtawa promised as Temmonin's ears sunk beneath the water's surface.

Temmonin glided into the tube staring at the ceiling.

The luminescence of the quartz grew strangely eerie. This coupled with the fact that he could hear nothing but his own breathing played strange games with his mind. The lack of oxygen in the air amplified the effect of the games. He was not sure if he was dying or being born. Perhaps he was with his brother smashing gourdfish seedpods on the shores of the marsh near the village. Certainly, he was with Zheva. He was wrapped in a warm, green gel of ecstasy and Zheva was with him and they were finally married. He was floating in liquid love. He was paddling his feet but he hardly noticed. And it seemed that he was not really moving and that it was taking forever. But he was exhausted. He hated this place and he never wanted to leave it. Then his head hit something.

Temmonin was suddenly alert. He reached past his ears and felt something heavy, yet not very hard. It was a foot. It did not react as he touched it. He inspected further, feeling the entire thing to get an idea of its size when he brushed past several sharp points. It was Mishchag's huge foot. He poked the sole to wake the beast but nothing happened. The quill-man was unconscious again. Temmonin spat out a curse. Then he stopped to think. The air here was not as thick as it was farther up the passage-way and this fact comforted him. The ceiling was only a hand away from his face, however, and this gave him very little room to maneuver. He decided to push the Ginginmarin the rest of the way.

Once Temmonin had gotten beyond the initial heave, it was actually quite simple for him to push Mishchag through the chute. Inertia did most of the work for him. Temmonin felt quite satisfied that something which looked as if it might be a big problem was so little trouble. Then they hit something.

Temmonin's shoulders rammed into Mishchag's feet and spread them to the walls. But although Mishchag had stopped, Temmonin could not keep himself from continuing a short distance between the hulk's calves. Again, quills pricked his shoulders. Fortunately, none pierced the skin.

The Ek-Birin hissed through his lips as he tried to picture how best to get the leverage to pull the porcupine-man back away from what was obstructing his free passage. Then he got a better idea. He clutched a couple of quills that were attached to the beast's legs and yanked them out. Mishchag did not react. Temmonin grabbed the hulk's left foot, searched for a spot on his sole with the least amount of calluses, and jabbed the quills into the foot with as much force as he could muster.

Mishchag jerked and kicked, splashing water into Temmonin's nose and mouth. The Ek-Birin coughed and let go of the huge foot he was holding. When he had cleared his sinuses and his throat, Temmonin called out.

"Mishchag?" No response. "Mishchag!" he screamed. The beast made no movement, no sound. Temmonin checked his foot and felt a strong pulse. "You big baby!! Can't you stay awake through anything?!"

Concluding that the tube must bend at this point and that the porcupine-man was caught in the corner, Temmonin attempted several times to pull Mishchag back from where he was wedged and to redirect his body. But every time he freed the hulk and began to push again, the walls of the tunnel forced him back into the same corner. Temmonin decided to get a view of the obstacle.

He took a deep breath and turned himself over. On all fours, he could maneuver better. He was barely able to raise his nose above the water level so that he could breathe. Of course, to do this, he had to press his forehead against the quartz ceiling. But this position allowed him a reasonably good view of the tube.

He could not see Mishchag's head. The tube had narrowed and the beast's huge chest and shoulders would not fit through. Damowan, in all of his excitement, had failed to mention this potential problem. Temmonin closed his eyes for a moment and took several deep breaths. Then, one of the Mitsa-Mitsa warriors was at his back.

"Hang on, brother," Temmonin yelled. "There's a problem."

"Wait a second," the warrior called back. "I can't hear you very well." He turned himself over onto his hands and knees and, as he did so, Temmonin turned around to face him.

"My neck is startin' to cramp up so I need to make this quick, okay?" Temmonin did not wait for an answer. "What's yer name?"

"Zemzarvosh."

"Okay, Zemzarvosh, the porcupine-man's pluggin' up the tube. All we need to do to get by is to pull him back out of the place where the thing

narrows down, let me get through, and then you
shove and I'll pull him through. Got it?"

"Yea," said the Salamander.

Temmonin pulled the beast's body back as he
pushed himself forward. It was not particularly easy
to get past the Ginginmarin because the water
caused all of his quills to float away from his body.
But, in spite of that fact, Temmonin managed to
avoid any major snags. He squeezed himself along
one side of the tube while Zemzarvosh gently held
Mishchag to the other side and away from him.
Soon the Ek-Birin's knees were at the beast's chest.
He felt around ahead of himself for the narrowing
of the tube. At this point, there was just enough
space between the surface of the water and the
ceiling for him to keep his nose in a position to
breathe. And he was forced to pucker his lips in
order to avoid taking in water. No wonder
Mishchag had fainted. Temmonin had no idea how
he himself was still able to function.

But, as he had hoped, this narrowing lasted for
only about an arm's length. After that, the tube
widened again and Temmonin's desire to panic
lessened. He started to turn himself around so that
he could help pull Mishchag through when
something brushed by his leg.

His whole body tensed and he cracked his
forehead against the quartz above him. Spitting and
panting in a fresh panic, he held himself as close to
the surface of the water as he could by pushing
against the sides of the channel with his arms and
legs. His face was smashed against the ceiling.
Damowan had not warned him about anything
living in this tube. It was probably only a harmless
fish, but the knowledge of this fact had had no
effect whatsoever on Temmonin's reflexes. As his

breathing slowed down, he decided to turn himself over and take a look.

It was a piece of seaweed. In the murky light, Temmonin could see many plants swaying below him in the channel. He was relieved that no one had seen this escapade. After a moment, he turned himself to his back again and made his way to Mishchag.

He was able to grab the hulk's arms and pull them over his giant head. This gave Temmonin good leverage. Zemzarvosh gently pushed as the Ek-Birin slipped through the narrow spot holding Mishchag's wrists. Once through, he was able to shift to his hands and knees and, with only a little work, pull the porcupine-man through.

He thought he might warn Zemzarvosh about the sea-weed. Then, he realized what it might make him look like and he decided not to.

Not far from the narrowing, the tube widened into a large cavern. Damowan and Jemalemin greeted Temmonin and helped him pull Mishchag onto a small, sandy beach.

"He fainted again," Temmonin grunted as he stood and stretched and looked around.

Damowan beat on the Ginginmarin's chest to wake him up.

The cavern rose to a place high above their heads and, within a stone's throw, opened out into a sheet of white fog. The sound of dripping echoed through the moss-covered hollow. The beaches on either side of the channel were wide enough to walk around on. Temmonin reveled in the space.

The others reached the bay within a few minutes and quickly oriented themselves to the new-found freedom to move and breathe. After Damowan had roused Mishchag, he sat down next to Jemalemin and his brother. Loudly enough for the entire group to hear, he apologized,

"Man, I'm sorry I fergot to warn you guys about the sea-weed back there," he laughed. "It scared the crap outta me when I first touched it. I thought it was an eel or somethin'!"

Everybody laughed. Temmonin had to chuckle at his brother's transparency. But he was too exhausted to chide himself for his own inhibition. He just stretched his neck and back muscles and tried to relax. He had a headache.

"Where are we?" Kashtawa asked.

"This is the world of the Chrebin, Kashtawa." Damowan was having a hard time not smiling.

"What're we doin' down here?" asked one of the Mitsa-Mitsa. He looked at Jemalemin. "Isn't yer brother out wastin' villages?"

"I believe this is to be very important," Mishchag stated. "His brother has already to did too much. We might to chase him for a long time and not to stop him. The Chrebin have to say a thing to us. We will go to them and to listen. The Chrebin race do not to do a thing for no reason."

The Ginginmarin's statement seemed to eliminate the need for any further objections.

"Well," Damowan took the opportunity. "What're we waitin' for?" He stood and walked to the edge of the fog.

Temmonin and Jemalemin joined him. As they drew near to the mouth of the cave, the fog above their heads cleared enough to reveal an oil black sky and a stark white, full moon. Wisps of fog curled around the scene. The small stream that they had followed down the tunnel flowed into a pool which filled the floor of the space in front of them. But the fog hindered the party from judging the dimensions of this place. Temmonin's chest swelled

with awe. Then he shuddered as the thought
occurred to him that they would again need to crawl
through the tube behind them in order to leave this
place. But the moon whispered to him and wooed
him from his dread.

They slipped into the water. It was warm like
a dream. The moon illuminated the pool so that no
one had trouble seeing what was ahead. In fact, the
floor of the pool was smooth, not full of stones and
pebbles like a stream, not sandy like the shores of a
lake--but smooth like molded and baked clay. After
a moment, Temmonin realized he did not have to
be careful of his step. He gazed around himself,
tantalized by the mystery of this place.

At random spots throughout this pond, steam
oozed up out of the water and into the thick air that
hovered around the group. The water became very
warm. Temmonin suddenly wished he could sink
into this pool and live here forever under this silent
sky that asked him no questions and gave him no
advice. The only sounds he could hear were the
soft roilings of the water just behind him. The pool
was now waist-deep.

Small islands began to appear. On some of
them, Temmonin could see evidence of some sort
of building. But the buildings did not seem to
intrude on the deep peace that rested here in this
place. He imagined that whoever had built them
must have done it so quietly that they had not even
stirred the water. All of the small huts seemed to be
made of the same stuff as the floor of the pool.
They rose seamlessly from the islands upon which
they had been built. For a moment, Temmonin
wondered if these were not natural formations. But,
although they were so well entwined with their
foundations, their style betrayed a less random
intent than nature typically displayed. What

appeared to be archways punctuated the sides of the huts near the surface of the water. Other rounded openings allowed steam to enter and exit. Temmonin imagined that these doorways and windows were designed less to keep the weather out of the dwellings as to give it and the inhabitants free access. Yet, no Chrebin greeted them.

The pool was as empty as it was quiet. And, although this fact did nothing to reassure the party that they were here for a good reason, Temmonin was not bothered in the least. He wondered if he should be.

Next to him, Damowan seemed as impressed as he was. In fact, the whole group showed no sign of protest. All of them gazed about in awe and held their tongues as if they had been instructed to do so. Steam and ethereal silence lead them forward through the maze of islands and sculptured huts around them. Soon, they wandered into a place where no islands interrupted the surface of the pool. This clearing was roughly circular and, above it, the fog dissipated and give a lucid view of the constellations. The moon flooded the scene with light. The floor of the pool glowed aqua and lime green and made Temmonin's legs look thick and heavy--heavy like his soul. The entire place seemed to have swelled his body until it was so thick that it could do nothing but wade slowly through the warm water and notice every detail of their surroundings.

He was entranced by the unearthly greens and blues of the floor. Then, after a while, he lifted his eyes to the sky. It was as black and silent as the night when they had danced with the Salamanders in the village on the shore of Moza-Imsaw. In such intense moonlight, Temmonin was sure his mother could find and pluck grey hairs from her head. And Temmonin began to see more of their surroundings.

He noticed the horizon. Below this line, the stars seemed to be swallowed into oblivion. Temmonin studied the shadows. Were they surrounded by mountains or very tall trees? He tried to remember what the mountains had looked like before they had entered the cave hours ago. No success. But then the darkness yielded somewhat to the moonlight and revealed more details to Temmonin. After closer study, he could see that they were encircled by cliffs.

"Zubzza," Damowan whispered an answer to the newly forming question in his older brother's mind.

"This far down?!" Temmonin's exclamation would have sounded like a sigh in any other situation. But here in the white hush, he was embarrassed that he had spoken so loudly.

He peered out through this fog that continuously concealed the Fat Gorge from those who looked down from the cliffs above. Temmonin could now make out the actual edge of the cliff and the silhouettes of the trees that pushed into the sky from that point. They were definitely at the bottom of the gorge.

Something drew his eyes back down to the water. The glassy surface had begun to tremble. The entire party suddenly became engrossed in the movement. It was all around them. For the first time since they had entered the gorge, Temmonin felt reason to be alarmed. But he did not allow himself to react. He knew he could trust the Chrebin at least as far as Damowan was concerned and Damowan was standing directly to his left.

The trembling grew. Soon, although the temperature of the water had not risen, the movement became a roil and seemed to gather at specific points. These points remained in the form of a circle around the party. The spots darkened and the roiling began to sputter and it became apparent that several objects were rising from the aqua.

They were heads. They were huge heads. They were Ginginmarin heads--maybe twenty of them. The water dripped from their hair and their quills as their shoulders and chests pushed up into the air. Temmonin and the others watched with blank faces as their massive torsos rose and towered above them, their feet eventually resting effortlessly on the surface of the water. They resembled Mishchag in every way except that their faces and arms were proportionately shorter in comparison to their bodies and that their fur and quills were a mottled ochre-green and mustard yellow. Temmonin was more numb than confused at the sight. He waited for what would follow like a child who has just been brought into a strange room. At the same instant, Damowan and Temmonin turned to Mishchag to see if the brute recognized these creatures. But the brown hulk stared with as much awe as the rest of the group.

Then a voice stirred the stillness. But it felt not so much like it was reaching him through his ears as through the water around his waist and up through his torso and into his throat and head. Yet this was no rude intrusion. Actually, it was quite soothing. It was as if the warmth of the water was saturating his entire insides.

"The world watches the moon and cries to see it eaten by the darkness only to laugh as it once again pushes its way into fullness and light. And we cry with the red clay and we laugh with the silver sand. We breathe in with the day and we breathe out with the night and, in so doing, we have found the world as those who live in futility can never find it. For the world is lost to these. But to us who know and who see, the world is found. And we have found our way with the world."

The green Ginginmarin stood around them like moss-covered tree trunks. They stood like pillars holding up the fog above them. None of their mouths had moved as the voice spoke. Temmonin noticed that all the others in his party were as entranced as he was--but none against his own will, it seemed. And, judging from their reactions, they had heard the voice just as he had.

"You who live in futility," the voice continued. "Do you now choose to listen to the voice of reason and absurdity?"

A long pause followed. Temmonin felt a strange mixture of emotions inside his chest. There was a slight urgency which demanded that he answer the question posed. But, at the same time, the situation had eased him into a state of absolute comfort and he felt almost unable to conjure up enough energy to speak. And the mild urgency he did feel did not gain any pressure. He remained quiet.

The voice again saturated his veins, "We have remained in the shadows long enough. We have felt that now the time is ripe that we should speak to those who live in futility that some--if even a few-- might come to know meaning and truth. Ours is not to persuade or to convict. Ours is simply to state the truth as the moon sheds its light and to watch as that truth is accepted and rejected. And ours is to know that, whether it is embraced or violently denied, that we have spoken it and, thereby, it continues to exist. For truth unspoken is, at the very least, a tragedy and, at the most, the end of the world."

There was little or no difference in the voice as it continued, yet Temmonin sensed that now the ochre giants were speaking as one. Still, their mouths did not move, nor did their bodies.

"It was truly long ago when the Chechemroo walked through the forests and the mountains in the land of futility. But at that time it was not the land of futility. The Chechemroo walked in peace with the eagle and the bear and the wolf and the fox. There was no reason to fear for the land was plentiful enough for all the creatures of the earth to satisfy their needs. The fox did not feast on the rabbit, nor did the grizzly fight with the wolverine. There was peace in the land of futility in those times--and it was not called the land of futility but, simply, the land. But one day, Tsishamantoo, the eel, prankster that he was, decided to cure his boredom by playing a trick on the Chechemroo. Tsishamantoo went to the place in the Great River where the Chechemroo used to gather seaweed in the springtime--for every year, the Chechemroo feasted upon the seaweed to thank the world for another winter past, another summer to come. Now, Tsishamantoo knew that his sweat would make the Chechemroo crazy when they ate it. And so, just before the Chechemroo went to gather the seaweed, Tsishamantoo swam up and down the river several times until he was dripping with sweat. And when he was finished, he went and rolled in the seaweed. He did this thing many times until the weeds were covered with his sweat. Then the evening came when the Chechemroo gathered the weeds and feasted. They had a very good feast and thanked the earth well and went to sleep with their stomachs bulging and their spirits satisfied.

But during the night, they had horrible dreams. Not a single Chechemroo could escape these nightmares. The next morning, when they woke up, something had changed.

Now, some of the Chechemroo had always been ochre-green like moss but most had always been deep brown like the bear, yet no one had ever seen a problem with such differences. Actually, the Chechemroo had always rejoiced that the world had given forth such variety. But this morning, something had changed--something had changed horribly. Tsishamantoo's sweat had made the Chechemroo crazy. It had made them very crazy.

Suddenly, the brown Chechemroo despised the ochre Chechemroo. Like lightning on a blue-sky-day, they turned on the ochre Chechemroo and persecuted them until blood stained the cedars. And Tsishamantoo laughed and laughed to see what a devious prank he had played on the Chechemroo. But what he thought might be a small and playful trouble became a bitter, horrible sentence of pain on the ochre Chechemroo.

The Ochres also supposed the insanity might last only a short time--perhaps one day or one week. But, when the beatings and the burnings did not stop after the entire spring, they knew that they must find a way to escape this wicked torture.

Now, the Browns had killed almost all of the Ochres when summer's heat entered the land. The rest of the Ochres had to use their magic to save themselves. One night, they gathered at a secret place in the forest and, under the light of the half-moon, they joined their magic together and became smaller and smaller. They did this so that they could hide from their Brown brothers and sisters--it was the most insane situation the Chechemroo had ever experienced. Yet, as they became smaller, they discovered that their magic had grown stronger. That entire night, under the light of the half-moon, they continued to grow smaller and stronger until they finally became small enough to hide in holes in trees and under large rocks and in very small caves. The process was very painful and many of them died before the night was over. When they had finished, they were all small enough to hide wherever they wished. Yet there was no longer any need to hide, for their magic had become strong enough so that they could easily defend themselves against their own people.

But the Browns' hatred for the Ochres did not weaken at all. They despised their brothers and sisters even more violently because of what the Ochres had done to themselves, saying that it was unnatural and even wicked. The persecution never stopped and, even though the Ochres were no longer physically vulnerable to their brothers and sisters, they grew tired of the constant hatred and insults. They moved to a place where no Chechemroo lived--near the southeast marshes. They lived there for a time in peace. But, it was not long before other brown Chechemroo settled near the Ochres and again began the work of hatred. The Ochres moved again. But the news of their presence spread throughout the entire land of the Chechemroo until the Ochres were welcome nowhere. Such an atrocity the world had never known before.

When there was nowhere else to turn, the Ochres found a place near the swamps where few Chechemroo lived. One night, by the light of the half-moon, they came together and gathered their magic and made the ground sink. They caused it to sink until they were sure that no Chechemroo would ever want to go to that place. Then they caused it to sink even farther to make sure they would have a safe place to raise their children free from the hatred of the other Chechemroo. For a hundred thousand moons and longer, the Ochres have lived here in Zubzza."

Suddenly, the giants disappeared. But where they had been, on the surface of the water, stood twenty Chrebin. The entire party stood stunned. One of the squirrel-men walked upon the water to Damowan and climbed his arm until it reached his shoulder. It was the one who always stood there. It stood there now as the voice again began inside Temmonin's head.

"The people of futility, the smooth-skins, entered the land of the Chechemroo many thousands of moons after the people you call the Chrebin had found their place in Zubzza. The Chrebin watched with sad eyes as the smooth-skins stole every single place the Chechemroo had ever called their own. The smooth-skins did not ask or apologize or discuss--they simply took. And the deepest insult was that the smooth-skins acted as if they had hardly noticed the Chechemroo. Later, we discovered that, in fact, they had not noticed them.

But the futility did not end there. After the smooth-skins pushed the Browns into the caves beneath the mountains, they turned against one another and killed each other just as the Browns had done to the Ochres. It was as if that prankster eel had sweat on the whole river and the smooth-skins had drunk that sweat and had become as crazy as the Browns.

Still the futility has not ended. It continues and the Chrebin continue as well. Yet the Chrebin have chosen against futility. We do not rejoice to see the Browns decimated by Chaneerem and his growing army of warriors but we know that such things will happen and happen again. The sweat of the eel has poisoned the land and all who drink

from its rivers have fallen into the futile insanity--
the insane futility. The Chrebin walk on with such
knowledge always before them. But they do not
drink from the rivers. They no longer live in the
land of futility. They now live in the other place
where the eel and the Chechemroo and the smooth-
skins do not come. And from their place, they
watch the moon as it is eaten by the darkness and
they watch as it pushes its way back into fullness
and light. They watch the futility but they do not
join in the futility. And the fog above them shields
them from the sad land of futility and each new
sadness in the land where the sweat of the eel
pollutes the rivers. We have found our place and it
is one of watching and one of much sadness yet it is
one of peace."

The silence that followed was as long and as
empty as the night sky. No one spoke. No one
moved. Temmonin could hardly think. After such
monumental words, he felt that it would be rude to
do so. For what may have been hours, the Ek-Birin,
The Chrebin, and Mishchag stood and soaked in all
that had been said until, in the end, the Chrebin
quietly turned and disappeared into the fog. The
Chrebin on Damowan's shoulder, however,
remained there and showed no sign that he wished
to leave.

Moon Beneath the Mountains

XVI.   Perhaps he can see farther than we can.
Perhaps the gift we have been given is far, far better
than the one we would have wished to receive.
Perhaps we have been moles crawling blindly
through tunnels, completely unaware of the world
above the darkness. Perhaps our eyes have grown
so accustomed to the pitch that any amount of light
seems to us harsh, strident, painful, and cruel. But
could it be that if we were to endure the pain and if
we were to grow accustomed to the little light we
can bear--could it be that we might enjoy the new
sights we would see? And could it be that we might
then desire more light? And could it be that that
desire might become hunger and that hunger
become yearning? And could it be that someday,
we who now stumble in deep grey, will revel in what
once was death to us? Will we then dance in the
light of the sun and the light of the moon that boils
the blood in our veins. And will our blood not then
wash onto the shores of history and stain its sands
with knowledge and hope? And should the giant
approach, could we not then die in peace, knowing
that he too has been given the same gift we have
been given and will feel the repercussions of all his
own choices. And we, in the path of his descending
heel, when so many would be frantic with the
bitterness of the wolfpack and the all-consuming
fear of the ultimate violence, might we then begin to
see the shadow of the vague memory. And as we
are raked across the rapids of death in our battered
canoe that we could not repair or steer to shore,
might that shadow not slowly take shape as the light
increases. And in our passing, will we not then see
the ultimate violence of death as the gateway to the
land where the trees never fall, where the vague
memory becomes lucid, livid life, and where hope
and history become things of the past?

Perhaps then we will truly see.

CHAPTER 16

Temmonin and Damowan walked with tired steps through a tired land under a tired sun. It seemed that the silence that had descended upon them in the Fat Gorge had gripped them and held them and intended to remain on them as long as it could. Temmonin's stomach ached like it never had before. The back of his throat felt as if it had been beaten by stones. The vulture of depression had pierced his heart with its infected claws and had died while doing so. And now, it hung limp and gangrenous from his side, dragging him closer and closer to despair.

It had been a week since they had crawled back up the thin tunnel that led to Zubzza. Temmonin and the others had hardly said a word to each other except when they needed to discuss some practical detail about their trip to intercept Chaneerem. At times, Temmonin could no longer see a good reason to chase the talon-licker. The Chrebin had stolen almost every bit of hope from Temmonin's soul and had replaced it with guilt and confusion. Everything he had been working for before the meeting with the Chrebin was in question. What could he do in the face of this avalanche of history? Was there no way to fight the futility and the insanity? Was the only answer isolation? His thoughts only pulled him farther from comfort.

"So now what happens when we do catch up to him?" Temmonin almost surprised himself that he had broken the deadness. Yet his attitude showed no attempt to lift spirits in any way. "I mean what do we do with the idiot? Take him back to the Island of the Council?"

450

"We kill the bastard," Damowan said flatly, his eyes never leaving the trail ahead of him.

"Damowan?" Temmonin's exclamation was the first sign in a week that he still had fire in his soul. "I can't believe you jus' said that!"

Damowan looked straight at his brother, "What else do you do with such an insanely selfish idiot? He deserves to die even if he only burnt one of those villages. Who knows how many he's burnt by now. He's a bastard and he deserves to die."

Temmonin's gaze lingered on his brother for a moment. Damowan obviously felt it and turned toward the elder Ek-Birin with an expression which told Temmonin that Damowan would ridicule any protest. Temmonin turned away slowly and retreated to his thoughts.

For Temmonin, the past week was worse than the three months they had spent in the cave tied to logs. At that time, he himself had felt the brunt of an injustice. Now, he had to carry the shame of two injustices his people had done to the Ginginmarin. And pressing itself over that enormous burden was the knowledge that even such a powerful race as the Chrebin had thrown up their hands at any solution to the problems they faced.

At this point, he saw almost no point in continuing but he had no better idea of what to do. He felt that if he stopped and went home, he would not be able to bear the weight of his thoughts. Somehow he pushed his way through the humidity that clung to his face. One more day. After they had made camp, he fell to sleep with no consolation from his brother. He hoped he could avoid dreams of death.

Still, he did dream.

The clatter of clam shells meandered through the forest. Then there was the drum beating--the sound steady and dull like the soft pulse of his own blood in his veins. Then, there was her voice again. He could never forget that voice.

"What is it you wish to know, Temmonin of the Ek-Birin?"

Her voice was like cool water running over his sweaty forehead. Was it eel's sweat? He was too groggy to know what he was thinking. The Flicker woman's costume was even more grandiose than it was the first time Temmonin had dreamed of her.

Tears suddenly filled Temmonin's eyes. "I should be happy to see you," he choked and was embarrassed. "But it jus' makes me feel like a fool." He sobbed in counterpoint to the drumbeat and the dancers that circled the Flicker spirit.

"And why are you a fool, my son?" she asked through the thin smoke that hovered above the dying fire. "What have you done that has made you into a fool?"

"Nothin'! That's the problem." In spite of the fact that he had blurted his answer loudly, none of the others woke from sleep. He expected nothing different. "Damowan and Jemalemin and I've been runnin' ev'rywhere tryin' to keep disaster from happenin' but it seems we're always jus' late enough to watch the results and feel like garbage." His face was wet with tears and it was difficult for him to speak but the bitterness in his jaws needed to be released.

"And this makes you a fool?"

"You told us we'd do so much fer the cause of righteousness. But we've totally failed. We're jus' watchin' unrighteousness have a field day. It seems like Chaneerem jus' can't be stopped. So many people're on his side. And he jus' keeps on killin' and killin'."

"And this makes you a fool?" Temmonin looked up at her. He wanted to be angry at her but the kindness and compassion in her eyes would not allow it. Then, he wanted her to take him onto her lap and hold him like his mother used to do. He could not stop himself from crying. In his mind were only visions of Ginginmarin villages roasted in revenge. Dying eyes. Pointless killing.

"So, you are a fool because you cannot control the actions of others?"

"No, it's not that," Temmonin shook his head. "It's just we haven't been able to do anything to stop Chaneerem from wipin' out the Ginginmarin."

The Flicker spirit did not say anything for quite a while. Perhaps she saw no need to point out that Temmonin's explanation of the situation agreed with hers completely. When she did speak, it was with a voice more stern than her usual tone. "Did you suppose that because I came to you before, that you were guaranteed success in everything you attempted?"

Temmonin was taken back by such a question. He did not know exactly what her point was. In fact, her sudden harshness was like an arrow shoved up under his ribs. "Well, no," Temmonin responded confused. "I jus' thought we would at least succeed in makin' this tie with the Ginginmarin."

"And you did not accomplish this task?" Her persistent questions only rammed the arrow farther into his heart. Temmonin could hardly believe he was hearing this.

He answered very carefully. "No. Do you think we have?"

Again, the Flicker spirit was quiet for a long time. Temmonin glanced at the others in his party.

They were all still asleep, just as they were during the other dream he had had.

"Look at those around you, my son," the compassion had returned to her silvery voice. "And ask yourself again whether or not you have succeeded. You are only one man."

Then she was gone and the six dancers with her and the beating of the drum and the clatter of clam shells. But his tears were still smeared across his cheeks and chin. And his brother and Jemalemin were still there at his side sleeping. Mishchag's fur and quills lay in a heap just next to Jemalemin. Kashtawa and the rest of the Mitsa-Mitsa were scattered around the far side of the dead fire. It was black night and a trace of smoke was still in his nostrils. He sat and felt the emptiness in his heart mix with the confusion he felt at the Flicker spirit's appearance and the minute sign of hope she seemed to have offered just before she left. His tears eventually dried but his mind was soaked through with thought. He remained sitting and thinking for more than an hour and, when he realized how his thoughts were twisting themselves farther into each other, he lay back down and slept until dawn.

They had already traveled quite a distance into Imnanaw-Kanat. As they advanced through each new village, they asked the inhabitants if they had seen Chaneerem's army. Mishchag used the map to lead them through Demnaza territory until they were headed in the direction of Wolverine country. According to him, many larger Ginginmarin villages were burrowed beneath these northernmost mountains. Temmonin caught a glimpse of the map and saw that the mountains were dotted with villages and that they were indeed concentrated there. Chaneerem was surely having a dark party beneath those mountains.

It was difficult for him to know what to think or how to feel. At this point, he wondered if anything could cause Chaneerem to give up his rampage. And he also could not guess how many warriors the talon-licker had swayed to his insanity as he made his way from village to village. Temmonin fully understood why they would follow the oath-taker. Actually, Chaneerem was brilliant in his wickedness. He always knew exactly when to apply guilt to someone, when to make people feel sorry for him, when to plow his way through a relationship with rage, and when to give praise when one of his accomplices did something as selfish as he himself was capable of doing. Of course, Jemalemin was the one trapped most effectively by his older brother. Amazingly, he was the only one Temmonin had ever seen break free of the talon-licker's grip.

But, weirdly enough, Chaneerem could also be quite warm and, at times, almost vulnerable. Once, he had watched the oath-taker stand in awe of a sunset. Of course, when Chaneerem knew that he was being observed, he was immediately embarrassed. But, at least the warmth was there inside him somewhere.

Still, in spite of all the confusion that was breaking Temmonin's brain, he knew he must try to stop Chaneerem from destroying more villages. If he succeeded in nothing else, he must accomplish this one task. He wished he could somehow reach into the talon-licker's spirit and persuade him to let go of all the stupid pretense and bitterness. It would be so beautiful to see him and Jemalemin relating like adults. Temmonin thought of himself and Damowan and how much better things were since Temmonin had been broken of his infatuation with himself. Maybe it was just a matter of time.

And now time was all Temmonin had. The party hiked through mountain valleys in the full sun and, although normally he would have enjoyed every new turn in the trail, at this moment, time itself had sucked him away from beauty and into this whirlpool of thought. He was depressed at the heat. He was depressed at the dry, tan grass that lined the trail. He was depressed at his failures and at all that the Chrebin had told them. He was depressed that they had gone into Zubzza at all and were now almost a week behind Chaneerem. He was depressed at the entire hike thus far. He was depressed that the spirit of the Flicker had come to him and had told him nothing. And he was depressed that he had to continue living in this hot, nauseating, fly-filled world.

The sweat on his back was attracting flies like rotten squash. The thought crossed his mind that he was fortunate the black flies were not out yet. But that gave him little consolation. Then he was depressed because he did not want to come out of his depression. Disgusting.

"Wonder how Mom and Dad're doin'," Damowan said without too much enthusiasm.

"Yea," Temmonin replied. "And Tutumora."

"Hope they're not killin' themselves worryin'."

"Yea," Temmonin grunted. "I know."

"Did you have a dream last night?"

"Yea." Temmonin's spirit lifted slightly. "You too?"

"Yea. Not much encouragement there, eh?"

"Yea. I don't know."

"So we made a couple of friends from different races," Damowan smirked. "What's that. The whole world's burnin' down and we made a couple of friends." Damowan blew out through his lips and made them rattle.

Temmonin had no desire to continue their discussion. It only shoved the arrow deeper under his ribs. He and Damowan went to sleep that night without saying another word to each other.

It was early dawn when they were woken by a group of older women and some children. Temmonin snapped from sleep. Next to him, Damowan rubbed his eyes for a moment, then remarked, "Wolverines."

"Yer right," Temmonin agreed. "What're Kumuchska grannies doin' this far east. We're not in Wolverine territory yet, are we?"

"Definitely not."

Some of the Salamanders had already been discussing something with the women and, as Temmonin and Damowan were getting to their feet, Kashtawa came over to them to inform them of the subject of their discussion.

"This is really bad, you guys," Kashtawa explained. "These old grannies're tellin' us that the Hitasha have attacked the Wolverines totally unprovoked." He shrugged matter-of-factly. "Of course, we all know that's jus' their side of the story."

"They've been waitin' for decades for a reason to nail the Kumuchska," Damowan interjected. "This whole thing with the mutants and the Ginginmarin's prob'ly given 'em more than a few excuses to start somethin'." Damowan's pessimism was burning his own throat.

"What village're they from?" Temmonin asked, suddenly thinking of Zheva and the rest of his cousins.

"I don't know," Kashtawa replied. "You could ask 'em."

Temmonin did not wait. He went to one of the old ladies. "I greet you my grandmother," he began. "I greet you in the name of my father who is a Wolverine--Amowz who married Semarda and lives now among the Flicker."

"My son, we have no time for formalities now," the woman said as she picked up one of the smaller children. "What do you need?"

"Sorry. Just which village are you from?"

"Shishootootamar."

"Is that near Demdegumshannatez?"

"Of course, just down the river." The old woman's eyes lit up for a moment. "Why, is your family there?" And before Temmonin could assent, the child in her arms began to scream. "Sorry, I have to go. But, just to let you know, that village was attacked too. I don't know how they fared though. Sorry I can't help you more." And with that, she passed by him and joined the rest of her group.

After the woman had left, Temmonin wanted to scream for having forgotten to ask her if she happened to know Zheva and her family. But now the woman had passed into the forest and he did not want to follow her. The others were already starting to eat breakfast and they would probably eat it all if he did not take some now.

The party encountered more refugees that afternoon. And they were fleeing from the same area. The entire territory had been attacked. Demnaza land was full of refugees. This was no typical war for the purpose of making coup. The Rattlesnakes were interested in blood. Temmonin smelled eel sweat.

That evening, as they entered the last Demnaza village on the border of Wolverine territory, he saw her.

"Zheva!!" Temmonin forgot that he was among warriors and ran off like a little boy to meet her. He could see nothing else but her gloss black hair and her soft auburn face. Then she recognized him.

"Temmonin!!" And she ran to greet him.

When they reached each other, Temmonin decided to bypass the usual rituals. He embraced her and lifted her from the ground. She did not seem in the least bit surprised by his action nor did she resist in any way. This thing they were both immersed in--this struggle, this war--was large and invasive enough to shatter every custom that was in use among the tribes. And it seemed to Temmonin that they both were suddenly filled with a passion for each other they could never have known had this thing not invaded their lives. They kissed and held each other. They melted into a warmth that flooded Temmonin's heart with an instant, all-encompassing joy. He was elated like he had never been in any of his dreams. This was real life--more real than he had ever known it. And he was living it.

But after a moment, they both realized that, if they continued, it would be embarrassing for the Salamanders and for those in the village who happened to be watching. They relaxed their hold on one another and began walking toward the village.

"How's the family?" Temmonin asked eagerly, afraid of what he might hear.

"Temmonin," tears rushed from her eyes and she stopped. "They killed Papa. He's dead. And a lotta warriors from the village. They surprised us. Shegra's still back fightin'. Dendaminek too. We had to leave."

Temmonin also cried, not as loudly as she, but he could not hold himself from mourning the uncle he so dearly loved. He suddenly did not care what anyone thought about him and Zheva. Encompassing her with his arms, he crushed her to himself and cried into her hair. After a time, he released his hold on her and they both turned and walked toward the search party. Neither felt the need to speak. But as they neared the party, she noticed that Damowan was separating himself from the rest to come and greet her. She smiled through her tears.

"Damowan."

"Zheva, my sister," Damowan spoke somewhat formally, yet warmly. "Peace and beauty."

"Peace and beauty, my brother."

Just then, Temmonin noticed a look of surprise pop into her eyes. She was looking over Damowan's shoulder. It was Mishchag.

"You've taken a prisoner?" she spoke softly so that only Damowan and Temmonin could hear her.

"You mean. . .what?" Damowan was a bit lost.

"She means Mishchag," Temmonin helped him, then turned to Zheva. "No, Zheva, this Ginginmarin is helpin' us track down Chaneerem and his war party."

"Oh," Zheva's face showed her confusion. "So you're not with him, I mean Chaneerem?" And, as Temmonin and Damowan both shook their heads, she continued. "But you guys've come to help get rid of those monsters, right?" Her face darkened with a bitterness that Temmonin found unattractive.

"Zheva, they're not monsters," Temmonin replied. "And only a few of 'em're really bad."

But that's how we got attacked. That's how Papa died. Because of them." The bitterness deepened.

"Whaddaya mean?" Damowan asked, his face twisted. "Uncle Nosh died?"

"Exactly, Damowan." She was having a hard time making her words understandable. But in spite of the fact that Damowan's face had just gone white with realization, she continued in her angry confusion. "The Hitasha accused us of sidin' with those monst. . .those things and so they attacked us. That's why Papa's gone--because of them!" She pointed at Mishchag, her anger filling her face with blood.

Thankfully, Mishchag was not looking in their direction when she pointed. Temmonin was frozen in his mind. The pain he saw in Zheva's eyes would not allow him to contradict her. But Damowan had no such problem. His emotions seemed to have collided inside him.

"Cousin Zheva, it's not what everybody thinks—Chaneerem's an idiot. We're tryin' to stop him. This whole thing is a huge mix-up. The Ginginmarin're peaceful people. They needed our help. But they didn't count on Chaneerem. But we had no idea Uncle Nosh died." His face twisted. They walked a moment in silence.

"Zheva," Temmonin began after a time. "Mishchag is our friend. He saved our lives and we've saved his from Chaneerem and his war party. They aren't all bad. You have to believe us."

Zheva's shoulders eased a little but caution remained on her cheeks. The three of them slowly joined the party and walked into the village.

The group was welcomed with suspicion. But, under such circumstances, Temmonin and the others were very happy to be accepted at all. They

461

needed information and this was the best source. It was necessary to explain some things about their mission but they avoided blatant statements about their relationship to Chaneerem's group. They had to guard themselves from giving out too much information about their intentions. These matters were so easy to misinterpret and to misunderstand. But that night, around the fire, they learned that Chaneerem was last seen not far from there.

Temmonin's heart began to race as he pictured apprehending the talon-licker. Depression was no longer the only fox in the den of his heart. For the first time in a week, he saw something besides vultures on the horizon. Zheva was here. Chaneerem was close. He had a reason to push through his lethargy. And the fire in front of them was especially inspiring.

"I haven't stopped thinkin' about yer family since last winter," Temmonin leaned in close and spoke in Zheva's ear. "It's so good to see 'em here." He nodded at her mother and grandmother as he leaned back away. In spite of the circumstances, the two women still seemed in good spirits about him and Zheva. They smiled subdued smiles. Temmonin stared at the fire for a moment. Then he leaned in again. "Actually, I couldn't stop thinkin' about you."

His comment noticeably impressed Zheva. In spite of the fact that she had just recently lost her father and was probably worried about her brothers, she still blushed enough for him to recognize her pleasure. But then her face dropped.

Temmonin was suddenly embarrassed. Had he said something stupid? Was she not ready for this? Was there some other man he knew nothing about? He felt sick.

For a while, he did not dare turn towards her. He stared at the fire and listened as one of the Demnaza elders continued a narrative. But his attention was deeply engrossed in the flames in front of him and in the flames that were singeing his throat. He could not bear to speak another word to her but, more than that, he could not bear the thought of not knowing why she had just lost her smile.

"If there's somebody else, I'll shut up right now and never say another thing to you."

Zheva turned and gazed up at him with glossy eyes that were orange with firelight, "No, Temmonin. It's not that. It's not that at all." And she delicately touched his knee with her fingertips. Then she returned her hand to its place in her lap and looked at the fire.

Temmonin could not tell if she planned to explain or if she felt she had said enough to relieve him. He was relieved. At least he still had a chance to marry this woman. Yet, did he? If there was no one else, then why was she holding back? She had not held back when they had embraced earlier that afternoon. And her looks were as rich and alive with love as the pine forest in spring. But why was she not responding to him like he hoped she would. He thought this subject would draw her away from thoughts of her father's death. It had certainly pulled his heart out of a black pit.

"When this thing's all over," he spoke with all of his emotion, "I mean when we figure out how to solve this problem with the Ginginmarin, I'm comin'. . ." Damowan poked Temmonin's ribs with his elbow and caught his older brother in mid-stream. Damowan said something that Temmonin hardly cared about. Irritated, Temmonin assented and immediately turned back to Zheva, his face transforming from bother to excitement as it swung. "As I was saying, when this thing's over, I'm comin' back and I'm gonna take care of you." Temmonin's face was so full of heat it rivaled the fire. He was elated and as proud as the dawn.

Zheva blushed a little bit. Then, her face turned sour, "Temmonin, don't say stuff like that at a time like this. Don't you know anything?" And she again turned to the fire.

Temmonin 's stomach tightened and shrunk. He had thought that his excitement would surely lift his cousin out of her sorrow. Should he have said something when they first embraced? Should he have waited until tomorrow before he left to follow Chaneerem's trail? Or should he not have mentioned his love for her at all while she was mourning? He wished he could be inside her mind for a moment--the questions were hot inside him. But he dared not speak again. When they parted that night, she gave him an uncomfortable smile that only added to his confusion.

The party woke early the next morning and Temmonin thought he might miss Zheva altogether as they left the village. But she was there to bring them breakfast. And she did not try to avoid him. Just before they left, he had a chance to talk with her alone.

"Zheva," Temmonin's eyes were as sincere as arrowheads. "I don't wanna say anything bad or stupid or anything. I wish I never said stupid stuff."

"I know," Zheva sighed as she spoke.

"It's just I want you to know that I care." He paused. "I wish I didn't have to go so soon. But, I'll be back to take care of you and your family." Heat again sweltered behind his cheeks. "I love you, Zheva."

They embraced once more before the party left.

Temmonin hiked with a heart that vacillated between hope and despair. He knew now that they would intercept the oath-taker within the next two days, perhaps even later that same day. He knew he should feel relaxed because this party of Salamanders came with the authority of the High Council of the People. But he pictured a tense encounter with the talon-licker's war party. From what they had just learned, Chaneerem's horde had grown exponentially. And since the Ginginmarin were so concentrated in this area, they were traveling quite quickly between massacres. Temmonin was afraid of Chaneerem's insane anger and his ability to infect others with the same.

But, at the same time, he was already dreaming of his return to the village that they had just left. He saw the wedding a thousand times over. He saw their first night together and how he would honor her with the expression of his love. He saw his family and hers rejoicing over them and their new place in the longhouse. Yet, always, there was Chaneerem.

That day, just after noon, they came across what must have been the last village the talon-licker had demolished. Temmonin and the others winced at the stench. The funeral pyre was still burning strongly. He could not help looking up at Mishchag. And when he did so, he immediately began to cry. The others around him did not notice but, in the light of such hideousness, he no longer cared if they had noticed. What was left of his composure was shattered by the sight of half-burned limbs and gasping mouths charred open in the blaze. The sight of babies torn in half and roasting in their own blood stole what was left of his reservation and transformed his sorrow into anger. His tears became hot acid that ate his face. Now he was ready to meet Chaneerem.

They searched the underground village from which the burning Ginginmarin had been dragged and found only one old porcupine-man still alive. He was badly wounded but had found a place to hide from the raiders. The Mitsa-Mitsa found him in the main tunnel. He could barely stand.

"Old man," Mishchag spoke in his native tongue. "When did they do this to you?"

"Last night," the old creature spoke as if he had just swallowed sand. "They got everybody. There's no one left, my son. Not even the little ones."

"I know, old man. They've done this to us all. We're trying to find the smooth-skins who did this to you. Can you help us? Did you hear them say anything about where they were going? Anything at all?"

"You're helping these smooth-skins?"

"Old man, you should know at your age, that there are good people and bad people in every tribe and village--and even every family." As Mishchag reasoned with the elder, he seemed to submit to the logic. "You're going to have to trust me on this one," Mishchag continued. "Now, did you hear them say anything about where they were going?"

"My boy," the old one said gruffly. "You know we all learned their language but us older folks saw so little reason to keep on studying and practicing. I couldn't understand a thing they said. We'll all be dying soon anyway. And it's been so long and never any progress on reaching the smooth-skins. Now I wish I had kept up my practice. But that's always the way it goes, isn't it?"

Temmonin had been translating the conversation for Kashtawa and the others but was becoming impatient. "Old man," he said in Ginginmarin. "Where is the closest village?"

The old porcupine-man gave a puzzled look to Mishchag.

"It's okay, old man," Mishchag reassured. "These are my friends."

The old man did not seem entirely convinced but answered anyway. "There are two not far-- Melunnim near the waterfall and Zegint just beyond this mountain."

"How far?"

"Either one not a day's walk."

"We got him now!" Damowan punched out his words. "There's enough footprints out there a blind man could find which way they went by touch."

"We should go then, right?" Kashtawa prompted. "We could catch up by nightfall"

The rest agreed and turned to exit the tunnel.

"Wait!" Mishchag had remained by the other Ginginmarin. "We cannot to leave here the old man," he said in Mokhamoyuba.

The rest of the party stopped and turned to look.

"Temmonin, he's almost dead," Damowan whispered. "He won't make it ten steps."

"I must to carry my old man." Mishchag leaned down and lifted the shag.

Kashtawa objected. "Mishchag, yer slow as it is. We can't afford any more delays. And we need you with us to talk to yer people--I mean, the survivors. You're gonna have to leave him here."

"I cannot to do that," Mishchag said sternly.

Temmonin was mildly surprised.

"You're gonna have to Mishchag," Kashtawa returned. "He's jus' one man and there're hundreds of lives to save. We can't waste time."

"I must to carry him. I must to."

"No!" Kashtawa commanded.

Mishchag stopped. Temmonin thought he saw anger in the Ginginmarin's face but he could not be sure. Kashtawa's tone would definitely have made Temmonin's neck stiff. Mishchag simply stood there quietly. Then he looked down at the old man in his arms. He released his arms and the old man crashed to the floor.

"He is dead now. We may to go."

Temmonin and Damowan looked at each other in shock. Mishchag stepped over the dead heap as if it were a pile of rotten pumpkins. Without a word, the beast walked up to the Ek-Birin and stood in front of them, his chest and his quills in their faces. They stared up at him for a moment until they realized he wanted them to leave. As the whole party turned to exit the tunnel, Damowan gave Temmonin a look that mixed confusion, surprise, and a touch of irritation and disgust. In any other situation, Temmonin might have laughed hysterically. But, Temmonin had just watched someone drop a dead elder and, whether the old man had died before Mishchag dropped him or as a result of the drop made very little difference to the people of the confederation. It was one of the most offensive things Temmonin had ever witnessed.

As they hiked from the charred belly of this mountain, new thoughts joined the thousand that were already boiling in Temmonin's brain. Mishchag's actions and reactions were so strange to him that he was forced to begin hypothesizing as to the reasons. But Damowan was in a more talkative mood that day.

"Tonight's the night," Damowan began. "What's he gonna do when we get there? That's what I'm burnin' to know."

"Typical Chaneerem stuff, I'll bet," Temmonin offered.

Kashtawa was hiking close by just next to Jemalemin. "What's typical Chaneerem stuff--I mean besides what's obvious from what we've been seein' in these villages?"

"Oh, y'know," Damowan stretched his face into a strange position and made huge hand gestures. "Manipulatin' the circumstances so he looks like an angel, makin' everybody else look like complete idiots, yellin', gettin' his way in everything, never admittin' he's wrong even if it kills him." He relaxed his face and arms. "Y'know, and other really obnoxious stuff that makes ya wanna give him an elbow in the gut when he's not lookin'."

"And that's on a good day," Temmonin added.

Jemalemin chuckled. So did Kashtawa. It was not much but it promised them all that the seriousness of this particular situation would someday be over and they could all laugh again without reservation.

"Seriously though, we should expect plenty of resistance tonight--not necessarily physical but . . ." Temmonin turned to Damowan as the younger Ek-Birin interrupted him.

"But we better not count that kind of resistance out!"

"Yea," Temmonin continued. "Chaneerem is one gigantic, disappointing surprise. The only thing you can be assured of is that he'll prob'ly do somethin' annoying or out and out offensive ev'ry time you meet."

"Is that right, Jemalemin?" Damowan called across Temmonin and Kashtawa.

"Yea," Jemalemin nodded his head strongly, "I lived with him my whole life, too!"

Temmonin felt a little embarrassed at Damowan's question. The last thing he wanted to be involved in was brain-washing or breaking up families. He knew the whole thing was true but he did not dare to encourage Jemalemin's hatred of his own brother.

"Should I be the one to talk to him when we get there?" Kashtawa asked.

"No offense," Temmonin answered. "But I don't know if that's the best idea. You're Mitsa-Mitsa, Kashtawa. Who knows what he'll do with that. I mean all of you being Salamanders might send him way off. Obviously, Kashtawa, we don't have anything against the Mitsa-Mitsa. I mean, you're one of our closest friends. But, Chaneerem? Ya jus' better watch ev'ry word ya say around him."

"Yea, but he's not gonna listen to us or Jemalemin," Damowan interjected. "And he sure as mornin' ain't gonna listen to Mishchag."

"Not much choice, eh?" Kashtawa said.

"Don't get me wrong, Kashtawa," Temmonin apologized. "I don't really know what he'll do if you talk to him. Maybe he'll stop." Damowan laughed at that. "It's jus' we don't know."

They were a long way from the next Ginginmarin village when they began to smell the smoke. Temmonin could see the adrenaline at the corners of Damowan's mouth. His younger brother always tightened his lips in this way when he was preparing for action. As far as Temmonin knew, he himself made no particular signal as his own excitement mounted. But inside, his stomach was sizzling. The last leg of the day's hike threatened to burn a hole in his gut.

In less than an hour, they came to the edge of the forest. From there, they could clearly see the beginnings of one of Chaneerem's atrocities. But they were not too late. The party unconsciously accelerated their pace. Kashtawa motioned to the others that they should hold themselves back.

Ahead of them, the heap of Ginginmarin was barely visible but easily recognizable. As they drew closer, Temmonin could see that many of the porcupine-people on the burning pile were still alive. Acid sliced his jaws. The depth of Chaneerem's cruelty should no longer have surprised him. But he continually remembered the night he saw the oath-taker staring at that sunset. It just seemed as if that same man could not sink this far into stupidity.

It did not take long before one of Chaneerem's warriors noticed the arriving party. He was binding Ginginmarin with ropes so that they could not escape the round-up. He immediately alerted the others near him and, by the time the Mitsa-Mitsa and the Ek-Birin were within earshot of the action, a group of warriors from several tribes was lined up to greet them.

"What is your business here? Have you captured this filth-bag for us to burn?" one of them asked, staring at Mishchag. Temmonin recognized his red and yellow face markings as Tanaka. He was from the Clan of the Lynx. In the distance, the heap of Ginginmarin moaned muffled moans as they roasted. Temmonin could hardly concentrate on the conversation.

Kashtawa chose to ignore the Lynx's second question. "I am Kashtawa of the Clan of the Salamander. My party and I have come as representatives of the High Council from the Island of Ojeb-Mawitez to speak with Chaneerem of the Ek-Birin. The elders have words for him."

Temmonin thought he saw plenty of suspicion in the eyes of these men, but the spokesman refused to betray his feelings. Yet he continually eyed Mishchag as he spoke. "What sort of message shall I relay to Chaneerem of the Ek-Birin. At present, he is occupied below ground organizing this cleansing operation."

Temmonin's eyebrows bent as he heard the word 'cleansing'. So Chaneerem had found his way to incite these warriors. He could picture the talon-licker convincing them of the disgusting inferiority of the Ginginmarin and the need to purify the land of such filth. He could hear him promising that nothing would ever be safe again if they did not eradicate the poisonous snakes from beneath the stones. Temmonin was sure he had appealed to their love for their families and especially their children. The thoughts shoved splinters under Temmonin's fingernails and spilled more acid into his jaws. He was so angry he almost superseded Kashtawa. But he held himself. Next to him, Damowan was obviously about to spit oil. Behind the Tanaka warrior, the moaning continued.

"The words from the elders," Kashtawa proceeded cautiously. "Deal with this very operation. We have been sent to inform him and those with him of the latest decision of the High Council. This is the most urgent of business."

Silence ruled the waiting air. Yet the silence was full of the murmurs of death. Temmonin could see Mishchag staring at his people bound and gagged and lying, faces down into the sand and gravel, some of them already on the heap and burning and groaning. The hulk was trembling. But

he obviously saw the need for patience. He stood
as calmly as he was able to next to Damowan and
Jemalemin. Temmonin could see that Damowan
had relaxed slightly. His younger brother knew it
was useless to waste his energy before it was time.
Yet Temmonin knew Damowan was ready to move
at any moment. Jemalemin looked as if he might
cry--not a hopeless, helpless cry but one of
compassion for these creatures. Temmonin thought
he could also see the birth pains of outrage in
Jemalemin's cheeks.

The scene seemed to hang in the air around
them as the Tanaka warrior chose his words. "I will
attempt to notify him."

"That will not suffice," Kashtawa spoke
sternly.

"And what will suffice?"

"You will lead us to where he is before any
new activity takes place here."

Temmonin could see something change even
behind the red and yellow on the Lynx's cheeks.
"You are correct." His lips quivered so slightly that
it was difficult to notice. "We will escort you to
him."

At least these men were accustomed to
submitting to authority. Kashtawa had reminded
them of their duty and they had responded well,
regardless of their personal feelings about the Mitsa-
Mitsa or the Ginginmarin. Temmonin could see the
familiar looks of disgust on their faces as they
glanced at Kashtawa and his fellows. But, in spite
of this, they had chosen to behave properly.

The warriors turned and led Temmonin's party
around the group of bound and gagged
Ginginmarin. As soon as they had cleared the
circle, Temmonin could see the cave entrance. It
was not extremely visible, but he was growing

accustomed to the way the Ginginmarin hid their tunnels. Temmonin could hardly bear to look at the pile of porcupine-people and the reek was intense here. It made him too angry. He looked back toward the cave entrance.

Someone was emerging from the hole. First, there were two Ek-Makatin warriors he did not recognize. Then Chaneerem crawled out and stood up. Temmonin's heart pressed into his ribs. The talon-licker was followed by several warriors dragging Ginginmarin with ropes. But Temmonin had no thoughts about those other men. Chaneerem was in front of him.

The oath-taker's face went straight when he saw their group. Temmonin thought he saw embarrassment among the black and red battle stripes Chaneerem had smeared across his cheeks. The killer had not expected this. But he was a quick-thinker, quicker than anyone Temmonin knew. He stood and waited at the mouth of the cave.

As the Ek-Birin and the Mitsa-Mitsa approached with their escorts, the warriors behind the talon-licker continued pulling captive porcupine-men from the passageway. Chaneerem's position just outside made it difficult for them to maneuver. Of course, their leader would not consider stepping aside to make their job easier. Temmonin saw in Chaneerem's eyes that he was aware of the others behind him. And, in spite of the fact that he had commanded these warriors to do what they were now doing, he did not move out of their way. Temmonin recalled times in his own childhood when he had acted in exactly the same way toward Damowan. Now, the sight made him shake his head. The oath-taker stood like a dead tree, his cold, dead eyes slipping farther into the black pit of himself with each new act of hatred. Temmonin stared directly at him, determined not to look away no matter how the talon-licker responded. Chaneerem matched his stare with what was probably intended to look like casual indifference. But Temmonin knew the kind of bitterness that was biting at the back of that mask. The stare-down continued even after the escort presented Kashtawa to the talon-licker.

"Chaneerem of the Ek-Birin," Kashtawa began. "As head of this service of the High Council, I, Kashtawa of the Mitsa-Mitsa, stand before you as the mouth of said council to bring you the most recent will of the Confederation." He paused, expecting an acknowledgment. Nothing came. Temmonin could see the hesitation in Kashtawa's eyes but he saw no sign that the Mitsa-Mitsa was the least bit threatened by Chaneerem's arrogant silence. Kashtawa continued. "The most recent decisions are now nearly fourteen moons old yet they are spoken with the full authority of the council. They concern the present activities now under your command"

Kashtawa would have continued but Chaneerem suddenly raised his arm. It was the one with the burnt forearm and the tiny red Chrebin brand. Temmonin had forgotten about the talon-licker's encounter with the squirrel-men. Surely, Chaneerem had not forgotten about it for a single moment since it had happened. And he had probably found a way to use the wound as a symbol of power. It was definitely a wound awesome enough to use as a symbol of power.

The Mitsa-Mitsa waited an uncomfortably long time before he resumed. "It is the. . ." Kashtawa stopped short again as Chaneerem moved his arm in an even more aggressive gesture for silence.

Chaneerem was looking into the forest with an unfocused look that told everyone he was listening to something.   He held his melodramatic pose until the instant Kashtawa began to speak again. Then the talon-licker's face melted into the most sincere expression he could muster.

"Wait, I think I hear something black and orange squirming under a rock somewhere." Chaneerem could not have said a more offensive thing to this group of Salamanders. Temmonin was truly appalled. Damowan's hair was about to ignite. Somehow, Kashtawa managed to keep his dagger in its sheath.

"The High Council has spoken," Kashtawa continued as calmly as he could. But his next sentence was naked and sharp. "You are commanded to stop this bloodshed!"

Chaneerem seemed to enjoy the power of his own silence. He pretended not to be shocked by this news. And perhaps he was not. Perhaps he knew his rampage would be a limited one. Perhaps he was able to be so calm because he had already had enough to satisfy his vengeance. Temmonin might never know.

"As a member of the Confederation myself and as a warrior, I do still retain the right to know the reasons for the High Council's decisions, do I not?" Chaneerem's tone irritated Temmonin. Kashtawa had said nothing about the talon-licker's rights being restricted yet Chaneerem had just painted himself violated. Typical.

"Of course." Kashtawa said, controlling his voice and his anger. "The Council has heard the words of Temmonin, Damowan, and Jemalemin in regards to the same issues which you yourself discussed only a short time before they reached the Island of the Council. The Council decided that the weight of these three testimonies was greater than that of yours. They have rescinded their blessing of your activities and wish to reconvene with the four of you and with representatives of the Ginginmarin."

"So, the Council has weighed the three against the one?" Chaneerem's anger slipped out between syllables. "Or they weighed one against one--brother against brother?"

Jemalemin looked uncomfortable but Temmonin felt secure in that the youngest Ek-Birin was next to Damowan. Chaneerem moved a little closer to his brother. Temmonin and Damowan both started forward to protect the boy but held themselves back when they could see that the talon-licker meant to keep a reasonable distance.

"What did my own flesh and blood have to tell them to convince them to reverse their decision?" Chaneerem spoke haughtily. Then he noticed the Chrebin on Damowan's shoulder. Fear and loathing entered the oath-taker's eyes simultaneously. Temmonin thought he saw words gathering in the man's jaws. But Chaneerem did not mention the squirrel-man. He turned back to Jemalemin. "Did my own brother have to give them a nice character sketch? Did he explain how, when we were cubs, the older brother did all the things older brothers're famous for. How he teased and tormented the younger brother and toughened his skin like nobody else's? Did he explain how his older brother never showed him any mercy so that he'd never become like a weak, whimperin' coward but, rather a brave, hardened warrior? Did he explain how the older brother taught him to fight, to hunt, and to think like a warrior 'cuz his father never had the patience? Did the younger brother tell of his older brother's tireless efforts?" He

477

paused, it seemed to Temmonin, simply for effect. "Or did he color his brother with another shade of red?"

"I told the truth!" Jemalemin protested. "The truth about the Ginginmarin and the truth about you!"

"The truth?!" Chaneerem's anger was losing it's control. "The truth about how so many times, I laid my body over yours and took the beatin' Dad meant for you?" At that, Temmonin saw Jemalemin's face go white. Chaneerem continued. "Not to mention all of the times I stole you away from home and spent whole nights keepin' you away from the longhouse because Dad was in the mood to make you bleed--even in the freezin' cold when I'd wrap myself around you while we were buried in the snow so you could stay warm? And then there's the truth about how my two middle fingers on my left hand have no feeling in 'em 'cuz of one of those extremely cold nights when I was protectin' you from Dad and there wasn't even enough time to grab enough skins to keep us warm!"

Jemalemin was obviously distraught at this outburst. It looked to Temmonin as if Jemalemin was forced to assent to the truth of every statement his brother had just spoken. Yet something red and hot was seething just beneath the boy's face.

"I told the truth about how you hate everybody who won't let you have your way!"

"And that reversed their decision? Ha!" The talon-licker moved forward and pressed in close to his brother. "Listen here!"

Damowan and Temmonin stepped up as Jemalemin retreated.

"What?! Now I can't talk to my own little brother?"

Temmonin and Damowan hesitated but allowed Chaneerem to pass between them. Suddenly, he stopped and pointed at the Chrebin.

"And git that thing outta here!" he growled as he turned to his brother.

Jemalemin seemed oblivious to all that was happening around him. He was concentrating on the next words he wanted to say. He was nervous but enraged enough to stand his ground and his face suddenly burned brighter than a bonfire. "I told 'em how you tried to kill me!" he screamed until his neck was maroon and had swelled thicker than his head.

Chaneerem looked as if he had expected this. His face hardened into granite. More quickly than Temmonin or Damowan or Jemalemin could predict, he drew his dagger and drove it deeply into his brother's chest. Jemalemin's face froze and lost its color. In the same instant, Chaneerem's face was flooded with regret. But his body and his brother's had become one. The talon-licker could not move. In that one moment, Temmonin thought he saw more tears in Chaneerem's eyes than he himself had cried in his entire lifetime.

But Damowan had not noticed the oath-taker's remorse. He slammed into Chaneerem with both of his fists balled together. He punched him twice before the talon-licker released his grip on the dagger. Jemalemin fell to the ground and Damowan leapt over him and rammed Chaneerem to the dirt. He pounded and pounded and pounded. The oath-taker did not resist in the least. But just before he died, Temmonin thought he saw a look of relief on his bloody forehead. And Damowan pounded more. Then Chaneerem's chest stopped moving and Damowan stopped pounding.

No one moved for a long time. Temmonin was still trying to understand what had happened when Damowan's sobs began. Temmonin slowly turned to Jemalemin. The boy lay dead where he had fallen, the handle of the dagger protruding from his chest. He turned back to his younger brother whose tears were now mixing with the blood that was streaming from Chaneerem's motionless face. And next to the talon-licker's head stood the Chrebin who had leapt from Damowan's shoulder as the fighting began. The squirrel-man had observed everything and now continued to observe as the tears fell. And Temmonin observed as well. But it all felt as if he were watching this from the top of a cliff and the two brothers had died a hundred feet below him.

Then, something like pain gripped his stunned heart and pulled him to his knees beside Damowan. His brother turned and fell into Temmonin's lap bawling and clutching Temmonin as if he were hanging from the cliff and Temmonin were the only solid rock to hold on to. Temmonin's tears began to wash over his cheeks. All he could see through the blur was Damowan's heaving back and, just beyond that, Mishchag's huge torso. The porcupine-man had bent down to look at Damowan. Temmonin's eyes met the Ginginmarin's with the same helplessness that shone through that huge face.

Temmonin felt something come to rest on his shoulder. It was Kashtawa's hand. As he glanced at the Mitsa-Mitsa's comforting eyes, he could not stop the flood that was gushing across his face. All around them were the warriors who had looked on as the two had died. They stood like a forest in winter, cold and lifeless.

Moon Beneath the Mountains

Somewhere, far beneath Temmonin's swollen eyes, he realized that, at least for now, his people had stopped killing the Ginginmarin.

EPILOGUE

Since Mishchag was too tall to enter the longhouse through the opening, Amowz proposed that they extend their family's quarters outward and upward. This way, the Ginginmarin could enter through a special doorway into a separate chamber that was connected to their section of the house. The extended family was accustomed to Amowz's attitude toward the Mitsa-Mitsa so this adoption of a foreigner into their longhouse was no surprise. Yet Temmonin sensed the reticence with which the others accepted the changes. Some of the men seemed fixated with the architechtural challenges the modifications would entail. They were very pessimistic about the chances of success. But he was sure they would be more than willing to make the necassary changes if one of their daughters were to have taken a husband and the longhouse needed to be expanded.

Once it was apparent, however, that enough people were willing to live with Mishchag, those who were reluctant found a way to hold their tongues. Temmonin knew that this was the best they could expect. He hoped that with time, the village would grow to befriend the Porcupine Man. He also hoped he would be able to understand this mystery of a friend. He wondered if he could ever accept his strange, offensive manner of dealing with embarrassing situations and, more importantly, with the dying and the dead. If others in his village were repulsed by Mishchag for no good reason, would Temmonin ever overcome his disgust at the Ginginmarin's harsh actions? Would he come to see things from that beast's point of view? And if he did, would he then alienate himself from his own people? For the time being at least, he was being led by his principles and not his disgust. He could only trust that all that his father had instilled in him would eventually prove itself to be true.

He knew that soon he and Damowan would need to begin considering how they would initate negotiations with the Ginginmarin. But Damowan was brooding so much that Temmonin was not sure he would be able to function in council. The elder shed many tears as well when he thought of how Jemalemin and Chaneerem had died. But he himself had not killed anyone so his sorrow was of a different flavor than Damowan's. Actually, he hurt almost as much for his brother as he did for the two who had died. And he completely understood why Damowan was in no condition to negotiate. Of course very few people blamed Damowan. Almost anyone would have reacted similarly given the situation. But most would have stopped sooner than Damowan had.

Zevil, on the other hand, minced no words regarding the death of his sons. Even though he was not there when they were killed, he spoke of the event as if he were an expert. And if no one else blamed Damowan for Chaneerem's death, Zevil did so with the vehemence of an entire village. In fact, he blamed Damowan and Temmonin for both deaths. Temmonin had never seen him express such emotion. He would not listen to anything the two said. He would not listen to anythig the village leaders said. He would not listen to anything the clan leader said. He had dug himself into a pit of bitterness and from there, he willed heavy spirit stones onto Damowan's and Temmonin's shoulders. And he took every opportunity to add to the load they carried. Temmonin never remembered encountering that man as often as during the days following their return. Now it seemed as if he were

seeking them out. It seemed as if the fact that the
village and clan leaders and the rest of the
confederation saw them as innocent only fortified
Zevil's accusations against them. He obviously
sensed that Damowan and Temmonin were
uncomfortable in his presence and seemed to enjoy
the power this afforded him. If he were unable to
satiate his thirst for revenge in a physical way, at
least he could punish them with guilt.

In the end, no one could create a worse
punishment for Damowan than for him to have to
live with what he had done. He wandered in a
stupor; an overcast that clung to his forehead from
the moment he woke each day until he fell asleep
each night. Fortunately, the council was not
pressuring Damowan and Temmonin. In spite of
the fact that the issue of the Ginginmarin was
urgent, the leaders of the confederation had pity on
them.

At this point, it seemed that most people
had accepted their story. This was at the same time
a blessing and a curse for even though the
confederation now trusted the two Ek-Birin, they
were also now very suspicious of the Porcupine
people. Temmonin did not look forward to
negotiating. It seemed to him that it was simply an
invitation to heartache.

This dread that congealed in his stomach
was mixed with the dull ache caused by the absence
of the people he had recently come to enjoy. He
missed Kashtawa. But he knew he would see that
jolly soul soon enough when the council
reconvened. He also missed his Uncle Nosh and
that pain lingered longer; burned deeper. He would
not see Nosh any time soon. And of course, he
longed for Zheva. But although thoughts of that
Wolverine woman caused him to suffer, they also

soothed his achings. He had promised her that
when he could, he would return to her. Yes, he was
needed at council. Yes, he would do all that was
necessary to help his people in this moment. But as
soon as he could go, he would go to Zheva and give
her his heart. He had found the woman with whom
he would spend the rest of his life. And he would
go to her and give her his heart.

IMPORTANT CHARACTERS (WITH AGE) AND PLACES

Amowz (45) Married To Semarda (47)

Shabba (65) Father Of Semarda

Sons – Temmonin (20)
       Damowan (18)

Eshtawana (80) High-Mother Of Longhouse

Daughters – Tutumora (14)

Ammon (44) Brother Of Amowz, Wife Died In Childbirth Along With Only Child

Nosh (40) Brother Of Amowz, Married To Zemma (38)

Sons – Shegra (22)

       Demdaminek (14)

Daughters - Zheva (20)

           Mezha (17)

Desh - High Chief Of The Clan Of The Flicker

Da - Chief Of The Flicker Village Of Kemkemmayam

Mayban - A Mitsa-Mitsa Warrior Living In Kemkemmayam, Married To Teshamasaw

Mok - A Daimadunva Chief

Shemshem - A Kumuchska Warrior Who Befriended Temmonin

Kemkemmayam - Flicker Village Where Temmonin And Damowan Live With Their Family

Demdegumshannatez - Wolverine Village Where Nosh Lives With His Family

Mestaumdelmez - Painted Turtle Village Where Mok Lives And Rules

Gamnashta - Elk Village Known For Its Hot-Springs

Semsaweva - Healing Plant

NOTES ON TRIBAL GOVERNMENT

This story takes place among a people with a highly developed, republican form of government. Within each village are several longhouses, each housing the extended family of a housemother. The society is a matrilineal one and so this eldest living woman of a particular family rules over such things as planting (of what limited agriculture they have), meals, and living situations. She is also consulted on trivial village matters and any matter involving only the members of her longhouse. When a man marries a woman, he leaves his housemother's longhouse and moves into his wife's longhouse. Each village also has a male leader or chief who oversees decisions concerning hunting, war, and ceremonial matters.

Several villages in a geographical location are linked together by a common clan totem. Clan councils are held when necessary. Five clans that live in similar habitat are organized into tribes. These include the marsh-dwellers (Mamarra), the mountain-dwellers (Kanattar), the swamp-dwellers (Shushunushu), and the forest-dwellers (Krim-Krim). (By no means is the geography of the land so segregated as to entirely indicate a tribal dwelling place. The tribal name merely reflects the overall character of the terrain in which they live. In fact, forest of some kind covers most of the land excepting some vast marshes.) These tribes also meet sporadically. Finally, the four tribes are linked to each other by a tribal confederation, the governing body of which is the Confederation High Council. This ruling body meets regularly only once per year and these meetings are characterized by a longevity of no fewer than ten days.

At these meetings, delegates from all twenty clans of all four tribes participate in ceremonies, games, and the exchange of news. When matters of extreme importance arise, additional High Councils are called.

I dedicate this book to the Medellín cartel. I do this with all my heart and by the love of Jesus Christ, who put this love for you in me. Through this book I give glory and honor to our heavenly Father, who, in 1983, while I was detained in Rikers Island jail in New York City, picked up the pieces of my life and put them back together and made a new person out of me.

To the Mafia With Love

All names, except those of the author, the Colombian cartel leaders, and selected organizations have been changed. Portions of the narrative and conversation have been edited for clarification and to provide continuity. All facts as presented are true.

Chapter 1

New York, July 14, 1983

S uddenly I was surrounded. I stood frozen, hemmed in by a ring of cars, the sirens cutting the quiet summer air. Plainclothesmen were crouched around me, guns pointing, yelling hoarsely.

The incredible speed and fury of the attack left me paralyzed, my heart slamming against my ribs in deep, thudding strokes.

I moved slightly, and the guns dipped. "Get your hands up!"

My eyes traveled around the circle, my mind in turmoil. Who had known I was coming? Who could have tipped them off?

"Get your hands up, ma'am. Get them up!" The voices crashed through my dazed consciousness. Slowly I raised my hands.

"What's in the bag, ma'am?"

I could not answer. My mind felt sluggish.

"What's in the bag, ma'am?" The question was repeated roughly.

"It's a radio…" My voice trailed off uncertainly.

"A radio?" The detective's voice rose slightly. He glanced over at his partner, his eyes mocking. "It's a radio, Joe. Guess we were wrong this time." He turned back to me, his manner apologetic. "We're going to have to take a look inside, ma'am." Slowly he opened the bag and reached inside, his eyes fixed on mine.

Sweat trickled slowly between my shoulder blades. I clenched my fists, fighting the sudden weakness in my knees.

He was watching my reactions, his eyes judging, calculating. Suddenly they hardened, widening in mock astonishment. "Well, well…What do we have here?"

A feeling of nausea washed over me. My eyes jerked toward the bag; I watched in sick fascination as the detective pulled his hand from the bag.

"What is this, ma'am? A radio?"

Several officers laughed.

The detective held the clear plastic bag up with the tips of his fingers, swinging it gently by the corner. He shook his head in apparent confusion. "No…What then? Is it flour? Or sugar?" His voice was dripping with sarcasm.

My cheeks were burning, my eyes fixed on an invisible spot on the ground.

"Or could this white stuff be cocaine?" His voice was prodding, insinuating.

I closed my eyes, blocking the tears. I had known this was going to happen. I had seen the signs and ignored them. I had not listened. Why? Only six more days and I would have been in Colombia.

The officer was watching me. "Ma'am, you have $30,000 worth of cocaine here. You say you didn't know?"

I shook my head mutely.

"Speak up, ma'am. We can't hear you."

"No, I didn't know."

He flipped his hand and made an obscene comment.

Indignation straightened my back. "Sir, I am a lady," I said, stiffly. "Please do not talk to me that way."

"A lady!" he sneered, his eyes hard. "You think you're a lady, selling cocaine in front of your daughter?"

My fingers curled, wanting to scratch the taunting face.

"Ben," another officer warned quietly, "that's enough." The detective turned his back. "Cuff her."

My head was throbbing. Johanna had warned me. Mama had warned me. My friends had warned me. So many mistakes, so many wrong decisions. Now I was going to pay. Tears gathered in my eyes. It was over. This time I was not going to get away. I was going to jail—for a very long time.

Chapter 2

Marta, you're next." My teacher rushed past, her hair flying. "Don't miss your cue."

"Death to the Granadinos," I whispered to myself. "Death to the Granadinos." I tiptoed to the corner of the curtain and peeked out. Three more lines, and it would be my turn. "Virgin Mary, don't let me trip," I pleaded. "Don't let me forget my lines." I took a breath and waited.

"Death to the Granadinos! Death to the Granadinos!" The furious shouts broke out on stage. It was my cue! I crossed myself and swept onto the stage, spurring my brave soldiers on to freedom.

But history had written a different freedom for my heroine. I stood in the middle of the stage, holding up the tattered flag. Soldiers swept past me, their long cloaks swirling. With a final sigh I wrapped the flag around my shoulders and sank to the ground, my eyes narrowing, then closing in death.

A soldier leaned over me, then straightened. "She's dead. Policarpa Salavarrieta is dead."

The soldier's sad pronouncement brought a rousing cheer

from the enemy forces. "The battle is over! Salavarrieta is dead."

Applause sounded from the audience, loud and long, and excitement coursed down my back. The play was over; the heroine was dead, but we were a success. The audience had loved us.

Dead soldiers sprang up around me. "Marta, get up." A ten-year-old soldier poked me irreverently with his wooden sword. "You're not dead anymore."

I ignored the jab, a peculiar feeling gripping me. I had lived every moment of my brave heroine's life. Policarpa—what fierce loyalty she had shown for Colombia, dying for her country, her name emblazoned forever in history.

Classmates stripped bands from their heads, the defeated soldiers taking retaliatory swipes at the enemy behind the teacher's back. I stood up, grasping the folds of the flag, its vibrant colors sending a rush of patriotic pride through me. "Someday, I will do something great for Colombia," I whispered fiercely. "One day I, too, will make my country proud."

"Marta, that was wonderful." My teacher's face was flushed with pleasure. "You played a beautiful Salavarrieta."

Others were pressing in, congratulating me and the revived cast. "Great play. Congratulations. *Fue buenísimo!*"

Offstage my mother's face was shining, her eyes proud. She beckoned me. "Come, Policarpa," she said. "It's late, even for a heroine. Let's go home."

We walked home through the streets of Medellín, the soft night air soothing my still-flushed cheeks. My young heart was burning with loyalty, lofty dreams of sacrifice forming in my head. I straightened my shoulders, my heart thrilling to the memory of Salavarrieta's noble sacrifices. I was only nine, but I was determined—one day I, too, would make Colombia proud.

* * *

Medellín, Colombia, was a pretty city in the 1950s, street corners bursting with baskets of blooming orchids and geraniums. Clean and friendly before the drug wars, Medellín waited, sleepy and sun-drenched, for night to fall. A fierce, midday sun beat down on the city, baking the streets and sidewalks, sending Colombians scurrying home for afternoon siestas. Only at night did the city come to life. Nightfall was the signal to awaken, drowsiness giving way to festive music and late-night dancing under the stars.

The streets of our *barrio* were busy in the morning. Children made their way to school, and parents headed for the buses and work. Women balanced large baskets on their heads, calling, "Avocados! Papayas!" Others brought *parva*, a tasty collection of buns, toast, and pastries, to sell on the street corner.

We were poor as a family, but we were happy. Sometimes my mother would send me to the little corner store to purchase cakes or buns. A special treat for me was the candy we could buy for one cent.

Mama was the dominant influence in our household, and we went to her for everything. She managed the money and took care of our schoolbooks and materials. She worked during the day and then took work as a seamstress at night to bring in extra money, so we didn't see her much—but she took good care of us. Each morning we were dressed and ready for school, our faces scrubbed and clean, our books tucked under our arms.

Papa was a quiet presence in our home, keeping his distance and staying apart from our activities. He was a good man, but he gambled.

Mama hated the gambling. When my brothers followed Papa's example and started playing cards, she beat them until they promised never to touch the dice or cards again. Cowed into submission, they kept their promise well into adulthood.

Through twelve years of school, I never lost my interest in the heroes of our country. I studied hard, working to keep my grades up. I was small and skinny but eager and determined. Partying with my friends was fun, but school always came first. If I was going to do something great for Colombia, I realized I was going to have to do well in school.

In 1962 I graduated from one of the best schools in the country. My family celebrated with abandon. There were dances held in my honor, and students from the universities came to dance and party until early in the morning.

Two months later I was teaching fifth grade in a small, quiet town in the Aburrá Valley just south of Medellín. I took my role as a teacher seriously, leaving the dancing and partying for weekends and evenings, refusing to smoke or use drugs, and drinking only when pressured. Every Monday morning I was back at school, alert and ready to face my students.

Soon I was transferred to a convent in Medellín where I began teaching first and third grades. When the Mother Superior asked me to start teaching the nuns themselves, I agreed eagerly; it was an honor to be asked to teach these women of the church, so selfless in their service to others.

Convent life was peaceful, and I loved the nuns; but when the Mother Superior talked to me about becoming a nun, I resisted. I did not enjoy the thought of sacrificing myself in service to God. I loved money and relished my freedom too much.

Life was full and rich in those first several years of teaching. Then one day I received an invitation from a friend in the United States. "Marta, why don't you come and visit me for a couple of months?" she wrote. "You can stay with me in my apartment, and I'll show you around New York. We'll have lots of fun."

New York! Broadway, Chinatown, the Statue of Liberty! I could not resist. In 1966, I landed in New York for the first time. It was December, I was twenty-two, and New York was bursting with energy. Excitement pumped through my veins like a drug. This big, beautiful city was everything I had imagined. I visited with friends and partied late, hitting all the night spots in New York. My friends laughed at me, enjoying my enthusiasm, watching with amusement as I danced with one partner after another. Finally, early in the morning, we staggered home to collapse in my friend's apartment.

By the end of January, I was ready to go home. The sparkling snow was beautiful and the frosty nights lovely, but my Latin blood longed for the heat of the Colombian sun. I missed the soft glow of the city street lights, the clear night sky dark above mountain villages, the peaceful countryside ribboned by slender dusty paths.

Anxious to see my family and students, I returned to Colombia and settled in again, happy to be home. The thought of financial success in the United States remained an alluring thought on the outskirts of my mind, but the homesick feeling I felt away from family and friends kept me from reapplying for a visa.

Still, the provocative thought persisted. Friends wrote, telling me of financial success in New York, and I wondered what would happen if I went back to the States and got a job. Once I had enough money to buy my own home in Colombia, I would never have to leave again.

The arguments see-sawed back and forth—until one day the argument was settled for me.

"Marta!" A friend of mine was flipping through my passport excitedly. "Did you know you have a multiple visa?"

"A multiple? You're kidding!" I reached for the passport. "Let me see." Astonished, I turned the pages. Sure enough, the visa was for five years. I looked up at my friend inquiringly. "How did this happen?"

Her eyes were sparkling with enthusiasm. "It must have been a mistake."

Mistake? Maybe—but what a fortunate twist of fate this was! I would not have to reapply for a visa. The decision was made for me. I was going back to New York.

In 1968, I took a leave of absence from teaching, boarded the plane to New York, and took a job as a baby-sitter and housekeeper for a Jewish family in New Jersey.

It did not take long for reality to set in. In Colombia I was a well-educated and well-respected teacher. In the States I scrubbed floors and washed dirty linen for wealthy Americans. I was a housekeeper in charge of four little children who spoke better English than I did.

The children were well-behaved and friendly, but I struggled with disappointment. The American dream I had heard so much about seemed to dangle constantly out of reach. The money I was saving inched agonizingly toward the mark I had set.

You can make it, Marta, I encouraged myself. *Just be patient. It won't be much longer.*

Six years later I was still in the States.

The price for financial independence seemed terribly high, but still there were rewards. Days off were spent with friends, going to discos and eating out, drinking and partying. My friends were loud and boisterous, and nights out became a little wild at times, but I enjoyed being with them. Small and lithe, I was rarely without a dance partner at the discos. We partied and drank until early in the morning, crashed at a friend's apartment long enough to sleep off the effects—then were up again and off to another disco.

The partying did not help my small stash of money, and my teacher instincts surfaced frequently during those nights out, but my friends teased me unmercifully. "Marta, loosen up—have a drink. Have a little fun. You only live once. You can't always be stuffy."

"I may be stuffy," I retorted, "but at least I have my self-respect."

One night, at a disco in Queens, I sat at a table, tapping a foot, unaccustomed to being without a partner. *I must have bad luck in this chair*, I thought impatiently. I moved to another chair and waited.

It was hot in the disco, and I waved a fan gently, the warm breeze lifting tendrils of damp hair from my neck. Sweating, gleaming bodies danced to the *cumbia* and *salsa* beats, temperatures rising as Latin blood clashed with summer heat.

I glanced sideways, allowing my eyes to drift casually over the crowd by the door, then stopped, my attention caught by a well-dressed man in dark trousers and white jacket, his black hair touched by silver. I stared, the dark eyes and quick smile raising my interest level alarmingly.

He raised his glass in a silent toast, and I grinned appreciatively. *Changing chairs must have worked*, I thought humorously. He started toward me, an eyebrow raised quizzically.

I swept my eyes down, avoiding my friends' amused looks.

"Excuse me..." The voice was deep and resonant.

One of my friends cleared her throat. "Marta, someone is here to see you."

I looked up into eyes that glinted, dark and amused. He held out a hand. "Would you like to dance...Marta?"

No use feigning disinterest. I slid my hand into his, a shiver touching my skin as his fingers closed over mine. "Yes, I'd love to."

His name was Esteban, and we moved well together on the dance floor. "Where are you from, Marta?" His deep voice sounded Chilean. "You look like you might be from Colombia."

"Medellín," I said. "And you? Chile?"

"Yes," he said, pleased I had guessed. "Chile..." His arm tightened around my waist, his eyes suddenly absorbed. "Marta, may I have another dance later this evening?"

I tilted my head, considering. If I moved too quickly, he might lose interest. If I showed too little interest, he might give up. "Yes," I said quickly, "of course."

Esteban deposited me at the table, leaving with a slow smile and a nod for my friends.

My friends were impressed. "Where did you get that one from?" they giggled. "If he comes back while you're in the ladies' room, we'll just say you went home and take him for ourselves, okay?"

I did not mind the teasing but wondered where I was headed with this smooth Chilean. I was more than a little interested.

When Esteban asked for my telephone number and permission to call, I gave it to him gladly.

That summer, our little group met at parks, beaches, and discos every weekend, laughing and playing through the warm, sunlit days of summer. Esteban was a welcome addition to our group, and I watched him with interest, intrigued by his slow smile and warm eyes. He was different from other men I'd known. He did not drink or go out with other women. He was a hard worker, he enjoyed the simple life, and he treated me with respect.

I was falling in love.

Chapter 3

Six months later, Esteban and I were married.

The whirlwind romance and weekend marriage did not change much in our lives. There was no honeymoon, and we saw each other only on weekends when I was off work, but we were happy and we were in love.

One year after we were married, I discovered I was pregnant. I had many fears about becoming a mother, and my anxieties were only heightened by the constant nausea I felt every day of the nine months. But our new daughter was beautiful, and it was charming to see the delight Esteban took in his little child.

What joy we felt as we pushed Lina's stroller through the park and to the zoo. I was fortunate to have a husband I loved, a healthy child, and the care of my mother, who had come from Colombia to help me.

In 1976, I was finally given legal resident status in the United States, and Esteban and I moved into our own apartment. He was a good husband and a devoted father. He worked hard at a factory warehouse during the day, then returned home early every night to be with his family. Those first several years were very happy. I began planning for the future—three children, a nice home, a good business—it all seemed possible. The American dream seemed tantalizingly close.

Then, one day, Esteban had a surprise for me. "Marta," he said, "I want to take you and Lina to meet my family in Chile. Mother wants to see her new granddaughter." He paused briefly, then added quickly, "And her new daughter-in-law."

The pause was barely noticeable. "Of course," I said eagerly. "You know I've always wanted to see Chile—and I would love to meet your family."

He looked relieved. "Good. I'll get time off from work."

I held out a hand. "Esteban…"

He lifted an inquiring eyebrow.

"Will your mother like me?"

"Like you?" A slight frown crossed his face. "Of course she'll like you. Why wouldn't she?"

"I…it's just that we never…we were married so quickly."

His lids lowered, hooding guarded eyes. "So?" He stood up abruptly. "Everything is going to be fine, Marta. Don't worry about it. She'll love you."

The nervous tingling in my throat left me feeling vaguely troubled and just a little tired, but I saw Esteban watching and smiled stiffly. "It'll be fun, Esteban. We'll have a good time."

I prepared for the trip carefully, wanting Esteban to be proud of me. We were scheduled to be in Chile for four weeks, but I knew the days would pass quickly.

We left for Chile on a beautiful day in December 1977. Chile was breathtaking, with shadowed mountains on one side and the sparkling ocean on the other. The airplane glided through the Andes to land on a concrete strip carved in the underside of the mountain, the lush green of the land touched by rich-blue shadows.

Esteban's family was delighted to see Lina, and if Esteban's mother seemed a little reserved toward me at first, I knew it would change once we got to know each other.

We spent our days visiting the sights and getting to know each other. Esteban's family treated me with respect, and they accepted Lina eagerly, but I noticed with increasing nervousness that Esteban's mother remained uncomfortable around me.

As the weeks passed, her manner toward me became frigid, an underlying antagonism bubbling closer to the surface. She jealously guarded time with her son, skillfully manipulating time alone with him and making me feel like an intruder. I was uncomfortable, but for Esteban's sake I tried to smooth over the tension. I was determined to make our stay pleasant for everyone.

While I was careful to ease the awkward moments that cropped up during our visit, I could not avoid the problems that seemed to leave Esteban irritable and preoccupied. The family business was not doing well. The shelves of the little grocery store were almost always empty, and there were few customers. Several times I wondered what had happened to the money Esteban had sent from New York.

Unanswered questions hung between us, but Esteban brushed me off, unwilling to talk. He seemed strangely distant, spending more time with his mother and his family than he did with Lina or me.

The weeks passed slowly, and I began to think longingly of home. I missed the closeness Esteban and I had enjoyed in New York and resented the relationship he now shared with his mother.

Several days before our scheduled departure, the tensions came to a head. Esteban drew me aside. "Marta," he said, "I've been thinking."

Why did my hands clench so suddenly, irrationally? "Yes? About what?"

He sat down beside me. "My mother's store. Why don't we stay in Chile for a while and see if we can make it work? We could make it a success if we worked on it together."

I uncurled my fingers, keeping my voice calm. "Esteban, you can't be serious. What about our resident status in the U.S.?"

"What about it? We're a family. We'll be happy wherever we are."

"I worked six years for that visa, Esteban."

"I know that." He waved a hand impatiently. "I know that, but my mother needs me here."

"Your mother!" I stared at him.

He looked away, unable to meet my eyes.

"Esteban…" I took a steadying breath. "I'm sure we can work this out, but if we stay here, we cannot live with your mother."

"Not live with Mother?" His voice rose. "Why not? Of course we can!"

I looked over my shoulder at the closed door. "No, Esteban, it just isn't right. If we stay, we'll have to live in our own house."

He changed tactics abruptly. "Marta, what about your savings?"

Thrown off balance, I looked at him, bewildered. "What about it?"

"Why don't you invest it in a small taxi business here? We could support our family with it."

Something was happening that I did not understand. I shook my head to clear it. "Esteban, you know I promised to buy a house for my parents with that money."

Esteban drew a silent breath, then looked straight at me, his decision mirrored in his dark eyes. "I'm staying in Chile, Marta; are you staying with me?"

Was this an ultimatum? Was he giving me a choice? I could feel the chasm widening. I answered blindly, instinctively. "Esteban, you know I want to stay with you, but if this marriage is going to work, we're going to have to live in our own house."

Esteban turned and walked out of the room.

The days that followed were filled with tension. Esteban was cold and reserved. When we spoke, he kept his eyes averted, his face set and sullen. Uncertainly, I waited for our departure date. Was he serious? Would he really give up his family to stay in Chile with his mother?

In the days before our scheduled departure Esteban avoided any contact with me, but the night before our return flight, he seemed to come to a decision. "Marta, we have to work this out," he said. "Give me a couple of months to help

Mother with the store. If it goes well..." He left the sentence unfinished.

"You'll come back?"

"I'll call you."

The ride to the airport the next morning was quiet. At the gate, Esteban took me in his arms. Suddenly we began to cry—softly, painfully. Something had gone wrong. But what?

Esteban took his little daughter in his arms and kissed her. "Good-bye, Lina," he said. "I'll miss you, *mi hija*." He took my face in his hands. "I'll call you, Marta. I promise."

With a curious dread in my stomach, I flew to Colombia to finalize negotiations on the house for my parents, hoping Esteban would decide to follow me.

Determined to keep the rift between us a secret, I steered conversation away from Esteban, avoiding questions that probed too deeply. Mama and Papa were curious about Esteban's absence, but if they suspected anything, they kept it to themselves. They were preoccupied with the purchase of the house and accepted my excuses without comment.

At night, alone in my room, I wept, remembering Esteban's parting words: *"If it goes well..."* The promise was unclear, the future uncertain.

As the days passed and Esteban did not follow me to Colombia, the curious dread began to harden into desperate certainty. Night after night I lay face-down on the bed, sobbing, Esteban's words running through my head. *"Give me a couple of months... I'll call you."*

Finally the deal was closed. I signed the papers, said good-bye to my family, and boarded a plane for New York, holding stubbornly to the slender hope Esteban had given me. "He'll come back," I whispered in Lina's ear. "Daddy will come back soon."

Back in New York I hid the truth from friends. "Esteban is fine," I said. "He just wants to stay in Chile a couple of months to get the family business going. He'll be coming back sometime around March."

March came and went, and Esteban did not come. Friends turned away in embarrassment as I tried to explain the situation. "He had some problems with the business," I explained lamely, "but he'll be back by June."

June slipped by, and still Esteban did not come. I pushed his date of return back to August, then to October. Curious, but not wanting to interfere, friends began avoiding me. They were good friends, but they felt uncomfortable around me. Gradually they stopped calling.

Too ashamed to tell the truth and afraid to let anyone see my emotion, I shut myself in the apartment, crying for days at a time.

Then, incredibly, one day in December the call came.

"Marta," Esteban said, "it's me."

"Esteban!" I gasped. "Where are you?"

"I'm in Chile, but I'm ready to come home. I miss you. I want to come back this week. Could you send me a return ticket?"

My heart settled in my stomach.

"Marta," he said softly. "I miss you."

I shoved back the tears. "I'll wire it tomorrow," I said. "I'll ask a friend for the money tonight and send it right away."

That night I could not sleep. "Daddy's coming home," I whispered in Lina's ear. "He's coming back to us. He loves us. He's coming home."

The following day I wired the ticket to Chile, then called Esteban's neighbor to leave the message.

"Sylvia, it's Marta."

"Marta!" Sylvia exclaimed. "Where are you? Why are you—"

"Esteban is coming home," I interrupted excitedly. "He's coming back! He called me yesterday." The excitement made my voice thick. "I need your help. Do me a favor and tell Esteban the ticket has been wired. He can pick it up tomorrow."

There was silence on the other end.

"Sylvia?"

"Yes?"

"What's the matter?"

"Esteban isn't here."

"I know that."

"And he isn't living with his mother."

"No? Where does he live?"

"Don't you know?"

"Know what?"

"Esteban has been living with another woman for ten months."

The words filtered through a haze. The floor started to spin toward me. I reached out a hand, steadying myself against the wall.

"Marta, are you there?"

"Yes, Sylvia," the words came through numb lips. "Yes, I'm here."

"He moved in with her almost as soon as you left Chile." She sounded embarrassed.

"Did his mother know?"

"Of course."

I was trembling. "Sylvia, promise me something."

"Yes?"

"Don't tell Esteban I called. I'm putting a stop on the ticket."

I hung up slowly, sickened and stunned. Esteban had lied to me. He said he loved me, and all the time he had been living with another woman. I had stayed faithful to him, praying for a reunion, and he had taken a mistress.

Anger was an anesthetic, deadening the pain but leaving a dry, bitter taste in my mouth. I felt the pain as though it were a death, yet I was not allowed to grieve as a widow.

The stop on the ticket went through the next day, and the anger dissolved into tears. Depression set in, each day a reminder of failure. A year passed, gray and barren. I worked steadily but avoided outside contact, sleeping and crying through months at a time.

That year, a chapter in my life came to an end.

I never saw Esteban again.

In the year that followed, I picked up the pieces, looking for a reality I could face. A year had slipped by in depression, but I found that time did bring healing. New friends invited me out dancing, and slowly I began to establish new friendships.

Life without Esteban was difficult at first. Mother was living with me in New York, taking care of Lina while I worked, and I found her presence a comfort—but it was difficult supporting all of us on one salary. I had a job working at a restaurant in Queens, but it did not pay well, and I struggled to make payments on the house in Colombia while paying my own rent.

While the work at the restaurant was tiring, it kept me busy and I enjoyed the time away from the apartment. The young men at the restaurant made me laugh, flattering me with their attention. They seemed genuinely interested in me, asking me many questions about my background.

"Marta, where do you live? Where do you study?"

The questions seemed innocent enough, and I thought they were being friendly. "Where are you from, Marta? Are you a resident?"

Then, one day, the real question came. "Marta, do you know what *corte* is?"

Corte! Of course I knew what *corte* was. Many Colombians do. A substance almost the same color and consistency as cocaine, *corte* is used to cut cocaine. Some of it is white, some a little yellow; but when mixed with the drug, it is difficult to detect and can stretch a pound of pure cocaine to a pound and a half.

Everyone knows what it is used for, but because it is not an illegal substance, the police cannot make an arrest if they find it on a suspect's body.

"Do you know where we could find some, Marta?"

"Why?" I asked carefully.

"We want to buy some."

I hesitated. Was it wrong?

"We'll pay well for it."

"I think some of my friends use it," I said reluctantly.

"Do you think they would sell us some?"

"They might."

"Will you bring it to us? We'll pay you well."

They would pay me? It was not drug dealing, and I could not be arrested for it—but was it wrong? The faint stirrings of unease were difficult to ignore, but I pushed them to the back of my mind. Bills were piling up at home, and I needed the money. I agreed to bring them a delivery of *corte*.

I got the *corte* from one of my Colombian friends and took it to José, the leader of the group. The delivery went smoothly and they were right. I was paid well for it. It seemed almost too easy. No one questioned me, and the police did not even glance my way.

Over the next several months I supplied José and his friends with several deliveries of the dust. The money they paid me helped with the bills, and it felt good to have a little extra money around the house.

I was beginning to feel confident, and things were going so well that when José asked me to make a delivery of cocaine to a customer, I barely hesitated. I would not be dealing, I reasoned—just delivering. They already had the customer; all I had to do was deliver the package and collect the money.

José gave me last-minute instructions: "Marta, make sure you get the money before you leave. If the customer doesn't want the merchandise, just bring it back—all of it." His smile glinted, his eyes holding an unspoken warning.

By now I knew I was dealing with the Colombian Mafia. José was friendly, but if anything went wrong, he would want an explanation. A chill slid down my spine. Drug cartels did not wait for long explanations. If you crossed them, they killed you. Simple as that. If I slipped up, I wondered how long they would let me live.

I made the delivery, but the customer did not want it. "It's too flaky, Marta," he said. "Next time bring me rocks."

Unsure of what to do next, I left his apartment. I already had the merchandise and I needed the delivery money, so I decided to take the package to another customer. Felipe was a friendly, outgoing Colombian who had purchased from José on several occasions at the restaurant. He was well-liked by the cartels because he was honest and he paid on time. He was a good prospect. I knew José would approve.

Jenny, a friend from Colombia, agreed to go with me. This time I decided against putting the drugs in my purse. I slid the package inside my sock, pulled my pant leg down over the package, and slung the purse strap over my arm.

Felipe and another friend were standing outside their apartment with three men in sports jackets when we drove up.

"Oh, good, Jenny," I murmured. "Felipe's right out front. We won't even have to get out of the car."

I rolled down the window. "Felipe!"

The three men in jackets turned around, but Felipe and his friend did not move.

"Felipe, come here a minute," I called.

He ignored us.

What's the matter with him? I wondered angrily. *Why doesn't he look at us?*

Jenny nudged me. "Maybe he didn't hear you, Marta. Call him again."

I opened my mouth to call again when suddenly two of the men were at the car, one pulling the key out of the ignition, another one opening the car door.

"Step out of the car, ladies." A badge flashed in my face. "We're going to have to take a look in your car."

The breath went out of my lungs in a crippling rush. Undercover cops! A search! Oh, God—the package!

Jenny's purse was emptied out on the car seat. Keys, makeup, pens, gum, green card, everything spilled out on the seat and floor. There was nothing to raise suspicion, but—my purse! There was nothing in it, not a penny, not a scrap of paper.

"Miss, you can go."

Jenny's eyes opened. "I can go?"

The detective's eyes crinkled. "Yes, you can go. We can't search you unless we have a policewoman. There's no policewoman, so you can go."

Relief surged through my body. They would not find the package. They could not search me!

The detective held out his hand for my purse. He turned the purse upside down and shook. Nothing. He shook it again, a little harder. Again, nothing. The officer glanced at his partner.

"Ma'am, there's nothing in here."

I felt my face flush. "Officer, I...my..." What would he believe? "I don't...I wasn't...We came out to buy some milk..." I faltered to a stop.

"Where's your green card, ma'am?" His voice sounded tired.

"At home."

"At home? You don't carry it with you when you go out?"

"No...yes, I just...I forgot." The sweat on the back of my neck felt clammy.

"I'm sorry, ma'am, we're going to have to ask you to take a seat in our car."

Fear tightened around my neck. If they called for a policewoman...

I followed him stiffly, hoping my pant leg did not ride up

above my ankle. Jenny was standing uncertainly in the street. "Jenny," I urged, "go to the apartment and get my green card. Hurry!"

"Ma'am..." The detective was holding the police car door open. "Watch your head." He placed a hand on my shoulder, guiding me through the door.

I ducked and slid over next to Felipe and his friend. The detective closed the door behind me.

The silence in the car was suffocating.

"Marta," Felipe broke the silence. He sounded vaguely uncomfortable. "They're investigating us for drugs. I'm sorry you had to get involved in this." His face was troubled. "We didn't know you were coming."

"Felipe," I stopped him. "Look."

I hiked my pant leg up several inches. Felipe's eyes swerved first to my face, then down to my leg, and fixed in fascination on the small package on my ankle.

"Marta!" His voice was a bare hiss, the panic making his voice unrecognizable. "*Madre de Dios*...What in the name of God are you doing with that?"

His hand grasped my arm. "Put it under the car, Marta." Frantically he fumbled for the package. "Get rid of it!"

He turned to his friend. "Nick, open the door and throw it under the car."

Nick's face blanched. "Are you crazy? They'll see us."

Felipe's breath was coming in gasps. "Marta, put it under the seat. Hurry! They won't look there."

"No, Felipe." I shook off his hand. "I can't! Who's going to pay? I don't have $8,000."

Felipe's voice was tight. "Forget the money, for God's sake. Worry about the time you'll get. *Dios mío*, forget it..."

"Ma'am..." The officer was opening the door, his face unreadable. "We're going to have to ask you some questions."

He turned down the car radio. The pounding in my ears made it difficult to hear.

"Where do you live?"

"Twenty-three Main Street." The control in my voice surprised me.

"Where do you work?"

"At 4564 Grand Avenue."

I could hear the stilted breathing of Felipe and Nick and the creak of the car seat as I shifted my cramped leg.

Dear God, I prayed, *get me out of this, and I will never do it again.*

"Okay, ma'am," the officer was holding the door open, "you can go now, but don't ever let me see you with these guys again."

I felt Felipe and Nick collapse beside me.

Calmly, Marta, I coached myself. *Calmly; don't over-react.*

I stepped carefully out of the car, praying they would not see the outline of the package on my leg. I was shaking so badly I could not walk straight. I saw Jenny's car returning several blocks down the street.

"Jenny!" I waved her to a stop. "Jenny, stop! Turn the car around. Quick!"

Jenny's face was white. "They let you go?"

"Yes…" I sank back against the seat. "Just get me out of here, please."

At home my family was in an uproar. "Marta, what are you doing to us?" Mama wept. "You almost brought the cops here. Your brothers had to run."

My brothers! They were here illegally. If the police had searched the apartment, they could have reported my brothers to immigration and had them deported.

"See the friends you are making?" Mama's anger was showing through her relief. "They're no good, Marta. No good! You're going to get us all into trouble if you keep on like this."

"I know, Mama," I said tearfully. "I will stop. I promise."

And I did stop. The near-arrest had frightened me badly, and I was ashamed of the actions I had found so easy to justi-fy. What had happened to the young schoolteacher who refused to drink in front of her students? What had happened to the young woman who had promised to make her country proud?

Selling drugs was a crime I hated, and I had walked into it with my eyes open, making excuses and ignoring the truth.

"God, help me," I prayed. "I promise I will never do this again. I will never sell drugs again."

Chapter 5

Still recovering from my breakup with Esteban, I met Víctor. A gregarious, outgoing Colombian, Víctor had served in the U.S. Marines for six years and spoke English without an accent.

When we first met at a club in Queens, Víctor was married but was having an affair with another woman. His marriage soured quickly, and neither Víctor nor his wife seemed willing to consider reconciliation. Víctor soon filed for divorce.

I reproved Víctor sharply for his infidelity but knew his actions were only the outward sign of an inbred selfishness and pride. He enjoyed the attention of other women and thrived on the danger of the illicit.

Eight months after the divorce, Víctor was married again, this time to a lovely girl named Diana. Although his first marriage had been a disaster, his second marriage came as a surprise.

"He's been divorced only eight months!" I protested to friends.

"So?" They looked puzzled.

"So, it's wrong. How could he marry again so soon after his divorce?"

His friends shrugged. "He likes women," they said indifferently. "That's just the way he is."

Our circle of friends closed rank quickly after Víctor's marriage, and despite his behavior, I hoped he had found happiness.

Six months later Víctor was back. "Where's Diana?" we asked, surprised.

"Well, we're having a few problems," he admitted sheepishly.

"What kind of problems?" I asked.

"She doesn't approve of my girlfriends."

"Girlfriends? I thought you got married."

"I did, but I couldn't give up the other women."

The men whooped appreciatively. "Víctor!"

Víctor's eyes brightened. "I don't know what it is. She has this problem with me and other women for some reason."

I watched him in disbelief. His eyes were glittering, moving back and forth, enjoying the attention, seeking approval. Inwardly I was repulsed; he was a married man and still he flaunted his affairs in front of his friends.

When we had a moment alone, I scolded him. "Víctor, that is no way to treat your wife."

He put his head down. "I know, Marta; I just don't know what to do. I can't seem to make it work."

I watched the transformation in amazement. He was faking it! "You might try giving up the women," I said a little caustically.

"Give up the women?" He looked horrified. "Marta, I couldn't do that."

He seemed genuinely stunned by the concept. I bit my lip, trying not to laugh. "Víctor, you're sick. If you want your marriage to work, you're going to have to try."

"I do try," he said unconvincingly.

"Really?" I looked at him skeptically. "How?"

"I buy her flowers."

"Flowers? After you've been with another woman?"

"Yes."

I stared at him in frustration. "You don't get it, do you?"

"Get what?" His face was blank.

"Never mind," I sighed. "Víctor, listen to me. Another divorce means the problem is with you. Go home and stay with your wife. Give up the other women. You've got to try to make your marriage work."

He nodded his head suddenly. "Marta, you're right." He brought his hands together decisively. "I'm going to try. I'm going to go back to Diana." He smiled ruefully. "I don't know if she'll be happy to see me, but I'm going to give it a try."

Two months later Víctor was back.

"What are you doing here?" I grilled. "What happened?"

"Diana's asking for a divorce."

"Did you stop seeing the other women?"

"Well, no—but I needed time to change."

I stared at him. Something was deeply wrong with him.

Over the next several months I tried to reason with Víctor, and several times he did go back to Diana; but each time he came back insisting she did not understand him.

I was having a hard time understanding him myself. He said he loved his wife, but he refused to give up the other women. He said he wanted his marriage to work, but he stayed out late with other women, drinking and flirting.

Incredibly, Víctor seemed flabbergasted when his attempts at reconciliation were rejected. "I don't understand it," he said sorrowfully. "I try to make it up to her, but when I bring her flowers, she starts yelling and kicks me out of the apartment."

"Maybe she knows why you're bringing the flowers," I said bitingly. "Maybe she knows you're just trying to ease your guilty conscience."

He looked at me appealingly. "Don't be so hard on me, Marta. I've tried; I just can't make it work."

I felt myself giving in. I did not approve of his actions, but I found myself making excuses for him. It was difficult to keep things in perspective when he smiled at me with that lopsided grin, winking wickedly at me through dark lashes. Somehow the truth took on a different slant when I was with him. Maybe Diana was to blame. Maybe she just needed to be a little more understanding.

Víctor seemed unaffected by his failing marriage, spending hours with his friends at the discos. Our own friendship was developing quickly, and we spent a great deal of time together. Our closeness caused me some concern when I was alone, but when I was with him, I shrugged off the discomfort. He was charming and attentive and treated me like a lady. Still smarting from Esteban's infidelity, Víctor's attention helped restore my confidence.

And yet, as much as I enjoyed being with Víctor, I knew I could never allow myself to fall in love with him. I knew too much about him. Underneath the polished smile was a personality hungry for attention and recognition. His charm hid a subtle danger that frightened me. I enjoyed being with him, but I did not trust him.

One day Víctor came to my house. I let him in, and he stood in the middle of the room, dazed.

"What happened, Víctor?" I asked, alarmed.

He sat down, holding his head in his hands. "It's over."

"What's over?"

"My marriage. Diana's gone, and she took everything, even the furniture."

"Where did she go?"

"I don't know." He sniffed noisily, reaching in his back pocket for a handkerchief.

I watched him speculatively. "Víctor, why are you crying?"

He did not answer.

"Are you crying for Diana," I asked suddenly, "or are you crying for the furniture?"

He looked up, startled.

"Because if you're crying for the furniture, stop it—you can buy more. But if you're crying for Diana, get up and go look for her."

He buried his head in his hands.

"You are crying for her," I said fiercely. "Get up. Go find her."

Slowly he shook his head. "No," he said finally. "I am not crying for her."

Appalled, I sat down. "What are you saying?"

"I don't love her."

"What do you mean you don't love her? She's your wife. You have to love her."

"No, I don't love her," he repeated.

His lashes were wet with tears, his hands restlessly loosening his shirt collar. I watched him, remembering the way his eyes sparkled when he laughed, watching the way his smile started in his eyes and moved to his lips.

He had handsome features. His mouth was a little spoiled but endearing, his hair dark and thick, curling slightly around his neck. He looked so young and vulnerable. I felt his gaze on my face and realized, suddenly, that I loved him.

Horrified, I stood up. I had counseled him through two failed marriages and several relationships with other women. I knew about his affairs and his indiscretions. I knew his girlfriends by name. I had fallen in love with a man who hurt the only women who really loved him.

"Víctor, please leave."

"Leave?" He looked up, bewildered.

"Yes."

"Why?"

"Just leave."

He saw my eyes, desperate and sick, and left without arguing.

Over the next several months, I fought for composure, struggling to regain control of my emotions. How could I possibly consider a relationship with him? I did not trust him.

When Víctor asked me for a relationship, I resisted, frantic, fighting for survival. "How can you ask me for a relationship, Víctor? You're still married."

"I'll get a divorce."

"But your girlfriends…"

"I'll leave them."

"You don't love me," I said weakly.

"That's not true. The first time I saw you I loved you."

He was lying. I backed away, avoiding his hands. "How can you say that, Víctor? You're still seeing other women."

"No, I'm not. I haven't looked at another woman since I met you."

I pulled my hands away. "You know it can't work. Forget it, Víctor."

"Marta, please," he said huskily. "Give me a chance. It can work. It can work because we love each other."

The fight went out of me. I leaned my head against his shoulder and nodded, a leaden weight in my stomach. "Okay, Víctor. I'll give you a chance."

I loved him. I would have to make it work.

Chapter 6

When my mother returned to Colombia several weeks later, I sent Lina back with her. She was only four; I did not want her to see me with a man who was not her father. The next day, Víctor moved into my apartment.

The first three months were a honeymoon. Víctor was faithful and attentive. He came home early most evenings, and we went out to discos together. He was responsible and thoughtful, calling to tell me when he could not make it home on time and apologizing when he had to work late.

Ashamed for doubting him, I hid my fears. As the weeks passed and Víctor remained attentive, I began to question my own judgment. I watched him at the parties, but he was a model of courtesy and attention. He stayed close to me, always at my elbow, bringing me drinks and fanning me solicitously when I complained of the heat. He spoke to other women but turned back to me, instantly attentive when I spoke.

At home, thoughts of Esteban brought occasional moodiness, but Víctor teased me out of the dark moods, making me smile, coaxing me out of depression. He was fun to be with, and his attention was reassuring. Slowly I began to relax.

You see, I chided myself, *there was nothing to worry about. He just needed a chance.*

Three months later, things started to change.

"Víctor," I asked tentatively. "Where were you last night?"

"Last night?" His eyes stayed fixed on his newspaper. "At work. I had some things to take care of."

I brushed a piece of toast from the table. "It took all night?"

He looked up slowly. "It wasn't all night, Marta."

"Three o'clock..."

He lowered his newspaper. "What are you saying, Marta?"

"Nothing," I said lamely. "I...nothing."

"You don't think I was working?" He lifted his coffee mug casually, the rising steam hiding his eyes.

I shrugged.

The coffee mug hit the table with force. "You don't trust me, do you?"

"Yes, of course," I said defensively. "I...It's just that I worry about you."

"Well, don't," he snapped. "I can take care of myself!"

He finished his breakfast in silence.

That night he stayed out late again.

For the next several weeks, I fought to keep my suspicions under control, hoping I was wrong; but the first time Víctor brought flowers home, I froze, looking down at the armful of roses.

"What are these for?" I asked carefully.

He watched me, his eyes a little wary. "They're for you—a gift."

"You aren't trying to hide something with these flowers, are you, Víctor?" I asked lightly.

"Hide something?" His lips tightened imperceptibly. "What would I be trying to hide?"

"Nothing." I turned to find a vase. "Forget it."

His face changed suddenly, lightening in teasing humor. "Marta, Marta," he said, "what am I going to do with you?" He reached for my hand. "I told you too much about myself;

now it's all coming back to me. When are you going to learn to trust me?"

"I do trust you," I faltered. My lips were smiling, but I felt a pinpoint of fear forming inside. He was seeing other women.

As the nights grew later and more frequent, my suspicions grew.

"Víctor, what is this?" I asked one night, pointing to the ashtray in his car.

"Cigarette stubs," he said, frowning.

"And this?" I picked out a cigarette stained with red lipstick.

"I...that's..." He appeared momentarily rattled. "Some of my clients..."

"Forget it," I said wearily, "you don't have to explain."

Several weeks later I found an earring in the car. "Víctor, whose is this?" I asked mildly.

"What?"

I handed him the earring. He examined it closely, turning it over several times, his eyes narrowing in concentration. "It isn't yours?" he asked finally.

"No."

"Well, maybe it belongs to Orlando's wife. I drove them home."

I looked at him thoughtfully. His face was open and guileless. Maybe he was telling the truth.

I wanted to believe him, but as the evidence mounted, I knew he was covering the truth. When Víctor returned late at night with lipstick stains on his shirt collar and perfume on his skin, I raved at him, hating him, my suspicions confirmed. He denied my accusations and swore at me for doubting him, but I knew he was lying.

The next time Víctor brought flowers home, I snatched them from him. "I don't want your guilt offering," I cursed.

He stood, frowning in concentration. "Marta, what are you talking about?"

"Your flowers. I don't want them."

"Why? What's wrong with you?"

"You used to bring Diana flowers too."

"Diana!" He was staring at me. "What does she have to do with us?"

"You used to bring her flowers when you felt guilty about your women."

Víctor took the flowers from me and jammed them in the vase, his eyes hard. "Don't be ridiculous!" He turned his back on me, reaching for the door. "I haven't looked at another woman since I met you."

"Liar!" The word ripped from my throat. I pointed a finger at his startled face. "You were with another woman last night!"

He looked at me, evaluating the extent of my knowledge, then decided I was guessing and smiled derisively. "No, I wasn't. I had to work late." He walked back toward the door.

Víctor's friends had already told me the truth. He had been at a party last night with another woman. Images of his wives and girlfriends flashed before me, and I burst into tears. "Get out!" I stormed. "Get out and take your flowers with you."

His face went still. "Get out?"

"Yes. Pack your things and get out."

He looked at me measuringly. "That's what you want?"

I did not say anything.

He turned wordlessly and left the apartment. I heard the apartment door slam behind him and burst into tears. He was gone.

The next week he was back.

Friends were horrified. "He's lying to you, Marta. He's seeing other women. Don't let him come back."

My mother tried to warn me. "Marta, Víctor is not for you. He's crazy. Leave him alone. You're going to get in trouble."

I smiled but refused to listen. I was bound by an attraction that refused to admit its sickness. I could not leave him.

Víctor played my emotions skillfully, enjoying the inexplicable control he had over me. "Marta," he whispered in my ear, "I love you. You're the only woman I've ever loved."

Torn between what I wanted to believe and what I knew

was the truth, I threw him out of the apartment one week, then let him back the next, struggling alternately between hatred and fascination.

Víctor's behavior worsened with each incident. He was very jealous and would not allow me to speak to other men, but his eyes wandered constantly, even when I was with him. He reveled in his popularity with the women, laughing and joking with my friends, then turning to watch me for my reactions.

One evening we went to a party together. I discovered Víctor in another room, his arm around a pretty blonde, his lips close to her face.

"So, this is where you are!" I announced loudly.

Víctor straightened, his face flushing. "Marta…"

I ignored him, pointing a finger at the woman. "Ma'am, that man you are kissing is my husband."

The crowded room grew suddenly quiet.

"Marta, shut up!" Víctor's face was red.

"Get away from him," I said. "You are no lady."

Víctor stood up threateningly, his eyes murderous. He took a step toward me, and I retreated, backing out of the room. His footsteps sounded behind me. Panting, I ran for the front door. Outside, the night air was quiet, the street deserted. A long, wickedly spiked wire rod lay on the ground near the street. Snatching it up, I whirled, my body in fencing pose, ready for attack.

Víctor's face was livid, his lips white with anger. He lunged at me, scratching for my wrist. "How dare you make a fool of me in there!"

"Stay back, Víctor," I said, slashing wildly at him with the wire. "Don't come near me, or I'll crisscross your handsome face!"

He cursed and took a swipe at me. "If you scratch me, I'll kill you!"

"Watch your face, Víctor," I warned, "or your little girlfriend in there might not want you back."

I whipped the wire away from his reaching hand, leaving a red welt on his palm. "Go home and get your things,

Víctor. I don't want you in my apartment anymore." I turned my back on him and walked inside with dignity.

Víctor moved out that night.

True to the twisted pattern of our relationship, he was back several days later. The smug look on his face brought a seething anger, but I was powerless to break the relationship.

One evening I waited in the apartment for Víctor to come home. He had promised to drive me to a party and was three hours late.

Finally, he sauntered through the apartment door with a friend, telltale traces of lipstick on his shirt collar.

"You're late!" I snapped.

"Calm down, sweetheart," he said with a grin at his friend. "Don't get so excited."

"You're three hours late, Víctor."

"Yes, well, I sort of got tied up."

"With another woman?"

"It's none of your business," he snapped. "I'm here, aren't I? Get in the car. I'll take you."

"Get out!" I screamed. "Get out and take your things with you." I jerked the door open. "I've had it with you. This time it's over." The words sounded empty in my ears.

Víctor made a careless gesture with his hand and started toward the kitchen. "Come on, César, let's go get a drink."

Infuriated, I spun on my heel and headed for the bedroom.

Víctor turned slowly. "Where are you going?" He followed me into the bedroom. "What are you doing?"

I ignored him, lifting his television set and dragging it toward the window. Víctor watched incredulously. It was a large set, and I had difficulty pulling it to the window.

"Marta, what are you doing?" he repeated.

I heaved the television onto the window sill, balancing it awkwardly with one hand and pulling the window open with the other.

"You're going to throw my television out of the window?" Víctor's eyebrows were dangerously high.

"No, I'm going to use it to prop the window open," I said sarcastically. I was struggling to hold onto the big set while jerking at the window.

"You wouldn't dare," he said.

"Oh, no?" I said, panting. "Just watch."

I was angry, but I had no intention of pushing the television out of the window; it was an expensive set, and we were four flights up.

"Do it," Víctor dared me suddenly. "Go ahead! I'm watching." He gestured toward the bed. "And maybe you should throw the bed out too while you're at it. We won't be needing it." He punched his friend playfully in the ribs, and they burst out laughing.

"Maybe I will! And maybe I'll throw you out with it." The words sounded childish, but I was close to tears, his taunting making me angry.

"On second thought, you'd better forget about the bed, Marta—you're having enough trouble with the television." Víctor and his friend doubled over.

I opened the window wider and inched the television closer to the edge.

"You don't have the guts," Víctor taunted.

"Oh, no?" I said.

"No." He started toward me threateningly.

"Get away, Víctor," I warned. "It's going out the window."

"So, do it then," he shouted.

"I will!"

"No, you won't," he sneered. "You're chicken." He turned away in disgust.

He had pushed me too far. I gave the television a quick shove, tilting it out the window as Víctor turned, lunging, too late. The television shattered on the sidewalk four stories below.

The sound of exploding glass only increased my fury. "Now get out, and take your friend with you," I yelled, out of control. "Your clothes are next. Run downstairs and catch them."

Víctor and César were leaping down the stairs, their feet pounding a flight at a time. The door slammed behind them. Suddenly I felt sick. What had I done? What if the television had hit someone on the street? I could have killed someone.

"Oh, God," I sobbed desperately, "please help me. What is wrong with me?"

I closed the window, pulled the curtains, and locked the door, sitting silently in a wash of emotion. I had to get out soon, or I was going to hurt someone. "Please, God, get me away from this man. Help me, please. I can't take it anymore."

The door banged in on its hinges, and I sat up, staring.

"Marta!" It was my mother. Mama had returned from Colombia several weeks ago and was not happy about my relationship with Víctor. "Guess what, Marta?" she panted. She had just climbed four flights and her chest was heaving, her eyes wide with incredulity.

I wiped my face. "What, Mama?"

"Somebody just threw a television out the window!"

"No, really?"

"Yes, really. Everyone is outside looking at the pieces. It's all over the sidewalk. Who could have done such a thing?"

I did not answer.

"You didn't hear anything, Marta?"

"No—who could have done it?"

"Some crazy person probably." She shook her head sadly.

"Yes, probably," I agreed weakly.

The next day, Mama came to visit. She went into the bedroom to turn on the television.

I waited, frozen, guilty.

"Marta, where is the television?" Mama was standing in the doorway, a puzzled look on her face.

I stood staring at her. The silence stretched interminably. She waited, curious. "Marta?" Slowly, awareness crept into her eyes. "Marta! Was it you?"

I shrugged sheepishly.

"Marta!"

"Yes."

"What happened?" she gasped.

"I had a fight with Víctor."

Suddenly, Mama started chuckling, an irrepressible grin

spreading over her face. "You're crazy, Marta! Do you know that? *Loca!*"

"Yes, Mama," I said, embarrassed. "I know."

"He's going to get you in trouble, Marta," she said quietly. "He's not for you."

"I know, Mama."

"Leave him, Marta."

I shook my head. "No, Mama...I can't." I had tried before and had failed. I could not leave him.

If I had known what was about to happen, I might have tried a little harder.

Chapter 7

M arta, who's in charge of the Colombian cartel?"
I looked up sharply. Víctor was tapping his fingers pensively, waiting for my answer. His eyes were narrowed, his eyebrows drawn together in thought.

It had not taken long for Víctor to move back into the apartment after our last fight. His control over me had deepened, and this time it had only been a matter of days before he was back.

"Why?" I asked slowly.

"I'm just thinking."

"About what?"

"Well, for one thing, those guys make more in one trade than I make in one year. It isn't fair."

"It may not be fair," I said forcefully, "but they go to jail."

He brushed my comment aside. "Just tell me, Marta."

"Which one? Medellín or Cali?"

He leaned forward, his body showing tension. "The Medellín cartel."

My answer came slowly. "...Pablo Escobar and the Ochoa brothers."

"Where do they get their drugs?"

Was he serious? Everyone knew that. "The coca plant."

"I know that," he said impatiently, "but where do they get the plant? Is it grown in Colombia?"

"Some of it is, but most of it is imported from Perú and Bolivia."

"What do they do once they get it?"

"They process it."

"Where?"

"In Colombian laboratories."

"In the open?"

I stared at him. "Of course not! It's an illegal operation. They process it in hidden laboratories."

"If you wanted to get cocaine, could you get it from someone else?"

"I suppose if you wanted to. There are independent dealers, but they usually get their deliveries from the cartels too. The cartels control everything." I was getting tired of his questions. "Víctor, why do you want to know all this?"

He waved a hand impatiently. "How much does a pound of cocaine cost, Marta?"

Warning bells sounded in my head. "Why do you want to know, Víctor?"

"How much does it cost?" he repeated.

"It depends," I sighed. "One pound in Colombia is $5,000. After reaching Miami it could go for $20,000. In New York, $60,000."

Víctor's eyes were gleaming.

I shifted uneasily. "Víctor, it's a dangerous business. You could be killed. If you lose the cocaine, you still have to pay—or someone in your family pays."

Víctor's eyes did not waver. "Marta, some of your old *barrio* friends are in the Mafia. Why don't you introduce me?"

I looked at him fearfully. "Are you crazy?"

"Come on, Marta," he said pleadingly. "You grew up with them. They're your friends. They'll trust you."

"Yes—but they won't trust you."

He frowned briefly. "Marta, please. Just introduce me. I'll take care of the rest."

I did not enjoy the prospect of introducing a young, hot-headed Víctor to dangerous cartel connections; but he was insistent, and I wanted to please him. Several months later we took a trip to Colombia to visit our families, and I set up a meeting with an old friend named Sebastián.

Sebastián was suspicious of Víctor from the beginning. "How serious is he about this business?" he asked me.

"I don't know," I answered, "but he won't cross you."

Sebastián considered me thoughtfully. "If you recommend him, Marta, and he talks too much..." He didn't finish the sentence.

A chill passed through me. "Don't worry, Sebastián, I'll make sure he doesn't do anything stupid," I promised. "I'll take care of everything."

"Alright," he agreed finally. "You and Víctor go back to New York and get the money together for one kilo. Once the kilo is shipped to Miami, I'll call you."

Víctor was elated. "Marta, this is great!" he crowed. "We'll go into business together and make lots of money. We're going to be rich!"

I wasn't so sure. There were too many things that could go wrong. Between the police and the cartels, someone always got hurt. "Víctor, please be careful. They'll kill you if you don't do business their way."

"Marta, Marta," he scolded affectionately, "you worry too much. Everything will be fine. I'm too smart for them. Don't worry about it."

But I did worry. God forbid that Víctor ever made a big enough mess to bring him to the attention of the cartel leaders—he would be dead in days.

The deal went through, and Víctor stayed close to home for several weeks setting up the details. Dutifully I helped him call friends, promising small quantities of cocaine in return for cash. When Sebastián's call came, we were ready with the money.

"Marta, this is Sebastián. Your package is ready. Bring $10,000 to Miami. You can pick up the merchandise. You'll have two weeks to pay the rest. Tell Víctor not to fly." His instructions were clear.

I passed the information on to Víctor and gave him careful instructions. "Come back by train or bus, Víctor. Don't fly. If you fly and are caught, you'll still have to pay."

Security on flights from Miami was very tight. Flying from Miami to New York with a kilo of cocaine was risky.

"Okay, okay," Víctor said, anxious to be gone. "Just give me the directions to the warehouse."

I handed him the directions. "Víctor, please," I pleaded, "don't do anything stupid. If the cocaine is lost…"

"Yes, Marta, yes," he interrupted. "I know. I've got to go. I'll call you from Miami."

I spent a sleepless night tossing restlessly in bed. Víctor could be so stubborn at times. He always had to do things his way, even when he knew the danger.

The next day I waited anxiously for his call. When the phone rang, I picked it up quickly.

"Marta…" It was Víctor. "I'm at Miami Airport. Meet me at LaGuardia at eight o'clock. I'll be at the baggage claim."

The line went dead.

He was coming by plane! "*Estúpido!*" I was so angry I was trembling. He was going to get killed one of these days.

At the airport I waited silently for him to get off the plane. He walked through the airport lounge, dark shades hiding his eyes, the swagger unmistakable. "Marta!" He waved enthusiastically. "Great news!" He put an arm around me. "Oh, God, Marta, we're going to be so rich."

I shrugged away from his hand. "Don't touch me, Víctor."

"Marta!" He peered curiously at my face. "What's the matter with you?"

"What's the matter?" I fumed. "You could have been stopped, Víctor! Don't you understand that? What's wrong with you?"

"Stopped? Oh, yes," he said smugly, "that's what Sebastián said, wasn't it? Well, I guess he just doesn't know what he's talking about." The swagger became more pronounced. "I wasn't stopped, Marta. No one even looked at me. It was so easy!" Víctor smiled expansively, throwing an arm over my shoulders. "I'm so good at this. We'll have the money to Sebastián by the end of the week."

I followed Víctor to the baggage claim, ignoring his steady stream of conversation. He seemed oblivious to the anger building inside me, chattering happily about the trip, turning to smile at me occasionally. The conveyor belt wound by with loads of stickered traveling bags. Luggage crate after luggage crate emptied onto the carousel.

"I just gave the password," Víctor said, "and they opened the door. We did the deal, and that was it! The police weren't anywhere around. I went to the airport, bought my ticket, got on the plane and—ya!" He dusted his fingers lightly. "It was done."

I glanced at my watch. The carousel was emptying quickly as passengers lifted their suitcases off the belt.

"Sometimes I wonder if those guys even know what they're doing," Víctor sneered. "They act like they know everything, but they're just uptight about everything."

Fifteen minutes passed, and still there was no sign of the suitcase. I saw Víctor sneak a quick look at his watch. "We could make a lot of money doing this, Marta," he said.

Twenty minutes ticked by, and Víctor threw a quick glance around the terminal. Small beads of sweat were standing out on his forehead. He thrust his hands in his pockets. I knew they were shaking.

He turned slowly, looking for signs of activity.

"Did Sebastián say anything to you this morning?" he asked casually.

"He didn't call."

"Oh."

The belt was almost empty, the floor clearing out as passengers left one by one. Víctor pulled a shaking hand out of his pocket and adjusted his shades. "Should be coming any minute now," he said. He coughed, trying to hide the tremor in his voice.

Finally I saw it. The suitcase spilled over the lip of the carousel and moved slowly down the belt toward us. It was the last one, and it was open. I saw it but could not move. We stood there numbly, stupidly, as the suitcase rumbled past us.

Leaden feet rooted to the ground, we stared at the bottom of the suitcase. It was empty.

Víctor reached a trembling hand toward the carousel then snatched it back. "It's a trap, Marta," he whispered hoarsely. "They set us up!"

"A trap!" I turned on him furiously. "It isn't a trap! Sebastián told you not to fly. I told you not to fly. You lost that package because you're stubborn. You always have to do things your way. It's your own fault. Now you're going to have to pay."

Víctor's face was chalk-white, his eyes blazing. "You sent me down there," he said wildly. "I went down there because of you. You told me to go."

"Oh, shut up!" I hissed. "Just shut up! This is your fault, and you know it."

Víctor's mouth was twitching. "What will he do, Marta? What will Sebastián do?"

"I don't know," I said, cold anger burning in my stomach. "Why don't you call him and find out?"

"No, Marta, please." Víctor's eyes were pleading, frantic. "You call him. He won't believe me; he'll think I stole the drugs."

I looked at him sharply.

He stared back at me. "What?"

"Did you?"

"Did I what? Steal it? No, I didn't steal it," he snapped, on edge. "Why would I do a stupid thing like that?"

He had already done a stupid thing, but I did not say anything. I would have to call Sebastián. The whole mix-up was my fault anyway; I never should have introduced him to Sebastián.

"Okay, Víctor," I agreed wearily. "I'll call him, but you're going to have to call Miami."

Relief spread over his face. "No problem; I'll call the warehouse tonight. They'll believe me."

Víctor called Miami that night to explain, and later that evening I placed the call to Sebastián. The long-distance connection to Colombia was faint, and I held my breath waiting for the call to be picked up. Finally I heard Sebastián's voice on the other end.

"Sebastián," I started, "this is Marta."

"Marta," Sebastián said warmly. "How are you? Did you get the package?"

"Well—yes...no," I said. "No, we didn't."

"No? What happened?" His voice was careful. "Didn't Víctor make it to the warehouse?"

"Yes, he picked up the package. It just never made it to New York."

It was quiet on the other end of the line.

"Sebastián?"

"Yes, I'm here."

"I don't know what happened, Sebastián. Víctor checked the baggage, and it was fine; but when we went to baggage claim, the bag was open and the package was gone."

I knew his next question before he asked it.

"He took the plane?"

I sucked air through dry lips. "Yes, Sebastián. I'm sorry. He just thought it was the best thing to do."

I jumped and snatched the phone away from my ear. Sebastián's voice was crackling through the receiver. I realized I was clutching the receiver and loosened my grip. I glanced over at Víctor. His face was sweating.

I placed the receiver gingerly back to my ear. "Sebastián, I'm sorry," I said, "but what can we do? It's gone."

The silence on the other end was sinister.

"Sebastián?"

"Marta, listen to me." Sebastián's voice was quiet. "I trusted you. Now the cocaine is gone. Someone is going to have to pay." His voice hardened. "You and Víctor have two weeks to come up with the money."

"Two weeks!" I quavered. "Where are we going to get $30,000? We already borrowed $10,000 from friends for the down payment."

Víctor's face was ashen. "Ask him for more time, Marta," he interrupted. "We can't get it in two weeks."

I hushed him, trying to hear Sebastián's voice.

"That's Víctor's problem," Sebastián was saying. "You have two weeks to get the money."

"Sebastián, please," I pleaded. "We'll get it, I promise, but we need more time. Please—trust me."

The phone went dead.

I looked at Víctor. He was wiping sweat from his face, the fire gone from his eyes. They were going to kill him. I looked at him, a sheen of nervous sweat covering his skin, and realized that I still loved him. I could not let him face Sebastián alone.

In a frantic attempt to raise the money, I flew to Colombia and initiated a wild scramble to mortgage the house I had bought for my parents three years before. The legal paperwork tied me up for two weeks, but finally I had $10,000 in my hand.

I placed the call to Sebastián that morning. "Sebastián, come and get your money."

"Who is this?"

"It's Marta."

"Where did you get the money?"

"Don't worry about it; just come and get your money." I slammed the phone down. I was furious. I had been forced to give up my life savings for something I would never see. I had worked six years for nothing. The waste was staggering. I sat down and cried.

That afternoon, Sebastián came to my house. I dumped the money in his hand. "This is the end of my responsibility," I said. "The rest is up to Víctor. If you kill him, no one will pay the rest."

Grudgingly, Sebastián agreed to give Víctor more time.

Víctor was forced to continue selling small amounts of cocaine to meet the bill, and it took several months, but finally it was paid.

This time I was sick of the business. I had promised never to get involved with drugs again. This time I meant it. I would never go near the cartels and their drug business again.

Chapter 8

"Marta, how many times do I have to tell you to keep your mouth shut when customers are in the house?" Víctor's face was thrust close to mine, his eyes boring angrily into mine. His lips were tight, his jaw clenched in anger. "I'm tired of warning you, Marta. One of these days, you're going to ruin one of my deals."

"Ruin one of your deals?" I shouted. "I'm not going to ruin one of your deals! The police are going to do that."

"The police?" His eyebrows rushed together threateningly. "The police?"

"Yes, the police!" I leaned away from him. "They're going to find out sometime, Víctor."

Lina's frightened face peered through the door, and I lowered my voice. She was with us in New York now, and I tried to shield her from as much as I could. I waited until she left, then turned back to Víctor. "You've paid Sebastián off, Víctor. Why can't you stop now? Now, before something else happens."

He glanced out the window toward the street, nervously adjusting the shade, then turned back to me. "What do you mean something else?"

"You know what I mean, Víctor. It's going to happen again—it always does. Why don't you stop first?"

He glared at me suspiciously. "Are you planning something?"

"No."

"Well, stop worrying so much then. You're making me nervous."

I knew I was upsetting him, but I could not stop worrying. With Víctor's brashness, I knew it was only a matter of time before something else happened to get us in trouble.

One day, Víctor set up a deal with some customers he had met at a bar. He knew I did not approve and warned me several times to keep my mouth shut. "I don't want you opening your mouth when they're here," he warned me. "Understand? Just keep your comments to yourself."

"You're going to be sorry, Víctor," I said, tight-lipped. "Those guys are either Italian Mafia or undercover cops. They're going to get you in trouble."

He sighed with exaggerated patience. "Yes, I know. The cops are going to get me. Marta!..." He crushed the white powder on the table viciously. "How many times do I have to tell you? They're my customers; let me worry about them."

That evening, Lina and I watched the deal from the bedroom. The customers were dressed in sports jackets and jeans, their muscles straining against tight-fitting shirts. They seemed slightly nervous.

Víctor slapped the bag of cocaine on the table and motioned with his hand. "It's good stuff," he said. "Try it. It's the best I have." He looked over at me and raised a warning finger.

Two of the customers checked the drug, tasting the powdery substance carefully. I watched them thoughtfully. Something was wrong. They were watching Víctor's actions, crowding him at the table, distracting him.

A slight movement caught my attention, and I glanced over at the customer standing behind Víctor. His hand was moving steadily toward his pocket, his body still, his eyes moving casually around the apartment.

I shrank back, my pulse beating in my throat.

He's going to kill us, I thought in panic. *He's going to shoot us for the cocaine.*

My skin felt cold, my palms clammy. *Think, Marta. Think!* If he made one move toward me or Lina, I was going to start screaming.

His eyes moved to the right, stopped, and then came to rest on me.

I exploded, my voice harsh with panic. "Get out! All of you! Out! Take your stuff, and do your business on the street."

Víctor's lip curled in anger. "Marta! Shut your mouth! This is none of your business."

"Yes, it is! I want them out of here, Víctor. Now!"

"Víctor, it's okay," the leader said soothingly. "We can go outside. Come on, let's go."

"Yes! Get out! Get out and don't come back!" My voice was loud and insistent.

Víctor snatched the bag of cocaine from the table and backed out of the apartment, his glittering eyes promising a fight. I sat on the bed, afraid to move. Somehow I knew what was coming next.

Down on the street, the men snatched the bag of cocaine from Víctor and jumped into a waiting car. Víctor was left standing in the middle of the street.

It took Víctor ten months to pay the dealers back.

"It's all your fault!" he shouted, furious. "If you had kept your stupid mouth shut, this wouldn't have happened!"

"If I had kept my stupid mouth shut, we would be dead!" I yelled back.

Víctor blamed me constantly for the loss, and over the next several weeks our disagreements became increasingly physical. I fought back, defending myself, but as the confrontations grew violent, I worried that Víctor would hurt me seriously.

Family and friends tried to convince me to leave. Mama begged me to get out for Lina's sake. "She shouldn't have to see that," she said. "Get out before he hurts you or Lina."

"Víctor is good to Lina," I protested. "He treats her like his own daughter. He won't hurt her."

"But she shouldn't have to see you fighting."

"She doesn't. She's always sleeping when we fight."

"What about when he punched you in the face? She saw your eye."

"It wasn't that bad."

"You quit your job because of that eye, Marta."

"Lina's too young to know that. She doesn't understand. She's only five."

Mama's eyes welled up with tears. "Marta, leave him before it's too late."

Too late? A curious dread crept through my body. "Mama, please; I've told you before—I'm not going to leave Víctor."

She turned away, disappointed.

Frightened, I watched her leave. A force stronger than my love for my own family kept me trapped in the relationship with Víctor. I wanted to leave but could not.

Depression, so foreign to my nature, began to lap at the edges of my consciousness as the initial stages of hopelessness began settling in. Friends noted the dark circles under my eyes and reacted with alarm. "You've got to get away from him," they insisted. "He's not good for you."

I shrugged off their concern. They did not understand. How could they? They were not in my position. At night, I pulled the covers over my head, burying my face in the pillow to shut out their voices.

Out of work and policed by an increasingly jealous Víctor, I became a prisoner in my own apartment. Víctor was possessive and would not allow me to leave the house without his knowledge. Several times a day he called the apartment to make sure I was home. If I went shopping for food, he gave me an hour, then called the house to make sure I was back.

Several times he stormed home from work, his face dark with anger, accusing me of calling my boyfriends. Depression made tears well up in my eyes. He was crazy. He knew I did not have any close male friends. He had seen to that months ago when his insane jealousy had forced me to cut off several close friendships.

Caught in a cycle of jealousy and suspicion, my nerves strained close to the breaking point. I prayed for an end to the relationship. Outwardly things appeared to be normal, but inside the frustration was growing. I flew easily into rages, breaking into tears at the slightest provocation.

Many nights I stayed at home while Víctor went out dancing and partying. "You can't go out anyway, Marta," he said. "Lina is sleeping, and someone has to stay with her."

With nothing to do and nothing to look forward to, I slipped into severe depression. Completely dependent on Víctor for an income, and too insecure to look for my own job, I stayed at home, cooking and cleaning, and then waiting for Víctor to come home.

At night I wandered through the apartment, cursing Víctor for the late nights, hating myself for staying. When Víctor finally returned in the early morning hours with lipstick on his face and shirt, I screamed at him, threatening to leave. The threats only angered him. "So leave then," he snapped angrily. "Why don't you just go? I'm tired of your threats."

He knew I would not leave. I had nowhere to go.

Feeling insecure, hating him, and yet powerless to break the relationship, I felt trapped. Vague thoughts of suicide began to crowd my mind. An awful emptiness gnawed at my insides. I was coming dangerously close to the edge. If something did not happen soon, I was going to take my own life.

Desperate for help, I went to see a psychiatrist at the hospital. One look at my sagging shoulders and sleepless eyes brought a look of sympathy to his eyes. "You're under a lot of stress," he said kindly. "You look like you haven't slept in a week. Here." He wrote on a slip of paper and handed it to me. "It's a prescription for sleeping pills. They should help. If you don't feel better in a week, come back and see me."

"Thank you," I said numbly. "Thank you."

I picked up the pills from the pharmacy and went home.

That night, Víctor came home late again. We had a terrible fight. Tired and defeated, I tried to think of one reason to stay alive. My family did not need me. Víctor did not care either way, and Lina would be better off without me.

In a daze, I took the bottle of sleeping pills and walked to the bathroom. Locking the door, I ran water in a cup and sat down on the floor. Tears ran down my cheeks as I swallowed the pills one at a time. It would soon be over. My family would suffer, but they would learn to live with my death. Lina would suffer, but she, too, would learn.

I heard Víctor in the other room. He was reading the note I had left—too late.

Death would be a relief.

Chapter 9

The banging on the door was making my head hurt. I was slumped on the floor, my body twisted at an awkward angle. My head felt heavy and swollen. I fought the effects of the pills, momentarily lifting my head off the floor, but it was too much of an effort, and I let it drop back to the floor.

"Ms. Estrada, please open the door."

The banging was louder now, irritating in its insistence.

I did not answer. My eyes focused and unfocused on the white tiles under my cheek. I was so dizzy. I rested my head on the floor. The cool ceramic felt good on my hot skin.

"Ma'am, open the door before it's too late," the voices urged.

I smiled briefly. Too late? It would never be too late; I wanted to die.

"Open the door, ma'am."

I was drifting in and out of consciousness, my eyes rolling in the back of my head as the effects of the pills spread through my body.

I thought of Víctor, and the mist cleared. Then I remembered—Víctor did not care what happened to me. He would never change. I hated him.

I relaxed again, my mind drifting.

"Open the door, ma'am." The doorknob rattled. "You need help."

I squeezed my eyes shut. "Go away," I mumbled. "Leave me alone. I don't want help." My tongue stumbled over the words.

"If you don't open the door, we're going to have to break it down." The voices outside the door were urgent, threatening.

It was useless. They were not going to let me die. Víctor—he must have called the police.

I reached for the door. Outside the door, the talking stopped. I fumbled with the lock. White spots swam dizzily in front of my eyes. My fingers felt numb. It was so hard to close them. The effort was too much...It would be so much easier to give up. Slowly I let my hand drop back to my side.

The voices started up again. "Don't give up, ma'am. Keep trying."

Slowly I closed my fingers over the lock and turned. The bolt clicked back in its chamber, and I collapsed, my mind sinking into unconsciousness.

Screaming sirens cleared the way to the hospital, paramedics rushing to save my life. Barely conscious, I fought for breath, trying to stay aware. I could hear the paramedics asking questions but was too groggy to answer.

At the hospital, the emergency room was chaotic. Medical personnel hurried in and out, the emergency team working quickly. Nurses pumped my stomach, forcing the poison out of my system. The white ceiling and bright lights faded, and I slipped into darkness.

When I regained consciousness, I was lying in a hospital bed with clean sheets stretched over me. I could hear faint sounds of activity coming from the corridor. I looked around at the white, sterile environment and started to cry.

"You're very lucky to be alive," the nurses told me. "Someone up there saved your life." They pointed mysteriously toward the ceiling.

"Someone up there should have minded His own business," I whispered bitterly.

The drugs in my system made me feel heavy and tired, and a sense of failure dragged at me. Thinking of the darkened apartment and the hours of depression spent at home waiting for Víctor made my stomach cramp. Fear flattened me in the bed. I could not go back to that apartment.

The following day, Víctor came to pick me up.

I turned to the doctor, pleadingly. "Please don't send me with him," I begged. "Please, I don't want to go with him."

The doctor pried my fingers from his arm. "I'm sorry, Ms. Estrada," he said firmly. "You're going to have to go."

One of the nurses walked me out to the parking lot, her arm supporting me. "Don't worry, Ms. Estrada," she said kindly. "Everything will be okay." She helped me into the car and closed the door. "Your husband will take good care of you."

Víctor slid in beside me, leaning across to close the window. "Thank you, nurse." He waved at her, smiling. "She's just tired."

I huddled in the corner of the car, crying. "Don't make me go back to the apartment, Víctor—please." My stomach was knotted and I was breathing hard. "Don't make me go with you," I sobbed. "Please, let me go."

"Shut up, Marta." His eyes were hard.

We drove home in silence. Víctor's hands were white on the steering wheel, his lips a thin line of cruelty.

Back in the apartment, Víctor put me in bed, then walked out. I watched the door close behind him and collapsed on the bed. Nothing had changed.

Hours later, I got out of bed and wandered through the apartment crying, the floor spinning beneath me. The effects of the pills had not worn off yet, and I was still high.

That night Víctor came home late. We fought again, and I felt a numbing depression seep through my body; it was starting all over again.

Víctor did not realize how deadly my depression had become. He goaded me viciously, playing on my jealousies, intentionally inciting me. Our nightly arguments became screaming matches, my voice rising to match his, insult for insult, the threats swinging violently from mild to extreme.

At night I sat in the living room waiting for the scrape of Víctor's key in the lock. I came to dread the sound of his stealthy footsteps outside the apartment door. The sound of his key in the door and the flip of the light switch in the hall were enough to bring a feeling close to nausea.

Trapped by my own insecurities and paralyzed by hopelessness, I waited for the breaking point. It had to come. The volatile mixture of depression and anger had become too much for me to handle. Finally, late one night, I snapped. Out of control, I grabbed a butcher knife from the kitchen and went after Víctor.

Angered, he knocked me down and threw me out of the apartment.

Locked out of the apartment and standing on the street alone, I cried in humiliation. "Víctor, open the door," I pleaded desperately.

"Go away," he yelled.

His voice carried down the block, and several lights went on. Curious neighbors peered through their blinds.

"Please, Víctor, just give me Lina," I whispered.

"Go away, Marta. I'm not opening the door."

Deep, wracking sobs of self-pity rose in my throat. He had no right to Lina. She was not his daughter. I banged on the door with my fists. "Let me in, Víctor. Let me in, or I'll call the cops."

His snort on the other side of the door made my fists ache. I walked away. I needed help. David—my mother's employer. Would he help? How many times had he tried to convince me to leave Víctor? How many times had he warned me to get out? I had never listened. Would he help me now?

I walked to the corner pay phone and dropped a coin in the slot. "David," I sobbed, "I need help."

"Marta?" He was wide awake. "What happened?"

"Víctor—he locked me out of the apartment."

"He what? Where are you?" he asked sharply.

"On the corner."

"Where's Lina?"

"Víctor has her in the apartment."

I heard him curse. "Don't do anything," he said. "I'll be right there."

David picked me up on the corner and drove me to the police precinct, his face set. "You should press charges, Marta," he said. "You could get Víctor in a lot of trouble."

"No, David, I don't want to," I said miserably. "I just want Lina."

An officer interrupted. "Is Mr. Vega the father?"

"No!" I shook my head emphatically. "He is not her father."

"Then he has no right to hold her," he said firmly. "Let's go get her."

I could not control the smile that spread across my face. Víctor had cocaine stashed throughout the apartment. He was going to have a heart attack when he heard the police.

A light was still shining from beneath the door when we arrived at the apartment.

The officer rapped firmly on the door. "Mr. Vega, open the door."

"Go away," Víctor shouted from inside.

I knew Víctor's friend, Oscar, was inside, and I pounded on the door. "Oscar, it's me, Marta. Open the door."

"I can't, Marta." Oscar sounded embarrassed. "Víctor said not to."

The officer stepped forward. "Mr. Vega, this is the police. You have thirty seconds to open the door."

I knew Víctor so well I could almost hear his heart stop beating. Inside the apartment, there was complete silence. For a moment I thought there would be no answer, then Oscar pulled the door open, his eyes tense.

One of the officers pushed his way in, surveyed the room, then motioned to me. "Okay, ma'am, go get your daughter."

I stepped through the door and walked by Víctor. I saw the tension on his face and marched past him defiantly, my nose in the air. Víctor slammed the door to the bedroom, cursing loudly from inside.

I woke Lina with trembling hands, gathering her warm form close to my body. "Lina, wake up. We're leaving."

Her eyes were closed, her breathing deep and quiet. I smoothed her tousled hair away from sleepy lids. "Wake up, sweetheart. We're going home to Colombia."

I walked out of the apartment, holding Lina tightly in my arms.

Víctor was still cursing from the bedroom, but I kept walking. This time I knew I had the strength to leave him. "I'm never coming back, Víctor," I said as I passed the closed door. "It's over. I never want to see you again."

Chapter 10

June 1982—Medellín, Colombia

S tepping off the airplane in my homeland into the warm, breezy summer air of Medellín, I nearly cried. The warmth and brilliance of the Colombian sun gave me hope for the future.

I did not have much money, but with the proceeds from some clothing I had bought wholesale in New York, I put a down payment on a restaurant and went into partnership with a friend.

It was not long before our little restaurant was prospering. Noisy, chattering Colombians packed the restaurant from early in the morning until late at night. *El Caribe* became a popular meeting place for young people. Some evenings I had to lock the doors to keep customers from overcrowding the little restaurant.

I had little time to brood about the life I had left behind. Lina was in a private school and learning under an English tutor, and it made me proud to see her dressed in her starched uniform, with her face scrubbed and clean, her schoolbooks tucked under her arm. She was a bright child and a delight to her Catholic teachers.

Colombia was a time for me to heal, a time to chase uneasy shadows from my mind. I went to mass every day, confessed my sins to a Catholic priest, and promised to stay away from Víctor and the drug trade.

I was invited to many parties in Medellín, and away from Víctor's suffocating jealousy, I found myself developing warm friendships with several men. Colombian men were charming, and I found their attention gratifying.

One evening, seven months after my return to Colombia, I glanced up from the dance floor and saw a young man I did not recognize. Something about his eyes made me pause. Warm and honest, they lacked the calculating ambition and desire I remembered so well in Víctor.

Careful not to stare, I watched him out of the corner of my eye. He was younger than Víctor, but he looked older, his strong, chiseled features giving him a look of maturity. His hair curled damply on his forehead, his eyebrows winged over darkly lashed eyes, white smile flashing in a deeply tanned face.

Feeling my gaze, he looked up and I turned away, aware that my face was reddening.

Several times that evening I felt his eyes on my face and turned away, feigning indifference. Chagrined, I realized he had seen my interest.

Ignore him, Marta, I told myself. *Just ignore him.*

A slight brush on my arm made me turn.

"I've been trying to get your attention all evening," the young man said, smiling. "You're ignoring me, aren't you?"

"Ignoring you?" I asked, flustered. "No, of course not."

"Why were you looking at me?"

"I didn't know I was." I searched desperately for my cousin.

"You were." He took my hand and led me out on the dance floor. "My name is Roberto," he said. "And yours?"

I looked down at his hand, confused. He was very sure of himself. "I'm Marta."

His face was calm and assured, his manner poised. He had all of Víctor's confidence but none of his arrogance. His eyes were clear and direct, with a hint of reserve.

He had a presence that I found intriguing.

"How long are you staying in Medellín, Marta?"

"I live here."

He smiled slowly. "Oh...good."

A tingle started in my fingertips. "And you, where do you live?" I asked.

"Medellín."

That night, Roberto walked me home through the soft darkness of a quiet city. I found his guiding hand on my arm oddly comforting. Outside my door he stopped. "Marta, I'd like to see you again."

I paused, as though thinking. "Well, I'm having a birthday party next month."

"May I come?"

I nodded. "If you'd like."

"Will you dance with me?"

I blushed. "Yes, of course."

"Then I'll be there."

Inside the house I tossed my purse on the bed and turned to glare at myself in the mirror. *What's wrong with you? Have you forgotten how to speak to a man?* I turned away in disgust. *You'd better think of something to say at this party, or you're going to lose him.*

Business continued as usual at the restaurant. The work consumed my day, but I could not hide my nervousness. Would Roberto come? What if he forgot?

The night of the party I dressed carefully, dusting make-up lightly over glowing skin and brushing my hair until it shone. The black dress I selected was tasteful, showing off my slender form and accentuating high cheekbones and sparkling eyes. Pearl earrings and a rosette with silk streamers completed the outfit.

My friends and family filled the house with laughter and festive music. I waited, tense and expectant. Would he come? My eyes wandered over the crowd, looking for him. There were several newcomers at the door, but Roberto was not among them. Disappointment was a lead weight in my stomach. It was getting late. He must have forgotten.

I saw some activity at the door and turned. Roberto was

standing just inside the doorway, his eyes searching the crowd. He saw me and stopped. "Happy birthday," he mouthed across the room, smiling.

I turned away abruptly, blushing like a schoolgirl.

I heard him come up behind me. "You promised to dance with me tonight." His voice was mildly scolding.

"I know," I stammered. "I didn't forget."

"You're not going to ignore me again, are you?"

"No," I laughed. I turned, hoping he would not notice my burning cheeks. "I won't ignore you."

There was something special about Roberto. His personality was magnetic but not controlling. When I was with him, memories of Víctor faded. Over the next several months Roberto and I became fast friends. Several times a week he came to help me at the restaurant, waiting until the last customer was gone, then cleaning up and walking me home.

During the evening hours Roberto kept a careful eye on the customers, watching me protectively from his seat in the corner.

"He likes you," my employees giggled. "Look at the way he watches you."

Several months passed happily, and I felt our friendship deepening. Roberto's warm eyes and whimsical smile tugged at my heart. He was so gentle, so thoughtful. I liked to watch his eyes, the irises darkening when he was upset, brightening when he laughed.

I did not feel any pressure from Roberto. He seemed content to be my friend, allowing me to dictate the pace and following my lead, but I wondered sometimes whether our relationship was developing into something more than friendship.

"Are you in love with someone, Marta?" he asked me one evening.

"No," I said, scarcely breathing. "Why?"

"I was just wondering."

He dropped the subject. Disappointed, I wondered whether he would ask again.

One morning, several months later, my phone rang. It was 2:30 in the morning. I reached for the receiver.

"Hello," I answered sleepily.

"Marta!" The voice sounded slurred. "Is that you?"

I sat up, fully awake, my skin constricting in horror. "Víctor!" I pulled the covers protectively up under my chin. "Where are you?"

"Marta, aren't you glad to hear from me?" He was drunk.

"Why are you calling, Víctor?"

"I missed you. Are you coming back to New York anytime soon?"

"Why?"

"I just wanted to know."

He knew I had to go back to keep my resident card updated. "Yes," I answered grudgingly. "Why do you want to know?"

"Can I see you when you come?"

"No." The single word came out flat and toneless.

Disappointment sounded in his voice. "Will you think about it?"

"No."

There was an awkward silence. "So, how are you doing?"

"I'm okay." What did he want? Why was he calling?

"Do you miss me?"

I did not say anything.

"I miss you, Marta."

"Víctor, I have to go," I said abruptly.

He hesitated. "Okay, but can I call you again?"

"No," I said and hung up.

Now I was frightened. Why had he called? I did not trust him. Already I could feel the subtle tug of deception.

Several days later the phone rang again, jolting me from a deep sleep.

"I went dancing tonight," Víctor was saying drunkenly. "I remembered how it was when we were together, and I got depressed."

"Víctor, you've been drinking," I said accusingly.

"Yes," he admitted. "I need you."

I gripped the phone, my knuckles whitening. "Víctor, I don't want to talk to you. I told you not to call."

"But, Marta," he insisted, "I feel so much better when I speak with you. Please let me call you again."

"No," I whispered desperately. "No, please—leave me alone. Don't call me anymore." I jammed the receiver back in its cradle.

The following week the phone rang again. I knew who it was and picked up the phone angrily. "Víctor, I told you not to call."

"Hold on, Marta," he interrupted. "Someone wants to say hello."

"Marta!" It was one of Víctor's friends. "Víctor hasn't been himself since you left. Come back to New York. He needs you."

"No, Francisco. Good-bye. Give me back to Víctor."

Víctor took the phone.

"Víctor, listen to me. If you call me again, I'll hang up on you. Do you hear me? I don't want to talk to you anymore."

"But, Marta, I've changed."

I hung up on him.

Bewildered, I sat staring at the phone. He sounded so sad—and he was drinking. He had never done more than drink socially before. Maybe he was in trouble; maybe he did need me.

The next time Víctor called, I listened, confused.

"Marta, I'm a different man," he said. "There aren't any more women. Ever since you left I've been faithful to you."

He had lied to me before. Why should I believe him now?

"Marta, come back, and you will see. When you come to the States, come to New York and stay with me in the apartment. You'll see that I'm different."

I was surprised by his offer. Would he offer to let me stay in the apartment if he was seeing another woman?

"Marta, let me pay for your ticket. The business is doing well, and I have a lot of money. I'll be in Miami when you're here for your residency. I could meet you there and drive you up to New York."

If Víctor paid for my ticket, I would not have to use any

of the money from the restaurant. It was a tempting offer.

"Marta, please, just give me another chance."

I had already given him many chances. Could I afford another one? "If I come, will you promise one thing?" I asked reluctantly.

"Yes, Marta," he promised excitedly. "Anything."

"When I'm there, no one must call the apartment—no women."

"Of course not," he said eagerly. "There are no more women. I'm a changed man. You'll see."

Was I crazy? Going back to him for even a month was suicidal. Maybe, but I needed to prove that it was over between us—and I needed the money. I would stay the month required to protect my resident status, tell Víctor it was over, then come right back to Lina and Roberto.

It was a good plan. Now I had to tell Roberto.

Roberto's face was still as I stumbled through my plan, carefully leaving Víctor's name out of the explanation.

"How long will you be gone?" he asked.

"Four weeks."

He took my hand. "May I ask you something?"

I looked at him, my eyes guarded. "What?"

"Are you going to see another man?"

My eyes fell. "No."

"Don't lie to me."

"No, Roberto," I protested weakly. "Of course not." I looked down at my twisting hands, hating the lie. "I'm going back for my residency."

How could I tell him the truth? I could not afford to lose him. I needed Roberto to anchor me to Colombia. If I lost him, I would lose my will to resist Víctor.

Several days later, Roberto took me to the airport. "I'll be waiting," he said. "Write or call."

Tears slipped down my cheeks. A familiar scene with Esteban flitted across my mind, and I shook my head angrily. "I'll be back," I said. "I promise."

Chapter 11

Víctor met me at the airport in Miami. Held close to his chest, I felt the old, inexplicable attraction stirring and struggled to free myself.

"Let me go, Víctor."

"Marta, I've missed you," he said huskily. "Promise you'll never leave me."

I was not ready to promise anything. Roberto was still in Colombia, and already I was having second thoughts about this visit. "We'll talk later," I promised vaguely. "Where are we staying?"

Víctor had made reservations in one of the most exclusive hotels in Florida. Whisked through the streets of Miami Beach in the gleaming rental car, I stared through the tinted glass. Víctor seemed to be doing well financially. Where did he get all this money? His moving company had never been that successful. He worked hard, but his trucks had never brought in much money.

Víctor was watching me intently. "Marta, what are you thinking?"

"Nothing," I mumbled.

I slid my fingers along the seat, fingering the rich leather. My eyes slid down Víctor's arm, lingering on the expensive watch then down to his tailored trousers and handmade Italian shoes. I shook my head wonderingly. He was certainly well-dressed.

At the door to the hotel, Víctor gallantly opened the car door and escorted me into the lobby. "I've reserved an entire suite, Marta," he said. "The best in the hotel." He kissed his fingers, bursting them airily. "It's *bellísimo*."

The suite was beautiful. The scent of flowers drifted through the spacious, sunlit rooms. Chilled champagne waited on the dresser, and a brightly wrapped gift sat perched on the bed.

Víctor waved grandly toward the bed. "I brought you a present, Marta. Come and open it." His eyes were intense, steady.

I sat down on the edge of the bed and pulled the present toward me.

Víctor nodded approvingly. "Open it," he urged.

The bright, reflective wrapping paper showed my face, cheeks flushed, eyes large and dark. I lifted the lid slowly. Out streamed a black nightgown, elegant and lacy. Confused, I stood up.

Víctor's eyes followed me. "Don't you like it, Marta?"

"What's in the briefcase?" I asked, pointing to a small case lying half-opened on the table.

"Don't you like it?" he repeated. His face was surly.

"Yes, it's lovely. What's in the briefcase?"

He turned away, disappointed by my reaction. "Open it; take a look."

I lifted the lid, then breathed in sharply. Rows of diamond rings lay winking in the sunlight, sparkling clear and hard.

A fist of fear curled in my stomach. "Whose jewels are these, Víctor?"

"Mine."

"Where did you get them?"

"A business payment." He walked to the wide, sunlit windows. "Go ahead; take two for yourself."

"Víctor!"

He did not look up.

I should have known. I had seen the signs. "You're dealing again, aren't you, Víctor?"

He slid his hands into his pockets, looking out over the beach below. "Does it matter?" A cloud passed over the sun and the room darkened briefly. "You won't be involved."

"You've said that before, Víctor."

Víctor reached out and opened the drapes wider, then carefully adjusted the flower arrangement on the table near the window. "It's different now, Marta. Things are going well." He lowered his voice. "I just need to pick up some merchandise here in Miami."

Merchandise...I turned away. What did it matter anyway? I did not need to know the details of his transactions. I would be gone soon, and he could do whatever he wanted.

I took one of the rings and slid it onto my finger, holding it up to the light. Exquisitely cut facets threw out a dazzling light, the inner core glowing with cold fire. It was beautiful—and obviously expensive. I selected two of the largest pieces and slipped them into my purse. They would help pay for the restaurant.

We stayed in Miami for five days.

Now that I was with him, Víctor seemed almost lightheaded. He dreamed out loud, making plans for our future. "Soon I'll have enough money to go back to Colombia with you," he said triumphantly. "We'll buy an apartment, put some money in your restaurant, and then start all over."

Víctor in Colombia? I shuddered. What would I tell Roberto? "We'll talk about it later," I promised quickly. Later—when I could think more clearly.

Víctor completed his business transactions in Miami and prepared for the trip back to New York. "We'll have to hide the merchandise," he said, thinking out loud. "We don't want any problems from the cops."

After some thought, he packed the cocaine in the doors of our rental car and sealed them tightly. "The police won't even think about stopping us," he said confidently, "and if they do, they'll never find the package."

With four pounds of pure cocaine at my elbow I was

tense and anxious, but I did not say anything. Chances were slim that we would be stopped, and I did not want to risk upsetting Víctor. Once we got to New York, I would make him stop.

In Washington, D.C., we stopped to see Víctor's sister. "Marta, you've got to talk to Víctor," she whispered. "They're calling him the biggest mafioso in Queens."

Mafioso! Víctor had always tried to remain independent, making sure he was not connected to the cartels. It was safer. Now they were calling him the biggest mafioso in Queens. Why would he start working with them?

"I'll talk to him when we get to New York," I promised. "He'll have to stop soon anyway—he says he's moving to Colombia."

We headed north through Baltimore and Delaware, then into New Jersey. Soon we would be home. New York! I loved New York with its exciting night life, restaurants, and theaters. I missed the late parties with friends. My friends! They were all in New York waiting to see me.

Víctor braked gently, and I sat up.

"What, Víctor? What's happening?"

Revolving lights flashed threateningly ahead. Police cars were parked along the side of the road. Officers were out on the highway with dogs, flagging down the cars.

I leaned forward, straining against the seat belt. "What are they doing?"

Víctor's eyes were tense, his knuckles taut on the steering wheel. "Sit back, Marta."

"What are they doing?" I watched as the officers opened the door to one car, holding dogs firmly in check. "Why are they stopping everyone?"

"Sit back, Marta," Víctor repeated tightly.

"Oh my God, they're looking for drugs!"

"I know what they're doing, Marta," he gritted. "I'm not stupid." His eyes were trained on the dogs. "Just sit back."

I leaned back, closing my eyes in disbelief. We had close to $120,000 worth of cocaine packed in the car doors and were being stopped by a police blockade. Five days with Víctor, and already I was going to jail!

Víctor looked at me briefly. "Marta, if they hear your accent, they'll have those dogs inside this car in a minute, so keep your mouth shut!"

An officer waved down the car in front of us, forcing us to a crawl. I heard Víctor's labored breathing beside me and screwed my eyes shut, praying rapidly. "Mary, Mother of Jesus, please get me out of this, and I promise I'll never get involved in this mess again."

Beads of sweat traced glistening lines down Víctor's jaw. Revolving lights made playful designs on my body, splashing color on the car doors. I could almost smell the cocaine next to me. If they stopped us now, it was over.

"Please get me out of this," I whispered. "Please."

Incredibly, the officer was motioning us on.

Víctor blinked, then accelerated carefully. I forced myself to stay calm. I turned slowly to look back at the dogs. They were sniffing eagerly around the car behind us. "*Cuídate*, Víctor," I cautioned. "They could still stop us."

He was not listening, his mind concentrating on the road. His breathing was short, the strain showing in his shoulders. A mile down the highway, Víctor pulled the car to the side of the road. His hands were shaking violently. "I can't drive, Marta," he said. "Take the wheel."

His face was pale, sharp lines of tension etched around his mouth. His skin was stretched tight over jutting cheekbones, an odd shade of gray showing through his darkened tan.

I wondered sadly how long it would be before he was killed. Someday the dealings would catch up to him, and he would have to pay the price.

I prayed I could make him stop before it was too late.

Chapter 12

Back in New York I realized that things had not changed. The calls started soon after we arrived. "Víctor loves me…He doesn't love you…You're dealing drugs with Víctor…I'm going to call the police."

Two weeks after our return from Miami, the old fights started again. Familiar anger burned in my stomach. "Víctor," I yelled, "your girlfriends are driving me crazy. They call here every day. Make them stop, or I'm leaving."

"Marta, you're just upset; calm down—I don't have any girlfriends."

"Don't stand there and lie to me," I screamed. "You were living with another woman while I was in Colombia."

"Who told you that?" he asked quietly.

"Carmen told me. You're sick, Víctor. You had another woman in this apartment, and you tell me you love me. Are you crazy?"

His eyes were glittering dangerously. "Carmen should mind her own business."

I stopped abruptly. "Leave her alone, Víctor."

"It's the truth, Marta," he insisted. "I could never live with another woman."

He was lying. I knew it—and still I believed him. What was wrong with me? Maybe I was the one who was sick.

We slipped easily into our old relationship, the arguments growing wilder. Memories of old fights crashed through my mind, and I wondered why I had come back. Was I blind? The emotional nightmare was worsening, and still I could not leave him. His control over me was frightening.

Three weeks after we returned from Miami I made a decision. I had to get out before his control became impossible to break.

"Víctor," I said, facing him defiantly, "I'm leaving."

"Leaving for where?"

"You know where, Víctor. Don't play stupid."

Anger darkened his face. "You're not going anywhere, Marta. You'll go when I have the money."

"I don't care about the money, Víctor. I want to go now."

"No!" he shouted, slamming a hand on the table. "You're not going until I'm ready. I have a deal to finish."

"A deal?" Now I was yelling. "You don't have a deal! You're going to see a woman! Why don't you just tell me the truth?"

He tilted his head suddenly, regarding me whimsically. "It's a business deal, Marta. Come with me, and you'll see for yourself."

Oddly, this time I knew he was not lying.

"Come with you?" I expelled my breath slowly.

"Yes."

A cunning thought slipped into my mind. "Víctor, if I agree to go with you, will you leave for Colombia as soon as it's over?"

He stayed quiet for a moment, looking at me. Finally he nodded. "If that's what you want." He lifted a finger. "But I don't want you ruining my deal. Jake is my best customer. If he asks you any questions, let me answer. You just keep your mouth shut."

I agreed, and Víctor quickly set up a meeting with the customer he called Jake in a parking lot behind the old Peacock Diner. He gave me the cocaine and told me to put it in my purse. "I'll call you over when we're ready to do the deal," he said.

The diner had been closed for several years, and the parking lot was deserted. Weeds and debris covered the sidewalks. A shiver touched my spine. What if Jake was an undercover cop? How much was in the package I had in my purse? One pound? Enough to get us both a lot of time.

An old sedan pulled slowly into the lot, and I strained to see the driver's face.

"*Cálmate*, Marta." Víctor's warning look was sharp. "Stay here until I call you."

The car door closed. Víctor's greeting was distant, and I could not hear his words, but the conversation seemed cordial enough. Finally, Víctor turned and beckoned to me.

"Jake," Víctor was saying, "this is my wife, Marta. She just arrived from Colombia."

"Hello, nice to meet you, Ms. Vega." The blue eyes were composed.

I smiled. "Hello, Jake." I placed the bag in his outstretched hand. "Nice to meet you." I shuddered slightly as his blue eyes held mine for a second. Why was he looking at me like that? My eyes dropped first, and I backed away, my heart beating a little faster.

Víctor jerked his head toward the car. "Wait for me over there, Marta."

I nodded gratefully and walked back to the car. I slid into my seat with a sigh of relief. It was almost over. Colombia was just a heartbeat away.

But it was not almost over. After the deal with Jake, Víctor seemed reluctant to leave New York. Several bad deals made him edgy, and my own growing fears were making him jumpy.

I pressured him constantly to return to Colombia, but he brushed me off. "No, Marta," he said impatiently. "I'm not ready to go yet. When I have the money, we'll go. Not before."

I was already well past my scheduled departure date, and when Mama called from Colombia she sounded upset. "Marta, what's going on? I thought you were coming home."

"I am, Mama. I just have some things to take care of first."

"Well, when are you coming back?"

"I don't know. Soon," I said, my voice non-committal.

"Are you with Víctor?"

I did not say anything.

"I'm sending Lina," Mama said firmly.

"No, Mama, please. I'll be back soon."

"I don't care, Marta. She needs you," Mama said determinedly. "I'm sending her."

I did not want Lina around for the final deals, and I did not want Víctor to have another hold on me; but Mama was insistent, and Víctor offered to pay for the ticket. Several days later, Lina joined me in New York.

Víctor's drug deals were getting larger, and as the amount of money involved continued to grow, I became increasingly nervous. I did not trust Víctor's customers. Jake especially made me uneasy. Jake was polite and treated me with respect, but something about the way he looked at Víctor made me uneasy.

I was with Víctor when he met Jake for the second time at a restaurant in Queens. When he talked about a rich friend who wanted to buy some cocaine, my flesh tingled. What was it that made me uncomfortable? Was it the smile he gave when Víctor asked to be introduced to his friend, or the too-casual interest he showed in Víctor's contacts?

"Víctor, be careful," I warned. "Jake is going to get you in trouble."

"Marta, please!" Víctor snapped. "Stop worrying so much! You're making me nervous."

"But, Víctor, I don't trust him."

"Shut up, Marta!" Víctor shouted. "Just shut up! I've had it with your negative thinking. Why don't you just let me worry about Jake?"

The tension was beginning to escalate in our nightly fights. I knew something was wrong but could not prove it. I was off balance now, distraught and crying constantly. I was frightened and wanted to get away but could not formulate a clear plan.

I worried constantly about Roberto. I was haunted by his face in my dreams, pleading, "Come back to Colombia, Marta. Come back before it's too late." *Too late*—the words echoed ominously in my mind.

I pressed Víctor constantly now, desperate ·to return.

Finally, one night Víctor exploded. "That's it, Marta! I've had it with you. I'm tired of hearing about Colombia. Did you leave someone over there? Did you leave a boyfriend? Is that why you're so anxious to go?"

I looked at him, sick inside.

He saw my face and threw up his hands. "Go then! Pack your things and go back to him. I'm tired of your whining. Go back to Colombia. I'll even give you the money. Just get out; you're making me crazy."

I looked at him uncertainly. Did he mean it?

He did. Víctor made arrangements to have $5,000 in cash released to me, then left the house in silence. I quickly called the airline and placed reservations to return to Colombia on the twentieth of July.

It did not take Víctor long to reconsider. "Marta," he pleaded several days later, "just give me one more month. One more month—and we'll leave together."

Together? "You're going too?" I asked carefully.

"Yes."

Now I was cautious, humoring him, bargaining for time. "I'm not changing my reservations, Víctor. I'll make reservations for you, but on the twentieth I'm leaving with or without you."

"Don't worry," he said. "I'll be ready."

That evening, Víctor left the house early. Late into the night I paced the apartment floor, thinking. I did not want Víctor in Colombia with me. I could not take him back with me. How was I going to explain him to Roberto?

Late that evening I called Colombia. "Roberto, I'm coming home soon," I promised. "I'll be back by the twentieth."

By one o'clock, Víctor still had not returned. My anger built to a fevered pitch. He had lied to me about his women. He had lied to me about his drug deals. Now he was lying to me about Colombia. I knew now that he was not going to let me go. Galled by my own stupidity, I cursed myself mentally. I had believed every one of his lies and had no one to blame but myself.

At two o'clock the phone rang. It was Johanna, a friend in Miami. "Marta, you must leave Víctor immediately," she said. "Something bad is going to happen to you. The spirits have told me."

I started to cry, the strain overwhelming me. "What, Johanna? What is going to happen?"

"I don't know, but leave him now. Get out before it's too late."

"I am—I'm leaving for Colombia on the twentieth."

"No, Marta," she said insistently. "You must leave tonight. You are in danger."

"Yes, Johanna," I cried, frightened. "I will. I'll leave right now."

I hung up, then paced the floor, crying, trying to decide. I could not leave tonight. Where would I go? It was too late.

At three o'clock in the morning, Víctor stumbled into the apartment, drunk.

Johanna's warning hung darkly in my mind. *"Something bad is going to happen to you. Get out before it's too late."*

I shook my head. I could not leave now. It did not make sense. I only had a few more days left. Wearily, I went to bed. I tossed for hours and finally slept fitfully. I woke up groggy, with a headache. The curtains were pulled and the room was dark. I glanced at the clock. It was 9:00 a.m.

I heard Víctor's voice speaking quietly from the kitchen. "Where do we meet? This will have to be my last transaction. We're leaving in six days."

I got out of bed, my feet quiet on the floor. Víctor's back was turned to me, his words slightly muffled. Johanna's warning sounded in my head, and I had a sick feeling in my stomach. I shook my head, trying to shake the impression of danger. Johanna's warning had upset me more than I cared to admit.

I left Víctor on the phone and went out to buy some medication for Lina. Outside, I noticed a van parked across the street. When I returned from the pharmacy, the van was still there. Unnerved, I went upstairs. "Víctor," I said quietly, "there's a van outside. Someone is watching you."

His eyes narrowed. "Where?" He lifted a blind and looked out, his lips tightening as the van sped away.

I was agitated now. "Víctor, the cops know about you. They're going to arrest you."

Víctor let the blind fall. "I'm going out," he said.

"Where are you going?"

"I'm meeting Jake for lunch."

"I'm coming with you," I said.

"No, Marta. You'd better not come."

"I want to," I said insistently.

Víctor rubbed his eyes wearily, and I wondered if he, too, sensed something was wrong. "Okay, Marta," he said. "Get Lina. We'll eat lunch and then take her to the park. You need to get out—you're looking pale." He looked abstractedly at his watch. "Let's go. I'm late."

We made a quick stop to pick up the cocaine, then drove to the restaurant in silence. We arrived a little early and parked around the corner. Víctor shut off the engine and took the keys out of the ignition. The street was quiet. The heat of the summer sun warmed the sidewalk and street asphalt.

Víctor handed me the box with the cocaine. "Put this in the bag with Lina's medicine," he said. "Wait five minutes, and then come in. We'll eat lunch and then give Jake the cocaine. Don't wait too long, and don't act suspicious."

Víctor slid out of the car, shut the door, and took a quick look around. He disappeared around the corner.

The minutes ticked by, and I planned my packing. There was so much to do before we left. The sounds of summer drifted through the window, and I began to feel drowsy.

Víctor had said five minutes. I glanced at my watch. It was time.

At 2:45 p.m., I opened the door, helped Lina out of the car, slung my purse over my shoulder, locked the door, and walked around the corner to the restaurant.

Chapter 13

The next few moments will remain among the most terrifying of my life. Suddenly, undercover police were everywhere, their shouted instructions smashing through my dazed consciousness. "Get your hands up! Get them up!" The voices were brutal, angry. Guns were pointing at me from every direction.

Stunned, I backed into Lina, my eyes swinging from face to face.

"Mama, what are they doing?" Lina's hands were clutching my leg.

I could not answer her. My breath was coming in gasps, my lungs straining against my ribs. Where had they all come from? How had they known?

My hands tightened spasmodically on the bag. *The cocaine!* They were going to find the cocaine! My eyes traveled wildly around the circle, searching, questioning. Their eyes stared back at me, cold and hard, their guns leveled in steady hands.

The faces blurred suddenly, and I swayed, close to fainting. The bag was snatched from my hand and opened, the cocaine pulled from the box. The detective's sneering face made my fingers curl.

"Mama!" Lina was crying, her hands grasping for mine.

She was only six years old—too young to witness her mother's arrest. *I'm going to lose her*, I thought numbly. *I'm going to lose my baby.*

"Do you use drugs, ma'am?" The detective's voice was clipped.

I shook my head.

"No, of course not," he snapped, shaking his head in imitation. He looked over at his partner. "They never use drugs, these Colombians. They're too good for that. They just sell the stuff."

"Okay," the sergeant ordered, "search her."

I looked around, startled. They could not search me unless they had a policewoman with them.

"Manos arriba, por favor." The voice behind me was firm and very female.

I turned in disbelief.

"Please put your hands up," the order was repeated.

A policewoman! They knew I was coming! They had been expecting me. I fought to stay calm, fighting the hysteria rising in my throat. Who could have told them? I saw a flurry of activity and turned. The police were leading Víctor out of the restaurant in handcuffs. Víctor's eyes met mine for a brief second then slid away, his face expressionless.

I stared over his shoulder, then frowned in concentration. Blue eyes gazed back at me, calm, detached—Jake!

Suddenly I knew. Víctor had been selling to the New York City narcotics squad the whole time.

Tears of anger and frustration slid down my cheeks. Six more days, and I would have been gone for good. Six more days, and I would have been back in Colombia—with Roberto.

"Oh, God," I cried brokenly. "Why did You let this happen? Why didn't You make me listen? Why did You let me come back to him?"

Víctor was walking past me, his eyes cold. He saw Lina next to me, and his eyes held for a second, then looked away. He lowered his head and kept walking. I stared after him. For one brief moment I thought I had seen shame cross his face.

I realized, suddenly, how many people were lining the sidewalks, watching. Painful, searing shame swept over me. Handcuffs were slapped on my wrists, the cold steel biting into my skin. "Let's go, ma'am. Get in the car. We're taking you in for questioning."

"Lina," I gasped, looking around wildly.

"Relax," the officer said, "she's coming with you."

I got in the police car and put my head down, hiding my face. It was quiet in the car, and no one spoke as we drove to the police precinct. Lina sat quietly beside me, shaking. I looked down at the top of her head. She was so small, so defenseless. Her little body was stiff, her eyes staring straight ahead.

"Lina," I whispered, "it's going to be alright."

She nodded, tears welling in her eyes.

The handcuffs pulled at my wrists. I shifted, adjusting my arms, looking for a more comfortable position. The officer looked over, watching me closely. I stopped moving, and the officer relaxed.

She thinks I'm trying to escape! I thought in disbelief. *She thinks I'm a criminal.* I sat back, the blood draining from my skin, leaving me cold and shaken.

"Do you use drugs, ma'am?" The detective's words echoed through my mind. *"No, of course not. They never use drugs, these Colombians. They're too good for that. They just sell the stuff."*

A mental picture of a nine-year-old girl on a school stage draped in a Colombian flag flashed through my mind, and I felt my chest heave. I stared out the window, unshed tears burning my eyes. I was almost forty years old. What had happened to my promises to do something great for my country? What had happened to my promises to bring honor to my nation?

Had I given the world another reason to curse my country and my people? Had I given the U.S. government one more statistic to chalk up against the account of the Colombian people?

A childhood dream died inside.

Hot tears trickled down my cheeks, and I turned my face away from Lina.

At the precinct I was helped out of the car and ushered through the lobby. Víctor had already arrived in the other car and was being led into another room.

"Ma'am, we're going to have to take your daughter," the officer said apologetically.

Lina's hand tightened convulsively in mine. "No! Mama, no, please."

"Ma'am, I'm sorry." The officer's face was apologetic. "You can call your family to come and get her, but she will have to go."

"I don't have any family," I lied. I saw Lina's confused look and squeezed her hand sharply, silencing her. I could not call my brothers. They were still here illegally.

"Then we'll have to take her ourselves, ma'am," the officer said.

Lina's nails bit into my palm.

"No," I said quickly, "please, I have a friend who will take her."

"Give us the number. We'll call her."

One of the officers left to make the call, and I knelt beside Lina. "Lina, listen to me. Bianca is coming to get you."

"No, Mama, I don't want to go." Lina's face was white, quivers of fear jerking at her mouth. "I don't want to."

"I know, Lina, but you must. They have to ask me some questions."

"Why can't I stay with you?"

"They won't allow it."

"But why are they doing this to you?" she sobbed. "You aren't a bad lady."

I looked at her face, streaked with tears, and felt my throat tighten. "Lina…"

"Why won't they let you go, Mama?" she asked. "Why? You didn't do anything wrong." Her voice was demanding, insistent.

How much did she know? Did she understand what was happening? She had seen some of the deals in the apartment, and I was sure she had seen Víctor preparing the cocaine several times.

"They want me to stay so they can ask me a few questions," I said. "Víctor has been doing something he shouldn't have."

"Is he in trouble?"

He was, but so was I. "Yes, he's in trouble," I said. I looked up from the floor. "Lina, listen to me. I can't tell you everything that happened here today—you wouldn't understand. But one day I will tell you everything, okay?"

Lina nodded, her lips quivering. "But will you come home soon?"

"Yes," I promised huskily. "I will—as soon as they let me. Right now I have to stay. You sit here and wait for me."

An officer tapped me on the shoulder. "This way, ma'am. They're waiting for you."

Víctor was sitting at a large table in the other room, his fingers drumming nervously on the surface. He swung around when he heard me, his eyes searching my face. "Marta..."

"Leave me alone," I said.

"Marta, listen to me," he said. "You can't tell them the truth. If you do, you'll just get in trouble."

"Be quiet, Víctor," I snapped. "Just shut your mouth. I don't want to listen to you."

I put my head on the table, depression seeping through my body. Shock had set in, and my body was shivering despite the heat. I could not think clearly, but I knew that if I spent time in jail because of Víctor, I would hate him for the rest of my life.

Víctor was whispering information in my ear. I moved away, not wanting to be close to him. "Shut up, Víctor. You're going to get us in trouble with your lies."

"Ma'am, come this way." The officer's hand was on my shoulder. "We're going to have to ask you some questions. Sir, you come this way."

They were going to question us separately! If Víctor lied, our stories would not match. I knew now I was going to have to tell the truth.

The questioning was difficult, and I wondered what answers Víctor was giving in the other room, but finally it was over. An officer motioned to me. "Ma'am, your friend is here for your daughter. She's waiting to say good-bye."

Lina was still waiting for me in the hall, and I took her small hand in mine. "Lina, are you ready to go?"

The dark eyes were frightened, but she nodded.

"Bianca will take care of you," I said. "Be good and listen to her. Give her these keys and tell her to get your clothes from the apartment. And don't worry; I'll be home soon." The words stuck in my throat.

Lina left the hall, clutching the officer's hand. She looked back, tears coursing down her cheeks, straining to see me over her shoulder.

I fought back the tears. Johanna had warned me; Mama had warned me; and still I had refused to listen. I had no one to blame but myself. Now I did not know when I would see my daughter again.

Chapter 14

We were taken to the holding pen in the Queens Court House at 8:00 that evening. Packed with angry, miserable human beings, the tiny holding pen was filthy and smelled of old urine.

Stale air hung over the pen. Poor lighting made the faces appear old and tired. The women in the pen could not have been over twenty-five years old, but they looked much older.

Their blouses were tight and low-cut. Tiny skirts strained above mid-thigh, showing slender bodies through strips of clothing. Bright makeup did little to cover the hardened look of the streets.

I crept to a corner bench and huddled on the hard cement, palms sticky and warm. "Oh, God, help me," I moaned. "Get me out of here."

Questions crowded my mind. Did I have any rights as a Colombian? Víctor's warning whipped through my mind. *"You're Colombian, Marta. If you tell them the truth, you're going to get maximum time, so don't tell them anything."*

How much time was I going to get? More than fifteen? In fifteen years, Lina would be twenty-one years old. She would be a woman by the time I got out. My mind recoiled from the thought.

"Hey, what'd they arrest you for?"

I closed my eyes, my heart beating wildly.

"Hey, I'm talking to you." The girl looked friendly under the lipstick and thick mascara. "Don't look so scared," she laughed. "We're not going to hurt you. What did they get you for?"

"Drugs," I mumbled. "Cocaine."

She raised an eyebrow. "Where are you from?"

"Colombia."

"Oh," she grinned. "I should have known."

My muscles contracted in anger. How dare she?

"Marta Estrada?" An officer was standing at the barred entrance.

I jumped up. "Yes?"

"You're being arraigned. Let's go."

The hall stretched before me. My footsteps sounded loudly on the tile floors. I stumbled several times, and the officer reached out a steadying hand. "Careful, Ms. Estrada."

The courtroom was large and well-lit, and Víctor was already seated with his attorney.

"Your Honor," the prosecution was saying, "we have charges against Mr. Vega, but we have nothing against the lady."

I looked around, bewildered. No charges? Was I being released?

"We should have her charges within several hours," he said.

Defeated, I slumped in my chair.

Prosecution had more than enough evidence to convict Víctor. Detectives had been following Víctor for more than three months before I returned from Colombia. When I stepped off the plane, I had stepped right into the middle of a sting operation.

No wonder Jake had been so anxious to meet Víctor's "wife." He probably thought I was bringing fresh drugs from Colombia. I saw Jake's eyes, deep-blue with a hint of suspicion beneath their cordial welcome, and groaned inwardly. How much time was I going to get?

The acrid taste of regret was bitter in my mouth, and I

felt the irony deeply. I had pushed Víctor to return to Colombia. Knowing it was Víctor's last transaction, the detectives had moved in quickly to catch us before we slipped away.

I was taken back to the holding pen late that night. I spent a sleepless night on the cement bench, listening to the obscenities swirling around me. The prostitutes stood on the benches to look at the men in the adjoining pen, and the men shouted vulgarities back at the women, suggesting unthinkable activities.

I heard Víctor's voice yelling above the noise, "Shut up so we can get some sleep."

But sleep did not come. I huddled on the bench and prayed for morning.

"Marta Estrada?"

I looked up wearily.

"Court time."

Again Víctor was the topic of discussion. I listened to the proceedings, dazed and confused. In my state of shock and exhaustion, I found the legal process impossible to follow. Finally, I heard my name.

"Ms. Estrada?"

I looked up. "Yes, your Honor?"

"You understand the charges being brought against you?"

I nodded uncertainly.

"Good." He motioned to his right. "Prosecution, you may begin."

"Thank you, your Honor." The district attorney adjusted his glasses, flipping through a stack of papers on his desk. "The incident for which Ms. Estrada was arrested was not the first time she was involved in one of Mr. Vega's deals. Ms. Estrada was filmed on two previous occasions during transactions with an undercover officer."

My mind whirled. *Filmed on two other occasions?*

"What are the charges?"

"Narcotics...ten felony counts."

The judge's face was grave. "Ten counts—for what?"

"Possession, sale, and conspiracy."

"You have evidence of these two encounters?"

"Yes, your Honor."

A scene flashed before my eyes—blue eyes watching calmly as I placed the bag of cocaine in his outstretched hand. "Nice to meet you, Ms. Vega," Jake had said.

I stared down at my hands, the tears frozen deep inside.

"In light of the evidence presented," the judge was saying, "it is the decision of this court that Ms. Estrada remain detained until trial." The gavel crashed, making me jump. "No bail."

I sat motionless, my mind spinning. Sale and conspiracy, possession—no bail.

I looked over at Víctor. His face was stony and cold. In that moment I hated him.

I was going to jail.

Chapter 15

I was taken to Rikers Island Correctional Facility in hand-cuffs at eleven o'clock that night. Hot, muggy summer air moved through the bus, occasional swirls of hot air gusting through the open windows. No one spoke. The silence in the bus was broken only by the clinking of the metal security dividers and the quiet voices of the driver and guards. I stared dully at the handcuffs on my wrists, twisting them to adjust the edges.

In the distance I could see the glint of barbed wire and chain-link fences surrounding the jail compound. Beneath us, the dark waters of the East River lapped at the shores of the island, the murky waters reflecting the lights of Manhattan on the other shore.

The bus rolled slowly across the bridge and eased to a stop outside a darkened building. The officers banged on the side of the bus. "Okay, everybody out! Let's go!"

After two days of sitting in the Queens holding pen, my muscles were aching. I stepped from the bus and shuffled into line, my swollen feet making it difficult to walk. The building lights were bright after the darkness of the bus, and I paused inside the doorway, blinking.

"Come on in, ladies," an officer called. "Have a seat. You're going to be here for a while."

We were shown into the holding pen. I sat down on the edge of the bench with my feet close together, my eyes fixed on my hands. My white pants were dirty, and I spread my fingers, trying to hide the stains. The heat inside the holding pen was suffocating. Beads of sweat broke out on my forehead. I ran a hand over wet skin, mixing sweat with tears.

Women settled on the benches around me, some standing, some sitting. I shifted to make room for one of the women. Her skin touched mine, and I moved away. Miserably I clenched my fists. How long would they keep me here? What if Víctor told them I had been involved? I had lived with Víctor. I had even been with him on several of the deals. Who would ever believe I had not been involved?

The sound of violent retching made me look up. A young girl was bent over in the corner, her shoulder braced against the wall, her legs half-bent. Limp hair hung around her face, but I could see her arms, dotted with needle marks. The short dress rode up above her knees, showing crusted needle marks trailing down her legs. She fell back against the wall, and I saw her eyes, half-crazed, the whites showing.

I looked at her in horror and growing awareness; this young girl was a drug addict. As I watched, a shattering realization hit me. This was what cocaine did to a human being.

"They never use drugs, these Colombians. They're too good for that. They just sell the stuff."

Suddenly sick, I bent over.

"Ms. Estrada," an officer called. "Please step outside."

I stood up, then shuffled past the girl, avoiding her eyes. "This way, please."

The heavy door slammed behind me. "Watch your step."

I followed the officer to the counter where the fingerprinting equipment was set up. Another officer slipped a card into the guide racks and motioned for my hand. "Right hand, please."

I held out my hand, ignoring the persistent throbbing in my chest, concentrating on the officer's motions. My heart was beating in quick, erratic strokes. I pressed a hand to my chest, the pounding bringing back memories—the sudden, terrifying moment when I knew I was surrounded—the real- ization that I was holding enough cocaine to put me away for years. Sweat slid slowly down my face.

"Okay, you're finished." The officer slipped the card out of the guide racks and handed me a paper towel. "Wipe your hands and stand up against the wall."

I wiped my hands obediently and backed up against the wall. The camera flash popped, and I blinked. I was now a prisoner of the City of New York.

The officer opened the door to the pen and motioned me inside, then called another name. I sat down, avoiding the curious glances of the waiting women. One by one, the other women were taken out for processing and returned to the pen.

I sat on the bench, my mind disoriented and confused. Over and over I replayed the moment in front of the restau- rant. *"Get them up! Get your hands up!"* I covered my ears, blocking the voices.

"Get in the car. We're taking you in for questioning..." The policewoman's eyes had looked sympathetic. Had she sensed my embarrassment?

"Ma'am, you have $30,000 worth of cocaine here...you say you didn't know?"

I ran my tongue over my lips, feeling the dry, cracked skin. My hands were shaking.

"You think you're a lady, selling cocaine in front of your daughter?"

Sudden tears burned my cheeks. Lina—her father had left her; now her mother was in jail.

"Ms. Estrada..."

I looked up, my heart jerking painfully. "Yes?"

An officer was holding the door open. "Step outside please."

This time I was shown into a large room off to the side of the holding pen. Several shower stalls against the far wall were occupied, hot steam billowing into the room. There were no shower curtains on the stalls, and the women in the showers were clearly visible. I looked away, averting my eyes, trying to still the fluttering in my chest. The thought of bathing in front of another person was humiliating to me.

There was only one officer in the room. I focused my eyes on her back, my eyes adjusting to the low light. I felt a wrenching pain in my back and adjusted my weight slightly.

"Get them up!" The angry voices and pointing guns flashed unwelcome across my mind. I swayed and took a step to catch my balance.

The officer looked up. "Ms. Estrada, please remove your clothing."

"Remove my…take my clothes off?"

"Yes, ma'am."

"Why…what are you going to do?"

The officer looked at me. "It's a search, Ms. Estrada. We can't search you with your clothes on."

I turned my head away, staring at the wall.

"Ms. Estrada."

I undressed slowly, helpless tears stinging my eyes. Standing naked in front of the officer, I felt the sobs building inside. If my mother saw me like this, it would kill her.

"Okay, squat down."

I wrapped my arms around my naked body, trembling uncontrollably. I felt sick.

"Ms. Estrada, please—squat down."

I bent my knees, squatting down in front of the officer.

She examined every part of my body for hidden drugs and weapons and then stood up. "Okay, Ms. Estrada, go take your shower."

I could not move. Shame spread through my body with numbing force. I was not a criminal. I was a businesswoman. What was I doing here?

"Ms. Estrada, we don't have all day." The officer's glance was impatient.

Something inside me snapped. I put a hand to my face, tears squeezing out between clenched fingers. I stepped to one side, avoiding the officer's guiding hand and, still naked, stumbled into one of the shower stalls.

I washed in a daze, the strong jets of water beating down on my face, the water mingling with my tears.

"Get them up!"

I threw up an arm to block the thoughts, fresh waves of fear coursing through my body. I was shaking uncontrollably. In the shock and fear of the arrest, I had urinated on myself. The memory of that one uncontrollable moment washed over me—the wet clothes, the dried urine. Forced to appear in court with the stains and the smell of dried urine still on my pants had shamed me deeply, and I scrubbed furiously, trying to erase the memory.

"Okay, that's it. Get dressed."

Eyes downcast, I dried off quickly, dragging the faded blue nightgown over my head, the thin material sticking to my damp body.

"Put your dirty clothes in the paper bag," the officer said. "You'll wash them tomorrow." She pointed to the side of the room. "Wait over there with the others."

One by one, the other women were brought from the holding pen into the room for their search and trip to the shower. I kept my eyes trained on the floor as the last few women were searched in front of everyone.

Finally everyone was dressed in nightgowns and thin slippers. We were taken upstairs for physicals. For the next several hours we waited on benches in the corridor as a medical doctor examined us one by one.

The hours dragged by. Sunken eyes glared back at officers, the women cursing and complaining. The faces around me were taut with fatigue.

I had not slept since the arrest, and my eyes strained with the effort to stay awake. Night hours stretched into early morning...five o'clock...six o'clock...

Finally, my head dropped in exhaustion.

I was jerked out of my doze by shouted commands. "Everybody up! Time to see your new home."

I straightened my aching back. Seven o'clock...We had been in processing all night.

The officers ushered us into a large room with rows of beds. "This will be your home until medical results come back," an officer announced. "Once the results come back, you'll wait until we find you a vacancy in jail population."

Slowly I lay back on one of the beds, shock settling into my body. My mind drifted. Exhausted, I slid into unconsciousness. Time passed without sensation. I had knowledge of my surroundings, but no sensation of time. I knew where I was, but I did not know how long I had been there. In a coma-like state, I slept through the day and into the night.

Sometime the next morning I sat up in the middle of the bed. Women were moving around the room, getting dressed. I sat still, waiting for my heart to slow.

I heard the whispers around me: "She'll probably get fifteen to life...She's Colombian. They got her for drugs."

I heard the whispers but felt nothing. I lay back on my bed as the voices drifted around me. Late into the afternoon I lay on my bed, not moving.

I heard someone stop by my bed and opened my eyes—the girl from the holding pen. "Wendy," I said dully, "what day is today?"

"Sunday."

I sank back, shaking. I had been arrested on Thursday. Today was Sunday. I had lost two days of my life and could not remember them. The sensation of lost time was frightening. Confused thought melted into bitter realization. My plane was leaving in three days. I knew now I would not be on it.

For days I lay in bed, my mind trapped in confusion. Late into the night I lay motionless, staring at the ceiling. In fifteen years, Lina would be a grown woman. Roberto would be married. If I was sentenced to fifteen years, I would have to kill myself. I had tried once before; this time it would be easier.

I heard a noise in the bed next to me and froze. It was dark in the dorm and the lights were out for the night, but some of the women were still not asleep. I turned my head slowly. The girl in the bed across from me was awake, her eyes open, staring at me in the dark. She was lying on the bed naked, her legs spread wide apart.

I dragged the pillow over my head, my stomach cramping with fear. I knew what happened to new inmates. The younger ones were raped, sometimes in gangs, and threatened with beatings if they screamed for help.

I choked down the nausea rising in my throat. "God, help me," I moaned. "Please, help me. Get me out of here."

"Marta," Wendy was shaking me, "what's wrong with you?"

I pulled the pillow away from my face. "That girl," I said, pointing.

Wendy looked over at the girl. "What's wrong with her?"

"She keeps watching me."

"Watching you?" Wendy's face tightened. "Has she touched you?"

"No…"

Wendy looked at me for a minute. "You're afraid she'll rape you?"

I nodded.

"Stay here a minute," she said. "I'll be right back."

I heard her searching for something in the dark, then heard her coming back. She touched me lightly on the arm. "Here, take this."

I looked down at her hand. A large safety pin lay gleaming in her open palm. It was long and viciously pointed. "If she comes near you," Wendy paused, grinning maliciously, "stick her with it—hard!"

For the next several days I felt safer with my safety pin, but it was not until Wendy complained to an officer that the girl was finally removed from the dorm.

After this incident, Wendy watched me carefully, keeping an eye on the other inmates and stepping in whenever I needed help. She was concerned about me but seemed confused by my reluctance to talk about my family.

"Why don't you ever call them?" she asked. "Don't they want to help you?"

"No…yes…they don't know," I finished lamely.

Her eyebrows lifted momentarily. "They don't know?"

I shook my head.

"They don't know you've been arrested?"

"No."

"Oh." She shook her head, bewildered. "What about your daughter?"

"She knows."

"Do you talk to her?"

"Sometimes." Bianca had already told me about Lina. "She sits by the window at night and cries when she thinks everyone else is in bed."

I lay back on the bed, sudden tears squeezing out behind closed lids.

"Marta," Wendy's voice was harsh. "Stop it!"

"Stop what?" I sniffled.

"Going over your mistakes!"

I turned away, shielding my eyes. "Don't you ever think about the people you hurt because of your mistakes?"

Wendy did not answer.

I threw my arm over my face, blocking the tears. "My daughter is going to suffer so much because of me. And my mother—she'll be so hurt when she finds out."

Wendy was quiet. I lay still for a moment, then rolled over and looked at her. "Wendy, what's the matter?"

She sat looking at her hands, her eyes red. "Marta, can I tell you something?" Her voice sounded strained.

"What?"

"My father is a corrections officer here in Rikers."

I stared at her, the words frozen on my lips. "Wendy—I don't…"

She wiped her eyes angrily. "Forget it, Marta. I shouldn't have told you."

"Does anyone else know?"

She shrugged. "Probably. I just don't want the other officers to find out."

Wendy's pain only added to my own anxieties. The depression and fear over my arrest were being compounded by legal and financial problems. Shortly after the arrest, I had sent Bianca to the apartment to get the money I knew Víctor kept stashed in the air conditioner. Bianca had found $50,000, and I decided to keep half for my legal fees.

As my co-defendant, Víctor was brought to court every time our case was called. When he found out what I planned to do with the money, he was furious. "That is my money," he hissed at me in court. "You have no right to take it."

"No, Víctor," I corrected, "only half is yours. The rest is mine. I need that money for my lawyer. You put me in here—you're going to pay."

Víctor leaned over and grabbed my arm, his fingers bruising my skin. "Where is it, Marta?"

I brushed his hand off my arm. "Don't touch me! You'll get your half. Don't worry."

But Víctor did not want half. The following week I received a visit from his lawyer.

"Ms. Estrada, where is Víctor's money?" he asked sternly.

I stared at him. "Sir, I don't know what you're doing here, but that money belongs to me. Víctor put me in here, and he's going to pay for my lawyer." I narrowed my eyes threateningly. "You can just go back and tell Víctor to leave me alone—or I'm going to keep all the money."

The threat did not work, but once I paid my lawyer and repaid the mortgage I had lost during the deal with Sebastián, the money was gone, and Víctor seemed to give up.

In July, my case was moved from Queens to Manhattan and assigned to a judge named Smith.

Judge Smith was considered one of the best justices in the system, so I was confused when other inmates looked away in sympathy.

"Wendy," I asked one day, "why does everyone look at me funny when I tell them I was assigned to Judge Smith?"

Wendy shrugged her shoulders. "I don't know."

"Wendy!"

"I don't know," she insisted. "Maybe it's because he goes kind of crazy when he gets a drug case."

"Crazy? What does he do?"

"Gives the max."

"Every time?"

"I think so."

"Why?"

Wendy looked at me, then away. "His daughter died of a cocaine overdose."

"A cocaine overdose…" I repeated the words slowly, the

full impact of her words registering slowly. "A cocaine over-dose."

I knew my verdict even before I was sentenced. I sat down on my bed and cried.

Chapter 16

After six weeks I received medical clearance and was transferred to my own cell. Four walls surrounded a cell the size of a large closet. A small iron bed with a thin mattress and some linen stood against the right wall. To my left was an open toilet and a sink with a tiny mirror. Against the far end was a small desk and chair pushed against the wall.

"All yours, Marta," the officer said. "You'll soon learn the ropes around here."

I stood there looking at the small, efficient cell. "Do I ever get out?" I asked.

"Sure. You can go to the television room, and you go to the dining room for meals three times a day."

"Can we work?"

"If you want to. You'll have to apply for one of the jobs—there's dish detail, laundry, some secretarial and janitorial…maybe a few jobs in social services."

"How many hours a day?"

"It varies."

"Do we get paid?"

"Sure."

"How much?"

"Anywhere from five to seven dollars."

"An hour?"

She laughed. "No—a week."

I could not speak.

"It's enough to send you to commissary," she said kindly.

"Commissary?"

"Personal items, cigarettes, cakes, soap..."

"How do I get out in the morning?"

"Yell. They'll buzz you out from the booth."

Miserably I walked to the window. The waters of the East River stretched off in the distance, rays of sunlight reflecting off the surface.

A sudden, violent longing for freedom swept over me.

Memories flashed through my mind—early afternoon walks in the park, my daughter's small hand tucked in mine, her dark eyes sparkling up at me.

An unbearable longing strained at me, and I turned away from the window.

"Breakfast is at five o'clock," the officer said. "If you want to eat, you'll have to get up."

Five o'clock! Depression already made it difficult to drag myself out of bed, and I knew I would come to hate that early-morning call.

The daily schedule soon became routine, however. Every morning at five o'clock the steel doors clanged open, and officers on duty yelled, "Breakfast!"

It was still dark outside, and I dressed using the light shining from the corridor. The dining room was usually quiet in the mornings. The women ate silently, then returned to their cells for a few more hours of sleep.

At nine o'clock, the officers walked through the corridors, shouting, "Everybody out! Work or television room."

Those with jobs went to work. Everyone else went to the television room. I did not have a job, so I went to the television room. With nothing to do but watch television all morning, I spent hours staring at the wall, my mind a blank, waiting for lunch.

At eleven-thirty we were taken to the dining room, then we returned to our cells for an hour to shower and rest. Later in the afternoon we were allowed to go outside for recreation time, and then at three o'clock we returned once again to our cells. For one hour we were locked in our cells while every inmate in Rikers Island was counted. If the count was off by one, we waited until the missing inmate was found. Sometimes we were locked in our cells for hours while officers searched for the inmate.

Following dinner at five o'clock, all those under medical treatment were taken to the infirmary for medication.

My heart had been beating in quick, painful thuds since the arrest, and after eight weeks of constant turmoil and uncertainty, I had finally asked to see a doctor. The jail psychiatrist had diagnosed my heart condition as stress-induced anxiety.

"You must try to relax, Ms. Estrada," he warned me. "Your heart is not going to slow down until you start to take it easy." He wrote briefly on his pad. "How long has it been beating like this?"

"Since my arrest."

"When was that?"

"Eight weeks ago."

He put down his pen and stretched back in his chair. "You're going to have to try to relax. The medication we prescribe will help, but your heart rate won't slow down until your stress level is reduced."

"Thank you, doctor," I murmured. "I'll try."

It was empty advice. I could not relax. My body was reacting to the stress of a situation over which I had no control and could not change. The medication slowed my heart rate but could not control the anxiety or depression.

Back in the cell complex after medication, the entire population was hit by a burst of energy induced by the pills. In a rush of euphoria from the high, the women cleaned and mopped everywhere, and for one hour the entire population was happy.

At seven o'clock, each inmate was allowed to make one outside telephone call. Each call was clocked at three minutes. If your call went longer than three minutes the officer in the security bubble disconnected the line.

After our calls, we were taken to the gym where we were allowed to mingle with women from other cell areas. Timid, and afraid to get into fights, I usually kept to myself. The threat of an infraction and time tacked on to my sentence made me reluctant to draw any attention to myself.

By ten o'clock we were back in our cells, with lights out by eleven.

All night long the guards came by with flashlights, looking in each cell, taking the count.

"They look for hangings," one inmate told me. "They keep the really depressed ones on suicide watch."

"Have they ever caught anyone?" I asked.

"Sure, but sometimes they miss."

I did not want to sound too curious. "How do they do it?"

"They wrap the sheet around the leg of the bed and pull it until they strangle themselves to death."

I shuddered.

"Sometimes they get a safety pin in through security and scrape their wrists to cut the veins."

The topic seemed to hold a morbid fascination for the women. Several noted my interest. "If you want to do it without pain, put your medication pill under your tongue," they instructed me. "Don't swallow it. When the nurse looks in your mouth, she won't see it. Once you have twenty pills, you'll have enough."

Somehow, the thought of dying before Mama found out held some appeal. I was crying nightly now. My nerves were stretched to the straining point, thoughts of suicide alternating with thoughts of escape.

I thought again about the pills. They would be painless... But what if the nurse caught me? The thought drained the blood from my veins.

"I can't take this place," I sobbed. "I can't take it here. I have to get out. God, help me get out of here."

One evening, one of the officers on night duty came into my cell and sat down on the edge of my bed. "Marta," she said slowly, "can I talk to you for a minute?"

Her gaze was direct, and I felt a little uncomfortable; her eyes were so piercing.

"Yes," I said, "about what?"

She stopped as though searching for words. "Marta, I know that you don't understand what's happening to you right now..." She paused again, looking at me steadily, "...but I think God has a plan for you."

Something unusual in her eyes held my gaze. There was a quiet warmth about her that made me feel peaceful, a genuine concern that made my eyes moisten.

"God loves you," she said. "You can know Him personally." She saw my hesitation. "Would you like to know Him?" she asked softly.

"Yes," I nodded uncertainly. "I guess so."

"Then ask Him to make Himself real to you," she said. "He will." She laid her hand gently on my arm. "Let me pray for you."

I lay there on the bed after she was gone, an unusual feeling of peace stealing over me. What was it about her that made me feel so different? I thought about the words she had prayed. *"Father, give Marta Your peace. Touch her life and show her Your love."*

The prayer had sounded so simple—almost as though she were talking directly to God.

It was a startling thought.

I tried to remember her words. *"Ask Him to make Himself real to you. He will."*

What would happen if I prayed those words? Would He talk to me? I closed my eyes. There was only one way to find out. "If You're real," I prayed, "show me; I want to know You."

I waited.

Was it my imagination, or did I feel a faint stirring of peace? I lay back on the bed, trying to sort out the questions in my mind. What if He was real? Could we really know Him personally?

It was a haunting experience, but I soon pushed the incident to the side. God had not spoken to me, and I had too many other things to think about. I was still jumpy from the medication I was taking, and Wendy was beginning to worry me with her constant warnings.

"Don't trust anyone!" she warned me several times. "You think everyone is your friend, but they'll turn around and stab you in the back. Don't trust them."

"Yes, Wendy," I said, "I'll be careful. I promise." I shook my head at her concern.

One inmate I knew I could trust was my friend Yvette. She was outgoing and fun, and we had become friends from the moment we met.

One day, Yvette approached me. "Marta, would you deliver this note to a friend of mine in the gym?" she asked. "I'm not going, and I need to get this note to her."

I was glad to help out. "Sure," I said. "No problem."

I delivered the note and returned to my cell. I was lying on the bed, dozing lightly, when someone rapped sharply on the security gate down the hall.

"Marta, you fool!" Wendy yelled down the corridor. "Come here!"

Frightened, I swung my legs over the edge of the bed and walked to the gate.

Wendy's lips were tight with anger. "Don't ever," she punched the word for emphasis, "*ever* deliver a note like that again!"

"Like what?"

"Like the one you delivered for Yvette."

"Why not?" I asked, puzzled.

"Because you could have gotten time." Her eyes were angry.

"For what?"

"For drugs, that's what!" She slammed a hand against the bars. "I warned you, Marta."

"Wendy, what are you talking about?"

"That note had drugs in it. You could have gotten big time."

Drugs! "I didn't know," I whispered tearfully.

"You didn't know?" Wendy was almost yelling. "Do you think they care? Do you think they want to hear your excuses? You delivered—you do the time. Next time don't be so stupid." She turned away. "Don't ever speak to Yvette again."

I was shaking. "I won't."

"And don't hold a package for anyone in your cell; they'll just get you in the raids."

The drug raids were another part of jail life I found impossible to adjust to. Without warning, corrections officers would pound on the cell bars, yelling, "Okay, ladies. Out in the hall! Move it! Let's go!"

The raids were conducted thoroughly and systematically. Mattresses were turned over, walls pounded, picture frames moved, and pillows thumped. During the summer we stood half-naked, dressed in underwear and skimpy nightshirts, until the search was finished.

The fights and beatings, the cursing, the raids were only adding to the emotional strain I was under. Thoughts of Lina crowded my mind. How was I going to care for her? Who was going to raise her? And my parents...Back in Colombia, Mama and Papa still did not know I was in jail.

"You'll have to tell them sometime," Bianca insisted. "You can't keep it from them forever. Your mother is going to be hurt."

"Bianca, please," I pleaded. "Don't tell her."

"She's your mother, Marta! You can't do that to her."

"Bianca, please..."

"Oh, alright," she agreed reluctantly, "but it isn't right."

Bianca and my brothers were able to keep the news from my parents, but they could not stop the friends who called Colombia to talk to their families. "Did you hear? Marta has been arrested for drugs! She was caught with Víctor!"

Several months after my arrest, Papa heard the news at the corner bar. At home that night he wandered around the house, a sick look in his eyes. Mama's sharp eyes followed him, but he avoided her, close to tears. She watched him closely, questioning him occasionally. Finally, late that evening, Papa broke down and told her everything. They sat on the couch together and cried.

When Mama called my brothers in New York, she was furious.

"Did you know Marta was in jail?" she asked.

"Yes, Mama."

"You knew she was in jail? You knew she was in jail, and you didn't tell me?"

"We couldn't, Mama."

"Why?" she wept in anger. "Why couldn't you tell me?"

"Marta told us not to."

"Marta told you not to?" Her voice rose. "Marta is my daughter! She had no right to tell you that."

"Don't yell at us, Mama. Yell at Marta."

"Who has Lina?" she asked abruptly. "Bianca?"

"No, we have her now."

"I'm coming to New York," she said curtly and hung up.

Bianca did not tell me about the call, afraid I would be upset. She was nervous and worried whenever we spoke by phone, but I did not notice. I had too many other things on my mind. Somewhere inside me a piece was missing. I felt a sensation almost like that of hunger but could find nothing to satisfy the feeling. I was strangely restless, an unusual feeling of desperation gnawing at my stomach.

"God, help me!" I cried. "Please help me. Save me."

If someone did not answer soon, I was going to kill myself.

Chapter 17

The morning of September 15, 1983, I woke up and looked in the tiny mirror over the sink. Dark eyes stared back. My cheeks were sunken, circles of depression darkening the skin around my eyes.

I had been in jail for nine weeks now. Nights were spent sobbing facedown in my bed, tears soaking the pillow. In the morning, my eyes were hot and swollen from crying.

I dressed slowly, then picked up a brush and ran it through my hair.

"Let's go, ladies!" The officer on duty called. "Everybody out—television room or work."

I had been given a job working in the laundry room but was finding it more and more difficult to go to work in the mornings. I washed and folded piles of sheets and towels for hours, the hot steam burning my face, the hiss of the steam irons hiding my sobs. I wept for Lina, for my parents, for Roberto. Bitterness against Víctor swelled in my stomach. "I hate him," I sobbed helplessly, "I hate him."

I thought again about suicide—the feeling of well-being, the curious sensation of relief. I wondered again how long it would take to get enough pills to kill myself.

Late that afternoon I returned to my cell and sat on the

bed, the sickened feeling of depression clutching at my insides. I stared at the floor, tracing patterns with my toe, listening to the announcement drifting from the loudspeaker.

"Ladies, there's an evangelical meeting tonight in the chapel. See your correction officer for a pass."

An evangelical meeting? It was not a Catholic service, and I did not know the group giving the meeting, but I needed to get out.

"I'll go and say a prayer," I mumbled. "Maybe God will hear me this time."

I applied for a pass, then waited for the call.

"Let's go," the officer called. "Everyone going to the service, line up."

I slipped on my shoes and ran my hands down my pants, smoothing out the wrinkles. The hall gate opened slowly, and the line of women shuffled through, then started down the corridor. I could hear the service already in progress and walked a little faster.

The chapel was well-lit and inviting. The woman at the piano smiled warmly at us as we filed into the aisles. She was an older woman, her eyes warm, her voice strong and sure. I could not understand her words, but there was a brightness, an indefinable quality in her smile that caught my attention. I watched her closely as I walked to my seat. She reminded me of someone, but who?

I sat down, crossing myself dutifully, my mind wandering. This was not a Catholic mass. Would God mind? I shifted nervously. Where were the candles? How could they pray to God without candles? I missed the familiar burning scent.

"To love only You, my Lord, and never look back. To follow in Your ways, my Lord..."

I looked back at the lady. I could hear her words clearly now. I sat back, analyzing her thoughtfully. There was something unusual about her. She looked full of life. Her eyes were luminous, her smile brightening her face.

"To walk and never fall, my Lord; to kneel before Your throne, my Lord..."

Someone else had looked like that. Suddenly I remembered—the officer who had prayed for me! I had seen that same look of joy on her face. And the peace when she had prayed for me—I was feeling it again.

"... *And never look back.*"

Never look back...Suddenly, inexplicably, I felt like crying. I looked around, bewildered. No one was looking at me. Everyone was watching the woman, absorbed, their eyes fixed on her face. I turned back toward the stage and swallowed hard. A sudden warmth poured over my head, and I felt my chest heave. Tears welled up in my eyes, and I blinked hard. The tears started trickling down my cheeks. I lowered my head, fighting back the tears.

"*To kneel before Your throne, my Lord, and never look back.*"

Now the strange warmth was enveloping me. My head was down. I breathed slowly, fighting for control. If she did not stop singing soon, I was going to burst out in sobs.

Mercifully, the singing stopped. I lifted my head and looked around cautiously. Surreptitiously, I lifted a hand, wiping the tears from my eyes.

The lady stood up and walked to the podium. She stood there for a moment, flipping through a large Bible propped on the podium, then looked up.

"How many of you have been here longer than a week?" she asked.

I concentrated on her words as she asked for a show of hands. Every hand was up.

"How many of you have had more than ten visitors this week?"

The hands went down slowly.

"How many of you have had more than five visitors this week?"

No one moved.

"Three?"

Still no one moved.

"How about one?"

A few hands went up.

Her eyes looked sad. "Ladies, where are your friends? Where are your families? Your boyfriends are out getting high, and your friends don't even remember who you are. No one cares enough to visit."

It was quiet in the auditorium.

"You think no one loves you. You think no one cares. No one takes the time." She paused, her dark eyes full of a wonderful light. "Today I want to tell you about Someone who does have time; Someone who loves you and cares about you; Someone who will never leave you."

I could feel the sobs starting inside again.

"He will stay with you when things are good and when things are bad. He will stay with you when you're hurt and when you're alone."

I blinked rapidly, tears falling in my lap, soaking my pants. My head was down again, hands clenched, nails biting into my palms.

"He loved you so much that He died for you."

Breathing hard, I strained to catch her words. Who was she talking about? Who loved me enough to die for me? Esteban loved me, but he left me. Víctor loved me, but he hit me.

"He will pick up the pieces of your life and make you a new person. He paid the price for your sins. Because of what He did, you can receive forgiveness and become a child of God." She walked to the edge of the platform, the worn Bible held between her hands. "Do you want Jesus to forgive you and make you a new person? Are you tired of living your own life?"

Trembling, I raised my eyes. How did she know?

She was still watching us with that peculiar glow on her face. "He's heard your prayers. You can know Him. All you have to do is ask."

Suddenly, I was out of my seat, stumbling to the front, blinded by tears I could not stop. Sobs were shaking my body, an incredible warmth spreading through me, a deep feeling of longing crashing over me in wave after wave.

"Do you want Jesus in your life?"

I looked up. It was the lady with the shining face.

"Yes," I nodded, an unspeakable yearning inside of me. "Yes, please."

"Then ask Him to make you a new person. Say 'Jesus, come into my life. Forgive me for my sins. Wash me and make me clean. Make me a new person.' "

I did not know what I was praying. I did not understand half of what I was saying, but the words that came from my mouth were a cry from the heart, a desperate, pleading cry for help. I needed Jesus more than I had ever needed anything else in my life.

"I'm sorry," I wept. "I'm so sorry. Please forgive me. Make me a new person. Make me clean."

Sudden warmth poured over my head and a feeling of joy swept through me. Now I was laughing and crying at the same time. Years of depression, loneliness, and emptiness slipped from my shoulders, and I laughed out loud. Tears washed down my face, dropping on my hands. I was drowning, floating in an indescribable pool of peace. I could not stop crying, but the longer I cried, the cleaner I felt.

I heard the lady saying something about being born again and looked up. Born again! That was it! I felt just like a newborn baby.

I felt a hand on my head. "Jesus, show her Your plan for her life."

There it was again! *The Lord has a plan for your life, Marta,* the officer had said in my cell. Now here it was again.

What did they mean? What plan could God have for me?

I returned to my cell in a daze after the service, clutching the Bible they had given me. I sat down on the side of the bed, a feeling of completeness wrapping around me.

I opened the Bible. "But as many as received him, to them gave he power to become the sons of God" (John 1:12).

As many as received Him—*I had received Him!* I had become part of God's family. The realization that I was His child burrowed deeply into my spirit, and I laughed for joy. I read the Bible until late that night, verses leaping out at me, the words burning in my spirit.

Lights were turned out at eleven o'clock, but I could not sleep. I sat by the window, looking toward the Whitestone Bridge, praying.

A flashlight shone through the bars.

"Marta, are you okay?" It was an officer making her rounds.

"Yes," I said, "I'm praying; don't worry."

She shook her head, chuckling. "And another one gets jailhouse religion."

Late into the night I sat by my window, praying, resting my hand on my new Bible, leaning my head against the window.

The next day I awoke, refreshed and eager. I looked in the mirror over the sink and took a deep breath. My face was different! My eyes were alive and vibrant. A curious glow shone on my face. *Just like the lady in the service*, I thought excitedly.

The following weeks passed in a blur of happiness. The Bible had always been difficult for me to read, but now I found myself reading entire chapters at a time.

Sometimes at night I felt something moving gently on my head like a feather; but when I reached up to touch it, nothing was there. *Maybe I'm going crazy*, I thought worriedly. *Maybe I've flipped out.*

I checked with one of the other inmates. "Nancy, do I look crazy?"

"Crazy?"

"Yes...*loca*—you know, crazy."

"No," she said doubtfully. "I don't think so." She looked me over from head to toe. "You look happier than before, but you don't look crazy."

Still the feeling persisted. One evening I read about Jesus' baptism where the Spirit of God came down on Him like a dove. I held my place thoughtfully. *A dove*. Was it possible? *A dove—feathers*. The thought sent shivers through me.

I bubbled with excitement and enthusiasm in those first few weeks. Everything fascinated me. The lady with the shining face invited me to come to her Bible study classes, and every Thursday I went to study the Word of God with her. Her name was Nilsa, and she prayed with me and encouraged me.

"You feel great right now, Marta," she said kindly, "but don't expect that feeling to be there all the time. Make sure that your relationship with Jesus is secure, because when the storms come, your love for Him will have to be based on faith—not feelings."

I took her advice and studied feverishly, reading the Bible, praying, and memorizing scriptures. I was not sure what the "storms" were, but I wanted to be ready when they came.

One day I noticed something different about my heart. I grabbed one of the inmates and pulled her aside. "Sonia," I said excitedly. "I think I've been healed."

"Healed? What do you mean, healed?"

"My heart; it used to beat so fast I thought I was having a heart attack."

"Weren't you taking medication?"

"Yes, but every time the medication wore off, my heart would start beating fast again."

"And now?"

"Now it stays the same, even after the medication wears off."

She was looking at me curiously. "When did this happen?"

I thought back. "I'm not sure. I think it happened when I met Jesus Christ."

I checked with the doctor, and he confirmed my diagnosis. "You won't be needing your medication anymore, Ms. Estrada. Everything seems to be fine. You've finally learned how to relax—that's good."

Learned to relax? I was sure it was something more. I stopped taking the medication and nearly burst with joy when I went through an entire day without one palpitation.

The joy radiating from my face was beginning to attract the attention of other inmates. "What happened to you, Marta?" they asked. "You look different."

"I *am* different," I said happily. "Jesus came into my life. He made me a new person."

Some inmates laughed at me. "You're crazy, Marta."

I did not mind their comments. If going crazy meant that

the awful depression would leave; if going crazy meant that my heart would finally start beating at a normal pace; if going crazy meant that I would have this absurd joy in my heart, then I wanted to be crazy for the rest of my life.

Chapter 18

Excited about my new relationship with Jesus, I studied the Bible, prayed for the other inmates, and readily answered questions about the changes in my life.

It did not take long for me to realize that not everyone was interested.

One day, an inmate sat down next to me in the television room. "Marta," she said, "I'm in love."

"Really?" I asked, looking up from my Bible. "Who's the lucky guy?"

She smiled widely. "That officer." She pointed toward the security bubble.

"Officer Brown? You're in love with Officer Brown? But she's a woman!"

"I know," she blushed happily. "A very cute one."

I looked at her in dismay. "Melinda, are you a lesbian?"

She shrugged, unconcerned. "I wasn't when I came here."

"So? What happened?"

"I don't know." She looked through the door toward the security booth. I turned, following her gaze. The officer was looking at Melinda. "You see?" Melinda smiled and wiggled her fingers at the officer. "She likes me." She leaned toward me confidentially. "She told me to meet her in the interview room."

"Did you go?"

"Yes."

"What happened?"

"She kissed me."

"Melinda!"

"Don't look so shocked, Marta," she said. "That happens here."

"But, Melinda, you're not a lesbian. Why would you do that?"

"Because I like her."

I choked back the revulsion. "Melinda…"

"She loves me, Marta," she insisted defensively.

"Melinda, Jesus Christ is the only one who will ever love you unconditionally."

For a brief moment Melinda looked at me, her eyes wistful, then she turned and looked back at the officer. "No," she said slowly, "Officer Brown loves me."

Several times after that I saw Melinda in the private room kissing the officer and turned away.

Several weeks later a beaming Melinda came into my cell. "Marta, look." She pulled up her skirt. "What do you think?" On her thigh was a heart-shaped tattoo with Officer Brown's initials stamped in the middle. "Do you like it?"

"Melinda, please," I pleaded. "Don't get involved with her. She's just going to hurt you."

"Hurt me?" she scoffed. "Officer Brown loves me. She won't hurt me."

Several weeks later, a beautiful new inmate came to our floor, and Officer Brown started taking her to the private room.

The look in Melinda's eyes brought back memories of my own mistakes. Like Melinda, I had wanted love. Like Melinda, I had looked in all the wrong places. Like Melinda, I had been too blind to see my own mistakes. It had taken the shock of my arrest to pull me up short and make me realize how much I needed Jesus Christ.

Melinda went to chapel with me several times after that,

but it was clear she was not ready to change. I could only pray for her, believing that one day she would choose to serve the Lord completely.

As the Lord continued to move in my life, I began reaching out to other inmates around me. One inmate had been crying in her cell for days. The constant wailing was beginning to irritate the other inmates. "She killed her baby," one inmate told me angrily. "She says it was an accident." Her eyes were cold. "Baby killer!"

"Maybe it was an accident," I suggested.

"Accident?" she sneered. "It wasn't an accident. That's what they all say. They just don't want to serve their time."

I walked to the cell door. "I'm going to talk to her. She needs help."

The inmate shrugged. "Yeah, whatever."

The woman in the cell was hunched over by the window, hands restlessly clutching her nightgown, hair limp around a haunted face. I tapped on the door tentatively. "Excuse me."

She looked up and I stepped back, stunned by the look in her eyes. "I'm sorry," I said, "but is there some way I can help you?"

"No." She turned her head away. "Nobody can help me."

"Jesus can."

She did not answer, but her body grew still.

"He helped me," I continued. "When I didn't want to live, He gave me peace."

She lifted her head. "You're the lady who prays."

I nodded.

"Would you pray for me?"

"Yes, of course," I said. "Jesus can forgive you."

She buried her head in her hands. "It was an accident," she moaned. "It was an accident. I didn't mean to hurt him. I would never do anything to hurt my baby." Her hands were restless, agitated. "I loved my baby. I was giving him a bath. My sister came in. I knew she had been sleeping with my husband. She said, 'Yeah, I've been sleeping with your husband, so what?' I lost control and started hitting her—I forgot all about my baby." Her face twisted. "When I came back to the bathtub...he was dead..."

The horror of finding that little body!

My heart ached for her. How many times had I come close to killing Víctor? How many times had I forgotten Lina in the other room while we fought? I shuddered. I loved her, but my fights with Víctor were so furious I might have forgotten Lina for a brief moment. I could so easily have been in this woman's place.

I said the only words I could think of: "Jesus, give her peace."

Many times after that I prayed with her. I remembered the officer who had prayed for me. "Rebecca, you need His peace," I said. "Ask Him to make Himself real to you."

Rebecca's story brought back unpleasant memories. Would I ever be a mother to my own daughter? She had suffered so much because of me. Would I ever be able to make it up to her?

In late October, three months after my arrest, an officer banged on the cell door. "You have visitors, Marta. Get ready."

Visitors? Bianca had visited me once in the first week after my arrest, and Víctor's lawyer had come to see me once, but since then I had not received any visits. Lina could not come by herself; Víctor was in jail; my brothers were here illegally; and my parents did not even know I was in jail.

"Let's go, Marta. Stop dreaming," the officer called.

I walked eagerly to the visitor's room, through the gates and through security. I felt a tremor of excitement. Who could it be?

I stood in the doorway, looking through the crowds of visitors gathered at the entrance. The cigarette smoke hanging in the sunlight made it difficult to see. I looked again, then stopped. A familiar form was flying toward me, her little face lit up. Lina!

Trembling, I scooped her up, burying my face in her hair. "Lina! What are you doing here?"

"Mama," she protested, wriggling to loosen my hold, "you're choking me."

"I'm sorry," I laughed. I stretched back to look at her

face. "*Mi hija!* It's so good to see you. Who brought you? Bianca?...Or did you come by yourself?" I chuckled, hugging her tightly.

"No, Bianca didn't bring me." She twisted her head, looking over her shoulder. "Gramma did."

My arms tightened convulsively. "Your grandmother..." I turned and looked where she was pointing. Mama was standing quietly, her face wet. She put her hands out, palms up. She was trembling.

I went to her, tears coming as her arms wrapped protectively around me. "Mama, I'm sorry..."

"Why, Marta?" she whispered. "Why didn't you tell me?"

I shook my head wordlessly.

"How could you keep it from me?" Her eyes were swimming. "Your father had to find out at the corner bar."

"Oh, God—I'm sorry, Mama."

She pulled away from me. "Three months, Marta! Three months!"

I led her to a table and sat down, holding Lina's hand in mine. "Mama..."

"Your brothers didn't tell me," she scolded, wiping her eyes. "Bianca didn't tell me. Your own father didn't want to tell me." She broke off, looking around. "Marta, this is a horrible place."

I had to smile. "Yes, Mama, I know," I said, "but I'm happy here."

Her lips quivered, and she burst into tears. "Why do you keep lying to me, Marta? I'm your mother. You can tell me the truth."

I took her hands in mine and said quietly, firmly. "Mama, look at me."

She looked up quickly, blinking back tears.

I held her eyes with mine. "I'm not lying, Mama. I *am* happy here."

She pulled away, wringing her hands anxiously. "They've made you crazy, Marta. You've been here too long. You've lost your mind."

"No, Mama, listen to me. I want to tell you something."

"Yes?" She searched my face intently as though looking for something. "What is it?"

Aside from Lina, Mama was the most important person in my life. I formed my next words carefully, wanting to get them just right. She had to understand. I said the words slowly, distinctly. "I'm happy here because this is where I found Jesus."

Her eyes were startled. "Jesus?" The name came out awkwardly.

"Yes," I said, "Jesus Christ."

"Marta, we'd better go." She stood up. "You need your rest. Come, Lina." She looked defeated.

I walked around the table and hugged her fiercely. "Don't worry about me, Mama. Everything is going to be fine."

She smiled, brushing my hair back with her fingers. Her eyes were tired. "We'll come again next week. Good-bye, Marta."

I kissed them both, then knelt to hug Lina. "Don't let your Gramma worry too much, *mi hija*." I cupped her face between my hands and planted a kiss on the top of her head. "I love you, Lina. Be good, and listen to Gramma."

They left, Lina smiling back at me over her shoulder. I remembered the last time I had seen her and felt a rush of happiness. This time I knew the Lord would take care of her.

Every Saturday after that, Mama brought Lina to see me. The first several weeks, Mama watched me warily, weighing my actions and words carefully. But as the visits continued, she started to listen, an arrested look in her eyes, a softening around her mouth.

"What happened when you met Jesus?" she asked me several times.

"He came into my heart and gave me peace."

"You do seem to be more peaceful," she admitted grudgingly.

I nodded happily. "It's because of Jesus."

I enjoyed Mama's visits and looked forward to seeing her seated with Lina in the visiting room; but when Mama suggested that she come to my next court hearing, I hesitated.

Mama had never seen me in court before, and I was not sure how she would react.

"I don't know, Mama," I said hesitantly. "I don't know if it's a good idea. It might be too hard for you."

"I'm your mother, Marta," she said insistently. "I should be there."

"But..." I saw her eyes and caved in. "Okay, Mama, I'll talk to Reverend Green. I'll ask her to bring you."

Reverend Green was the founder of an organization called Women's Advocate Ministry and had already helped me with several case-related problems. She agreed to bring Mama to my next court appearance.

The following week I sat in the holding pen, tense and anxious, waiting to be called down. Mama had never seen me in handcuffs. If she got too emotional, Judge Smith would make me leave the courtroom until she calmed down.

Late that morning I was called down to the courtroom. Careful to avoid eye contact with the audience, I sat down next to my lawyer, keeping my head down.

My lawyer leaned over. "Marta, you have visitors." He nodded toward the audience.

I turned and looked. Mama and Reverend Green were sitting in the third row. Mama's eyes were red.

I turned back, staring woodenly at my hands. "She's going to cry, Mr. Sullivan...She's going to cry. Judge Smith isn't going to like it."

Sullivan looked sympathetic. "Don't worry about him. He'll be alright." He glanced at my mother, then looked back at me inquiringly. "Do you want me to set up a visit?"

If I did not request the visit, Mama would be hurt. I nodded wordlessly.

Sullivan spoke with Judge Smith, and a quick court visit was approved. Sullivan leaned over my chair. "Five minutes, Marta. Remember, if you touch each other, the visit's over."

A court officer brought a chair over to the partition, and I took a seat in front of Mama. She was staring at my wrists.

"Mama..."

She looked up slowly. Her eyes were full of tears.

"I'm sorry," I whispered.

She raised her hands brokenly. "Why, *mi hija*?" she wept. "Why?"

The courtroom grew quiet. The judge looked down at his papers.

"Mama, please—I'm sorry."

She was weeping openly. I looked helplessly at Reverend Green, and she came forward. There were tears in her eyes. "Come, Ms. Estrada," she said gently. "Let's go." She put an arm around my mother and helped her out of the courtroom.

I sat down by my lawyer and waited stiffly for the proceedings to end. Mama's reaction had hurt more than I anticipated; I could not allow her to come again.

Back at Rikers I made my decision. "Reverend Green, please don't bring Mama to court anymore. It's too painful. It would be better for her if she didn't come."

Reverend Green nodded, understanding. "We must pray for her."

And I did pray for her. Every night I petitioned the Lord for my mother's salvation. "She needs to know You," I pleaded. "She needs Your peace. Most of all she needs You as her Savior. Help her."

Despite the emotional pain of this time, I felt excitement stirring in my heart. I felt an unusual and distinct impression to pray for my release.

Was I going to be released soon? Impossible! My bail had been set at $250,000, and I was facing felony charges on ten counts of criminal sale, possession, and conspiracy. Six of the counts were Class A felonies with *each one* of those counts carrying a minimum sentence of fifteen years to life! There was no way the courts would release me; the charges were too serious.

Still the feeling persisted.

I thought for a minute. If my case stayed with Judge Smith, I would be sent to prison for a long time. If my case stayed in his court, the odds were high that I would receive the maximum sentence. But what if my case was transferred to another judge?

With a different judge, there was the possibility that the courts would consider my case with more leniency. With a different judge, there was always the possibility that I might receive a lighter sentence. But was it possible? No, how could it be? Cases were rarely transferred from one judge to another.

Unless there was a good reason, Judge Smith would not give up my case. My case would remain in his court.

Finally one night, I knelt by my bed. "Lord, if this is Your will—if You want me out of here—give the courts a reason to transfer my case. If this is Your plan, give the courts a reason to give my case to a more lenient judge."

It would take a miracle.

Chapter 19

November 1983

My lawyer was looking concerned. I had been waiting in the Manhattan courthouse all afternoon, and still my case had not been called.

"Your Honor," my lawyer stood up. "My client is on the calendar today, but her name still has not been called."

Judge Smith looked up over his glasses. "You're sure she's on the calendar?"

"Yes, your Honor."

Judge Smith glanced down at his desk, checking the court listing. "If she's on the calendar, where is her file? Why isn't it here?"

"I don't know, your Honor. It was sent up." Sullivan peered at his notes.

Judge Smith shuffled the papers on his desk, irritated. "Well, it isn't here." He looked over at the court officers. "Is that file over there?"

The officers sorted busily through stacks of files piled on their desks. "No, your Honor; we don't have it."

"Well, where is it?" he snapped. "If it was sent up, where is it?" No one volunteered an answer.

He looked at my lawyer. "Find it, Sullivan."

"Yes, your Honor."

Sullivan left the courtroom, and Judge Smith continued looking through the folders on his desk. He was frowning. I sat patiently, waiting. Cases were postponed for any number of reasons, but rarely because a file was lost. Judge Smith seemed upset about the missing file. Would he penalize my lawyer for the oversight?

"Your Honor?" Sullivan was back.

Judge Smith looked up. "Yes?"

"I found it."

"Where?"

"In Judge Phillips's court."

"Judge Phillips's court!" Judge Smith stood up. He was furious. "What's it doing over there? Her case has not been transferred. Mr. Sullivan, come with me."

They left the courtroom together. Court officers huddled in the corner, waiting. All cases were put on hold. Fifteen minutes later Judge Smith and Sullivan were back.

"Ms. Estrada, come to the front." Judge Smith's words were clipped.

I walked to the front, my heart pounding.

"Ms. Estrada..." Judge Smith looked angry. "I don't know what happened here. There's been a mix-up with your file." He glanced at Sullivan, his eyes like chips of ice. "Your case is being transferred to a different courtroom. Your new judge is Judge Phillips." He banged the gavel and motioned for the next case.

I stood there stunned. *Transferred!* My case had been transferred! I had a new judge!

"Oh, thank you, your Honor." I smiled brilliantly at Judge Smith. "Thank you."

Judge Smith glanced at me, puzzled. "You're welcome."

I turned away, holding back tears of joy. No one could explain the error—not even Judge Smith. It had to be a miracle.

"Congratulations, Marta." The court officers were smiling warmly at me.

"For what?"

"Your new judge—he's nice."

The tears spilled over. "It was Jesus," I smiled mistily. "He made them lose my file."

It was an exciting answer to prayer, but still I knew the battle was not over. As naive as I was about the criminal legal system, I realized that my lawyer was not doing all he could to prepare a strong defense. Many times he showed up late for the hearings. Other times he did not show up at all. He told me it was useless to fight.

"You'd better take fifteen to life," he advised me one day. "It's really the best we can do."

"Fifteen to life?" I was horrified. "But that's the maximum! I could have done that without you."

He tapped his pencil on the bench, irritated. "Fifteen to life is good for what you did, Marta. You were guilty."

"But, Mr. Sullivan, this is my first offense!" I protested.

"Marta, you don't understand our legal system," he said firmly. "Why don't you just leave the legal thinking to me?"

I shook my head stubbornly. "Mr. Sullivan, Víctor admits I wasn't involved with his business. How could I possibly get fifteen to life for something I didn't do?"

"Because you were his accomplice!" Sullivan snapped. "You were there. You were holding the drugs. Look, Marta, just take the time and forget it."

But I could not forget it. By this time I knew the Lord was working for my release. He would get me the deal He wanted. I dug in my heels. "I'm sorry, Mr. Sullivan. I can't accept the deal. Fifteen to life just isn't good enough. You're going to have to do better."

Sullivan was furious, but I knew I had made the right decision.

"Jesus is my lawyer," I told Mama on the phone. "If He wants me out of here, He'll take care of my case. He'll get me the deal He wants. I'll just have to be patient."

During this time of waiting, there were many wonderful Christian people who encouraged me and prayed with me. Sister Hershey was one person the Lord sent my way. Her face shone just like Nilsa's, and she always seemed to be laughing. She brought me teaching books and talked and joked with me.

People thought she was a nun because of the little white Mennonite covering she wore on her head. When inmates asked if she was a nun, Sister Hershey would grin and say, "I'd better not be—I have five kids."

Sister Hershey was over fifty years old, but she had a fearless disregard for her own safety that made me laugh. She and her husband, the pastor of an inner-city church, lived with their five children in the Bronx. They all shared the same lack of fear.

We laughed for hours about her experiences in the Bronx. One night a young man broke into their home while Pastor Hershey was away. Sister Hershey tackled him, jumped on his back, and tried to throw him to the ground. By the time the police arrived, Sister Hershey and her youngest son had tied up the young man with a towel and a jump rope and were sitting on his back. The four police officers stood around them, trying not to laugh.

"Anytime we catch someone in the house," Sister Hershey explained kindly, "we send them to jail. If they want to go to a Christian program, we ask the judge to release them. If they don't want to go..." she shrugged and smiled sympathetically, "you know what they say: If you can't do the time, don't do the crime."

Her friendship meant a lot to me. She was fun and could not stay serious too long, but she was serious about the Lord. Her encouragement and smile buoyed me through many low times.

Sister Hershey prayed for my family many times, and with her and Nilsa and Reverend Green all praying for Mama, I knew it would not be long before my mother found Jesus.

One night, several weeks later, Nilsa came up to me. Her eyes were sparkling. "Marta," she said, "I have some good news for you."

"Yes? What is it?"

"Your mother went to church last Sunday—Genesis Church."

I held my breath. "And?" I could not read Nilsa's expression. "Did she..."

"Yes," Nilsa laughed. "She did; she accepted Jesus."

I could hardly wait to see Mama. Would I see a change in her? Would she be different? That Saturday I walked into the visitor's room and felt my heart burst. Mama's eyes were sparkling, and she had a mischievous smile on her face.

"Marta, guess what?"

"What?" I asked, feigning innocence.

"I went to church last Sunday."

"Really?" I saw her eyes and started laughing. "I already know, Mama. Nilsa told me."

She hugged me. "I feel such peace, Marta."

"I know, Mama," I smiled.

She folded her hands and pressed her lips together firmly. "Marta, we have to pray for the rest of the family. They're calling me *loca*. They're laughing at me because I'm just like you."

"Let them laugh," I chuckled. "Soon they'll be *locos* just like us."

The change in Mama was apparent, and it was exciting to see still another answer to prayer. Several days later, I received more good news. Sullivan told me the prosecution was willing to offer me three years to life.

Once again, I refused the deal.

This time Sullivan was incredulous. "Marta, this is ridiculous! Three years is great for what you did! You can't turn it down. It's the best you'll ever get!"

"It may be good for you, Mr. Sullivan," I said calmly, "because you are not the one doing the time. But it's too much for me. I cannot accept the deal."

It was clear to me now that Sullivan was not going to do any more than he had to on my case. I wanted to fire him but lacked the courage; he was too powerful and knew too much. Still, I felt the Lord's leading. If Sullivan missed three more court appearances, I would fire him.

One month later I called him at his office. "Mr. Sullivan, you're fired."

"Fired? What do you mean, fired?" he spluttered.

"I don't want you for my lawyer anymore. You're fired."

"You can't fire me," he said indignantly.

"Oh, yes, I can. You aren't fighting for me. You're only taking my money. I don't want that kind of lawyer. You're fired."

I knew I had made the right decision, but now I had a problem—I did not have a lawyer.

"Marta," the Lord told me, "I will take care of you, but first you must clean your house."

Clean my house? What could He mean? Confused, I searched the Scriptures for understanding. Finally, late one night I came across a passage in my Bible:

"Let no one be found among you who... practices divination or sorcery, interprets omens, engages in witchcraft, or casts spells, or who is a medium or spiritist or who consults the dead. Anyone who does these things is detestable to the Lord" (Deut. 18:10 –12 NIV).

I stopped reading, horrified. Divination... sorcery... omens. Was it wrong? What about *santería*? Johanna had practiced *santería* for me many times.

I went back and read again, ticking the items off the list one by one. Witchcraft...spells...consulting the dead. How many times had I used the Ouija board to talk to the dead? And spells—how many times had I asked Johanna to give me special potions to ward off evil spirits, or to say special chants to break the spells placed on me by others? I was guilty of almost every one of the practices listed in the verse.

I mulled over that scripture for hours. Divination and witchcraft were both such accepted parts of Colombian life. Was this verse saying they were wrong? My mind fought to reject the thought. The good-luck charms, the candles, potions, and chants—all displeasing to God?

I remembered suddenly that Johanna had given me a painted Indian statue and some little amulets to rub for good luck. I remembered with horror that the amulets were still in my pocketbook at the apartment. My heart started beating faster. I had to get rid of them!

The next day I called my mother. "Mama, you have to clean the house today!"

"Clean the house?" She sounded offended. "It's already clean."

"No, Mama," I said. "Listen to this." I read the verse to her.

"So?" She sounded confused. "What about it?"

"*Santería*, Mama. Divination, witchcraft—it's all wrong! The Lord doesn't like it."

"Marta, what are you saying?" Mama's voice grew hushed, frightened.

"It's a verse from the Bible, Mama. I'm not making this up."

Mama's voice went stiff, years of tradition warring with her new belief in Jesus. "You're overreacting, Marta. There's nothing wrong with a little good luck. Not all spells are bad."

"That's not the point, Mama. God is jealous! He wants to take care of us. He wants to be the one who protects us. Those spells and chants are said to other spirits, and the Lord doesn't like that! He wants us to trust in Him, not in some other spirits."

She gave in, and that night, Mama went through the apartment, looking for anything that matched the Bible description. She did a thorough job, and between the two of us, I knew we had gotten rid of everything.

Satisfied now that the house was clean, I relaxed.

Several days later, an inmate from Colombia pulled me to the side. "Marta, I know you're looking for a lawyer," she said. "There is a lawyer you should talk to. He's good. I was up for kidnapping, but he got me good time."

"How much?"

"One year."

"One year—for kidnapping?" I could hardly control my excitement. "What's his name?"

"Charles Maxwell."

"Is he Jewish?" I asked.

"Yes."

Warm memories of the Jewish family I had worked for in New Jersey came to mind. "He's the one," I said excitedly. "I know he is. I'll call him tomorrow."

As soon as I saw Maxwell, I liked him. Competent and honest, he cut straight to the facts, promising nothing but delivering a great deal.

"Ms. Estrada," he said, "if I can get you less time than Sullivan, I'll take the case. If I can't, I won't. Call me Wednesday. We'll talk."

For three days I paced back and forth in my cell, praying. If the Lord wanted me out, He would take care of my case and my lawyer.

Wednesday afternoon I dialed Maxwell's number.

"Marta, I've reviewed your case." Maxwell's voice was warm.

My heart turned over. "And?"

"And I've decided to take it."

"Does that mean you can get me less than three years?"

"Yes, I can get you less than three years."

"Thank you, Mr. Maxwell," I said politely.

I placed the receiver back in the cradle and turned around.

"What happened?" an inmate asked.

"He took it!" I shouted. "He took my case!" I jumped around the room, laughing and crying.

Eight days later, my bail was reduced to $50,000.

Things were moving so quickly now that I knew something was about to happen. The Lord wanted me released for a reason. I was being prepared for something in the future—but what?

I would soon find out.

Chapter 20

December 31, 1983—New Year's Eve

Inmates stood at the cell doors, tense and excited, yelling as the countdown began.

"Ten, nine, eight, seven..." How many things had happened to me in the last twelve months? My return to Víctor, my arrest, my incredible experience with Jesus Christ.

"Six, five, four, three..." Sad moments, happy memories, exciting growth in my walk with the Lord.

"Two, one! Happy New Year!"

"Happy New Year!" The cries bounced off concrete and steel, echoing through the corridor. A new year...a new life.

Suddenly, the mood changed. Down the corridor an inmate cried out, "My children!" Another inmate burst out, "My mother!" All around me sobbing broke out.

I knelt down in the middle of my cell. "Thank You, Jesus, that I know You. This is the happiest time of my life." Tears rolled down my cheeks. "Keep my family safe," I prayed. "Protect Lina, and be with my mother."

I thought about Víctor. What was he doing tonight? The Lord had taken my bitterness toward Víctor away. Víctor had put me in jail, but the Lord had healed me of my anger.

Víctor's friends—were they out selling? It was a cold night, but the dealers would still be working. Suddenly, I felt sorry for them. It was a brutal life.

"Protect them, Jesus," I prayed. "Change their lives. Do what You did for me."

What were the Mafia leaders doing tonight? Memories flashed through my mind. New Year's Eve—fireworks, liquor, good food, orchestras, live entertainment. Tonight they drank and partied on their country estates while we sat in jail.

I felt a touch of anger. How many widows, how many orphans—how many had been destroyed while the Mafia bosses partied?

"Bring them to Me, Marta!"

I looked up, startled.

"Bring them to Me, Marta!"

Suddenly, a feeling of compassion swept through me. The Mafia—hated by foreign governments, sought by their own government, reviled by nations and countries around the world—and loved by God.

"Bring them to Me, Marta!"

They controlled the drug trade but could not control their own lives.

They had such wealth—but such emptiness inside. Without Jesus they were lost; without Jesus they were nothing.

When they died, they would leave their wealth behind to face their Creator with empty hands. Names began to come to me one at a time.

Pablo Escobar. One of the richest men in the world, Pablo Escobar owned properties and businesses throughout Colombia. His private mansion and estate, *Hacienda Nápoles*, had become a tourist attraction. The Robin Hood of Medellín, Escobar had built a *barrio* for the poor, and soccer fields and playgrounds for the youth.

Gustavo Gaviria. Escobar's cousin and right-hand man, Gaviria was a very rich and powerful man. Like Escobar, he had earned his wealth through the drug trade.

The Ochoa family. The names were coming to my mind with increasing clarity. The Ochoas were known in the seventies for their horses. Later they became known as the ruling family of the Medellín drug empire.

"Bring them to Me, Marta."

Was this the plan Nilsa and the officer had been talking about? Was this what the Lord had been preparing me for?

"They belong to Me, Marta. Bring them to Me."

The pressure on my heart grew stronger. "Yes, Jesus," I wept. "I will. I will bring them to You."

Through the night I wept for Escobar, the Ochoas, the Medellín cartel, the tears flowing as I felt God's love for them. "I will," I repeated over and over. "I will bring them to You."

The next morning, reality set in. I could not reach the Mafia. I was in jail. The impossibility of the plan overwhelmed me.

For days I struggled with the questions, reasoning with the Lord. "How, Lord? How can I reach them? Look where I am." At night, I tossed in bed, the questions running through my mind. How could this call possibly be from the Lord? I was in jail, awaiting sentencing on very serious charges. I was not going to be released any time soon.

Finally one night, I slipped out of bed and knelt on the concrete floor. "Father, I know You are working for my release. If this call is from You and You want me out of here to reach the Mafia, please do something about my case."

On January 17, 1984, my bail was reduced to $7,500.

"Get the money together," Maxwell said, "and I promise you will never come back here again."

I called my mother. "Mama," I yelled, "my bail was reduced to $7,500. Maxwell says that if we get the money together, I'll never come back here again."

"Marta, what did you say?" she whispered.

"Maxwell! He got my bail reduced! If we get the money, I'll be released."

She started crying.

"Oh, Mama," I wailed, "don't start crying now. It's good news."

"I know," she sobbed.

"Can you get the money?" I asked.

"Of course!" she said, still sniffling. "I'll borrow it from friends."

My bail reduction came as a surprise to many of the other inmates. "How did you do it, Marta?" they asked curiously.

"Do what?"

"Get bail at $7,500. Colombians never get low bail."

"They don't?"

"No. They always jump."

"Not this Colombian," I laughed.

One night, several weeks later, an officer called me to the security booth. "Marta," she said smiling, "get your things together, you've been bailed out."

I stared at her. "Bailed out?"

The other inmates started screaming. "Congratulations, Marta! Congratulations!"

I started screaming myself, jumping around the security booth. The girls were yelling down the corridor, the news flying from cell to cell. "Marta's leaving! She got bailed out!"

Quickly, I went back to my cell and started gathering my things. The girls crowded around, wishing me well. Officers stopped by to shake my hand. "Congratulations, Marta," they said. "We don't want to see you around here again. Understand? Don't come back here."

I nodded my head, tears in my eyes. "I won't."

I was fingerprinted in the office, the security box was opened, and I was given back my belongings. I waited as the officers went through endless stacks of paperwork, searching the computers for any missing information on me. Finally, at one o'clock that morning, I was released.

On February 8, 1984, just five weeks after the New Year's call to reach the Mafia, I walked out into the cold New York air, clutching my Bible and a small bag of personal belongings.

I would never walk through those bars in handcuffs again.

Chapter 21

I walked into my old apartment at two o'clock that morning. Laughing and crying, my family crowded around me.
"Marta, what took so long? We've been waiting all day."

I looked around. They were all there—my two brothers,
Carlo and Iván; my sister, Rosa; her husband, Héctor; my
two cousins, Edwin and Hernán; my niece, Vicky; and Lina.

Lina was hopping from foot to foot in her excitement,
her dark eyes sparkling happily, shouting above the noise,
trying to get my attention.

"Sit down, Lina," Rosa scolded. "You're shouting."

"Marta, we have to celebrate," Carlo said. "Let's have a
party. We can invite all your friends."

Lina jumped up. "You mean with balloons and presents
and everything?"

I laughed out loud, enjoying her excitement. "Yes, with
balloons and presents and everything. Let's do it. Give me a
pen."

"Who are you going to invite?" Rosa asked, thrusting a
paper and pen in my hand. "If you invite everyone, it might
get a little crowded in here." She looked around the small
apartment.

"Well, let's see," I said, taking the paper. "We should

probably invite Joe and Ben...and Carmen...and we can't forget Wess, or Jeff..." I paused, a thought striking me. "Carlo, did Joe ask about me while I was in Rikers?"

He thought a moment. "No."

I looked at the next name on my list. "How about Ben? Did he ask for me?"

"No."

I read through the list, checking off the names one by one. "Carmen? Wess?"

"No..." Carlo looked embarrassed.

Ten names, ten great friends. We had been through a lot together. They had not cared enough to write or visit while I was in Rikers.

I stood up, crumpling the paper. "There isn't going to be a party."

"Marta!" They looked at me in alarm. "What do you mean?"

"I don't want a party." I picked up the crumpled piece of paper. "Jesus was the only one who stayed with me through everything. I won't turn my back on Him now. I don't ever want to dance again."

They stared at me, stunned. Rosa broke the silence. "You're tired, Marta. Go to bed. We'll talk about it in the morning."

I smiled tiredly. They did not understand. How could they? Jesus Christ had changed my life completely and irrevocably.

The next evening, Bianca came to visit. I saw her and Rosa whispering in the kitchen and sighed. What were they plotting?

"Marta," Bianca looked around the door, "may I come in?"

"Of course."

She looked determined. "Marta, I've been talking to Rosa."

"I know."

She sat down next to me. "Get up. Let's go dancing."

I shook my head stubbornly. "No, Bianca. I'm not leaving this house."

"Marta!" She stood squarely in front of me and folded her arms. "You have to get over this complex."

I stared at her, perplexed. "Bianca, what are you talking about?"

"This complex—you think everyone is looking at you because you've been in jail, but no one knows where you've been. You don't have a sign on your forehead that says, 'I've been in jail.' "

I shook my head wearily. "That isn't it, Bianca. You don't understand; I just don't want to go."

"Yes, you do," she said firmly. She went to the closet and picked out a colorful skirt and blouse set. "Here, this is nice. Get dressed."

Bianca had been Lina's family when I was first taken into custody. She had stood by me even when she knew it might get her in trouble. Resignedly, I held out my hand for the skirt and blouse.

Bianca's look was triumphant. She scurried around the room looking for earrings. "You've been in jail so long you've forgotten how to have fun," she said. "Here, put these on."

She tilted her head, looking at me consideringly. "You need makeup—lots of it." She held up a bright red lipstick, pushing my hand aside. "No, I'll put it on. You probably don't remember how to do it anymore."

I sat quietly, my hands lying listlessly in my lap. What was wrong with me? I used to love dancing; tonight I felt indifferent. I thought about the drinking at the discos. Would the men try to touch me? I felt slightly nauseous.

Bianca turned her back, and I rubbed some of the eye shadow off my eyelids. "Bianca, all I can say is, no one had better touch my body tonight."

Bianca leaned back for a final look, ignoring my comment. She brushed a little more blush on my cheekbones, then nodded, satisfied. "Okay, that's good enough. Let's go."

The disco Bianca selected was one of my favorites. The music was loud, the dancing frenetic. Sweating bodies crowded the floor. Bright, flashing lights swirled over exposed skin.

Suddenly I felt sick.

Nothing had changed. The same faces slid by, bodies twisting to the music, colored disco lights disguising the emptiness in their eyes.

I walked out to the lobby and stood there, my heart pounding. *I had changed!* I was not the same person I had been.

"Marta, what are you doing out here?" Bianca looked angry.

"I want to go home, Bianca."

"Home? You can't go home! It's still early."

"But I don't want to be here."

"What do you mean you don't want to be here? What's wrong with you?"

I shrugged my shoulders in mute apology. Bianca stood there, looking at me helplessly. I felt sorry for her but could not change the way I felt. "I'm sorry, Bianca; it's just that things are different now. I don't belong here anymore."

Bianca's face softened. "Marta, you've had a hard time in jail. You just need time to get back in the swing of things. Come on, let's try another disco."

It felt like the night would never end. When would my family and friends believe that I was a different person, that I really had changed?

We tried two other discos. Bianca was determined to find one I enjoyed. The third one was Colombian. Bianca's face was alight with anticipation. "Come on, Marta! Let's go! We're going to have a great time."

"Bianca," I whispered miserably. "Take me home."

She swung around, still holding the car door open. "What did you say?" Her eyes were hard.

"I said, take me home."

"Home? We just got here!"

"I don't care; take me home."

She stared at me. "Marta, something is wrong with you."

"No, I'm just not comfortable here anymore."

"You're not comfortable..." She threw her hands up. "It's your stupid religion, isn't it?" she asked. "*Aguafiestas*! I can't fight you anymore. You've spoiled my whole evening."

Unmoved, I sat waiting.

She gave in, resignedly. "Fine then! Let's go home."

Oddly enough, I was not fighting temptation. I was not struggling with a desire to go back to the old life-style. Why should I? I had given up fool's gold and found pure gold.

I would never go back.

Chapter 22

My feet sank into the rich carpet of the small, affluent Manhattan bank. Warm sunlight filtered through the windows, spilling over the dark mahogany desk, picking out deep tones of gold in the furnishings. Shadows chased lightly through the room, briefly darkening the sunlight flitting over leafy plants.

"You've been with us for several weeks now, Marta..."

Sunlight always reminded me of Colombia—the warmth of the sun, the sweet, fragrant smell of flowers, the explosion of colors on street corners, the feelings of nostalgia.

"...Your supervisor says you're one of our best temporaries." The personnel director's words drifted past me.

I nodded dreamily. Roberto was a part of Colombia. His dark, gleaming eyes held promise of a different future. Soon I would go home.

"...and we like your work."

Feelings of nostalgia sharpened briefly, then disappeared, swept before the tumbling, rising tide of the vision that had flashed in my soul since before my release. How many nights had been spent in prayer, weeping for the cartels, their families, their children?

"We'd like to interview you for a full-time job."

I was jerked back to reality. "A full-time job?"

"Yes." The personnel director opened her desk and pulled out two sheets of paper. "Would you be interested?"

"Oh, yes!" I breathed. I needed a full-time job.

"Good." Ms. Samuels looked satisfied. "The first thing we'd like to ask you to do is take a typing test." She held out the sheets of paper. "Here's the test. Take as much time as you need."

I focused on her outstretched hand. "A typing test?"

She nodded. "When you're finished, just bring the papers back here—and good luck."

I took the papers and walked slowly to the other room. Good luck? I did not need good luck; I needed a miracle. I had never learned to type faster than thirty-five words a minute. I rolled a blank piece of paper into the typewriter and looked over at the applicant sitting next to me. His fingers were flying over the keys.

I pulled my seat closer to the table and peered at the test. I tapped an experimental key, and the other applicant sped up. I looked over at him again. He was hunched over the typewriter, his fingers punching the keys rapidly.

I took a breath, shoved the hair from my eyes and started the test in a flurry of key strokes. I was shaking so badly I could hardly keep my fingers on the keys. In a panic I realized I was hitting all the wrong keys. I struggled through the test, knowing I was typing words that did not exist. I finished the test and glanced down at the paper. My eyes glazed. I could not read what I had typed.

I rolled the sheet of paper into a tight cylinder and went back to the personnel director's office. "Ms. Samuels?"

She looked up from her desk. "Yes?"

"I'm finished."

"Already? My, that was fast." She put on her glasses and held out a hand. "Let's take a look." She looked at the paper, blinked, then looked again. "Uh, Marta, what is this?"

I did not answer.

"Marta?"

A teary chuckle squeezed through my throat. "It looks a little like Chinese, doesn't it?"

"Well, yes, sort of," she said. "What happened?"

"I was scared."

"Why?" She peered at me over her glasses. "I didn't give you a time limit." She folded the paper and handed it back to me. "Why don't you try again? This time try to slow down a little."

Only someone who has been in jail can understand the total loss of self-esteem, the shattered confidence that an inmate experiences after release. After only seven months in jail, I had absolutely no confidence in myself. I could not take that test again.

"Ms. Samuels, please," I stammered, "I don't think I can take it again. I don't think I would do any better."

Ms. Samuels watched me a moment, then thrust the paper into a folder. "Well, let me talk to some people. I'll see what we can work out. Why don't you come back and see me tomorrow?"

The following day I was called back to her office. She smiled warmly at me, and handed me some forms. "Here, fill these out, and then come see me again. I have something you might want to hear."

I took the forms to the other room, filled them out, then was shown into a private room with a staff processor.

"Wash your hands with some of those wipes over there," the processor said. "We'll need to take your fingerprints."

I stood staring at the ink and pad on the table.

"Ms. Estrada…"

It was a process I would dread for the rest of my life. I reached for the wipes and cleaned my hands slowly. They were going to find out.

"Let's start with your right hand," the processor said. He rolled my fingers in ink. "Ms. Estrada, please try to relax."

I looked at my fingers. They were crooked, curled in a tight ball.

"Relax, Ms. Estrada, you have nothing to worry about."

I closed my eyes. *Nothing to worry about?* The fingerprint check would turn up my record in less than a week.

"Okay, Ms. Estrada, left hand."

I would have to leave. I could not wait for them to find

out. I would have to find a job somewhere else—somewhere that did not require fingerprints.

"Okay, Ms. Estrada, wash your hands and go see Ms. Samuels."

I walked into the other room, and Ms. Samuels shook my hand. "Congratulations, Marta," she said. "We'd like to offer you the job."

My heart sank. "Thank you," I said. "Thank you."

"You're welcome," she smiled. "We're looking forward to having you here with us."

"Ms. Samuels…"

"Yes?"

I looked at her friendly face and changed my mind. "Nothing," I said.

At home, I sat down at the kitchen table, deep in thought. "Mama," I said slowly, "I have something to tell you."

She looked up apprehensively. "Oh, Marta. What happened?"

"The bank gave me a permanent job."

"A permanent job? But, Marta, that's wonderful!" she said excitedly. "When do you start?" She saw my face and stopped. "What? What happened?"

"They took my fingerprints."

"Oh…" She sat down.

I twisted my fingers together. "Mama, what am I going to do? I'll never be able to find a good job. My record is always going to follow me."

Mama watched me, tears of sympathy in her eyes. "No, *mi hija*, don't…"

"How am I going to take care of Lina? How? No one will hire me because of my record."

Mama leaned forward. "Marta, do you believe Jesus had you released from jail?"

"Yes."

"Do you believe He loves you?"

"I know He loves me."

"Do you believe He loves you enough to take care of you?"

I nodded. "Yes, I do."

"Then trust Him, *mi hija*. The Lord will take care of everything. Pray about it and then leave it to Him."

She was right. I was going to have to trust Him.

The next several weeks I did my work conscientiously, waiting for the report to come back from Albany. My supervisor seemed pleased with my work and smiled when he handed me my first paycheck. "Good work, Marta," he said. "We're glad you're with us."

The check was small, but it was clean money in the eyes of the Lord, and I was grateful. It was enough to support my little family.

Things were going well for me now, but there was still one thing I had to do. With the money from my first paycheck, I took a roll of quarters and went to the corner telephone booth to make a call I had been waiting to make for seven months.

The distant ring was faint, but it was picked up on the other end almost immediately.

"*Aló?*" It was Roberto's voice.

My throat was suddenly dry. "Roberto?"

"Yes. Who is this?"

"Marta."

"Marta?" A pause. "Marta Estrada?"

"Yes," I said with a shaky laugh. "Marta Estrada."

There was a brief silence. "Where are you calling from?"

"New York."

"What are you doing in New York?"

"I live here now."

"What happened to you?" He sounded distant. I wondered if it was the connection. "Why didn't you call?"

Was it possible he had not heard? Surely the rumors had reached him? "You didn't hear anything about me?" I asked cautiously.

"No…" He paused. "Your cousin said you got married."

"Married?" I winced. "No, I didn't get married."

"Then why didn't you come home?"

This was not going to be easy. I took a breath. "I was in jail."

The silence on the other end was frightening. The seconds ticked by. I wondered if he had heard me. I could hear my pulse beating through the receiver.

"Is that why you didn't call?" he asked finally.

I let out my breath slowly. "Yes."

"Where are you now?"

"With my mother."

I anticipated his next question and braced myself.

"Marta..."

"A friend of mine was dealing to an undercover cop," I interrupted. "I was with him when he was busted."

Another pause. "Why didn't you write?"

"I didn't want you to know."

Roberto's voice was low, regretful. "I'm sorry. Are you coming home soon?"

"I...I can't; I'm not allowed to leave the country until my case is decided." My last quarter clunked in the box. "Roberto, can I write to you?"

"Yes, of course," he said. "And I'll write back."

We talked until the line disconnected, then hung up. Confused, I walked back to the apartment. He had sounded happy to hear from me, but underneath the concern was a reserve that was frightening.

I walked into the kitchen, and Mama looked up. "Marta..." She pulled out a chair and patted it. "Here, sit down."

"I called Roberto," I said.

"I know," she said compassionately. "Marta, don't dream about him. He's not for you. Forget him."

"Mama!"

"He's seeing another woman," she said abruptly.

I turned to face her, the feeling draining from my body.

"He started seeing her when you didn't come back from New York." Mama's eyes were regretful. "I saw him with her before I came to New York. Last week your cousin called and told me they were still together."

I had not imagined the reserve in his voice. "I should have written to him," I said bitterly. "I should have told him sooner."

"No, Marta, please," Mama pleaded. "It's in the past. Forget him."

I tensed. Forget him? I shook my head stubbornly. I had lost him once. I would not make the same mistake again. As soon as my case was decided, I was going back to Colombia to fight for him. *I'll get him back*, I promised myself silently. *And this time I won't give him up*.

Work at the bank helped keep my mind off Roberto. I worked long hours, and as the months slipped by, I settled into a routine. My skills were growing, and my supervisor seemed pleased with my progress.

Occasionally I remembered the fingerprints and wondered what had happened to the reports. The prints had been submitted for several months now, but still nothing had been said to me. Puzzled by the delay, I worked hard, waiting and praying.

Finally, one day, things took a sudden turn. My supervisor reached for the ringing phone. He said a few words into the receiver, then turned to look at me. "Marta?" he repeated. "Yes, she's right here." He paused, then nodded briefly. "Sure, I'll have her bring them right up."

He hung up the phone, pulled two client folders from the cabinet and handed them to me, his eyes curious. "That was Mr. Jones," he said. "He wants you to bring these two files to his office."

I stared at the folders. Mr. Jones—the vice president. The report must have come back from Albany.

I walked to the executive offices, my mind whirling. Mr. Jones had always been very courteous to me. Several times he had seen me studying my Bible during lunch break and smiled. I felt my eyes sting. It must have been a shock to hear about my arrest.

Ms. Samuels—she had pushed for my job, hiring me even when she knew my skills were not strong. What had she thought when she saw the report? I stopped at the end of the corridor and wiped my eyes. This was not going to be easy.

The door to Mr. Jones's office was open. He saw me and motioned me inside. "Come in, Marta," he said cordially. "We've been waiting for you." He motioned to a chair and then nodded toward his right. "You know Mr. Torres, of course?"

I looked over at the man in the adjoining chair. Mr. Torres—the company's security director.

"Yes," I murmured, "we've met."

Jones closed the door behind me and walked to his desk, smoothing a hand over his forehead. He sat down and adjusted his seat. He seemed reluctant to start, looking through a thick file on his desk. "Marta," he said finally, "we have a report here from Albany…" His voice trailed off.

"Yes?" I said quietly.

"It says…" He stopped, then continued. "It says you were arrested for drugs."

I did not say anything.

Jones looked embarrassed. "Marta, is this true?"

There was silence as they waited for me to speak. I lowered my head to hide the tears.

Jones was clearly uncomfortable. "Marta, we can talk about this later if you want."

"No." I raised my head. "I'm sorry. It's true."

They looked at me, speechless. The mid-afternoon traffic noises faded outside, leaving it quiet in the office.

Finally Jones stirred, glancing over at Torres. "Mike, what's the bank's policy?"

Torres did not look happy. "Marta, bank policy will not allow us to hire someone with your record."

I nodded slowly.

Jones ran a hand through his hair, looking helplessly at Torres. "Now what do we do?"

Torres shrugged and gestured back to Jones.

Jones put his hands on the desk and clasped them together. He seemed to be thinking. He watched me quietly for a moment, then leaned back in his chair. "Marta, is there anything we can do to help?"

I paused, then answered his question quietly, confidently. "Mr. Jones, I know I made some mistakes in the past and I will never stop regretting my actions—but I am a new person now. Now I just need a chance to support myself and my daughter in a decent and honest way. If you want to help me, call my lawyer or my probation officer and let them explain what happened. They'll tell you the truth."

They looked at each other. "That's it?"

"Yes, that's it."

Jones stood up. "Okay, Marta, we'll need to talk this over. Why don't you take a break before you go back to your desk? We'll call you when we come to a decision."

That night I paced back and forth in my bedroom, praying. The Lord was going to have to take care of this one. There was nothing I could do but pray.

The next morning I went to work, tired but resolute. If they fired me, I would still trust Him.

Late in the afternoon I was called into Mr. Jones's office. The two men seemed quieter than the day before. I took a seat again in front of the mahogany desk.

"Marta." Jones's face was unreadable. "We spoke to your probation officer about your case."

I sat still, praying.

"And we have decided to ask you to stay with the bank. We like your work. We want you to stay."

I jumped up in tears. "Oh, thank you," I whispered. "Thank you."

"You're welcome." Jones was smiling.

I hugged him, then turned to Mr. Torres. "Thank you, Mr. Torres."

He smiled sheepishly. "You earned it, Marta. You're a good worker. We owed it to you to give you a chance."

My heart swelled with gratitude. The Lord had protected my job and my reputation.

He was about to protect something that meant even more to me.

Chapter 23

Carlo was my younger brother, impudent and fun-loving and, in typical little-brother style, was always teasing me about my "new religion."

"You found God in jail?" he asked. "Don't worry; you'll get over it. Once you've had time to relax, things will get back to normal."

After Héctor and Rosa accepted the Lord, Carlo seemed a little quieter, an uneasy look in his eyes, but he never stopped the teasing.

"Marta!" Carlo stuck his head through the doorway, grinning. "*Loca*, Marta!"

I waved back at him. It was Sunday, and I was on my way to church. Since my release, I had been attending Genesis Church where Mama had received Jesus Christ and Héctor and Rosa had come to the Lord. Now they were praying for Carlo.

"Carlo, what are you doing here?" I asked.

"I came to get the girls." He looked at my purse on the couch. "Hey! Where are you going? Aren't you coming with us?"

"What's today, Carlo?"

"Sunday." He slapped a hand against his forehead. "Oh, church."

"Why don't you come along?" I asked.

"Church? Are you kidding? You know I don't go to church." He looked down at his little daughter. "Julie, where are we going today?"

"To the beach," she sang happily.

"And where are we going next Sunday?"

"To the park!"

He looked back at me smugly. "See, *loca*?"

I shook a finger at him, grinning. "Call me *loca*, Carlo, but one of these days you're going to be just as crazy as I am."

He opened his eyes in mock terror. "Oh, no! Please! One *loca* in this family is enough. Two *locas* with Mama—definitely too many." He rolled his eyes toward the ceiling. "And now Héctor and Rosa."

I laughed. "Anything else?"

"Yes." He tapped a finger against his forehead. "This Mafia thing—it's going too far. God gave you a vision?" He shook his head. "The cartels aren't interested in this God stuff. What are you going to do? Walk onto their estates and tell them to stop selling drugs?" He whistled and made a slicing motion across his neck with his hand. "They're too powerful for you, Marta. They'll never listen to you. They don't need God." He paused, then looked at me for my reactions. "I don't need Him either."

"Carlo," I said abruptly, "come here a minute."

"What?" he asked, suddenly cautious. "What's wrong?"

"I want to talk to you about something."

He sidled into the room and sat down on the edge of the chair. "What? You look serious. What's the matter?"

"Carlo, I know you're dealing drugs."

He lifted an eyebrow in surprise. "So? Everyone knows that. It's how I make my living—a very good one," he added with satisfaction.

"Carlo, I know you think you're a big shot with all your money and your cars, but your five cars don't impress me."

"Eight."

"Your eight cars don't impress me. Carlo, you're going to get in trouble with those drugs. Don't you remember what happened to me?"

"That was you. I won't get caught." Carlo was grinning again, unconcerned.

I forced myself to stay calm. "Carlo, I can't allow you to come here anymore."

He looked up, surprised. "Why not?"

"Undercover cops are parked on the corner, Carlo. They're watching me. If they think I'm dealing drugs again, they'll send me back to jail to do my fifteen years."

Carlo stood up and called for Julie. He left without a word.

When Mama found out, she was upset. "Marta, he's your brother! How can you do that to him?"

"Because he's dealing drugs, Mama. If he keeps coming here he'll get us all in trouble." I paused for a moment, thinking. "Mama, I'm going to start praying that Carlo's business goes wrong."

"Marta!" Mama's eyes were shocked. "He's your brother. Pray for him, don't make trouble for him."

I closed the Bible on my lap decisively. "No, Mama. Carlo is stubborn. He's not going to listen as long as things are going well. I'm going to pray that the Lord will get him in trouble. Then, maybe he'll listen."

Mama looked like she was going to cry. "But, what if he's arrested?"

"If that's what it takes to make Carlo listen, then we have to be willing to let it happen. Remember what happened to me."

It did not take long.

Several months later I walked into my apartment. Carlo was sitting on the couch, his face ashen. Mama was sitting beside him, her breathing shallow. She looked badly shaken.

Frightened, I looked at Mama. "What happened?"

Mama pointed to Carlo. "Ask your brother."

I turned to him. "Carlo, what happened?"

"They're after me."

"Who's after you?"

"The police."

"The police? Oh, dear..." I could feel the corners of my mouth twitching. "What did you do, Carlo?"

"Nothing. I missed a deal. My partner was busted—now they're after me." He wiped a hand across his forehead. His hands were shaking.

I put a hand up to hide my eyes. If Mama saw the laughter in my eyes, she would not be amused.

"Tell her the rest," Mama said.

Carlo dropped his head in his hands. "One of my clients split with $150,000 in cocaine."

I choked and sat down. "Oh, no—that's too bad. Do you have to pay it back?"

"Of course I do."

"Do you have that much?"

He frowned irritably. "Marta, please."

I watched him for a moment. "Carlo, can I say something?"

"What?"

I walked over and grabbed him by the front of his shirt. "God has been trying to get your attention for a long time, Carlo. He's been calling you, but you've been so busy trying to be a big shot. You said you didn't need God; now you're in trouble—big trouble." I tightened my grip on his shirt. "Are you ready to listen now?"

"Yes." He was quiet, his face strangely subdued.

"Come here." I took him by the hand and led him to the other room. "Kneel down. I'm going to pray for you."

Carlo knelt beside the bed, and I took his hands in mine. They were shaking. "You've been joking around too long, Carlo," I said. "Now the joke is over. It's time to make a decision. Close your eyes."

He closed his eyes.

"Jesus," I prayed, "I consecrate these hands to You and to Your service. From this moment on, do not let these hands touch any more drugs or dirty money. Give him peace and protect his life. Clean his mind and his heart; change his life and change his heart."

Suddenly, Carlo started crying.

Mama came into the room; I heard her sharp intake of breath.

"Carlo, do you want to receive Jesus?" I asked. "Do you want to change as I have changed?"

He was weeping. "Yes."

"Do you want to have a new life?"

The single word came out in a choking voice. "Yes."

Mama was kneeling beside us now, her tears mingling with Carlo's. "My son," she whispered brokenly, "my son."

I put my hands on Carlo's head. "Carlo, say this prayer with me: 'Jesus, come into my life. Change my heart. Make me a new person.' "

Carlo repeated the words, Mama weeping silently beside us. There was silence as we stayed on our knees, the presence of the Lord filling the room.

Finally, Carlo stirred. He looked up. His eyes were red.

I smiled at him tearily and sat down on the bed. The change was already showing in his eyes. "Carlo, you're going to have to make some decisions now," I said.

He wiped his eyes. "Like what?"

"The drugs—if you're going to serve Jesus, you're going to have to stop dealing."

"Marta!" He licked suddenly bloodless lips. "I can't do that! I owe $150,000. They'll kill me if I don't pay it!"

"So pay it," I said.

"Pay it?" he said hoarsely. "With what? Where am I going to get $150,000?"

"Get a job."

The color came rushing back to his face. "Marta, be serious. You know I don't know how to do anything but sell drugs."

"Why don't you ask Héctor for a job? He'll give you some work."

"Héctor?" Carlo looked appalled. "Construction work?"

I looked at Carlo's polished and manicured nails and laughed. "Yes, construction work. What's the matter, Carlo? Don't you want to dirty your nails?"

Carlo loved fine clothing. He was always immaculately groomed and wore only the most expensive clothing.

"You've got to start somewhere, Carlo," I said.

Carlo stood up. His face was set, his lips taut with determination. "Fine," he said. "I'll ask him."

Héctor and Rosa were sitting in the living room when Mama and I came out of the room with Carlo. They stared at Carlo's face.

Carlo cleared his throat nervously. "Héctor, I need a job."

"A job?" Héctor raised an eyebrow. "Doing what?"

Carlo grinned. "Construction."

Héctor's eyes traveled down Carlo's expensive clothes, ending up on his handmade Italian shoes. "Construction?" He looked back at Carlo's face. "You're serious?"

Carlo nodded.

Héctor's eyes did not leave Carlo's face. "You'll need to be here early."

"What time?"

"Seven o'clock."

"Seven o'clock!" Carlo swallowed.

"Take it or leave it."

Carlo nodded. "No problem. I'll be here." The door closed behind him.

It was quiet for a while, then Mama looked over at me. "Will he—do you think he'll come?"

Héctor snorted. "Carlo? Don't believe anything that happened here today. He hasn't changed. He's not going to show up."

The next morning, the entire family was up, waiting.

"He's not coming," Héctor said. "Just forget it."

Mama's eyes were indignant. "Give him a chance, Héctor."

At seven o'clock the doorbell rang. The entire family turned and stared in disbelief. It was Carlo. He was standing in the doorway dressed in work clothes and old sneakers. "Hi, everybody," he waved. He looked around. "What are you all staring at?" He smiled over at me. "I'm going to do it, Marta. I'm going to earn an honest living."

I hugged him, my heart bursting. "You're doing the right thing, Carlo. The Lord will take care of you."

The next several weeks Carlo worked hard, surprising everyone. Even Héctor seemed faintly pleased with the new Carlo. "Maybe he'll do alright," he said grudgingly.

Then, one night, Carlo showed up at my apartment, his face creased with worry. "Marta, I'm in trouble."

"Now what?" I asked anxiously.

"They've put the hit out on me."

"The hit? How do you know?"

"The dealers—they left a note in my house. They want their money back."

"Well, tell them to cancel it," I said. "Tell them you'll pay it back."

He looked at me incredulously. "Pay it back? With what?"

"You have a job. Ask them to let you pay back fifty dollars a week."

Carlo's face was frozen in disbelief.

"I know, Carlo, I know," I said, "but just try. We're going to have to trust the Lord in this."

"They're going to kill me, Marta." Carlo's shoulders were tense.

"And then you'll go straight to heaven," I smiled. I stood up. "I'm going to call Nilsa and Genesis Church right now. We'll get everyone to start praying for you."

He shrugged resignedly. "Alright. I'll go talk to them tomorrow."

The prayer chain started that night.

The next day, Carlo called me. "Marta…"

"What happened?" I asked excitedly.

"They threw me out."

"Oh." I sat down.

"They said they were going to kill me."

"I see…" I thought for a minute. "Well, there's only one thing to do now."

"What?"

"Keep praying."

Over the next several months, Carlo sold his cars, pawned many of his belongings, and paid off as much of the debt as possible, but still it was not enough. Finally, he told the dealers he could not pay any more. "If you kill me, kill me," he said, "but I don't deal drugs anymore, and I don't have that kind of money."

Inexplicably, some of the dealers started giving Carlo money to pay off the debt.

While the dealers seemed to respect Carlo's decision to stop selling drugs, there was nothing we could do about the hitmen. They were under contract and would not stop until Carlo was dead.

"There's nothing we can do about it," Carlo said. "The contract is out. It can't be canceled. The Lord will just have to take care of them."

The Lord did take care of them—in a rather final way. Several weeks later, both hitmen were killed.

Chapter 24

July 18, 1984—New York

Ms. Estrada, please stand."
I stood up, my hands clasped tightly behind me. After seven months in jail and five months out on bail, my case was finally going to be decided. I was about to be sentenced.

Judge Phillips looked at the file in front of him. "Ms. Estrada, on the fourteenth of July, 1983, you were arrested for possession of cocaine in the amount of one pound and charged with ten counts of felony. Those counts have been reduced to attempted possession of a controlled substance in the third degree. On June 25, 1984, you entered a plea of guilty to that charge." He held my eyes for a moment. "Are you ready to be sentenced?"

The tremor in my voice was barely noticeable. "Yes, your Honor."

He paused. "In the case of the people of the City of New York against Marta Estrada, this court hereby sentences the defendant to five years' probation."

Maxwell did not move.

Judge Phillips looked up, his face a kindly mixture of

encouragement and warning. "Ms. Estrada, you have been given a very light sentence, but do you understand that if you are arrested again on any of these charges, you will be sent back to do your time?"

"Yes, your Honor."

"And do you understand that if you are found involving yourself with drugs or violating your probation in any way, you will come back here to serve your time?"

I would never go back to that jail again in handcuffs. "Yes, your Honor." My voice rang out. "I understand."

Judge Phillips smiled. "Good. See your probation officer before leaving this court." The gavel cracked the silence. "Next case."

I stood there in a daze. It was over.

Maxwell took my arm and guided me out of the courtroom. In the corridor, he turned to face me. He was smiling. "You'll need to report to your probation officer," he said.

"I know."

"And you'll need to make sure you don't do anything to violate probation."

"I won't."

"But you are free."

"Yes," I said mistily. "I know."

His eyes were serious. "Do you know this is a miracle?"

"Yes," I said, "I do know that." I hugged him with tears in my eyes. "Jesus used you to help me. Thank you."

At home, the celebration started. "It's a miracle, Marta! A miracle!" Mama caught me in her arms, her face shining.

"Yes, I know," I said, dancing around the apartment. "Jesus took care of my case. He took care of my family..." I grabbed Lina and hugged her. "And He took care of my daughter."

Five years' probation—it was far better than anyone expected. After just seven months in Rikers Island, I was free.

As the celebration continued, a single thought crept into my mind. Roberto...

"Marta, what are you thinking?" Mama's eyes were perceptive.

"Mama, do you know that I'm not allowed to leave New York City until my probation is up?"

"New York City!" Carlo interrupted. "The five boroughs?"

Héctor's eyes were fixed on my face. "You mean you can't leave New York City for five years?"

I looked down. "If I leave, I'd be violating probation."

"Five years!" Mama was trying to smile. "But that's not that long..."

Not that long? In five years, Roberto would be married.

"Ms. Estrada, do you understand that if you are found involving yourself with drugs or violating your probation in any way, you will come back here to serve your time?"

Violating probation was a serious offense. If I was caught leaving the country, they would send me back to serve my time.

But what if I was not caught?

The thought slipped in, catching me by surprise. What if I left without telling anyone? Once I reached Medellín, the U.S. government would not bother looking for me. If I got out of the country without being caught, I would be safe. Once I reached Medellín, I would never have to come back.

But what would happen if I was stopped? Horrified, I thrust the thought away. It was wrong.

Still, over the next few months, the questions haunted me. Five years was a long time. What if Roberto married someone else? What if I waited too long and I lost him again? Was I willing to risk it?

No, I decided, I was not.

Finally, in December 1984, I made my decision. I was going home to Colombia.

I kept my arrangements a secret, knowing my family and church would be horrified. Mama would cry. Nilsa, Reverend Green, the Genesis pastor and church members—they would all be shocked. Sister Hershey—I could almost hear her: "Marta, that is the stupidest thing I ever heard of! Why would you even think about doing something so dumb?"

I did not even want to think about Pastor Hershey. He had always treated me like a daughter. Those blue eyes would snap with anger when he heard the news. He might even come to Colombia and drag me back to prison himself.

Angrily, I closed my mind to the thoughts. My mind was made up. I was going.

Lina's papers were already in order. All I had to do was get my passport and green card back from my first lawyer, buy the airplane tickets, and pack. I would resign from my job at the last possible moment, just in case. Once I had my passport, Lina and I could be out of the country in hours.

I made an appointment with Sullivan's secretary to pick up my documents, then spent a restless night worrying. Sullivan's secretary was an inquisitive woman. What if she started asking questions? Worse, what if Sullivan suspected something? He was a lawyer. Would he pick up on my nervousness? What if I let information slip by accident? Would he piece the facts together?

Sullivan was standing in the doorway when I walked into the office the next day. I felt my face redden.

He looked up, then looked back again. "Marta..."

"Hello, Mr. Sullivan." I swallowed nervously. "I came for my passport and green card."

He motioned for me to sit down. "I know. My secretary told me."

I sat down on the edge of the seat, hugging my purse tightly. "I...It's just that I never got them back from you before," I explained lamely.

He looked at me curiously. I saw the question forming in his eyes and felt my pulse quicken. Did he suspect something? He knew I was Colombian. He also knew I could not get out of the country without my passport.

"Are you out on bail?" he asked casually.

"Yes...no...I'm on probation," I said tightly.

"Oh, really? How much time did you get?" he asked.

"Five years' probation."

Sullivan's face showed a flicker of surprise. "Five years' probation? You got good time."

I could not help the brief surge of satisfaction. "I know."

"Who was your lawyer?"

"Charles Maxwell."

"Well, congratulations," he said. "He did a good job." He lost interest abruptly and turned away.

I wondered what he would say if he knew I was about to jump probation.

I signed the release forms, slipped the documents into my purse, and slung the purse strap over my shoulder. A quick feeling of guilt tugged at me and I shrugged it off irritably. *I'm not doing anything wrong*, I reasoned. *I'll still be serving the Lord. In fact, I'll be able to serve Him better because I can reach the Mafia directly in Colombia.* The argument sounded weak even to me.

I threw the purse strap over my shoulder and left the office. I walked back to the apartment, going over my plans. I would buy the tickets, pack, then resign from my job. My passport and green card were legitimate, so no one would ask any questions. At the airport they would not have time to pull up my record, and by the time anyone realized I was gone, it would be too late.

Maxwell—I paused momentarily. He had believed in me. I crossed the street and turned the corner, thinking. Maybe I should tell someone. Maybe I should tell Mama—or Carlo. No. I shook my head silently. It was too dangerous. It would be safer to leave and call from Colombia.

I reached the front of the building and stopped. The courts—what if they found out? I shuddered. After Judge Phillips's words of warning, I knew they would not give me a second chance. This was not a minor offense. If they caught me, I would go back to serve my fifteen years.

I stopped mid-thought, caught in a swirl of conflicting thoughts. And then, in one incredible moment, the issue was settled for me. A sudden violent tug on my shoulder threw me to one side and I whirled, off balance, to stare into the faces of three young men. In one stunned moment of disbelief I watched as they ripped my purse from my shoulder and fled down the street, the broken strap dangling from the clasp.

For an instant I could not move. Then sudden realization broke through my daze and I leaped after them, my high heels pounding the sidewalk. *My passport!*

They disappeared around the corner, and I stood in the middle of the sidewalk, my hands hanging at my side, tears of frustration staining my cheeks. "Not today," I whispered. "Oh, God, not today."

"Ma'am, are you alright?" Two officers were watching me from a squad car.

I looked up, then shook my head wordlessly.

"What happened?"

"Someone stole my purse."

The officers opened the doors and climbed out. "Anything valuable in it?"

"Yes."

"Money?"

"No…" Ironically, my money was in my pocket.

"What?"

I could hardly get the words out. "My passport and green card."

"Alright, ma'am, get in the car. We'll take you around the neighborhood and see if we can spot them."

We drove around the neighborhood for half an hour looking for the men, but they were gone. Finally, the patrol car pulled over to the side of the street. "I'm sorry," one of the officers said apologetically. "There isn't much else we can do. We can have you fill out a report at the precinct, but that's about all."

"I understand," I said dully.

"And don't worry about the stolen documents," they said kindly. "You can always have them replaced. It only takes a few weeks."

I smiled, feeling the irony. "Thank you."

I filled out the forms, filed the police report, and went home.

Inside the apartment I walked to my room and closed the door behind me. I stood staring at the suitcase I had pulled out.

Deep, heaving sobs shook my body, and I fell on my knees. My hands were still shaking from the shock. "Why?" I cried, rocking back and forth. "Why did You let this happen? Why? I would not have stopped serving You."

I felt, rather than heard, the Lord speaking to me: *"Marta, I called you to reach the Mafia. You almost gave up your right to that call. Is that what you want?"*

The full impact of what I had nearly done hit me. In one moment of selfish ambition, I had nearly jeopardized my right to the call the Lord had placed on my life. I had come very close to choosing Roberto over the Lord.

I collapsed in tears. "I'm sorry," I wept. "I'm so sorry. Please forgive me."

I had come so close to losing what I had found in Jesus. A shiver went through me. *Nothing was worth that!* Nothing was worth losing my relationship with Jesus Christ—not my family, not my friends—not Roberto. I would have to give him up.

Chapter 25

I sat staring out the window, the rain running down the window pane, sheets of rain blanketing the streets.

"Ms. Estrada...do you understand that if you are found involving yourself with drugs or violating your probation in any way, you will come back here to serve your time?"

The rain was falling in earnest now, large drops of water beating on the glass. A fine spray misted the window sill. I stood and lowered the window.

"Did you hear the judge?" Maxwell asked. "If you get involved with drugs in any way, you will come back and do your time."

I traced designs in the fogged window panel, small rivulets running down the glass, drops of water spinning away from my fingers.

It had been a year since my release. With memories of Roberto safely buried away, the burden for the Mafia had resurfaced to burn brightly, steadily, but still the questions remained. How was I going to reach the Mafia? The penalty for seeing anyone associated with drugs was clear.

"Marta, what are you thinking about?" My mother's voice broke through my thoughts. "The phone has been ringing. It's for you—it's Nilsa."

"Oh, I'm sorry," I apologized. "I didn't hear it." I took the phone from her. "Nilsa, how are you?" I said warmly.

"Fine. Marta, it's been six months since your case was decided." Nilsa never wasted time.

"Yes," I said, puzzled.

"And you're on probation for five years?"

"Yes."

"You know, you can go back to jail if you want."

"Go back to jail! I...Nilsa, what are you talking about?"

She chuckled, enjoying my bewilderment. "Your testimony—you can go back in and give your testimony."

"After only six months?" I asked.

"Well, you're supposed to wait a year, but they might be willing to work something out in your case."

The prison system was packed with drug traffickers and Mafia hitmen, and I knew there were mafiosos scattered among the population. I could give my testimony without jeopardizing my case.

"Oh, Nilsa, I would love to," I said. "I've been praying about this. I think it's the Lord's answer. When do I start?"

"Well, it isn't a job interview," she laughed. "You can start anytime. How about next week?"

"Next week? I'll be ready!" I could hardly contain my excitement.

The following week, Nilsa picked me up at my apartment. I felt my heart skip a beat as we drove across the bridge to Rikers Island. We stopped at the security checkpoint on the other side, and I glanced down at my wrists. Maxwell had promised I would never come back in handcuffs. He had kept his promise.

"How do you feel, Marta?" Nilsa smiled.

"Wonderful!" I breathed. "This is beautiful."

I walked into the brightly lit security area. Eleven months ago I had walked through those doors promising never to return. Now I was back, eager to tell others what had happened to me.

An officer looked up, then looked back again. "Hey," she said in surprise, "I thought we told you never to come back here again."

I laughed, holding up my visitor's badge. "I'm here as a visitor."

"Oh," she smiled. "Good—congratulations."

Other officers were crowding around now, congratulating me. "Marta, you look great. How much time did you get?"

"Five years' probation."

They stared at me. "Five years' probation?"

Long, drawn-out whistles of disbelief brought a delighted grin to my face. "It was Jesus," I said. "He gave me a miracle."

"So what are you doing back here?"

"I'm preaching the gospel."

No one laughed. "Really? That's great! Go for it!"

I followed Nilsa through the security checkpoints and walked into the chapel. Girls were already beginning to file into the auditorium. Several of them looked up, their eyes widening in recognition. "Marta!" They waved at me.

I smiled broadly and waved back.

Nilsa went to the piano and started playing. She looked over at me briefly, and sudden emotion flooded me.

She looks just the same, I thought. *She's still shining*.

The women were now in their seats, waiting, a palpable sense of excitement in the auditorium. Nilsa was standing at the podium. She reached back and held out a hand, motioning for me to join her at the podium. "Ladies," she said, "some of you will probably recognize this young lady on the stage with me tonight. A year ago, she was released from Rikers Island. Tonight she's back with an exciting story. Marta, come here and tell us what the Lord has done for you."

Nilsa adjusted the microphone, then took a seat behind me on the stage.

I stood looking out over the audience. Little more than a year ago, I had been sitting in this auditorium, bitter, angry, thinking of suicide. Tonight I was a new person, sharing the hope I had found in Jesus.

I traced my life from the arrest to my incredible experience with Jesus Christ, reliving the moment when I had heard that Jesus died for me. "I had heard about Jesus all my life, but I never knew Him personally. I did not understand what was happening to me, but in that moment I knew I needed Jesus."

I saw several girls put their heads down.

"I asked Him to come into my life. That night Jesus gave me a new life and filled me with joy. Today, because of Him, I am a new person."

Many times after that I visited Rikers Island. I wept to see drug dealers broken and crying before the Lord. I wept to see drug addicts released from the power of drug addiction.

"They never use drugs, these Colombians. They're too good for that. They just sell the stuff."

The words came out of nowhere. I winced. How often had I tensed when I heard those words, resenting the detective's tone and the implication? How often had I defended my country, fighting the surge of anger? Now I heard the truth in his words and wept.

American prisons were full of young Colombians. For love of money they had thrown away the respect of their country and the love of their families. Now they were behind bars, their future reduced to four walls and a barred window. Some of these men would not see their families for twenty... thirty years. Some of them would spend the rest of their lives in prison. The results to both society and their families would be devastating.

The passing months brought an ache to my soul. Nothing, it seemed, could stop the drug trade. Back in Colombia, the cartel leaders had become bold, almost flamboyant in their drug transactions, amassing incredible fortunes while controlling the flow and distribution of cocaine throughout the world.

The United States government pressured Colombian officials to stop the flow of cocaine to the States, but as the stranglehold tightened, the flow increased. The business exploded, bringing in millions for the cartels.

Through the drug trade, Medellín had spawned a literal hierarchy of drug families. The Medellín cartel boasted some of the richest families in Colombia. They were the drug lords, the aristocrats of the drug trade. One prominent financial magazine had listed Pablo Escobar, the leader of the Medellín cartel, as one of the ten richest men in the world, figuring his wealth at close to *two billion dollars!*

The thought was staggering.

The Colombian Mafia—famous, powerful, and fabulously wealthy. Would they listen? Could they be reached? My knees weakened at the thought.

It did not seem possible.

* * *

While the prison ministry at Rikers continued to grow, I could not avoid the obvious conflict that was beginning to develop in my own family.

Papa had joined us in New York several months before and was not happy. He missed Colombia and resented the changes he found in my home. He had smoked two packs of cigarettes a day for over forty years and was not about to give it up just because his daughter had found some "stupid religion."

"I'm not going to stop smoking just because you're religious now," he said. "I'm a good person. There's nothing wrong with smoking."

I was still a new Christian, but I knew I did not want to do anything that would damage the place where Jesus was living. "Please, don't smoke in the house, Papa," I pleaded. "If you want to smoke, go outside."

Papa reacted angrily. "You can't tell me what to do!" he said. He lit a cigarette defiantly. "If I want to smoke, I'll smoke."

Several months later, Papa collapsed and was rushed to the hospital.

"You're very sick, Mr. Estrada," the nurses told him sternly. "You're going to have to stop smoking. If you don't, you're going to kill yourself."

"Has my daughter been talking to you?" Papa asked suspiciously.

"No, why?"

He pursed his lips and did not answer. But when I came to the emergency room, Papa confronted me. "I know what you're doing, Marta!" he said. "You told those nurses to talk to me."

"I did what? Papa, what are you talking about?"

"You told those nurses to make me stop smoking."

I stared at him in amazement. "Why would I do that?"

"Because you don't want me smoking!" he said. "You and your stupid religion! Why don't you just leave me alone, Marta? If I want to smoke, I'll smoke."

His words hurt, but that night I gathered the family together. "Listen to me," I said. "Papa is very sick. He has lung cancer. The doctors have given him a medication that reacts to the nicotine in cigarettes. If he smokes, the reaction could be fatal. *No one* is to give him money. Understand? No one!"

They nodded, understanding.

"If you give him money, he'll just use it to buy cigarettes."

When Papa found out about the meeting, he was livid. "Did you tell my family not to give me money?" He was shouting.

"Yes."

"Why? Why did you do that?"

"Because you'll just spend it on cigarettes."

"So?" His face was turning red. "What about it? It's my life. If I want to smoke, I'll smoke."

"Papa, you can't," I wailed. "It could kill you."

He threw his newspaper down on the table and stormed out of the house. I followed him to the window, my heart breaking as I saw him picking cigarette butts off the sidewalk.

That night I tried to reason with him. "Papa, please don't do that. You're only hurting yourself."

He turned his back and walked out of the room.

The next several weeks, the situation worsened, accusations growing bitter on both sides. I found it impossible to reason with Papa. At night, I collapsed in bed, worn by the constant struggle.

"I can't take it much longer," I complained to the Lord. "He's driving me crazy."

Soon Papa began demanding that I send him back to Colombia. "I don't want to stay here anymore, Marta," he said. "Send me back to Colombia."

I shook my head. "Papa, you know I don't have any money."

He looked at me speculatively. "Don't lie to me, Marta. I know you have money."

We had been over this before. I rested my head wearily on my hand. "Papa, I don't sell drugs," I said. "You know I don't have much money. I'll send you when I save enough to buy a ticket."

He slammed his hand on the table. "No, Marta! I want to go now!" His eyes narrowed cunningly. "Send me back, Marta, or I'm going to throw myself off a train!"

I looked at him incredulously. Was he serious? This was ridiculous! I flung up a hand. "You want to kill yourself?" I shouted. "Go ahead then! Go ahead and throw yourself off a train."

His face registered shock. "Marta!"

I sat down on the couch, my hands shaking. "I'm sorry, Papa," I whispered, sick with regret. "I'm sorry."

"You're a Christian?" he shouted. "You're a Christian and you're telling me to kill myself?"

For days after that, Papa sulked. I tried to talk to him, but he would not listen. I tried to apologize, but he ignored me. As the days dragged by and Papa still refused to speak to me, I began to struggle with resentment.

At night in my room, I wrestled with the Lord. "I have feelings too," I argued. "I'm a Christian, but I'm also human. How much am I supposed to take?"

I felt the Lord nudging me gently, asking me to forgive Papa, but I could not; Papa had hurt me deeply.

Finally, I had enough money to buy one ticket to Colombia. Relieved, I bought the ticket, took him to the airport, and put him on the plane for Colombia.

Chapter 26

With Papa gone, I found life returning to normal.
I was attending Sister Hershey's English-speaking
church in the Bronx by this time and was excited to
see the warmth and concern they showed toward others. Joy
Fellowship was a small, inner-city church with a big vision
and a heart for missions.

Steve, the assistant pastor, had a strong burden for missions and seemed a little impatient with the petty squabbles
and material selfishness of American churches. "People are
dying around the world," he preached one Sunday, "and all
we're concerned about is what 'so and so' said to hurt our
feelings. Christians in China are dying for their faith, and
American churches can't decide whether they should have
red or purple chairs in the sanctuary."

It was very quiet in the auditorium.

"Chinese Christians are dying, risking their lives to get
Bibles, and we don't even read the ones we have!" Steve was
pounding his hand on the pulpit, his voice rising.

"When are we going to grow up as Christians? When are
we going to give up our rights and do the things we know are
right? Do we have time for petty disagreements? Do we have
time to get upset because someone looked at us wrong? No!"

Now he was shouting. "People are dying around the world, and all we want to do is make sure we get out of church by noon so we can watch the Dallas Cowboys." He stopped and wiped his forehead. "Matter of fact..." He looked at his watch. "They play at one o'clock—let's wrap this up."

The laughter was a relief. Steve was getting much too close to the truth.

He looked around, serious again. "We have an opportunity to go to China and take Bibles to the believers on the mainland. How many of you would like to go?"

Hands flew up all over the auditorium.

"How many of you would like Pastor Hershey to pay your way?"

Laughing, we all raised our hands. Then I remembered. I was still on probation. I could not leave the country for another three years. Embarrassed, I put my hand down.

After the service, Steve pulled me aside. "Marta, if the Lord is telling you to go, He'll make a way."

"I can't," I said. "I'm still on probation—and I never had my green card and passport replaced. Even if I got permission to go, I'd never get them replaced in time."

"Well, pray about it," he said. "If the Lord wants you to go, He'll work it out."

The next time I went to see my probation officer, I approached the subject tentatively. "Ms. Hale, can I ask you a question?"

"Yes."

"Can I go to China?"

She blinked. "China?"

"Yes."

She looked at me mildly. "Well, I guess so."

Startled, I repeated the question. "China, Ms. Hale. China, the country—not Chinatown."

"I know," she said, smiling faintly. "I heard you—and I don't see why not."

"But it isn't a family emergency."

"No? What will you be doing there?"

I grinned, enjoying the moment. "Smuggling Bibles."

She looked at me blankly. "Smuggling Bibles?"

I nodded.

"Well, I don't know," she said slowly. "It certainly sounds exciting. I'll have to ask the judge."

One week later I was on a plane headed for Hong Kong.

In one week, I had received a tax refund for the exact amount I needed to buy my plane ticket, my stolen passport and green card had been replaced, and the judge had given me written permission to go. *All in one week!*

Steve joked about his little Colombian drug smuggler turned Bible smuggler, but I was too nervous to respond. I had read several books on the Christians suffering in China and was more than a little worried.

"They torture them," I told my mother tearfully. "They torture the Chinese who believe in Jesus. The government sends them to labor camps."

"What if they arrest you?" Mama asked worriedly. "Will they send you back here to prison?"

I had already asked Ms. Hale that question. "No, Mama, whatever I do over there will not affect my case here."

The eighteen-hour flight from New York was long but fun with my wonderful, rowdy church and group leaders laughing and joking the whole way to Hong Kong.

Once there, ministry workers prepared us for crossing the border. "First of all," they said, "we need to tell you that methods do not work. We can show you several fairly successful ways to pack your Bibles, and we can demonstrate techniques for avoiding the scanner. But in the end everything will come down to trusting in the Lord. There are no proven methods. Even the best couriers get caught—often."

"What do we say to the guards if we're caught?" someone asked.

"That's between you and your conscience. In the Bible, Rahab told a lie to protect the Hebrew spies hiding in her home. Should you lie to protect your Bibles? That's between you and the Lord. We ask only that you not give away specific information about this ministry."

"Are we allowed to pray in public?"

"If you do, you'll only bring attention to yourself. We

suggest that you pray with your head up and your eyes open."

"But that's lying." Some of the other church groups were offended. "That's denying Christ."

"If you feel uncomfortable with the policy, then pray openly; but please disassociate yourself from the rest of the groups until the Bibles are delivered safely. Let's remember our purpose here: We're here to take Bibles to our Chinese brothers and sisters, not to prove we are Christians."

It was clear there were going to be many uncomfortable decisions to make on this trip.

That night we locked the doors to our rooms and began packing for the border. Late into the night we packed and repacked our bags, praying for God's protection.

"The Lord will create diversions for you," experienced couriers assured us. "Just keep your eyes open and move when He says move."

He would create diversions. Would He? Would I know the diversion when I saw it? My mind was busy, working the angles. I was exhausted, but consumed with excitement.

The next morning we filed silently out of the hotel with our bags and piled into waiting taxis. Several minutes later we were on the train, heading toward the border. The border was only twenty minutes away, but it felt like hours.

At the border my legs were rubber as I filled out my immigration forms and walked slowly to the back of the customs line. Guards were on either side of the scanner, checking forms and loading bags on the belt. Tourists were moving through the line quickly, waiting for their bags on the other side. I wiped a bead of sweat from my lip.

"Move up, please."

I shuffled forward, keeping a safe distance between myself and the front of the line. The custom form went limp in my damp hands. A few more minutes and the guards would be loading my bags on the belt. I prayed under my breath, looking for the diversion, waiting for the opening.

"Next."

I leaned over and checked the front of the line. There were still several people between me and the scanner. I looked over at the exit. It was on the far side, beyond the guards, but I looked at it consideringly. If I could just slip by without being noticed...

For one brief second, the guard looked away and I was out of line and heading toward the exit door. My eyes were down, my bags slamming against my legs. I heard the commotion behind me but kept walking. If I could just make it to the exit door—

A khaki-clad arm blocked my way, and I looked up into the face of one of the guards. "Miss, I'm sorry," he said courteously. "You missed the scanner."

Embarrassed, I followed him back to the scanner and placed my bag on the belt, biting back tears as the bag rumbled through the scanner entrance and emerged on the other end. I heard the shouts and closed my eyes. They had seen the Bibles.

The guards were moving toward the scanner quickly. The bag was dragged off the belt, and a guard motioned to me, "Miss, please come."

There was chaos around me. I saw several others in my group, but they looked away, some walking past the belt in the confusion, ignoring the shouted commands.

I turned and followed a guard into a large room off to the side. It was empty. The supervisor held out her hand. "Your forms, please."

I handed over my papers reluctantly, watching helplessly as my Bibles were taken out of the bag one by one.

"Who are these Bibles for?"

My heart lurched. I heard Steve's voice: *What you say during questioning is between you and your conscience.* What should I say? I could not lie, but how could I answer honestly? I might be endangering the lives of others.

"*Lo siento, Señora*," I said hesitantly in Spanish. "*Español, Español.*"

"No English?" The supervisor looked angry. "No English?"

I pulled out my Colombian passport. "*Spanish, Señora—Spanish...Español.*"

She threw my papers on the table. "Stay here!"

I closed my eyes. If they found an interpreter, I was in trouble.

Several minutes later the supervisor came back scowling. She was alone. "Take her Bibles," she said roughly and walked out.

I was left alone with the guard. My Bibles were still stacked on the table, my bag lying empty beside them. I looked over at the guard. She was standing off to the side writing on one of my forms. She looked nice.

I watched her for a moment, then cleared my throat. "Excuse me," I said quietly in English. "Would you please give me some of those books back?"

Her head jerked up.

"They are my books," I said. "May I have some of them back?"

She was smiling now, amused, but shaking her head. "No, I'm sorry. You can't have any."

"Maybe just a few?" I suggested.

"No," she insisted out loud. But looking around to make sure we were alone, she took three Bibles from the stack, tucked them into the bottom of my bag and said, "Go."

I went. I carried my three little Bibles across the border to the meeting point, left them at the checkpoint, and returned to Hong Kong. Back at the hotel I locked the door to my room and collapsed in tears.

I had flown several thousand miles from New York, taken time off from work, and paid my own way. I had fasted and prayed for days that the Bibles would make it safely across the border into the hands of believers on the mainland. After all that, I had only carried three Bibles into China.

I cried for two days.

"Marta, it happens to everyone," Steve chided me. "Don't take it personally. You've got to leave the results in the Lord's hands."

Steve's wife was a little stronger. "Marta, don't question the Lord's methods. He used you to create the commotion needed to get the other Bibles through. You were the diversion! Everyone else around you got through."

I was too crushed to care. I curled up in my bed, crying.

Finally, late the second day, I felt the Lord speak to me in gentle rebuke. *"Marta, I am going to use you to do My work—but you have to learn to trust Me. Just like David used that small stone to kill the giant Goliath, I am going to use you. You are going to be that small stone in My hand."*

I sat up. Encouraged and strengthened, I went to find Steve. I was ready to go back in. This time I would leave the results to the Lord.

The next trip was scheduled for a different border, and our group leader reminded us of the procedure. "If someone gets caught, don't stop. Go through and wait on the other side. If the guards are watching, leave immediately. We'll meet you at the hotel. Jessica, you're first."

Jessica left—a natural New Yorker—mingling easily with the crowd. We all dispersed, walking quickly to different points in the customs building, brushing casually past each other.

I looked down at a small bag several feet away— Jessica's. It was full of Bibles. If someone found it, they might be able to trace it back to the ministry.

I picked up the bag and slung the strap over my shoulder. I struggled to walk normally, the heavy luggage dragging at my shoulder. I already had two bags of my own and was puffing by the time I reached the first checkpoint. I dropped the bags and picked up a pen to fill out the forms.

Suddenly, panic hit me.

They're going to get my Bibles, I thought frantically. *I can't go through this again!*

I saw a guard watching me and looked down quickly. A thin film of sweat coated my palms. *He knows something is wrong*, I thought. *He sees my hands shaking.* The pen slipped, and I looked up again. The guard was still watching me.

I looked down again, scribbling furiously on the paper.

"Please step this way, ma'am." The guard was reaching for my papers.

He had not noticed! I picked up my bags and moved toward the scanner. The guard moved away, and I took five steps toward the scanner, then stopped short. I felt a sudden, very distinct impression to move to my left. I looked around, confused. The feeling grew stronger.

I moved one step to my left and waited. No one stopped me. I took another step and waited. Still nothing. There was a corridor to the side, and it looked empty. Something said quietly, *"Go."*

I sidled past the guard, took a quick turn to the left, and walked rapidly down the corridor, looking straight ahead. It was a private corridor, and it was empty. Incredibly, no one stopped me.

Thank You, Jesus! I exulted. *Thank You!*

Then I saw him. Halfway down the corridor, a guard was watching me. Too late to turn back, I remembered the words of a famous Bible smuggler. "Lord," I prayed, "You have made blind eyes to see. Now make seeing eyes blind. Please don't let him see me."

He did see me, but he pointed to the exit door. The next moment I was out in the bright sunlight, dragging my bags behind me.

I glanced around slowly, casually, looking for the rest of the group. No one else was in sight. My heart sank. Had they all been caught? All I had was the name of a hotel in Canton. I saw Jessica standing alone just outside the customs building. "Jessica," I waved excitedly. "Jessica!"

She saw me and rushed over, relieved. "Marta! Where's everyone else?"

I looked around. "They must have been sent back to Hong Kong." I looked down at her empty hands. "Jessica…"

Her face fell. "They got them, Marta."

I held up her bag, smiling. "Not all of them."

She broke into a broad grin. "Marta! Where did you find that?"

"On the other side. I saw it after you left." I took a quick look around. There was still no sign of anyone else in our group. "Jessica," I said nervously, "maybe we should pray."

She nodded and we prayed together silently, our eyes wide open and our heads up. I had three bags of Bibles safely inside China, and no one was going to take them from me.

We boarded the bus to Canton, nervous but determined—we were not going back to Hong Kong until our Bibles were delivered.

Once, along the road, our bus was stopped. Armed guards peered in through the door of the bus but did not search us. The situation was almost ludicrous—two women, alone in China, with three bags packed full of Bibles. It was humorous, but I was not laughing. Tense, and afraid to talk, we bounced along the dusty roads avoiding the questioning glances of the other passengers.

The trip was long, and by the time we reached Canton it was night. Tired and thirsty, we stumbled out of the rickety bus.

"Jessica, remind me not to complain about New York City transportation," I groaned. I looked around. "Now what?"

We were stranded in the middle of downtown Canton. We did not know where we were. We did not know how to get to the hotel, and we did not speak any Chinese. "Let's pray again," I said.

Again we prayed with our eyes open and our heads up.

If we aren't careful, we could build a doctrine around this, I thought, amused. *Praying with our eyes open seems to work.*

"Send us someone who speaks English," I prayed, a tinge of desperation coloring my prayer. "It's getting dark, and we're alone in China. Please send someone to help us."

We looked around casually. A young Chinese man was walking toward us, smiling.

"Hello," he said in flawless English. "Do you need help?"

We looked at him incredulously. "You speak English?"

"I used to live in San Francisco."

"You're kidding!" We burst out laughing. How typical of Christians. We pray for something, and when the Lord actually answers, we are surprised.

Our new friend flagged down a taxi and gave careful instructions to the driver. An hour later we were at the hotel. I heaved a sigh of relief when the bags full of Bibles were safely transferred to the Chinese couriers. Within days, those

Bibles would be making their way through China to be placed into the hands of Chinese believers.

The trip to China was a lesson in trust for me. I had seen His hand and learned to listen for His voice. The Lord had kept His promise and made me a stone in His hand. *They had not gotten my Bibles!*

The trip back to the United States was uneventful, and we reached customs in Los Angeles without any problems. I gathered my bags and moved to the back of the line.

We would be home in several hours. The line moved, and I shuffled forward, slipping my passport out of my purse. The pages fell open, and I looked down at the foreign stamp showing an entry into China. A sudden thought struck me. I was Colombian, living in the Bronx, and coming back from China. It did not look good. I felt my lips begin to quiver. This was going to be interesting.

"May I see your passport please?" The customs official was holding out his hand.

I handed it over, looking apologetically toward Steve and the rest of the group standing on the other side of the partition. My Colombian passport had given me problems throughout the trip, and they had grown accustomed to waiting for me.

"Where are you coming from, Ms. Estrada?" The official was looking through my passport, his face impassive.

"Hong Kong."

"And where are you going?"

"The Bronx."

The muscles in his face did not move. "You're Colombian?"

"Yes."

He flipped through the passport, stopping briefly at the stamps showing entries into China. "Ms. Estrada..." He looked at another entry, his tone casual. "May I ask what you were doing in China?"

He had a right to be suspicious. I almost laughed myself. "Smuggling Bibles."

He looked up slowly. "Smuggling Bibles?"

"Yes."

The customs official turned and called another official. "Hey, Brannon, could you come here a minute?"

I looked over at the group. They were crowded around the partition, watching me. They were not talking.

"What?" Brannon took my passport, looking briefly at my face. "What's the problem here?"

"Ms. Estrada here is from Colombia."

"So?"

"She's coming from China."

Brannon suddenly looked interested. "Yes?"

"And she lives in the Bronx."

"I see."

Brannon turned several pages, stopping at the China entries before handing the passport back. His lips were twitching. "Ms. Estrada, what were you doing in China?"

He was going to laugh. I could see it in his eyes.

"Smuggling Bibles."

Brannon choked. "No! Really?" He turned to his colleague. "I think maybe we should search her bags."

"Yes, I think that would be a good idea," he agreed.

Brannon turned to me. "Ms. Estrada, we're going to have to ask you to open your bags. We'd like to take a look inside."

I shrugged, throwing a bemused glance at Steve and the rest of the group.

I dragged the bag toward me and pulled at the zipper. The sides of the bag were bulging, packed tight. The zipper did not budge. "I'm sorry," I apologized. "I guess I must have packed too much in this bag."

The two men exchanged amused glances.

I felt a chuckle building inside. They were going to be so disappointed. I tugged again. The zipper gave way abruptly, and my Bible came up through the opening.

Brannon leaned forward, startled. "Is that your Bible?"

"Yes."

"Oh."

He seemed speechless. I waited for them to say something.

"Do you want to look through the bag?" I asked kindly.

"Yes." Brannon nodded halfheartedly. "I guess we'd better." It was clear he had lost his enthusiasm.

"I really was smuggling Bibles," I said, smiling.

"We believe you." He closed the bag and nodded sheepishly at his colleague. "Go ahead. Let her through."

I rejoined Steve and the group, taking the good-natured ribbing with a smile. I thought back to the day in 1983 when undercover cops had pulled that bag of cocaine from the box. I thought back to the moment when they had led me to the car in handcuffs, people lining the streets, watching curiously. I remembered the pain I had caused my family and my daughter.

This time I was innocent. The feeling of freedom was exhilarating.

Chapter 27

Back in the Bronx, I continued visiting inmates and praying for the Mafia. Joy Fellowship picked up the burden for the Mafia and ran with it. My heart swelled with joy as I saw black and white, Hispanic and Asian Christians all praying for the salvation of Pablo Escobar and the Medellín cartel.

Pastor Hershey urged the congregation to pray. "God is placing a call on Pablo Escobar's life," he said. "Pray that the Lord will protect his life until he has a chance to hear the gospel and make a decision to serve Jesus Christ."

I continued ministering in the prisons, and as the burden for the Mafia spread, I began to receive letters from inmates across the state.

One day I received a letter from an inmate in a prison upstate. I read the name in the upper left-hand corner and felt my skin pucker with fear. Víctor! How did he know where I was? Fearfully I opened the letter.

"Marta, I miss you," he wrote. "I want to see you. Please come and visit me."

I pushed the letter away. Mama would not be happy to know I had heard from him. "Mama, Víctor wants me to visit him," I said cautiously.

"Víctor?" Her face sagged.

"Yes, he sent a letter."

"What does he want?"

"I don't know. He says he wants me to visit."

"Where is he?"

"Upstate."

"Don't do it, Marta," she said pleadingly. "He's dangerous."

"I know, Mama." Even now I could feel the subtle tug of his personality. "I don't trust him either, but he sounds different. Maybe he needs help."

She looked at me helplessly. "Marta, not again. Please."

She was right. I was not ready to face him yet. Instead, I wrote a long letter telling him about my experience in Rikers Island. I included several tracts explaining how to be born again then sealed the envelope, hoping it was over.

Several weeks later I got a letter back in the mail. "Marta," Víctor wrote, "Guess what? I'm a Christian too. I received Jesus Christ as my Savior. I'm serving the Lord and helping the chaplain here."

I reached for the table lamp, flipping the switch on to see better.

"Jesus came into my life," he wrote. "I'm a Christian. I'm doing very well. Come and visit me. We have so much to talk about."

I sat back, staring at the scrawling signature. Was it possible? Víctor—a Christian? I put the letter down. If he really had accepted Jesus Christ, he would be a different person.

"Mama," I said cautiously, "what would you say if I told you I was going to visit Víctor?"

Her eyes flew open. "Marta, you're crazy."

I pointed to the letter. "He says he's born again."

"He…" she looked at me incredulously. "Is he?"

"I don't know," I said. "That's what I want to go and find out."

"Well, can't you just write and ask him?" she asked.

I raised my eyebrows sardonically.

"Alright, so he lies," she conceded, "but maybe he's telling the truth this time. Maybe he did accept the Lord."

"Maybe, but I won't know until I see his face, Mama."

She lifted her hands, then let them fall in concession. "Do what you have to do." Her eyes were worried. "Just be careful."

I asked my probation officer for permission to visit, and the following week I took the four-hour trip upstate. It was a long trip, and I could feel the dread in my stomach. I shook myself, fighting the sense of control. This was ridiculous. Why was I still afraid of him?

In the visiting room I waited anxiously, my hands clenched behind my back, my feet tapping nervously. I heard Víctor's voice behind me and turned, my eyes jumping to meet his. He looked older and thinner than I remembered. The washed-out prison clothing did little to hide the weight loss. His hands were held out in welcome, his mouth curved in a welcoming smile. I looked at him, remembering the pouting lips, the dangerous, still-charming smile.

"Look at his eyes," Mama had told me. "They'll tell you the truth."

He moved close to me, his body brushing mine. "Marta, how are you?"

I stepped back, repulsed. "I'm fine."

"How's Lina?"

"Fine…"

I had always been able to judge Víctor's moods by his eyes. Now they were cold and strangely flat. I fought down the disappointment. He had lied.

He looked at my Bible. "Oh, Marta, I'm doing some work with the Bible too. I'm helping the chaplain here in the prison."

"Yes, I know. You told me that in your letter." I sat down, deciding to force the issue. "Víctor, tell me—how did you receive Jesus Christ?"

An uneasy look came into his eyes. "I…He came into my heart."

"When?"

"I …" He looked nervous, his eyes shifting. "Well…"

He moved away, and I smelled nicotine on his breath. "Víctor, are you still smoking?" I asked quietly.

192 / *To the Mafia With Love*

"Of course not," he said indignantly. "I'm a Christian. I don't smoke."

A middle-aged man was walking toward us. He called Víctor's name and we both turned. "Hello, Víctor," he said. "I don't want to interrupt your visit..." He looked at me apologetically. "I just wanted to congratulate you on your party yesterday. It was wonderful. Your mariachi friends played wonderfully."

"Thank you, Father George." Víctor looked away, avoiding my eyes.

"Not at all. Thank you. Hope you do it again real soon."

I watched Father George walk away. "Víctor, you didn't tell me about this party."

"There was nothing to tell," he snapped.

I watched him curiously. Why was he so nervous? "Víctor, what are you trying to hide from me?"

"Nothing—what would I be trying to hide?" he asked defensively.

"I don't know—why don't you want to talk about the party? Are you ashamed of it?"

"Of course not!" he said angrily. "I'm not ashamed of it. It's just not worth talking about."

I looked at him calculatingly. What had gone on at that party to make him so reluctant to talk? Which one of his women had been at this party? "Víctor, you're still the same person you always were," I sighed. "You haven't changed."

"So? What about it?"

"Have you seen a change in your life since you accepted Jesus?" I asked suddenly.

"What do you mean—change?" he asked suspiciously.

"Have you changed? Are you different?"

"No, of course not!" he said irritably. "Why would I be different? I'm the same person you used to know."

"Víctor, when Jesus comes into our lives, we won't do the things we used to do; we won't say the things we used to say. If there hasn't been a change in your life, something is wrong."

"Yes, I've changed," he said.

"How?"

He was sweating now.

"How, Víctor?" I repeated.

His eyes shifted. "What is this, an interrogation?"

"Víctor, God is not a fool. You can lie to me, but you cannot lie to Him." I turned away and gathered my things. "It's over between us. Please don't write to me anymore."

I left, but back in New York the letters continued. Now they were threatening. "Marta, I want my money. You stole that money from me. If you don't give it back to me, I'm going to reopen your case."

Reopen my case! My mind spun. Could he do that? In his court statement, Víctor had admitted I had nothing to do with his drug deals. If he changed his statement, would it affect my case? Could they send me back to prison?

"Mama," I said softly, "Víctor's threatening me about the money again."

"Ignore him," she snorted.

"I can't."

"Why not?"

"He says he's going to reopen my case."

She went white. "Marta—can he?"

"I don't know," I admitted. I was frightened now. If Víctor changed his testimony and lied, what would that do to my case?

The next day, I placed a panicky call to Mr. Maxwell. "Mr. Maxwell," I said, "I need help."

"Why?" His voice sharpened. "What's the matter?"

"It's Víctor—he's threatening to reopen my case and testify against me."

Maxwell expelled his breath sharply. "Víctor doesn't know what he's talking about." He sounded a little impatient. "Víctor can't reopen your case, Marta. Tell him to forget it. Your case is closed."

Relieved, I put Víctor's letters in the garbage.

One night, several months later, the bell in my apartment rang. I looked at my watch, then at the guests in my living room. It was too late to be someone else for the prayer meeting. Had I forgotten someone? I slipped out to the kitchen and pushed the intercom. "Yes? Who is it?"

There was a pause, then I heard Víctor's voice, low and disguised. "Open the door, Marta. It's Nacho."

"Víctor!" I gasped silently. What was he doing here? I flew back to the living room. "Listen to me, everyone," I said panting. "It's him—Víctor. He's out of prison. Don't leave me alone with him—please. Don't anyone leave this house until he leaves."

Eyes lit up around the circle. "Leave? Are you kidding? We've always wanted to see this guy."

Víctor was knocking on the door.

"Coming!" I called breathlessly. I walked down the hall and peered through the eye hole. I saw Víctor's face staring back at me and shuddered. Unlocking the door, I pulled it open. "Hello, Víctor," I said coolly. "Would you like to come in?"

He looked a little embarrassed. "Yes, thank you." He followed me unsuspectingly to the living room. "I want to talk to you."

He stepped into the living room, then took a step backward, his eyes smoldering.

"Why don't you have a seat," I said generously. "We're just getting ready to start a prayer meeting."

Víctor sat down on the edge of the sofa, his hands on his knees. His eyes were burning. The meeting was long, and I watched him squirm uncomfortably in his seat. Several times he looked over at me, his eyes locking on mine. I looked away, praying. Would he force a fight in front of everyone?

Finally, I brought the meeting to a close. Careful to follow instructions, no one left. I looked around the circle, trying not to laugh. All eyes were set, flinty in their determination.

"Coffee anyone?" I asked.

There were nods all around. "Yes, please."

They're going to need it, I thought, grinning to myself. They looked determined to stay all night. Still chuckling, I got up and went to the kitchen.

I heard Víctor behind me and turned quickly. "What do you want, Víctor?"

His eyes were bright, feverish. "I want my money."

"Your money!" I repeated, stalling for time.

"Yes, my money. Give it to me, now." He spread his arms, blocking me in.

Out of the corner of my eye I saw someone leaving to get help. Pastor and Mrs. Hershey lived in the same building. Pastor Hershey would be upstairs in minutes.

I bit my lip nervously. Would Víctor be foolish enough to try something? "Víctor, I told you before, I don't have your money. It went to pay your legal fees and my legal fees."

A vein swelled on the side of his neck. "You were guilty, Marta. You had friends who were involved with drugs. You know you were guilty. I'm going to reopen your case, and I'm going to testify against you."

"You can't, Víctor. You know I had nothing to do with your deals."

"You were with me."

"So?" I whispered. "I was not selling with you." I was close to panic.

Víctor's face was thrust close to mine, his eyes dark with barely controlled anger. "Marta, give me my money!"

"I don't have it," I said desperately. "Leave me alone, Víctor. You destroyed my record. You're the one who put me in jail."

Víctor's hands moved down, pinning me against the wall.

"Excuse me…what's going on here?"

I whirled. Pastor Hershey was standing in the doorway. Tearfully, I flew to his side.

"What's going on, Marta?" His blue eyes looked ready to skewer Víctor to the wall.

"Víctor wants his money, but I don't have it anymore."

"Where is it?"

"It went to pay for our lawyers and to repay the mortgage on my parents' house in Colombia."

Pastor Hershey turned toward Víctor. "Víctor, Marta doesn't owe you any money. You're the one who put her in jail. Besides, that money was made illegally. Forget about it. Start over and earn your money honestly."

Víctor was backing up, looking at me menacingly. "Marta, are you going to report this?"

If I reported him, the courts would take away his prison leave privileges. "Just leave, Víctor," I said wearily.

"Are you?"

I did not answer.

He turned and left.

That night I could not sleep. Víctor's sudden visit had brought back memories: the inexplicable control, the fear and depression, the anger and violence of our fights. I thought back to the days immediately following my arrest. I was in shock, I was suicidal, but I had actually smiled when I saw the walls and wires of Rikers Island around me. Those wires and bars were a protection against Víctor.

Puzzled, I sat up in bed. What was wrong with me? Why was I so afraid of him? Even after I accepted the Lord, Víctor had remained a threatening presence. The old memories pressed in again, the feeling of dread rising.

The next morning the bell rang at seven o'clock. It was Víctor. I punched the intercom button ferociously. "Go away, Víctor, or I'm calling Pastor Hershey."

"Pastor?" Víctor sneered. His voice sounded distorted through the intercom. "He isn't your pastor. He's an undercover cop. You're just trying to set me up."

It was useless to argue. I went to the phone and called Pastor Hershey. When he went outside, Víctor was gone.

I went into the living room and sat on the couch. In that moment I realized that Víctor was frightened by the changes he saw in my life. He was frustrated by the peace he saw in my eyes. My emotions were no longer his to manipulate. The threats and intimidation might continue, but Víctor's control over me had been broken and replaced by the power of Jesus Christ.

After years of fear and control, I realized it was finally over. I never had to be afraid of Víctor again.

I leaned my head on my hand and cried.

Chapter 28

July 1987—Medellín, Colombia

I gazed out the airplane window and felt my heart quicken. Colombia! How many years had it been? My friends had not seen me since before my arrest in 1983. They would have so many questions. Would they see a difference in me? The Lord had changed me in so many ways.

Roberto! I felt a touch of shame. I had never given him up completely.

I looked out through the thick glass as the plane touched down gently on the runway. I had called Papa from the States. His response to my call from New York had been cool. Would he want to see me now that I was back in Colombia?

The plane taxied to a stop and eased into the gate, passengers stretching and pulling luggage from the rack.

Outwardly, Medellín appeared the same. Small children played barefooted in the streets. A soft breeze rustled through the trees, the mid-afternoon heat drying the morning dampness.

The city seemed peaceful on the surface, but something was different. Undercurrents of hostility throbbed beneath a civil exterior, dark undertones of fear shading the eyes of Colombian citizens. Even the air felt thick with danger.

Television stations in New York had been carrying reports of clashes between the Mafia and the government. There were signs that Colombia was in the initial stages of a full-blown drug war.

The Mafia was beginning to dominate the evening news, and Pablo Escobar's name was appearing more and more frequently in the reports.

While the prison ministry continued to grow in New York, the Colombian cartels remained unreachable. Brief attempts to pierce the security surrounding the cartels had been unsuccessful. The leaders, especially, were hard to reach. Protected by bodyguards and living on private estates, they remained unapproachable. Three and a half years after the vision, I was no closer to an answer than before. It was disturbing.

My visit to Colombia was for a sad occasion. I was still on probation, but Judge Phillips had given me permission to return briefly to attend my cousin's *novena*. John—fun-loving, outgoing—shot in a quarrel over a woman. He had fought for his life for months, but the injuries were too severe. He had died several days ago.

The sounds of the old *barrio* burst on my senses. I breathed in deeply, loving the warm, sweet air and the sounds of spring so peculiar to Medellín. It was good to be home.

Papa's greeting at the door was cool. The smell of cigarette smoke was strong in the house, and Papa eyed me warily, but I did not comment. I was preoccupied. Roberto lived just two blocks away.

I unpacked, washed, and sat thinking for a moment. I had permission to be here. I was not breaking any law—but would the Lord approve? Was Roberto part of His plan? I left a message at Roberto's home and spent a sleepless night worrying. What if he did not return my call?

The next day, the phone rang.

"Marta! When did you get in?" Roberto's voice was warm.

"Yesterday afternoon." My pulse was racing. "I'm at Papa's house."

"May I come and visit?"

I nodded, too excited to speak.

"Marta?"

"Yes, of course. Please. Come anytime."

"How about three o'clock?"

"Three o'clock would be fine."

I dressed carefully for his visit, deciding on a black jumpsuit and pink turtleneck. Was I too old for him? I looked anxiously in the mirror, smoothing the wrinkles around my eyes. Would he still be interested? What if he was still seeing another woman? I wandered around the house, straightening furniture, whisking dust from window sills.

The waiting stretched interminably, and I looked out the window. He had said three o'clock. Maybe he had forgotten—maybe he did not want to come.

I heard a knock on the door and jumped up. I took a quick look in the mirror. My face was flushed and warm. I touched my face with trembling fingers, practicing a composed look. No use. My eyes were anything but composed.

There was another knock on the door.

"Coming!" I called. I pulled a brush through my hair, patting loose curls into place and taking another look in the mirror. It would have to do. I peered through the window. It was Roberto, as young and handsome as I remembered.

I opened the door and held out a hand. "Roberto!"

He ignored my hand and kissed me on the cheek, looking down at me. "Marta, you look very elegant."

"Thank you. And you look...You are...It's good to see you." Flustered, I ushered him into the living room.

We sat there looking at each other.

He spoke first. "You look well."

"Thank you."

"You look happy."

"I am."

"Marta..." He paused, a curious look in his eye. "There's something different about you. Did something happen to you in New York?"

I felt a flush of joy. He had noticed! I leaned forward eagerly. "Yes, it's Jesus. I met Him when I was in jail."

"Jesus Christ?"

I saw the look of interest in his eyes and started from the beginning. We sat and talked late into the afternoon. The sun cast deepening shadows across the living room floor, and Roberto's eyes became absorbed. I felt the tug of physical attraction and kept my hand on my Bible.

That night, Roberto was the only thing on my mind. I paced the floor in my room, praying, grappling with my emotions. How could I justify a relationship with a man who did not know Jesus Christ, the most important person in my life? How could I fall in love with a man who did not share my burden for the Mafia?

The next morning I wandered around the house, waiting. Roberto had promised to call. I stayed near the phone, willing it to ring. My peace was gone, and I felt oppressed at the thought of waiting for him to call—but I was stubborn.

Finally, the phone rang. I snatched it up on the first ring.

"Hello?" I said breathlessly.

"Ms. Estrada, this is Reverend Rodríguez."

Disappointment was sharp. "Yes?"

"We're having a Bible study at three o'clock this afternoon. Would you come and testify?"

"A Bible study?"

"Yes, at three o'clock."

If I accepted, I would miss Roberto's call. If I missed his call, I might not be able to see him again before I returned to New York.

"Yes," I agreed reluctantly. "I'll come."

I hung up the phone. Several times I picked up the phone to cancel the appointment; each time, I placed it back on the hook. I stood there baffled. Something was wrong. The peace I knew so well was gone. Was I trying to force something that was not in God's plan?

I went to my room and shut the door. A feeling of grief swept through me, and I knelt on the floor, burying my head in my hands. It was a struggle I had never completely given to the Lord. The Lord had called me to reach the Mafia—and still I held to my hopes for this relationship. Was Roberto that important to me? Was he so important that I would once again compromise the call the Lord had placed on my life? The knot in my stomach twisted.

"Take him from me," I pleaded. "Take him from my mind. I can't do it on my own."

I became keenly aware of the Lord's presence and knew I would have to end the relationship. I loved Roberto, but I loved the Lord more.

I got up, washed my face, and left the house for the Bible study.

The next day was difficult. The grief of John's death was compounded by a strong sense of loss over Roberto. I tried not to think about him, but his face slipped across my mind often.

Over the next several days I began holding Bible studies in my home. Friends and relatives came to the studies, and lives were committed to Christ. I saw the change in their eyes and felt the familiar joy bubbling inside again.

One afternoon as I sat preparing for the Bible study, I heard a knock on the door. I looked at my watch. It was too early to be someone coming for the Bible study. Maybe it was Pastor Rodríguez coming early to pray.

I walked to the window, lifted the curtain, then dropped it. *Roberto!* What was he doing here? I rushed to the door and pulled it open.

"Hello, Marta." Roberto's eyes were warm.

"What…what are you doing here?" I stuttered.

"I came for the Bible study."

"The Bible study?" I stood there, stunned.

"Aren't you having a Bible study here today?" he asked gently.

"Yes…yes, of course," I said "Come in."

That afternoon, Roberto came race to face with the Lord. I watched with tears in my eyes as he prayed to receive Jesus Christ. In obedience, I had given Roberto to the Lord—in love the Lord had given him back.

Now I discovered something I had not expected: Suddenly, inexplicably, I found that I had lost interest in

Roberto. With my own ambitions safely out of the way, I was able to see Roberto through different eyes. Suddenly, I knew he was not for me. Smiling, I closed the chapter on this part of my life. When I left Colombia this time, it would be without regrets.

* * *

With Roberto safely out of the way, there remained just one more relationship that needed the intervention of the Lord—Papa.

Papa was still angry with me. He never spoke to me unless absolutely necessary and remained cool and reserved toward me. He sat on the sidelines and watched as the house filled up for the daily Bible studies. He did not speak to me, but his watching eyes unnerved me.

Marta, you're a hypocrite, I told myself. *How can you stand up here preaching about God's forgiveness when you can't even forgive your own father?* I knew I had to forgive him but could not. Papa's treatment of me in New York still rankled.

Friends insisted he was proud of me. "He sees a difference in you," a friend told me one day.

"Why do...how do you know that?"

"He said so."

"He said what?"

" 'Marta really has changed.' "

The words made me thoughtful. "He said that?"

"Yes. He used to see this house full of people partying and drinking. Now he sees it full of people studying the Bible. He sees the change."

I groaned. How could I refuse to forgive my earthly father when my heavenly Father had forgiven me so many times? "Jesus, help me," I cried. "Please heal this bitterness. Help me to forgive him."

Just before I returned to the States, I sat and visited with my father. In a time of healing and forgiveness, I led Papa to the Lord. God took years of anger and resentment, turned them around, and brought life and forgiveness.

Several days later I was ready to return to the States. Papa promised to open the house every week for Bible studies and promised to write. With a heart lightened by God's forgiveness, I prayed with Papa, kissed him good-bye, and waved to him as the taxi pulled away from the house.

Six weeks later Papa was dead.

Chapter 29

September 1988—Medellín, Colombia

The walk up the prison driveway was difficult. Unseasonable rain had made the unpaved road a muddy battlefield for my thin shoes. The bleak gray walls, barbed wire, and dark steel of the Colombian prison loomed ahead, an unlikely goal for our small group.

The bus driver, seeing the prison surrounded by military police, had dropped us off at the foot of the road leading to the prison, refusing to take us any closer. My four friends from America seemed unnerved, looking over their shoulders at the disappearing bus.

I walked ahead to avoid their nervous chatter, my feet slipping on the soggy ground. I thought back a year ago to my father's funeral.

I had received the news of his death in shock. Papa...I had just been with him. What if I had not spoken to him about his relationship with Jesus Christ? What if I had held onto my pride and refused to forgive him? My fingers shook at the thought.

I had flown back to Medellín for Papa's funeral. During the funeral service, I had preached and given my testimony, holding back tears of gratitude. The Lord had restored our relationship—just weeks before Papa died.

Many came to the Lord as a result of my father's new life in Jesus, and by the time I returned to the United States, a small church had been established.

Now I was back in Colombia for a two-week visit. The courts had granted me an early release from probation, and I was in Medellín making final arrangements for my return.

I wiped rain from my face and looked ahead at the prison. Pastor Omar, the Colombian pastor who had invited us, led the way, his broad back pushing stolidly ahead.

I could not ignore the pounding of my heart. The pounding grew louder as each step brought us closer to the imposing structure.

I saw dark smoke moving slowly across the drenched sky, crowds of people swarming around the military checkpoint, blocking the entrance to the prison. The military presence was unusual. Armed guards stalked the front of the prison, machine guns slanted, rounds of ammunition slung over their shoulders.

We stopped at the checkpoint, easing our way to the front of the crowd. Family members of inmates were milling around, asking questions of harried-looking guards.

Pastor Omar beckoned one of the guards. "*Señor, perdón*, what's happening?"

The guard looked at my American friends and scowled, waving us back. "There's been a fire. No one will be allowed in today. Please stand back."

"Sir, excuse me," Pastor Omar said apologetically, "my friends have come a long way to visit. Couldn't we possibly have just a few minutes to meet with some of the men inside?"

"No, I'm sorry," the guard said, turning his back. "It's too dangerous."

Pastor Omar was persistent. "Would you allow us to speak to the director to get permission?"

The guard turned back impatiently. "Sir, please try to understand. The inmates just had a riot. It's very dangerous inside; you could be harmed."

I glanced at the dark clouds of smoke hanging over the prison and thought of the men inside. "Lord, you've brought us so far," I prayed out loud. "Please don't let them turn us back now."

"No, no, that's okay," my American friends insisted. "Really, we don't mind. We can just go home." They laughed nervously, eyeing the machine guns. "We can come back some other time."

Attracted by the commotion, an officer walked over casually. "Is there a problem here?" he asked.

The soldier snapped to attention. "No, sir!"

"Then what's the holdup?"

"These people want to visit with some of the men."

The officer looked us over curiously. "For what?"

I could see his point. Why would anyone voluntarily ask to visit a prison during a riot?

"They want to preach and pray with the men."

"I see." The officer turned crisply on his heel, nodding at the soldier. "Go ahead, then. Let them in."

A thrill slid down my spine. We were in!

We walked through the checkpoint alone, passing the crowds of people waiting in front of the prison, then walked through the front gate. With few windows, tiny exercise courtyards, and cold steel and concrete on every side, how could more than 3,500 inmates possibly be incarcerated here?

I realized suddenly how vulnerable we were to attack. With an average of three murders a week among the inmates, conditions were volatile. What if one of the inmates chose to make a statement by killing an American?

"Father," I prayed. "Please keep us in Your hand. You are the only one who can protect us." My heart was pounding again, but I realized that it was from excitement, not fear.

We stopped at an iron gate dividing the administrative area from the recreation area and followed Pastor Omar upstairs to the chapel. It was a pleasant room where we could talk and pray for a few minutes. Everyone seemed to relax.

"No one will be allowed to come to chapel today because of the riot," Pastor Omar said.

"Oh, too bad," my friends smiled happily.

"So why don't we go to *La Guayana* instead?"

"*La Guayana*?" My friends shifted nervously. "What's that?"

"Maximum security, where they hold the most dangerous inmates."

One of my friends stood up, muttering darkly under his breath. I thought I heard him say something about life insurance. "Did you say something, Bart?" I asked solicitously.

Bart shook his head morosely, and we all chuckled, feeling the tension.

Pastor Omar continued. "They won't give us much time, but we should be able to talk to some of the men. Let's get started."

We followed him upstairs, filing one by one through a dark, narrow passageway, emerging at the end of the corridor into a small area patrolled by a single guard. The guard held up a hand, barring the way.

"*Pare*! Hold it!"

I hid a smile. Where did he think we were going in a maximum-security facility?

"Why are you here?"

"We've come to visit and pray with the men," Pastor Omar said.

"You have permission?"

I swallowed another chuckle. How did he think we got this far?

"Yes," Pastor Omar said patiently, "we do."

The guard nodded briefly. "Okay, just be careful. It's dangerous. I'll let you in one section at a time. You'll have fifteen minutes. Stand back, please."

He unlocked the gate. We filed past slowly, crowding each other into the narrow, dimly lit corridor. I looked around at the steel gates facing us on four sides. Beyond each gate was a row of cells with a cement wall at the end.

The guard closed the gate behind us and turned the key in the lock. Bart's eyes followed the guard's actions, his eyebrows inching up his forehead.

"Don't worry," I whispered, pulling him toward the first cell. "The Lord is protecting us."

I stopped in disbelief at the first cell. Barely enough space for one, this cell housed four men. Some of the men wore nothing but a pair of trousers. Others, with help from family members, had a blanket or mattress to lay on the concrete. There were no toilets, only plastic jars and newspapers set in the corners. The smell was thick and nauseating.

We moved from cell to cell, section by section, greeting the men. Many of them seemed happy to see us; others withdrew, scowling. My eyes lingered on the younger faces. Some of them had been hitmen for the Mafia. For a few thousand pesos they would kill anyone marked by the cartels.

"Marta, why don't you give your testimony first?" Pastor Omar suggested.

I nodded silently, then cleared my throat.

Several men looked up, interested.

"Hello—my name is Marta Estrada," I started. "I'd like to take just a few minutes to tell you what Jesus Christ has done in my life."

Eyes shifted away, interest lost. Conversation resumed.

Undaunted, I continued. "Five years ago I was arrested in the United States on charges of drug trafficking and taken to Rikers Island jail in New York City. I was facing fifteen years to life on ten counts of felony for conspiracy, sale, and possession."

Eyes swung back, some surprised, others openly skeptical.

"In Rikers Island I did not care if I died. I hated the man who was responsible for putting me there, and I hated myself for allowing it to happen."

No one looked away.

"It was in Rikers Island that I met Jesus Christ." After five years, my throat still tightened with emotion. "He took the pieces of my life and put them back together. He gave me a new life and gave me a love for other people I never had before. I never thought I would be here today preaching the gospel, but He has sent us here to talk to you about the plan He has for your life. Jesus Christ changed my life—He can change yours."

I stepped back and looked for Pastor Omar. As Pastor

Omar invited the men to receive Jesus, I thought back to my brother, Carlo. Like these men, he had not wanted to listen. He had laughed at me and my "religion"—until he had hit bottom. Then, when his life was in danger, he had knelt on that bedroom floor and cried out for help.

Pastor Omar's invitation was simple and direct. To become a child of God we must first be born into God's family. To become a part of God's family, we must accept Jesus.

As hands went up around the complex, I thought of the Colombian Mafia. In an odd way these men seemed to represent the cartels. Regardless of what they had done, the Lord owned the rights to their souls. Regardless of what they had done, He was going to fight for them. Lovingly, tenderly, He was going to bring them to His feet.

Now it was just a matter of timing.

Several weeks later I returned to the United States.

The next time I returned to Colombia, it would be as a missionary to the Mafia.

Chapter 30

I returned to Colombia in March 1989 to pastor a growing church. Colombia was on the verge of a full-scale drug war, and the tension in the air was palpable. Medellín was a powder keg waiting to go off.

Several weeks after I arrived in Colombia, the powder keg exploded. The newscaster's face was grim as he read the news. "The Colombian government has announced that it will begin extradition of cartel members to face drug charges in the U.S."

Extradition—the thing the Mafia feared most. "That's it!" I said. "It's over. Medellín's going to explode."

And explode it did—violently, viciously. Medellín became a war zone. Mandatory curfews were imposed by the Colombian police. Army troops were ordered in to patrol the streets. Anyone out on the streets after ten o'clock at night was shot. Every night the city morgues were filled to capacity, an already overburdened police force taking up to six hours to respond to reports of a shooting.

The war rocked back and forth for much of 1989. Every night I watched the news and listened to the reports: "Mafia related—more bombings ordered by the cartels—killed by the Mafia."

The reports were brutal: government officials killed in cold blood, police cars rigged to explode, buses blown up in the streets.

Fear of the Mafia remained deep-rooted.

"Marta, did you hear?" a friend asked.

"What? Is it the Mafia?"

"Yes. Listen to this—they cut up two guys, put the pieces in a box and sent it to the mother with a note."

I swallowed the nausea. "What did the note say?"

"Sure you want to hear this?"

"Yes," I gulped. "What did it say?"

" 'We'll be watching you at the funeral. The first one to cry is the next one to die.' "

I stared at her in horror. "Dear Jesus..."

Every day the papers were filled with stories of brutality. Some of the reports were enough to make me physically sick, but through it all I heard the words in my mind: *"Bring them to Me, Marta. They belong to Me."*

The war raged on through 1989 and 1990.

Resentful of the United States' role in the extradition process, the Mafia began threatening to kidnap Americans in exchange for cartel members extradited to the States. The U.S. government asked Americans to leave Colombia, and American missions boards began calling their missionaries home.

Friends warned me to be careful. "Marta, tell your American friends not to come down here anymore. Escobar hates Americans. He could have them kidnapped."

"Escobar may hate Americans," I said, "but American churches have been praying for him for years. If my friends want to come, I can't keep them away."

Friends called and wrote often from the States, asking about Escobar and the cartels, but I did not have good news. Things were getting worse in Medellín.

I was struggling with the loneliness of the vision and experiencing some problems with the congregation. The church was growing, but there were problems, and I was forced to struggle through many difficult decisions alone.

I knew the Lord was preparing a church where Mafia

families could feel at home, but I wondered sometimes whether I would make it through to the end of my three-year commitment to the congregation. At night I threw myself across the bed in tears, weeping from pure exhaustion and frustration, the struggles with the congregation sapping my strength.

"Isn't there a pastor in Medellín who can pray with you and help you make decisions?" Pastor Hershey asked from New York. "You need to talk to someone who has experience in that area."

I knew he was right. I desperately needed the godly counsel and years of experience of the other pastors in Medellín. But I was so new here. Would they accept me? Missionary to the Mafia! Would the other pastors accept a woman with so bold a claim?

I felt suddenly alone and powerless. Fulfillment of the call seemed improbable, almost impossible. "Jesus, send me some pastors to help carry this burden," I prayed. "I need people to help me pray."

Several weeks later, Pastor Omar pulled me aside. "Marta, there's going to be a pastor's retreat in Medellín. There will be over two hundred pastors at the retreat. It's sponsored by two organizations, *Asociación de Ministros Evangélicos de Medellín* and *Cristo Para La Ciudad*. Would you like to come?"

Two hundred pastors in one place at one time? "Yes, of course!" I said. "I'd love to come."

Eagerly, I packed for the weekend. This was too much of a coincidence. The Lord must have set this one up.

The retreat was a refreshing time of fellowship, and my heart swelled to see so many pastors and leaders united in prayer for their city. One day, Medellín would feel the impact of those prayers.

For the next several days I soaked in the teachings and godly wisdom of the pastors, waiting eagerly for the opportunity to share. I kept my eyes open, waiting and praying for an opening, but as the days slipped by, I realized with a sinking heart that I had made a mistake. I had not anticipated the tight scheduling of the weekend. Every meeting was structured and well-planned, and there was little time for anything but the scheduled events.

The final night of the retreat I sat in the audience with a heavy heart. I looked down at my Bible, bitter disappointment welling up inside. How could I have missed the Lord's leading so completely? Blindly, I stared at the pages in front of me. I had been so sure.

"May I have your attention, please?"

The president of the organization was standing at the podium, going over the notes in his hand. He waited until the crowd quieted, then looked up.

"I know this isn't on the program tonight," he said, "but I think that now might be a good time to hear from some of you in the audience. Why don't we take the next fifteen minutes and hear what the Lord is doing in some of the ministries in Medellín?"

My heart started pounding so hard I thought it was going to punch a hole right through my chest.

The president looked around, then pointed to a pastor on my left. "Brother, let's hear from you."

I put my hand down slowly. The thought of American and Colombian churches united in prayer for the cartels made tears well up in my eyes. If these pastors caught the vision, the course of Colombian history could be changed forever.

The pastor on my left spoke briefly, then sat down. The president looked over in my direction inquiringly. "Did I see a hand over here somewhere?" he asked.

I waved my hand.

He looked at me and nodded, motioning for me to stand.

"Thank you," I said. I stood up, clutching my Bible with cold hands. "My name is Marta Estrada. I've only been pastoring for a short time, so I don't know very many people in Medellín, but I'm very happy to be here. I would like, first of all, to thank the Lord for the things He has done in my life. He has always been there, even when I have failed Him, even when I have disobeyed Him."

There were several sympathetic nods and a few understanding smiles.

"Six years ago, I was arrested for dealing drugs."

Several pastors turned around in their seats.

"I was searched and handcuffed and sent to Rikers Island jail in New York City to await sentencing. It was there in Rikers Island that I met Jesus Christ. Since that moment, my life has never been the same. He took the depression and fear, and made me a different person. He took the anger and bitterness, and gave me a new life."

I stopped and took a breath. As I looked around at the years of spiritual wisdom and sacrifice represented in that room, I could not control my emotion, and my voice started to tremble.

"There, in my cell on New Year's Eve, 1983, the Lord gave me a burden..."

Please, Jesus, let them see Your hand in this calling.

"...A burden to reach the Colombian Mafia for Jesus Christ."

The words seemed to hang in the air. Several people in the back stood up. Others leaned forward to see. In the sudden quiet, I said the words I had been waiting to say for five-and-a-half long years.

"Brothers and sisters, we know that the Colombian drug cartels will never be stopped by the police. We know that it isn't by military power, or by the might of the government that the Mafia will be stopped, but by the hand of the Lord. And when the Colombian Mafia turns to Jesus Christ, this country will be known, not for its drug trafficking or violence, but for the move of the Holy Spirit."

I sat down. It was not much, but it was all I had to say. I kept my head down, afraid to look up.

For a brief moment, there was complete silence. Then suddenly, they were applauding, those in the back standing on their feet, those in front nodding and smiling at me. I looked around at those dear Colombian pastors and felt my heart burst, fighting the tears, touched by their unspoken support.

After the service, the pastors crowded around, shaking my hand and hugging me. "You're very brave...God bless you...We don't know anyone else who has this burden... They need to be reached...God bless you."

The Mafia—hated by foreign governments, persecuted by their own country, forgotten by their countrymen, *but remembered by God's people!*

Chapter 31

The tension in the plane was discernible. Passengers glanced nervously through cabin windows as ground crews worked quickly to service the large plane resting on the tarmac. Thousands of gallons of fuel poured into the plane, the servicemen keeping a close eye on the gauges. Faces tensed as the plane doors were locked and sealed, the massive engines whining sluggishly to taxiing speed.

It was one week after the crash of a Colombian airplane in New York. In a tragic miscalculation, the plane had run out of fuel a mile and a half from Kennedy Airport, crashing and killing seventy-three people.

As this was the only international airline providing direct service between Medellín and New York, passengers on this flight were noticeably edgy.

The steward's voice crackled over the sound system. "Ladies and gentlemen, please fasten your seat belts in preparation for takeoff. Return all trays to the fastened and upright position."

The sounds of snapping seat belts clicked through the plane. I snapped my buckle in the clasp and settled back in my seat, excitement churning in my stomach. New York was just five hours away. Joy Fellowship was waiting to hear a full report on the work in Colombia; I knew they would not be disappointed.

"Marta, get up and tell these people about Me."

I put my head down. The pressure in my heart was familiar, and I groaned inwardly. "Preach on a plane?" I protested. "I can't do that. What would I say?"

"I'll give you the words."

"But what if they won't let me?"

"I'll take care of it."

I put my head down. This was going to be embarrassing, but I would have to trust Him.

I leaned forward and beckoned to an attendant. "Ma'am, excuse me. Do you think it would be possible for me to speak to the captain for a minute?"

"About what?" She sounded annoyed.

"I'd like to ask his permission to pray for a safe flight."

A tinge of red crept up to her hairline. "Pray? Here on the plane?" She looked around the cabin. "We've never had anyone pray on the plane before."

"Well, to be honest with you, I've never prayed on a plane myself," I said smiling.

She paused, a reluctant smile tugging at her mouth. "Well, I guess we could all use a little prayer right now. Wait here. I'll ask the captain."

She was gone for several minutes, then came back, nodding her head in friendly assent. "The captain says it's okay. I'll give you a few minutes after the emergency procedures."

Flight attendants took the passengers through the standard emergency procedures, noting the emergency exits and demonstrating proper use of the oxygen masks. Passengers were unusually attentive during the demonstration, and I noted wryly that the Lord had picked a good time to have me pray.

The explanations seemed to be taking longer than usual, but finally the attendant motioned for me to stand. I stepped out in the aisle, smoothing wet palms on my skirt. Rows of faces stared back at me.

My knees started to quiver.

"I know that we're all a little frightened by what happened last week," I started tentatively.

The faces looked back at me blankly.

"And I know that many of you are worried about this flight."

Still nothing.

I swallowed and continued. "Today I want to remind you that our lives are in the hands of God—He is the one who protects us. I want to pray for protection for everyone on this flight; but before I do, I'd like to say something."

I hoped I had heard the Lord correctly. If not, I was going to remember this as one of the more embarrassing moments in my life.

"Some of you on this plane right now are carrying drugs."

The attendants stood frozen. No one moved.

The passengers appeared immobile, carved in stone, staring at me.

"Six years ago, I was arrested in New York City and taken to jail. I was fingerprinted and photographed and given a number. I became just another criminal, another statistic in the system."

Several young men turned to stare through the plane window, but the strain in their shoulders and the tilt of their heads showed they were listening closely.

"I have never stopped regretting the actions that led me to that moment. Because of drugs, I now have a criminal record. I cannot erase what happened to me. I cannot change what I did—but you still have time. If you have drugs on you, get rid of them. Stop what you are doing before it is too late. Stop shaming your country and stop shaming your family. Change your lives and repent before Jesus Christ."

I prayed briefly for protection, then sat down. There was complete silence in the plane. The gentle whirring of the air conditioning filled the silence. The person in the seat next to me shifted to look at me. I kept my eyes fixed on the seat in front of me.

I heard a stirring in the aisle and looked up.

Several people were leaning over my seat. "Excuse me—do you work in the prisons in the U.S.?"

"Yes."

"Do you visit people in jail?"

"Yes, of course," I smiled.

A woman leaned over, holding out a slip of paper with a name and address written on it. "Would you visit my son?"

I nodded wordlessly, taking the slip of paper from her hand. Others were handing me pieces of paper. "Would you visit my brother?...My sister is in jail; would you visit her?...My grandson..."

Throughout the flight, passengers came to give me names of children, brothers, sisters in American prisons. I sat back, overwhelmed by the beauty of God's plan. Was this the beginning of an international ministry to the Colombian Mafia and their families? Was this His plan?

It had to be. In one act of simple obedience the Lord had laid the groundwork for a ministry that would set in motion the call placed on my heart six years ago.

My eyes filled as I traced the simplicity of His plan. Everything was in His timing.

"Soon, Marta. Soon it will be time."

Chapter 32

The trip to New York had ended in excitement. Contacts were made in the prisons, and many of the young mafiosos received Jesus Christ. When I returned to Colombia, it was with a full heart and a notepad full of names and addresses.

Back in Medellín, things were heating up for the Mafia. Clashes between the government and the cartels were intensifying. In the dramatic crackdown the government began seizing the property of cartel leaders. Network news features showed confiscated property of the drug lords—gold faucets, marble floors, lavish decorations, impeccable grounds.

Pablo Escobar's estate was one of the properties confiscated. I felt a twinge of anxiety. What if he disappeared completely? This action could only drive him further underground. "Put him somewhere safe," I pleaded. "Protect his life until someone can tell him about You."

As the cartel leaders and their families went underground, I felt the pressure of the burden growing. One night, I felt a strong and distinct impression to write a letter to Escobar.

A letter? I laughed out loud. Escobar was the target of one of the most extensive manhunts in history. His was the most famous, the most recognized face in Colombia. The Colombian and U.S. governments, the police, and the army were all searching for him.

He's in hiding, I reasoned. *He'd never get it.*

The impression persisted.

But why? I protested. *I have no way of delivering it.*

The feeling grew stronger.

Resignedly, I took out a pen and paper and sat down. *Lord, if this is Your plan, You're going to have to find a way to deliver the letter.*

I pulled my seat up to the desk and started writing. As I wrote, the words seemed to flow onto the paper. The concern I felt seemed to come from the Lord. I finished the letter, signed it, and laid it on the desk.

A week later I felt impressed to write another letter. Again, the words came—quickly, easily. When I finished, I folded it and laid it next to the other one. "Now it's up to You," I said. "You're going to have to make the way."

He did. The following afternoon I sat in my living room visiting with a friend from another church. She looked up at me with a satisfied smile. "Marta, I have something to tell you," she said.

"Yes? What is it?"

She leaned toward me. "There's a lady living with me whose husband used to work for Pablo Escobar."

I looked up, startled. "Pablo Escobar?"

She nodded. "I thought you might find it interesting. I know you've been praying for him."

My eyes were fixed on her face, my mind spinning. "Maritza," I said slowly, "can I ask you a question?"

"Of course," she said. "What is it?"

"Do you think your friend would be willing to do me a favor?"

"What kind of favor?" She looked a little anxious.

"Deliver two letters to Pablo Escobar."

"Pablo Escobar?" Her eyes went wide.

"Yes, Maritza," I grabbed her hand excitedly. "I've been praying for a way to get the letters to him but couldn't think of anything. Do you think your friend would do it?"

I knew my eyes were shining.

"I don't know," she said doubtfully. "I suppose I could ask her."

"Will you bring her to visit me?"

"I can try." She smiled reassuringly. "I'm sure she'll come. I'll bring her tomorrow."

That night I could not sleep. The answer, coming so soon after the second letter, seemed too much of a coincidence.

The next morning, I welcomed Maritza and her young friend into the living room.

Maritza turned to me. "Marta, this is Elena."

I shook Elena's hand warmly. "Elena, did Maritza tell you why I wanted to see you?"

"Yes." Her pretty face was thoughtful.

"Do you think it's possible?"

"I don't know," she said softly. "I can try. I know where his office is. I don't know if the letters will get to him, but at least they'll have a chance." She looked at me hesitantly. "Ms. Estrada…"

"Yes?"

"I need to ask you a favor."

"Of course," I said, "what is it?"

"Ruth Rasmussen…"

"Yes," I said cautiously. "What about her?"

"I'm having problems with my house," Elena said. "Do you think she would help me?"

Ruth Rasmussen and I had shared an apartment in New York years ago. When her niece married one of the most powerful men in the Mafia, Ruth had moved back to Colombia to be with her family.

"What do you need?" I asked Elena.

"Permission to build in the *barrio*."

"Escobar's *barrio*?"

"Yes; do you think your friend would help me?"

Mafia families were under constant government surveillance, and I had not wanted to involve Ruth in the delivery of the letters, but Elena's situation would require little more than a referral. She might be willing to help.

"I'll do what I can," I promised. "I'll call and ask if we

can come and see her. After we deliver the letters to Escobar's office, we'll go see Ruth. If you explain your situation, I'm sure she'll help you."

That afternoon I set up an appointment to see Ruth at a beauty parlor in El Poblado, then called Elena to let her know it had been arranged.

"Meet me at my house," I said. "We'll go together."

The next day, Elena met me at my house. We decided to make photocopies of the letters before we took them to Escobar's office, then go to the beauty parlor in time for our three o'clock meeting with Ruth.

I was sick with an infected throat, and my voice was gone, but I was burning with excitement. We made the photocopies and left the building. Outside it was pouring rain. I looked up at the dark clouds. The skies had been clear when we left the house, but now they were dark and angry. The wind was whipping my clothes around my legs, drops of rain stinging my face.

"Elena," I croaked, "I don't have an umbrella."

Elena peered at me with concern. "Marta, you don't look well. You're too sick to be out in this rain. Why don't you go home? I'll deliver the letters to the office myself."

"But what about our meeting with Ruth? You wanted to meet her."

"Don't worry," she said firmly. "We can always see her another day."

"You wouldn't mind?" I asked gratefully.

"No...go, we'll make another appointment this week."

"Thank you, Elena," I said. "I'll call Ruth tomorrow."

Suddenly exhausted, I struggled home and crawled into bed. My fever was high and I tossed in the bed, my body burning. I was sorry I had not gone with Elena, but I was too sick to get up.

Three o'clock came and went, and I slept fitfully. The rain was still beating on the windows, the room darkened. I was slowly drifting into sleep when I heard someone at the front door.

"Marta!" The banging was insistent. "Open the door. Hurry! Please!"

I dragged myself out of bed, wrapped a robe around my body and went to the door. "Who is it?" I asked.

"It's me—Elena. Open the door."

"Elena!" I unlocked the door and pulled her into the house. Her face was pale, her hands shaking. "Elena, what are you doing here?" I asked, alarmed. "What happened?"

"The letters..." she said. "I went to deliver them. It all started happening so quickly. Someone ran into the room and started yelling, 'They just killed Guillermo and Edwin at Rosie's Beauty Parlor.' "

I gasped. "Rosie's Beauty Parlor!"

"Yes—they started slamming and locking doors and closing everything up. They rushed me out and locked the doors. I didn't know what to do. I didn't want to stay, but I didn't want to leave until they promised to give the letters to Escobar."

"Elena!" I sat down suddenly. "Rosie's Beauty Parlor is where we were supposed to meet Ruth."

She stared at me, the color draining from her cheeks. "Rosie's Beauty Parlor?"

I nodded weakly.

Elena's eyes were fixed on my face. "Marta, they were shot at three o'clock."

"Three o'clock..." A shudder passed through me. "Elena, are you sure?"

"Yes, I'm sure. I didn't get to the office until three o'clock. It was 3:15 when everyone started rushing around. The guy said it had just happened."

"Elena," I said slowly, "do you know what that means?"

She nodded, her eyes wide. "We were supposed to be there when the shooting happened..."

"...and the Lord made it rain so we wouldn't go," I finished.

Shaking and crying, we hugged each other.

I flipped the television set on and got the first report. Three men had been shot and killed in Rosie's Beauty Parlor. It had happened at three o'clock that afternoon.

I felt tears coming to my eyes. The Lord had protected us, but others had died. He had protected us this time, but how long would it be before life was taken from someone close to me? The violence that had become a part of our lives was tearing at the fabric of Colombian society. How long would it be before it touched my own family?

Doubts fed my fears, fed my concern for my family and for the congregation. Was I really doing the Lord's will? Had the Lord really called me to reach the Mafia?

One afternoon I was coming back from a meeting in the city when I heard my name being called. I recognized the voice and turned. Juan was an old *barrio* friend. We had grown up together and been through many childish scrapes together. Since my return to Medellín, he had been watching me closely, but keeping his distance.

"Juan!" I greeted him warmly. "How are you?"

"I'm fine." He looked slightly nervous. He fiddled with his shirt collar, straightening it in the humid air. "Marta," he said finally, "I think you're doing a good thing here—preaching the gospel and helping people."

"Thank you," I said gratefully.

"And I'm glad you're here."

I smiled and waited.

"Marta," he said, "do you remember that big drug loss you had back in New York?"

"You mean when Víctor took the plane?"

"Yes."

"Of course I remember," I laughed. "It took us forever to pay it back."

Juan watched for my reaction. "Did you know they had a contract out on you?"

"A contract? You're kidding!" I said. "Who set it up?"

Juan's eyes widened. "Marta!"

"I'm sorry," I apologized. "I know you can't tell me." A quick thought crossed my mind. "Juan, do you know what this means?" He looked confused, and I answered my own question: "Jesus Christ protected me even when I didn't know Him."

Juan looked suddenly defensive. "I'm the one who protected you, Marta." He scuffed a foot against the curb. "I defended you when they put the hit out on you." He looked down at the sidewalk, suddenly embarrassed. "I did it because I believed in you."

Humbled, I took his hand. "Juan, that's beautiful. I'm glad you believed in me—but there's Someone else you need to believe in."

He backed away, suddenly wary. "Yes, Marta—maybe I'll come to your house sometime and you can pray for me."

Juan never did come to my house. Today, he stands in the back of the crowd during our street meetings and watches but does not come forward. He is afraid of the cartels.

With the question of protection settled, I turned to the other question that was troubling me. Was I really called to reach the Mafia? Or was I wasting valuable time pursuing a vision that would never be fulfilled? Would the cartels ever be reached? *Could* they be reached? It was a difficult question to ask. I had been in Medellín for one year now and still there was no sign that the Lord was ready to open any doors. Six and a half years since that night in Rikers Island—and still nothing.

One morning, at a Wednesday morning prayer meeting with the pastors from *Asociación de Ministros Evangélicos de Medellín*, I sat listening to the president of the organization. Since the pastor's retreat a year ago, Pastor Carrión had become a dear friend and adviser. I had come to respect him for his godly advice and sincere concern for others.

Toward the end of the meeting, Pastor Carrión stood to introduce a visiting pastor. "Pastor Molina is originally from Colombia," he explained, "but he's now living and ministering in California. Pastor Molina, why don't you come and share with us for a few minutes? Tell us what the Lord is doing in California."

Pastor Molina stood up. "Thank you, Pastor Carrión. It's always good to come back to Medellín, and it's always exciting to see the things the Lord is doing here in this city." He pulled a small notebook from his pocket and flipped back the front cover.

"Last year, I was at a conference in California. There were over five thousand pastors and leaders from all over America at the conference. During one of the services, a prophecy was given." He glanced over at Pastor Carrión. "I'd like to share that prophecy with you, if that's alright."

Pastor Carrión nodded encouragingly.

He paged through the notebook until he reached the back. "There were several different things said in this prophecy. First of all, it said that the Lord is going to move in ways we have never seen. People around the world will be touched by the Lord in ways we have never seen. Children will stand outside hospitals and raise their hands, and sick people will be healed."

He flipped a page. "Our young people will go around the world preaching and testifying, and many will come to the Lord as a result of their witness. The third-world countries will enter into revival, and there will be a time of great spiritual revival." He paused. "And the Mafia..."

Chills swept down my arms. The pastors turned and looked at me.

"The Mafia will be put in jail, but in jail they will receive Jesus Christ and will become witnesses for Him."

I put my head down, tears gathering.

"...And as the Lord continues to move among the Mafia, they will be used by Him to bring healing and deliverance to thousands around the world."

The pastors at that conference in California could not have known I was questioning the vision. They could not have known the struggle I was having. They could not have known I needed a confirmation of His call to reach the Mafia—but the Lord had known.

It was all the confirmation I needed.

Chapter 33

With renewed vision, I gathered the congregation together, encouraging them to pray for the Mafia. It had taken time, but they were united now, banding together, weeping and praying for the Mafia. Churches in the United States had been praying for the cartels for years. Now the churches in Medellín joined the battle. "Pray for Escobar," the pastors urged their congregations. "Pray for his salvation. And pray for the Mafia."

I thought back to a seminar I had taught in Joy Fellowship several years ago.

"Are you pregnant?" I had asked. *"Is there a vision or a goal that the Lord has birthed in you? Are you praying for your spiritual baby to grow and develop? Be patient. When it is time to deliver, you will feel the labor pains, and the baby will come."*

The Mafia! My spiritual "baby"! The weight of the vision pressed constantly on my heart, growing and developing. His word had been confirmed. I knew the doors would open in His time.

While we waited, the Lord began to move in the community in a powerful way. Word began to get out that at

Casa de Oración lives were being changed through the power of Jesus Christ.

Paco was one example of God's mercy.

Paco was well-known in the area. During the day he wandered around the neighborhood, eating from the garbage and begging for money to buy alcohol. At night, he slept in the pigpen by the brook.

"Why, Paco?" I asked. "Why do you live like this?"

"Like what?"

"Drinking and begging on the streets."

"I don't drink that often," he said defensively.

"You don't?"

"No." He ducked his head. "Only when I don't have enough money for drugs."

I stared at him. "Paco…"

He looked embarrassed. "The drugs help me sleep at night. It's cold."

"But why do you sleep in the pigpen, Paco?"

"I don't have anywhere else to go."

"What do you do when it's cold or raining?"

He shrugged. "I get wet."

"Paco," I said softly. "Do you want to change that kind of life?"

He stared at his feet.

"Paco?"

He looked up, a sudden longing in his eyes. "Yes, Sister Marta. I do."

"Then why don't you let Jesus help you?" I asked. "He can change your life."

I smelled the alcohol on his breath and saw the unfocused gaze of the crack addict and knew I had to get him away from the neighborhood. If he stayed here, it would be too easy for him to return to old habits.

"Paco, let me send you to a program."

He shifted his eyes away. "A program—what will they do to me?"

I smiled at his nervousness. "It's a Christian drug program, Paco. You'll study the Bible, and they'll train you to get a job."

His eyes brightened. "A job?"

"Yes, they'll help you learn a skill so you can get a job."

"How long is it?"

"Seven months." I held his bleary eyes with mine. "Paco, you know you can't keep living like this."

He looked down at his clothes, ragged and smelly from months on the streets. Something clicked in his eyes, and he nodded slowly. "You're right, Sister Marta. I can't keep living like this. I'll go."

Before he left for the program, Paco accepted the Lord, and I smiled at the new look of determination in his eyes. "I can make it," he said grimly. "With Jesus, I can make it."

Several months later Paco came home a changed man. The people in the community were stunned to see Paco dressed nicely, clean-shaven and on his way to work. "Didn't you used to eat from the garbage?" they asked.

"Yes," Paco nodded happily.

"Weren't you the one who slept in the pigpen?"

He nodded again.

"What happened to you?"

"Jesus changed me."

The entire community was amazed.

"Ms. Estrada, you're doing a good job with that man," a mafioso told me. "I'm glad to see what Jesus and you have done for him. I think it's good that you are trying to help people."

"Thank you, Luis, but Jesus wants to do the same thing for you."

He looked away. "I don't sleep in the garbage, Ms. Estrada."

"We all need Jesus," I said gently.

"Yes—maybe sometime." He smiled politely and backed away. "I just wanted to say you are a good lady to help Paco."

Paco did well for the first several months then started drinking again. I knew I had to get him back into a structured and disciplined environment and quickly sent him off to the program again. When he came back, he did well for several months, then slipped back into his old patterns.

"Paco," I said firmly, "God is not playing games with you. You have to get your life straight with Him."

He nodded, ashamed. "Yes, Marta, I know—I will."

He tried, but could not stay away from the alcohol. Several times I saw him on the streets. Each time he looked away, embarrassed. I prayed for him but did not pressure him. The Lord would have to intervene.

One day, several months later, Paco showed up at my doorstep, his eyes wide and staring. "Marta," he panted, "that crazy man tried to kill me."

"Who?" I asked.

"That mafioso who comes around here."

"Luis?" I asked incredulously. "Luis tried to kill you? Why would he do that?"

"Because he saw me using crack."

"He saw you…" I broke off. "I don't understand."

"He had a gun. He was yelling, 'What are you using drugs for? Don't you know that lady is killing herself for you? Don't you know you are blaspheming the name of Jesus Christ; I'm going to kill you right now.' "

A mafioso threatening to kill Paco for using drugs! It was too good to be true. I bit my lip, trying to hide my laughter, fighting to control my quivering lips.

"He's crazy!" Paco's eyes were bulging. "He pointed the gun at me and started pulling the trigger. I jumped in the bushes to hide. When I tried to run, he got in his car and started chasing me."

I could not hold the laughter in anymore—a mafioso defending the Lord's honor with a gun. It was too much. I burst out laughing. "That's wonderful," I said, choking.

"Marta, I have to get straight with the Lord," Paco said. "Send me back to a program. I'm going to get off drugs. I have to repent."

"Okay, Paco," I said, still chuckling. "Get your things together. I'll send you back tomorrow."

Many came to the Lord during this time. Others left and went back to the streets. It was painful to see former members on the streets, using drugs or prostituting, the empty look back in their eyes.

We watched some people weep tears of repentance, then saw them back on the streets the next day, selling their new Bibles for drug money. Some of them came back. Others were killed on the streets, shot or dead from an overdose.

Despite the disappointments, I remained convinced of God's mercy.

I never grew tired of seeing the glowing faces, the changed lives. People in the neighborhood came for Bible studies and prayer. Others came for counseling and ministry, turning my house into a bustling center of activity.

I was learning, growing as a pastor, but there was still one area of ministry I had not encountered. One night, I read the verse: "And these signs will accompany those who believe: In my name they will drive out demons" (Mark 16:17 NIV).

I put down the Bible. *Those who believe?* If I was His follower, I should be doing the same. I pursed my lips thoughtfully. *I don't know how to deal with something like this. I need help.* I bowed my head. "Jesus, help me to study Your Word. Help me so that I will be ready to handle this situation when it comes."

The "situation" came sooner than I expected.

Vicente was a good-natured young man. He was fun and personable—but subject to uncontrollable bursts of anger. He had accepted the Lord but seemed to have no control over his temper.

"Vicente, why do you do these things?" I asked. "Why don't you change?"

"I don't know," he said, hanging his head. "The voices tell me to do it, and I have to listen."

I grew very still. "What voices?"

"The ones in my head."

"What do they say?"

"They say, 'Kill...kill.' " His eyes turned cold.

Was he telling the truth? "Do they do anything to you?"

Vicente looked away, embarrassed.

"What, Vicente?" I asked. "What do they do?"

He shook his head. "Nothing."

"Do they hurt you?" I asked.

"No, not really." He lowered his voice, ashamed. "They scratch me."

"Scratch you! Where?"

"On my chest."

"Can I see?"

"No!" He backed up. "You can't see anything. They're gone."

I looked at him consideringly.

"I'm not lying," he said defensively. "They do scratch me."

I was not sure he was telling the truth, but several days later Vicente called me. "Marta, they did it again last night. Come to my house."

I dressed quickly and went to his house. Vicente's grandmother opened the door. "He was screaming again," she said, her voice trembling. "He needs help, Marta. Please pray for him."

"Where is he?"

"In the bedroom." She cupped her hand. "Vicente, come to the living room. Marta's here."

We waited until we heard his footsteps. He came in quietly and stood in front of me. He did not look up.

"Vicente, what happened?" I asked.

"They scratched me."

"Can I see?"

Reluctantly, Vicente pulled his shirt up. I stepped back. The scratches on his chest were raised and ugly, dried blood crusted on the edges.

"Vicente, you need help," I said firmly. "You have to do something. Do you want help?"

He did not answer.

"Vicente, answer me," I pressed. "Do you want help?"

"Yes," he said reluctantly.

"Okay, then let's pray."

His face changed suddenly. "No, Marta," he pleaded, backing up. "Not today. Please."

I was stunned by the terror in his voice. "Okay, Vicente," I said, backing off. "Not today, but will you call me when you're ready?"

"Yes," he said hoarsely.

Over the next several weeks I waited for Vicente's call, but the phone did not ring.

The torment continued. "He screams," his grandmother said tearfully. "He screams, and I can't help him. Marta, please, you've got to do something."

"I can't," I said. "He has to want help. When he's ready, he'll call."

Finally, one day, Vicente called my house. "Okay, Marta," he said. "I'm ready." His voice was ragged. "Come to my house."

All morning I prepared for the confrontation, fasting and praying for protection for myself, my daughter, and the congregation. A student from the local Bible seminary agreed to come with me, and that afternoon we went to Vicente's house. I sat down next to Vicente and took his hands in mine.

"Vicente," I said, "Jesus came to deliver the oppressed. He wants to set you free. Do you want to be free?"

He nodded.

"Good. First we're going to pray for you," I explained, "then we're going to ask the Lord to set you free. Okay?"

Again he nodded.

Ernesto and I laid hands on him, and Ernesto began to pray. "Jesus, we know that You came to set us free. We know that You are more powerful than any demons in Vicente. We know that You want to set him free. We ask You, in the name of Jesus..."

Suddenly, Vicente's voice changed. His face twisted, and he jerked to one side, away from our hands. "Don't touch me," he snarled.

My hands tightened on his shoulder. It was not Vicente's voice.

"Be quiet," Ernesto ordered hoarsely. "In the name of Jesus. Answer only when we ask you questions. How many of you are in there?"

The answer was ripped from his throat. "Just a few."

"Blood of Jesus!" I whispered. *They were answering!* I reached for my Bible.

"Why are you bothering Vicente?" Ernesto asked.

Silence.

"Why are you bothering Vicente?" Ernesto repeated the question firmly.

"Because we want him to kill." The answer came back cold and angry, the voice full of hatred.

A chill passed through me. "Spirit of death," I said, "I rebuke you in the name of Jesus. Get out of this body right now."

Something went out of Vicente's body with a yell and Vicente slumped forward, then sat up again, his eyes cold and hard. I backed up, alarmed by the hatred in his eyes.

Ernesto looked over at me. "Does Vicente have any weapons in this room?"

"I don't know." I looked over at Vicente. He looked back at me, his eyes calm. "Vicente, do you have a gun?" I asked.

He pointed to a night table.

"Bring it to me."

He went to the desk and pulled out a gun. Grasped in his hand, it gleamed, sleek and evil-looking in the muted light from the shaded lamp. He held it lovingly, stroking it gently, then turned and pointed it directly at me.

My heart jerked, then slowed. "Put it down, Vicente."

He hesitated, and I reached out a hand, pushing the barrel to the floor. His eyes stared into mine.

"Let go, Vicente."

I saw the struggle in his eyes and said the name of Jesus. Reluctantly, his grip loosened.

"Now, take the bullets out," I ordered.

He took the gun, emptied the chambers, and handed the gun back.

My knees were weak. "Vicente, this voice that keeps telling you to do these things—you must resist it. You must tell him to go. Tell him to leave in the name of Jesus."

Vicente shook his head.

"Say it!"

"Leave in the name of Jesus," he repeated weakly.

"Tell him you are protected by the blood of Jesus."

"I'm protected by the blood of Jesus." His voice strangled on the last word.

"Say it again, Vicente."

"I'm protected by the blood of Jesus."

"Now tell him to get out and leave you alone."

Vicente's voice was stronger now. "Get out and leave me alone!"

He started saying the name of Jesus over and over, and we saw the peace begin to steal into his eyes. It took more than an hour, but finally Vicente was completely delivered.

I called his mother. She came into the room and hugged Vicente. There were tears in her eyes.

"Vicente, look at me," I said gently.

Vicente looked at me and smiled. He looked weak and shaken, but his eyes were clear and alert.

Today Vicente is a new person. He has completely turned his back on his old ways and teaches the Bible to his aunt and his mother. Many members of his family have come to the Lord as a result of his dramatic testimony.

Chapter 34

A s the dramatic crackdown on the Mafia continued, the Colombian government began shipping many hitmen, dealers, and mafiosos to prison. With a shiver I remembered the first part of Pastor Molina's prophecy: *"The Mafia will be sent to jail..."*

The prophecy had been frighteningly accurate so far. *"...but in jail they will receive Jesus Christ."* If the prophecy were true, we could be standing on the threshold of a mighty move of God among the Mafia.

Foreign media began to pump the news back to eager audiences. "The members of the Medellín cartel are turning themselves in to the Colombian government in unprecedented numbers. Rather than face drug charges in the United States, these men have chosen to turn themselves in to their own government."

Still, the top leaders remained on the loose.

"Marta, they're getting a prison ready for Escobar and his men," a friend told me.

I had already seen the news clips. The small prison in Envigado was a fortress. Heavily guarded and off-limits to the public, the prison would house the top leaders of the Medellín cartel. Security was extremely tight; once the men were captured, they would be guarded by some of the most highly trained officers in Colombia.

News reports speculated that Escobar would kill himself before he gave himself in to the government.

"He's a proud man, Marta," friends warned. "He won't give himself up. He'll kill himself first."

The words cut deep. "Don't let him kill himself," I pleaded with the Lord. "Don't let him die yet. Keep him safe until he has a chance to turn to You."

While we waited for developing news of Escobar and his men, I continued visiting other prisons in Colombia.

With the help of Pastor Omar, I gained access to a prison many considered to be the most dangerous in Colombia. Averaging three murders a week among the inmates, this prison had earned a reputation as one of the most violent in the country.

In maximum security, where each cell was meant for one person, there were often five, six, even seven men crammed into one cell. If an inmate managed to get a knife through security, the results were deadly. In the crowded cell, with nowhere to go, the other cell-mates were stabbed repeatedly, some bleeding to death before medical help could arrive.

Even in prison, the Mafia influence was far-reaching. If an inmate was marked by the cartels, there was little the prison officials could do to protect him. The hit could come at any moment—and very often the hitman was a cell-mate.

On weekends the inmates were allowed to visit with friends and family in open courtyards called *patios*. One *patio* in particular held my attention. Where the other courtyards held as many as six hundred inmates, this one held no more than twelve or fourteen men. They were from the Mafia.

Knowing my burden for the cartels, Pastor Omar pointed the *patio* out to me several times. I passed it often during my visits, but each time I kept walking. No one visited that *patio* unless invited. The Lord would have to create the right moment.

Finally, late one afternoon I felt the Lord saying, *"Now, Marta."*

This was it! Heart pounding, I walked over to the group of men gathered by the soccer field.

"Pardon me," I said politely, "may I speak to you for a minute?"

The men looked at me in surprise.

I found myself staring into the narrowed eyes of a large, well-dressed mafioso. He looked at me with raised eyebrows for a moment and then moved over, making room for me.

"Thank you," I smiled.

He crossed his arms and waited.

I did not have an opening, so I said the first thing that came to mind. "You know...I was in jail at one time too."

The mafioso's eyebrows raised a fraction higher. Several of the men shifted positions, leaning forward to see me, their glances skeptical. "Really? What jail?"

"Rikers Island in New York."

"New York—what were you in for?"

"Drugs."

Their eyes widened briefly. "Cocaine?"

I nodded.

Glancing at my Bible, they nudged each other, smirking. "Are you still dealing?"

"No, I'm preaching the gospel."

"Do you need help getting the drugs into New York? We can help."

"No, I'm not involved with drugs anymore," I said.

"Do you make good money?"

They were not listening. I had lost control of the conversation. Laughing and slapping each other on the back, they ignored my attempts to speak.

Embarrassed, I bowed my head, praying.

"Where do you get the cocaine?" they laughed. "We know where you can get a good deal on a kilo."

I looked up. "How many of you cry at night when your friends are not looking?"

The question fell like a bomb in silence. Some turned away. Others looked down, faces red. No one said a word.

"How many of you cry at night because you're alone and afraid? You're afraid because you know your wives and children are in danger. You know they can be kidnapped or killed at any moment because of the life you are leading."

They were listening.

"Your lives are in danger," I said, "but Jesus Christ can protect you. He can give you the power to change the way you are living. He can make you a new person—but you must repent and give your life to Him."

I stopped, feeling the Lord tell me it was enough. The Lord was preparing the way, laying the groundwork for a move of God that would reverberate across Colombia, sweep through the prisons, and into the streets of Medellín. One day, even the top leaders of the drug cartels would hear the message of God's love. I could only pray it would happen in my lifetime.

At Pastor Omar's urging, our small church began bringing teams into the prison where he was chaplain. At his request, we began holding special services in the *patios*.

One afternoon, we decided to hold a service in one of the larger *patios*.

"We'll have to get permission from the *cacique* to have the meeting," Pastor Omar said, "but it shouldn't be a problem. Wait here, I'll go ask."

As the unofficial leader of the *patio*, the *cacique* held a great deal of influence. If we wanted to give a special service in one of the *patios*, we had to ask not just the director of the jail, but the *cacique* as well.

Soon Pastor Omar was back. "Ten minutes," he said.

"Ten minutes?" I protested. "That's not enough time. It'll take that long just to set up!"

"That's all he'd give," Pastor Omar said, "and he didn't seem too happy to give that. When you preach, be careful what you say; he's touchy."

Lina and some of the young people from the congregation were with me. We set up the sound system quickly, fully aware that the *cacique* was keeping track of the time. I saw him talking with some of his men in the corner and swallowed nervously. He was not going to like what I had to say.

The men gathered around, watching, and finally we were ready. I opened with a quick prayer and then started the message. "Today I have a message for the Colombian Mafia."

The sudden quiet was testimony to the power of the Colombian Mafia. The *cacique* turned and stared at me, his face startled. The inmates looked at me nervously.

"Last year a prophecy was given at a pastor's conference in California; part of that prophecy was for the Mafia. Here's what it said: 'The Mafia will be put in jail, but while they are in jail they will receive Jesus Christ and will become witnesses for Him.' "

The *cacique* still had not moved.

"Many of you know that only a few months after that prophecy was given, the government began arresting the Mafia. Soon the Lord is going to fulfill the rest of that prophecy. He is going to touch the lives of hundreds of drug dealers and *narcotraficantes*."

The *cacique* was walking toward me, his face red.

"In 1983 I was arrested in New York for dealing drugs. I was facing fifteen years to life, and $250,000 bail. I was without faith or hope, and I wanted to kill myself."

The *cacique* was making motions for me to stop. I looked away, my heart pounding. My mouth was dry, my lips sticking to my teeth.

"Then I met Jesus Christ. He changed my life and gave me joy. He gave my daughter back to me and gave me a new future. Because of Him, I have a reason to live. Today, Jesus is calling you. He wants to use you to bring this country to Jesus Christ, to bring your families to Him. He wants this country to be known as a holy nation of godly men and women—not a country of drug traffickers."

The *cacique* was behind me, tapping me on the shoulder. "Miss, you must stop now."

The sunlit courtyard was quiet. Six hundred men packed the corridor where I was preaching. Their faces were intent, listening. I could not stop now.

I clenched my teeth to keep them from chattering and motioned to Lina to start the drama. The young people had their face paint on already and did not need much time to set up. Quickly they started the first skit.

Out of the corner of my eye I saw the *cacique* signal to

one of his men. I put the microphone down and picked up my Bible. I was bold, but I was not foolish. "Okay, it's time to go," I said briskly. "Let's go."

"But, Mama, we're not done," Lina protested.

The young people were looking at me, confused.

"I'm sorry," I said. "We have to go. Come on, pack up."

That night the *cacique* was removed from the *patio* and taken to maximum security and solitary confinement. No one gave us a reason for his removal, but I knew the Lord had him removed. The Lord has a plan. He is going to reach the Colombian Mafia, and He will remove anyone who stands in the way of that plan.

As the prison ministry continued to grow, we saw hitmen, drug dealers, Mafiosos, and *caciques* come to the Lord. Under the leadership of Pastor Omar, that prison was turned upside down with the gospel of Jesus Christ.

One service in particular will remain forever branded in my mind.

I was standing in front of a group of inmates, giving my testimony, when I felt an unusual heaviness press on my heart, a sense of urgency prodding me. I kept talking, tears pricking my eyes. My eyes wandered over the crowd, searching.

Then I saw him—a young man standing in the front of the crowd, his eyes dark and sad, his face still. I looked away, an inexplicable feeling of sadness holding me. My eyes wandered back to the young man's face. His head was down. Suddenly, I stopped talking and turned to him.

"Young man, what is your name?"

He looked up, startled. "Me? Antonio."

"Antonio, God is calling you."

He looked bewildered, his eyes almost frightened. "Me? Why?"

"Because He loves you." I moved closer and took him by the hand. "Antonio, you must accept Jesus today."

He looked down at my hands, his body shaking. "Why?"

I looked into his eyes, searching for an answer. The heaviness became almost a physical pain. "Because tomorrow might be too late."

Antonio's chest was moving rapidly, his breathing shallow. "Too late?"

The prodding urgency became more insistent. Suddenly, I started to cry. "Yes, Antonio, you must receive Him today."

He was trembling. "How? What do I have to do?"

As simply and as urgently as I could, I explained the gospel to him, sensing the need to make it very clear. The hand of God was on this young man's life in a very unusual way. As we prayed together, the tears began to trickle down his cheeks. When we finished, he lifted his face. His cheeks were wet with tears. "I can feel Him, Ms. Estrada," he said shakily. "I can feel Jesus in my heart."

The heaviness was lifted from my heart.

That night, Antonio was killed by another inmate.

Chapter 35

The prison in Envigado remained empty.

The Medellín cartel declared war on the U.S. and Colombian governments, and the violence intensified. Many cartel members had already been shot and killed. Those that survived were sent to prison.

Still, the leaders refused to surrender.

The violent climate in Medellín remained unchanged. The death rate climbed steadily, and Medellín became known as one of the most violent cities in the world—second only to Beirut.

Edison was one young man who seemed to represent the darker side of Medellín. Shot several times in the chest, stomach, and legs, Edison was not expected to live.

His aunt called me from the hospital. "He's dying, Marta," she said. "Would you come and pray for his soul?"

The prayers of those left behind can never change our place in eternity. Once the soul leaves the body, eternity is fixed. If Edison died before he made a decision to accept Jesus Christ, it would be too late. I could not pray for his soul, only for his salvation.

"Yes, Nydia," I said heavily. "I will come."

The hospital room was crowded, the grieving family

gathered around the bed, murmuring relatives pressing in to look at the dying man's face. Death hung in the still air, the life ebbing slowly, reluctantly from the broken body. Edison's eyes were closed, his skin sallow, his jaw stiffening in death.

I placed my hands gently on his forehead, my fingers feeling the damp coolness of his skin. He was slipping fast, the coma deepening. If he lived through the night, it would be a miracle. I anointed him with oil, smoothing it into his skin, praying for healing. If he lived, they would know it was God.

"Thank you, Marta," his mother whispered. "Thank you for coming."

With a heavy heart, I turned and left the hospital.

Life is never promised to us. In our pride and ignorance we live our lives, failing to count the cost of a life without Jesus Christ. God is merciful, but He is also just. All of us are given the opportunity to be born into God's family. If we reject that opportunity, we must pay the price in eternity.

Sadness pressed on my heart. "Father, have mercy," I wept. "Be merciful to this family. You can preserve life and reverse death. Give this young man his life. Give him a chance to know You."

I paced the floor of my room, weeping for Edison and for Colombia. So many young people were dying; so many of them were losing their lives before they reached twenty. There was so much to do and so little time. "Spare their lives," I pleaded. "Give them a chance to hear the gospel."

The phone was ringing, loudly, insistently; someone knew I was home. Tears still damp, I picked up the receiver. "Hello?"

"Marta!" It was Edison's aunt. She sounded out of breath.

"Yes? What's the matter?"

"You're not going to believe this, Marta." Her voice was tight, incredulous.

My heart turned over. "What happened?"

She started to cry. "Marta, when you left the hospital, we knew it was over. Edison was so still, so cold. The doctors said he would die before the end of the night." Her breath started coming in gasps. "We were standing around the bed, crying..." She stopped, fighting for composure. When she spoke again, her voice was shaking. "Edison opened his eyes and said, 'Who was that lady who prayed for me?' "

"He's a merciful God," I said shakily. "He's giving Edison another chance."

Many of Edison's friends and family came to the Lord as a result of his miraculous healing, but his story was only beginning. When the doctors told Edison he would never walk again, I went to visit him. "Edison, do you want to walk again?" I asked.

His nod was emphatic. "Yes, Marta. I do."

"Do you believe the Lord can give you another miracle?"

"Yes!" His face was shining.

"Then let's pray."

Edison did walk again, returning to work with his father a few months after being released from the hospital.

Several months later, Edison turned his back on the Lord.

I was stunned. How could he leave the Lord after what he had been through? How could he leave what he had found in Jesus Christ to go back to a life-style that had almost caused his death?

Fear for Edison's life gripped me. Serving the Lord is not a game. God is not a toy to be picked up when we want to be amused and discarded when we lose interest. Frightened, I begged the Lord for mercy. "Spare Edison's life," I prayed. "Bring him back and show him Your mercy."

Julián was an answer to the bitter disappointment I felt at Edison's defection. Julián was a delight to me. A new Christian, he showed remarkable maturity in the Lord. He was strong and stable, and I watched him hopefully, praying for him to develop a true calling to the ministry.

Julián loved the Lord, and he loved the congregation. He had a steadying influence on many of the young people and demonstrated a youthful integrity and spiritual hunger that encouraged me. He was close to me, and I loved him as a son. The leader I had been expecting to find in Edison was now developing in Julián. I watched the promise of strong, mature leadership and knew the Lord had great things planned for Julián's life.

Then, one night, the call came.

"Marta, Julián's been shot."

"Shot?" My knees went weak. "Where is he?"

"By the bridge."

"Is he okay?"

"I'm not sure. You'd better come."

I ran out of the house with Lina, grabbing a sweater on the way, forgetting the curfew. We hurried through the deserted streets, wrapping our arms against the night chill. The shootings were so common now. Who could have shot Julián? He did not have any enemies.

A crowd of neighbors stood around Julián's body.

"They shot him, pastor. For no reason."

He was dead. I looked at his youthful body sprawled in the street in his own blood and choked back tears. I had loved him for his smile, his laugh, his encouragement, the promise of life. He had been the son I never had. Now his dead body lay useless in the street.

I heard Lina sobbing next to me. I stumbled home through the streets, clutching Lina's cold hand in mine, my mind numbed, dazed.

How could the Lord have taken him? How could He have allowed this young life to end so violently?

I put Lina to bed, then sat on the edge of my bed. I could hear Lina crying in the other room. I knew she blamed God. Hot tears splashed on my hands, grief twisting in my stomach. Edison had turned his back on God, leaving me with an empty sense of betrayal. Now I had lost another one.

The next several days passed in a blur, my mind drifting to Julián and his family. The day of the funeral, the small house was packed. The gleaming casket was lined with flowers, the scent faint but fragrant in the warm Colombian air. Julián's dark head rested on the pillow, his young face calm and still in death. Family members wept softly, the sounds of grief echoing through the house.

I looked again at that young face and felt an encompassing sense of loss.

During the nine days of mourning that followed, many of Julián's friends and relatives received the Lord. Still I struggled with the questions. How could the Lord have allowed this to happen?

With Julián gone, I found my thoughts returning once again to Edison. Despite his blatant rebellion, I knew the Lord could forgive him and bring him back. He may have turned his back on God, but the Lord still loved him. I could not help feeling that Edison was still marked for God's service.

Edison's mother became a special joy to me during this time. She loved her son but would not allow his life to influence her relationship with the Lord. She was determined to serve the Lord and seemed very serious about ministering to others.

One day she called me. "Marta, would you visit a friend of mine? She's in a wheelchair and in a lot of pain. She wants someone to pray for her."

"Of course," I said. "When would you like me to come?"

"Is tomorrow too soon?" she asked.

"Of course not. Is she expecting me?"

"Yes, I told her I was going to invite my pastor."

"I'll be there," I promised.

The following day I went to visit. The woman in the wheelchair was close to my age but looked older. Her face was pinched with pain, her eyes tired. She was sitting by the doorstep, staring sightlessly at the street.

I looked down at the address written on the slip of paper, then back at her. "Excuse me," I started tentatively. "I hope I'm not disturbing you, but your friend…"

The woman turned her head abruptly and looked at me intently. Suddenly her eyes widened, and she straightened in her chair. "Marta? Marta Estrada?"

I looked closer.

"Marta!" she said. "*You're* the pastor?"

Suddenly I recognized her. Nelly! We had gone to elementary school together and been close friends. Shocked, I glanced down at her legs, covered with a thick blanket. "Nelly, what happened?"

She lifted her shoulders painfully. "I was shot."

"Shot?" I could hardly get the words out. "But—why? Who?"

"Dora's husband."

Stunned, I sat down. "Dora's husband? When did this happen?"

"Six years ago." She shifted in her chair, her lips tightening briefly as a look of pain crossed her face. "Dora was visiting me. Her husband was upset about some fight they had had..." She pulled the blanket up around her waist. "We heard him yelling downstairs. There was a lot of noise and some shouting, and then we heard him coming up the stairs. We tried to hide under the bed, but he saw us." She lifted her head and looked at me. "He stuck the gun under the bed and started shooting. Dora was killed—I was left paralyzed."

"Dear Jesus," I whispered.

She slid a hand across her face. "On the way downstairs, he saw my son on the stairs." Her lips grew white around the edges. "He killed him—my only son."

I sat still, my mind grasping for answers. "Dora's children...?"

"They were in the car, waiting." I saw reflections of horror in her eyes. "He shot them too."

"He killed them?"

She nodded.

Incredibly, Nelly's story was not finished. "A couple of years later, some men came looking for information. They thought I knew something about some guy they were looking for. They put me in the back seat of a car and drove for hours. When we stopped, they took me into a house..."

A slight sweat broke out on the palms of my hands. "What did they do?"

"They tortured me."

I looked at her crippled body. "Why? What did they think you knew?"

She smiled sardonically. "Who knows? It took them all night to find out I didn't know anything. I almost died in the process. When they finally realized I was telling the truth, they gave up."

"They let you go?" I asked incredulously.

"No, of course not. I knew they had to kill me."

"Looks like they botched the job."

She chuckled. "Well, not really. They took me to an empty lot and shot me in the back. They must have thought I was dead because they left me there. The next time I opened my eyes, I was in a hospital bed."

I looked at the crumpled body in front of me and prayed for wisdom. I could so easily say the wrong thing. "Your friend told me you're in a lot of pain," I said gently.

She nodded, her eyes clouded.

I took her hand and looked into her eyes. "Nelly, listen to me—you know there's only one thing more important than the condition of your body, and that's the condition of your soul."

"I know," she said. "My sister in New York has been telling me the same thing. I prayed with her to accept Jesus." She curled her hand over mine. "Pray for me, Marta. I do want to serve Him."

We prayed together, and every week after that I went to teach her the Bible. I saw the smile and the easing of pain.

"I love Him," she told me. "He has given me so much peace."

One night, several months after our first meeting, Nelly attended an all-night prayer meeting at the church. My heart swelled to see her weeping for the cartels, praying for their salvation and protection. She was new in the Lord, but she had been quick to catch the burden for the Mafia. She was still in pain, but the peace and the concern for others shone through.

Edison's mother watched Nelly's transformation with joy. Her new life gave both of us new hope for Edison. Her shining face somehow represented the hope we had for Edison. Somehow we knew the Lord was going to bring him back.

Two weeks after the all-night prayer meeting, the phone rang. I looked at the clock. Lina and I were already in bed. The luminous digits on the clock read 11:00.

Wearily I reached for the phone. "Hello?"

The words came quick and straight. "Marta, they killed Edison."

I sat bolt upright, my mind going into a slow spin. I heard the words but could not process them. I was quivering, shock waves passing through my body.

"He's dead, Marta. They shot him." The voice was strained, broken.

"Who is this?" I hardly recognized my own voice.

"Ligia."

Edison's sister! "Where are you?"

She was hysterical, sobbing. "He's dead, Marta. They shot him to death."

I was out of bed, dressing quickly, fumbling in the dark. "Yes, *hija*," I said soothingly, fighting for calm. "Where are you? Tell me where you are."

"In the mall."

"Are the police there?"

"Yes."

"Is your family there?"

"Yes...Marta, please come."

"I am; I'm getting dressed. I'll be there as soon as I get Lina."

Hurrying, trying not to tremble, I woke Lina and called for a taxi. Lina's eyes were large, frightened. "What happened, Mama?"

"Edison was shot."

"Is he dead?"

"Yes, Lina," I said. "He's dead."

"Did he die with Jesus?"

It was the first question I had asked myself. I had no answers. I sat in the darkened cab, tears of shock on my face.

I had been so sure that Edison would return to the Lord. I had been so sure that I had stopped praying for his protection. I sank back against the seat, shaking.

A small, lonely group huddled around the body on the ground outside the darkened mall. The police were turning the body over, counting the bullet holes. His body was still warm, the blood seeping through his clothing.

Edison's sisters saw me and flew to me, crying. I hugged

them, staring at the body on the ground. Edison's blood had soaked into the sidewalk, turning the police chalk lines crimson. Lina pressed close to me, trembling. I turned her away, shielding her.

I stood, transfixed by the sight of Edison's body lying in the street, the young life wiped away, his years cut short. The violence of Medellín once again had robbed Colombia of one of her young people.

The voices broke through my thoughts, and I looked at the three girls still weeping quietly at my side. "What did you say?" I was not sure I had heard right.

Ligia repeated herself. "He was at church tonight."

"Who was at church?" I asked urgently.

"Edison."

"Edison?" I repeated the name slowly. "Edison went to church tonight?"

"Yes. He said he wanted to get his life together."

Lina's hand tightened in mine. I could feel my fingers shaking.

"He kept asking Jesus to forgive him. He was crying; everyone was crying. He rededicated his life to the Lord. Everyone was so happy." Ligia's voice broke. "Then he went to the mall. They found him here...dead."

I held them close, the words not coming. Edison! God's miracle! Shot to death just one year after the first shooting that had left him in a coma. Shot three hours after he had once again dedicated his life to the Lord.

The Lord had been merciful, giving Edison one more chance; still, I could not shake the grief. Two deaths, two funerals—how much more could I take? It had been a hard year—a year of change, of pain, and of great loss. The pain burrowed deeply into my spirit. It was too much. Discouragement dogged my footsteps.

When a pastor invited me to join his church at a convention in Ecuador, I accepted. I was emotionally exhausted, weakened by the constant drain on my emotions. I had to get away.

Ecuador was a time to regroup, a time to reorder my priorities. Julián's death; Edison's dramatic return, his violent death—I might not ever understand. I might not ever know why. But I did not have to. The Lord was in control. He would do what was best for His children.

I returned to Medellín with renewed fervor. I arrived at the church just as the Sunday service was finishing and stood in the back as the guest pastor closed in prayer. The congregation seemed quieter than usual, but it felt so good to see familiar faces. I realized again how much love the Lord had put in my heart for this congregation.

The service dismissed, and I turned to hug those closest to me.

"Marta..."

I turned. A group was gathered behind me, waiting. I looked inquiringly around the circle. "Yes?"

"We have some news for you."

"Oh, yes?" I said smiling. "Is it good news?"

"Maybe you should sit down."

My hands went cold. "Why?"

"It's Nelly."

"Yes?" I looked around again at the faces. "What happened?"

"She was shot."

"Oh, no," I groaned. "Not again—how bad is it?"

"She's dead, Marta."

Stunned and reeling, I backed into a chair, looking from face to face, my mind slipping into shock. Nelly—dead? Impossible. I stared at the faces around me—my mind numbed, drained. How could she be dead? Just weeks ago she had been at Edison's funeral.

The energy drained from my body. Who could have shot her? I clenched my hands, then forced the question. "Was it the Mafia?"

The shrugs were cautious. "They don't know. Someone came up to her on her doorstep and pointed a gun at her chest. She said, 'Oh, my dear—you're going to kill me?' almost like she knew him. Then he shot her."

The total disregard for life was chilling; the total lack of respect for human life frightening. I went to my room and sat down on the bed, stripped of emotion. Nelly—my Nelly, so full of life since she found Jesus—gone. I wept, feeling the bitter loss of the families. I wept, feeling the hurt of the families. I wept for the children of Colombia, for the young people, for Julián, and Edison and Nelly.

What had Colombia become that our young people could not live to see twenty? What had Colombia become that our people would shoot an old woman in a wheelchair?

I felt a small ball of cold fury begin to form in my stomach. Were we breeding cowards in Colombia—cowards hiding behind their guns, their power, their money? Where were the men who would stand up for decency and honesty, for truth and honor?

I loved my country and my countrymen, but God was going to bring justice on a nation that treated life with such contempt.

One day, Colombia would answer to a just God.

Chapter 36

On June 19, 1991, Pablo Escobar turned himself in to the Colombian government.

The news flashed around the world. I sat with other students in the *Seminario Bíblico de Colombia* and watched as the helicopter landed on the roof of the government building and took off with Medellín's most-wanted citizen, now a prisoner of the Colombian government.

I watched, holding the tears in check.

I thought back to the letters Elena had delivered to Escobar's office. "Be thankful to the Lord," I had written, "because He has protected you. You have been close to death many times, but the Lord has spared your life. Many people all over the world are praying for your salvation and protection."

Had Escobar ever received those letters? I could not be sure.

Several months ago I had picked up a magazine, my eyes drawn to an interview with Pablo Escobar. The words leaped out at me.

Escobar: There have been many attempts on my life; I have been close to death more than sixty times.

Interviewer: Why do you think you're still alive?

Escobar: Because God has spared my life, and because many people all over the world have been praying for my protection.

I sat, stunned. Coincidence? He had quoted almost word for word from one of the letters. If not my letter, then someone had managed to communicate the concern of God's people to him. "Thank You, Jesus," I whispered. "Let Your people minister to him. Send someone to give him the gospel."

Over the next month and a half, Escobar's men turned themselves in to the Colombian government.

Just one year after Pastor Molina shared that prophecy with the group of *AMEM* pastors, every top leader of the Medellín cartel was in prison.

* * *

December 1991—Bronx, New York

Steve was standing in his office, the sunlight throwing strong shadows on his chiseled features. "What about Escobar?" he asked. "What's happening with him?"

"He's still in prison," I said.

"And the ministry?"

"For the Mafia? I won't be able to open the office for at least a year."

"Why not?"

I looked at him, my stomach tightening in anticipation. "Because..." I leaned forward eagerly. "I think this is the year."

"The year—for what?"

"To finish the book."

Steve ran a hand through his thick hair and leaned back in his chair. "Isn't it almost finished?"

I bit my lip, embarrassed. "No."

He looked at me thoughtfully. "How much did Barbara get done?"

"Mostly research."

For the last three years, Barbara, a friend from Joy

Fellowship, had been working on the book, gathering information, researching dates and details, but the story was still incomplete. Now, ironically, she and her husband were leaving for China. They had accepted teaching positions in Inner Mongolia and were taking the entire family to China for two years.

I looked back at Steve. "Why would the Lord send Barbara to China just when it's time to finish the book?"

"Why don't you ask Him?"

I smiled.

He smiled back. "Can't she finish it before she goes to China?"

"No. It would take at least another year to write it."

Steve considered me for a moment. "Why don't you ask Tina to finish it?"

"Tina?" Steve's suggestion startled me. Pastor Hershey's daughter? I looked at him uncertainly. "Would she do it?"

"I don't know. She might. Why don't you ask her?"

Tina Hershey. She might be the Lord's answer. But would she do it? Would she take on the challenge of a year-long project?

Several other people had already recommended Tina. In fact, my friend, Michelle, had been adamant. "She can do it, Marta. She's the one. Ask her."

I decided to ask Sister Hershey, Tina's mother. She would be honest with me.

Later that week, I sat down with her.

"Tina?" Sister Hershey did not look too sure. "She's pretty busy. I don't know if she'd take a year off to write a book."

Suddenly, I knew Tina was the right person. I felt a lump in my throat. "Sister Hershey, the book has to be finished this year," I said. "I think Tina is the one."

"Really? Well, pray about it," she said soothingly. "If it's the Lord's will, I'm sure she'll do it."

While I waited for the right moment to approach Tina, I set up prayer chains for Escobar and his men. We had not seen much success in reaching the cartel leaders over the years; I wondered now whether this book was part of the

Lord's plan—maybe this was His way of reaching them. Only time would bring an answer.

Several days later I received a call from my sister.

"Marta!" Her voice sounded breathless over the phone.

My heart stopped momentarily. "What, Rosa?"

"Your house was robbed yesterday." The tension in her voice made the words sound slurred.

"Robbed? How do you know?"

"Laura called. Three guys got into the house."

My heart pulsed in my throat. "Where was Pastor Manuel?"

"In the living room. They put the gun to his head. Laura was there praying with him and his wife. Laura started screaming, 'Don't kill the pastor! Please, don't kill the pastor!' She was screaming so loud they left the pastor and went after her."

My heart lodged in my throat. "Where did she go?"

"To Lina's room."

I groaned. "Lina's room?" The door to Lina's room was so weak that it had fallen in on Lina several times. "Why did she run there? Didn't she know about the door?"

"Yes, but Marta, listen to me." Rosa's voice held a tinge of excitement. "They couldn't break it down. They kicked it and kicked it, but they couldn't break it."

I could not speak for a moment.

"That's not all, Marta." Rosa was laughing. "Listen to this—you know that little glass window in Lina's room?"

"Yes."

"They started banging on it with the gun."

"And what happened?"

"Nothing. They couldn't break it."

My hands were shaking now.

"They kept yelling at Laura, 'Come out, or we're going to kill the pastor.' Laura started crying and praying. She said, 'Please don't kill the pastor, but I'm not coming out.' She knew they would kill her if she did. Finally they gave up. One of them held the pastor and his wife; the other two took the television, the VCR, and some of the office equipment and threw everything in some blankets and carried it all out."

My voice was quiet when I asked the next question. "Rosa, who were they?"

"Laura didn't say, but she says you know them."

Laura was right; I did know them. When I heard the names, I felt a terrible pain in my heart. They were drug addicts from the area—and they had been given information by someone in the church.

Five weeks later, three of the men involved in the robbery were killed. All three were killed on the same day, in three separate incidents.

December 1991—Joy Fellowship, Bronx, New York

I had her cornered in the church. She had heard the rumors and was looking at me out of the corner of her eye, the set of her head defensive. "What, Marta? What do you want?"

"Tina," I said, "I want you to finish the book."

She eyed me warily. "Why me? I don't know how to write a book. I've never written one before."

"The Lord will help you."

"No, Marta," she said firmly. "I can't do it. I'm sorry."

"Why?" I felt my heart sink.

She looked at me, grinning. "I have my reasons."

"Reasons? What reasons? Can I pray about them?"

"Sure," she said generously. "If the Lord wants me to write this book, He'll take care of the situations."

"Can you tell me what they are?"

She laughed. "Well, okay. One of them is my house in Virginia. If I write the book, I'll have to get rid of that financial responsibility first."

"Is it on the market?"

"It's been there for several months."

"I'll pray about it. We'll see what the Lord wants to do."

January 1992—Bronx, New York

I looked at the tape recorder and microphone propped up on the table between us and grinned at Sister Hershey.

"Where do we start?"

"Well, let's see—Tina wants us to start from the time you first met Víctor, and then work backward. She'll fill in the blanks later."

I heard Tina working in the other room and smiled at Sister Hershey.

Sister Hershey smiled back. "You realize this means she won't eat for twelve months?"

"Yes, I'm sorry," I grinned.

"Don't worry," Sister Hershey said. "She'll enjoy it."

I thought back to several days ago. Tina's real estate agent had called her. "Tina," he said, "you're not going to believe this. I met a guy last night who's interested in your house. He wants to sign a contract; can you believe it—on New Year's Eve!"

I put my head back and laughed. Eight years ago I had been given a call on New Year's Eve that had burned in my spirit for eight long years. Now I had my writer—supplied by the Lord on New Year's Eve. The timing of the Lord was perfect.

For the next several weeks I poured my life onto tape, recording every detail, reliving experiences, jogging my memory for dates. It was an exhausting time for Tina as she struggled to develop a story line from the mounds of information. She was going to need months to finish the book.

In February I returned to Colombia. I tried to send cassettes of information to Tina in New York; but surrounded by the distractions of the ministry, I found it impossible to sit down and talk into a tape recorder. After several months of struggling, I gave up. I would have to go back to New York. This time I would not leave until the book was finished.

June 1992—Bronx, New York

"Tina?"

Tina's back was turned toward me, but I did not need to see her face. The tension was in her shoulders. She had been quiet for several hours, staring at the computer screen.

"The Lord has everything under control," I said gently.

Tina did not say anything.

"Tina, we have to trust the Lord."

She tapped a few keys sharply then turned around. "I don't think I can make it, Marta." Her face was tense.

I lowered my reading glasses, laying them on the manuscript. Tina was insistent on accuracy. I had been reading for hours, correcting slight inaccuracies, recreating the stories, trying to recapture the flavor of the moment without distorting the facts. Now I could see the stress on her face.

"Tina, this book will be written when the Lord wants it to be written. Everything is in His timing."

"But what about Escobar?"

"The Lord will take care of him," I said confidently. "Don't worry; you'll make it."

She smiled briefly. "What makes you so sure?"

Should I tell her? Several days ago I had been struck by a sudden thought. Would it encourage her, or put more pressure on her?

"Tina, in December it will be nine years since the Lord first gave me my spiritual baby."

Her eyes widened. "Nine years...nine months..."

"Yes." I felt goose bumps. "It may just be a coincidence," I said carefully, "but the Lord has been telling me this is the year. If it is His will, you'll make it because He's in control."

Tina nodded and went back to work determinedly.

For hours each day we worked on the book, pressing to finish the manuscript, recording my life, transcribing the results, editing, rewriting, adding, and deleting.

Tina struggled with the story line, fighting to keep the story uncluttered. "We have too much to choose from," she said. "What am I going to do with all this information?"

I knew I was there as a sounding board and kept quiet.

"What am I going to do with Chico?" she asked, staring at the computer screen. "It's a great story; it just doesn't fit the story line." She pulled her legs up under her chin and glared at the screen. "How am I supposed to decide what to use?"

I waited patiently while she sorted out the facts in her

head. Finally she blacked in a large section, looked at it regretfully, then hit the delete button. "It's gone," she said. "I'm leaving it out."

The late nights became early-morning editing sessions, and Tina's brothers and sisters were added to the team. "I need them," she said. "They're all good writers, and they'll be honest."

The next week she was upset with her small cadre of editors. "They're destroying me," she said wearily. "They want perfection."

Late into the night we worked, shaping and reshaping the manuscript. Tina ordered in Chinese food and we pushed ahead.

One night, Tina pushed the keyboard back and ran her fingers across her eyes. "Marta, I know you want the book finished this year…" She rubbed her forehead wearily. "But what if we don't finish it in time?" Her eyes were suddenly strained. "Marta, what if I don't finish it in time, and Escobar is killed?"

I did not want to think about that. "Don't worry," I said reassuringly. "The Lord will take care of him. If we don't get to him in time, the Lord will use someone else to reach him before he dies."

She cleared the screen and started a new chapter, typing in the opening line. "He gets the only copy?"

"Yes, the first one."

She tilted her head, reading the line she had just typed. "Then what?"

"Then, when the Lord says it's time, we'll print the next ones for the entire Medellín cartel."

"Seems like an awful lot of work for one man."

"The Lord loves him," I said gently.

She nodded, chastised, and kept working.

Late that night I left her and went upstairs to pray. I was staying with Michelle while I was in New York. I walked into the apartment and heard her call my name. "Marta, is that you?"

"Yes," I answered.

"Come here a minute."

Something had happened. I flew into the bedroom, my heart beating. "What?"

"Call Colombia."

Call Colombia—it could mean only one thing. It was not Lina—she was with me in New York. It was not the congregation—I had just heard from them. It had to be Escobar. I dialed my cousin's house with shaking fingers.

"What happened?" I asked.

"Escobar's been kidnapped."

"From Envigado?" I gasped. "What happened?"

"They don't really know. It's all so confusing. There was some shooting, and they think some of the guards were killed. It's so chaotic they haven't been able to sort it out yet."

"My baby," I wept. "They're going to kill my baby."

Could I have been wrong about the Lord's timing? Had I waited too long? Were they going to kill him before he had a chance to accept the Lord? I flew downstairs.

Tina was still working when I banged on her office window. She looked up, startled. I was shaking, almost in tears. So many years of prayer...so many hours of patient work and research for the book. For what? Were we too late?

"Tina," I said, "Escobar has been kidnapped."

Her heart was in her eyes. "Kidnapped? When—by whom?"

"They don't know yet. The reports are so confusing."

"Is it on the news?"

"Yes."

"Maybe the first stories weren't true," she said. "Turn on the television."

Over the next several days the story unfolded. In the wild scramble to report the news, reporters had jumped to conclusions. The reports were inaccurate. Escobar had not been kidnapped. He had escaped—along with several of his top men.

"Which is worse?" Tina asked.

"I'm not sure," I said worriedly. "They won't be able to hide very long."

Escobar's face was known everywhere in Colombia. Old photographs were being pulled out of files and dusted off as the dramatic news of his escape flashed around the world.

We discussed the advisability of continuing. "There's still time, Tina," I insisted. "He's still alive. We have to finish it. We can't wait any longer. His life is in danger."

The developments were difficult to keep up with, but I was receiving the latest from many different sources. People were calling from everywhere with bits of information. "Marta, his last words were, 'The war is back on.' Escobar says he'll never give himself up again. He hated prison; he'll never go back. Escobar says he's going to start kidnapping Americans again."

Through it all, I knew we had to keep going.

We pressed on, working against time.

On October 9, 1992, news flashes carried the news around the world: Pablo Escobar and the men who had escaped with him were going to turn themselves back in to the Colombian government.

"The Lord is putting him back where we can reach him," I told Tina excitedly. "Remember the prophecy? The Mafia will receive Jesus Christ in prison."

"That includes Escobar?"

"All we can do is pray."

By December, Escobar still had not turned himself in, but after years of planning and months of writing, the book was finally finished. The manuscript would be reviewed one last time, the changes entered, and the final manuscript prepared for translation.

My mind turned once again to that school stage and the young girl wrapped in the Colombian flag. Nine years ago the childhood dream had died when New York City detectives snapped handcuffs on my wrists. Today I was a new person, changed through the power of Jesus Christ. The young girl had become an adult. The dream had become a vision—a vision to see the Colombian Mafia turn to Jesus Christ. The greatest thing I could do for my country was to bring the message of God's love to the Colombian Mafia.

As I prepare to return to Colombia, my heart remains burdened for my country. How can we sleep at night, knowing we have allowed our country to turn from God; knowing we have taught our young people to worship money and power? How can we have peace in our hearts when our young people are dying around us?

Colombia, it is time to wake up!

It is time to stop the killings. It is time to stop the hatred and the revenge. Colombia does not need more hitmen or drug addicts; Colombia does not need more homosexuals or prostitutes. Colombia needs holy men and women of God who will listen to and obey His voice.

Before God and before my country, I have asked for forgiveness for the lives I destroyed through my participation in the drug trade. I ask for forgiveness for bringing shame to my country.

In the last several years I have seen, vividly and often, God's hand of mercy on my life. I have seen the Lord's protection, guidance, and love in many ways. The church, *La Casa de Oración*, is located in an area known for its drug addicts, hitmen, and prostitutes. We have been given the privilege of ministering to these people.

In the future we will open an office to work with the families of *narcotraficantes*. We will offer information about jails and prisons in other countries and help families translate legal documents to be sent to lawyers in those countries. We plan to send bi-monthly newsletters to inmates, hold Bible studies, and minister to the families of incarcerated men and women. And when it is time, we plan to open a drug rehabilitation program for men and women from the streets of Medellín.

These are exciting times for Medellín. It is just beginning, but Medellín, the city known for its violence and drug trafficking, is starting to be shaken by the preaching of the gospel.

It has been a long journey from that New Year's Eve in 1983 when the Lord first gave me the burden to pray for the Mafia. There have been many difficult times, but the Lord has been faithful. He has given me the strength and the courage I needed in every situation. I know there will be many hard times ahead of me, but I know the Lord will protect my life until His work is done.

It is my prayer that one day soon we will see changes in the lives of hundreds of cartel members and their families. God is good and He will do it. He loves them, and they are precious in His sight.

Epilogue

December 1993

As we were going to print with the first edition of *To the Mafia With Love*, we received the news: On December 2, 1993, Pablo Escobar was shot and killed in Medellín, Colombia.

As the world celebrated the news of his death, churches in Colombia and the United States grieved for the loss of the man they had come to see through the eyes of Christ.

After ten years of prayer and tears, Escobar's life ended in a shoot-out on a rooftop in Medellín.

The final paragraph of the manuscript delivered to Escobar in March 1993 read as follows:

History has not yet written the final chapter of this book. We do not have the information we need in order to finish it. The book is written, and my job is finished. It is time to return to Colombia.

Pablo Escobar, the final chapter is up to you.

It is with sadness and pain in my heart that I rewrite the final paragraph.

This book has many chapters. Many are still waiting to be written.

Today is the day of salvation.

The final chapter is now up to you.

To the Mafia With Love

The Bible tells us that the wages of sin is death.
For the love of money, many have given up their lives.
For the love of money, many have left their families and their children. But is it worth it? Is it worth it to lose your education, your position, and your reputation to spend the rest of your life in prison?

Do you want to see your children grow up to be drug addicts, your daughters become prostitutes, abused, beaten, and sick with AIDS and venereal diseases? Do you want to see your sons in prison and your parents killed because of the drug business?

Stop what you are doing! Go back to your wife. Go back to your family. Go back and make your country great. Rebuild your city and your country. Stay in Colombia and raise your children and grandchildren. Work honestly and find peace with God.

The Lord has called you to serve Him. He created you, and He is merciful, but He is also just. One day you will be before God and He will be your judge. What will you say to Him then—"I gave money to the poor"?

Remember that the good things you do mean nothing to God. The money you give to the poor, the prayers you say, the holy communion you take—all mean nothing without Jesus in your heart.

The Bible says that nothing impure will enter the king-dom of God—only those whose names are written in the

Lamb's Book of Life. Is your name written in that Book? Have you asked God to forgive you for the things you have done?

God has seen every sinful act you've committed, but He can forgive you. Admit that you are a sinner, and ask for His forgiveness. Ask Him to help you start a new life and make you a holy person for His glory. Open your heart to Him and give Him control of your life.

Look up; humble yourself before God. He is ready to forgive you and to protect you.

If you want to know God, ask Him to change your heart and change your life. He hears you when you pray. Pray this prayer, believing in your heart:

"Dear Father, I know that I have sinned against You. I confess my sins to You and ask You to forgive me. Please, Lord, come into my life. I open my heart to You. I want to be Your child and to do Your will. I want to live for You and bring honor to Your name. Help me to live my life the way You want me to, in a way that is pleasing to You. I ask You to be my Lord. Thank you for making me Your child. In Christ Jesus, Amen."

It is a simple decision to turn your life over to Jesus, but it is not easy to live life His way. There will be many hard times ahead as you try to live for Him, but He will protect you, and He will guard your footsteps. Look to Him and He will bring you peace.

Obey Him and bring honor to His name.